White Buffalo

(New Beginnings)

Series

Series and Books written by
Lauretta Beaver

Series #1: White Buffalo (New Beginnings)

Book #1: Passionate Alliance
Book #2: Raven & the Golden Eagle
Book #3: Revenge of the Silver Fox (Coming Soon)

Series #2: The Curse of the Celtic Dragon Medallion

Book #1: Dream Dancer & the Celtic Witch
Book #2: Twin Destinies
Book #3: The Seeker & the Shadow Hunter

RAVEN
And The
GOLDEN EAGLE

Written by: **LAURETTA BEAVER**

To contact the Author for reviews, send email to; mlorettabeaver@gmail.com

Published by Lauretta Beaver, Falher, Canada.

ISBN Paperback: 978-1-77354-384-0
ISBN e-Book: 978-1-77354-385-7

Publication assistance by

PageMaster
PUBLISHING
PageMasterPublishing.ca

This book is dedicated to my late husband,
Edward Milton Beaver
Born April 21, 1958... died May 20, 2008.
It was a tragic tale that someday I might be able to tell.

Also, to my two beautiful daughters, Pamela Lynn Ryman and Jessica Alexandria Oper, who stole my heart the day they were born. I loved you then and I will love you two forever. I thank you both from the bottom of my heart, for the love the two of you have shown me over the years. As well as your patience, while putting up with my constant writing.

I would like to thank my hairdresser at Zahaira for the beautiful hairstyle for my back cover. Also, to Tracy Gagne for the gorgeous pictures especially on such short, notice... thank you, ladies.

A special thank you goes to my mother, Irene Chaisson, for her help with some of the editing on both of my books.

Extreme gratitude and love, goes to my partner Michel Pelletier; for his help getting all my books redone. Thank you!

I would also like to thank The Great Spirit for the enduring Love, even though at times it doesn't seem as if I AM cares. I would like to share a short story with my readers of my grief, if I may.

Edward died a month before we were to be remarried. I lost my job a year later then to make things worse I hit a deer and totalled the front of my car. This all happened in less than two years, I was depressed... it seemed God hated me at the time. I put on a DVD that Edward bought before he died, called the Isaac's. A song they sing called 'Stand still and Let God Move' sent shivers down my spine. I looked up imploringly. "Okay, obviously you are trying to tell me something! If that's what you want; I will stay still, but please tell me... what do you want from me?"

While I waited for The Great Spirit to tell me what I needed to do next, I picked up my pen and finished two books that I had started when I was twenty-four. Passionate Alliance and the second book to the series Raven and the Golden Eagle. Wouldn't you know it, I sent the first one in, and it was published! Just because the Almighty gives you hard times, doesn't mean he hates you even though it seems that way at times. Remember, if you stand still and let, I AM move in your life after such tragedies something good usually follows. Not when we want it to, but when the Lord says it's time! I pray that your dreams come true as mine have.

The Rise of the Shaman

The Prophecy

One arises more powerful than any shaman in a
hundred years!
Able to walk in dreams;
his powers will exceed all before him!
What he becomes in the future hangs in the balance,
as the choice between his powers and life...
looms ever closer!

Montana

Hearing a tinkling laugh of delight behind him; Devon Rochester, couldn't help smiling. He moved his rifle before turning in his saddle, to see his youngest sister's pleasure as a startled doe with a fawn, jumped in front of the horses pulling the wagon she was on.

Janet, Devon's older sister was riding beside him side-saddle. It had taken a lot of time to find her one. In Montana they were less common since women rode astride most times. Malta's Mercantile would have had to order one in, which would have taken at least a month... they didn't have time to wait for it. Luckily, the owner's wife had one she was willing to part with; as long as Lord Rochester bought her a new one, from Smith-Worthington Saddlery. He had agreed of course, anything to make his sister happy. Plus, he ordered one for his younger sister, Tiffany. The saddler promised to send him a message when it arrived.

Disillusioned by court life, plus the death of Devon's father had led up to this trip. Two weeks after his dad died; a letter from someone in North Dakota changed everything. He wanted to buy the Englishman's property in Montana. Lord Rochester wrote him back and advised him that because of the conditions of the will, he couldn't sell until he had lived on it for a year. The man wrote back then said he was willing to wait. So, the young lord started preparing to go to Montana... willing to try something new.

Devon's sisters found out where he was going and asked to go. He said no, but changed his mind after he thought about it. His older sister was widowed, with nothing left; since their father stole it from her. She was adamant that she wanted to start a life elsewhere.

Tiffany, Devon's second sister was a year younger than he was and had always been sick. The doctor said his sister had a weak heart, so she would never be able to get married because she couldn't have children... it would kill her. She begged; when that didn't work, she pleaded. But what convinced him to take her was her belief that she would die in the next two years. She wanted to go, so she could see something new before she died, even if it killed her to come.

With both sisters standing in front of him declaring they would rather die anywhere but England. Devon choice agreed unwillingly.

The trip across the Atlantic had taken over a month because of the brutal storm that blew them off course. Thankfully, finally getting to Boston relatively intact but late; they had to rebook passage to Cleveland by stagecoach. It took two days to get there then they had an overnight stay before being able to board the next stage that would take them to Grand Forks, North Dakota. The three dishevelled travelers disembarked, two weeks too late causing them to miss their wagon train that had left without them. A frustrated Devon spent four days searching either for a guide or another wagon train going to Montana. He did find one heading out in two days. Rushing around, he found a wagon and the three travelers were on their way.

Getting to Malta Montana a week ago, Devon couldn't help feeling that this trip was more than he had bargained for; his sisters seemed to be enjoying every experience and waved away his concerns.

It took some time before Devon could find guides; most, refused to take two white women into Indian Territory. Thankfully, Lord Rochester had lucked out yesterday while in the saloon and found two brothers willing to lead them.

Shrugging off his straying thoughts, Devon turned back to face the front before smiling at his older sister... inquisitively. The laughter behind him made all the frustration melt away. "Any regrets?"

Shaking her head no, Janet opened her mouth to answer; but all that came out was a squeak, as the one ahead fell off his saddle dead!

The last thing Devon heard was the screams of his sisters, and the blood curdling shrieks of a dozen Indians. The Englishman's horse reared in fear, but he did get a shot off before more hideously painted Cheyenne surged out of the trees. Instantly, they were surrounded then everything became blurry as he hit the ground.

North Dakota

The five people riding for the North Dakota border were two days from their ranch. The man leading was tall, with broad-shoulders; a white man with salt and pepper hair. On his chest pinned to his vest was a deputy marshal badge. Jed was ahead by half a horse length.

The person riding behind his left shoulder; on his horses left flank, wasn't as tall with narrow shoulders that tapered down to a slim waist. With distinct feminine features, his wife wore a black hat to conceal hair that was pure white. On Melissa's vest, was a marshal's badge.

On the other side of the deputy marshal past his shoulder, on his horse's right flank was Pam. She had black eyes and an olive complexion, with dark blonde hair that was done in two braids. With such high cheek bones, one could tell she was half Cheyenne.

Behind the deputy marshal, between Melissa and Pam was a white male leading a packhorse. He was riding on the left side of the native woman. He looked like the man leading, but with blonde hair. Daniel wore a silver cross; proclaiming to all his profession as a Baptist Pastor.

Next to him was another white woman, Jessica. Her fiery red hair was done in a braid down her back. She was leading a white two-year-old stallion. She was riding on the right side of the marshal, past her sister's shoulder. Having called of her wedding, she begged Melissa to come. Jess needed to leave after catching her fiancé with another woman.

Melissa nudged her horse forward then looked at her husband curiously, she motioned in question. "Jed, how long will it take us?"

Unsure, Jed shrugged. "It should take twenty days if we push hard."

Anxiously, Melissa couldn't hide her worried expression.

Reaching over, Jed took her hand gently; he gave it a reassuring squeeze before letting go. "We will make it in time Mell... I promise!"

Melissa gave her husband a smile of relief before dropping back. She glanced across Jed's horse's rump at her daughter-in-law in concern.

Pamela or Morning Star to her father's Cheyenne people, smiled before turning to face the front; not wanting her mother-in-law to see the fear in her eyes. Silently, Pam prayed to Ma'heo... the Cheyenne's Great Spirit. "Please help us reach my father in time... I beseech you!"

CHAPTER ONE

MONTANA

The sun was topping the mountains when the rider on a roan mare stopped to admire the view. It was breathtaking to watch them change colours as the sun emerged above them. The rider stiffened in alarm then looked left, at the sound of horse's hooves coming from the cliffs above... just as a ringing challenge pierced the air. Before relaxing, knowing the sound of that defiant squeal as the eyes of the human and horse collided.

The rider held still as the black stud snorted testing the air for a scent. When the sun materialized over the mountains, it shone on the brawny stallion... making his coat seem as red as the mares. At other times, his hide appeared blue. The mare neighed in response to the stallion's challenge then started shifting in anticipation.

Soothingly, the rider stroked the horse to calm her, while watching the stocky black paw the air as he reared. The stud turned before disappearing heading back into the canyon where he came from. Nudging the mare forward, they rode toward the same location that the stallion headed for.

If one didn't know about the crevice behind the rocks ahead, you would ride right past it. Missing one of the most beautiful hidden valleys, the rider had seen. They had stumbled on it about four and a half years ago when the idea of catching the black stud first occurred. It took a year to apprehend the horse, but after six months of trying to get the stallion to breed; they gave up when the horse became sick. Knowing that the stud would die if kept in captivity, they brought the animal back to the valley then set the stallion free... some horses were not meant to be tamed!

The rider desperately needed another stallion for the big herd of mares at the ranch. So, they decided that if you couldn't bring the stud to the mares, the idea of bringing them to him was tried.

Every spring this horse was brought here for breeding before they got busy with the cattle drive. There were two reasons; one was because she was the alpha mare. The second was that the rider knew that this particular horse would stay close even if her life is threatened. One whistle is all it would take. Nothing would stop this mare from getting to her rider; she was that reliable.

The mare and rider would spend two or three days with the stallion. One-week later, they would bring twenty-five mares into the valley and leave them with the stud for one month. Afterwards, these mares were herded back to the ranch then another twenty-five were brought in... until all seventy-six horses were bred.

It was a nerve-racking challenge two years ago when they first tried it, because the stallion kept trying to steal the mares... only half of them got pregnant. But with the roan mare on guard, plus two herd dogs working together; last year everything went off without a hitch, with only two losses. Lots of the foals promised to have their sire's height, and muscular build.

The rider had come to an understanding with the stud; as long as they didn't try to catch him again, and he didn't try to steal the mares... everything worked according to plan. Somehow, the black seemed to know when they were coming, because he was always on that particular ledge waiting.

When the mare entered the valley, she stopped obediently as her rider pulled her to a halt so that they could admire the view. All that could be heard from the pair was a deep intake of breath then the release of air in a great sigh of relief. This was the only time of relaxation permissible from the everyday pressure of running the largest ranch in the Montana territory.

Smiling in satisfaction, the rider looked around pensively; it was incredibly beautiful here, with trees and lush vegetation. A pool fed by an underground spring was on the right of the cliffs. The hills circled all the way around enclosing this oasis except for this opening. They are the reason people didn't know about the valley.

Nudging the mare forward into a gallop without a trace of fear... the rider knew the stud wouldn't be here if there was any danger within miles. The mare stopped at the edge of a cluster of trees, just before the bottom of the far cliffs; it was the only trees in this valley so the perfect place for a camp. Familiar with this routine, the horse knew her rider would set her free here.

After dismounting then unsaddling the horse, they stood for a few moments listening to the sound of the stud's hooves as he galloped towards the pond. The mare's ears perked forward, but she didn't move otherwise... waiting for permission to go. Stepping back with a quiet murmur of approval, the rider gave a low chuckle as the mare eagerly spun on her hind legs before galloping towards the black.

The rider watched the horses run around the valley in pleasure. Finally, turning away knowing the camp needed to be readied. Walking over to a cairn of rocks to dig up the supplies hidden underground to protect them from scavengers, the rider took them to the fire pit then set up camp. Once done, decided to take a swim so ambled over to the edge of the lake.

The transformation that took place at the lagoon would leave a stranger stunned in open mouth shock. The rider shook waist length raven black hair out from under her light brown hat. Only after her clothes were removed did one see her lush body... she was stunning; she stood five-feet-five-inches tall with a muscled body that was every man's fantasy, with large firm breasts. She had a touch of a slant to her light green eyes with black luscious eyelashes. High cheekbones with a dusky complexion gave away her Indian heritage. She stood bold and proud against the shadows of the cliffs then dove gracefully into the water. Swimming until her body felt refreshed as well as relaxed, she hoisted herself up and out of the lake.

Raven sat in the warmth of the sun to dry her golden bronze body then shook out her ebony tresses; hoping her hair would dry faster.

Lying back, Raven thought about her parents... which she hadn't done for some time. Her mother, Morning Dove had been a full-blooded Cheyenne. If you saw both of them together, you would swear they were twins; except for Raven's green eyes that went with her lighter skin. Her grandfather on her mother's side was Giant Bear, a Cheyenne Chief of the wolf tribe. Her father had been half-Cheyenne and half-British. Her grandfather on her father's side was full British, an Earl of the realm in Britain. He had been a general in the army stationed at the fort, which is how he met his Cheyenne wife. They were married by the Cheyenne first then later he had taken her to the fort, where he had married her in the white man's way. It had caused a scandal here, and in England she was told. They had one child Everett to the whites or Red Fox to the Cheyenne.

Raven's Cheyenne grandmother died giving birth to Everett, so her English grandfather quit the army then bought a thousand acres of good fertile land. He started what was to become one of the largest wealthiest ranches in the area. It wasn't until the earl died that his son, Everett decided to go find the Cheyenne and meet the rest of his family. There he met Raven's mother. They fell in love then returned to Everett's ranch where they got married by a white preacher.

They had two children, Raven who was twenty-three, as well as a boy Edward Williams Charles Summerset named after his British grandfather. She affectionately called him Ed; he was known to the Cheyenne as Dream Dancer.

Five years ago, both their parents died in a stagecoach hold up on one of their rare trips to Boston. Raven eighteen at the time had to take responsibility of a grieving eleven-year-old boy; plus, a thriving ranch that she had to learn to manage on her own.

One thing that Raven would like to thank her parents for was keeping their Indian culture alive. Since she was three, she had spent six months out of every year with her Cheyenne grandfather, Giant Bear.

The first three years with the Cheyenne were spent playing with the other children, learning their customs and language. When Raven was six, the women took the rambunctious youngster in hand and taught her how to cook, tan hides, plus make buckskins.

At the age of eight, Raven was banished from the women's presence before being taken in hand by her grandfather; and one of the six warrior societies of the Cheyenne... known as the shields. From that day forward, she learned everything a warrior did. The young Cheyenne maiden learned to hunt with a rifle, plus how to track game or humans. She mastered the art of using a tomahawk, the proper use of a bow, then knife fighting and how to use a coup stick; everything a warrior learned was passed on to her.

This Raven didn't understand because in the Cheyenne society, females weren't even permitted to touch a warrior's weapon. She was the only woman to learn both that she was aware of anyway. After her parents died, she had approached the shaman curiously then asked him why she was allowed to be a warrior when she was a woman.

What the shaman told Raven amazed her, but it made her proud...

The shaman eyed Raven for a moment speculatively before nodding, as if deciding she was now ready for the truth. "At your naming ceremony, I had a vision of you and a boy; Dream Dancer, who wouldn't be born for another seven years. It's highly unusual to have a dream of siblings together, especially when one isn't born yet. Both of you were standing protectively over your ranch then over the Cheyenne village... instantly the vision changed. You stood alone like a warrior with Indian buckskins, war paint, plus a gun. A raven was in the background protectively keeping evil spirits away from the ranch and village. So, you were trained as our first Cheyenne warrior woman. A different vision was shown to me about your brother. He would also stand protectively over both the ranch and village. He had on the white man's clothes with a book that had scratches on it. I saw him standing on a giant canoe."

*****

So far, Raven mused, the visions had proven to be true. The Cheyenne wintered in a canyon that was part of her ranch, so nobody bother them. She had men patrolling that sector of the sprawling ranch to make sure her people remained safe.

There was one Cheyenne brave from each band that kept the young braves in control; because one of the rules was that as long as the Cheyenne stayed on Raven's land... no war, killing, taking white captives, or horse stealing from town was allowed.

There was one exception made. The young braves who were close to becoming warriors were given a description of a horse that was hidden on her land. They were told that if they could find that horse without being discovered, they were allowed to keep it. This was their final test before they become warriors... Raven never made it easy for them.

Prior to Raven's father death, they went to a town meeting to let the townspeople know they planned to have the Cheyenne winter on their land. There was outrage and apprehension at first; but after six years of peace, the town accepted even traded with them.

As word got around to other Cheyenne, that Raven's family was living in peace so close to a white town; more groups asked to join the winter procession. Where once there were fifty tepees, now there were two hundred and fifty. Every year more tribes asked to join.

All white captives brought onto these lands were questioned before being released. Or they could stay with the Cheyenne then be adopted. Only one problem surfaced with a band that refused to give up a prisoner when she wanted to return to her own people. She happened to be owned by a war chief who refused to give her up. There was much arguing at first, but the band was finally asked to leave; which Raven was grateful for, since she knew that they would have caused problems.

The main issue when other bands started joining... was food. Raven, her grandfather, and all the other chief's that already joined the band deliberated for days. It was eventually agreed that two months before winter hit, all the groups would show up then every available hunter would hunt... until the snow started falling. It was also decided that two warriors from each band would work on the ranch as wranglers to earn the right to fresh beef, and other supplies needed during the winter months. Every warrior had to take their turn.

Some older Indian women, plus a few men that couldn't keep up when the bands were moving; with no family, stayed at the ranch year-round. So, they could contribute to their tribe's well-being.

So, the town wouldn't feel slighted, there were fifty year-round cowboys. There were two camp cooks that stayed out on the range. Several people from town were hired to assist in the gardens, barns, as well as the forge.

It was also decided that all the trade goods of the Cheyenne were sold for cash then this money was given to Raven. It was becoming apparent that another thousand acres would be needed soon, if any more bands were going to join. She kept this money in a separate account, she even added funds from the sale of her cattle and horses. Next year she would be able to pay cash for the thousand acres that was against her property.

So far, this system worked remarkably well for Raven.

Thinking about the other part of the vision, Raven sighed dejectedly... it was also coming true. Her brother was leaving for university in the fall to become a lawyer. He said it is unjust how the white man takes advantage of the Indians, so becoming a lawyer would help him fight for Indian rights. Edward decided to go to school in England, so he could take over the title and lands that belonged to him through their English grandfather. She knew the task her brother chose wouldn't be an easy one. Being three-quarters Cheyenne, in a white community would be hard to overcome. Thankfully, Edward didn't look native so that would be to his advantage.

Exhaling noisily, Raven got up to get dressed then went to set snares for fresh meat. She decided to walk around before the sun went down. As the young woman walked, the Cheyenne maiden spotted her mare with the stallion. She watched as the stud's penis came out and he mounted her horse. The mare squealed in pleasure when he entered her.

Since Raven took over the ranch, she had watched horses, cattle, dogs... as well as pigs breed. She hadn't thought much about it; it was only to increase her herds. But two years ago, when she first brought this mare here to be bred, something changed. She started to feel shivery sensations whenever she watched the stud cover her mares.

It wasn't long after Raven's first stirrings that she began having dreams about a man she couldn't see fully... only a shadowy image.

The first time that it happened, Raven woke up feeling hot, flushed, and scared. She also felt frustrated because she couldn't remember the entire dream; all she could recall when awake is a shadow of a man. She had gone to the shaman to ask him about it...

The shaman smiled in satisfaction as he chuckled knowingly. "Raven, you are becoming a woman; not just a warrior!"

The shaman would say no more after that, Raven left his tepee still confused and without answers. The dream returned often, but she tried to ignore it without much success.

Raven finished her walk then turned back to her camp to check her snares. She was in luck when she found two rabbits. While they cooked, the young Cheyenne maiden scraped the hides automatically... without thought. She tried to ignore the shivery feelings she was still experiencing from watching the horse's mate before crawling into bed.

As Raven slept her dream lover came to her again, but this time it was different. The dream was so intense that it seemed as if she was actually there then she saw him for the first time. He was riding a white horse straight towards her at full gallop. Just as the man came abreast of her, he leaned down then swept her into his arms.

Turning, Raven looked at him for the first time. He had eyes that would rival the storm clouds that swept in from time to time, with light hair almost white. The man's head started to drop for a kiss.

'Neigh'... Raven was awakened by a ringing challenge from the stud, and the sound of her mare's hooves galloping toward her in excitement. She jerked into a sitting position then grabbed her revolver, which was never far from her side. The Cheyenne warrior maiden sprang to her feet instantly awake before gathering a handful of her mare's mane; she vaulted onto her horse, in one swift motion.

Raven turned her horse before galloping towards the opening of the valley, to see what was upsetting the stallion. The mare stopped beside the black and they waited for whatever was coming. She looked up, thankful to see a hint of twilight lighting up the sky; it was just enough so that she could see the opening coming into the valley.

The only sound that could be heard at that moment, was the faint sound of another horse then the cocking of Raven's revolver. She had to strain hard to hear the soft tread of the other horse, so she knew it couldn't be a white man's... this one wasn't wearing shoes; it was probably another stallion. Just as the new horse came into view, a raven's call floated through the stillness.

Sighing in relief, Raven put her gun away when she heard that call. When she saw her cousin Running Wolf, a shiver of anxiety shook her. She knew he wouldn't come unless there was an emergency. He would think it beneath him as the next chief to be a messenger.

Running Wolf and Raven clasped arms in the traditional warriors greeting then she turned her horse to take the brave to her camp. She peeked at her half-cousin speculatively out of the corner of her eye; thinking how much he looked like his father Black Hawk or Tommy as his mother Mary sometimes called him. He had his father's and grandmother's blue eyes, with their grandfather's husky build. He did have the darker skin with the long black hair of his mother people who were also Cheyenne, but from a different tribe.

Like Raven, Running Wolf was three-quarters Cheyenne, and a quarter white. His father, Black Hawk was Raven's half-uncle; he had lived with Melissa Brown most of his life before Giant Bear even knew he had a son.

Giant Bear's second wife; Mary, found out she was pregnant after her Cheyenne husband left to pursue the killers of his first wife. Being white and not growing up in the Indian ways, she got scared so ran off to her brothers to have her baby. She learned quickly she made a mistake. He hated Indians then tried to kill his nephew when he was born. Later, he attempted to kill Giant Bear when the lovers were reunited.

Dismounting, Raven's contemplation was cut short. She slapped her mare's rump to send her back to the stallion before indicating to Running Wolf that he should sit. She put fuel on the fire to heat up coffee and the rabbit she had cooked earlier; thankfully, she hadn't finished it.

Sitting across the fire from Running Wolf... Raven served him the remainder of her rabbit as any Indian maiden would do. While he ate that; she took out her peace pipe, as tradition dictated must be smoked before anything serious can be discussed between two warriors.

Running Wolf belched in appreciation then Raven lit her peace pipe. She took two deep puffs; she blew smoke towards the Great Spirit, and at the ground to Mother Earth before turning to blow more smoke to the west then to the east because that is where the sun rises and sets... it gives precious light, plus life in an otherwise dark world. She handed the pipe to her cousin. He repeated the ceremony.

After the pipe was smoked, Running Wolf sat forward intently. "I bring greetings to the Raven, 'protector' of our tribe, and a message of urgency to come to the winter camp as soon as possible!"

Speechless for a bit... stunned; Raven finally motioned in apprehension. "But the winter camps been empty for two weeks. Why would Grandfather bring the tribes back there?"

Exhaling noisily in irritation, it's all the emotion Running Wolf would allow to show. "I can't say why Nam-shimi' chose to return to the winter camp. It was only the wolf tribe that needed to go back; the other tribes had left already. All I can give you is Grandfather's message. He said to tell the Raven, she must hurry to the winter camp or many deaths would occur... only she can stop it. He said you must come as an Indian with no white man's trappings. Nam'-shimi will explain when you get there."

Raven knew by the way her cousin pronounced nam-shimi' that he was saying grandfather, and when he used the other nam'-shimi he was saying, grandpa. She shook off her distracted thoughts before mussing over the cryptic message... frowning baffled. She gestured curiously at her half-cousin. "Do you have any idea as to what is going on?"

Running Wolf scowled in annoyance before shaking his head negatively. "No, I don't! All I can tell you is that seven moons away from our winter camp; we came across a wagon that had been wiped out. Only two white survivors were left... one was a woman the other was a man. The woman died despite all the medicine man's attempts to save her. The man was unconscious when we found them. The medicine man didn't think he would live either. The shaman and Nam-shimi' argued. Then the shaman went into seclusion to meditate and ask the Great Spirit what to do. He came out then called Giant Bear to him and they argued again. When Grandfather finished talking to the shaman, he advised everyone that we would be returning to the winter camp. Nam'-shimi approached me then asked me to come give you his message of great importance."

Raven grimaced in anger. It only took her a few minutes to figure out who was responsible, but asked anyway just to make sure. "Do you happen to know which Cheyenne band?"

Nodding decisively, Running Wolf waved grimly. "Yes! Slippery as an Eel was among the dead. He's from the tribe you turned away."

Inclining her head grimly, Raven's suspicions were confirmed... she waved anxiously. "Go tell nam-shimi' I will come right away, but I must go home for my Indian pony. I'll meet you at the winter camp."

Getting up, Running Wolf jumped on his gelding and left.

Standing there thoughtfully, Raven watched him leave before giving a shrill whistle for her mare; while waiting, she broke camp.

Brandy galloped in when she heard the urgent whistle from her mistress; she stood as Raven saddled her for the trip back.

Patting her horse in sympathy, Raven frowned grimly. "Sorry, girl, it looks as if your love life is going to have to be put on hold for now."

The mare nickered as if she understood then waited.

Mounting, Raven bent down close to her horse's neck. "Come on girl get me home as quickly as possible!"

As if the mare understood the urgency, she pinned back her ears then spun on her hind legs towards the cliffs and the shortcut home.

As Raven's horse flew across gullies then through streams at a gallop her thoughts were flying as fast. It's evident to her that the other group of Cheyenne was setting up her family, but until she learned all the facts; it would be impossible to figure out what they were up too.

Raven was mystified by her grandfather's insistence that she come as an Indian... instead of as she was; she knew though that nam-shimi' wouldn't tell her to do it if it were not necessary for some reason.

Shaking off thoughts of her grandfather; Raven tried to remember her dream. She recalled seeing her dream lover's face, now it was gone... again! Sheesh, the Cheyenne maiden couldn't help thinking that sleeping longer might have helped. Someday she knew they would meet, until then she must put him out of her mind.

Sighing in aggravation, Raven shook off all thoughts. She needed to pay attention to where they were going. She leaned closer to her mare's neck for more speed urging her on as her anxiety increased.

CHAPTER TWO

Raven and her mare crested a hill, which gave her a clear view of the sprawling ranch. She slowed her horse, as she looked down in pleasure then kept them at a walk for the last quarter mile to cool the mare down. Unable to help it, the Cheyenne maiden thought of her father and mother again; she knew her parents would be extremely proud of her if they could see how much the ranch had grown... since she took it over. Not only was she going to expand to two thousand acres next year, which her father had talked about before he died. But in the last five years, she had built a second bunkhouse for the men then one for the women.

Three cottages were built then a second barn; before a bigger forge followed, with additional stalls for sick or quarantine animals.

The cattle herd increased from one thousand head to two thousand. Three more bulls were bought to improve the conception rate... plus boost the quality of beef she was selling. Now there were twenty bulls, which was another reason more land was needed.

The horse herd also doubled, now there were four pastures not two.

Frowning thoughtfully, Raven knew that another stallion would have to be found soon because it was just too hard on the black stud. They had been really lucky last year that most of the mares conceived. She finally saw one that she had instantly fell in love with several months ago... he would be coming here next year. He was a stunning silver white thoroughbred stud colt from Melissa Brown's ranch in North Dakota.

At one time, Melissa was a sheriff in a town called Smyth's Crossing, but now she's the marshal of North Dakota. Raven met her and her husband Jed through her grandfather Giant Bear. She had grown up on stories of her nam-shimi teaming up with Jed Brown before meeting Melissa Ray. The three of them defeated a group of cold-blooded murderers. Unfortunately, she hadn't seen them in years; it wasn't until last year that the Cheyenne maiden was able to visit them.

Melissa showed Raven a colt that she was selling when she found out the young rancher needed a stud. He was the last son from her white stallion, Lightning. He would make an excellent addition to the Cheyenne maiden's herd. The marshal promised to keep him for her.

Shaking off her thoughts; Raven frowned, it was almost suppertime... they had galloped all the way home. Both were extremely exhausted. They only stopped a couple of times to eat and to give her horse a needed rest. She reached down then patted her mares sweat encrusted neck in apology. "Sorry about that, girl!"

Raven guided her mare over to the lower pasture where her Indian pony Brave Heart was kept. She gave a sharp, shrill whistle... calling him to her. Jumping off her mare, the Cheyenne maiden loosened the saddle before tying the reins around her neck so the mare wouldn't trip on them. Moving to the side, she slapped her on the rump to send her on her way. "Okay girl, go to the barn; Steve will look after you."

The mare turned to the stables where she knew oats would be waiting for her before trotting off obediently... familiar with this routine.

Galloping up to the fence at his mistress's call, Brave Heart waited.

Opening the gate wide, Raven let her stallion out; not one bit worried he would take off. While she was closing the gate, he turned to face his mistress without budging from that spot... waiting patiently. She turned to him and walked around checking his legs then his hooves, making sure her horse was ready for a hard journey.

Brave Heart was a beautiful stallion; standing fifteen hands high with perfect markings. Highly prized by the Cheyenne, he was a black and white pinto. The Mustang was wild when Raven first saw him staggering around with a bullet crease in his neck... even being shot, he managed to evade capture. It took a long time to get him to trust her enough to treat the wound, but eventually she was able to help him. They have been inseparable ever since.

Grabbing her horse's mane, Raven hoisted herself up bareback then walked him to the barn for her Indian tack. Jumping down... she turned to him in command. "Stand!"

Going into the barn, Raven had no worries leaving Brave Heart. She knew her horse wouldn't budge from that spot... neither would anyone get close; mustangs were volatile, so they avoided him at all costs.

Entering, Raven looked around expectantly but didn't see anyone. "Steve, where are you?"

"Over here!"

Raven saw Steve's head pop up from behind her roan mare, so she walked over to the stall. She leaned against it studying him carefully.

He had golden blonde curly locks, and was shorter than she was; with brown eyes that were so light in colouration, they appeared golden. The stableman was a little overweight, but not fat. He was the best horse wrangler Raven had ever met, except for the Cheyenne of course. She paid good money to keep him around here.

Steve was bent putting a wrap on the back leg of her horse.

Sighing in regret, Raven eyed her mare. "Is her leg injured?"

Inclining his head distractedly, Steve continued working on Raven's mare. "She was limping a bit and it feels a tad hot, so I decided to wrap it for the night in case. You sure rode her hard, I have never seen a horse you were riding this wore out before... what's up?"

Scowling in worry, Raven shrugged unknowingly. "There's trouble at the winter camp! Not sure what the problem is, it doesn't sound good."

Looking up at Raven perplexed, Steve's eyebrows rose in surprise before looking back down at what he was doing. "I thought they were gone; shouldn't they have left already?"

Scratching her chin irritably, Raven grimaced resignedly. "Yes, but they had to come back for some reason. I had to come here for Brave Heart before I could go find out what's going on up there. You might want to watch my mare for a while; the black covered her a few times before we left so hopefully, she's pregnant."

Nodding, Steve got up. "Okay, I'll keep her in here for a bit."

Smiling in thanks, Raven pointed behind her at the barn doors in warning. "I'm leaving Brave Heart outside the doors; can you please take some oats out to him?"

Inclining his head, Steve left the mares stall and went to get the oats.

Raven unhooked her Indian rifle holder from her saddle then grabbed the rest of her Indian tack. All three she made herself; the bridal had no bit. The saddle blanket had a few modifications, there was a girth strap... plus a wooden saddle horn was tightly woven in for mounting at a run.

Walking out of the barn, Raven put the saddle on Brave Heart. He was still standing exactly where she had left him. She walked up slowly, praising him in Cheyenne for standing so patiently.

Steve nearing the barn doors started whistling a tune loudly, to let both Raven and Brave Heart know that he was coming out. Only once had he made the mistake of walking outside without warning the stud first. The stableman would carry the scar on his hip forever.

Brave Heart's ears went back in anger then he tried to back away from the barn. A sharp command from his mistress was the only thing keeping him from bolting. It took him a few minutes to smell the oats, when he did instantly his nostrils flared.

Smiling when Brave Heart nickered, Raven chuckled in delight then called out. "It's okay Steve; he knows that you are coming."

Sticking his head out the door cautiously... Steve checked; when he saw the stallion standing with ears perked up, he slowly walked out the door. He set the bucket down close to his boss, but stayed away from the horse.

Finished putting her Indian tack on Brave Heart; Raven grabbed the bucket then let her horse eat. She turned to Steve inquiringly as she motioned hopefully. "I have to go up to the house, can you just stand here for a few minutes?"

Nodding calmly, Steve was not worried now. "Sure, you can go; I will make sure nobody comes and spooks him."

Inclining her head in thanks, Raven turned and sprinted to the ranch house. She vaulted up the three steps then rushed through the door. She paused as she looked around; on the left side of the house was a dining room and a kitchen, with the maid's room past that.

On the right was a sitting room then a small hallway that brought you to the stairs leading up. If you walked past the little entrance with the stairs, you would reach the den and just beyond that was the cook's room. There was a door at the end of the hallway; it led into a storage area then down to the root cellar. The root cellar ran the entire length of the house.

Going past the sitting room, Raven turned right; she didn't stop to take off her outer footwear. She hurried to the end of the short hallway then turned left before taking the stairs two at a time. Once upstairs you were facing a blank wall which was Edward's rooms, behind her was the library. But to get into either place you had to turn left and go down this short hallway to the end. Which would lead you to a T then you could turn left or right into a large hallway. Once you turned left down that hallway, there were two guest rooms on the right. They would be over the dining room as well as part of the kitchen. On the left was access to the library.

If you turned right down the bigger hallway instead, and go that way, it would take you to her rooms on the left. That would make her bedroom directly over the maid's room, plus part of the kitchen. It was across from Edward's rooms that would make his bedroom above the cook's room as well as the den.

Once at the T she turned left, went about ten steps before turning left again to enter the library.

Raven rushed through the door out of breath from the steep stairs. She scared her brother so bad that he jumped from his seat in fear, which caused his book to tumble to the floor in his panic.

Edward stood with his mouth hanging open in shocked surprise for a moment before managing to get words past the tightness in his throat. "Raven; what on Earth are you doing home and why did you try to give me a heart attack?"

Laughing at the astonished look on her brother's face, Raven wasn't in the least worried by his admonishment. She sat down in a chair as she studied him silently in affection. Edward at the age of sixteen was a half an inch away from reaching six feet already. He was powerfully built for his age, thanks to his training with the Cheyenne; plus, the hard work he did around the ranch to help his sister. His hair was shoulder length a light brown with auburn streaks throughout. In the summer, his hair turned lighter almost a strawberry blonde.

Their father always said that Edward looked so much like his dad, the late earl that it was eerie. He had the same aristocratic nose as well as the strong, stubborn chin. Raven's brother had eyes that were a deep green. They were so dark they sometimes appeared black; especially when her brother was upset or angry. He had the high cheekbones of the Cheyenne with a dusky look to his skin, but much lighter than hers was... except in the summer when he tanned.

Sighing, Raven shook off her reflection before getting up and pointed down the hallway. "Come on, Ed. I will explain while I pack."

Nodding perplexed, Edward followed his older sister dutifully. He watched her grab an Indian dress that she rarely wore. Moccasins, buckskin pants, with a matching shirt soon ended up in the pile on the bed. He frowned in puzzlement before showing his youth in his impatience. "What's going on Raven? Grandfather and all our people left for the summer; what do you need your Indian clothes for?"

Jumping a bit in surprise; Raven had been so busy trying to find everything as she mumbled under her breath, she forgot about her brother standing there impatiently... waiting. She grimaced in exasperation at herself then sat down on her bed before looking up at Edward in apology. "I'm sorry, I forgot you were there."

Edward inclined his head, pacified by the sincere apology. "It's okay; now please explain to me what is going on!"

Raven told him everything that had happened since she left.

Frowning uneasily when she finished; Edward motioned in apprehension. "Should I go with you in case I'm needed?"

Shaking her head negatively, Raven gestured calmly. "No, I need you here! You will have to take my mare and a few hands then drive those horses into the valley for me. Don't forget to take Lady and King; they will keep the stallion from running the mares off."

Scowling in forewarning, Edward leaned forward intently. "Okay, but I have to warn you there's a late winter storm coming; it's going to be a bad one. I was going to send Josh later to warn you, it should be here... "

Stopping, Edward looked off into the distance before turning back to Raven... troubled. "In three, four days at the most I would say!"

Nodding calmly, Raven didn't even ask him how he knew this; for as long as she could remember, her brother had been able to predict storms. He even knew that there was something wrong with their parents before anyone else. When she questioned the shaman about her brother, he told her that Edward could have been a powerful shaman or medicine man if he decided to stay. However, he refused to teach him since he was leaving them to go to England.

Sighing in aggravation, Raven waved decisively. "I will take my wolf fur with me, but I still have to go storm or no storm!"

Grimacing knowingly, Edward waved grimly in caution. "I know you do; just be careful, okay!"

Grinning reassuringly, Raven got up before stuffing her extra clothes in her saddlebag then handed it to Ed before pushing him towards the door.

Leaving the room, Edward let his sister get dressed.

Raven took her hat off before dropping the Stetson on the bed. She plaited her hair into two Indian braids then grabbed her wolf pelt out of the closet. Immediately, she put it on the bed so she wouldn't forget it. She turned back to change into her buckskins.

Once done, Raven turned back to her closet. She took out an intricately designed arrow carrier that she made herself. She checked all twelve of her arrows, for breaks or missing raven feathers. Satisfied, she put them back into her carrier and strapped it to her back. She turned to her bed then picked up her headband with her raven society beaded and proudly displayed, she tied it on; next, she put her fur over her shoulders. Turning back to the closet, she grabbed a long chest that held three hunting knives... all intricately made by her. She stuck one in each moccasin before putting the last knife inside a sheath on her belt, strapped to her waist. When she was done, she grabbed her bow that was propped against her closet wall and turned to leave.

This transformation was even more dramatic than the one at the lake. Instead of looking like a man, Raven now looked like an Indian... except for the eyes. Her expressions and mannerisms from this point on would reflect her native heritage, until she changed herself back. She rushed out the door then down the stairs.

Edward was waiting with her saddlebag. He had added mittens, and a beaver hat. On one side of the saddlebag, he had put in matches, jerky, a little chopping axe, and hardtack... just in case she needed it. On the other side was the gift she was making for their grandfather. He looked deeply into Raven's eyes, guessing she had already changed he switched to Cheyenne. "May your journey be swift and without hardships!"

Locking arms with her brother in farewell as tradition dictated; Raven then grabbed him and gave him a sisterly hug. She turned to leave, but not before tucking the mittens with the hat inside the saddlebag. Swiftly, she was out the door whistling for Brave Heart.

*****

Steve hearing the whistle, backed away from the stallion.

Brave Heart reared before spinning; he galloped towards his mistress.

While Raven was standing there waiting for her horse; she put the bow over her shoulder. Grabbing the two ropes that she had added to each saddlebag so she could tie them tightly under her chest, like a belt... she quickly secured them. Not only did it free up her hands but it also kept her wolf fur, bow, as well as her arrows in place.

Raven waited expectantly. When it looked as if her horse would gallop right past her... she took two running strides; reaching up, she grabbed his mane and the extra-large saddle horn before vaulting onto his back.

At a full gallop, Raven untied her saddlebags from around her waist. She turned before securing it behind her saddle blanket, to the ties that were meant to keep it there. She turned around and lifted her bow over her head then attached it to the strap on her blanket, under her left knee; made to hold it tight, so it didn't bounce against her horse. Leaning forward, she asked her stallion for more speed as she urged him on.

Walking over to Edward, Steve shook his head in awe before turning to Raven's younger brother. "Every time I see her do that, I wonder if one of these days she will miss and fall flat on her face."

Edward laughed in amusement before he slapped Steve on the back in reassurance. "No, my friend. I don't think she will ever miss. As for me, I have tried to learn that trick. I am so inept at it, though; I get dragged for a couple of feet before I can manage to get on my horse."

They both laughed at the image of the sixteen-year-old being dragged along the ground.

Sighing, Edward's face sobered in question before motioning inquisitively at the stableman. "How long before Ravens mare is ready to be ridden again?"

Shrugging in concern, Steve pictured the mare. "Not for two or three days at least, Raven rode her pretty hard."

Nodding thoughtfully, Edward waved in caution towards the North. "Well, there's a big storm coming in a few days, so I guess we have to wait to go to the valley until afterwards."

Steve inclined his head without questions, familiar with Ed's predictions. He turned away to go back to the barn so he could check on the mare.

Edward stared after his sister a bit longer, extremely concerned before turning to the house with a worried frown. Something wasn't right; he felt a shiver of foreboding, he had a strange feeling he should have gone too.

*****

Raven rode hard for the rest of the night. The direction she was taking would require at least three or four days of hard riding to reach the village. Two extra days then the direct route, but she needed to tell her men to drive the cattle closer to the ranch... just in case. Her brother was never wrong and she didn't want to take any chances.

Reaching one of her herds of cattle around nine o'clock, Raven sighed in relief. She had only stopped once to water her horse before grabbing a quick bite. She saw three of her men turn their horses to meet her, so she gave her ravens call to let them know who was approaching. Two men stopped to wait; while one turned then rode back to camp to give them warning.

Halting, Raven inclined her head in greeting at the two men; both were brothers, identical... even though they weren't twins. One had blue eyes, the other grey. They were the same height at five foot nine, with brown hair. Paul was skinnier than his brother, but Jake was more muscular.

Turning to the younger brother, Raven motioned anxiously. "Paul, call in the rest of the boys and meet us at camp."

Paul nodded without questioning why then rode off.

Jake eyed Raven in concern before beckoning. "Follow me."

Riding into camp beside her foreman, Raven warily dismounted before turning Brave Heart loose to graze. She walked over to the fire then knelt down as she patiently waited for the camp cook to dish her up beans with pork and biscuits. He handed the plate to her then poured her a strong cup of coffee. She smiled gratefully at the hefty black haired typical camp cook, and ate hungrily as the men started coming in.

Waiting until everyone was there, Raven gestured at Jake in warning; she included all the men in her discussion, though. "There's a storm coming in three or four days, so I want you to drive the cattle closer to the hay sheds. You will have to let Shorty know for me, so he can get his cattle closer too."

Nodding in agreement, Jake wasn't surprise having noticed that the cattle were a bit restless today.

Changing the subject, Jake waved inquisitively at her clothes in surprise. "What's up Raven you are dressed to go see your grandfather, but I know he left already? John and Adam are both here; they didn't leave their post until all the Cheyenne were gone."

Raven retold the story to the men.

Jake frowned grimly when Raven finished... he motioned anxiously. "This could cause you lots of problems with the townspeople if they find out. You know that they only tolerate your people and even you because they have benefited too. We both know that there are still some, especially your neighbour; who keeps trying to get the townspeople to drive you out or call in the army. The only reason they haven't done it yet is that they don't know how many Cheyenne are actually out here. If they ever find out, they will bring in the soldiers for sure!"

Scowling knowingly, Raven waved in aggravation. "I know! That's why I'm going there now, and why I need you to make sure all hands stay on the ranch until I get back. I wouldn't want anyone to say anything by accident. Running Wolf said that they found Slippery as an Eel, so we know who did it. Unfortunately, the white man was unconscious when my family rescued him, so he won't be able to help clear my family of any wrongdoing. First, I will have to prove it wasn't them then track the real killers and bring them to town to hang. Or the townspeople might still try to blame my people... just because they are Indians!"

Gesturing decisively, Jake leaned forward earnestly then pointed at her. "If you need me to help track down the killers, send for me! I will be watching for your signal."

There was a murmur from all the men as they each vowed to help Raven and her family if she needed them. She thanked every one of them for their support then got up and turned away. The young woman walked towards her horse not wanting them to see her misty eyes. She knew all of her hands would die to protect her, as well as the ranch if need be.

Walking around Brave Heart; Raven wanted to make sure the hard journey wasn't affecting him. It gave her the time she needed to get her emotions under control. Once satisfied, she mounted before turning back to Jake. She gestured in hope. "Have you seen Bruno?"

Looking towards the men, Jake saw them shaking their heads no. He turned back to Raven then waved towards the North. "I saw him once about a week ago, with a female wolf."

Nodding in disappointment, Raven shrugged dismissively. "If he's around here, he will find me."

Jake inclined his head before turning to his men. "Mount up boys; it's going to be a long night. Paul, go let Shorty know about the storm."

Turning to look at Raven one last time, Jake concerned expression was glaringly evident. "You be careful, I will watch for your signal. Don't be stubborn about it either!"

Reaching down, Raven took his hand in gratitude. "Thanks Jake, you take care of the boys."

Turning Brave Heart, Raven galloped away without another word spoken. They maintained that pace for the rest of the night. At dawn, she slowed to a trot then to a walk to allow the stud to cool down so they could stop for a rest.

Raven wanted to stay at one of the established campsites that were hidden from strangers. There were four of them... they had passed one at dusk. At each one; there was a cairn of rocks with blankets, food, flint, water, coffee and pot, plus oats for the horses. Everything was buried in waterproof containers so that nothing spoilt. Twice a year, one of her men took a wagon then replenished the sites. That is why she hadn't bothered with a packhorse.

Unpacking the cairn; Raven gave Brave Heart some oats then a little water before grabbing a sack with dried jerky and cakes for herself. Finished eating, she grabbed her blankets then rolled into them. She was just dozing off when Brave Heart gave a loud snort and pawed the ground in warning. The warrior maid turned over then stared up into a pair of yellow eyes. Unexpectedly, she felt a rough wet tongue lick her face. She smiled in pleasure as she reached up and patted the silky soft fur. "Hello Bruno. I knew you would find me if you were around here... where's your girlfriend?"

Bruno looked behind him.

It wasn't until then that Raven saw the second pair of eyes.

The female turned and disappeared.

Giving Bruno a final pat, Raven waved her hand at him in dismissal. "That's okay boy, you don't have to go this time."

Turning back, Bruno gave Raven another sloppy kiss in goodbye before disappearing with the female wolf. She sighed dejectedly as she turned to go back to sleep wondering if she would ever see him again. Raven had raised him from a pup; he was half wolf and half dog, the only one that had survived out of the litter. They were inseparable, until he started wondering looking for a mate. She was glad he had found one.

Yawning, Raven fell asleep; she slept for two hours before jerking herself awake and broke camp. She saddled Brave Heart then turned back to make sure everything was back the way she had found it. Satisfied, she mounted and galloped away. It wasn't long before Bruno caught up then loped along beside her. She looked behind them and saw the female following. Grinning down at Bruno, she nodded in pleasure. "Okay boy, you can come along too."

Raven stopped twice to feed and water the animals then she was in the saddle again. Dawn was on the horizon when they reached the fourth campsite, she was getting worried now; the young woman could smell the snow coming. Unfortunately, they were all exhausted... sleep was a must at this point. It would still be another day until she reached her grandfather's, if she could keep up this pace. Maybe two if the snow slowed them to much, but it wouldn't help if she killed them before they could get there. She stopped reluctantly and fed the animals then curled up beside Bruno and fell asleep instantly.

Raven didn't wake up until snowflakes fell on her face. Instantly, she sat up and knew that she had slept too long. She hurriedly got up and broke camp as fast as she could... not taking the time to eat, she mounted. They were in a race for their lives now; the animals sensing the urgency broke into a gallop.

They maintained that speed until Raven felt it prudent to slow down, not wanting to hurt one of them in her haste. It was now a full blizzard, impossible to see two feet in front of them. She bent towards Bruno in urgency. "Find Grandfather, Bruno!"

Bruno trotted ahead, while Raven tied herself to the saddle; so exhausted now, she could barely keep her eyes from closing. The animals knew the way they would get them safely to the canyon without any help from her. They were still a day away at this speed, but she was chilled to the bone as the temperature dropped dramatically. She knew that if she didn't tie herself on, she could fall off then freeze to death.

Raven hunched under her wolf fur before dozing in the saddle for the rest of the day. Twice she almost fell off; thankfully, her bound hands saved her. She didn't wake up until Brave Heart stopped then Bruno started barking insistently at something. She tried to release herself, but the bonds had shrunk... they wouldn't budge and they were cutting painfully into her wrists.

Running out of the tepee, Giant Bear hurried over to help his granddaughter. He was a bit wary of the stud, but too worried about Raven to let that stop him.

Brave Heart shifted uneasily; luckily, he was too exhausted to fuss.

Barely able to speak, Raven managed to get a few words past her chattering teeth. "Bruno... find Spotted Owl and bring him."

Bruno lopped off with a little yelp.

Getting Raven's bonds severed, Giant Bear caught her as she fell from her horse... too exhausted and frozen to walk. The chief was lifting his granddaughter to bring her inside when Spotted Owl arrived with Bruno.

Giant Bear turned to the brave in concern. "Take Brave Heart to the corral, you are the only one that can touch him then bring the shaman here... quickly now!"

Spotted Owl nodded in confusion, wondering why the chief didn't want the medicine man instead. He shrugged and picked up Brave Heart's reins then talking to him soothingly in Cheyenne, he turned and trotted off. He stopped short in surprise when he saw their spiritual healer coming towards him.

The shaman motioned inquisitively. "How is she?"

Spotted Owl shook his head unknowingly. "It doesn't look good; the chief had to carry her in!"

The shaman inclined his head in thanks before hurrying to the tepee in concern. The spiritual healer rushed in and went straight over to his chief, without even looking at the white man huddled in the corner. All his attention was on Giant Bear as he lovingly pulled the hide off his granddaughter.

The white man sitting in the corner sat huddled in silence fearfully. He finally woke up today with his arm bound, and tied to his chest. The pain was excruciating; he knew by the feel that it was broken in more than one place. When the medicine man probed at his ribs, he thought that at least one of them might be cracked. His face was in horrible shape, since his nose was broken with both his lips swollen. Devon could feel some cuts in his mouth they were stinging something fierce, and there was a distinct metallic taste of blood when licking his lips. Both his eyes must be swollen because he needed to squint to see, they hurt like a bugger.

The medicine man tried to straighten his nose, Devon wasn't sure if the man had succeeded or not. All he knew was it had hurt like bloody hell. He had been given food, water, as well as medicine then told to stay. Why he was still alive, he didn't know. He asked about his sister's doggedly, but the medicine man didn't understand English. Although, he must have guessed at the question because he gave a sad shake of his head so the Englishman figured that both were dead.

Devon sat in this spot all day afraid to move or speak, remembering all the horror stories he heard about Indian torture; he wondered when they would get around to killing him. Sitting here quietly, he watched the chief secretively whenever he came into the tepee.

The chief was sitting beside the fire when a dog started barking; Devon stared in disbelief when the older man jumped up then rushed outside. The Englishman heard someone speak, but it was too low to understand or make out whether it was male or female. The white man was astonished when the chief came back into the tepee carrying what looked like a wolf, until he noticed the long legs dangling.

A moment later, a wolf did walk in. Devon jerked in shock, and groaned in pain as his ribs throbbed in protest at his movement.

The wolf looked over at the petrified white man curiously then went over to investigate. As the animal sniffed him, Devon sat still holding his breath in dread. The Englishman tried hard not to let the animal feel his panic. When Bruno was satisfied, he licked the man's hand before lying down beside him.

Devon released the breath he had been holding; he tentatively reached out to pet the animal with his left hand in wonder. The wolf let the Englishman touch him for a minute before getting up then went over to the chief to watch him.

Looking up in exasperation, Giant Bear spoke harshly in rebuke. The wolf whined plaintively and went back to the white man then laid down in a sulk, but continued to watch the chief.

Giant Bear saw Bruno slink over to the white man, and trustingly settled down beside him. He watched the Englishman tentatively reach out to stroke the animal's soft fur in awe. The chief nodded in satisfaction, when the terrified white man overcame his fear to pet the large wolf. The man had courage, maybe this crazy plan would work after all.

Turning to the shaman when he knelt beside him... Giant Bear motioned in question. "Are you sure your vision was correct? We don't know who this man is, are you positive he is the one we talked to my blood-brother about?"

The shaman sighed in exasperation as he gestured in reassurance. "Yes, I'm sure. In the first vision, I was told to find the owner of the neighbouring lands then bring him here to meet Raven. The Great Spirit didn't warn me that his sister and the guides would be killed! If I had known, I wouldn't have told you to ask Grey Wolf to find him. When we stumbled on the massacre and I meditated again, the vision changed. If she doesn't marry him now, all of us will die... including Raven. The vision told me that the man must become a white Indian, without knowledge of Raven's ranch. He must accept us before he can leave! Remember, at Raven's naming ceremony, the golden eagle had also been present, but so distant I had a hard time distinguishing what it was. At that time, I didn't understand why he was there. Now I know that those two were destined from birth to become one."

Musing over the shaman's words, Giant Bear continued to lift the wolf hide off his granddaughter. They still must have done something to cause this, but he couldn't figure out what. Even if it was true that the two were fated from birth for each other, something wasn't right. The Great Spirit wouldn't tell them to do this then change it.

Checking his chief's granddaughter over carefully, the shaman sighed before looked at Giant Bear. "She isn't hurt, so you don't need the medicine man; Raven's just exhausted from her ordeal."

Giant Bear nodded relieved, glad his granddaughter was okay then turned to the shaman. He waved irritably concerned that this was their fault. "How are we expected to make the two marry, you know Raven and the white man will fight this to the end! Not only that, but how am I to explain this to our people! I have forbidden the warriors to make war on the whites or take captives for twenty-seven years. We have changed completely, now over half of my people are part bloods or whites, what am I supposed to tell them?"

The shaman shrugged thoughtfully; their 'protector' had always been difficult. As for the others... secrecy was the key. "I know they will fight this! Just tell the white man, his life will only be spared if he marries your granddaughter. Tell Raven that she has to marry him to save us or he will go to the army. Don't tell her we arranged for this man to come here; she would be furious. As for the others, don't tell them a thing we must keep it a secret!"

Sighing in irritation, Giant Bear wasn't sure he liked this situation or if it would work. He turned, beckoning the white man to come forward impatiently... wanting to get this over with.

Before the white man got to them, the shaman covered Raven up again so he wouldn't be able to see her.

Devon got painfully to his feet then limped to the chief. Curious, he wondered what they would want him for. He sat facing them. He looked at the bundle of fur wondering if the person was dead.

Jerking his head upwards at an annoying snort, Devon hoped he hadn't offended the chief. He stared in shock when the man started talking in English, until now he figured nobody knew his language.

Scowling angrily at the stunned look in the white man's eyes... Giant Bear shook off his irritation. He pointed towards himself then the shaman before talking in English; afterwards, he translated the conversation into Cheyenne for the shaman's sake. "I am Chief Giant Bear and this is our shaman. What's your name? Why were you travelling on my land?"

The white man frowned surprised. He had been told he was on the late earl's property, which now belonged to his grandson Edward. He scowled puzzled then pointed to himself. "My name is Devon Rochester, I'm from England. I have property I come here to sell. I didn't know I was on your land; I was told, I was on Earl Summerset's property."

The conspirators looked at each other; Giant Bear nodded in apology at the satisfied, I told you so look on the shaman's face. The chief turned to Devon curiously. "Why would you come here to sell land?"

Devon shrugged bewildered by the questions the chief was asking, but answered anyway. "The property was bought on speculation years ago by my grandfather. The late Earl Summerset talked him into buying it. My father inherited it, but there were stipulations attached. One was that he couldn't sell it, only give it to his second son... which happens to be me. I could sell it if I wished, but I had to come here first then live for one year on the property. Only after my time is up, could I sell it. A man named Jed Brown got in touch with me last year wanting to buy my land. When I told him about having to live here, the man said he could wait. When my year is done, he will come to discuss the sale of my property."

Giant Bear nodded musingly pretending he didn't know that. Listening to the Englishman talk, a solution to his dilemma triggered a sigh of relief. He motioned calmly towards Devon. "We now know you had no bad intentions when you came to this land. Even though it wasn't our band that killed your people they were still Cheyenne, so we will give you a life for a life."

Scowling in disbelief, Devon's fear vanished as a feeling of rage took its place... he waved incredulously. "What do you mean not your band? You are the only Indians I have seen since I came to this godforsaken land. It was you who killed my family, and it's you who will be punished when I leave!"

Sighing in disagreement, Giant Bear shook his head grimly, he pointed decisively at Devon. "No, it's you who doesn't understand! I didn't say you could leave. I said you will get a life. You must marry my granddaughter."

Jerking back as if slapped, Devon thundered in shock without thinking of the consequences. "Marry a murdering Indian Squaw... I would rather die!"

Jumping up with a roar of rage, Giant Bear reached across the bundle for the Englishman's throat.

The wolf sensing the anger in the air jumped between the men; protectively covering the bundle of fur in warning, Bruno growled.

Devon fell back in surprise when the wolf sprang between him and the chief. The Englishman lay on the ground groaning in pain; he held his side as his tortured ribs throbbed in protest at the movement.

The bundle of fur whimpered plaintively then thrashed about; Raven didn't wake up though, still too weak from her ordeal.

Giant Bear dropped back down beside the wolf fur before lifting it. He bent then spoke in a soothing whisper; until his granddaughter stopped thrashing around. He put the hide down... calm again. He turned to the shaman grimly. "I don't think this is going to work at all, did you see the look of disgust on his face at the idea of marrying an Indian?"

The shaman reached out and patted the hand Giant Bear still had resting on the wolf fur. "We both knew it wasn't going to be easy; you are aware that he would be as prejudiced as any other ve'ho'e. That is why he is to become a white Indian before he can leave here. The vision stressed that he must marry your granddaughter to save us!"

Nodding in resignation, Giant Bear turned towards Raven's wolf-dog. He spoke reassuringly to the animal. "Bruno it's okay, lay down!"

Bruno looked at both men intently, wanting to protect his mistress. Sensing the danger past, he went then settled back down. He didn't go far, still cautious... he watched them closely.

Once the wolf left, Devon slowly sat back up painfully and watched the chief warily. Not sure what would happen to him now; he wondered if his careless words had just signed his death warrant.

Giant Bear faced the Englishman again, but this time a hint of menace entered his voice as he motioned decisively with determination. "Listen to me Devon, you have two choices! You can be given to the squaws as you put it to be tortured to death; or you can get adopted by the shaman then married to my granddaughter. Either way... you will not leave here!"

Devon opened his mouth to speak angrily, but snapped it shut again when the chief lifted his hand for silence.

Continuing as if there was no attempt at interrupting him, Giant Bear frowned. "Don't get me wrong, marrying my granddaughter won't be easy. Normally, in our culture women are submissive... she is different! There's been rare occasions in our history when a woman becomes a shaman or healer. My granddaughter is unique because she's a warrior, our first one in history. You will have to prove you are worthy of her, my warriors will be watching you. My granddaughter will fight to avoid this marriage, but here my word is law; she will marry you when I insist."

Staring hard at Giant Bear stunned, Devon saw anger, plus a steely resolve painted on the man's face. The Englishman sighed dejectedly in frustration. He looked down at the bundle thinking fast, not wanting to offend the chief again; he would probably kill him next time. Why would he be trying to get rid of his granddaughter? Maybe, it was because she was a warrior making her grotesquely muscled; there had to be something wrong with her!

Grimacing in resignation, Devon looked at Giant Bear hopefully. "You don't leave me much choice, but I would like to think about it."

Looking at the shaman inquisitively, Giant Bear translated and saw him nod in agreement. He turned to Devon then inclined his head in consent... he got up. "We will leave you to think about it; you have one night to resign yourself to marrying my granddaughter. Néxahe, which means my grandchild... is sleeping, but she will wake soon. I will be back with food for the both of you."

Watching in amazement, Devon was speechless as the two men left without another word. He looked down, wondering why the chief would trust him not to hurt his granddaughter while he was gone. The Englishman looked fugitively to the side at the dozing wolf, remembering how fast the animal had jumped between them. He knew the wolf would kill him if he tried it.

Tentatively, Devon lifted his hand to move the wolf skin aside so he could see the woman he might have to marry to save his hide. When it fell away from her face, he sucked in his breath in shock... she was beautiful; midnight black braided hair framed an oval face that was perfect, not a blemish or even a spot marked her skin. Her cheekbones were high with a complexion that was a dusky brown, but not as dark as her grandfather's. The Englishman hand reached out to remove the rest of the fur, but stopped suddenly.

The woman's green eyes sprang open in bewilderment.

Devon stared down at the lightest green eyes he had ever seen. Apparently, she wasn't a full-blooded Indian.

*****

Raven woke slowly to the feel of someone watching her intently. When she managed to open her eyes fully, it took her a moment to focus on the strange ve'ho'e sitting in front of her. She gasped in stunned shock then panic before rolling away out of reaching distance. Pulling her knife out of her moccasin instinctively... without thought; she squatted with her blade held out threateningly. The three-quarters Cheyenne warrior maid was ready to defend herself as she waited for the white man to make the first move.

Bruno sensing his mistress's alarm woke quickly. Instantly he crouched, readying himself to jump at the horrified confused white man before growling menacingly at him in warning.

Toppling backwards again in alarm; this time Devon lost consciousness from the excruciating pain.

CHAPTER THREE

Raven, crouched in confusion; ready to defend herself should the white man attack, watched in disbelief as the stranger fell backwards and passed out.

In confusion, Raven looked around at the familiar tepee and wondered how she got there. Then it came back to her; the visit from her cousin telling her to hurry and her wild ride through a blizzard.

Bruno quieted when he realized Raven was no longer in danger. He walked over and whined at his mistress before going over to sniff curiously at the white man.

Giant Bear walked in with two bowls of the stew then stopped short at the scene inside. Raven was squatting there with a knife drawn, and the ve'ho'e was lying on the ground out cold.

Putting the bowls down by the fire swiftly, Giant Bear rushed over to Devon. He looked at his granddaughter in reproach as he passed her before bending to check on the Englishman. "What have you done to him? I swear if you caused his death after it took us so long to heal him, I will kill you myself!"

Scowling perturbed, Raven quickly sheathed her knife; she stood up then grabbed her fur off the ground before draping it over the white man to keep him warm. She sat down across from her grandfather with the vi'hoi in between them.

Looking down, Raven studied the white man curiously. She had never seen him before, nor was he from town.

Telling her grandfather what happened to make the Englishman pass out; Raven spoke in English automatically, since Giant Bear liked to practice with her from time to time. When she finished her explanation, she looked up and opened her mouth to ask her grandfather about the white man then snapped it shut in surprise.

Quickly, Giant Bear raised his hand for silence when she looked up at him. "Raven, I don't want you to speak in English for now. I don't want the ve'ho'e to know yet that you can."

Nodding in confusion, Raven switched to Cheyenne. "Okay, Nam-shimi', but I would like to know why? I would also like to know what's going on around here! Who is this man?"

Sighing, Giant Bear motioned in dread not looking forward to that discussion; thankfully, he was able to put it off longer. "I will speak to you privately about what happened later. As for his name, its Devon Rochester... he's from England."

Frowning in surprise, stunned; Raven broke in incredulously. "Lord Devon Rochester who owns the neighboring thousand acres that I want to buy... do you know why he's here?"

Grimacing in annoyance, Giant Bear hadn't realized that Raven knew the white man's name. He just hoped she didn't know about the conditions of the will that Devon's grandfather left. Or found out that it was because of him that Englishman was here in the first place. Everett had gotten a hold of Earl Rochester before he died because he wanted to buy his land... that's how the chief found out about it. But at that time, Devon was too young to come here. When the shaman told him about a vision that he had of Raven and the neighbor getting married; Giant Bear suggested getting in touch with his friend Jed Brown then he could arrange it so Devon would come out here right away.

Giant Bear stared through his granddaughter distantly, thinking quickly. He finally noticed that she was scowling in annoyance at him, wondering why it was taking him so long to respond. He quickly cleared his throat then shrugged; he avoided Raven's glance by looking down at Devon. "No, I don't know why he came here! I haven't asked him yet, since he only just woke up today and found out his sister is dead. So, I left him alone to grieve."

Nodding in approval, Raven frowned at her grandfather in confusion when he continued insistently.

Looking at Raven for a quick second, Giant Bear sternly gave her an ominous warning; before he looked down at the Englishman again... hiding his guilty look. "I also don't want you to ask him either, not for a while anyway. He needs time to heal and get over his sister's death."

Raven thought it over, wondering what her grandfather was up too. It wasn't like him to avoid her glance. She sighed thoughtfully then inclined her head, knowing he would tell her eventually; they were too close to keep secrets for long.

Giant Bear reached over and grabbed one of the bowls of stew before handing it to Raven. "Here eat this; it will warm up your insides. You gave us quite a scare."

Taking the bowl, Raven smiled in thanks... half starved. "I'm sorry I scared you, Nam'-shimi; I was exhausted more than hurt. I had to go all the way home first, since I was with the black stud. While I was there, Edward told me about the storm. That's why I was prepared in the first place. Then I had to go warn the men."

Giant Bear motioned inquisitively. "How's Dream Dancer?"

Looking down at the white man with a pensive frown, Raven studied him curiously as she ate. She didn't hear her grandfather's question as she stared down at Devon wondering what he would look like once his face healed. It was rugged, with what looked like some laugh lines around his eyes; it was hard to tell with both of them so swollen and black. He had a hawkish nose that was broken. It was almost but not quite straight again, with a lump in the middle that probably would never go away. His lips looked full. Yet again, it was difficult to tell because they were swollen plus badly cracked.

Reaching out, Raven touched Devon's hair curiously but it was greasy and it looked like he had a lot of dirt or soot mixed in. If she had to guess, she would say it was probably a light brown or possibly blonde. He looked vaguely familiar. She wondered if his grandfather's portrait was somewhere at the ranch... he had been a friend of her English nam'-shimi.

Nodding to herself, Raven remembered one in the library with both men standing together. That would make him an earl, or the next one if his father wasn't dead. It disturbed the young woman deeply. He could go to the army and insist that her family were the ones that attacked his wagons. She wouldn't be able to do anything about it; they would take his word over hers, even though she was an earl's daughter because in their eyes she was an Indian. Three quarters, but it didn't matter to them.

How could Raven stop this man from going to the army and demanding justice? The only way was to keep him here; but keeping him captive, wasn't the answer either. Eventually, they would have to let him go... or he would try to escape. If he succeeded, it would only make things worse for them.

If Giant Bear could hear his granddaughter's thoughts right now; he would be ecstatic because he had the solution all planned out.

Raven scooped up the last of the stew still staring the ve'ho'e. She looked at her grandfather inquisitively as he cleared his throat to get her attention.

Giant Bear gestured to the north side of the village. "Go to your tepee and sleep for a while. I will come tomorrow to discuss what happened when we found the white man."

Nodding without argument, Raven got up slowly... exhausted. She looked down wondering if she should take her fur.

Grinning up at Raven, Giant Bear waved permission... guessing at her thoughts. "Take it; I have lots here."

Inclining her head wearily, Raven took the fur before whistling to Bruno. "Come on boy, let's go."

Devon woke to see Giant Bear putting an extra fur on his bed... the whistle had disturbed him. He looked around wondering where that she-devil had gone, but was relieved when he couldn't find her or the wolf.

Walking over, Giant Bear sat across from the Englishman.

Painfully, Devon sat up; still looking around suspiciously, waiting for the she-devil to jump out at him again.

Smiling in reassurance, Giant Bear waved towards the entrance. "She's gone if you are looking for my granddaughter. I sent her to her own tepee to get some much-needed sleep. I'm sorry she scared you so badly, but you frightened her just as much. You shouldn't have lifted the wolf fur to look at her."

Shaking his head in horror, Devon gestured angrily. "That's the woman you want to marry me too... she tried to kill me. No wonder you want to get rid of her. I can see why you have to give her away; nobody would want a she-devil as a wife!"

Pausing for breath, Devon geared up to continue berating the chief... he stopped in astonishment; staring incredulously at Giant Bear as he roared with laughter. The Englishman watched in puzzlement as the older man tried to stop laughing, but he was having quite a hard time of it.

Getting himself under control, Giant Bear wiped tears away. When he looked into the younger man's disbelieving eyes, the chief sighed before motioning in explanation. "Devon, try to think of it this way; my granddaughter arrives at my tepee half dead from the cold and unconscious. As she is waking up, she expects to see another Indian or me. Instead, she wakes then sees a ve'ho'e, which means white man in English. Who just so happens to look like death since your eyes are black, your nose is twice its size and crooked, plus your lips are badly swollen, and you are as white as a ghost from fear... as well as pain. If you are honest, you will realize that her reaction is no different from what yours would be under the same circumstances. If I remember correctly when you first woke and saw us, if you had a knife, you would have done the same. Just because she's a woman, doesn't mean she has no right to protect herself when she feels threatened."

Giant Bear watched the amazement leave Devon's eyes to be replaced by a pensive look as he mulled over what the older man had said. The chief smiled pleased then nodded in satisfaction as he realized that the Englishman wasn't averse to new ways of looking at things. He let Devon think about it for a few minutes before handing him the still warm stew.

Devon looked at it suspiciously. He sniffed it cautiously before tentatively taking a small amount of meat and tasting it. Surprise showed on Devon's face at the tangy taste of the beef stew. He wondered where the beef came from. It didn't matter where really; he was so hungry that he shrugged off his suspicions then hastily ate every bit of it.

Grinning in approval, Giant Bear watched Devon devour every morsel. He chuckled, remembering the Englishman's account of his first experience with Raven. The chief wondered if telling the Englishman that half the men here, at the ranch, and in town were in love with Raven would help. No, even better, he would keep quiet and let the man find that out for himself. He waited until Devon finished off the stew then cleared his throat and pointed behind him. "I put extra furs on your bed; because of the storm it's going to be cold night."

Nodding his thanks; Devon put the bowl down and stared intently at Giant Bear. He wondered if he dared to ask the chief questions or if that would just get him into trouble.

Seeing the uncertainty on Devon's face; Giant Bear waited patiently for him to overcome his fear enough to ask the questions that the chief knew the Englishman needed... as well as wanted to know. However, the first question he asked shocked the old man completely.

The startled look on Giant Bear's face almost caused Devon to change his mind; he pushed his fear away then asked curiously once again, when the chief didn't answer him right away. The perfect English, as well as the laughter earlier had him immensely curious. From all that he had heard about Indians since he got here, the chief was definitely not how he had pictured them being. "How did you learn to speak such good English?"

Grinning in delight at the question, Giant Bear decided to answer honestly except for names. His face sobered sadly, as he remembered the death of his first wife. "A white man taught me... a long time ago. I won't bore you with all the details. I will tell you though, about the three white men that killed my first wife. They were going around raping and killing any woman or child in their path. No matter what colour of skin they had. They were known as the Shadow Killers of Montana. I had taken my family from our tribe to go on a special hunt. When I got back to the camp that we set up, my wife was dead; they killed her after they finished raping her. My sister had also been raped but wasn't dead. Fortunately for me, my wife hid my daughter before the killers got to them. After telling me what happened, my sister took her life before I could stop her since she couldn't stand the shame. I went back to my tribe and took ten braves with me to hunt the men responsible."

Giant Bear paused for a moment trying to decide whether he should go on. Devon had listened the whole time; the expressions on his face went from outrage at the killings to shame at what the white men were capable of doing. The chief frowned thoughtfully, wondering if he should tell him about Mary... or if he should leave that out.

Quickly, Giant Bear made a decision to take a chance that Devon would understand then forgive him for his mistakes. Besides, if he wanted the Englishman as his grandson by marriage to accept him, he had better be as honest as he possibly could. Even when it showed him in a bad light. He took a resigned breath, and his face became expressionless. "Two weeks later we came across three white men camped with a white woman. She was separate from the men crying. We didn't ask questions; we just went in then killed all three men. The white woman screamed hysterically and ran into the trees... I went after her in concern. I didn't know many English words at that time, but I did understand some. After I had calmed her down, I was able to convince her that I wasn't going to hurt her. It was then that I found out we had made a mistake. The white woman hadn't been crying because those men hurt her or were even going too. She was crying because her brother had forced her to marry someone she didn't know. Her new husband made her leave everything and everyone behind without being able to say goodbye."

Giant Bear sighed in sorrow for killing innocent men... even if they were white. He stared intently at Devon watching for his reaction; his face was incredibly expressive. At first, there was outrage then disgust for what Giant Bear had done. However, much to the chief's surprise the Englishman's expression turned to sorrow and acceptance that although Giant Bear was a chief of his people, he wasn't infallible to mistakes.

Devon looked at Giant Bear in understanding... he waved consolingly. "I can't condemn you for that. At first, I was going to; but after I thought about it, I realized that if it was me. I might have made the same mistake. I would like to know what happened to the woman, and I don't understand where this man who taught you English comes in?"

Getting over his astonishment; Giant Bear was pleased that Devon was sensitive and intelligent enough, to see both sides. He also realized that although the younger man had blown up at the idea of marrying an Indian woman, the Englishman wasn't as intolerant as he had at first thought. If he were prejudiced beyond redemption, Devon wouldn't have understood at all. The Englishman would have just condemned the chief for killing white people regardless of the reason.

Smiling in delight, Giant Bear thought of his second wife then his expression sobered. "Well, I couldn't leave the woman wandering around by herself with nowhere to go, so I brought her to my tribe. I planned on finding a way to send her back to her brother. Even though we couldn't communicate all that well... we did manage and fell in love in the process. We were married a month later, in that time I learned to speak English better but not by much. We spent a month together; unfortunately, I knew I would have to leave again. I had to avenge my first wife and sister before I could have a good marriage with my second wife. I didn't want to make the same mistake that I had made when I took my warriors with me last time, so I decided to go alone. Besides, the men that I was chasing had two months to get to wherever they were going, which probably included a few towns. I certainly couldn't take my dog soldier's there, or the army would come looking for us without asking any questions. So, I gave my daughter to my second wife to look after then left the shaman in charge until I returned. Before I left, I had a vision that I was to look for a cabin there I would find a man that would help me. Without his help I would never reach the killers. Without him, I got shown that I would die within a year."

Pausing needing a break to gather his thoughts, Giant Bear got up then went and got his pipe. He filled it with tobacco before sitting then lit it. He offered it to Devon first, but the Englishman shook his head in refusal. Shrugging, the chief took another puff and continued his story as if he hadn't stopped at all. "As the killers travelled across the country, they hit every cabin or small community that they could find. They were killing every woman or child that they found alone, plus some that weren't. Of course, that wasn't too many since Montana at that time was only thinly populated with not many women around. But it was still enough to make you sick. For three months, I followed those men trying to catch them or find the cabin in my vision. I had almost caught them when I found the place I was looking for. It looked deserted, so I waited hoping to use it since the weather had turned ugly... we were in for quite a severe lightning storm. I was about to go to the cabin when a man on a horse leading a string of mules behind him showed up then disappeared inside. I waited for a bit and finally decided that I should introduce myself as the storm worsened. Suddenly, the door flew open. He came out and marched over to a huge tree with a shovel then started digging a hole. Leaving again, he came out with a white bundle next. He carried it over to the freshly dug grave. I hid in the trees and patiently waited; I didn't want to intrude on his grief. I knew who this man was. Not personally, you understand, I had heard of him though. He was the white man that the Indians called Grey Wolf, I had the feeling that the bundle he was carrying over to the grave was a woman, a child, or maybe even both. When the man finished filling in the grave, he bellowed out some loud words in rage. I didn't understand what he was saying. Sadly, I realized though that the three men I was chasing must have found this cabin too. I waited until his words were spoken before stepping out. The Blackfoot had named him after the immense grey timber wolves because he was just as silent and deadly as the wolves when he was hunting. It didn't matter either if you meant an animal or a human. Thankfully, Grey Wolf teamed up with me to pursue the killers after I told him about my sorrow. On our journey, he taught me your tongue and customs. I'm not going to tell you the whole story because it is a long one. I will finish it by telling you that it took us nine years to track down those men. We finally did catch them though then they paid for the death of our wives with their lives."

Devon shook his head in disbelief, he gestured curiously. "Why did it take you so long to find them; you said that when you met this Grey Wolf you were catching up to them... what happened?"

Giant Bear was extremely pleased that Devon was so interested in his story that he wanted to know more. He sighed irritably and looked sad, trying to explain further without getting into the whole story. "We don't know why it was taking so long, after we left the cabin; the men just disappeared suddenly... without a trace. We searched for a long time, but we couldn't find them anywhere. Once they started killing again, we continued the pursuit. They did this more times than I care to remember. Sometimes, the killers would be behind us when they surfaced, at other times they were ahead of us. When that happened, we would lose them altogether for a short time, usually a week or two; sometimes they would disappear for a month or more. Twice for over a year, there didn't seem to be any pattern or reason for what they were doing. We knew that in the end, they were going to Dakota. Unfortunately, we didn't know whether it was South or North Dakota. All we knew was that they were looking for a woman who had killed two of their brothers. We had no idea who she was or where she lived. All we could do was keep tracking them hoping they messed up somehow, so we could get them or that the law would catch them and do the job for us. Sadly, it took us nine years before we could put an end to all the killings."

Shaking his head in amazement, Devon waved inquisitively. "Didn't you or Grey Wolf ever think about giving up?"

Looking at Devon solemnly, Giant Bear pointed at him intrigued... wondering if he was wrong about this Englishman. No, he was sure he wasn't mistaken about the man's character; he had to ask to be sure though. "Would you have quit if it had been your wife and sister?"

Opening his mouth to say that he would have; Devon snapped it shut again grimly. He looked the chief in the eye deadly serious. "No, I guess I would have done the same thing as you two did."

Hiding a smirk of satisfaction, Giant Bear knew he was right about Devon. The Great Spirit would never match Raven with a weak minded, snivelling, coward. The chief was sure of that.

Taking a deep breath, Devon hardened his courage to ask his next question; wondering if the chief would be as open for this one. "I want to know why you attacked us then killed everyone, but left me alive!"

Shaking his head in denial, Giant Bear sat forward intently; waving seriously, he tried to convey his heartfelt sincerity to his future grandson. Anyone else he wouldn't have cared whether they believed him or not, but this man one day soon would be Raven's husband; which meant he would spend a lot of time here. "We didn't kill your people, I assure you. It was a different Cheyenne tribe that did it."

Scowling, Devon stared angrily in disbelief at Giant Bear before gesturing decisively. "I don't believe you, why would they do such a thing? No! I know it was your tribe and sooner or later I will escape then you will regret it!"

Hiding a frown, Giant Bear shook his head at the furious Englishman. Settling back, the chief tapped out the tobacco against a rock; in a way he felt responsible since he had sent for him. "I'm sorry, you won't be leaving and you will marry my granddaughter."

Carefully, Devon got up... holding his ribs in obvious pain. "I promise that you will all pay for what you have done! I have a lot of influence in England; I will make sure that the army hunts you down! As for that story about those white men, I think you just made it up so that I would feel sorry for you. It would make it easier to convince me that you didn't kill my family, but you haven't fooled me. I have also decided that you are bluffing about marrying your granddaughter, so I'm going to decline your offer of marriage to her!"

Giant Bear stood up instantly in rage then took a menacing step forward; he jabbed a finger towards Devon to get his point across. "You have not been listening to me! When I said you had no choice in marrying my granddaughter, I meant every word! YOU WILL MARRY HER... or you will DIE! As for not believing me about how I learned to speak English, I don't care whether you believe me or not. Now though, since you choose to be so obstinate, you will be confined to this tepee unless one of us is with you. You had better hope that I can find a way to prove that we didn't do it! Or you will NEVER leave here, do I make myself clear!"

When Giant Bear had taken that menacing step toward him... Devon stepped back hastily in anxiety. This was the first time since he woke that the Englishman felt real fear. Even after he insulted the chief's granddaughter, the white man hadn't felt any actual threat to his life. He had no illusions that the older man meant every word that he said.

Devon knew that eventually he would give in because he didn't want to die, he wanted revenge! Suddenly, an idea came to him and he frowned thoughtfully. "Giant Bear earlier you said that I was to marry your granddaughter as payment for a life. Does it mean that after we are married, I can decide I want my revenge by taking her life... is it my, right; or will I have the whole village in arms against me?"

Flabbergasted for a moment, Giant Bear was surprised by that question. He was amazed that Devon was smart enough to figure out that a life for a life meant just that. Once the two were married, he could kill her if he wished. Or even tell her in front of a crowd that she had to kill herself... honour would require that she do so. The chief was sure the Englishman didn't know about the last part. He definitely wasn't going to tell him; this was not what they had in mind. The shaman waved away his chief's concern when he had mentioned it; figuring Devon would not find out about that custom until after he fell in love with Raven.

Eyeing Devon searchingly, Giant Bear tried to decide if he needed to lie or if he should chance that the Englishman was too soft hearted to kill a woman. Then he thought of Raven, his beautiful... headstrong granddaughter. He was so proud of her managing a large ranch all by herself, plus still found the time to spend part of each year with them.

Every year Raven won the archery contests, knife throwing, and horseback riding tests; the only ones she had problems with was tomahawk throwing and long-distance running; his grandson Running Wolf always won them. The chief smirked in smug gratification then stared at the white man calmly.

Devon saw the smug look cross Giant Bear's face for a fleeting moment before it was gone. The wily old chief regarded him gravely; the Englishman knew he was up to something, but had no idea what it was.

Giant Bear stared at the white man for another couple minutes, watching the Englishman's eyes narrow in suspicion... in amusement. He cleared his throat so he wouldn't laugh aloud then motioned calmly. "Well Devon, I must say you catch on quick; I would never have thought that you were ruthless enough to kill a woman. But you are correct in our culture a life exchanged for a life means that you can kill for revenge and not pay for it. But you can't kill my granddaughter until after you are married then you must convince her you are allowed to do so. I think you might have a problem with that!"

Grimacing in annoyance, Devon realized the chief was right. He distinctly remembered Giant Bear's granddaughter jumping out of that fur with a knife in her hand... ready to kill him if he threatened her. He had full confidence in himself though, the Englishman was no weakling. He had boxed, as well as fenced most of his young life. However, there was the other problem. Sure, he had shot a couple of men before in fair duels but never a female. He could also remember just how beautiful that woman looked before she woke up; he was exasperated when his mental picture of her caused a surge of unwanted desire.

Hardening his heart to the image... Devon banished it from his sight. He sighed in relief when he remembered that although he had to marry the woman here; in England the union wouldn't be binding. So, when he escaped from this place, he would still be available to marry someone from home. Sighing, thankful he wouldn't have to kill her after all!

Smiling, Giant Bear watched the conflicting emotions flirt across Devon's face. He could see that the Englishman was trying to figure out how to get out of this wedding without having to kill Raven. The chief also knew by his expression that he thought he wouldn't have to honour the marriage, but the old man had a surprise for the white man... even his granddaughter would be shocked when she found out.

Looking at Giant Bear, his mind made up... Devon nodded decisively before waving irritably. "I will marry your granddaughter, but of course you knew that I would give in if I want to live. I still haven't decided whether I will kill her after the marriage or if I will make her life a living hell. So, when do you want us to get married?"

Turning aside, Giant Bear didn't want Devon to see the smug look of satisfaction on his face as the Englishman gave himself an out... not wanting to kill the beautiful Raven. The chief succeeded in hiding his amusement then wiped all expression off his face as he turned back to the white man. "You will be married a month after your side and arm heal; the medicine man says your ribs should be better in two to three weeks. In that time, you will learn our language and all our customs. After your arm heals which should be in about three weeks or so after your ribs, you will be trained as a warrior."

Dumbfounded, Devon's stare was genuinely confused as he gestured incredulously. "You want to train me as a warrior, even though I might kill your granddaughter... why?"

Giant Bear eyed Devon pensively, wondering how much he should tell him. He shrugged before deciding it wouldn't hurt to explain it to him. "Well, there are a few reasons... I will tell you a couple of them. First, as I told you earlier my granddaughter is a warrior. So, for you to be happy with her you must match or at least come close to her skills; otherwise, you will never come to terms with your new life. The second reason, which is the most important one for you; even though you don't believe me, is that we will be going after the Cheyenne that killed your family. I know you will want to be there for that!"

Devon tried to interrupt the chief angrily.

Holding up his hand for silence, Giant Bear knew the Englishman was going to argue that point.

Shutting his mouth with a 'snap', Devon fumed in silence.

Grinning at Devon's sulk, Giant Bear motioned knowingly. "I know you don't believe me right now, and it doesn't matter if you do or not. But this is how it is going to be, my wife will be here in the morning to start your lessons. Then my grandson, Running Wolf, will take over training you once you're healed enough. Oh, one other thing, you will have dealings with my granddaughter. She wasn't here when we found you, so she doesn't know anything about it. Until I permit you to speak of it, I don't want you to tell her anything. Except about the actual attack, not why you came here or about our talks. If I find out you told her anything... I WILL, slice out your tongue; you don't need it to marry her! If she asks for details use your grieving as an excuse for not talking about it, am I understood?"

Nodding, Devon shrugged off his confusion at the chief's insistence; it didn't matter to him before waving curious. "Do they speak English?"

Giant Bear inclined his head yes; his first plan had been to lie then say Raven couldn't, so the Englishman would have to teach her to draw them closer. He knew though that she wouldn't agree to it. It was better to let them talked, as long as Devon remembered to keep his mouth shut. Of course, the chief would never cut out his tongue. As long as the white man believed that he was that ruthless though... it served its purpose. "Yes, my wife is white so speaks English. She is another one I don't want you to talk to about why you came here or about our conversations. My granddaughter speaks your language too. Running Wolf can speak when he wishes, but refuses to lower himself by talking in the white man's tongue. He won't even teach you until you have learnt our language."

Scowling confused by it all, Devon didn't care one way or the other... he just wanted to get out of here. The Englishman nodded before clearing his throat curiously. "Giant Bear can I ask what your granddaughter's name is. In all our conversations about her, you have never told me."

Frowning thoughtfully for a moment... thinking back; Giant Bear finally gestured in apology as he grinned sheepishly. "You are right, I'm sorry, my granddaughter's name is Raven. I might as well tell you my wife's name as well; her English name is Mary and her Cheyenne name is Golden Dove."

Silent for a time; Devon tried out Raven's name with his first mental image of her jumping out of that fur with a knife drawn, ready to attack him... it suited her.

Giant Bear pointed to Devon's sleeping pallet. "You will sleep there until you are married. I arranged for my wife to stay with Raven tonight. Go to bed now; you have enough to think about, we will talk more tomorrow."

Devon turned then went to his bed, obediently. As he was drifting off to sleep; unwillingly, an image of Raven was his last thought.

*****

Leaving her grandfather's, Raven draped her fur over her shoulders making sure to cover her lower face as she braved the pelting sleet and snow. Even though it was freezing out; the first thing she did was go to the corral to check on Brave Heart. He nickered a greeting when he saw his mistress then walked over for a scratch.

Materializing beside Raven; Spotted Owl pointed at the stallion as he leaned close in order to be heard above the wind. "I wiped him down before checking his legs. He is fine, no damage from the storm."

Inclining her head in thanks, Raven turned to Spotted Owl curiously. "Have you met the ve'ho'e yet?"

Spotted Owl shook his head negatively. "No, I only saw him from a distance. They beat him up pretty bad, the chief wasn't sure he would make it at first."

Nodding in disappointment, Raven turned to leave.

Touching Raven's arm to get her attention; Spotted Owl continued when she turned to him inquisitively. "Your grandmother is in your tepee waiting for you. She asked me to come and find you then tell you that after you are finished checking on your horse, she would have stew waiting for you."

Raven smiled before chuckling at the image of her formidable grandmother that popped into her head. "Thanks, Spotted Owl. Please give Brave Heart extra oats and put a warm fur on him for me... I better go see her right away."

Releasing Raven's arm, Spotted Owl left.

Turning, Raven pushing against the wind trudged towards her tepee. Just before she entered, Bruno gave a yip to say goodbye to his mistress. Now that she was safe, he could go. She squatted to pat the wolf in farewell. "Okay Bruno you can go back to your girlfriend; thanks for leaving her to help me."

Bruno licked Raven's face, turning he left.

Watching him go, Raven sighed. She turned away and entered her tepee. She was immediately enveloped in a hug; laughing Raven squeezed her grandmother back.

Mary or Golden Dove as she was known here, held Raven at arm's length. She looked her up then down making sure her granddaughter had suffered no damage. Mary waved for her to come and sit.

Raven laid her fur on the ground then sat on it obediently before accepting a bowl of food gratefully; she didn't dare refuse even though she had already eaten. The younger woman watched as her grandmother moved about cleaning up the tepee. She knew better than to say anything until after she finished all the stew in her bowl, Golden Dove wouldn't respond until she ate every bite. Her grandmother hadn't changed since Giant Bear brought her home twenty-seven years ago. Her hair was still a golden blonde, without even a hint of grey anywhere. Of course, she wasn't Raven's real grandmother. Her nisgii had been Giant Bear's first wife.

However, Golden Dove was the only grandmother Raven knew; she didn't love her any less then she would have her other nisgii. Finishing her stew, she sighed in pleasure as the warmth of the fire and food warmed her insides.

Watching her grandma for a few more minutes, Raven couldn't help commenting. "Nisgii, you look beautiful. Actually, every time I see you, I think you get even better looking."

Turning to her granddaughter at that remark, Golden Dove blushed in pleasure. "Well thank you, Raven; that is such a lovely compliment."

Nodding thoughtfully, Raven sighed sadly before motioning in apology. "After almost freezing to death today, I realized that I have never told you how much I love and admire you."

Golden Dove sat down beside Raven then took her hand in hers in concern. "We were all worried about you, the storm hit so suddenly; thankfully you are here now that's all that counts. How is your brother doing, by the way? He hasn't been out to see us this year... we miss him?"

Smiling at her grandmother's abrupt change of topics, Raven impulsively hugged Golden Dove then sat back to regard her lovingly. "Dream Dancer is fine; he's just busy getting ready to leave for England, he hasn't had time to visit. I will make sure he comes to see you before he leaves... I promise."

Grinning in delight at the thought of her rambunctious grandson, Golden Dove changed the subject. "I fixed your bed up then put furs on it. I hope you don't mind if I stay here. I got banished from my tepee until tomorrow."

Raven was extremely surprised by this; ever since Giant Bear brought Golden Dove and their son home. He hadn't let his wife out of his sight for more than a few hours. After all these years, he still took her everywhere.

Seeing the shocked look on Ravens face, Golden Dove shrugged her shoulders... as perplexed as her granddaughter. "I was just as amazed as you are; he's definitely up to something. The shaman and your grandfather had their heads together since we found the white man alive. Actually, that's not entirely true; the two of them have been scheming something for the last two years. But every time I try to find out what they are up to, they say that it's nothing for me to worry about."

Pondering her grandmother's words for a moment; Raven waved incredulously. "You don't think that whatever they are up to has anything to do with that man... do you?"

Golden Dove thought about it for a moment; finally, she shook her head negatively. "No, it's highly unlikely. We have never seen that white man before we stumbled across the massacre. Giant Bear and the shaman were just as shocked as the rest of us were. Although, they seemed more upset about it than anybody else was. Both of them did have a great deal of relief on their faces when we found the Englishman alive. They decided to come back here after the shaman had his vision. I don't know, maybe it just made whatever they were up to impossible now... that's why they were so upset."

Frowning, Raven sighed before motioning curiously. "Yeah, you're probably right. What did they do with all the bodies?"

Not so sure that was all there was to it; Golden Dove let the matter drop. "We brought them with us for a decent burial. Giant Bear figured the white man would want it that way. We also cleaned up everything so nobody would suspect anything. We brought all the evidence with us so you could look at it before deciding what to do next. Slippery as an Eel was among the dead, so was Squatting Dog."

Sighing thoughtfully, Raven inclined her head in approval. "That's good I will look tomorrow. Slippery as an Eel is with the Eagles tribe. Squatting Dog is with the Badger tribe. I wonder if they have banded together, or if it is just a coincidence. Squatting Dog might have left his own band to join the Eagles. I will have to find out for sure one way or the other."

Golden Dove nodded then shook a finger at Raven in warning. "Not tonight, go to bed; by morning the storm will have past and you should be recovered."

Raven grumbled good-naturedly under her breath before going towards her bed obediently. She stopped and turned back inquisitively. "Is my saddlebag here, nisgii?"

Inclining her head, Golden Dove pointed. "Yes dear, it's there."

Grinning in relief, Raven didn't want to lose that gift; she climbed into her furs. Her last thought was of the white man.

CHAPTER FOUR

At first light, Giant Bear left Devon sleeping; he slipped out to see Black Hawk. He stopped in front of his son's tepee then scratched on the door and waited for permission to enter. The chief was about to leave when the flap was pushed aside.

Black Hawk's wife Gentle Doe was putting coffee on, so Giant Bear sat down across the fire from her; he waited for his son to sit in front of him.

Giant Bear spoke to his daughter-in-law in Cheyenne first. "Good morning, Gentle Doe. How are you this fine day?"

Bashfully, Gentle Doe peeked over at her father-in-law. "I'm fine ni-hoi, how is your morning?"

Giant Bear smiled tenderly, even after all these years Gentle Doe was shy when he came around. He motioned inquisitively. "It is going well; thankfully the storm is over and didn't cause too many problems in the village. Is my son treating you good, not asking too much of you?"

Gentle Doe turned to Black Hawk before saying anything.

Nodding, Black Hawk gave his wife consent to tell his father.

Looking at them curiously, Giant Bear wondered what was going on.

Turning back to Giant Bear, Gentle Doe smiled in pleasure. "No, I will be glad to give him another Ni-a."

In shock, Giant Bear's mouth fell open in disbelief at the mention of a son. He grinned after he shook off his shock and gestured in pleasure. "You are pregnant again? Congratulations, I know you have been disappointed about not having another baby since Running Wolf."

Beaming shyly at Giant Bear... Gentle Doe waved confidently. "I will get breakfast; you will stay of course, will you not?"

Inclining his head yes; Giant Bear watched Gentle Doe get up then go out. He turned to Black Hawk and saw the sad look on his son's face. He switched to English so his daughter-in-law wouldn't understand if she came back. "You don't think she will survive, do you?"

Shaking his head anxiously at his father, Black Hawk sighed dejectedly. "I don't know Ni-hoi. She has had so many miscarriages since Running Wolf, but this is the longest she has gone without losing it. I'm afraid for her! She's so tiny and frail... plus she is twenty years older now. I would rather she loses the baby then my wife!"

Frowning in sympathy, Giant Bear motioned consolingly. "I know you don't want to hear this, but the Great Spirit has plans for us. If Gentle Doe is fated to die giving you a baby, don't throw the sacrifice away. Go talk to the shaman; see if there's anything he can do, how far along is she?"

Black Hawk grimaced dispiritedly. He knew that his father was right, but he was still afraid. "Two weeks into her seventh month. She didn't want to tell Mom until she was sure she wasn't going to lose it. Ni-go-i gets so upset when Gentle Doe loses another baby. Especially since she couldn't have any more after Morning Star was born."

Giant Bear scowled remembering some of his fights with his daughter; in the end, she still got her way. She had wanted to go to a white school. He wanted her to stay here then marry one of his braves. It wasn't until Golden Dove interfered on her daughter's behalf that the chief gave in before getting in touch with Jed and Melissa Brown. He arranged for Morning Star to stay with them so that she could go to school.

Morning Star went by the white name of Pamela. After she finished school, she married Jed's oldest son who then went on to become a Baptist Pastor. The two of them took over Golden Dove's ranch in North Dakota. He smiled in pleasure, that was the only good thing to come of Morning Star's desire to go to school. Now he was related to Jed and Melissa, by marriage.

Shaking his memories away, Giant Bear looked at Black Hawk in speculation. "I was going to ask a favour, but with the news of a baby maybe I will talk to Running Wolf instead."

Gentle Doe came in, so the two men quieted. She handed each of them a bowl of porridge. Giant Bear and Black Hawk smiled their thanks before digging in; Gentle Doe poured coffee then handed one to each of them. She turned to the door leaving silently.

The two men quietly ate, both immersed in their thoughts; afterwards, they drank the coffee in companionable silence.

Black Hawk took out his peace pipe and lit it then handed it to his father to begin the ritual.

After the pipe was done, Giant Bear sighed in contentment. He patted his ample belly in gratitude. "You know, before we came here and started living on Raven's ranch we never ate so well. I remember days when we would be half starved before winter finished. Living here has brought many changes to this tribe; we owe her so much. I never thought when we first started coming here that this would work out. We only came because of her father, Everett."

Pausing, Giant Bear smiled sadly thinking of his older daughter Morning Dove; he missed her so much at times. Shaking off his distracted thoughts, the chief continued. "After Everett found his Cheyenne family, he suggested having our rituals or celebrations on his ranch... where no one would bother us or interfere. So, Everett's grandfather sent runners to all the tribes with directions on how to get here. We all came then he met my first daughter Morning Dove. You know the rest since you were here for that celebration."

Nodding thoughtfully, Black Hawk remembered when he first came here. He had been scared to death to meet so many Indians but thrilled at the same time that he had a father, after not knowing who he was for so long. His mother had never told him, always terrified that her brother would find out that her Cheyenne husband wasn't dead like Brian thought. For most of those years he had lived with his foster aunt, Melissa. She wasn't actually his nha-i, but Tommy always thought of her as such since she had looked after him for most of his younger years. It hadn't taken him long to learn the customs and language of his new family after he got here. For the first time in his young life, he found complete acceptance. The colour of his skin, the shade of his hair or eyes didn't matter. All that was important was what he made of himself... it didn't take Tommy long to become Black Hawk. Especially with the training Mell had given him in the art of knife fighting. He had won every knife contest after arriving here, until he taught Raven that is.

Musingly, Giant Bear was still thinking about the past. His people were known as the Bear tribe at that time. Everett's grandfather's band was the wolf tribe. They had both stayed after the celebration so that they could marry Everett to Morning Dove. Afterwards, both chiefs promised to come again on their first anniversary.

As promised, they showed up the following year. Not only did they celebrate their anniversary, but the birth of their first granddaughter and great-granddaughter. Just before they left, Everett's grandfather died unexpectedly. There was considerable confusion at first because his grandfather had nobody to replace him. After Giant Bear had everyone calmed down, he suggested they join his band.

The oldest among the tribe deliberated for a day, finally they agreed on the condition that Giant Bear would adopt the name of their tribe. So instead of being the bear tribe, they were now known as the wolf tribe. The other condition was that they kept their medicine man for healing, so Giant Bear's medicine man became the shaman dealing with the spirit world only. Everyone was happy with the new arrangement.

Giant Bear made plans with Everett to meet in this valley every summer so Raven, when she turned three could stay here with them to learn the other side of her heritage.

This went on for years, in all that time his daughter hadn't conceived again. In the seventh year, Giant Bear arrived right on schedule. He was greeted by an ecstatic Everett and Morning Dove, with a squirming bundle. A boy they named Edward William Charles Summerset after his white grandfather, Earl Summerset; or Dream Dancer as he was to become known to the Cheyenne.

Remembering back, Giant Bear pictured the sheriff who had arrived with a half dozen townspeople to discuss their concerns at having so many Indians close to their town. Everett, having his father's charm managed to talk them into accepting them so close. He gave his word to the townspeople that there would be no horse stealing, murders, or kidnapping. So, it was agreed and everything had been peaceful until now. The deaths, especially the two from town would create a full-scale panic. It wouldn't be long before the army showed up... he was sure.

Black Hawk watched his father in speculation, wondering what he was up too. The scheming had started about two years ago, at a powwow on the border of North Dakota. Melissa, accompanied by her husband Jed had shown up to celebrate with them. It wasn't unusual for them to come to their powwow's when held so close to their home. However, it wasn't like them to go into hiding with Giant Bear then leave two days later before it was over.

Black Hawk hadn't paid much attention at that time. But just after they got to the winter camp that year, a rider from Dakota showed up... sent by Jed no doubt. The messenger talked to Giant Bear and the shaman for an hour then left. For a week, his ni-hoi and the shaman huddled together scheming.

Inquiring curiously, Black Hawk was told to mind his own business. He was crushed by the rejection... until he saw his mother staring at him; Tommy realized he wasn't the only one being shut out, his mom was also told it was nothing. He had talked to her about it, but ni-go-i would shrug and say to him that when his father was ready to confide in them, he would. Until then, they could spend time together.

It wasn't until they came across the massacre that Giant Bear started acting weird again... first by arguing with the shaman not once, but twice. Afterwards, he brings everyone back here with the white man and the dead bodies. Then he sends for Raven, who has a ranch to run to fix things; how she's supposed to do this nobody knows. The final act of madness, is that his father sends his wife away so he could stay with the white man alone. Not once since he was reunited with Golden Dove had he slept alone or left her behind when travelling. Now, he sends her away because of a vi'hoi. This whole thing was odd and it was time to find out what was going on.

Watching a guilty look cross his father's face, Black Hawk cleared his throat loudly to get Giant Bear's attention. "Ni-hoi you know I care for you and would do anything to help, but if you don't tell me what the problem is... I can't. I know you have been up to something for the last two years. Does it have something to do with the white man we found?"

Giant Bear looked at his son in surprise; he hadn't thought he was so transparent, but he needed another ally right now. He just hoped Black Hawk didn't get angry with him for trying to arrange this marriage.

Taking a steadying breath, Giant Bear shrugged in apology for his thoughtlessness. "I guess I have been a bit obvious. I wasn't going to get you involved after hearing about the baby, but I need your help. I will start at the beginning; you already know why Raven was trained to be a warrior since it is no secret. In a dream the shaman had when she was three, Raven was to be the 'protector' of this tribe, it has all come true. Your niece keeps us fed and protected all through the winter months, and not once has my granddaughter ever asked for anything in return."

Smiling in thanks, Giant Bear accepted another coffee but didn't stop his explanation. "Two years ago, just before we left for the powwow, Raven came to the shaman worried about a dream she had about a man that she could never see. Well, our spiritual healer sent her off with reassuring words. Wanting to help her, since she has done so much for us; the shaman spent the last days of our stay here meditating on her dream, asking the Great Spirit to help her. On the last day, he finally got a vision. In it, your niece with a white man was standing close together holding hands as they surveyed their land. They were standing on a cliff wall looking towards her ranch. Behind them was the valley she uses to breed her mares to the black stallion too. That land she wants to buy since she doesn't own it. Raven, and the man she was with turned towards the valley still contemplating all the property that they owned. Then right behind them, two images appeared. Ravens, was a raven. Right behind the white man was a golden eagle. That is where the vision ended!"

Gentle Doe ducked into the teepee, causing Giant Bear to halt his explanation as he waited for her to gather her clothes then leave again before he continued. "The shaman had to interpret the dream, so he came to me asking my opinion since he didn't understand the vision. We figured out right away that Raven was supposed to marry this man, but who was he? The shaman asked me since both of them were surveying her land then the thousand acres that she wants to buy together, if it might be significant. At first, it made no sense to me. Suddenly, I remembered a conversation that I had with Everett before he died about trying to buy the neighbouring thousand acres. My son-in-law had thought it bizarre that his father would convince his friend in England to buy that land. It was even stranger that he got him to make a will that stated his firstborn son wouldn't inherit it; the old Earl's second grandson would though. Now his grandson could sell it if he wished, but he had to live here for a whole year before he was allowed to sell. Well, when I remembered that conversation it didn't take us long to figure out that the man in the dream was the owner of the thousand acres. All we had to do was get him down here from England so the two of them could meet and fall in love. How to get the white man here was the next problem we had to solve... Jed of course, was the first one I thought of to help us. He could contact the Englishman then pretend to want to buy his land, which would mean that the white man had to spend a whole year here. Since there was no house at the Englishman's place, he obviously would have to stay at Raven's. As the late Earl's granddaughter, she would have to let him stay for the whole year. We were sure that by the end of it, they would be madly in love. Last winter after we got here, my blood brother sent me a message. The white man would be coming this spring. His name was Devon

Rochester; he's the second son of Earl Rochester in England. You can imagine that we were thrilled that everything was going according to plan."

Giant Bear stopped talking as he paused to put tobacco in his pipe. He gathered his thoughts together unhappily.

Black Hawk waited patiently knowing his father wasn't done yet. He wasn't sure how he felt about what his ni-hoi was telling him. Tommy figured that allowing his father to finish would give him a better understanding, he hoped.

Taking a fortifying sip of coffee, Giant Bear continued talking. "When we left here two weeks ago for our summer camp, I was still pleased how events had turned out. Then we came upon the massacre, I figured everyone was dead. I knew this group was the one with Devon in it. I was heartsick every time I turned over a body. It was my fault the Englishman was here! How could the Great Spirit steer us so wrong, why did Ma'heo'o want us to bring this man here if all he was going to do was let him die? The shaman was the one who found the Englishman and his sister. Both were alive when we found them; unfortunately, within an hour the woman died. As for the white man, he was pretty beaten up. I argued with our spiritual healer thinking we had been wrong about the vision. The shaman was adamant saying we were right, but something obviously went wrong. So, we set up his tepee so he could try to find the answers. An hour later, he called me to him. He had been shown two visions. The first one was the same as before with the two happily surveying everything they owned, with both birds over their heads. The following vision scared the shaman badly. He saw Raven and Devon standing apart glaring at each other in rage. In-between them, were dead white men plus Indians lying everywhere. The shaman interpreted the dream like this... either the two would get married or we are all dead. Including Raven and Devon, since she had a dead raven over her head... he had a dead eagle over his. So, I sent Running Wolf to get your niece then I brought everybody here, including the dead. I gathered all the proof I could find to convince the white man that we didn't do it. When we got back the shaman and I came up with a plan. We would tell the white man he had to marry my granddaughter in payment for a life. We would tell Raven that she had to marry the white man to save us so he can't go to the army. I told Devon last night. He agreed to marry Raven to save his life. I will tell Ni'-khi later. What I want you to do is stay with the white man while your mother is teaching him our customs. You will be guarding him and protecting her!"

Black Hawk stared in disbelief at his dad, speechless. If he hadn't been present at the discovery of the massacre then been a witness to some of Giant Bear's descriptions, he would think the chief was trying to pull his leg. He knew his father was deadly serious though.

Shaking his head in bewilderment, Black Hawk wasn't sure what to say. "I'm not sure how to take this story; I will think about it and let you know. While I'm thinking, I'll go stand guard to protect my mother. As for making Raven marry this man, I think you might be making a mistake. Instead of pulling them closer, it might backfire then pull them apart."

Getting up, Black Hawk turned to the entrance. "I'll go check on Devon. If he's still asleep, I'll go get Mother. If he's awake I'll take him with me; some exercise would be good for him."

Giant Bear nodded then watched Black Hawk disappear out of the tepee. His son might be right when he said forcing Devon and Raven to get married could backfire. Unfortunately, he was committed; it was too late. The chief got up to go tell Raven she had to marry the white man.

*****

Devon woke up a half hour after Giant Bear left. Since it was dark in the tepee, he didn't get up. The Englishman had slept great, considering everything that happened. He thought of his home, now so far away in England where his ancestral castle sat... it wasn't far from London; actually, it wasn't his. It was his brother's now that their father had died. Then again, it never felt like home just a place he had to go to once a month as a duty.

After Devon grew to manhood, was when the feelings first started. He watched his father and older brother mistreating the servants, but it was the serfs they treated the worst. All his life the young lord watched them shame or beat the serfs; why baffled him. It wasn't until he grew older that Devon questioned the conduct of his father and brother.

One day when he was about sixteen, Devon caught his father trying to rape a female serf... he had received a severe beating for trying to stop him. Since then, the young lord had stayed away from his home whenever possible. When Devon's father died; he tried to get his older brother to lighten up on them. All his brother did was laugh at him before telling him that he should consider trying a female serf. It might change his tune then make him a man.

Leaving in a rage, Devon had not set foot in his home since. Lucky for him, his father had willed him an estate in Sussex where he now lived. Of course, the young lord owned a thousand acres here in Montana too. He also had a trust fund that his grandfather willed to him. Being smart, Devon knew that eventually he would cut all contact with his brother the new earl; so, he took his trust fund then invested it. His father had given Devon a living allowance while he was alive, so he lived on that while continuing to invest his inheritance. Now the younger lord was prosperous in his own right, but still wasn't happy... something always seemed to be missing. The older he got, the more disillusioned he became in regards to the way the Royalty treated the poor. It bothered him more each year. He figured there must be more to life somewhere, but it never got better.

After his father died, Devon began thinking of the land he owned in Montana. Should he sell it or should he go start a new life? The Englishman had enough money now to do or go anywhere in the world he wanted. Questioning some of the army generals that had been stationed in the new world; he was told so many horror stories of people disappearing, tortured, or murdered... it made him leery of coming here. Some described the fierce Indians as honourable and misunderstood. Other people he talked to said the Indians kept breaking their treaties. If you talk to a different group, they tell you it's the whites that keep breaking the agreements so the army can take their land. It was hard to determine who was right. The young lord knew that if he went it would be up to him to find the truth of it.

His mind made up; Devon decided to go to Montana when he received that letter... longing for a better life. The young lord unfortunately gave in to his two sisters when they begged to go with him. Now they were gone; their desire to die somewhere other than England was granted. It still hurts unbearably even though he knew it was what they wanted. He would never be sorry though as he remembered his younger sister's pleasure at every new experience. Like the day that the dolphins followed them. Her tinkling laughter as she watched them dance and frolic in front of their ship would be etched in his memory forever. As well as the sheer joy she experienced in Boston when he took her all over the city to see the sights. Then her blissful appearance as they travelled through the serene, but harsh and rugged landscape of Montana. He would never forget that he gave her so much joy before she died. One thing he did wish for was that he could see them and give them a proper burial.

*****

Black Hawk opened the flap on Giant Bear's tepee before closing it immediately when he heard the white man grieving. He didn't want to intrude, so he turned heading to Raven's to get his mother. He met his father in front of the tepee, they scratched at the door to be let in.

Golden Dove turned with an ecstatic smile of welcome before rushing over to give her husband a passionate kiss.

Turning away, Black Hawk and Raven moved off respectfully; politely giving their backs to the lovers, so they could have a moment.

Grinning at Black Hawk, Raven motioned curiously. "How are you Uncle, I haven't seen much of you lately."

Embracing Raven warmly, Black Hawk stepped back. "I'm fine, I just came to get Mom; I'm supposed to protect her while she is with the white man. I also have good news, but I'll tell you at the same time as ni-go-ii so it will wait until the lovebirds are finished their greeting."

"What good news?" Golden Dove walked over and asked as she gave her son a loving embrace of welcome.

Returning his mother's hug gently, Black Hawk kept his tone light. "Well, it seems you will be a grandmother again."

Stepping back in anxious surprise, Golden Dove held her son at arm's length. "Gentle Doe's pregnant; how far along is she?"

Wincing at his mother's anxious voice, Black Hawk remembered all the miscarriages. "It's all right Mom, she's two weeks into her seventh month; she should carry it full term."

Sighing in relief, Golden Dove waved in reproach. "Why didn't you tell me sooner? I could have been helping her with the chores."

Frowning, Black Hawk shook his head. "No, ni-go-i; Gentle Doe didn't want you to know, you get too upset when she loses it. She wanted to wait until she was past her seventh month."

Knowingly, Golden Dove eyed Black Hawk shrewdly. "You are worried that she has carried the baby this long, aren't you?"

Nodding, Black Hawk frowned sorrowfully. "Yes, I am; I don't think she will survive. If she doesn't, I don't know what I'll do!"

Hiding her concerned expression, Golden Dove hugged her son in support. "It'll be all right. I'll help her as much as I can."

Hugging his mother, Black Hawk looked at Raven over Golden Dove's shoulder. "I know it will be; I'm sure Gentle Doe will be glad to have help."

Stepping back, Golden Dove gave her son a reassuring look. "Come have some coffee. Did you both eat yet?"

Walking to the fire with his mother, Black Hawk sat beside her. He waved away the offered food. "Yes, nis-gi-i we ate."

Golden Dove nodded pleased. "Okay, we can bring some to the white man. Do you know if he's awake yet?"

Black Hawk grimaced with a frown of concern. "Yes, he's awake but he was occupied; I decided to come get you first. I'm sure Father and Raven won't miss us too much."

Getting up, Golden Dove dished up a bowl of porridge.

Turning to Giant Bear, Black Hawk waved towards his father. "Do you want me to tell the white man his sister's here; he might want to see her before we help her on the way to Ma'heo'o?"

Giant Bear inclined his head in consent. "Yes, but wait until the sun reaches its highest point. I need to speak with Raven; plus, we need to go over the evidence we collected before deciding what to do."

Nodding, Black Hawk got up to help his mother. "Here, ni-go-i... let me take that porridge and coffee."

Smiling, Golden Dove gave them to her son. On the way to her tepee, Mary looked at him curiously. She waved in demand wanting answers. "Tommy, did your father tell you what's going on?"

Grimacing knowingly, Black Hawk sighed resignedly. The only time his mother called him Tommy was when she was mad at him or wanted to know something that instant; whether you wanted to give an answer or not. Of course, it usually worked... except this time. "Yes Mom, I know. But I can't tell you, so you will have to wait until Dad decides to tell you!"

Opening her mouth to demand he tell her; Golden Dove snapped it shut when Black Hawk held up his hand. He frowned unhappily before scowling. "I'm sorry, Mum. I never keep anything from you so this is hard, but I'll make you a promise. If Dad doesn't tell you by the time the moon is full, I'll tell you. That's the best I can do!"

Golden Dove nodded her assent. She waved angrily in impatience. "Okay Black Hawk; I'll wait, but tell your father to confess to me himself soon! I want to know what the white man's name is, no one told me?"

Black Hawk nodded; he would give father her ultimatum. He sighed relieved when his mother called him by his Indian name. "I'll tell him. The vi'hoi is Devon Rochester, he's the son of an Earl in England."

Pacified by her son's promise, Golden Dove nodded thanks at getting a name for the white man. They reached her tepee, so she scratched at the flap in warning to let Devon know they were coming. They looked at each other in dismay at the subdued response from inside. "Come in."

Going in, Black Hawk held open the flap for his mother. When they were inside, they turned looking for the white man. The first thing they noticed was the cold then the darkness, no one had bothered with a fire or the lamps.

Shaking her head in angry disapproval, Golden Dove tsked in aggravation. "Tommy, make a fire while I open this tepee up."

Wincing at his mother's use of his white name, Black Hawk hurried to do as he was told. You never argued with Golden Dove when she was in this mood... no matter how old you were; even his father hurried when she used that tone. He got a good fire going before lighting the three lamps. Next, he put the coffee pot on a rock and set the bowl of porridge down to heat them up again. He also pushed open the smoke hole so that the sun would shine in.

Tying up the door flap, Golden Dove went to open the windows. When she first come here to live, she made Giant Bear cut out two windows so it wasn't so dark inside. She turned once done to inspect the man curiously.

Devon was sitting on his bed; the Englishman wondered if he should get up to greet the white woman. However, his manners got the better of him. He stood up then gave a bow of greeting. He grinned devilishly at Giant Bear's wife. "To see any woman as beautiful as you are when a man wakes up, even when a prisoner... is all a man could ask for."

Blushing in pleasure, Golden Dove smiled shyly at the white man. It had been forever since anyone flirted with her. At first, she felt flustered wondering if she still knew how; it didn't take her long to recollect. She lowered her eyes in modesty, and held out her hand so Devon could take it then touched his lips against the back of her hand.

Black Hawk chuckled in delight at his mother's blush then walked over to the white man; he held out his hand in greeting. "My white name is Tommy and my Indian name is Black Hawk. My mother's name is Mary... her Indian name is Golden Dove. You may use our English names until you become familiar with our language."

Inclining his head in greeting, Devon grasped Black Hawk's hand firmly with his good one as he joked. "My white name is Devon Rochester... I don't have an Indian name."

Chuckling, Black Hawk smirked teasingly at Devon. "I wouldn't be too sure of that if I were you!"

Devon let Tommy's hand go then looked at him in surprise.

Grinning, Black Hawk waved at Devon to sit without comment.

Golden Dove checked the porridge to make sure it was hot and handed it to Devon. She poured coffee for the three of them then sat back to watch the Englishman eat.

Hesitantly, Devon took a bite of the porridge before looking up in stunned appreciation. "Porridge with nuts and raisins... this is great! But where did you get them at this time of year?"

Pointing to the North, Golden Dove smiled at Devon mysteriously. She wasn't allowed to disclose to this man anything about Raven's ranch. Her husband had been extremely clear about that last night, so she shrugged then fibbed a little. "We collect the nuts at our summer camp, sometimes if it's a good year we still have some left over in the spring. As for the raisins... we trade for them. When I first came here; I insisted on having porridge with raisins, so my husband always manages to find me some."

Nodding at that explanation, Devon finished the porridge with gusto. He picked up his coffee and sighed relieved, he had been starving. The Englishman sipped it then grimaced at the bitter taste... used to tea. He looked at Mary in hope. "Your husband wouldn't happen to get sugar?"

Shaking her head negatively, Golden Dove motioned in apology. "No, sugar is harder to get here. We do harvest honey though... would you like some? I forgot that you are English, so prefer tea; I do have several kinds, I make my own tea so I will prepare you some later."

Devon nodded in delight as Mary promised him tea.

Getting up, Golden Dove went to the area where her trunks were.

Surprised to see the trunks, Devon hadn't noticed them last night then remembered Mary wasn't a prisoner; she was here of her own free will.

Walking back with a jar, Golden Dove opened it then took a small spoon and scooped out some honey to put in his coffee.

Frowning, Devon raised his eyebrows in surprise.

Golden Dove shrugged as she put the spoon back in the jar. "I did bring a few things with me from my old life. When you get to know us better, you will find we are more inclined to accept the useful white inventions. Neither will it take you long to realize this group of Indians is not as averse to change as some of the other Indian tribes. Most of our people here are mixed bloods with a few whites. We keep to ourselves trying to get along with both the white men and the Indian tribes that surround us. The next chief after my husband is three-quarters Cheyenne and a quarter white, so there are some white customs we follow."

Confused, Devon was surprised by this conversation as Golden Dove settled across the fire from him. He heard that Indians hated the whites so wanted nothing to do with them. He was told that Indians tortured then killed any white person they found. Except on some rare occasions when a child is stolen and kept. A few white women were adopted, later they willingly married an Indian like Mary had.

Black Hawk saw the astonishment on Devon's face; he shook his head in annoyance. He hadn't thought by looking at the Englishman that the white man would allow gossip or others prejudices to rub off.

Seeing the disappointed look that Tommy flashed his way, Devon remembered how the Royalty in England always degraded the serfs and servants. He recalled how frustrated it made him feel when trying to stand up for them. Maybe he was wrong in his thinking, could it be possible that he was doing the same thing now that he had stood against back home. Just because, someone was different didn't mean that they were wrong. It only meant that they had unconventional ways of looking at things or other customs to observe. He had come to this country to get away from prejudice and here he was doing the same thing. Well, this was his chance to learn the other side of life in this country. Perhaps it was time to be quiet then listen instead of thinking only of himself and his losses. His sister's died the way they wanted; it was time to put them away in his heart then go on living.

Black Hawk watched the conflict on Devon's face as he debated with himself on opening his mind to new ideas; or if he should shut himself off. Tommy was relieved when the Englishman's face became open.

Devon inclined his head, now ready for Mary to continue.

CHAPTER FIVE

Raven and Giant Bear sat across from each other staring wordlessly. The only sound in the tepee was the crackling of the fire, as well as an occasional voice from outside.

Giant Bear was the first to turn away with a guilty look.

Concerned, Raven frowned in surprise; usually her nam-shimi could outstare anybody. She remembered when Giant Bear had a staring contest with a chief from a different band. It went on for two days, finally the other man looked away.

Taking a sip of her coffee reflectively, Raven stared over the rim of her cup at Giant Bear... he refused to look up. Putting her cup down with a clatter, she grabbed her peace pipe and tobacco pouch. As she was filling the ceremonial pipe, she peeked at her grandfather but he was staring into the fire intently; he didn't seem to notice what she was doing. She wasn't fooled at all, knowing that her grandfather was aware of every move that she made. He used this tactic to confuse his opponent, that he was using it on her didn't bode well for her peace of mind... that, she was sure. She passed the pipe to him first, to begin the ritual.

Looking up finally, Giant Bear took the pipe from her before taking two puffs and blew the smoke into the air, towards the ground, right then left and passed it back to Raven.

Putting the pipe down after she was finished, Raven looked at Giant Bear intently as she motioned sharply in demand. "Nam-shimi' are you ready to tell me what is going on?"

Wincing at Raven's angry tone, Giant Bear sighed wearily before telling his rehearsed story. Once finished, he continued grimly. "We didn't understand at first what was going on; it wasn't until we found Slippery as an Eel then Squatting Dog that we figured it out. When we followed their tracks, we realized that they followed the wagon for a long time; it wasn't until they were on your property that they struck. They didn't seem to want any of the other tribes that stay with us involved because they waited until we got past the spot White Antelope's tribe usually leaves us. They stay with us almost to the end of your land, about six miles from your border. I think they left the two dead braves there to let us know who did it... wanting to taunt us. I'm not sure that Squatting Dog was involved."

Inclining her head, Raven had already thought of that earlier. Squatting Dog was from a different band. She waited for her grandfather to go on, not saying a word... knowing he wasn't finished.

Clearing his throat, Giant Bear waved beseechingly. "Well, we still didn't realize the full danger to ourselves. Not until the shaman went into seclusion to get a vision from the Great Spirit, did we get uneasy. I send Running Wolf to get you after the shaman said we had to return to the winter camp."

Raven mulled over everything her grandfather told her suspiciously. Running Wolf had told her the same thing, almost as if it was rehearsed. She shrugged off her doubts as her mind whirled with plans. Well, the first thing that needed to be confirmed was Squatting Dog's involvement, was it intentional or involuntary. Suddenly, she looked at her grandfather sharply in reproach as she realized that he hadn't said anything about the shaman's vision at all. She knew he had one it was written all over the chief's face.

Giant Bear looked away guiltily as Raven stared at him.

Pointing at Giant Bear in demand when he looked back at her... Raven asked in irritation. "Grandfather, what did the shaman say about his vision?"

Harrumphing to clear his throat uneasily, Giant Bear wasn't sure this was a good idea. He opened his hand in anxiety imploringly, trying to stall knowing if he continued there was no going back. "You aren't going to like it!"

Frowning in exasperation as her grandfather tried avoiding the issue; Raven sighed sure she wouldn't... she needed to know, though. "I figured that out already, now tell me!"

Reluctantly, Giant Bear told her about the vision. He left out the image of the golden eagle and the first vision. He watched his granddaughter's face go from disbelief to outright refusal then to resignation at the trap she was in.

Raven couldn't believe it; why? She sacrificed her whole life to look after her Cheyenne people and never asked for anything in return. Now she was being forced to give up the only thing she had left, her freedom! It wasn't fair; how could the Great Spirit ask for more!

Raven contemplated Giant Bear's description of the carnage that would occur if she didn't marry this white man. She knew that she would do it to save her family... no matter the cost. "Grandfather, you do realize that this white man will not recognize our marriage?"

Giant Bear smiled in relief at Raven's calm voice. He had expected hysterics; this was going better than he had thought it would. He shrugged dismissively as he waved that problem away... not bothered by that at all. "Don't worry about that right now, he has agreed to marry you. We will just have to trust in the Great Spirit for the rest."

Pinching the bridge of her nose, Raven felt a headache brewing... she dropped her hand and frowned dejectedly. "Nam-shimi', you know that if he does decide to stay with this marriage that I'll have to move away. I can't see an Earl wanting to stay here; he has other responsibilities in England."

Solemnly, Giant Bear shook his head in reassurance. "No Raven; I forgot to tell you that when Devon woke up, he told me he was the second son so has nothing holding him in England."

Sighing in relief, Raven gestured curiously. "Good, but why did you not want me to talk in English around him?"

Grimacing uneasily, Giant Bear had hoped she had forgotten about that. "I thought you could pretend not to know English, so he had to teach you; I hoped it might draw him to you."

Sputtering, Raven stopped when Giant Bear held up a hand.

Shaking his head knowingly, Giant Bear dropped it. "No, don't say anything. I had already decided it wouldn't work. In the first place, your grandmother is white so speaks perfect English. He wouldn't believe you were never taught. The second reason, is you will need to talk to him about what happened at the massacre. The final one and most important is that you are too honest. Sooner or later, you would say something; I think this Devon fellow is also honorable."

Agreeing, Raven inclined her head grimly. "You're right I would never have even gone along with it. Did you happen to ask Lord Rochester, why he came here in the first place?"

Giant Bear quickly nodded his head. He hated to lie to her, so wanted to get it over with... he answered in a rush. "Yes, I did ask, but he wouldn't tell me. I think it had something to do with his sister because every time I enquired about it; he would get angry. I don't want you to be asking him right now either, it just upsets him. There will be time later for questions."

Raven frowned in agreement; she would wait for now.

Sighing in relief, Giant Bear looked sheepishly at Raven. He fidgeted in dread not wanting to tell her this, but she needed to be prepared in case he was wrong about the Englishman. "There's one other thing

I have to warn you about; you have to realize that just as you are being forced to marry this white man, so is he being forced to marry you. I got his agreement in two ways. First, by telling him that he had to marry you or he would die. The second is by telling him I was giving him a life for a life. I didn't realize he would know what that meant!"

Shocked, Raven's mouth fell open in stunned indignation as she leaned forward in ominous foreboding. "You told him that you were giving me to him as payment for the death of his sister? Nam-shimi' why would you do that; now, if he demands my death, I will have to kill myself!"

Jumping up in a rage, Raven stormed around the tepee furiously. "Grandfather, how could you do this to me?"

Getting up as well, Giant Bear grabbed his granddaughter by her shoulders. "I'm sorry Raven; if I had known that he would guess correctly at what that meant I wouldn't have told him. He only figured out part of it though, he thinks that he has to kill you himself. He doesn't know that all he has to do is tell you to do it. If I thought that he would demand your death, I would never make you marry him... I would rather die!"

Looking at her grandfather, Raven needed reassurance. "Are you sure he won't order my death, Nam-shimi'?"

Letting Raven go, Giant Bear sighed dispiritedly as he shrugged. "No, I'm not absolutely sure that's why I warned you, but I did tell him he had to convince you. He didn't seem to be anxious to try it."

Staring off into space for a few moments desperately, Raven tried to think of a way out of this. "Grandpa, do I have to marry him now or can I have some time to think about it?"

Fortunately, Giant Bear shook his head. "No, you don't have to marry him yet; he has to be a white Indian before you do. You have a month to find his sister and resign yourself to your marriage."

Raven nodded in relief; maybe she could get out of this yet, with a little patience and a lot of work. If she could find the killers before the month was up... she might not have to sacrifice her freedom. She frowned grimly then looked at her grandfather in question. "Grandmother told me that you brought all the evidence and bodies back with you. I would like to see them now before I decide what I'm going to do next."

Giant Bear turned silently then beckoned Raven to follow him outside. He led his granddaughter to the south side of the village.

As they walked, Raven's mind was turning over possible courses of action that might work for proving her family's innocence; she hadn't come to any conclusions by the time they arrived at the spot.

Walking over to Squatting Dog and Slippery as an Eel; Raven could see that both had been shot by a rifle, but she couldn't tell whether it was from the same gun. She turned to her grandfather hopefully. "Did the vi'hoi say anything about the massacre that might help?"

Shrugging, Giant Bear shook his head negatively. "No, I haven't really asked him too many questions yet. I figured you would want to ask him yourself before you go anywhere."

Inclining her head in approval, Raven walked over to the two guides then groaned in dismay. She knew both of them, brothers Patrick and Scott from town. They had wives and several children, plus both had been staunch supporters on her behalf. She stroked Scott's hair tenderly then whispered softly. "I'm so sorry, I promise to look after your families; they will never want for anything, I swear!"

Turning to her grandfather angrily, Raven motioned in demand. "I want two coffins made for them. If you can't do it, contact Dream Dancer he can bring out two... no make that three coffins; the white woman should also have one."

Frowning thoughtfully, Giant Bear gestured in agreement; it would be too inconvenient right now to make them. "I'll send Spotted Owl to the ranch with your message."

Immediately, Giant Bear turned before trotting away.

Walking to the white woman; Raven studied her curiously... she was beautiful and young. The Englishwoman had no wounds that she could see. Turning the blonde to check her back, nothing. She was easing the woman down when a harsh voice made her spin around.

"DON'T TOUCH HER... you filthy squaw!"

Drawing herself up angrily, Raven watched the white man storm towards her with a look of rage plain on his face.

Walking beside Devon, Black Hawk reached over then grabbed the vi'hoi. He spun the unlucky Englishman around furiously before he could reach Raven. The half Cheyenne warrior hissed warningly, infuriated. "You will be careful how you talk to my niece, or you might find yourself lying on the ground with another broken arm."

Devon stepped back in shocked surprise. This side of Tommy the Englishman hadn't seen yet; it was easy to forget that the mild-tempered Black Hawk was a Cheyenne warrior at heart.

Pushing between the two men; Raven turned to Black Hawk in reassurance as she spoke in Cheyenne. "It's okay Uncle, he's upset. I need to question him come back in an hour to take him back."

Black Hawk scowled a warning at Devon before he left.

Spinning around, Raven glared at Devon angrily as soon as her uncle was out of sight. She jabbed a finger hard into his chest menacingly. "I will ignore your insult this time because I know how upset you are, but if you ever call me a squaw again, you will regret it... do you understand me?"

Frowning furious, Devon nodded... ashamed of himself; although, he hid it well. He waved anxiously towards the bodies. "What were you doing to my sisters, haven't your people done enough already?"

Stopping his tirade, Devon scowled in confusion at the stunned look on Raven's face. "Why are you looking at me that way?"

Raven scowled in uncertainty. "Did you say sisters?"

Scowling, Devon motioned grimly. "Yes, I brought both my sisters out here with me, why?"

Sighing grimly, Raven moved aside so Devon could see all the bodies. "There was only one at the massacre."

Walking over to his youngest sister, Devon looked around but didn't see his older one. He spun around anxiously as he waved in wild demand. "Where is she; my older sister Janet is not here!"

Rushing, Giant Bear rounded the corner quickly. He looked from one to the other in apprehension. "What seems to be the problem here, the whole village can hear you two shouting?"

Turning to her grandfather thoughtfully, Raven gestured at the young woman. "It seems that there should have been one more sister. Are you sure you got all the bodies?"

Giant Bear looked at Devon in surprise... he nodded decisively before turning to Raven. "Yes, we searched everywhere there was nobody else; could the killers have taken her as a captive?"

Nodding thoughtfully, Raven shrugged. "They must have, it's the only explanation."

Devon looked from one to the other suspiciously. He waved furiously in demand. "You must have her here somewhere, what have you done with my other sister?"

Raven shook her head sadly in sorrow. "My people haven't done anything to them; didn't my grandfather explain to you that it was not our tribe of Cheyenne who did this?"

Snorting in contempt, Devon waved angrily. "Do you expect me to believe that? I don't trust anything your grandfather told me. Indians attacked us, and they are holding me prisoner! I see no difference."

Grabbing Devon's left arm, Raven hauled him towards the bodies of the warriors furiously.

Trying to pull away, Devon was shocked when he couldn't. Raven was stronger than she looked... not many people could hold him.

Holding onto Devon until they reached the two dead Indians, Raven let him go as if burned. It had taken almost all her strength to pull him; apparently, he was no weak white man. The young woman had a feeling that the only reason she had been able to manhandle him was that he didn't have his full strength back yet. She pointed at the dead warrior's legs... ignoring the strange feeling in her hand. "Look at the moccasins of both these men and tell me what you see?"

Scowling at Raven suspiciously, Devon did as he was told. At first, he could see no variation between the two so he bent closer. The pattern on both moccasins was different... but not by much. He looked at the woman as he shrugged dismissively.

Frowning at the shrug, Raven waved impatiently... even a fool could see the deviation. "Now look at their weapons."

Looking at them carefully, Devon spotted the differences this time on the design and colours of the knife sheaths. The arrows were even more noticeably different; he looked at Raven inquisitively.

Raven nodded at the questioning look. "They are from two different Cheyenne tribes."

Beckoning to her grandfather, Raven spoke in Cheyenne.

Giant Bear nodded and left again.

Scowling in annoyance at being surprised, Devon hadn't even realized that the old chief was right behind him.

Bending over, Raven took off one of her moccasins and handed it to him. "Now look at my moccasin, do you see the differences now?"

Devon saw the variation right away now that he knew what to look for. He reached out then touched Raven's knife sheath before handing her moccasin back. While she put it on, he turned and watched Giant Bear coming him with a quiver of arrows, plus paint on his face.

Standing up, Raven pointed at the dead warriors. "Now look at the war paint on both of these men and look at my grandfather's face."

Looking at all three faces, Devon took the arrow that Giant Bear handed him then studied it. He handed it back before the chief turned and left again... without saying a word. The Englishman looked back at Raven then shrugged in exasperation. "All you have proven is that there were three Cheyenne tribes instead of two!"

Folding her arms under her breasts in anger, Raven was just to tempted to slap that arrogant look off Devon's face; she tried to explain again... she shook her head in exasperation. "No, we know there was one tribe for sure but we aren't certain Squatting Dog's was involved yet. He could have broken off from his people to join the others, or he was captured then killed before being left to try throwing us off the trail."

Frowning, Devon shook his head in puzzlement. "How do you know this; couldn't it have been the other way around? Maybe it was Squatting Dog's tribe and the other Indian was left."

Shaking her head, Raven sighed sadly. "No, Squatting Dog's tribe would have no reason to do this; Slippery as an Eels tribe on the other hand hates us for shaming them."

Scowling in frustration, Devon motioned in anger. "Are you telling me all this was done to get back at you? It just happened to be our misfortune to get caught in the middle!"

Nodding unhappily, Raven waved in apology. "Yes, it looks that way... I'm still not sure though. I needed to question you first before I ride to Squatting Dog's camp and make sure they are not involved too. Afterwards, I have to track down Slippery as an Eels tribe; when I have done this, I will be back to gather a war party to go after them. Grandfather says you will be ready to come along by then. I will also try to find your other sister. If I can safely get her out without help, I will. If not, we will go get her when I get back."

Devon turned to look at his youngest sister sadly. He reached out and tenderly stroked her hair then sighed in resignation. "I don't have any choice but to trust you and your grandfather."

Turning back to Raven, Devon clenched his good hand into a fist of rage as he shook it threateningly. "I do promise you this, though! If you don't return in a month with Janet or the whereabouts of my sister, I will find a way to escape. When I do, I will make sure the army wipes every last one of you out. For now, you have my promise that I won't run."

Raven clenched both her fists in impotent rage. Who did he think he was anyway threatening her? Who was the prisoner here... her or him?

Watching the conflicting emotions on Raven's face in interest; Devon couldn't help a surge of desire that shot through him. She was undoubtedly one of the most beautiful women he had ever seen. He quickly squashed that emotion before turning towards his sister to hide the evidence of his need.

Getting her emotions under control, Raven moved closer to Devon... she gazed down at the beautiful blonde. "I wasn't trying to hurt your sister earlier. I was only trying to find a wound to see how she died. I couldn't find anything; do you happen to remember what killed her?"

Shaking his head sadly, Devon stared down at his younger sister reflectively. "No, I didn't see what happened; my guess is that her heart gave out... she was born with a defect. The doctor didn't think she would make it to her first birthday, but she fooled him and everyone else."

Looking over his shoulder, Devon saw that Giant Bear had returned and was watching him grimly. He turned to Raven at the chief's warning scowl. "All I remember is talking to my older sister before the guide in front of us dropped from his saddle then a dozen riders shooting arrows came out of nowhere. Janet fell out of her saddle that's the last I saw of her. My younger sister and a guide were behind us in a wagon; I heard her scream. I did shoot the one you call Slippery as an Eel then two Indians pulled me out of my saddle and started beating me. I passed out from the pain. When I woke up... I was in your grandfather's tepee."

Raven nodded in sympathy. "Could you recognize them?"

Devon shrugged grimly. "I don't know for sure, maybe the ones who beat me so bad, but I won't know until I see them."

Frowning, Raven stared at Devon intently... she waved in promise. "I will find them, I promise! If I can, I will bring your sister back with me alive. You must not get your hopes up too high, she could still be dead; or be a totally different person when we find her."

Waiting for Devon's nod, Raven turned before walking to her tepee. She passed Black Hawk and nodded, but didn't stop.

Entering her tepee in a rage, Raven started throwing extra clothes and things together for the trail. All the while she mumbled under her breath about stubborn men who couldn't see the proof right in front of them... even if they got bashed in the head with it.

Stopping short, Raven stood staring off into space with a pensive look on her face. Remembering how she had grabbed Devon's arm then nearly dropped it at a tingling sensation. However, being stubborn she held on; the feel of the hard muscles under his shirt had shocked her. She shook herself in impatience, she didn't know the man... she certainly didn't like him. It was just a surprise to realize he wasn't a weak vi'hoi.

Finally, Raven finished packing her saddlebags then put them in the corner for tomorrow. At least the storm had quit; thankfully, the intense sun should have all the snow gone soon.

Giant Bear walked in then saw the saddlebags in the corner. He turned to Raven before motioning calmly. "I see you are already packed. I will have a packhorse readied for you with enough provisions to last you a month. I would like you to stay for a couple more days though."

Disagreeing, Raven shook her head before frowning in frustration at her grandfather. "I want to get started right away; the sooner I find the killers and the white woman, the faster I can get rid of the white man."

Giant Bear scowled grimly before gesturing decisively. "Look a few more days will not hurt anything. You know where both tribes are at; it isn't as if you have to follow a trail. Besides you are the best at breaking horses, so I want you to teach him."

Raven glared in aggravation at her grandfather. "It will take more than two days to teach him. I would need three weeks... I don't have the time."

Frowning, Giant Bear shrugged placatingly. "Take the rest of the week to show him everything you can. Whatever you can't teach in that time Black Hawk will show him while you're gone. Besides, you two need to get to know each other; plus, we will have Devon's adoption ceremony before you go."

Fretfully, Raven waved sharply in anger. "I don't want to marry him! That's why I want to find the killers then I don't have to!"

Grabbing Raven by the arms, Giant Bear shook her furiously. "The Great Spirit said you must marry him... or we will die! The vision didn't say that if you find the killers, we would live. Only through marriage will we survive."

Pulling away heatedly, Raven stood with tears streaming down her face. She hastily wiped them away, livid that she had let her emotions take control of her. "I don't want to marry him, Nam-shimi'! The Great Spirit can't ask me to do this, it's not fair! I want to marry for love, just as my parents did... as you did. Why should I have to sacrifice my life to a loveless marriage? Has Ma'heo, our Great Spirit turned away from me; what did I do to deserve this?"

Harrumphing uneasily, Giant Bear turned away so his granddaughter couldn't see the guilt on his face. "I'm sorry Raven; we must make sacrifices we don't like sometimes."

Turning back once he got his face under control, Giant Bear opened both hands in supplication... he pleaded. "Please don't close yourself off, give Devon and yourself a chance to get to know each other. Maybe you will come to love him in time. The Great Spirit does things for reasons we don't understand. All I ask is that you give this a chance to work."

Inclining her head sadly, Raven sighed in resignation. "I will try Grandfather, but I can't promise I will love him. It is just too much to ask of me! I think we will both end up hating each other in time."

Exhaling noisily, Giant Bear motioned helplessly. "For all our sake's, I hope you are wrong. All I can ask is for you to try."

Hugging her grandfather in reluctant agreement; Raven moved back so he could see her nod before changing the subject. "Which horse will you be giving Devon?"

Giant Bear grinned mischievously. "I'm giving him Devil."

Raven stood there with her mouth open in stunned surprise for a moment; suddenly, she snapped it shut incredulously before gesturing angrily. "Why would you give that mean brute to Devon?"

Chuckling, Giant Bear smiled smugly at his granddaughter's shocked reaction. "Devil isn't beyond hope, he's just never been tamed. I have been watching Devon; I think that stallion suits him."

Grimacing in distaste, Raven thought of the stud. She had been the one to give him the name Devil. The grey stallion stood sixteen hands plus, with a muscled body that was perfect. He was undoubtedly made for speed; he was so powerful that none of the other horses that were kept with him could outrun him. But he also had a nasty temperament to go with it... he hated people. So far, only Spotted Owl could get near enough to handle him.

Snickering again, Giant Bear smiled knowingly at Raven's scowl. "I figured Devon could give it a try. If I'm wrong and he hasn't made any headway with the stallion in a week, I will give him a different horse. I had Spotted Owl bring him in from the pasture before he left to see Dream Dancer."

Inclining her head reluctantly, Raven walked over to the corner then grabbed her training whip... plus a rope that she used as a halter. "I will meet you and Devon at the corrals. Oh, can you ask Black Hawk to bring that mare I gave him last year? Tell him to put her in the corral beside the stud, but not together. I don't need him trying to mount her while I'm working with her."

Nodding, Giant Bear left before Raven change her mind.

Gathering her lariat then bridle, even though Raven didn't think she needed them. She walked out of her tepee before going to the larger pasture and whistled for Brave Heart.

Unlatching the gate; Raven waited for her stud to come before letting him out. She turned to lead him towards the breaking pens with a soft whisper. "Come, Brave Heart."

Brave Heart nickered obediently as he followed his mistress. He made sure not to crowd her, keeping his nose near her left shoulder but not too close.

Giant Bear and Devon were already standing by the corrals watching Devil frisk then paw the air angrily.

Turning, Devon stared in amazement as he watched Raven leading another stud without any ropes or restraints that he could see. He took a step towards her to help, but stopped short when Giant Bear grabbed his good arm to stop him... not wanting him to get hurt.

Raven took her stud to the opposite side of the corral where nobody would get too close to him then softly commanded. "Stand, Brave Heart!"

Leaving her horse, Raven went to the gate.

Quickly, Giant Bear moved to open it now that the stallion wasn't with her.

Smiling in thanks, Raven walked to the centre; she put everything down except the whip.

Devon went in as well, but stood with his back to Raven; staring in awe at the stud standing there looking at them. The horse hadn't moved an inch from where he was told to stand.

Walking over, Raven stood beside Devon as she motioned towards her Mustang. "Magnificent, isn't he?"

Nodding, Devon grinned in admiration. "How do you get him to follow you like that and stay when you tell him to?"

Smiling, Raven shrugged dismissively. "It takes a lot of patience, plus weeks working with a horse to teach them that. Indians believe that for every warrior, there is one horse that will suit his or her personality. My grandfather, thinks that grey stud over there will be your perfect match."

Devil picked that moment to rear then paw the air in a challenge at Brave Heart, but Raven's stud ignored him.

Grimacing, Devon looked over at the grey in stunned disbelief. He turned back to Raven shaking his head grimly. "I don't think that stallion will let anyone near him!"

Both studs interrupted Devon as they loudly neighed enticingly. Devil raced to the end of the corral with his neck arched. Brave Heart also arched his neck and pranced in anticipation, but he didn't budge.

Devon looked at where both stallions were staring then smiled at the palomino mare that was led towards the pen.

Raven touched the Englishman's arm to get his attention. "I'm going to teach you to break your stud, but I will do it with the mare. I brought along my stallion to show what you can accomplish with patience and training. I need to explain a few things about him first. I was out hunting in the foothills when I heard a horse neighing in extreme frustration. I followed the sound then came to a gully where that stud was trapped. There was blood on his neck and he was staggering around badly. There was no food or water down there, so I hobbled my mare before gathering as much grass as I could then threw it down. I took my two water bags and slid to the canyon bottom then made a camp on the opposite side so that he wouldn't get too upset. I put the grass and a bowl of water in the middle of the canyon. This went on for a week, the stallion on his side... me on the other. I finally decided he was strong enough to get out by himself, so I broke camp. I wasn't entirely sure but figured a bullet had creased him. I scrambled up the bank then saddled my mare. When I was up on her back, I looked behind me and there was the stud watching me. I talked to him a lot while he was getting his strength back. I always called him Brave Heart so continued doing so. He followed me all day but stayed at a distance. I decided to make an early camp to see if he would stay. He did, but well back watching me. I took the bowl that I had used for watering him plus some oats that I had stashed away in my saddlebag then went to the edge of camp. I sat with the bowl in front of me singing softly. We did this for two days; on the third day, he came to me and ate the oats. The next day when I brought the dish I didn't even have to sit down. I finally got to touch him then was able to treat the crease in his neck. He has been with me ever since, but he won't let most near him. There are a few exceptions, Spotted Owl is one. He brought your horse here; he seems to have a way with all horses; although, he has never owned one. Remember, if you need help with Devil in the future, to ask him. So, while I do this demonstration, you will have to stand outside the corral."

Devon nodded and left with Giant Bear following. The two men took positions away from the gate. The Englishman watched silently as Black Hawk brought the mare in then handed Raven the rope.

When her uncle was out of the way, Raven gave one a shrill whistle. Brave Heart galloped into the pen obediently.

Black Hawk shut the gate before going to Devon so he could watch. Raven freed the mare and let her sidle up to Brave Heart.

The only response Devon could see the stud make was the ears twitching and his nostrils flaring. Other than that, the horse never moved from in front of his mistress.

Brave Heart lowered his head wanting a scratch. Obliging him, Raven smiled in delight at her horse. She stepped back and shook the whip out then lifted it so he could smell. She walked around him and moved the whip along his sides touching him everywhere with it.

Familiar with this routine, Brave Heart never even twitched. Pleased, Raven stood in front of him. She pointed the whip to the right then crooned. "Walk."

The horse turned right and walked around the corral. Raven moved in a circle with him as he went around keeping the whip pointed in the direction, she wanted him to go. She gave two whistles so her horse would pick up speed. He trotted two circles around the corral then Raven gave a low chirp.

Brave Heart broke into a canter immediately. She gave one loud whistle, and he went back to a walk. She lowered the whip then took a step-in front of him. The stallion stopped and turned to her instantly... waiting patiently.

Pointing to her left with the horsewhip, Raven gave a long low sharp whistle. Brave Heart spun to the left and went directly into a gallop. He maintained this pace for two full circles of the pen.

Dropping the whip on the ground, Raven gave a loud... sharp, intense whistle. The stud spun on his hind legs and in a full gallop bore down on his mistress. She waited patiently then reached up and grabbed his mane before vaulting onto his back in one running step.

Raven directed Brave Heart to gallop down the middle of the pen, she jumped down and grabbed the whip off the ground then was back on her stallion within two strides. She slowed her horse and stopped in front of Devon then gave a command. The stud rose up on his hind legs pawing the air squealing as he did so. Feeling another nudge, he dropped onto all fours again before bowing deeply to the Englishman.

Devon was impressed; he had never seen a horse so well trained or so eager to please. Black Hawk smiled proudly at Devon as he waved towards his niece. "Raven is our best horse trainer. Of course, we all know how to train our own horses. If we can convince her to do it though, the value on our horse doubles. She is known all over Montana as the best."

Leading Brave Heart out, Raven took him to the spot he had been at earlier. She beckoned for Devon to enter the corral when she did.

Going in, Devon stood beside Raven; they watched the mare. She ignored the two people as she pranced around the corral; first facing the grey stud then going over to the pinto.

Scooping the whip up in preparation, Raven turned to Devon. "See how the mare ignores us. The first thing we want her to learn is that when she is in this pen or around people, she's to pay attention. I will take this whip and run her until she stands still facing me, no matter the distractions. Every trainer is different, some use whistles or words, and some use body language with no sound. Black Hawk uses whistles, not many words. Because this is his horse; I will not use too many either, unless I have to. Try to stay close so I can explain as I go but I will be moving fast, don't get in the way."

Nodding in understanding, Devon followed close behind.

Walking towards the mare, Raven clucked but got ignored. When nothing happened, she cracked the whip to get the mare's attention. The horse jumped then spun away from the loud noise and went into a gallop. She let the mare run without any direction, but every time the mare would try to stop in front of one of the studs; Raven would crack the whip to keep her running. She called over her shoulder to Devon as she explained. "Now I want her to go the other way, so I will step in her path and point the whip the way I want her to go. If she doesn't turn, I will crack it until she does."

Taking a step, Raven pointed the whip in demand before clucking at the horse in urging. When she didn't turn, the whip snapped with a vicious crack; startling the mare... instantly she spun away. Twice she tried to turn wanting to go the other way, but each time Raven stopped her. She turned the mare twice then dropped her arm and stepped in front of the horse. "Whoa Lady!"

The mare stopped then turned to the stallion. As soon as she did, the whip cracked loudly and the mare was running again.

Raven called back over her shoulder explaining what she was doing to Devon as she halted the mare. "What I'm doing now is letting the mare stop, but even while she is resting, I want her attention to be totally on me. Every time she turns away or neighs at one of the studs, I will force her to run again. Some learn fast, others take a day or two to learn this. When she decides she has had enough, she will stop then turn to face me. When she does, I will praise her and let her rest."

The mare turned to the woman ignoring the stallions this time; she stood there quivering in exhaustion watching Raven.

Squatting, Raven patiently waited; letting the mare rest. One of the studs neighed, causing the mare to turn away. Instantly, Raven jumped up then started running the horse around again.

Devon stayed where he was holding onto his side and watched... in too much pain to keep up. When the mare stopped then turned to Raven, the Englishman went over and squatted beside her. It took three tries before she would stand, ignoring the stallions.

Smiling in approval at the mare, Raven turned towards Devon. "Now I will get up then walk towards her talking soothingly, if she backs up or turns away, I will rerun her until she lets me pet her."

Waiting where he was, Devon watched Raven as she walked towards the mare talking soothingly in Cheyenne. It took her another hour before the mare would stand then let the woman walk to her. She touched the horse and handled her feet; the mare didn't twitch.

Smiling at Devon, Raven beckoned him to come closer. He got up and walked toward her. He was almost there when the mare turned away from him. Raven spent another half hour running the horse until she stood still.

Raven then beckoned to her uncle to come in.

Climbing over the fence, Black Hawk walked to them. The mare didn't twitch. Raven smiled at her uncle. "What did you name her?"

Black Hawk grinned at Raven cheekily. "Her name is Lady."

Raven chuckled in delight. "I think she has had enough. We will work on her tomorrow afternoon at around the same time."

Nodding, Black Hawk left immediately.

Turning, Raven looked at Devon. "I'm going to take Brave Heart back to his pasture, when I get back, we will talk about your horse."

Devon watched her walk away without comment.

Walking over, Giant Bear looked at Devon proudly as he motioned inquisitively. "Well, what do you think about your first lesson on breaking horses Raven's way?"

Shrugging, Devon walked out of the corral towards Devil's pen. "I'm not sure yet, I never saw anyone breaking horses this way before. I will have to let you know after the mare is broke."

Giant Bear nodded; the two stood watching the grey pace angrily.

Trotting up to the men, Raven watched the stud in interest for a moment then turned to Devon... she waved towards the stallion. "I named him Devil but now that he's yours, you can call him anything you want. He will remain in this pen until you have trained him. I want you to come every morning before you start your lessons and talk to him. Always stand by the fence so that you can watch him, make sure that he can see you too. After lunch, we will meet here so that you can continue to help me break the mare. Every night before you go to bed, I want you to come out here again then do the same thing. We want the stallion to get to know you and rely on you. You need to realize that out here trust is the most crucial component in a human and horse relationship. If you don't have confidence in your horse, you can never be sure of him when your life gets threatened. I have been fortunate that way I have two horses I can depend on with my life. If you can break that stud, he will be your friend and companion until he dies. He is meant for one person; whoever has the nerve to win him over will have one heck of a horse."

Raven waited, for Devon to nod his head in understanding. She then turned to her grandfather; she gestured decisively. "You don't need to keep a watch on Devon, he promised not to run until I come back with the whereabouts of his sister. Show him where everything is and where his boundaries are."

Giant Bear nodded without an argument then beckoned to Devon.

Devon looked at Raven in amazement at the faith she was showing in him before following Giant Bear without comment.

After the men left, Raven turned to the grey stallion. "Well, you handsome devil you; I hope you can keep the Englishman so busy breaking you; he won't even think to run."

Raven went and gathered her things before going to dinner.

CHAPTER SIX

Devon woke the next morning and stretched experimentally, but his ribs only hurt when he overstretched. The Englishman lifted his left hand then touched his face; it was really sore.

Rolling out of his blankets, Devon quietly got dressed so he wouldn't wake Giant Bear or his wife. He picked up the bag Mary gave him on his way out then headed to the corrals to visit his horse. The Englishman approached the corral watching the stallion run in awe.

Devil saw the strange man so stopped abruptly; he tested the air cautiously. He could detect no fear, but he squealed in challenge anyway... pawing the ground in warning.

Smiling at the horse calmly, Devon wasn't intimidated by the stallion. He was in awe at owning such a stunning animal. The Englishman loved horses and had never been afraid of one in his life; he decided to sit up on the top rail to see what his horse would do. Mindful of his broken arm, he made his way up before sitting.

The stud pawed the ground again; Devil snorted irritably then pinned his ears back as he tested the air again. There was a strange smell, but it wasn't unpleasant so he didn't charge.

Giving a whistle of command, Devon tried to call Devil to him.

The stallion's ears tilted forward, otherwise he was ignored.

Caulking his head thoughtfully, Devon smiled in glee. "You are a handsome devil... aren't you? I think your name suits you just fine, so I won't change it."

Snorting, Devil bobbed his head up then down in agreement.

Laughing softly in pleasure, Devon tried to talk to the horse instead of whistling. "Come here Devil, come on boy."

Blowing through his nostrils testily, Devil ignored him.

Eyeing the beautiful stallion in pleasure, Devon chuckled not discouraged. The Englishman lifted the sack he still held. "Well, I brought you a treat; I will leave them here for you."

Taking out three apples, Devon rolled them around in his hand. He did this so the stud would get his scent off the apples. He put them on the fence and watched Devil hopefully.

Devil tested the air again then took a hesitant step forward at the enticing scent of the apples. Suddenly, the stallion stopped short and spun away before running to the end of the corral.

Grinning encouraged by that step; Devon got down off the fence. He dug into his bag and pulled out a handful of oats then put some in between the apples before turning and leaving. When the Englishman was far enough, he peeked over his shoulder then saw Devil eating the apples. Smiling in pleasure, he didn't go back but continued towards the chief's tepee.

Taking a deep breath of the mouth-watering smells that were coming through the tepee, Devon realized he was starving. He ducked inside once permission was given before putting his sack by the door. He walked over to the fire and sat down.

Mary turned with a smile and handed him a plate of pancakes. She poured him a cup of tea that she made for him then put honey in it; next she passed him the jar to put some honey on his pancakes.

Appreciatively, Devon grinned gratefully between mouthfuls. "Thank you, Golden Dove. Where is Giant Bear?"

Golden Dove beamed in delight at Devon's first use of her Indian name then sat down. "Giant Bear is closeted with the shaman, but he did ask me to tell you what to expect at the burial of your sister and the guides."

Devon frowned in surprise. "I didn't know Indians buried their dead. I heard they put them up on a platform then burn them."

Shrugging, Golden Dove inclined her head pleased with his knowledge. "Most Indian tribes burn their dead, but not all; we will discuss that later... eat your breakfast. Afterwards, we will talk about who the Cheyenne are."

Nodding, Devon dug in; he was almost finished when a scratching sound was heard at the door.

Getting up, Golden Dove went over to open the flap. Letting Black Hawk in; she warmly hugged her son in welcome.

Returning the hug; Black Hawk walked over to the fire... he sat down beside Devon. "How are your ribs and arm today?"

Smiling gratefully at his mother, Black Hawk accepted a plate then turned his attention back to the Englishman inquisitively.

Devon grinned before shrugging casually. "My ribs are better, only a slight twinge if I move too fast or overstretch. I don't think they are broken just bruised or maybe cracked. My arm still hurts like the dickens, but hopefully not too much longer."

Black Hawk sighed relieved that Devon was feeling better as he motioned curiously. "Did you go visit your new horse this morning?"

Chuckling at the picture of the stubborn Devil... Devon inclined his head eagerly. "I did, but he would have nothing to do with me. I did leave three apples that your mother gave me, plus oats on the top railing of the fence. As I was walking away, I peeked over my shoulder, Devil was eating them."

Nodding not surprised; Black Hawk laughed in humour. "Well, nobody said Devil was stupid only stubborn. I put some hay in his corral; there were no apples or oats anywhere."

Smirking in agreement, Devon chuckled. "You will have to show me where you keep the hay so I can feed Devil myself."

Inclining his head, Black Hawk agreed; he finished his breakfast in silence.

After they ate, Golden Dove sat across the fire from the Englishman and began his lessons while she worked on a pair of moccasins for him. "Devon yesterday you learned a few words in Cheyenne, but I think today I will tell you about the Cheyenne as a whole. I will also tell you how this tribe came to stay here. I have to go back in history, so please bear with me."

Golden Dove waited until Devon inclined his head that he understood then continued. "The Cheyenne were originally farmers they planted corn, squash, beans, as well as other vegetables. They migrated to the Sheyenne River in eastern North Dakota around the seventeen hundreds; they lived there for about a half a century. There the Sioux and the Cree surrounded them. They lived in Earth lodges most of the year, which was situated further up towards the northern region. Once they acquired the horse, around seventeen-sixty they ranged further out. They had their own political system as well as their own religion. It was believed that they are the direct descendants of the creator, which they call Ma'heo, sometimes Ma'heo'o, both mean Great One; some also use Heammawihio with many other variations that mean Great Spirit. They have different societies some of them included the dog, wolf, fox, and bull societies or soldiers as the whites come to call them. They also have the red shield as well as many others. Rivalries developed between the societies, which caused some of the tribes to break off then head into Montana. The constant fighting with the Sioux also contributed a great deal to the move. They crossed the Yellowstone River before slipping around the Blackfoot people. As they travelled, groups continued to break off and they branched out more. All Cheyenne tribes have their own Sun Dance at the beginning of the summer. Every five years though, they have a powwow where all the Cheyenne come together as an entire nation again. The Cheyenne refer to themselves as Tsis-tsis-tas. It was not until the white people started settling in Montana that the Cheyenne started going on the warpath again, except for a few tribes that kept to themselves refusing to go to war. Giant Bear was one who kept his tribe friendly, but then three white men killed his first wife so Giant Bear put on war paint. You already heard this story from my husband I have been told, so I'm not going to go into details. I will say that because of the white man Giant Bear was travelling with he learned to trust white people once more. When Giant Bear brought Black Hawk and me home, we started looking for a place where we could live in peace. I can't tell you how we came to settle in the Bear Paw Mountains because it's not my story to tell. But I am sure Giant Bear will tell you either before you marry Raven or after. Anyway, we winter here then every spring we go to the Bitterroot Mountains where we stay until fall. Normally we would be gone before now, but finding you changed that. Now my husband has decided to stay here instead of going to our summer camp. When we first came here to stay for the winters, we had fifty tepees in total. As word spread to other Cheyenne that we lived here in peace, more tribes came to join us and ask permission to winter here with us. Giant Bear agreed on the condition that all white captives were to be released back to their people. If they wanted to stay, they would be adopted into a family and treated like a Cheyenne. This of course was Raven's doing; she won't admit it, but she can't stand to see anyone suffer. Now we have four tribes of Cheyenne who live here! In total, we have two-hundred-fifty tepees' that remain throughout the winter months. You will find that we have adopted many of the white man's ways, but don't be fooled all Indians are dangerous... even peaceful ones. This is all for now, it should be time for you to join Raven at the corrals. After you finish with her, we will talk about your sister's funeral and your adoption then I will include more customs."

Devon nodded and left the tepee; he hadn't even realized what time it was. He was so engrossed in the story Golden Dove was telling.

Black Hawk caught up to him then touched his arm to get his attention. "Well, what do you think of us so far?"

Frowning, Devon shook his head baffled. "I don't know what to think, I heard many horror stories; I'm finding this hard to believe."

Sighing, Black Hawk shrugged grimly. "Some of the stories you hear are true, some are not. All the Indians want is to live in peace, except the ones that have always been on the warpath like the Sioux. Regrettably, the whites keep breaking their promises so they can steal land. Take scalping for instance; it was the white man who started it!"

Forehead puckering, Devon shuddered at the mental image of someone scalping another. "I didn't know that; I had heard it was the Indians way of proving their courage in battle."

Grimacing, Black Hawk shook his head with a harrumph of distaste. "No, I think it was the French who first started it. They paid the Indians a bounty on any scalp they brought in of their enemies, which were the British I believe. After it started, the Indians quickly took up the practice. They figured it was the white man's way of keeping their enemy's out of heaven, as you whites call it. The Indians always used counting coup as a means of showing bravery on the battlefield. Counting coup means that you ride up to an enemy and touch him. If you use your hand only, it is considered the ultimate bravery test, or you can use a spear. We also have a special staff made up especially for this purpose; a brave will put a notch on it every time he is successful. In the old days, after counting coup you ride away without hurting anyone that was how we showed our courage... not by killing. It wasn't until the white man came that bloodshed became our way of life."

They arrived at the corrals a half hour later than planned; Raven was standing near Devil's pen waiting impatiently.

Black Hawk went over then hugged Raven. "I'm sorry we are late, but you know Mother, you better not budge until she is done talking."

Raven snorted in agreement and squeezed her uncle before turning to Devon. "How are you feeling? I see the swelling went down on your face, but it's turning interesting colours?"

Devon touched his face experimentally. "It feels better; my ribs too, only a twinge if I move fast. My arm is the worst off."

Nodding in sympathy, Raven turned to indicate Devon's horse. "You spent time with Devil this morning, how did it go?"

Sighing with a frown, Devon shrugged regretfully. "Not great! I sat on the top railing, but he wouldn't come near me."

Raising an eyebrow in surprise, Raven looked at Devon in disbelief for a moment. "He didn't charge?"

Grimacing, Devon shook his head negatively. "No, but I didn't go into the corral. I sat on the top railing and talked to him."

Frowning thoughtfully, still amazed; Raven turned to Black Hawk before pointing at the corral. "Uncle, go sit on the top railing for me please."

Snorting reluctantly, Black Hawk grumbled. "Do I have to?"

Raising an eyebrow at Black Hawk chidingly, Raven folded her arms across her chest impatiently.

Holding up his hands, Black Hawk gave in reluctantly. "Okay, I'm going!"

Watching uncertainly, Devon wondered what that was about.

Walking over hesitantly, Black Hawk climbed the fence. He straddled the top railing half in and half out of the pen... ready to make a getaway.

Devil stood watching Black Hawk with his nostrils flaring to catch a scent just like the horse had done with Devon. Suddenly, he reared then screaming a challenge he charged the fence where Tommy sat.

Quickly jumping off, Black Hawk almost ran over to them.

Chuckling in delight, Raven turned to Devon. "Now you see why I was surprised Devil let you sit on the fence. If I tried sitting there, he would come after me too; only Spotted Owl can handle him."

Devon watched the stallion go back to the middle of the pen.

Devil stared in their direction irritably pawing at the ground.

Intrigued, Devon slowly walked over to the fence.

Watching the man approach, Devil tested the air for a scent. Again, he smelt something... unusual; it wasn't unpleasant. The stallion pawed the ground before bobbing his head.

Carefully, Devon climbed up onto the top railing mindful of his injured arm. He had no fear or hesitation at all; since he was a child he had an affinity with horses, it even amazed his parents. He hadn't realized that it was anything special, until now... because he had never been around wild horses before.

Watching the white man, Devil remained where he was.

Experimentally, Devon gave a sharp whistle. The stud's ears perked up, but he didn't move.

Climbing down, Devon walked to Raven... awed by it all. He smiled in disbelief. "Will Devil let me train him?"

Raven shrugged unknowingly. "It's too soon to tell; the stallion lets Spotted Owl handle him, but will not let him ride or train him. Keep coming here and talking to him. Later we can see if he will let you go in the pen with him."

Inclining his head in agreement, Devon turned... they walked to the other pen. Lady was standing at the opposite end of the corral staring at the grey stud ignoring the humans.

Handing her whip over to Black Hawk; Raven had noticed the problems Devon had yesterday with keeping up, so decided it was too much. "We will stay here and watch. I want you to get that mare to pay attention to you then follow you. I will explain everything to Devon as you go along."

Taking the whip, Black Hawk entered before walking towards the mare; she ignored him until he cracked the whip.

Knowingly, Raven chuckled as the mare spun away from Black Hawk refusing to face him. She turned to Devon then waved at the mare. "His horse shouldn't take as much time as yesterday. If she is a quick learner, she should only take half the time. Tomorrow, she should pay attention as soon as we walk into the corral. After my uncle gets her attention, we will go in and make noise until she does not flinch from anything. I brought my rifle because we want her to stand still, even when somebody is shooting at or around her."

Devon waved incredulously. "You are going to shoot at her?"

Raven grinned before shaking her head negatively. "No, but I will shoot in the air. We won't shoot at her until she is trained."

They stood together watching Black Hawk work the mare. It took two hours for the horse to stand then face Tommy and another hour to walk up to the mare without her turning away.

Raven grinned in satisfaction. It took almost half the time. She stood up on the corral fence then hollered at Black Hawk. "Uncle, cluck to her and walk away; if she doesn't follow you, run her again."

Black Hawk nodded then turned clucking at the mare, but it wasn't until the third time she had to run around the corral that she followed him obediently.

Eagerly, Devon smiled at Raven in excitement. "So that's how you train a horse to follow you without a rope."

Nodding, Raven smirked before chuckling at Devon's enthusiasm. "Yes! Now let's go in and walk up to the mare."

They opened the gate then strolled towards the horse. The mare took off running, so the two stopped then waited until Tommy quit running her. Finally, she let them come to her.

Raven smiled at Black Hawk. "She's a quick learner; she will make a good horse for Gentle Doe."

Inclining his head, Black Hawk nodded but didn't comment.

Satisfied with the mare's progress, Raven turned to Devon. "Okay let's go get our noisemakers to see what she does."

They spent the next hour working with the mare until Raven was satisfied then she called a halt until tomorrow.

While Black Hawk wiped the mare down; Raven and Devon gathered her stuff together to take back to her tepee.

Inquisitively, Devon looked at Raven as they walked. "Where's your wolf? I haven't seen him around lately."

Raven pointed to the west. "He went to be with his girlfriend, I imagine... he's only half wolf. I probably won't see him again."

Devon walked ahead to push the flap aside then followed her in. He looked around curiously after handing Raven her things.

The tepee was almost empty, except two lamps hanging for light; plus, a sleeping pallet and some cooking items. Devon looked at Raven suspiciously. "You don't live here all the time?"

Looking at Devon for a moment, Raven quickly turned away again guiltily. "No, I only live here part of the year."

Scowling in puzzlement, Devon gestured in demand. "Where do you live most of the time?"

Turning, Raven ignored his question. "I have something for you."

Taking a step towards the corner; Raven halted when Devon grabbed her arm. The Englishman spun her around angrily.

Furious, Devon snarled in anger. "Answer me! Where do you live?"

Pulling her arm away, Raven glared at Devon irritably. "It is none of your business where I live. Now get out of my tepee!"

Meeting Raven's glower with one of his own, Devon gladly stormed out in a rage.

Sitting down on the ground in a huff; Raven glared at the tepee opening, wishing Devon would come back so she could punch him in the nose. Who did he think he was anyway demanding answers? She got up then walked over to the package that was lying against the back of the tepee before opening it. She had made them for her grandfather, but had decided to give them to the Englishman instead.

Inside the bundle was a buckskin shirt, a loin cloth with leggings, moccasins... plus a sheath with a knife in it. Raven spent nearly a year making them. She only finished them last night. About a year and a half ago, while in the valley that she used to breed her mares, an unusual albino buck had wandered into the valley. She had killed him for the meat and his hide.

The leather was soft, supple; the interior had a light, fluffy feel to it. The shirt was beaded, but the leggings were painted because beads didn't stay on them long. The designs on them were spectacular. The knife blade she had bought in town, but Raven had made the handle... out of the antlers of the elk. She had spent two weeks scraping then filing it until it was smooth.

Once done Raven had carved a design on it, which gave it a unique appearance... plus a good grip. When she first started making this outfit, she was only going to put a horse and cow. However, once she had begun a vision of a golden eagle, with a wolf in the background had come to her. Putting the raven on everything was only natural, since it was her personal symbol.

Raven had gotten the idea yesterday of giving them to Devon instead of her grandfather. Since according to her nam-shimi', she had to marry the man whether she liked him or not. At least the Englishman would have some decent clothes for his adoption and their wedding; that way he wouldn't embarrass her by wearing rags. Her mind made up she bundled everything back up then left the tepee with it under her arm.

Marching into her grandfather's tepee angrily, Raven spoke to Golden Dove in Cheyenne so Devon wouldn't be able to understand. "I'm sorry Nis-gi-ii; I just need to give this vi'hoi something. I have to go meet Dream Dancer and bring up the caskets for the burial. I don't want the Englishman to meet my brother."

Golden Dove frowned troubled at the furious look on Raven's face; guessing it had something to do with the matching scowl on Devon's. She got up then brought a bowl of stew to her granddaughter. "Okay, but eat lunch first."

To upset to argue, Raven ate; not looking at the Englishman.

Devon looked from one woman to the other waiting for one of them to say something. He frowned even more infuriated when neither would talk to him.

Handing the bowl back, Raven gave Golden Dove a hug.

Turning irritably to Devon at last... Raven glared. "I will be away for a couple of days so you and Black Hawk can work on the mare. I did bring the gift that I was going to give you before you became so rude."

Throwing the parcel at him, Raven stormed out of the tepee. She ran to the pasture and whistled shrilly for Brave Heart. Letting him out, they went to her tepee for his tack and gear. She was galloping out of camp when she heard her name called, but she didn't slow down.

Upset, Raven rode hard for the next two hour in frustration; finally, she pulled up and slowed her horse to a trot... calm once more. She wasn't in any real hurry, so she slowed to a walk. It was a beautiful afternoon. The ground was almost entirely dry now with no snow evident at all. It was as if the snowstorm had never happened.

Raven had decided to ride out to meet her brother. It was a spur of the moment decision, done more out of anger. She took a deep breath of the mountain air then slowly relaxed for the first time since she left the valley. She felt calmer now and knew this was a good idea. The young woman needed time alone right now. She would camp at the first campsite which was half a day away from the village and wait for her brother; it would be another day before Edward arrived, so it would give Raven time to herself. It probably wouldn't be him anyway. Dream Dancer should have driven the mares into the valley for her. If it wasn't him then it would be one of her ranch hands. She certainly didn't want Devon to see one of them yet.

Raven had no worries about missing whoever came, because a wagon could only get through this way. The way she had arrived after leaving her men the night of the storm, was passable only by a horse; it was generally a four-day trip to the village. Coming this way was a day and a half by horse or two days by wagon... it was much shorter.

Undoing the strips of rawhide that held her hair in two braids, Raven reached behind her and unravelled one coil than the other. She reached up to dig her fingers into her scalp massaging deeply in pleasure; before running her fingers through her hair spreading it out, so it surrounded her in a cloud of raven black. When the young woman was at the ranch, it was coiled up and tucked under her hat so it wouldn't get in the way. When she was in the Indian village, she wore it in two braids as tradition dictated an unmarried maiden wear her hair. Only when alone could she let her hair fall loose around her. It was so long it covered Brave Heart's hindquarters then fell down his side. The stallion was so used to this ritual of his mistresses; he didn't even flinch at the feel of her hair tickling him.

Unhooking her bow, Raven reached down and took out two arrows. One she put in her mouth. The other one was notched on her bowstring so it would be ready to fire at a moment's notice. She was hoping to flush something before dusk arrived; she looked up at the suns position... a couple hours she figured.

Riding along leisurely, Raven kept a bit of pressure on her bow; using her knees to guide her horse. She halted her stallion suddenly in anticipation then turned to her right at the sound of a bark. She automatically drew her bow and waited to see what was being flushed out for her. A buck charged out in front of Brave Heart wildly, trying to get away from the wolves.

Not even hesitating, Raven aimed then shot in a single motion. Her second arrow was notched in preparation before the buck took another step. Fortunately, she didn't need it so released the tension as the deer dropped dead immediately.

*****

When Raven had thrown the bundle at him, Devon had automatically reached to catch it... not thinking. He doubled up in pain as his severely bruised ribs protested at his quick reflexes.

Golden Dove rushed over to him to make sure he wasn't hurt before eyeing the package Raven had thrown in surprise. She knew what was in it and was shocked that her granddaughter would give it to the white man. She hadn't seen the finished garments but had watched Raven work on it several times.

Sitting up straighter, Devon untied the rawhide string awkwardly... one-handed. When the package sprang open, he was greeted with a shirt first. His mouth dropped open in stunned admiration; the Englishman reached out in awe and felt the velvety texture of the white elk hide. He looked up at Golden Dove pleadingly. "Can you hold it up for me so I can see what they look like?"

Nodding, Golden Dove reached down to pick up the buckskin top.

Devon gasped when the shirt fell open to reveal a golden eagle. Its wings were outstretched with the eagle facing forward as if it were just about ready to take off in flight. He noticed a raven under the left side of the eagle. Its wings were outstretched with the tip of one wing just touching the golden eagle. The raven was staring at you intently with its beak part way open ready to scold you. Under the right eagle wing was the head of a wolf, it looked as if it were about to snap its powerful jaws at you! The beadwork was extraordinary, how she had managed to find so many different colours way out here was fantastic.

Turning it around, Golden Dove watched Devon's expression change to astonishment in satisfaction as he looked at the rearing black stallion; under the horse's front hooves was a black and white cow. Both were done as a side view. She folded the shirt then handed it to him before picking up the leggings and let them drop, so he could see all of it.

Gazing at the pinto foal in admiration, Devon looked at the black and white calf... this time they were painted instead of being beaded. On the other leg, there was a wolf cub, a baby raven, as well as a golden eagle chick. The raven was prominent with both wings outstretched so that they would go part way around your thigh. The wolf cub, with the eagle chick was below the raven. They were staring up intently at the raven mouths open. The Englishman frown thoughtfully, it almost looked as if they were waiting to be fed by the raven. He shook his head at his foolishness, it couldn't be that.

Golden Dove folded the leggings then handed it to Devon. She reached down to pick up a pair of moccasins before gathering a loincloth and headband then displayed them. Kneeling, she rummaged inside the bundle then brought out two sheathes with a knife inside each... one was quite a bit bigger than the other. The footwear, headband, and knife sheaths were all beaded with the raven society designs on them.

Putting down the clothes, Devon reached out tentatively and took the larger one then pulled out the knife so he could examine it. The blade was long, it was obviously for hunting. The handle was unique, made out of the antler of the elk by the looks and feel. Each knife had a carving of a raven on one side and an eagle on the other. The small one must be for eating.

Devon gripped the knife in his hand experimentally, trying to get a feel for it. The Englishman was surprised that it didn't slide right out of his hand since Raven had worked it until it was so smooth... it shone. However, with the carvings on either side of the handle; it made for a sturdy, secure grip. If she had left the designs off, it would have been too slippery to hold.

Returning the knife to its sheath, Devon put them with the clothes before looking at Mary in speculation. "Did she make these herself?"

Nodding, Golden Dove smiled in pride. "Yes, she's been working on it for a year. She must have finished them recently because they weren't done last month when I saw them last."

Nodding thoughtfully, Devon wondered why she would give them to him. "They are magnificent; I understand why she would put the ravens, the eagles, the wolves, and the horses. But why a cow, what significance do they have to an Indian?"

Thinking quickly, Golden Dove couldn't tell him the truth then an idea came to her and she grinned in relief... she hated lying. "Well, all animals are sacred to the Indians, since they were given by the creator; even domesticated ones."

Devon nodded in understanding at this simple explanation.

Sitting back, Golden Dove waved enticingly. "I will take you to the lake after lessons so you can bathe; then, you can try on your new outfit."

Inclining his head in thanks, Devon listened attentively while Golden Dove continued his lessons.

*****

Grimly, Giant Bear yelled at Raven in demand as she galloped away but she didn't look back. He turned to Black Hawk angrily as he pointed in rage at his retreating granddaughter. "Now where is she going in such a hurry? She's supposed to be teaching Devon how to break his horse!"

Black Hawk shrugged perplexed. "They went to Raven's tepee alone while I was rubbing down the mare. Maybe he said something to set her off."

Giant Bear sighed in irritation. "Let's go find out!"

Storming into his tepee angrily, Giant Bear growled at Devon without looking at his wife... interrupting her in mid-sentence. "What was said to my granddaughter that made her mad enough to leave without a word?"

Golden Dove got up then frowned at her husband in censure at his offensive behaviour before switching to Cheyenne. "Raven went to meet her brother. She said she didn't want Devon to meet him yet."

Nodding, Giant Bear spoke in English wanting Devon to understand him. He motioned down at the white man distrustfully. "Perhaps, but he must have said something to upset her. Raven flew out of the village like a mad woman!"

Feeling at a disadvantage, Devon stood up to faced Giant Bear defiantly. "I helped her bring her stuff to her tepee. When I looked around, I could tell she didn't live there permanently. I asked her where she lived, she wouldn't tell me, so we argued."

Looking at Devon imperiously, Giant Bear gestured decisively. "Well first off, it's none of your business where she lives. Raven is a warrior so can live anywhere she chooses!"

Harrumphing angrily, Devon waved at the chief sarcastically. "That might be true now, but she is going to be my wife. Or so you say; that gives me the right to know!"

Shaking his head negatively in warning, Giant Bear pointed at the Englishman threateningly. "No! Until you are married you will not ask any more questions regarding my granddaughter... do you understand, Devon?"

Nodding irritably, Devon balled up his left hand in an impotent fist. "Loud and clear!"

Devon turned then stormed out without another word.

Eyeing Giant Bear angrily in irritation, Golden Dove turned to Black Hawk; she waved in demand after the retreating Englishman. "Tommy, go find Devon and show him where he can bathe!"

Black Hawk sighed plaintively when his mother used his English name; he gave his father a sympathetic look before leaving. He didn't want to be around for this conversation.

Golden Dove turned to her husband once alone. She pointed in demand at Giant Bear. "It's time you told me what is going on, now!"

Grimacing resignedly, Giant Bear knew that there was no getting around telling her this time; if he ever wanted to sleep in his own tepee again that is. Only once before had she used that tone with him. It was when their daughter wanted to go live with the whites so she could go to school. He had given in then and he knew he would give in now. He sighed in resignation then sat.

Giant Bear's hand brushed the package Devon left behind. Curiously, he opened it and examined the contents. He looked up in stunned admiration. "Where did these come from?"

Grimly, Golden Dove watched Giant Bear's reaction; curious to see what he would think of their granddaughter's gift to her future husband. "Raven made them then gave them to Devon."

Looking up at Golden Dove in amazement, Giant Bear picked up the shirt to examine it. When he saw the prominent golden eagle on the front, he smiled widely in pleased satisfaction.

Observing Giant Bear grimly as a look of glee come over his face; Golden Dove cleared her throat noisily to get his attention as she sat down. She stared intently at Giant Bear in demand. "Okay, what's going on? You had better not leave anything out either. I want to know all of it this instant!"

Giant Bear folded the shirt then put it back. He took a deep breath to gain some courage as he faced his angry, wife. He told Golden Dove the truth, the whole truth; leaving absolutely nothing out, as he had with all the others.

*****

Hastily gathering her hair over her left shoulder, Raven jumped off her horse. She unsheathed her hunting knife as she walked over to cut the buck's throat. Chanting her thanks to the Great Spirit; she let the deer bleed out. Looking around expectantly in anticipation once done, the young woman smiled as Bruno came loping over to her and gave her a wet sloppy kiss of greeting. She ruffled his fur in affection and appreciation. "Good boy, but where is your girlfriend?"

Looking at the edge of the woods; Raven saw the female pacing back and forth impatiently. Hungry, but too scared of the woman to come any closer. The Cheyenne maiden smiled then turned away before she pulled her hair into a ponytail. Swiftly, she put knots in her hair which raised it up so it wouldn't drag on the ground.

Getting down to business; Raven cut the buck's belly and pulled out the intestines then the guts. Usually, she would keep most of it for use later, but she figured Bruno and his she-wolf deserved a reward for helping flush out the deer. The only thing she wanted was the liver and heart. The rest she took to the edge of the trees then threw it as far as she could.

The female grabbed an intestine and dragged it away to eat in privacy. Bruno stayed with the buck then watched his mistress clean out the buck's cavity waiting patiently.

Taking the liver, Raven cut it into four. She quickly dug a hole then chanting her thanks to the buck and the Great Spirit... she buried two pieces in the ground. She usually ate the other two parts but since Bruno had shared in the hunt, she gave him one piece while she ate the other one. The eating of a raw piece of the liver was a tradition to acquire the animal's strength and spirit. She groaned in pleasure as the still tepid liver slithered down her throat; when the warm blood dribbled down her chin, she ignored it.

Once done, Raven went to her saddlebag; she pulled out a waterproof hand weaved container that was designed to keep the heart or any parts that you wanted to take with you. This way it wouldn't make a mess. She dropped the heart inside before sealing it and put it in her saddlebag.

Taking out her chopping axe; Raven walked around until she spied two saplings that were strong enough to keep the buck off the ground. Once back at her horse, she reached into her saddlebag then pulled out rawhide ropes that were kept for this purpose.

Fastening a rawhide rope around each pole, Raven put one on each side of Brave Heart's saddle horn. She took a third rope out before bringing the two ends of the poles together. She tied them so they wouldn't catch on anything.

Raven clucked to Brave Heart in command, he dutifully walked up beside the deer. She heaved the carcass onto the travois before taking the rest of her rawhide and tied the deer onto the poles securely; then to Brave Heart's tail so the body wouldn't slip off.

Brave Heart bore this treatment with a snort of indignation.

Chuckling, Raven gave her stallion a consoling pat before hoisting herself up into the saddle. She smiled down at her wolf-dog and saluted him. "Goodbye my friend, thank you; until next time we meet."

Bruno barked then left Raven to go eat what his mate left him.

Urging Brave Heart on down the trail, Raven tied her bow where it belonged. She took out her rifle then laid it across the saddle, so it was convenient. The scent of fresh blood would attract predators and the gun would be used to scare them off.

*****

Black Hawk went out searching for Devon, he found him at Devil's paddock. He was sitting on the top rail talking to the stallion dejectedly. The horse was in the middle of the pen watching the Englishman with his ears cocked forward curiously. Tommy chuckled then cleared his throat noisily to get Devon's attention. The Englishman turned in surprise at the noise and carefully climbed down off the fence.

Smiling in approval, Black Hawk waved at the horse. "I think Devil likes you. He sure pays attention when you talk to him."

Shrugging, Devon turned and looked at the stud. "I'm not too sure of that yet, but I like him."

Nodding knowingly, Black Hawk turned to Devon before beckoning him to come with him. "I'm supposed to take you to where we bathe, so follow me."

Grinning in anticipation, Devon fell into step beside Black Hawk. He motioned towards the end of the village curiously. "Why haven't they buried my sister or the guides yet?"

Sighing unhappily at not being able to be honest, Black Hawk frowned; it went against all the training his aunt Mell gave him when younger. "We are waiting for something, which is all I'm aloud to say. You will see for yourself in a day or so, we will have the funeral for the braves tonight."

Devon inclined his head sullenly.

Taking Devon to the north side of the village, Black Hawk followed a path until he reached a lake at the bottom of a hill. He searched along the lakeside until he found a particular weed then waved the Englishman over. Breaking off the bottom, the brave passed it to the white man. "When you are in the water and wet, take this root then crush it in your hand. It will foam as you rub the fluid into your skin. It cleans better then the soap you white's use."

Pointing down at his bound arm eagerly, Devon asked for assistance. "Can you help me with these bandages and my clothes?"

Black Hawk nodded then helped Devon unwrap his arm from his chest. He took off the Englishman's ripped shirt so he could unwind the binding from his ribs. Tommy took the bandage off the white man's arm; it was grotesquely swollen and turning interesting colours.

Stepping back, Black Hawk pointed over his shoulder towards the village. "I will bring you some clothes; mine should fit you."

Devon inclined his head in thanks and finished undressing. He picked up his root then walked into the lake carefully, mindful of his injured arm. The Englishman shivered when the icy water hit his warm skin. Still, he sighed in ecstatic pleasure as he lay back in the water... tired of being filthy; it didn't take his body long to adjust.

*****

Raven reached the camp two hours later. By that time, it was getting dark as dusk deepened. She jumped off Brave Heart; she untied the buck from her horses tail then unhitched the travois and dropped the poles on the ground. The Cheyenne woman warrior took out two rawhide ropes to hang the deer up into a tree, so scavengers couldn't get to it.

Looking up wistfully, Raven eyed the platform above her; way up in the top branches of the tree... even flies wouldn't go up that far. If

Raven had help, it would have been hoisted up there but it was too high. There was no way she could get him up there, even with her stallion's help.

Shaking off her wishful thoughts; Raven tied one rawhide rope to each of the buck's legs before throwing the loose ends over the highest thickest tree branch that she could reach. She went then gathered the two trailing ends and wrapped the rawhide around Brave Hearts chest, so he could help her pull. Slowly, she encouraged her horse forward... inching the deer up gradually. The buck finally reached the right height, now off the ground.

Satisfied, Raven went then grabbed the dangling rawhide that she had used earlier to attach the deer to her horse's tail; she tied him securely in place. Walking over, she untied the rawhide that was around her stud's chest then went back and tied it to a lower limb... just in case.

Unsaddling Brave Heart next, Raven wiped him down before making camp. She got the fire going then went over to unpack the cairn of food and blankets that was always there. She found three sticks to use as a spit then took out the deer's heart and skewered it; before putting it over the fire to cook. While it was roasting the Cheyenne maiden made herself a bed then coffee... waiting impatiently for her dinner.

When the stick holding the heart was lifted off the fire, Raven held it in front of her and ate it without removing it. When she ate her fill, she put it on a rock beside the fire for breakfast then sat back to enjoy her coffee and gazed up at the stars reflectively as the sky darkened.

Finishing her coffee, Raven stretched sleepily. She banked the fire for the night before curling up in her blankets. The young woman was too tired mentally and physically to bother with the deer tonight. Slowly she dozed off, enjoying the delightful sounds of the gentle warm breeze rustling the leaves as well as the crickets chirping. Just as Raven was falling into peaceful dreams, the frogs joined in as they started croaking their nightly song.

Unexpectedly, a deadly silence fell. Raven's eyes popped open in concern. Instantly, she was wide-awake as the nightly songs halted in mid-croak. Straining, she heard a distinctive grunt of an animal that she had hoped never to hear while alone.

Reaching over, Raven grasped her rifle that thankfully she had kept close; just as a massive grizzly bear rushed into her camp then went after Brave Heart. She rolled out of her blankets as fast as she possibly could as her stallion screamed a challenge at the monster.

Rearing up on his hind legs, Brave Heart desperately struck out at the enormous bear. All that Raven could hear was a mighty thwack, as her horses' front hooves connected with the bear's thick skull. The Cheyenne warrior woman quickly lifted her rifle and sighted on the grizzly, but couldn't get a clear shot as the stallion got in the way.

Brave Heart spun around in a frenzy to hit the huge bear with his more powerful back legs.

In satisfaction, Raven saw the grizzly stagger back at the impact when both Brave Hearts hooves connected solidly.

The grizzly raging now rose to his full height; with a savage growl, he took a swipe at the stallion.

Staggering, Brave Heart cried in pain when the bear raked his back leg.

Screaming at the black monstrosity in desperation, Raven tried to distract it as she ran forward. The grizzly turned to face the woman in a fury before dropping on all fours as it charged the smaller prey.

Raising the rifle, Raven shot the beast in the head twice in quick succession; regrettably, it was too close by that time. The silver-tipped grizzly leaped as the second bullet ripped through its skull killing him, but the momentum carried it straight into Raven. Screaming in shock, she fell backwards... blackness overtook her.

CHAPTER SEVEN

Raven came to half an hour later with the massive grizzly lying on her. She groaned in pain; its claws had scraped her thigh. She could feel her leg throbbing with infection. Luckily, her buckskin pants provided some protection, but not enough. When she tried to move, she winced at the sharp stinging sensation in her leg.

Hearing Brave Heart give a snort with a distinctive pained vibration to it, Raven frowned in alarm; she lifted her head when her horse limp over to her. She managed to get on her elbows then tried to push the black monster off her legs. The injured woman fell back in frustration unable to budge the animal. At least she managed to hold onto her rifle, it had four bullets in it, so she wasn't entirely helpless.

In frustration, Raven looked up at her horse in concern. He was standing not too far from her with his head hanging down in exhaustion; he had his left leg lifted a bit in obvious pain. Suddenly, she heard another menacing growl of an animal. She swore in exasperation as she cocked her rifle in fear then glanced around wildly. She couldn't see anything at first. Unexpectedly, she heard a familiar low whine and sighed in relief... she eased her grip on the rifle. "Bruno, come here boy!"

Bruno slunk slowly towards her with his hair all bristled, growling fearfully at the grizzly laying on top of his mistress.

Calling out in encouragement, Raven snapped her fingers impatiently. She couldn't help the sound of distress in her voice. "Bruno, come here!"

Finally, the wolf-dog managed to ignore the bear at the urgent plea of his mistress then rushed to her.

Sighing thankfully, Raven reached up and grabbed his thick fur then pulled his head down close to hers; she gasped out in beseeching demand. She could already feel the blackness of unconsciousness coming again. Desperately, she tried to keep it at bay. "Go find Black Hawk, Bruno... bring Black Hawk!"

Barking sharply in understanding, Bruno turned away and raced towards the Indian village when his mistress let him go. He ran past his mate, but paid her no attention to intently focused on finding Black Hawk. Rarely did his mistress use that high-pitched, desperate voice with him; when she did, the wolf-dog knew something was terribly wrong. His strides lengthened as he ran flat out nothing would stop him now... except death!

Raven thanked the Great Spirit that she had the foresight to teach him to get certain people when she asked. As a pup, they made a game of him finding her grandfather, Black Hawk, the medicine man, or Spotted Owl. By the time the half-wolf was a year old, he could find all four then bring them to the woman... no matter where she was. It would be quite a few hours before Bruno would return. She pulled the rifle in closer to her for reassurance and knew no more as blackness claim her.

****

Black Hawk brought Devon some clothes then walked down the trail carefully. Dusk was deepening with only a half moon to see by; thankfully, he knew this trail like the back of his hand. He reached the lake without incident. He called out knowing the white man was still in the water. "Devon, I brought you some clothes, come here I will re-wrap your arm and ribs."

Devon got out reluctantly, even though it was getting too cold anyway then made his way over to Giant Bear's son.

Smiling, Black Hawk couldn't help teasing him. "If you stay in there any longer you will turn into a fish or maybe even an iceberg since it is still pretty cold at night."

Shrugging, Devon chuckled in agreement. "It felt so good to stay in the shallows soaking. I didn't really want to get out yet even though I was starting to freeze."

Nodding, Black Hawk made no comment then put his bundle down within easy reach. He took a fresh bandage from the pile and wrapped Devon's ribs. Then took the other rawhide strip and wrapped the Englishman's arm before helping him put a clean shirt on. Tommy picked up the last buckskin cloth then wrapped the white man's arm tight against his side so he wouldn't bump or use it.

Black Hawk helped Devon put on his buckskin leggings and handed him an extra loincloth before stepping back then looked the Englishman up and down in approval. "Well, my clothes fit you good. You can keep them if you like I have more. The loincloth we usually sleep in, which is why I gave you an extra one. Some Indians will only wear a loincloth in the summer no leggings."

Grinning, Devon stroked the buckskins appreciatively. "Thank you; I like the feel of this better than itchy wool."

Black Hawk inclined his head knowingly with a chuckle. "I felt the same way the first time I wore them."

Turning, Black Hawk led the way back to the village. It had taken a good two hours to get Devon dressed it was dark now. They were almost there when the older man stopped before spinning to his left listening intently.

Devon cocked his head curiously, but couldn't hear anything. Just as he was opening his mouth to ask Tommy what the problem was, he heard a bark.

Whistling in response, Black Hawk waited.

Bruno came running towards them; he jumped on Black Hawk in demand then licked his face with a pleading whine. The half-wolf got down and trotted away before coming back. He leaped on Raven's uncle again with another woeful desperate whine.

Anxiously, Black Hawk turned to the Englishman as he pushed Bruno away. "Sorry, Devon you will have to find your own way. There's something not right with Raven... I have to go!"

Without waiting for Devon to answer, Black Hawk was sprinting towards his tepee.

Shrugging, at Tommy's strange behaviour; Devon went to Giant Bear's to sleep.

Black Hawk quickly grabbed his tack out of his tepee before sprinting to the big corral to call for his horse; thankfully he wasn't too far away. He let him out then saddled his gelding. He raced out of the village with the wolf-dog leading. Tommy pushed his horse as fast as possible in the dark. He prayed to the Great Spirit as he rode, hoping they would not be too late or that his horse wouldn't step in a hole and kill them both.

It was close to three in the morning when Black Hawk heard a horse whinny painfully in challenge. He slowed his horse then took out his rifle cautiously. Tommy's horse snorted in panic at the scent it caught; he sidled sideways refusing to go any further before backing up.

The wolf growled uneasily as his fur bristled, but Bruno slunk ahead anyway.

Jumping off his horse, Black Hawk tied him securely to a tree and advanced cautiously on foot. Thankfully, dawn was beginning to lighten the sky. He could smell the grizzly before he saw the ugly behemoth lying on top of Raven dead. Tommy rushed forward apprehensively, going past his niece's horse with only a brief glance at Brave Heart. He saw the horse holding his leg up, but didn't stop to see why.

Quickly, Black Hawk bent then heaved the grizzly over out of his way. He knelt down then ripped open the tear in Raven's buckskin pants so that he could examine the claw marks closely. They were festering already and burning to the touch.

Black Hawk jumped up; he built up the fire that was still smouldering before running to where he had left his horse. He untied him then led him into camp. His horse tried to balk once, but Tommy spoke harshly to him in Cheyenne; obediently, the gelding settled down and followed. The older man tied him near Raven's stallion before taking out buckskin bandages, plus a medicine bag that he carried in a pouch attached to his saddle.

Taking it over to the fire, Black Hawk went and pulled Raven's blankets closer to the firelight; now he would be able to see better. Going back, he picked his niece up then carried her over to the blankets. Tommy put her down and touched her forehead. She was burning up; if he didn't get that poison out of her immediately... she would die.

Hastily, Black Hawk poured out the coffee then filled it with fresh water from Raven's canteen sitting beside the fire pit. He dug into his pouch and pulled out two different types of bags; he didn't need to see them, just by the feel of the leathery hide he knew what kind of leaves were inside. He took three from one and only one from the other before crushing them into the pot to steep. Tommy took out one of his knives next then laid it in the fire to sterilize it.

While Black Hawk waited, he bent over so he could remove his niece's buckskin pants before examining her wounds critically. He knew just by looking that it would need stitching, so took out an awl plus a piece of fine thin sinew that would be used to sew up the gaping wounds. Tommy had learned this technique from his aunt's maid in North Dakota.

Waiting for the tea and his knife to heat up; Black Hawk took the opportunity to run his hands over both Ravens legs to make sure they weren't broken. Tommy sat back with a sigh of relief at finding no breaks... her knee looked a bit swollen though.

Leaning forward again, Black Hawk ran his hand through his niece's hair to check her scalp for any lumps or cuts. He noticed one bump, but not too large. After pulling his hands away, Tommy leaned closer to the fire to examine his fingers critically, but there was no fresh or dried blood. That was good, so he didn't worry about it after that. He lifted each eyelid to check her reaction but she never moved, and it was still too dark out for him to see anything.

Black Hawk added more wood to the fire then checked his knife, as well as the tea water. Neither was ready yet, so he got up and walked over to the grizzly then slit its throat with his other knife to let it bleed. He dragged it over to the edge of the camp, but not out of the light. Raven would want the skin and maybe even the meat. He walked over to Brave Heart next, chanting soothingly to him in Cheyenne; he cautiously advanced needing to see how severe the stallion was hurt.

Brave Heart snorted in warning, but let the man check the wound in too much pain to put up a fuss.

Sighing in relief, Black Hawk was glad to see it wasn't as severe as it looked; there was only a small amount of festering. He decided it could wait a while for treatment. Tommy backed away from the horse then went over to Raven. He would need a poultice for the stallion, but until the sun came up enough for him to identify the right plants it would have to wait.

The tea was ready, so Black Hawk poured some in a cup and blew on it steadily until it cooled down enough not to burn his patient. He lifted Raven then forced some down her throat. She choked, so Tommy put the cup down to free up his hand; tenderly he stroked her throat wanting her to swallow. He did this several times, until he got enough in her to satisfy him before laying her back down.

Taking the awl and sinew waiting, Black Hawk put it into the rest of the tea. He pulled his knife out of the fire, satisfied at the red-hot glow... he poured some tea over the blade. Tommy nodded in approval as the knife blade hissed before letting off a bit of smoke. He straddled Raven backwards to hold her down, he gently inserted the knife tip into her festering wound then quickly withdrew it to treat the other four gashes.

Raven tried to sit up as she screamed in agony; before mercifully passing out once more.

Grimly, Black Hawk held her down not relenting until he had drained all the putrid wounds of pus. When satisfied that all the poisoned fluid was out and only fresh blood was flowing, Tommy poured some tea into the open wounds. He took the awl with the sinew attached from the bottom of the cup so that he could sew her wounds up. She would have five nasty scars later to tell the tale, but Raven's uncle was sure now that she would survive. He turned back when finished then made her swallow more tea.

Black Hawk looked up at the sky in satisfaction it was almost dawn. He would have to leave the wound open until he could find what he needed for a poultice. He got off Raven before looking down at Bruno, who had not moved a muscle since they had gotten there... he sighed wearily. "Well, I have done everything I can; it's now up to her."

Bruno whined in anxiety and thumped his tail in agreement before laying his head back on his paws watching Raven intently.

Going over to his horse; Black Hawk stripped him of his saddle blanket and saddlebags. He took his bedroll over to the fire then made a bed beside Raven before putting his hand on her forehead... she had a bad fever. Tommy moved his hands further down and laid one on each side of her gashes then sighed in relief when there was no heat.

Turning away from Raven to pour the last of the tea into the cup, Black Hawk filled the pot with fresh water for coffee. He frowned at the sight of a heart lying on the rocks; he was too busy earlier saving his niece's life to see it. He looked around keenly, until he found the buck hanging in a tree. So that's what the grizzly was after; being that it was so early in the spring it was probably just out of hibernation... the scent of fresh meat would have drawn it here. Grizzlies loved salmon, but sometimes you would get a bear that preferred meat to their regular diet of fish, berries, ground squirrels, fruit, grain, grass, marmots, birds, and bugs.

It was light enough out to see better so Black Hawk walked over to the grizzly first. He checked its mouth to make sure it wasn't rabid; if the bear was, they were in big trouble. Thankfully, he found no foam around its muzzle. Tommy pushed the bear onto its back then noticed that it wasn't a he... but a she, and nursing a cub by the looks of it.

Walking over, Black Hawk looked down at the massive bear tracks... he slowly followed them into the trees. If she had a cub, it wouldn't be too far away; probably up in a tree waiting for its mother. Tommy looked down every once in a while, as he tracked to make sure he was still going in the right direction, but most of his attention was up in the trees. He stopped when he saw a black bundle clinging to a tree bawling loudly for its mother.

Well, Black Hawk had two choices; he could either shoot it, since it wouldn't survive without its mother... that would be the humane thing to do. On the other hand, he could cajole it down and take it home. He had raised a bear cub before, but this would be the first time he tried raising a grizzly cub. They were more unpredictable than a regular bear, so it would be interesting to say the least. He stopped at that thought and chuckled to himself. He had made up his mind without even realizing it.

The easiest way to get the cub out of the tree would be to go back to camp then skin the mother and bring the hide here. He could wrap the fur around himself, so the cub would smell its mother. Hopefully, it would come down then Black Hawk could take the cub back to camp. His mind made up he turned and headed back.

As Black Hawk walked along, he looked for the plants needed to treat his two patients; Tommy was just about back at camp before spotting what he needed. He took enough for a two-day treatment for Raven, as well as some for Brave Heart.

When Black Hawk got back, Raven was thrashing around moaning pitifully. He rushed over then held her down; Tommy picked up the cup of tea and made her drink the rest. The tea did the trick as she settled back into a deep sleep.

Black Hawk fixed the paste then put some on his niece's wounds before wrapping her thigh. He picked up the rest of it and the awl then walked towards Brave Heart talking soothingly, hoping the stud would allow him to treat his wound. The stallion surprisingly stood still and let him drain the infected scratches. Before Tommy put the paste on, he touched around the area to make sure it wasn't hot. Satisfied, he smeared the stuff on then backed away slowly.

The stud snorted and bobbed his head as if saying, thank you.

Laughing in disbelief; Black Hawk shook his head in amazement. "Sometimes, I think you understand humans."

Brave Heart just stared at him. Black Hawk shook his head at his foolishness then took out a knife from his moccasin and started skinning the enormous black silver-tipped grizzly.

Bruno trotted over then whined pleadingly.

Black Hawk nodded guessing what the half-wolf wanted and slit the belly of the bear open then pulled out all the insides. He smiled at Bruno in permission. "Go ahead boy you can have it all, you deserve it."

Yipping, Bruno grabbed an intestine then dragged it into the trees. A few minutes later, he came and got more before dragging it off.

Watching Bruno in puzzlement, Black Hawk caught a flash of silver fur and grinned in understanding. Bruno's mate must have been out of sight all night watching them, but she hadn't once shown herself.

Turning back to the grizzly, Black Hawk carefully skinned it. Raven would have his head if he wrecked the hide. It took him two hours since she was monstrous; when standing at her full height, she would be around eight feet or so. She probably weighed over a thousand pounds. It was small compared to a male grizzly. He would stand about ten feet and weigh between fifteen hundred to two thousand pounds easily.

When Black Hawk finished, he walked over to his pack then pulled out some rawhide ropes and hoisted the bear up into a tree. Without its hide, the grizzly was much easier to hang up, but it made him shudder; a skinned bear looked too much like a human carcass. He left the skin where it was for the moment then walked over to the cairn of rocks where the supplies were kept.

Grabbing a bucket that was left there for water, Black Hawk walked into the trees. He walked until he came to a creek... thankfully it wasn't too far. Tommy washed himself off first then filled the bucket with water, before looking along the bank until an overhanging shelf called to him. He dropped down onto his stomach before putting a hand in the water and waited patiently.

All of a sudden, Black Hawk's arm shot out as a big plump trout flew through the air then lay thrashing about on the grass trying to get back into the creek. He did this twice more before getting up; he carried the fish and the bucket of water back to camp with him. Tommy looked down at his clothes then over at the grizzly hide and grimaced. He would have to go naked... except for his loincloth.

Black Hawk hadn't thought to take any clothes with him. He shrugged dismissively... naked would do. Tommy put all but one fish by the fire then turned looking for Bruno, knowing the animal was here. Spotting him lying beside his niece again, he shook a warning finger at him. "Stay here with Raven, and don't touch the fish."

Bruno looked up and whined then put his head back on his paws.

Stripping, Black Hawk went then picked up the skin before putting it on; he couldn't help a grimace of distaste at the wet slimy feel, but left with it on. With a trout in his hand, he trotted to the place where he found the cub. He looked up and sighed relieved to see it there. He squatted then grunted and put the fish in front of him, enticingly.

The cub stopped crying instantly then slipped down the tree before halting undecided. He was confused by the scent he was getting. He could smell his mother and the fish, but there was a strange odour. Finally, his hunger drove him the rest of the way to the ground.

Picking up the fish, Black Hawk made grunting sounds in reassurance as the cub came towards him. Once the cub was close enough, he brought the fish closer before holding out his hand for the cub to smell him.

The cub hesitantly smelt the hand held out to him then walked closer. He squatted and ate the fish to hungry to care.

Letting him eat, Black Hawk made sure to run his hands all over the cub so that he would get used to being touched. The cub finished eating before snuggling up to his strange smelling mother.

Lifting the cub, Black Hawk carried him back to camp.

Jumping up, Bruno growled in warning when another bear came into camp... protecting his mistress.

"Oh shush, it's just me."

Whining, Bruno immediately laid down again at the familiar voice coming from the grizzly.

Hearing a chuckle, Black Hawk turned in relief to face his niece.

Raven propped up on an elbow eyed her uncle. "I knew she attacked for a reason, trust you to figure it out then save the cub."

Black Hawk grinned as he brought the cub over to her before laying the sleeping baby in her arms. "Well, if he was older, I would have left him there or shot him; fortunately, he's only about two weeks old and was up in a tree all night. So, it didn't take much to get him down."

Grimacing as the wind shifted, Raven got a whiff of Black Hawk then looked him up and down teasingly. "I think you better go wash; don't forget to put clothes on... you're a mess!"

Scowling down at himself; Black Hawk wrinkled his nose in disgust as he caught the scent. "Don't I know it, I stink too!"

Taking the hide off, Black Hawk threw it over a low hanging branch; he would work on it later. He grabbed his clothes and trotted to the creek for a much-needed wash.

Watching her uncle disappear, Raven settled back down with the cub curled up against her. She turned her head and saw Bruno staring at the bundle of fur curiously, so snapped her fingers. "Come here."

Crawling over to his mistress, Bruno licked her in greeting.

Raven brought her hand up with the scent of the cub on and pointed at the cub when he licked her hand. "Smell, Bruno!"

Bruno leaned over then smelt the cub and wagged his tail.

Smiling, Raven nodded at him as his tail wagged. "He's a friend."

Hearing a noise, Raven stiffened wearily before relaxing in relief with a grin; she couldn't help teasing her uncle when Black Hawk trotted back into camp. "Well, you look better with your clothes on."

Black Hawk laughed in delight. "I don't think my wife would agree with you. Stay still while I check your wound. How do you feel?"

Shrugging, Raven chuckled as she waved in jesting. "Like I got ran over by a grizzly, but not bad considering; I do have a slight headache though and my leg is throbbing. Mostly, I feel thirsty and hungry."

Kneeling, Black Hawk checked the wound then inclined his head thankfully... hunger was good. He looked at the swollen knee in concern before turning his attention to the neat stitch work as he talked distractedly. "Well, I have coffee on, so I can help you with the thirsty problem right now. I will use the rest of your deer heart and make you some soup too. That will take care of your hunger, just before you go back to sleep, I will brew up some tea for your headache and for the pain in your leg. Can you wiggle your toes then move your feet and legs for me?"

Raven did as instruct then watched him nod in satisfaction.

Black Hawk glanced up at Raven for a moment chidingly before looking back down at what he was doing. He decided to leave the wound open for a moment to give it some air. "You are very fortunate you didn't end up with two broken legs. You must have wrenched your knee when the grizzly knocked you over because it's swollen a bit. You are so lucky I got here when I did, or you might have lost your leg to poison or gangrene."

Sighing, Raven nodded with a grimace of agreement before waving at her knee... it didn't hurt. "I know, but I couldn't get the grizzly off of me to clean it. I am glad I trained Bruno to get someone when I'm in trouble. How's Brave Heart doing, did he let you treat him?"

Smiling in reassurance, Black Hawk walked around the fire to sit across from her. "Yes, he let me clean his wound and yes he's fine. His scratches were superficial, so they weren't as festered as yours. He will have a scar, but not as bad as you will have. I had to reopen your wounds then drain the pus before I could sew them closed."

While Black Hawk talked, he cooked then poured his niece coffee.

Propping herself up on her elbow, Raven tried not to disturb the cub and sipped it gratefully. She looked at the black bundle then chuckled at the ball of fur. "Well, he sure must have been exhausted he hasn't moved. What are you going to call him?"

Shrugging undecided, Black Hawk looked over at Raven. "I'm not sure yet. Oh, by the way, I hung up your grizzly. I wasn't sure if you would want anything besides the hide."

Looking towards the tree's, Raven frowned before waving irritably. "Keep the hide and head then throw the rest in the trees. I never thought of reaching out to cut its throat. The meat is no good, but it won't go to waste with Bruno and his mate around. This is the second time my wolf-dog has come out of nowhere then saved my life."

Black Hawk looked over at Bruno gratefully without comment; he handed Raven a fish for the cub. She held the trout to his nose then let him smell her hand before he dug into the fish.

Bruno stood up and reached around Raven so he could smell the cub again, but got growled at; he lifted his head away then cocked his head inquisitively and eyed the cub curiously for a moment before trying to sniff him again. When the cub looked up to see what was bothering him, their noses touched briefly.

The black ball of fur pushed back against Raven with a frightened cry. The half-wolf jerked back at the howl then bent again to sniff.

Raven laughed in delight as she looked at Black Hawk. "I think he remembers the last cub you had and wants to play."

Turning, Raven swatted at Bruno reproachfully. "Okay, he doesn't want to play right now, lie down and let him eat."

Whining in disappointment, Bruno did as he was told.

Waiting, Raven let the cub settle back down then pushed the rest of the fish towards him and watched him eat; afterwards, she looked over at Black Hawk. "Can you pass me some water the cub is probably pretty thirsty."

Getting up, Black Hawk found a bowl in his saddlebags then put some water in it before bringing it over and setting it down in front of the baby.

The cub drank it thirstily then curled up to Raven and went to sleep.

Turning away, Black Hawk went over then rummaged inside Raven's saddlebag for a bowl and filled it with soup then gave it to her. He washed out his bowl and put the rest of the soup in it before rinsing out the pan then put some fresh water in to boil. Tommy took out leaves from his medicine bag and crushed them into the water to steep. He sat down to eat hungrily; it had been a long day for him... and it wasn't over yet.

When the tea was ready, Black Hawk poured some into a cup for his niece to drink. Afterwards, he dipped a soft buckskin cloth that he used to disinfect wounds with into the rest of it.

Black Hawk picked up the paste before going towards Brave Heart. He talked soothingly to the stud in reassurance then gently cleaned the dry stuff off and checked the wound. Nodding in satisfaction, he put paste on then backed off. Tommy turned and walked back to the fire before squatting then washed the cloth. He dropped it into the tea to purify it.

Finished, Black Hawk took the pan off the fire and let it cool down before taking the cloth out of the liquid. He walked over to Raven then removed the blanket and cleaned her wounds with the soft buckskin. Tommy put paste, as well as leaves over the wound then smiled at her before looking down as he bandaged it. "It looks good; all the infection seems to be gone. I made a paste for the stud because I knew there was no way he was going to let me put a bandage on him."

Raven laughed at the image of her uncle trying to get a bandage on her stallion and sipped her tea; she shuddered in distaste. "This is awful!"

Nodding, Black Hawk smirked with a grin of agreement. "I know, but I want you to drink every drop. It will help your headache, and the pain in your leg. It will make you sleepy, which is the best medicine right now."

Reaching over, Black Hawk touched her brow in concern. "You still have a fever; until it's gone, you will stay right where you are. Now, before you fall asleep on me do you want me to skin your deer?"

Settling back, Raven nodded sleepily; the tea was already working. "Yes, please. I gutted it, so you don't need to do that."

Smiling knowingly, Black Hawk made no comment aware of that.

Finishing her tea, Raven curled up around the cub. With the half-wolf resting against her, she was too hot; it wasn't long before she slept.

In satisfaction, Black Hawk smiled at the picture of the three of them sleeping contentedly. He picked up her cup then put it beside the fire before going over to start the butchering.

CHAPTER EIGHT

Devon left quietly so he wouldn't wake Giant Bear and his wife. He made sure to grab the bag of goodies for his horse on the way out; the Englishman walked over to the permanent Earth lodge, it had bundles of dry grass cuttings for the horses when they couldn't forge.

After putting the sack down, Devon grabbed an armload then took it over to the corral before pushing it under the fence. Trying to do this one handed was extremely difficult, but Black Hawk was probably still absent or sleeping; so, he had to do it himself.

Frowning in thought, Devon hadn't mentioned Black Hawk's leaving to the chief, should he have? The Englishman shrugged; if it was serious, Tommy would have asked him to tell his father.

Going back to the shed, Devon finished feeding his horse. The Englishman went back and closed the door before grabbing his bag off the ground then went to the corral. The white man climbed up the fence and sat on the top railing again... watching the stallion in admiration.

The stud snorted then walked over to eat, ignoring him.

Grinning from ear to ear, Devon was pleasantly surprised; this was the first time Devil had come this close to him. He wasn't near enough to touch of course, but he was only a few feet away. He sat quietly not wanting to scare him off.

A few moments later the mood was shattered as Giant Bear came around a corner with a young boy, who had a bucket of water.

Devil squealed angrily then raced to the other end of the corral and stood there watching them.

Sighing in disappointment, Devon carefully climbed down. He pulled out a couple of apples and some grain then put it on the fence.

The boy brought the water and set it in the corral before leaving.

Giant Bear beckoned for the Englishman to follow him. "The medicine man wants to check your ribs and arm."

Devon nodded agreeably then walked beside the chief.

Giant Bear looked at Devon sideways in speculation. "You look different after a bath. Your hair is light, more golden than my wife's."

Devon grinned as he touched his hair. "You should see it in the summer it turns lighter, and in the winter it's different again... darker. It all depends on how much time I spend in the sun."

Nodding, Giant Bear changed the subject... he motioned curiously. "Did you see Black Hawk today; his wife said he never came home last night and she's worried?"

Shaking his head negatively, Devon gestured towards the other end of the village. "No, he was walking back with me last night when Raven's wolf came out of nowhere. Black Hawk took off running; all I heard was something about Raven needing him."

Swinging around with a look of anger and reproach, Giant Bear gestured grimly. "Why did you not tell me this last night?"

Shrugging, Devon frowned troubled at the chief's distressed look. "Well, you were already in bed; Black Hawk never said anything about telling anybody. So, I didn't think it was that important."

Glaring at Devon for another moment, Giant Bear finally sighed in annoyance; it wasn't the Englishman's fault. He didn't know the meaning of the wolf coming here for help. He turned away grimly, more irritated at himself than at the white man now though.

Relieved, Devon gave a thankful sigh when Giant Bear turned his angry stare elsewhere. The Englishman scowled in anxiety and gestured inquisitively. "Why did the wolf come here to get Black Hawk, if you don't mind me asking?"

Shrugging resignedly, Giant Bear grimaced bleakly; worried now, but continued leading Devon over to the medicine man's tepee. "If the wolf came looking for help, it could mean Raven is hurt."

Grimacing, Devon didn't want to marry the woman but that didn't mean he wanted to see her hurt either. Not right now anyway, he needed her to find his sister for him. After that, the Englishman wouldn't care what happened to her... he kept insisting to himself. He waved in demand apprehensive now. "Well, aren't you going to go find them to save your granddaughter then?"

Giant Bear shook his head negatively. "No, they could be anywhere. Black Hawk will find and help her."

Getting to the medicine man's tepee, Giant Bear scratched on the door.

The healer opened the flap and beckoned them to come in.

Devon followed then copied Giant Bear and sat cross-legged.

The medicine man undid the binding that held his arm to his side before helping him remove his shirt. The healer unwound the bandage from around Devon's chest and probed at his ribs. They were turning fascinating colours, but weren't broken.

Wincing at a few sensitive areas, Devon obediently drew in a deep breath; he let it out without any significant pain.

Nodding in satisfaction, the medicine man threw the binding into a corner. The old crusty looking Indian appeared at least a hundred years old, with a face that was so full of deep wrinkles you couldn't tell if he were frowning or smiling. His hair was snow white; it was so thin that Devon could see most of his pink scalp. The old man undid the binding from around the Englishman's arm then said something in Cheyenne... Giant Bear translated for him. "Wiggle your fingers."

Frowning in concentration, Devon tried to move them. He got a couple to wiggle but then groaned as searing pain shot up his arm unexpectedly.

Probing at Devon's arm for a few minutes more, the healer finally satisfied... re-wrapped it. The medicine man cackled then spoke in Cheyenne to his chief; he poked his finger into Devon's chest and bicep for emphasis.

Chuckling in agreement, Giant Bear dutifully translated. "He said your ribs are not broken, only badly bruised so you don't need to bind them anymore. Your arm is healing well, so you shouldn't need to fasten it to your side any longer. Keep it in a sling for another two weeks, but try not to use it yet. You should wiggle your fingers every morning for a few minutes if you can though. He also said you have nice muscles for a vi'hoi, a white man... Raven will be pleased."

Scowling in annoyance at that last comment; Devon didn't comment knowing it would do him no good to protest. The medicine man helped him on with his shirt.

Giant Bear turned to Devon then waved towards his tepee after the healer made him a sling. "Golden Dove is waiting."

Devon nodded sullenly and got up then left.

*****

Sighing in exhaustion, Black Hawk sat back and rested for a moment. He could hear Bruno and the female feeding in the distance in satisfaction. The Great Spirit can get extremely angry when you kill his animals then left them to rot.

The grizzly's head was hanging from a tree, and the claws were collected. Black Hawk put them by the fire to dry. The hide was stretched out and scraped clean of fat, with no membranes evident that he could see. The three-year-old buck was done; they would need to be reworked once at the village... this would do until then.

Black Hawk looked down in displeasure, naked again. He frowned distastefully, it was time for a bath before Raven woke.

Getting up, Black Hawk put fresh coffee over the fire; he looked over and smiled at the picture of Raven sound asleep with the grizzly cub curled up against her belly. Tommy grabbed his rifle then turned to leave, but stopped when he heard the rumble of wheels.

Brave Heart stared in that direction and called a challenge.

Raven woke instantly. She looked up at Black Hawk in reassurance. "That will be Dream Dancer or one of my men."

Inclining his head in agreement, Black Hawk handed her his rifle. "Here, I need to go bathe."

Taking the rifle, Raven wrinkled her nose. "You stink!"

Laughing in delight at her face, Black Hawk gestured towards the hides teasingly. "Well, if I wasn't reduced to doing women's work, I wouldn't need a bath."

Waving her hand towards the creek in encouragement, Raven grinned reassuringly. "Go I feel better, even my fever is gone!"

Giving a relieved sigh, Black Hawk grabbed his clothes then trotted off towards the creek without any more urging.

Experimentally Raven ran her hands down each leg; feeling no other injuries she lifted her dressing then looked at her wounds. Nodding in satisfaction at the neat stitches and healthy skin... she moved her legs experimentally. Only feeling a twinge when her stitches pulled a little, she slowly stood up then put some pressure on her injured leg. It held her up with just a little bit of pain in the knee that was swollen.

Raven could hear the wagon getting closer, it was travelling pretty fast. She limped over and slipped into her torn buckskin pants... like the men she wore a loincloth. Although the men only wore leggings with theirs, she made herself a full pair of pants. She found the thin supple leather more comfortable than the cotton bloomers the white women wore.

Going to the underground cairn; Raven gathered two cakes before going to the buck to cut off a chunk of meat. She limped to the fire then cut up the piece of deer and cakes, she threw them in the skillet to cook. She stood up and turned as the wagon came into view.

Black Hawk trotted into camp with four fish then dropped them into the bucket of water. He walked over to Raven and watched the wagon coming. "How's the leg feeling?"

Smiling gratefully at her uncle, Raven sighed plaintively. "Sore, but not bad thanks to you."

Jumping down in a panic, Dream Dancer rushed to Raven for a hug. "Are you hurt? I felt your need for me, but couldn't get here faster!"

Chuckling with pleasure, Raven patted her brother's cheek tenderly. "I'm just fine Ed. I had a run in with a she-grizzly, but Black Hawk came then patched me up. I thought you were taking the mares to the valley for me?"

Dream Dancer shrugged guiltily as the three of them walked over to the fire. He stopped short and eyed the black bundle still sleeping on top of Raven's blanket. He turned to his sister with a knowing look as he motioned incredulously in warning. "Trust you two to kill the mother then look for the baby. This is not just any bear cub though... it's a grizzly cub, are you sure it is wise to try raising it? They can be so unpredictable at times."

Smirking teasingly, Black Hawk pointed at the cute black bundle of fur. "Well, I'm not sure it's wise, but I couldn't leave the adorable little fellow to die now... could I?"

Snorting, Dream Dancer grinned. "No, I suppose you couldn't."

They sat around the fire eating Raven's hastily made meal.

Dream Dancer filled them in as they ate. "I sent Steve with the mares because the sheriff showed up at the ranch. Did you know Scott and Patrick disappeared with no trace?"

Raven sighed sadly then nodded grimly. "I know; they were the guides that were travelling with the white man."

Frowning in concern... Dream Dancer sighed resignedly. "I was afraid of that! The sheriff put a posse together, so now they are out looking for them. The town is supposed to have a meeting in a week. If the men aren't found by then, they are going to vote on sending the army to grandfather's village and drive them out. They figure if the two men are dead that the Indians did it. There are a few people demanding action now, but the sheriff said he talked them out of doing anything hasty. He will try to stall them at the meeting to give you an extra week to get our people out; he's not going to be able to stop them for long, he said."

"Darn it!" Raven swore in frustration. "I knew I should have left grandfathers immediately. Now I have less time than I first thought."

Scowling suspiciously, Dream Dancer waved in demand. "So, tell me what is going on in the village?"

Grimacing dispiritedly, Raven sat back and told him everything.

****

Jed kept them at a walk for half an hour then judging the horses rested enough, he picked up the pace. He slowed the animals to a walk again an hour later and looked back. "There's a good site ahead for a camp; we can have lunch there. We need a brief rest... especially the horses. There is a creek behind it for water, so we can refill canteens."

Melissa nodded without arguing, they had been riding hard since sunrise; the rest would be appreciated.

Finding the camp that Jed had used long ago; they set up a quick temporary camp. Mell, Jed, as well as their son looked after the horses while the others cooked a light meal.

Everyone settled around the fire then ate quietly. Once finished, Jed looked around and smiled in encouragement. "So far we are making excellent time. If we keep this up, we could be there before the twenty days are up, but don't count on it, we still have a long way to go! We will be travelling through Indian Territory after we pass this next town so I would like to stay there for the night. It will mean stopping an hour early, but the horses need a rest. We all could use a bed for at least one night. Once we leave this town, we will not see another one for three or four days until we reach the Montana border. I want Jessica as well as Pamela to hide their hair as Mell does, Indians will be less likely to attack five men then two men and three women."

Everyone agreed; they were all looking forward to a bed as the camp was dismantled quickly. They rode on once Jed was satisfied that there was no trace left of them ever being there.

****

When Raven finished explaining everything to her brother, there was a stunned silence. Dream Dancer leaned forward intently... he shattered the silence by growling furiously in denial; he gestured sharply in finality. "They can't make you marry this man!"

Shrugging dejectedly, Raven lifted her hands impotently. "Well, unfortunately, it looks like I don't have a choice."

Dream Dancer frowned shrewdly, knowing his sister the way he did; he knew there would be consequences. He waved uneasily afraid to ask, but Edward did anyway. "If you have to do this what will happen later?"

Raven shook her head sadly in sorrow. "I don't know for sure! If the Great Spirit forces me to marry a man I don't love, it might be the last time I ever go back to the village... or follow my Indian heritage. My people will always be allowed to remain on this land; I will not protect them anymore, though!"

Black Hawk shared a concerned look with Dream Dancer. Raven had never talked like this before; it scared both men.

Getting up painfully, Raven waved towards the ranch. "Well, I must hurry back! I have to find the killers, plus Devon's sister as soon as possible. I need to prove to everyone that my people didn't do it. Dream Dancer you go back to the ranch and look after things for me."

Shaking his head firmly, Dream Dancer waved decisively. "I can't, I didn't bring my horse; besides, if you must marry this man I want to meet him. Maybe the Great Spirit will give me a vision that will help."

Looking at her brother solemnly; Raven nodded in consent... she gestured in warning. "Fine, but on the condition that you leave for the ranch when I'm ready to go find the killers."

Dream Dancer grinned with a nod and helped clean up camp. They loaded the wagon with the hides and the deer meat then headed out.

*****

Devon sighed in relief as he slipped away from Giant Bear's and walked to the storage lodge to feed his horse. His head was spinning; Golden Dove had drilled him hard today. His adoption ceremony would be held tomorrow night, so he had learned what to expect for that. Then she had quizzed him on the Cheyenne words he learned already... plus, added more. She was angry with her husband, and taking it out on everyone. He chuckled in pleasure to himself, but not as hard as she was taking it out on the chief. Giant Bear had slept by himself in a corner last night.

Taking three armloads of hay over to his horse, Devon put them in the corral before climbing up on the fence. He sat quietly hoping the stud would come over and eat with him sitting here again.

Devil frisked a little before cautiously walking over to eat.

Smiling in pleasure, Devon sat still not wanting to spook him.

Suddenly, the stallion lifted his head before calling out a challenge as he rushed to the opposite side of the pen. Devil stared towards the west.

Seeing two riders coming followed by a wagon, Devon climbed down then squinted in the fading light. The Englishman recognized Black Hawk and Raven then looked behind them anxiously watching the cart. As it got closer, he noticed three coffins in the back. He looked at the driver and sighed in disappointment; it was only a kid, sixteen or seventeen maybe... not old enough to help him.

Raven rode past Devon without even looking down to acknowledge him. The Englishman stared after her miffed then followed curious to see what was going on.

The strange procession went to Raven's tepee and stopped. Black Hawk jumped down off his horse immediately... before rushing over to his niece; he lifted his hands to help her down.

Watching, Devon saw Raven look down at Black Hawk; she seemed about to bat the offered help away. The Englishman watched her uncle gestured angrily then he said something harshly in Cheyenne that he didn't understand. She finally nodded reluctantly before slipping off her horse into his arms.

Devon was puzzled by this exchange for a moment, until Raven tried to stand and her leg buckled under her. She would have fallen if Black Hawk hadn't been holding her up.

*****

Black Hawk scowled up at Raven... his irritably was obvious. "Don't be a fool; you've been in the saddle for hours. Your leg won't hold you if you try to get down on your own. I can see that your fever has returned, as well. Let me help you before I go get the medicine man!"

Raven nodded in exhaustion and grimaced in pain as she lifted her injured leg over her horse. She sat sideways for a moment before slipping into Black Hawk's arms. He held her stead as she tentatively put pressure on her injured leg... she gasped in pain as it buckled beneath her.

Sweeping Raven into his arms, Black Hawk turned to his nephew. "Hurry, go get the medicine man and your grandmother then bring them."

Dream Dancer nodded grimly and jumped out of the wagon instantly then hurried past the white man before disappearing.

Seeing Black Hawk Carry Raven into her tepee, Devon turned away and left for the chief's. The medicine man with the shaman following closely rushed past him. A moment later Giant Bear, Golden Dove then the youth all hurried by him. He continued on to the tepee... he stopped short remembering the bag lying by the corral. He shrugged irritably; he would get it tomorrow. He went inside to bed knowing he wouldn't be welcomed at Ravens.

****

The marshal's party slowed their horses for the last half hour of their ride. Dusk was deepening as Melissa rode up beside Jed. "We have not been in this town for a while; I hope it's quieter than the last time we were here!"

Jed grimaced grimly in agreement. "I'm hoping it is too; we will go to the sheriff's office to get a rundown on what's happening in town."

Melissa nodded thoughtfully. "Good idea, I need to get his reports anyway; he hasn't sent us one in a while. I also need to let him know that he will have to call on the other deputy marshals if he has any trouble while we are away."

Looking over at his wife, Jed smiled teasingly. "I know."

In the last twenty-seven years as marshal and deputy marshal, they had worked well together. The first year had been a bit rough though. They had argued quite a lot, but they had come to an understanding finally... after that, things had gone smoothly. Now they hardly ever fought, plus they knew each other so well now that they didn't need to ask the others opinion; they just knew what the other was thinking.

Melissa sighed in disgruntlement as the party came into sight of the town. It was aptly named, Wild Rose, they called it. Every time they went to town, they were pierced by a thorn... it never failed! It was extremely wild, most of the time they had to fight their way in; being only four days to the Montana border, it was a haven for outlaws, as well as gunfighters.

Jed had suggested they try sneaking into town a few times over the years to clean out the vermin; regrettably, somebody always gave away the fact that they were coming. Which is why, they had to fight their way in but this time no one knew they were here. So hopefully, they wouldn't have any problems getting in or away in the morning.

They rode into town looking around nervously. It was too quiet!

Taking off her white buffalo robe, Melissa put it behind her saddle with her bedroll. She turned back then unfastened the strap holding her gun in its holster when she was riding... just in case. She took out her repeater rifle next and laid it in front of her across the saddle.

Following Mell's lead; Jed, plus the two other women in their party took out rifles too. The only one who didn't was their son; he did have one... although, he swore that he wouldn't use it.

Shaking her head, Melissa sighed in annoyance. Maybe she should have left Daniel behind; it worried her that he wouldn't protect himself. Although, he had the same training as the rest of her children... plus was even faster with a six-shooter then Mell was. He absolutely refused to lift a gun anymore.

They got to the sheriff's office and dismounted before loosely tying their reins, just in case they had to make a fast retreat. Melissa took the lead at this point. Jed and Jessica stayed close protecting her back. Pamela was beside her husband so she could protect him as they brought up the rear.

Entering, Melissa hastily looked around. Within seconds, she had the whole room mapped out; plus knew that there was someone in the cell and only an unfamiliar deputy at the desk.

The deputy jumped to his feet in fear as he eyed the group coming towards him suspiciously.

Melissa pushed her vest aside so he could see her badge.

Dropping down heavily into his chair with a sigh of relief... the deputy wiped sweat off his forehead. "Am I ever glad to see you, Marshal; I was just writing a telegram of urgency to you!"

Nodding knowingly, Melissa had spotted the paper in front of him then motioned curiously. "What is going on around here; I don't know you! Where is the sheriff or the original deputy?"

The new deputy ran his hands through his hair in agitation. "Both are dead earlier today! I'm Deputy Mitch Carlile. We had a band of desperado's ride in several days ago. The deputy caught the sheriff taking a bribe, so he shot him and the man giving the bribe. The outlaws shot the deputy later when they were robbing the bank. We tried to stop them, but they got away except for the one that killed the deputy. I shot him out of his saddle; luckily, he had the money, so the town's people elected me as their deputy. The leader came about an hour ago, said if I didn't release his man by sunrise... he would be back. Oh, before I forget to tell you the deputy left you a message. He said to tell you that he had suspected the sheriff of tipping off the outlaws as to when you were coming. He didn't want to say anything until he had proof."

Sitting down grimly, Melissa sighed thoughtfully. "Well, I was getting suspicious, but I wasn't sure who was doing it. It looks like we got here in time. Continue that telegram, but send out two... one to Deputy Marshal Dusty and one to Deputy Marshal Tyler. They should be in Smyth's Crossing."

Turning to Pamela, Melissa motioned towards the hotel across the street. "Pam, you and Daniel take the horses to the hotel... book three rooms; then stable the horses, except mine and Jed's leave them tied in front of the hotel."

Gesturing at Jessica after receiving Daniel's nod, Melissa pointed towards the hotel. "Jess you can also go to the hotel then bring us something to eat, please; it's going to be a long night!"

After the three left, Melissa turned to the deputy then pointed down at the paper. "You can finish the telegram and send it out right away. Then go get a couple of hours of sleep, but be back here before midnight. I doubt very much that the outlaws will wait until dawn, they will probably hit right at midnight."

Deputy Carlile frowned anxiously; he hadn't thought of that. Hastily, he finished writing before leaving.

Looking at her husband, Melissa sighed. "No rest for us tonight!"

Frowning, Jed nodded in agreement then sat.

****

Dream Dancer then his grandparents rushed into Raven's.

The medicine man with the help of the shaman, were already checking Raven's wound.

Golden Dove hurried over to help them.

Giant Bear and Dream Dancer went over to Black Hawk. The chief grabbed his son's arm in demand. "What happened?"

Black Hawk grimaced at his father's scowl before pulling his arm away then waved to his nephew hopefully.

Turning, Dream Dancer trotted out of the tepee knowingly.

Looking back at his father, Black Hawk told him everything except Raven's forewarning. He wasn't quite finished when his nephew returned with the grizzly cub. Tommy pointed towards Raven without stopping his explanation to his father.

Taking the cub to his sister, Dream Dancer laid him down beside her. The ball of fur was crying when he went out to get him, but the baby grizzly quieted when he was deposited beside Raven. He snuggled against her contentedly before going back to sleep.

Raising her eyebrows at the addition of the cub, Golden Dove wisely didn't say anything.

The medicine man smiled in relief then turned to Golden Dove. "The wound looks good, but she does have a fever. I will give you medicine, it should be gone by tomorrow. She is more exhausted than anything else, a couple days of rest and she will be good as new."

Accepting the herbs, Golden Dove nodded her thanks.

Turning, the medicine man left the tepee.

The shaman relieved, also got up then went over to the men.

Golden Dove turned to her grandson in delight. "It's nice to see you Dream Dancer, I thought Raven wasn't going to let you come here?"

Moving to his grandmother, Dream Dancer hugged her in greeting. "I didn't bring a horse, so Raven had to let me come. Besides, I insisted after I found out she had to marry a vi'hoi. I want to meet him!"

Pleased, Golden Dove beamed; glad he would be staying then stroked his cheek tenderly. "Well, I'm happy you're here. Soon you will be leaving for England then I won't see you again."

Smiling reassuringly, Dream Dancer motioned decisively. "I wouldn't have left before coming to see you to say goodbye... I promise. I'm going to help the men unload, after we can visit."

Without protest, Golden Dove let Dream Dancer leave.

Gesturing, Black Hawk asked his nephew curiously, as they walked out of the tepee. "Where is Spotted Owl hiding?"

Grinning, Dream Dancer waved to the northeast. "I asked him to help Steve with the mares since he's so good with horses."

Black Hawk pointed towards the paddocks. "Can you take Brave Heart and put him in the empty breaking pen for me? His wound is healing, but we need to keep a close eye on him for a few days."

Frowning, Dream Dancer didn't like handling Raven's stallion at all. "I will try, but he's only let me come near him once."

After Dream Dancer left, Giant Bear pulled out the grizzly head; he eyed it in disapproval before shaking his head in amazement. "Fool woman could have gotten herself killed."

Sighing grimly in agreement, Black Hawk couldn't argue with that it was all too true. He unhitched the horses before taking them to the pasture. Returning, Tommy helped Giant Bear and the shaman unload the deer then the bear's head. It went into Raven's tepee.

The buck was taken to a structure Raven built for them; it was used to hang meat before being butchered. There was a wooden trap door by the back wall. When opened, stairs went down to the cellar; it ran the length of the building. Once the meat was cut, it would be taken underground to keep it cool and away from disease infested flies.

Once everything was put away, they all gathered at Raven's.

Raven was obediently sipping the tea her grandmother made of the herbs the medicine man gave her. She sighed as everyone gathered around. "I'm too tired to explain, but I will be leaving tomorrow."

The chief and the shaman both shook their heads negatively. However, the shaman spoke first. "No! The medicine man said at least two-day's rest. You must stay off that leg for the fever to go away, the wound will not heal properly otherwise."

Giant Bear waited until the shaman was done then gestured in grim determination at his granddaughter. "Besides, tomorrow we will bury the dead in the white man's way. We will also be having Devon's adoption ceremony tomorrow night, and you need be here for that."

Grimacing resignedly, Raven looked at both men in warning. "Fine I will stay tomorrow, but I'm leaving the day after first thing in the morning. Black Hawk can finish teaching Devon."

The shaman and Giant Bear looked at each other in dismay; both knew that they couldn't hold Raven any longer, so they nodded grudgingly.

Smiling at her brother invitingly as he came back in, Raven waved towards the corner. "You can sleep here with me."

Dream Dancer inclined his head in agreement before going out to gather his pack and bedroll. He came back and made his bed.

Good nights were said then everyone left.

****

Melissa sighed before pushing her plate away; she just finished her meal when the new deputy walked in.

Mitch sat down with a sigh of irritation. "I couldn't sleep anymore; every little noise would make me jump."

Jed pulled out the pocket watch that Melissa had given him before they were married... he looked at it speculatively. "It's almost midnight; we should take our positions."

Jed and Melissa picked up their rifles then went to sit on the porch.

Jessica crooked her finger at the deputy, he followed her out.

Turning away obediently, Mitch took his position when the marshal pointed him towards the opposite end of the building.

Pamela sat at the only window then broke open a pane of glass so her rifle could be fired from there.

Daniel went into the prisoner's cell. He had a gun, but it was for show. Pastor Brown brought a chair with him; he sat tensely watching the prisoner before looking at his wife. Pamela promised not to use her rifle unless given no choice.

Melissa frowned then called to the deputy curiously. "How many are there in total?"

Mitch peeked around the corner of the building at Melissa. "There was six when they came to town, but I'm not sure if that's all of them."

Grimacing knowingly, Melissa heaved a sigh resignedly... of course there would be more. Mell sat back in the chair and lounged back as if she didn't have a care in the world.

Not fooled, Jed knew that she was wound tighter than a spring. The deputy marshal sat not far from Melissa and propped his rifle across his knee. He took out his watch again to look at the time when they heard the sounds of horses. It was two minutes to twelve... just as Mell figured. The outlaws had planned to spring their comrade all along.

The outlaws came into sight, but they didn't see the marshal or deputy marshal until they were at the hitching rail.

Jed and Melissa stood up and walked to the edge of the porch cradling their rifles. The marshal was right again there were now ten of them. She nodded cordially at the group. "What can I do for you?"

The men looked at each other in confusion. They heard that there was a woman marshal in North Dakota but hadn't believed it. The leader looked at her badge in contempt then spat on the porch ahead of her. "You have my friend locked up; I want him released; NOW!"

Looking at the insolent outlaw in anger... Melissa didn't flinch or back down. "Sorry to disappoint you, but your friend robbed the bank. He also killed a deputy, so he will be hung for his crimes. If you are smart, you will turn around then ride away; since we have recovered the money, you are free to go. If you don't ride out of town, you will be arrested."

Melissa and Jed had decided to encourage these men to leave instead of trying to capture them. Her deputy marshals could chase them later; right now, they didn't have time to waste. Their crimes weren't severe enough to warrant killing them outright, unless given no choice.

Jed let the safety off on his rifle, as the tension in the air grew heavier. Finally, one of the outlaws made a mistake as he pulled his gun; the rest followed. Within seconds, the outlaws lay dead.

Walking off the porch, Melissa sighed dejectedly. "Well, I did try to give them a reason to leave."

Going to his wife, Jed reached over and squeezed Mell's hand in sympathy knowing how she hated to kill.

Turning without another word, Jed lead everyone across the street for some much-needed sleep before entering the hotel.

CHAPTER NINE

Getting up Devon went to grab his bag, but remembered he forgot it by the hay shed. He left the tepee and hurried to the paddocks... wondering where the boy had slept last night. The Englishman walked around the corner then stopped when the man saw the object of his speculation walking towards the second paddock; carrying hay, he threw it into the pen for Raven's stallion.

Devon watched in fascination as the boy began singing softly in Cheyenne before climbing the fence then jumped in with Raven's stallion.

Intrigued, Devon observed the stud in apprehension when Brave Heart snorted and pawed the ground in warning. The boy continued crooning softly almost as if hypnotizing him. The stallion stood then let the youth walk up to his hindquarters. The youngster took a cloth from the pouch at his waist and wiped the horse down before putting it back then took out a small container and opening it; he smeared whatever was in it on the stud's hind end. Backing away carefully, he tucked the item back in his pouch then went to the fence; climbing he sat on the top railing watching the horse.

Glad the stallion hadn't hurt the boy; Devon continued on his way. He went to the shed then grabbed hay for his horse. The Englishman whistled loudly to let the boy know someone was here, so the youngster wouldn't get a scare.

Turning still whistling, Devon walked towards Devil's pen. The Englishman looked at the boy out of the corner of his eye as he walked, but didn't stop. The white man awkwardly put the hay under the fence and turned to go back.

The boy was gone when Devon looked, so he quit whistling then went for more feed. When he got there, the kid came out with an armload and smiled at him before taking it over to Devil's pen without saying a word.

Grabbing a load, Devon awkwardly gathered his forgotten sack then went to the paddock. The boy helped him dump the hay over the fence before turning and trotted off, still not saying anything to the Englishman.

Watching him disappear, Devon sighed in disappointment then climbed on the top railing. The Englishman had hoped to talk to the boy; he shrugged before turning to Devil. He whistled trying to get his horse to come to him.

Devil took a couple steps, but stopped before snorting a warning; letting his new master know someone was coming.

Devon turned towards Brave Heart's corral at a noise, and saw the boy coming back with two buckets of water. He stopped at Raven's horse first then put one in there before grabbing the other one and walked over to Devil's pen. He put the bucket beside the hay.

Dream Dancer walked over then leaned against the fence not far from Devon. He smiled in admiration at the beautiful grey stallion and started crooning softly in Cheyenne.

The stud perked up his ears then took a hesitant step forward before rearing in anger, and ran to the opposite end of the paddock.

Chuckling at the horse, Raven's brother looked up before extending his hand to Devon. "Name's Dream Dancer."

Taking the hand, the Englishman squeezed it gently before introducing himself. "My name's Devon. How did you get the stallion to react like that?"

Grinning cheekily as Devon, Dream Dancer let go of his hand. He waved toward the stud in explanation. "It's not really a secret; you just need to remember that the horse you are talking to has been here all his life. So, the only language he knows is Cheyenne. If you want before I leave here to go home, I can teach you the words to that song."

Eyeing the boy speculatively, Devon cocked his head curiously. "And where is your home?"

Shrugging, Dream Dancer motioned vaguely towards the west. "That way one and a half days by horse; two by wagon unless you are in a hurry, you can make it in less than two, if you push the horses hard."

Gazing at the youngster inquisitively, Devon hoped that he could get more information from him. "And who are you?"

Chuckling in amusement, Dream Dancer waved towards his sister's teepee. "I'm Raven's brother, of course! Who are you?"

Looking at the boy more closely, Devon finally nodded. Yes, he could see the resemblance now. Although, Dream Dancer was fairer in colouring then Raven; they both had the same high cheekbones of the natives... the same nose, and face structure with an arrogant chin. Both of them had green eyes as well, but Ravens were much lighter in colouring. Her brothers were a brilliant dark green, very unusual... almost black looking. Where did he see eyes like that before? The boy was close to six feet now; by the time he reached full growth, Devon was sure he would be around six-foot-one or so.

Dream Dancer was studying Devon just as intently then smiled thoughtfully; yes, he wasn't a meek man by any means. The Englishman was powerfully built, but would he be able to handle his sister... Raven. He wasn't too tall about six feet. It was hard to say what his face and eyes looked like because they were pretty swollen in some places, with bruises covering the rest. His handshake had been firm, not overpowering.

Finished his inspection, Devon finally answered Dream Dancer's question. "I'm Lord Devon Rochester from England."

Cocking his head intrigued, Dream Dancer motioned inquisitively. "Why are you in Montana if your home is in England?"

Devon sighed in aggravation. "I have some property next to Earl Summerset's somewhere out here in this Godforsaken land. That is all I'm allowed to say right now... if I want to keep my tongue that is!"

Frowning, Dream Dancer was puzzled by that statement but didn't push the matter. Edward felt guilty enough at not being able to tell the Englishman that he was Earl Summerset, but Raven had forbidden him to mention it.

Smiling enticingly down at the boy, Devon hoped to get a few more questions that he had resolved. Although, the Englishman did feel a bit ashamed using Dream Dancer's open honesty to get answers nobody else wanted to give him. He pushed his guilt away and continued optimistically. "Does your sister live with you and where are your parents?"

Grinning knowingly, Dream Dancer was well aware that Devon was using him; he shrugged not seeing any harm in telling him the truth. "My parents are both dead, they were killed in a stagecoach hold up. My sister lives with me sometimes, at other times she lives here."

Nodding in anger, Devon had hoped for information; with none imminent, the Englishman changed the subject. "Why do they call you Dream Dancer?"

Raven's brother shrugged gravely. "The shaman says it's because when he had his vision of me, I was holding a dream catcher and dancing by the fire chanting. The moon was full, as I chanted black clouds with a touch of mauve interwoven throughout covered the moon; when I was finished the misty clouds dissipated almost instantly."

Devon looked confused. "What is a dream catcher?"

Dream Dancer chuckled at Devon's curiosity then tried to explain as best he could. "A dream catcher is exactly what its name implies. We make a hoop with wood fibre and weave into a pattern... symbols, using sinew or nettle fibers. Usually, the patterns are circular but not always. A shaman or a dreamer weaves an enchantment into the dream catcher as he is making it. You put this dream catcher over your sleeping pallet, it's supposed to keep away evil dreams or nightmares. It also helps us to remember them; Indians place great significance in their dreams, so we always want them interpreted properly by a shaman. Since I'm a dreamer, my dream catchers hold greater power. According to our spiritual leader, that is."

Grimacing in disbelief, Devon didn't truly believe in all that nonsense; he did not want to hurt the boy's feelings, though. It reminded him too much of the rumours of witchcraft in England, which he never believed either. He motioned teasingly. "Maybe you can make me one after I marry your sister?"

Sobering inquisitively, Dream Dancer pointed at Devon curiously. "Are you going to marry Raven?"

Shrugging, Devon's smile slipped away. He scowled angrily before looking away. "I don't have much choice, do I? I either marry her or die!"

Uneasily, Dream Dancer sighed at the livid rebelliousness in Devon's voice.

Hearing the anxious sigh, Devon looked down at the boy. Raven's brother was staring at the stud with a worried look. The Englishman cleared his throat to get the boy's attention then changed the subject. "What happened to your sister while she was gone?"

Glad to get off that delicate topic, Dream Dancer gestured calmly in explanation. "Well, she came to meet me..."

Raven's brother told Devon the whole story before grinning in humour. "She's fine now, but she will have another scar to add to her many others."

Dream Dancer grinned at the Englishman mischievously; he had forgotten to mention the cub. He beckoned Devon to follow him enticingly. "Why don't you come along, I need to check on her anyway? I can show you what we brought back with us."

Devon climbed down off the fence immediately, not suspecting a thing as he followed Raven's brother curiously.

Opening the drape, Dream Dancer stuck his head inside to make sure Raven was decent. Edward smiled pleadingly at his sister, who was sitting up sipping her coffee. "I brought Devon with me to see the grizzly head, is it all right if I bring him in?"

Raven set her cup down and eyed the wicked gleam in her brother's eyes hesitantly, wondering what he was up to then nodded consent.

Grinning, Dream Dancer ducked back out before motioning to Devon... they entered. He pointed to the corner where the grizzly head was displayed. Devon examined it then shivered in fear. "Good Lord, that animal is huge!"

Nodding in agreement, Dream Dancer waved at the other end of the village. "It was, and after we are done here; I will take you over to where the women are working on the hide."

Grabbing the Englishman's arm eagerly; Dream Dancer pulled him to his sister's pallet. "Can you show Devon your wound... please!"

Frowning at her brother distrustfully, Raven knew he was up to no good; curiously she nodded, wanting to see where this was leading. She pulled the blanket away so they could see.

Both of them squatted for a closer look. When Devon leaned forward... Dream Dancer grinning at Raven innocently before poking the grizzly cub hard. The black ball of fur jumped up with an angry yowl at being so rudely awakened.

The unsuspecting Devon cried out in panic before falling backwards then landed hard on his rump. He had such an expression of startled amazement on his face that Dream Dancer and Raven both doubled up in hysterical laughter... unable to help themselves.

Watching the two having hysterics at his expense, Devon couldn't help but grin at the trick Raven's brother had pulled.

The offended cub settled down once more, and curled back up against Raven then went back to sleep.

Eyeing the animal distrustfully, Devon got up and sat beside Dream Dancer. He watched Raven intrigued; this was the first time he heard her laugh. It was deep and robust lighting up her face. It took his breath away watching her.

Dream Dancer chuckled as he wiped tears away before poking his gullible victim in apology to get his attention. "I'm sorry; I just couldn't help myself."

Devon grinned in delight at the guilty Dream Dancer. "Well, I must have looked funny. I'm sure if I could have seen my face, I would laugh too."

Pointing at the cub in demand, Devon asked. "Tell me what that is?"

Raven answered Devon instead of her brother. "He's the reason that the she-grizzly attacked my horse. She could smell the blood from the buck that I had killed, so figured to get an easy meal for her cub. Usually, bears won't attack humans unless they have a good reason; like protecting young ones, being provoked, or are starving. She had left her cub up in a tree to keep it safe, not far from my camp. Black Hawk went looking for it as soon as he realized she had a baby then coaxed it down, but he seems to have adopted me. If the cub had been a little older, Black Hawk would have left him in the tree or shot him depending on his age."

Fascinated, Devon frowned. "Why, what's the difference?"

Beaming at the inquisitive Devon, Raven was pleased that he wanted to know more. "At this age they are easy to fool into adopting you. If they are young enough, they can be trained. An older cub would fight you all the way, they would be nearly impossible to manage. At five or six months old he would have had to be shot; it would be the humane thing to do, since he would be too young to survive and too old for training. If there is a female grizzly around, sometimes they will be adopted if not too old."

Nodding, Devon shrugged in apology. "I will take your word for it; I don't know much about animals out here."

Changing the subject, Raven pointed towards the paddocks. "How's it going with your stallion, any progress yet?"

Waving, Devon sighed forlornly not being a horse trainer he had no idea. "I'm not sure; yesterday when I fed him, I went and sat a little distance away from the hay on the top railing. He came over then stood not far from me and ate while I watched him. This morning when I whistled, he took two hesitant steps towards me, but stopped and backed away."

Raven smiled satisfied that he was getting better results than anyone else ever had with that stallion. "Good, you are making progress; after your lessons I want you to go into the pen. If he doesn't chase you out, take several steps and sit on the ground. If you have apples left, put them with some grain in front of you... stay there for a bit. Afterwards, come back here and let me know what happens. If the stud does chase you out, don't get discouraged. He might not be ready so try in a few days."

Devon nodded then got up and turned to Dream Dancer. "We will have to go see that hide later; I'm late for my lessons."

Dream Dancer inclined his head in agreement then watched him leave. He got up and made Raven coffee before settling down across from her... he asked curiously. "Devon seems like a nice man. He didn't get mad at being tricked by an Indian, most white men would. Don't you like him?"

Waving irritably, Raven shrugged dismissively. "I don't know him, so I can't say whether he's nice or not."

Frowning, Dream Dancer looked at his sister shrewdly. "Are you fighting this marriage because you dislike Devon and find him repulsive? Or is it the fact that you are being forced that's making you hate it?"

Putting her cup down, Raven eyed her brother in surprise before gesturing angrily. "Why would you ask such a question; of course, I hate being told that I have to marry someone I don't even know! How dare the Great Spirit or our grandfather demand this of me after all I have done for my people! I want to marry for love, not to save myself or others!"

Leaning forward intently, Dream Dancer took her hand pleadingly. "I know Raven... I would hate it too; you need to think of it in a different way, though. If we had been born in England, as we should have been... it would be worse. Not only do your parents pick out who you marry, but most never meet their intended until the wedding day. At least you have a chance to see Devon and get to know him before you marry him. It's good too that he's not old or ugly."

Raven grimaced reflectively knowing her brother was right, but didn't want to talk about it so changed the subject. "Go find me a walking stick; it should be time to go out for the funeral."

Dream Dancer nodded not wanting to push her too hard, she would just fight it more if he did. Edward squeezed her hand in reassurance before getting up to leave.

Sitting there stroking the cub absently, Raven couldn't help thinking about her brother's question.

****

Jed and Melissa met the rest of their party in the dining room for breakfast. Jed critically inspected Pamela then Jessica as they sat down. He grinned in approval at their clothes; both were now wearing buckskin pants. They had also bound their chests tightly to hide the fact that they were women. They had changed into matching fringed buckskin shirts with their hair tucked away under their hats... they had also added revolvers.

Pamela must have loaned Jessica a set of buckskins because she didn't have any of her own. From a distance they would pass as men, but up-close nobody would be fooled.

Nodding in thanks when the waitress brought them breakfast; Jed accepted the coffee, but didn't say anything as he ate. Once they all finished, he sat back then sighed contemplatively. "Okay, it's a hard four-day ride to the border between Dakota and Montana. There are no more towns until we cross into Montana. We must keep a close watch for Indians and any outlaws like last night. We have one fast flowing river to cross two days after the border town, that's dangerous. If we are careful, we should have no problems. We will stop at the store first for provisions, any questions?"

They all shook their heads no.

Nodding decisively, Jed stood up. "Good, let's go!"

They went to collect their belongings, plus made a stop at the store before heading out of town.

****

Dream Dancer was helping his sister up when their grandfather stuck his head in. "It's time you two, let's go!"

Raven grimaced at the rush. "Be out shortly, Grandfather!"

Dream Dancer helped Raven then held out the walking stick... she smiled in thanks then took it. Silently they left, walking together they reached the spot for the funeral then went to the front of the crowd; Giant Bear, Devon, Golden Dove, and the shaman were waiting for them.

Giant Bear stepped forward then raised his hands for quiet. He spoke in Cheyenne before repeating it in English so everybody would understand. "Since this is a vi'hoi... a white man's funeral, Devon will speak; some of you know English, but for those of you that don't I will translate so everyone can follow along. We will need silence please."

Nodding to Devon to go ahead, Giant Bear stepped back.

The shaman chanting, blessed the dead... with Giant Bear translating. Two warriors lifted each coffin into the ground, with more helping fill the graves.

Saying a prayer to finish it off, Devon said goodbye to his youngest sister; it was a beautiful service... the first time this Cheyenne band allowed the dead to be blessed not only by the white man's God, but by Ma'heo'o too.

Raven hobbled over to Devon then touched his arm, but snatched her hand back at the weird tingling sensation. "I just want to say that was a beautiful service, I'm really sorry your younger sister died."

Nodding in thanks for the words of sympathy, Devon turned away without saying anything. He walked to the creek; needing to be alone... he never looked back.

Sighing in distress at the rejection; Raven turned to her grandmother. "I better go back and feed my cub before he wakes up, he's liable to rip apart my tepee looking for food."

Golden Dove smiled in sympathy, having seen her granddaughter's distressed look before kissing Raven's cheek. "Okay, I will be there shortly with lunch. We won't have supper until the adoption ceremony."

Inclining her head in agreement, Raven turned away then walked towards Black Hawk. She motioned hopefully. "Did you go fishing this morning? My cub should be hungry by now."

Black Hawk chuckled in delight. "Oh, now it's your cub, is it? It's good that you feel that way because my wife refuses to have anything to do with him. So, he will have to stay with you; yes, I went fishing. I will bring them to you."

Grinning gratefully, Raven left. Her leg was feeling better and she was only limping slightly by the time she got to her tepee... she ducked inside.

The cub was awake walking around sniffing everything curiously. Raven beamed in pleasure at the cute ball of fur. She sat on her blankets as she regarded the cub thoughtfully.

The grizzly cub came trotting over to Raven and sniffed at her then cuddled up as he went back to sleep.

Raven reached down to stroke the cub tenderly as a name popped into her head, which made her chuckle. "I think I'll call you Cuddles."

Golden Dove ducked into the tent, followed by Black Hawk then Dream Dancer. Raven's uncle carried a half dozen fish, and her brother brought a pot of stew. A few minutes later, Giant Bear with Devon arrived then they all sat around the fire eating lunch together.

Giant Bear turned to his grandson curiously. "When are you going?"

Dream Dancer shrugged dejectedly. "Tomorrow, at the same time Raven does; I have some work I have to do."

Devon looked at Raven in surprise. "You are leaving tomorrow, what about your cub and helping me break Devil?"

Sighing plaintively, Raven looked down at the black bundle of fur; wondering what condition her tepee would be in when she returned. She looked over at Devon then pointed to her uncle in explanation. "Black Hawk will finish teaching you. The cub, he will have to stay here. Black Hawk's wife won't let him take Cuddles to their tepee."

Sitting up straight, Devon put a hand on his chest pleadingly. "I can stay with him, that will give Giant Bear time with his wife."

Looking at her grandfather, Raven saw him nod in agreement. She turned back to Devon. She inclined her head in thanks. "Okay, that would be a great help. You must take him out during the day. There are trees in the back that Cuddles marked as a scratching post, and a place to do his business. You will find bears seldom go to the bathroom in their own caves. They are clean animals so take him down to the creek for a bath. The reason a bear stinks is because they eat carrion. If there is water around, they prefer swimming and playing in it, as well as fishing. You can feed the cub... fresh fish, nuts, fruit, berries, eggs, birds, snakes, and they like ground squirrels. Grizzlies like carrion more than regular bears, but we don't want to feed him any; since he will be living inside and will start to stink after a while. Being so young, he will sleep a lot. You need to keep him occupied when he isn't."

Grinning enthusiastically, Devon sighed in pleasure... anticipating time by himself. He was surprised that they were going to let him stay alone, since technically he was their prisoner; although, he didn't really feel like one. The Englishman sat back and surprisingly enjoyed the rest of the visit.

*****

Five hours later, Devon sighed in pleasure as he tried to look down at his finery. The buckskins Raven gave him fit perfectly; unfortunately, he couldn't see what he looked like. Golden Dove had commented that she loved the look of his new clothes, but they felt funny to him. The Englishman sat down on his blankets so he wouldn't get them dirty then ran through what he had to say at the ceremony. Thankfully, the Cheyenne language was getting easier for him to understand... as long as they didn't speak too fast.

Devon smiled in delight as he thought of the afternoon he had spent with Dream Dancer. They went to see the she-grizzlies hide first. He found it hard to believe that Raven and Brave Heart had survived being attacked by that enormous monster. Afterwards, they went to the creek where his new friend taught him the crooning song for his stallion.

Once they finished bathing, Dream Dancer proceeded to teach Devon how to catch fish for the cub using his hands. It totally amazed him... never having seen it done before. Raven's brother explained that they tickled a fish's belly until they were docile, and quickly grasped it by the gills; once caught, you had to throw them on dry land.

It worked; Devon would never have thought of trying such a thing. They had laughed uproariously together as the Englishman tried to learn. Twice he ended up in the water, instead of the fish winding up on dry land.

Afterwards, they went over to Devil's pen; Devon went in then sat down crooning softly. The stallion did let him come in and sit, much to everyone's surprise. After a hesitant step towards him at the start of the song, the stud refused to come closer. He grinned ecstatically in anticipation, glad to be getting such good results. Even that one-step towards him is progress... at least he wasn't charging him.

Devon sighed in trepidation. He would meet all the Cheyenne tonight. After the ceremony was finished, they would come over to introduce themselves... plus their families. He wouldn't meet the other bands until fall, if he remained here that is; of course, he didn't plan on staying. He was hoping to be on his way to England before fall. The Englishman surprisingly felt disappointed.

Remembering his grandfather's will suddenly... Devon groaned grimly; unfortunately, the Englishman wouldn't be able to go anywhere until next year. Hopefully, he could use his time here as part of his year. Maybe this little incident would work out for him after all, and he wouldn't have to build anything on his property to live in... or impose on the Earl of Summerset.

*****

Smiling in approval at her brother, Raven gushed in affection. "You look absolutely gorgeous tonight!"

Dream Dancer blushed in pleasure. "Well, I did bring a variety of clothes with me, I wasn't sure what was going on; I'm glad that I did."

Raven hugged her brother affectionately. "I'm glad you're here. Devon likes you; he's been more relaxed and calmer since you came."

Grinning in delight, Dream Dancer thought of their first fishing expedition. "I like the Englishman too. It's just too bad he was caught in the middle of this. I think if he had made it to the ranch, you would have liked him too."

Scowling in warning at her brother, Raven didn't say anything. She walked over then put a fish beside the sleeping cub for when he woke.

Trying to look innocent, Dream Dancer ignored his sister's angry glare. He didn't tell Raven about his dream last night, since he wasn't sure what it meant. All he could see was a white buffalo leading people... it kept repeating in a feminine voice. 'I'm coming'; other than that, the Great Spirit was quiet on the subject of Raven's marriage to Devon.

There was only one female named White Buffalo that Dream Dancer knew of... that was his grandfather's friend Melissa. Did the dream mean that she was coming here to help? If so, was he supposed to delay the wedding until she arrived! On the other hand, there could be another meaning to the vision. Most of the time, his dreams meant two or three different things. It was trying to figure out which one he was supposed to use that always confused him.

Dream Dancer had talked to the shaman several times, but he couldn't actually help him. All their spiritual leader would say is that the meaning had to come from within. As he grew older, interpreting the dreams would come more naturally to him.

The shaman refused to teach him since he was leaving for England soon. That worried Dream Dancer, what if he interpreted it wrong. He could hurt someone unintentionally.

Raven watched her brother's expression go from a teasing smile, to a fierce frown of apprehension at his thoughts. She cleared her throat to get his attention wondering if he had a dream. "Has the Great Spirit given you any hint about what I'm supposed to do about Devon yet?"

Shaking off his anxiety, Dream Dancer shook his head negatively at his sister... it wasn't meant for her. "No, I'm sorry nothing yet."

Sighing dejectedly, Raven went over to refill her cup.

*****

Black Hawk sighed in apprehension as he watched Gentle Doe move around the tepee. She had been in her seventh month of pregnancy for two weeks now, and she wasn't looking good. But no matter how he tried, Tommy couldn't convince her to stay off her feet. Maybe he should talk to the medicine man, see if he would mind coming over then ordered his wife to take it easy... she might take their healer's advice. He would talk to his mother about keeping his wife with her so Golden Dove could keep an eye on her.

Gentle Doe walked over to pick up a pail of water.

Jumping up, Black Hawk rushed over before she could pick it up. "Don't lift anything; I will do it!"

Gentle Doe nodded at her worried husband, but didn't say anything.

Black Hawk picked up the pail then put it beside the fire. He turned and looked at Gentle Doe in concern; he motioned in demand. "I want you to go see the medicine man tomorrow."

Looking at her husband sorrowfully, Gentle Doe shrugged dismissively. "I will go if you insist, but I will die giving you another child and there is nothing anyone can do. I want you to promise me something though."

Staring bleakly at his wife in shocked surprise, Black Hawk shook his head vehemently. "You will not... I won't let you!"

Sighing, Gentle Doe knew he would be difficult but she had already resigned herself to her death. She sat down before telling him what she wanted. "I have seen my future; I will die giving birth to a healthy boy child, this I have accepted. But someone comes who will love you as I do, so all I ask is that you do not turn away from our son... or a new love. It will ease my mind if you give me your promise!"

Gazing at his wife incredulously, Black Hawk knew that look on her face... it permitted no refusal from him. He nodded reluctantly. "I promise!"

Choking back tears, Black Hawk rushed out to see his mother once his wife let him go... satisfied with his answer. Tommy rushed into the tepee without knocking.

Golden Dove looked up then started to smile in welcome, but sobered at her son's grief-stricken face. She turned to Devon and waved towards her granddaughters. "Go see Raven, show her how your clothes fit?"

Devon looked from Golden Dove to Black Hawk in concern; he nodded when he saw the stricken look on the older man's face. The Englishman left immediately without argument.

Waiting until Devon left; Golden Dove patted the spot beside her so her son would sit.

Dropping down heavily in distress, Black Hawk grimaced before looking at his mother imploringly. "Gentle Doe said she is going to die in childbirth."

Sighing, Golden Dove used her finger and thumb to wipe her eyes in distress sadly; not surprised by that disclosure... dropping her hand she looked at her son; she nodded unhappily. "It looks that way! The medicine man and I discussed her the other day. We also feel that she will not survive the birthing. Our healer figures the baby is way too big for her. The shaman had a vision, but we were going to wait until after the adoption ceremony to tell you. We know it will come down to a choice, of either saving the baby or saving your wife. You will have to make that decision yourself, I'm afraid."

Black Hawk jumped up in agitation as he raged... all the while shaking his head in denial. "I can't let her die, I love her?"

Golden Dove sighed sadly. "I know you do, but what does she want?"

Halting his frantic pacing, Black Hawk turned to his mother distressfully. "She wants the baby to live, and she made me promise not to turn away from him. She said a woman was coming who will love me like she does. I don't want another woman or a child. I want my wife alive and healthy!"

Frowning in disapproval, Golden Dove wished Gentle Doe hadn't told him that. Getting up, Mary took Black Hawk's hands and squeezed them compassionately. "I'm not sure if she's right about another woman or not; but you must realize that even if we let the baby die, Gentle Doe will probably still die. If it's time for her to go to the great hunting grounds there is nothing you can do to stop it. If you let the baby die and your wife survives, she will hate you. I know her well enough to know that she will take her own life if she thinks it is her time to die. If the baby dies too then all that you will have accomplished is losing both of them."

Scowling dejectedly, Black Hawk waved grimly. "I know, but I can't watch her die. It will tear me up inside, I will hate my child for killing her."

Shaking her head negatively, Golden Dove knew her son better then that... it was the grief talking now. "I don't believe that for a moment; you could never despise a child, especially your own! You have time yet to spend with your wife. Don't throw away her sacrifice or the time you have remaining by letting your feelings of anger and resentment get in the way. We all must go when our time is up, there's no way to stop it. At least you are prepared, so can tell her how much you love her. Most people don't have any warnings."

Black Hawk grimaced in thought then smiled appreciatively at Golden Dove for the excellent advice. "You are right of course; I must spend as much time with Gentle Doe as I possibly can. Thank you, I love you!"

Golden Dove grinned in relief as the despair eased on Black Hawk's face. It wasn't gone entirely, but manageable now. She hugged her son in encouragement. "I love you too; now go hug that pretty wife of yours."

Sighing in relief, Black Hawk nodded at peace and turned before sprinting home; not wanting to waste anymore time away from his wife.

*****

Devon strolled towards Raven's wondering what had upset Black Hawk. He still hadn't figured it out by the time he got to the tepee. The Englishman scratched on the door then waited.

Dream Dancer popped his head out and smiled in greeting at Devon. "Well, hello there, come on in."

Walking in, Devon saw Raven sitting on her bed patting the cub. He stared at her in approval; Raven was wearing a gold-coloured buckskin shirt that dipped low in front showing off her breasts and a dark skirt. It had hundreds of beads with unique designs and was fringed.

Turning away to hide his desire, Devon noticed Dream Dancer staring at him with his mouth hanging open in disbelief.

Raven's brother turned a shocked look at his sister. "You gave Devon the buckskins you've been working on! Weren't they for grandfather?"

Shrugging dismissively, Raven ignored her brothers knowing gaze. "Well, I wasn't sure who they were for; I was thinking of giving them to you as a going away present, but they ended up being too big for you."

Snapping her mouth shut, but too late; Raven bit her lip in annoyance at giving away this information to the Englishman.

Leaping on her mistake immediately, Devon looked at Raven's brother speculatively in surprise. "Oh, where are you going?"

Grinning at Devon, Dream Dancer replied in anticipation. "I'm going to school this fall; I am taking law to help my people."

Chuckling in delight at the excited Dream Dancer, Devon gestured curiously. "Well congratulations, I hope you make all your dreams come true. Where are you going to take law?"

Looking at his sister, Dream Dancer answered truthfully, he turned to Devon. "I'm going to school in England; I'm enrolled for next fall."

Raven's mouth tightened in disapproval, but she didn't say anything; Edward wouldn't listen to her anyway.

Devon stared at Dream Dancer in surprise, impervious to the dispute between brother and sister. "Well, England has the best schools; it is expensive though. How are you planning on paying for tuition?"

Dream Dancer bit his lower lip not sure what to say. He looked at his sister, getting an idea; he grinned devilishly... he waved towards Raven. "My sister is paying for some of it. She started saving money for my schooling after our parents died. My father left me a small inheritance."

Shaking her head, Raven scowled in anger at her brother for involving her so he could get himself out of the tight spot.

Looking at Raven in question, Devon shrugged dismissively when she refused to answer. Remembering Black Hawk saying that she trained other people's horses. He turned to Dream Dancer with enthusiasm. "When I get back to England I will visit; if you need help while you are there, let me know."

Frowning intently at Devon, Dream Dancer hoped to convey how serious he was. "Whatever happens between you and Raven has nothing to do with me. No matter what you discover, I hope you stay my friend."

Smiling in promise, Devon motioned reassuringly at Dream Dancer's pleading expression. "Well, I hope so too. No matter what happens here, you will always be welcome in my home."

Clearing her throat in aggravation, Raven gestured irritably. "Now that you are done proclaiming your undying friendship; can you turn around Devon and let me see how the buckskins fit."

Nodding as he turned for her, Raven was satisfied that it looked good on him... it was a perfect fit. He was taller than her nam-shimi was and broader in the shoulders. She frowned uneasily at how well it fit. She eyed Devon broodingly in suspicion. "Why are you here, I thought you weren't supposed to leave my grandfathers until the ceremony?"

Devon shrugged in bewilderment. "I thought so too, but Black Hawk came storming into the tepee. He looked upset. Golden Dove told me to come here to show you how the buckskins fit."

Raven shared a sad look with her brother.

Looking from one to the other in confusion, Devon impatiently asked. "Well, are you going to tell me or must I guess."

Shrugging sadly, Raven sighed in sorrow. "I suppose you will find out sooner or later, Black Hawk's wife is pregnant again. She is now two weeks into her seventh month."

Frowning perplexedly at the looks, Devon gestured irritably. "Well, what's so upsetting about that? You should be happy."

Inclining her head forlornly, Raven explained to the baffled Devon. "Well, Black Hawk and Gentle Doe have been married for twenty-three years. The first three, she had one miscarriage after another. Finally, his wife managed to get pregnant; this time she went the whole term. Both were thrilled when she delivered a healthy boy. After he was born, the miscarriages started again. Until now, she couldn't hold a child past her fifth month. We all know that this baby will kill her, she must know it too and told Black Hawk tonight that she wouldn't survive."

Devon sighed dejectedly. "You're right it isn't good; poor Black Hawk I know what it's like not having a mother."

Devon was interrupted when Giant Bear popped his head into the tepee. "Oh, there you are Devon; it's time to start... come on."

Dream Dancer helped his sister up then followed Devon out.

CHAPTER TEN

Nudging her horse forward, Melissa rode up beside Jed. "I think we better stop. The horses need a rest, and someone is following us."

Jed slowed his horse; he looked at his wife in surprise. He wasn't aware of that then motioned curiously. "When did you notice?"

Melissa grinned at her irate husband. "A couple of hours after we left town, they are riding hard trying to catch up."

Shaking his head in exasperation, Jed gestured in anger. "Why didn't you tell me before?"

Shrugging dismissively, Melissa smirked unperturbed. "Well, I wasn't sure they were following us... and I'm still not absolutely certain. It could be someone on their way to Montana like us."

Sighing in irritation at his wife's logic, Jed looked for a camp that was in a defensible position. He found what he was looking for ten minutes later. It was approachable one way with a creek running through it for water if they had to stay for longer.

They quickly made camp and Jessica started dinner as they waited tensely for whoever was coming. When they could hear horses, Melissa grabbed her rifle then walked over to Jed.

Two horses came into view, but only one rider. The slight man approaching slowed before taking off an old floppy Mexican sombrero, so they could see. Releasing her long midnight-black hair; she let it fall in a cloud of silk around her shoulders.

Looking at Jed, Melissa grinned in relief as they turned back to watch their daughter in disapproval. Patricia having her mother's piercing turquoise eyes with her father's coal black hair was a striking woman.

Patricia squealed with pleasure before she jumped off her horse, and raced over to envelop first Melissa then Jed in a big hug. "Shame on the both of you for running off on an adventure without telling me first; I was only a day behind you to start with, but I just couldn't seem to catch up to you at first. It wasn't until you stopped in town that I almost caught up you guys. I was only about two hours away by that time."

Melissa grinned unperturbed by Patricia's chiding voice. "Well Pat, if you hadn't been out of town at the time, we would have told you. Speaking of town, who did you leave in charge?"

Patricia smirked at her mother in delight. "John is looking after things."

Groaning in horror, Melissa waved dramatically in incredibility; as she pictured her youngest rambunctious son. "The town will be in shambles when we get back!"

Laughing in glee at her mother's theatrics; Pat was enveloped in a gigantic bear hug without any warning, before she could respond.

Daniel lifted Patricia off her feet and chortled in delight. "I knew that you were coming sis, I could feel you getting close."

Sighing in irritation, Melissa threw her hands up in defeat. "That's why you stalled us this morning in the store then again when we stopped for lunch."

Grinning devilishly, Daniel was not in the least concerned that his mother disapproved. "Well, I couldn't very well ruin the surprise or make it too easy for Pat to catch up now... could I?"

Chuckling at his mother's stern expression; Daniel turned back to his sister with a wink of devilment before changing the subject; he motioned inquisitively. "Where's your dog?"

Smiling at her twin teasingly, Patricia whistled.

A massive black monster of a dog came running at the whistle, and stopped beside Patricia then sat down; waiting patiently... she looked up at her mistress adoringly. She was one of the biggest dogs they had ever seen, her shoulders when on all fours where past her owner's waist and Pat was as tall as her mother, at five-feet-eleven. With her neck and massive head added, she almost reached her owner's chest. She could put a child's head in her mouth without leaving a mark.

The dog was pure black with silver on the tips of her hair. Her fur was long, like a sheepdog with a slight curl at the ends. She had a stub for a tail, nobody cut it off either that is the way she was born they figured.

None of them had any idea what kind of a dog she was. She looked exactly like a miniature grizzly bear with the silver tips on the ends of her hair. When the dog stood up on her hind legs, she was taller than Jed was. She stood at seven-feet plus a bit. However, she was one of the gentlest dogs they had ever owned. Unless you threatened her mistress that is then you had better run for the hills.

Patricia found her when she was a pup, starving and wandering the alleys of the town; so, had brought her home. She now used the dog as a deputy, they worked well together.

Smiling down in approval at her dog, Patricia nodded in assent. "Okay Silver Tip, you can greet everyone now."

Silver Tip went to Daniel first, her second favourite person; she stood on her hind legs then the dog put her front paws on his shoulders, for a sloppy wet kiss.

Daniel laughed and grabbed her around the neck for a hug.

Jumping down, Silver Tip went to Jed next. She greeted him ecstatically, her whole back-end wiggled back and forth as her stub of a tail wagged furiously. The dog butted against him insistently; almost knocking him off his feet, until he bent over with a chuckle for a hug.

Going to the two younger women who were sitting, Silver Tip sat before whining eagerly as she lifted her giant paw for a shake from Jessica first then Pamela next. Once they finished shaking it, both bent to give her a hug.

Only Melissa got different treatment. She squatted waiting for her turn. Silver Tip crept towards Mell on her belly, whining plaintively. The huge animal sat up when close to her before carefully enclosing the marshal's chin in her jaws, but didn't bite down. After releasing the female leader, the dog rolled onto her back; waiting for an approving rub on her stomach.

Silver Tip had done this since she was a pup. The only explanation anyone could come up with, is that the dog figured Melissa was the female alpha of their pack. So always treated her as such, afraid to be driven away. If it had been a male dog, it would have probably done the same to Jed... instead of Mell. This treatment suggested to them a wolf breed, but they had never heard of a wolf that looked so much like a bear.

Jessica called them for supper, everyone sat around talking laughing together enjoying Patricia's company.

After dinner was eaten, Pat turned to Melissa inquisitively. "Well, where are we going in such a hurry Mom, and how long till we get there?"

Smiling fondly at her daughter for a moment. Melissa's expression sobered then she frowned in concern. "Pam came to me upset several days ago, she was having nightmares of her grandfather and her people dying. I was having similar dreams of Giant Bear in trouble. Mine starts out with a white female buffalo running towards him, sometimes she goes to him and tells him something then all is fine.

Other times she doesn't. As the white buffalo turns away... blood, and death appear around him! In the dream she keeps repeating that they must not be forced to marry. An older white man comes into the picture then the white buffalo tells him something very important. Unfortunately, I can't hear what she says to him; it's really quite confusing."

Melissa touched her white buffalo medicine bag that she was never without; she knew that she was the white buffalo in the dream... she must find a way to help Giant Bear.

Pamela shuddered in dread when she thought of the visions that she had before gesturing apprehensively. "All I ever saw was blood and death, with an urgent feeling to go to my father immediately... it's really weird. I still don't understand who my dad would be able to force into marriage; or how would two people being forced could cause so much death. I still think my father would have contacted us if he was in danger!"

Melissa shrugged as she mused reflectively. "Maybe, but like I said before he probably doesn't know he is in danger yet."

Pat scowled decisively then motioned imploringly. "Okay, I see your urgency; I want to come too and help Uncle Bear."

Melissa smiled in humour at her daughter; Patricia had called Giant Bear, 'Uncle Bear' since she was five years old.

Laughing in delight at Patricia, Jed reached over and ruffled his daughter's hair affectionately. "Well squirt, I don't think we will be sending you back now that you have come this far."

Looking up at the three-quarter moon, Jed nodded in relief as he looked back at the others. "We have plenty of moonlight, so I want to keep going for another couple of hours. There's a good place to camp that I stayed at years ago with Giant Bear; it's further down, we will camp there tonight."

Nodding in agreement, there was lots of laughter as everyone mounted.

Jed rearranged their order, so they were now riding in a diamond shape formation. He was still out in front by three-quarters of a horse length. On his right riding on his flank was Pamela she was leading a packhorse. On his left was Patricia she had taken over her mother's place with her dog loping along beside her. Directly behind Pat on her horse's right flank was Jessica, she was leading the white colt. Beside Jess, riding on Pam's horses left side was Daniel who also led a packhorse. In-between Jessica and Daniel, but behind them half a horse length back was Melissa. Mell would protect their back trail.

****

Raven was sitting beside Devon with Dream Dancer on her right as they ate the feast the women had made. There was a pot full of nourishing beef stew, plus they had roasted a hindquarter of the buck she had killed over an open fire. There were potatoes with corn that they bottled, both from her ranch, as well as a dessert made out of last year's bottled fruit.

Sighing in satisfaction, Raven sat back. The ceremony had gone well. Devon had done everything right, even remembered everything he was supposed to say in Cheyenne. She frowned disgruntled as she looked at him out of the corner of her eye. It had been a complete surprise to everyone, especially her when the shaman named him Golden Eagle. The fact that the eagle was prominent on the buckskins she made then gave to him, caused goose bumps to appear all over her body in reaction.

Grimacing, Raven remembered back to the time she started making the buckskins; she had put the rearing horse and the cow on the back first to represent her ranch. Then she was going to put a bear standing on its hind legs, as well as a wolf because it was supposed to represent Giant Bear's Cheyenne tribe on the front. They are called the wolf tribe now, but they had been the bear tribe before that, so she wanted to show the difference between now and then.

Almost finished the back design, Raven had an inspirational dream that came to her of a golden eagle with its wings outstretched. A wolf head staring intently at you was under the right wing of the eagle. A raven... wings outstretched, with one touching the eagle was looking at the wolf staring relentlessly. It was under the left wing of the golden eagle.

The golden eagle was shielding both animals as if protecting them. Its stare was piercing, almost compellingly so. Inspired, Raven put the design on the front of the buckskin shirt instead.

Shuddering, Raven felt manipulated by the Great Spirit. She grabbed her glass of corn whiskey that had been made by the Cheyenne before downing it. It burned all the way down, causing her to almost choke.

A girl came around refilling everyone's cup. After getting more, Raven took a cautious sip of the strong alcohol. She turned to Devon sarcastically. "Well, Golden Eagle; how do you feel now as an adopted Cheyenne and named too."

Golden Eagle looked at Raven in concern... she seemed upset about something, but he couldn't figure out what it was. He smiled in pleasure as he gestured in amazement. "Actually, I'm quite surprised at the feelings of being whole. Like a part of me was missing all this time, that I hadn't realized until now was not there. As for being named Golden Eagle, I like it; it even fits with the new clothes you gave me."

Laughing in delighted satisfaction, Golden Eagle stroked the soft buckskin shirt in pleasure.

Raven just scowled fiercely back then took another hefty swallow of the alcohol... not in the least amused.

Golden Eagle stopped chuckling immediately, and frowned in confusion as he eyed her sour expression apprehensively. He watched her take a large gulp of the fiery liquid then motioned cautiously. "You are drinking a lot of that stuff; don't you think you should ease off a little?"

Furious, Raven waved decisively at him in anger. "It's none of your business how much I choose to drink!"

With that fuming statement, Raven turned her back and started to talk to Dream Dancer... ignoring Devon completely.

Sighing in uncertainty, Golden Eagle shook his head at Raven's foolishness before going back to eating.

The food was finally cleared away.

The shaman added more wood to the fire, until the flames were so high it looked as if they were touching the ceiling of the ceremonial tepee. Dressed in his best and most impressive outfit, the spiritual leader of the Cheyenne danced around the fire as the drums beat a rhythmic cadence... keeping pace with his spectacular awe-inspiring dance. He finished then sat down; the braves began chanting steadily then got up, except for the ones beating on the drums.

A few minutes later, the women joined in. They all danced together around the large crackling fire. Occasionally sparks popped loudly, sending shooting flames everywhere; it added suspense, with a touch of magic to the spectacular scenes happening around the fire. Suddenly all the braves sat, but the women remained.

Several minutes later the women sat; one brave got up to dance alone. Now the men told of their skills as well as their bravery, one by one. They tried to outdo each other as they showed off their storytelling abilities to the newest member of the Cheyenne.

Golden Eagle watched spellbound until the last brave sat.

Instead of the chanting stopping though, it got louder and louder then changed in tempo in demand. When that didn't produce the desired results; the chanting got accompanied by sticks and rocks being pounded together, until the noise was deafening.

Raven sighed in defeat beside him then got up unexpectedly.

The braves all cheered when Raven walked to the fire; she was a little unsteady, having drank way too much.

Dream Dancer scooted closer to Golden Eagle. He smiled before pointing at the retreating Raven. "I will interpret the dance, if you like?"

Nodding eagerly, Golden Eagle didn't look away from Raven.

In satisfaction, Dream Dancer smiled knowingly at Golden Eagle's rapt attention fixed on his sister. He began as he waved around at all the braves hunkered around the circle surrounding the firelight, as they beat on drums continuously. "Every Brave that you have seen so far has told his story of the last heroic deed they had done, so Raven will do the same. She will dance of her courage in facing the grizzly to save her horse, which was her last act..."

Golden Eagle listened to Dream Dancer distractedly as he told the story, but continued to watch Raven closely throughout the dance. He couldn't help feeling a surge of intense passion when he saw how gracefully she moved. The Englishman had never seen anything like it... it was incredibly beautiful. When done, a thundering cheer arose from the braves then three of them surrounded her; talking and gesturing earnestly. She shook her head firmly.

Frowning uneasily, Golden Eagle turned to Dream Dancer. "What are the braves discussing with Raven?"

Deviously, Dream Dancer smiled wickedly. "They are asking her to come to their tepee; if she agrees then goes, that means she has chosen him as her possible husband."

Stopping what he was saying; Dream Dancer chuckled as Golden Eagle jumped up and stormed towards Raven.

Surprised to find himself on his feet, Golden Eagle almost ran to Raven. The surge of jealousy he felt was shocking to him. When he got close, a bunch of Indian maidens converged on him then wouldn't let him go past.

One woman who spoke broken English, but not particularly well; gestured around at the five other women surrounding him, trying to explain. "We all think you are um... hand...some."

She stammered the word unsure if it was right. She tried again not deterred by the Englishman's frown of confusion. "We want the Golden Eagle to share blankets with us."

Before the woman could finish, Raven stormed into their midst and said something harshly in Cheyenne that Golden Eagle didn't understand. The woman, unrepentant smiled at the Englishman invitingly then left.

Raven was fuming; she rounded on Golden Eagle in a furious temper. "How dare you flirt with those women when you are marring me? If you went with one of them, you would have had to marry her if her father insisted."

Golden Eagle was taken aback by her angry ravings then smirked. "I wasn't bantering with them; they were flirting with me! Are you jealous?"

Closing her mouth with a loud 'snap'; Raven was surprised by Golden Eagle's question... she snorted in angry denial. "No, absolutely not!"

Turning, Raven stormed off without another word.

Confused, Golden Eagle watched Raven leave; he went to Dream Dancer.

*****

Dream Dancer watched Golden Eagle go storming off towards Raven in a fit of jealousy. He chuckled in glee, when a bunch of women waylaid his friend then wouldn't let him go. He couldn't help laughing uproariously as he watched Raven storm into the group in a rage. She not only admonished the women, but then she turned on the Englishman as if it were his fault. Edward watched his sister storm away; even more infuriated now, at whatever Devon had said to her.

When Dream Dancer's friend sat beside him, he had himself under control. Edward didn't want Devon to know he was laughing. The Englishman might take it the wrong way.

Sitting grimly, Golden Eagle looked at Dream Dancer glumly. "Can you explain the Cheyenne customs on marriage?"

Still finding it extremely difficult not to laugh, Dream Dancer had to clear his throat a couple of times before he could answer. "It's a little complicated, but I will try. A brave who is not married can ask a maiden who is untouched to go to his tepee. If she agrees, the warrior will go to her family the next day then offer whatever he feels that she is worth, since it is assumed that they will marry. If the father doesn't agree to the bride price, the brave must come up with a better offer, if he wants the maiden that is. Now a warrior who is married already can decide he wants another woman. If he is rich enough to afford a second wife, he doesn't have to ask the first one for permission. He can just go ahead and get one; although, not many braves will do this without asking their wife's permission first... if he wants peace in his tepee that is. Sometimes a warrior will take a maiden to his tepee then decide they don't want to be married afterwards. This happens infrequently, and it's frowned on; unfortunately, it does happen occasionally. If it does, the brave must make up for taking the girls maidenhood. Sometimes, a maiden's family wants their daughter to marry a certain warrior. If she doesn't want to the parents can pressure her into accepting, but the maiden can't get forced into marriage. A woman can refuse a brave if she wants, he can't take her against her will. If he does, he is banished from the tribe then marked so all who see him will know of his shame. A warrior who wants to share a blanket for one night with another man's wife can do so, only if her husband agrees. It's rarely done, since most men don't want to share their wives. If a brave has three or four wives, he might encourage them to find another warrior's when he wants to be alone with a certain wife. Take the woman who was talking for the others. They are all married to one man. He must have permitted them to ask you to share their blankets. You could have picked one of them or all of them."

Golden Eagle snarled decisively. "I couldn't take a man's wife or share mine; I don't want more than one wife either."

Dream Dancer chuckled and held up his hand to quiet his friend. "I'm not quite finished yet, so let me tell you one more thing. Now, in our culture women are generally not allowed to do anything the men do or vice versa. But some women do go to war with their husband, they stay on the edge of the battle watching; some even participate, if the war is going badly. The Cheyenne call these women, brave hearted women. In our culture, there has only ever been one woman who became a shaman, two who became medicine women. We also had one chief named Godasijo. She was the very first leader in our recollection. She was the only woman ever appointed as a chief, that

I am aware of. Now Raven is the first woman in our history to become a full-fledged brave. So, there is some confusion by the braves on how to approach her for marriage. She is highly sought out because not only is Raven the chief's granddaughter, but she has her own wealth... plus has proven her bravery repeatedly. She is also known as the 'protector' of her people, which is a first also. I guess you could call her a war chief, but then that wouldn't be the right term for it either. She doesn't take them to war, but she prevents conflicts. She is the buffer between the whites and the Indians. At one time, we had dog soldiers plus other societies that protected our people or went to war for us, but they were disbanded when we moved here. Now they are called the Raven Society, protectors only. So, my grandfather has had to fend off more offers than he knows what to do with... from every tribe of Cheyenne there is, Raven has refused them all."

Golden Eagle scowled puzzled then motioned bewildered. "If the chief can't force Raven to marry me, why is she going along with it?"

Dream Dancer shrugged in confusion. "I don't know; if she absolutely refuses, she doesn't have to marry you. He is our chief, so he does have certain rights if he feels the tribe is endangered... when this occurs his word is law."

Sighing in frustration; Golden Eagle watched the chief and Raven standing together arguing. Throwing her hands up, she finally stormed away heatedly.

*****

Raven marched to her grandfather in an infuriated rage, the nerve of the man implying she was jealous of those women.

Giant Bear saw Raven coming; he frowned anxiously at his incensed granddaughter, wondering what Golden Eagle said to set her off.

Halting in front of Giant Bear, Raven didn't even look at her grandmother she was so angry. She waved in finality incensed. "I absolutely refuse to marry that white man now or ever!"

Grimacing enraged, Giant Bear motioned in fury. "Oh, yes you will... that's final! As your chief, I'm ordering you to!"

Raven scowled; she pointed a finger at her grandfather; deadly serious. "If you make me marry him, you will regret it!"

Giant Bear growled then sputtered infuriated when Raven stomped off without another word.

Stepping in front of Giant Bear, Golden Dove planted her hands on her hips in warning. She glared at her husband and shook her head in bewilderment... she jabbed a finger into his chest for emphasis. "You will stop this madness now before it's too late! Or so help me, you will sleep on the other side of the tepee by yourself for the rest of your days!"

Golden Dove turned away instantly, not letting Giant Bear say a word; she hurried towards Raven's tepee to try calming her down.

Throwing up his hands in dismay, Giant Bear watched the two most important women in his life leave him... he stood there fuming by himself. He sighed in regret; the chief couldn't stop this even if he wanted to. All he could do was pray to the Great Spirit for help to get him out of this mess. He left for his tepee dejectedly, not feeling like celebrating anymore. With shoulders slumped in hopeless despair, he shuffled grimly back to his tepee. Looking very old at that moment, he rubbed his left chest irritably at a sharp pain.

*****

Mumbling an excuse to Dream Dancer, Golden Eagle followed Raven to her tepee and stood outside for a bit... chewing his lip in indecision. He wasn't sure why he had followed her in the first place, except that she lied to him about having to marry one of those women since they were already married. The Englishman entered then feigned surprise that she was there. "Oh! I'm sorry, I thought you were still at the party; I came to check on your cub."

Raven scowled at him angrily before swiping at her face, trying to hide her tears. Unfortunately, she had lit her lamps; so, there was nowhere for her to hide. "What do you care... go away, and leave me alone!"

Golden Eagle stepped forward in concern at the tears running down Raven's face. He reached out then gently touched a teardrop as it rolled down her cheek, and put it in his mouth.

Staring confused, Raven was taken aback at his actions.

Brows wrinkling apprehensively at her pain, Golden Eagle gestured curiously. "Why are you crying? You aren't hurt are you; or is your leg bothering you that much, did the dance strained it?"

Grimacing distraught, Raven motioned sharply in anger. "I'm crying because I hate you... I don't want to marry you!"

Raven was taken entirely by shocked surprise when Devon grabbed her around the waist with his left arm; he ground his lips onto hers unceremoniously... without warning.

*****

Golden Dove slowed when she saw movement in front of Raven's door; stopping, she stared as Devon stood there.

Once Golden Eagle went inside, Golden Dove smiled knowingly before turning away to go to her tepee. She looked up towards the heavens with a pleading look; she lifted both her hands in supplication... praying desperately. "Ma'heo'o, please make it right between them. They desperately need each other. However, as long as Giant Bear keeps interfering, they will never come to grips with their love. There has to be a way to stop my husband but so far, I'm unable to figure out how. I implore you to help me!"

Sighing grimly, Golden Dove dropped her hands. She grimaced dejectedly and ducked inside her tepee; it would be a sleepless night Mary knew... not use to sleeping alone.

*****

Raven struggled half-heartedly... unwilling at first. Unexpectedly, she started to respond before finally melting against Golden Eagle in surrender. Her traitorous body quivered ecstatically when Devon pressed her so intimately into his hard muscular body; her arms crept up and went around his neck then she was kissing the Englishman back.

Golden Eagle groaned deep in his throat in pleasure when Raven finally responded. Devon brought his hand up under her buckskin shirt, and stroked her bare back. The Englishman moved his hand around to caress her breast for the first time.

Pulling back a bit, Golden Eagle tried to remove Raven's shirt with one hand. Thankfully, he had taken off the sling for tonight's festivities; so, didn't need to fuss with that. She batted the Englishman's hand away then did it herself.

Devon gently lowered her to the furs that were spread out against the wall before straddling her; awkwardly, he tried to remove his shirt... she sat up impatient then helped him strip if off.

Pushing Raven down; Golden Eagle carefully laid on her, making sure to keep his broken arm above her head out of the way... plus, his weight off her injured leg. Devon ran his lips down her neck then continued to her upper chest, until he reached her engorged breast. He gently sucked and licked her nipple before nipping it playfully.

Raven gasped in pleasure then held his head against her.

Golden Eagle lifted his head away from Raven's insistent hands, with a chuckle. He started kissing his way down her stomach before running his good hand up the inside of her thigh... he was careful not to touch her wound. Reaching her inner heat. He tilted his head, wanting to watch her expression as he touched her intimately.

Unable to help herself... Raven groaned before raising her hips up encouragingly. Taking the hint, Golden Eagle stroked her bud of pleasure harder. She pulled Devon's head back for a kiss. She whimpered against his lips in surprise; pushing against his hand, she erupting deep inside.

Smiling in satisfaction knowingly, Golden Eagle broke the kiss. While she was recovering, Devon rolled over to remove his leggings then loincloth before lying on top of her.

Propping himself on his arm, Golden Eagle looked at Raven solemnly. "I want you desperately, but if you say no... I'll leave."

Surprised, Raven looked at Golden Eagle's earnest expression before ignoring his question... she pulled his head down for a demanding kiss. She locked her legs around Devon's waist without answering; not wanting to talk.

Moaning in understanding against her lips, Golden Eagle probed with his manhood until he found her moist opening. He lifted, so he could see her face as he gave one hard thrust. He stopped in shock at the extremely tight fit, which told him that she was still a maiden. The way she had encouraged him, he figured she wasn't a virgin.

Raven cried out in surprise at the uncomfortable snug fit which caused her a bit of pain; she watched Golden Eagle's expression turn to disbelief. She tightened her legs around him, and pulled his lips down to hers... not wanting questions. He wouldn't know of course, that several times over the years she had to encourage a stallion to cover a mare.

Without a word, Golden Eagle obliged Raven; he sighed regretfully. Devon brought his mouth down to hers for a kiss before the Englishman pushed his hips harder against hers.

Groaning, Raven lifted up to meet him.

Golden Eagle lost control as he surged up then ground his hips against hers... frantically. Devon could hold back no longer; reluctantly, the Englishman let his seed fill her.

Pushing against Golden Eagle; Raven wanted to feel that rush of intense pleasure again. Once she released control, it triggered an intense climax. She would have screamed, if Devon didn't pick that moment to fuse their mouths together stopping her cries of ecstasy.

Unable to move, Golden Eagle lay gasping for breath on top of Raven. Devon lifted himself up a bit then looked at her in apology. "I'm sorry; if I had known, I would have gone slower."

About to continue, Golden Eagle's words halted in surprise when Raven put her finger to his lips for quiet. She hushed him, not wanting to think; she whispered wistfully. "Please, don't say anything."

Surprised by that request; Golden Eagle nodded agreeing and bit Raven's finger... she jerked her hand back in surprise.

Chuckling at Raven's stunned look, Golden Eagle bent to kiss her tenderly. He gently stroked her nipple before bringing his mouth down. Devon was quite taken by surprise when he felt his manhood harden inside her... rising to the occasion.

Lifting up to watch Raven's reaction, Golden Eagle laughed in delight at her expression. As his manhood filled her, Devon made love to her again but much slower this time. Finally, exhausted they slept.

*****

Dream Dancer slipped away then went to his grandfathers to sleep in Golden Eagle's bed. He smiled in satisfaction, relieved at witnessing Devon and Raven coming together as they let their emotions lead them. Edward reached his grandfather's tepee then ducked inside to sleep.

****

Jed and his family wearily dismounted when they arrived at the camp he wanted to use. He smiled in pleasure when he looked around, recalling Giant Bear sitting here with him talking about the white man's customs; it seemed so long ago, a lifetime. He sighed forlornly praying they would make it.

Melissa sensing Jed's anxiety came over then put a reassuring hand on her husband's shoulder. "Come to bed dear, Pat will take first watch. We have a long day ahead of us tomorrow."

Nodding, Jed allowed his wife to lead him away.

A quick camp was hastily made by the others; afterwards, they all fell into their bedrolls in fatigue. There was no laughter or joking now; they were all too exhausted to even smile.

CHAPTER ELEVEN

Raven woke before the sun was up then slipped out of the blankets. They had ended up in her brother's sleeping pallet, which is why the cub hadn't bothered them. She got dressed, fed the cub a fish and gathered her things.

Standing over Golden Eagle, Raven watched him sleep for a few minutes. He looked different this morning... more peaceful; shaking herself, she quietly slipped out of the tepee. She went to the paddock where Brave Heart was then whistled for him. She let the stallion out and saddled him.

Brave Heart snorted then pawed the ground, in warning.

Spinning, Raven saw Dream Dancer bringing a packhorse with supplies. She turned back to finish saddling her stud.

Turning around, Raven took the lead for the packhorse from Dream Dancer; before tying it to a loop on her saddle blanket designed for this purpose. When done, she took a step towards Edward for a parting hug then mounted.

Curiously, Raven frowned before looking at her brother. "Where did you sleep last night?"

Dream Dancer smiled up hesitantly, not sure of Raven's mood yet. "I slept at Nam-shimi' tepee. I quickly left this morning before they realized it was me, not Golden Eagle."

Nodding her thanks, Raven motioned calmly. "You can stay for a few days if you like, but go back no later than a week to check on the ranch. Get a list from Nam'-shimi on what he will need to stay here for the rest of the year. Tell Jake to butcher a steer, a pig, and half a dozen chickens; oh, don't forget eggs. Whatever else Grandfather needs, bring. There's a lot left over from last year's harvest, so go into the cellar then get what he wants. Try not to go to town if you can help it right now. If the sheriff comes back to the ranch, tell him that I'm looking into the disappearance of the men from town. I will let him know what I find out when I get back. Tell him to try to stall the townspeople, as long as possible."

Inclining his head without comment, Dream Dancer waved goodbye as Raven galloped away. Edward never said a word about what he saw last night, and she never volunteered any information on the subject either.

Dream Dancer turned then headed to his grandmother's; he entered when permission was given.

Turning to Dream Dancer, Golden Dove smiled knowingly in satisfaction. "Golden Eagle stayed with Raven all night?"

Sighing fretfully, Dream Dancer nodded; you couldn't hide anything from his grandmother... he sat. "Yes! Raven just left and wasn't looking happy. I hope Devon didn't do anything foolish."

Beaming reassuringly, Golden Dove was glad to hear that. "Raven is just confused; she will need time to think."

Shrugging, Dream Dancer frowned in bewilderment. "Nis-gi-i, I think I won't ever get married or fall in love; it is way too confusing."

Chuckling knowingly; Golden Dove did not believe that. "Yes, it can be very complicated sometimes, but if you can sort it all out... it's worth it in the end."

Frowning, Dream Dancer shrugged... unconvinced. "Maybe!"

Golden Dove handed him two bowls of porridge, tea, as well as a small jar of honey. "You can take this to Golden Eagle, tell him that he can keep the honey for his tea."

Nodding, Dream Dancer got up to go. He stopped and turned back to his grandmother. "Oh, I almost forgot; can you tell Nam-shimi' to make a list of everything he needs to stay here for the rest of the year. Raven already told me what she thinks is needed. She said we still have lots left from last year's harvest, so whatever you need."

Relieved, having been worried about food; Golden Dove smiled thankfully. "I'll tell him then start one immediately."

Leaving his grandmother's reluctantly; Dream Dancer wasn't sure if he wanted to be there when Golden Eagle woke up, and discovered Raven gone. He shouldered his way inside... relieved to see no movement from his side of the tepee, Edward busied himself getting the fire and breakfast ready.

When Dream Dancer judged the fire was hot enough, he grabbed the porridge and put it on a rock beside the fire to keep it warm. Edward got up then brought one of the fish over to feed the cub.

The cub was eating noisily when Golden Eagle woke up. He sniffed at the smell of porridge, and turned around. Devon smiled at Dream Dancer sleepily before looking around. Not seeing Raven, he frowned perplexed then looked at her brother suspiciously. "Where is she?"

Dream Dancer sighed unhappily. "Raven left to find your sister."

Golden Eagle scowled angrily. "She didn't even say goodbye!"

Fidgeting, Dream Dancer shrugged consolingly. "I wouldn't take it personally; Raven doesn't say goodbye often. The only reason I know is that I had to bring the packhorse to her. Grandma said she is probably confused."

Grinning, Dream Dancer expression brightened. "But my sister did give me permission to stay for another week."

Eyeing his young friend's eager expression; Golden Eagle's frown of discontent disappeared then he nodded thankfully. "Well, that's good news. Do I smell porridge burning?"

Yelping, Dream Dancer grabbed the porridge from the fire.

Smiling, Golden Eagle sat up before tucking the blanket around him.

With a chagrin expression, Dream Dancer handed Golden Eagle the bowl of porridge then poured him a tea. "I almost forgot; Grandma sent over a jar of honey with some tea."

Smiling his thanks, Golden Eagle dribbled honey into his tea then put some on his porridge. Devon ate it, scorched taste and all... too hungry to care.

Relieved, Dream Dancer sighed thankful at Golden Eagle's calm reaction to Raven's leaving... he grinned enticingly. "If you hurry up and put on your clothes, I'll show you something. It should be about the right time, but you have to be quiet."

Suspiciously Golden Eagle looked at Dream Dancer warily, remembering his passion for playing jokes then finished eating. Devon swiftly put on his clothes from last night... at Raven's brother's insistence that he hurry. The Englishman would have to make a stop at Giant Bear's, and grab his other two changes of clothes. He looked down at the bear cub still eating his breakfast then figured the cub would be a while yet, so they should have time before he needed to be taken out.

Golden Eagle followed Dream Dancer out and into the woods.

They walked on a pathway for about ten minutes; Dream Dancer put a finger to his lips, indicating to Golden Eagle that he should keep quiet before leading him into the trees away from the path. They came to a clearing and squatted down waiting, for what Devon had no clue.

A few minutes later Black Hawk came striding into view only wearing a loincloth, as well as his moccasins. He walked to the middle of the opening then put down the two things he was caring. Tommy stood still for a moment, and closed his eyes.

Golden Eagle watched in amazement what could only be called a dance, but one he had never seen before. Black Hawk flowed from one move to the next gracefully, without missing a step. He did high kicks, low kicks then a roundhouse kick. The brave did forward rolls, backward rolls, his hands and arms were always moving at the same time. Every move, flowed into the next one in a dance-like pattern.

Black Hawk took out his hunting knife from the top of his moccasin then redid the dance. Finished with the knife, he put it away before picking up a large stick. It had, intricate designs painted on it; he danced with it, as well. The brave's last dance was completed with a tomahawk. When he finished, Tommy stood in the same position he had started in... facing the same direction.

Dream Dancer touched Golden Eagle's arm to leave, but they both stopped short when Black Hawk spun around then pointed straight at them.

Sighing in aggravation, Black Hawk crooked his finger demandingly. "Come out here you two!"

Grimacing, Dream Dancer and Golden Eagle shared a surprised look then left their hiding place.

In disapproval, Black Hawk scowled as he put his hands on his hips impatiently. "Well, I'm sure I don't have to ask which one of you had the bright idea of spying on me."

Looking directly at his nephew, Black Hawk stared at Dream Dancer accusingly. Edward flushed guiltily then looked away.

Immediately, Golden Eagle stepped forward trying to take the blame away from his young friend. "It's partly my fault for encouraging him; it won't happen again, I promise!"

Thoughtfully, Black Hawk eyed the two of them then sighed appreciating the confession... letting them off the hook. "Your apology is accepted; as for you Dream Dancer, I have felt you watching me before. I have waited hoping you would come and see me if you wanted to learn, but you never did."

Red faced; Dream Dancer shrugged embarrassed. "I'm sorry Uncle I did want to, but I was afraid you would be mad at me for watching you."

Black Hawk smiled then pointed at both of them. "Fine since the two of you are together... I will teach you both."

Dream Dancer and Golden Eagle looked at each other ecstatically; the two grinned and turned back to Black Hawk nodding eagerly.

Knowingly, Black Hawk smirked at their identical looks... he waved at the ground. "Okay, sit; I'll explain a few things."

Both walked over eagerly and sat.

Gracefully, Black Hawk sat too then looked at Golden Eagle. "Dream Dancer knows most of this, but I will start from the beginning for your benefit."

Golden Eagle inclined his head as Black Hawk waited for his nod of acknowledgement. Tommy sighed as he thought back, missing his aunt so darned much at that moment. "Believe it or not, I learned this dance from a woman sheriff named Melissa. She looked after me for most of my young life... until I was ten. My dad found my mom and me quite by accident. You already heard that story from my father so I won't go over it again, but before I left to come to the Indian village... Mell gave me two gifts. One was the new repeater rifle; the other was her knowledge of the art of knife fighting."

Both leaned forward then listened eagerly to Black Hawk.

****

Raven rode hard for the next few hours; her plan was straightforward so far. She would journey to the edge of the Bitterroot Mountains and visit the Badger tribe. There she would find out whether Squatting Dog had left on his own... or if Chief Spitting Badger had sent him.

After that, Raven would go into the mountains and look for the Eagle tribe to make sure that they were still at their summer camp.

Once there; Raven also had to find out if the whole tribe was involved or if it was just the War Chief Howling Coyote. Hopefully, she would find Golden Eagle's sister as well... alive!

Usually, the trip to the Badger tribe would take a week, but Raven was hoping to make it in three days. The challenge would be to get the chief alone to find out if he had any knowledge of Squatting Dog's activities; without accusing him directly... not wanting to start a war.

Afterwards, Raven would ride hard for the Eagle tribes summer camp, which would take four days of hard riding to reach. Then she needed to get Chief Red Eagle alone to see if he was involved.

Hopefully, with Golden Eagle's sister Janet in tow, Raven would be able to take the shortest route here and try to get back to her tribe within five days... if Janet was able to ride that is. Therefore, if everything went well; she needed fourteen days with no trouble before she could get back.

Raven's thoughts turned to Golden Eagle, but she quickly banished that thought; not ready to think of that yet.

Hearing a bark, Raven turned to her right; Bruno was loping along beside her. She smiled down at her wolf-dog then looked behind her shoulder and saw the female wolf keeping pace, but not getting too close. The young woman grinned down with delight. "I didn't think I would see you again, you are both welcome to come if you wish."

Silently, Raven bent urging her horse for more speed.

****

Melissa's group broke camp at first light then galloped off.

Patricia rode up beside Jed inquisitively. "How far is it to the Montana border, Dad?"

Smiling over at his daughter, Jed sighed thoughtfully. "Three days at the most, two days if we are lucky!"

Nodding, Patricia fell back in satisfaction at having her hunch confirmed. They were still riding in a diamond shape; it wouldn't change until after they left the next town and got into the Montana wilds... although, only slightly. They would still be in a diamond formation, but a tighter one with Daniel and Pam in the middle leading the packhorses with the white colt.

Jed would be further out in front; Patricia as well as Jessica, would take positions on either side of Daniel and Pamela to protect them... plus, their supplies. Melissa would still be riding behind to protect the rear.

Pamela hadn't liked the idea of riding in the centre, but she had two children who needed her to come home safe... Pam had agreed reluctantly.

Silver Tip was keeping pace with Jed's horse; she would remain there after the formation changed. The deputy marshal slowed the horses for a while then picked up the pace, once sure the horses were rested enough.

****

Black Hawk finished talking before getting up. He searched until he found two sticks the approximate length, and weight of a good hunting knife. Tommy went back then sat facing Dream Dancer and Golden Eagle again. "These sticks are to be used for your wrist exercises."

In warning, Black Hawk looked at Golden Eagle with caution before gesturing at the Englishman's busted arm. "You will have to do the exercises with your left hand, try exercising your bad one when you can."

Golden Eagle inclined his head in agreement.

Taking out his knife, Black Hawk went a quarter of the way up the makeshift hunting knife; using his blade, he carved a circle on each one. Finished, a notch where the handle would end and the blade began could clearly be seen; when done he passed them each a stick. "Now take the stick in your hand then hold it like a knife... below the circle is the hilt. Turn your knife so that you are holding it hilt first with the blade against your arm. Put your thumb on the end of the stick, the blade should still be against your arm. Twist your wrist to the right and left, but keep the stick pressed against your arm. Now twist your wrist in a circle to the right then turn it to the left. Make sure you go both ways completely around in a circle. I want you to twist your wrist around and bring the stick up horizontally. Good, now tuck the stick back against your arm. There is another exercise that I want you to do, but you will need to find a longer stick for this one. When you find one, I want you to grasp the stick in the centre then twirl it on the left and right of your arm. I also want you to weave the stick between your fingers. Rest the stick on the back of your hand after twirling it through your fingers then flip your hand over, and catch it with that hand... or even the other, to continue doing the exercises with that one."

In approval, Black Hawk nodded in satisfaction. "Good, now watch me; I will show you what it should look like when you get good enough to use a knife."

Sitting forward intently, Golden Eagle watched avidly as Black Hawk passed the knife from one hand to the other. Tommy's wrists were always in motion, but he never once moved his shoulders or any other part of his body.

Finished, Black Hawk put his knife away. "Now put the sticks down, I will give you exercises to do with your hands, as well as your wrists. Make a fist then bring it down and up as far as you can, it should look as if you are nodding. Open your fist then do it with your hand open. Always go as far back as you can, if you have to push your fist or open hand back further with your other hand... hold it there for a count of ten. Make circles with a closed fist then an open hand. You want to supple up your wrists so your knife will go in any direction you want. Do these exercises with an empty hand then with your sticks. Most people when they knife fight, hold their weapon straight out and use their body to lunge forward to stab. That means their wrist and arm is locked; so, all they can do is stab straight ahead then hope their foe doesn't have a longer reach. If you learn my technique, you will find that you have better control on how deep and at what angle you want the knife to enter your opponent."

Black Hawk paused, remembering the first time he had seen this unique way of training. Tommy grinned as he remembered the awe he felt watching his aunt Melissa perform her dance like exercises.

Shaking off his thoughts, Black Hawk turned to his students and continued. "Every person who learns the dance has a different way of doing things... no two dances are the same. For instance, Mell can kick straight up then touch her knee to her nose for a second. I can't do that, but I can stand sideways and balance on one foot then control my kick. Starting at waist height, I bring my foot up higher then higher until it's over your head. There I can stay for several minutes, without touching the ground. So, what you need to do is discover your weaknesses and your strengths. You learn this by pushing your body beyond its limits. You have to train your body to go further than it has before. Only with practice can you do this. It can take a year to perfect your dance, at first all you will be doing is exercises. When you find your limits, with all your stretches being done fluidly with no pain or effort then you know it is time to begin your dance. It took me six months before I began putting mine together, and a year to perfect it. Raven took less time; I think she learned faster because she was younger. Right from a toddler she would come here then watch me, afterwards we would play at it. That woman can do things with her body that I didn't think was possible. When she gets back, you will have to watch her. For now, I will give you exercises."

Black Hawk turned to Devon. "Golden Eagle because of your arm and ribs you will not be able to do all the exercises right now, but do what you can. Later you can add to the ones you can do now. So, up both of you lets started."

Dream Dancer and Golden Eagle stood up, watching eagerly.

****

Raven slowed her horse then looked for a camp; they had ridden hard most of the day, so all of them needed a break. She reached down then touched her injured leg, it hurt like heck but it wasn't hot to the touch.

Relieved that her fever hadn't returned, Raven knew she needed to stop and change the dressing then take some medicine... or it could return. She found an excellent defensible place, and made a camp.

Before seeing to her own needs, Raven fed Brave Heart and the packhorse then threw raw meat to the wolf, and Bruno. She built a fire after her animals were seen too then made lunch for herself.

While waiting for her food, Raven changed the bandage on her leg and made her medicine. Once done, she broke camp; taking one last look to make sure all signs of her were gone... she galloped away.

****

Dream Dancer and Golden Eagle limped painfully back to Raven's tepee. They went inside then stopped short; they both forgot about the cub... the tepee was in shambles. Cuddles had gotten into everything.

The furs were scattered from one end of the tepee to the other. Cooking utensils, as well as pots, had been dumped then spread around; the water bucket had also been pushed over and was now empty. Unfortunately, Dream Dancer's clothes were all over the place. The cub was sitting in the middle of the tepee with his mother's grizzly head lying beside him... bawling loudly.

Golden Eagle heaved a sigh of regret. "Well, I guess this will teach us not to forget about him again. This place is a mess, but I think we should leave it and take Cuddles outside now. We can clean it up later."

Dream Dancer nodded with a chuckle then walked to the cub, and picked him up. He stopped crying instantly then snuggled against him.

Golden Eagle laughed in humour. "I think he was lonesome. Come on, we will go behind Raven's then you can take him to the creek for a swim while I go for my lessons. We will meet at the corrals later, and I will try to get Devil to come to me again. Afterwards, we can clean the tepee."

Nodding forlornly, Dream Dancer walked towards the door. "Okay, I will look after the baby while you are gone."

Chuckling, Golden Eagle grinned at Dream Dancer's put upon expression; but didn't feel sorry for him as he followed him out.

****

Jed slowed and looked for a camp; he spotted one then rode towards it.

Groaning in pain everyone dismounted, a quick camp was made before all of them gathered around the fire to eat lunch. Once everyone finished, they all sat around talking sipping their coffees.

Clearing his throat, Jed waved in praise. "We are making excellent time, and should make it to town a day earlier than I first thought. I think we will be in the border town late tonight; if everything goes well, and we continue pushing hard. It will mean riding most of the night, but since the moon is almost full it should be bright enough for us to see. If we can reach it tonight, we will have one night in a bed... otherwise we will keep going."

Waving, Jed turned to his wife curiously. "What do you think?"

Melissa nodded thoughtfully; unwilling to lose a whole day. "I agree we should try to reach it tonight, or we will have to bypass the town."

Chuckling, Jed smiled sympathetically at the groans of distress at the idea of having to avoid the town; it was their last chance to sleep in a bed. He grinned in encouragement. "Okay, let's mount up then get going."

They hastily broke camp and were galloping away within minutes.

****

Golden Eagle left Giant Bear's with a sigh of relief. Golden Dove had growled at him for being late then grilled him hard today; she was still upset at her husband. Devon didn't know what the chief had done, but the Englishman wished the old man would make up with his wife soon.

Quickly, Golden Eagle carried his extra clothes to Raven's tepee. He hadn't seen Dream Dancer at the corrals so decided to bring his clothes here first. Devon ducked inside then laughed at his young friend; he was comfortably sprawled on his blankets, patting the sleeping bear cub.

Golden Eagle looked around; he grinned in appreciation over at Dream Dancer. "Thank you for cleaning up the mess; your grandmother wouldn't let me leave... sorry I'm late."

Dream Dancer smiled not in the least put out by his friend's tardiness then got up. "Well, I didn't have much else to do, so I figured I would clean up while I waited. Black Hawk was here a few minutes ago; he said we are to come to the paddocks when you got back."

Inclining his head in agreement, Golden Eagle put his clothes down.

Careful not to disturb the cub, Dream Dancer put a squirrel beside him.

Frowning, Golden Eagle eyed the squirrel in disapproval. "I thought Raven didn't want the cub to eat meat?"

Gesturing at the food, Dream Dancer shrugged nonchalantly. "Well, he can't eat just fish; the berries were the last of our winter storage. So, he needs something to eat until the berries are ready. I cooked the squirrel, so I don't know if he will eat it. Since it's cooked, he should be okay."

Nodding in agreement, Golden Eagle followed his friend out.

Black Hawk was standing beside the paddock watching his mare running around the pen. Dream Dancer then Golden Eagle walked up to him. They stood quietly watching the horse.

Turning to Golden Eagle inquisitively, Black Hawk motioned curiously. "Well, how are the lessons going?"

Grimacing unenthusiastic, Golden Eagle waved in irritation. "Tough, your mother is mad at your father, but she's taking it out on me!"

Smirking knowingly, Black Hawk waved grimly. "I know, I can always tell when she's mad or upset because she starts calling me Tommy; she's been calling me by my white name continuously for the last couple of days. That's why I have been staying away!"

Golden Eagle motioned in aggravation. "Don't I know it; she has been calling me Devon too. I wish your father would do something to make up with her before she drives us all crazy."

Black Hawk sighed forlornly. "Until he tells you and Raven that you don't have to marry, I think we will have to live with her mood. I'm pretty sure Father isn't going to do that!"

Taken aback, Golden Eagle looked at Black Hawk in scepticism. "Is that what she's upset about? I'll talk to her later about it."

Surprised, Black Hawk raised his eyebrows in inquiry. "Oh, are you going to marry Raven now without a fight?"

Shrugging angry, Golden Eagle grumbled crossly. "I don't know."

Not wanting to push too hard; Black Hawk frowned at Golden Eagle then changed the sensitive subject. "Okay, today I'm going to go in with the mare and see what the horse has learned. If she's a quick study, she should turn to face me as soon as I walk in. If she is stubborn, I might have to run her around again, but it shouldn't take as long only once or twice then she should stand. I want you two to come into the pen and bring the noisemakers in, make as much noise as you can. She should stand still faster today. If she does, I'm going to put a saddle blanket on her then a bridle. If she doesn't take long getting used to something on her and we have time, I will put those two big sacks on her for weight. They are tied together to give her the weight of a person on her back. Plus, the rope tied between the bags is long enough that they rest against her sides. That way if she runs the sacks will bounce against her, and she can get the feel of someone's legs on her sides."

Relieved to get off the subject of Raven, Golden Eagle nodded then watched Black Hawk gather his things before going into the pen.

*****

Three hours later finished with the mare, Black Hawk beckoned to the two waiting before turning to face them when they joined him. "She has had enough for today; I'm going to walk her before I put her away. Can you take my things to my tepee? I will meet you at my mothers for supper."

Seeing Dream Dancer nod his assent, Golden Eagle turned to Black Hawk before inclining his head in agreement. "Sure, I have to check on the cub anyway so we will meet you there."

Golden Eagle with Dream Dancer's help grabbed everything then walked away. They stopped at Raven's tepee first, but the cub was sleeping, so they went over to Black Hawk's place.

Dream Dancer scratched on the flap. He waited for Gentle Doe to open it. When it did, he smiled at Black Hawk's wife; switching to Cheyenne. "Hi, Black Hawk asked us to put his things in your tepee."

Gentle Doe nodded then backed away; she held open the flap for them. They ducked inside and put everything in the corner.

Turning to face Gentle Doe, Dream Dancer smiled gently. He indicated Golden Eagle, making introductions. "This vi'hoi is Golden Eagle; he will be your nephew by marriage soon."

Looking at Golden Eagle, Gentle Doe smiled shyly. "I hope you like it here. I think you will make Raven happy."

Confused, Golden Eagle had understood some of what she said, but not all... he turned to Dream Dancer to translate; Edward obliged his friend as he told him everything she said.

Smiling, Golden Eagle turned to Gentle Doe then hesitantly answered her in Cheyenne. "I will try."

Earnestly, Golden Eagle turned to Dream Dancer. "Please, tell her congratulations and I hope she has a healthy baby."

Nodding, Dream Dancer interpreted for Golden Eagle then watched Gentle Doe smile. He added his own wishes of goodwill as they left.

Forlornly, Dream Dancer turned to Golden Eagle and sighed then waved as they walked towards his grandfather's tepee. "Black Hawk and all of us are fearful for Gentle Doe."

Solemnly, Golden Eagle grimaced pensively. "She is so tiny; no wonder everyone thinks she won't survive."

Grimacing, Dream Dancer nodded sadly then gestured grimly. "The Great Spirit has given the shaman a vision; Gentle Doe will die! The baby will survive... it will be a boy."

Puzzled, Golden Eagle shook his head confused. "I don't know what you mean by visions; you will have to explain it to me."

Getting an idea, Dream Dancer smiled enticingly. "If you want, I can help you have a vision of your future. Although, I can't guarantee that you will have one or even like it. The Great Spirit comes to us when he chooses. Except for our spiritual leader, he can get visions when he wants them. He also dreams as he sleeps about the future or the past. The shaman says if I want to stay, I could become the most powerful spiritual leader the Cheyenne have seen in generations. I saw my future though. I am destined to go to England... there's something important I must do there that will protect my people. When I try for a vision after I go to England, I see a future where I will return. Why I believe that, is because I have seen two women in my dreams; the first one is white, the second is Indian. I don't know whether I will love them both or only one, but I will meet them. In some way, they will affect my life."

Dream Dancer stopped talking as he shuddered in fear, recalling some of his more disturbing dreams lately. Suddenly, he waved for emphasis as he continued fretfully. "When I try to see a vision of my future if I stay here, I see and feel nothing! All I get is a grey wall as if I'm no more. No, that's not the right description it's more like nothing is out... 'THERE', at all! So, no future is possible; not just for me, it's as if the world is empty. I feel no life anywhere! It has scared me badly enough that I must go. I know that I'm the only one who can stop the future of nothingness! You were also in my visions, but I don't know what significance you will have other then marrying my sister."

Golden Eagle grimaced in doubt, still not believing in that other worldly or witchery nonsense. Suddenly, he stopped; he turned to look at Dream Dancer sceptically in shock. "You saw me in your dreams before I even came here? That's hard to believe, how long ago did you have this dream?"

Turning, Dream Dancer smiled at Golden Eagle's stunned expression. "Well, my visions still come in bits and pieces; I don't always know what they mean yet. I dreamt about you two weeks before I came here. I saw great turmoil surrounding you... as well as Raven. She was holding your hand one minute then turning away from you a moment later. I saw the death of many Indians and white people if Raven turns away from you. Then I saw her death or that is what I thought I saw at the time. A conversation I had with her the other day before I met you made me rethink that scene. She will not die physically, but her Indian self will die, and she will turn away from her people. I don't know if you will cause this reaction in Raven or if her being forced to marry you will cause it."

Thoughtfully, Golden Eagle stood there thinking about Dream Dancer's vision then looked at him in shock at a troubling thought. "Do you think the shaman had the same dream, that's why I'm being forced to marry Raven? If he interpreted it like you did, about Raven dying... could it be why your grandfather is forcing me to marry her."

Mulling over his dream, Dream Dancer frowned then nodded hesitantly as he gestured uneasily. "Yah, that's a good possibility. Maybe after they found you, he had the same one."

Intently, Golden Eagle stared at Dream Dancer. "So, if we go by your dream, it could be that since in one part, she is holding my hand willingly that we can assume she falls in love with me. In the second part where she turns away, we can presume that she doesn't fall in love with me, but is still forced to marry me. So, she comes to hate me then turns away from her heritage. If we put the two visions together... it would be worded like this. I have to make Raven fall in love with me to save her and your people; is that right?"

Dream Dancer looked at Golden Eagle in disbelief at his uncanny reasoning then waved inquisitively. "You could be right; I never thought of it that way, are you willing to try?"

Sighing, Golden Eagle gazed at Dream Dancer musingly. "I don't know! I think your idea of helping me with a vision is good; later, I will let you know."

Gesturing in caution, Dream Dancer nodded decisively. "Okay, but don't say anything; I'm sure they won't let me do it."

Pensively, Golden Eagle inclined his head in agreement; they started walking again. They ducked inside, both wondering and worrying about what they would find out tonight.

CHAPTER TWELVE

Raven frowned not wanting to stop yet, but it was getting too dark to see. The moon was almost full, but with so many trees here it didn't help her much... she started looking for a defensible camp. It wasn't long before the young woman found what she was looking for; it was surrounded on three sides, with only one way in. Unfortunately, there was no water but it would do.

Unsaddling Brave Heart; Raven checked his feet, legs, and his wound. Everything looked good, so she rubbed him down then gave him oats before turning to the packhorse. She took the geldings pack off, and checked him for saddle sores before wiping him down then gave him a treat as well.

Finished with her horses, Raven saw to her own needs; she gathered wood for a fire. While it was becoming established, she grabbed her snares then walked into the bushes and set them before heading back.

Digging around in her pack, Raven brought out her skillet and a piece of meat from the buck she killed the other night. She sliced some for her dinner and threw it into the pan before cutting open a can of beans then added it too.

While Raven's supper was cooking, she went to check her snares and nodded in satisfaction at the rabbit caught in one. She took it out of the trap then reset it before going back to camp, and skinned it; when finished, she cut it in half then threw part of it to the wolf and gave the other half to Bruno.

Scraping the hide automatically without thought, Raven rolled it up to be tanned later. She ate her dinner and had a cup of coffee before she got up to saddle the packhorse again, just in case she had to leave in a hurry. The only thing she kept out was her coffee pot and the pan with the rest of her supper.

Reaching over, Raven grabbed her bedroll then made up her bed. After banking the fire for the night, she curled up in her blanket with a tired sigh... her last thought before sleeping was if Devon regretted last night.

****

Golden Eagle and Dream Dancer left Giant Bear's together then strolled toward Raven's place.

Turning towards Dream Dancer, Golden Eagle gestured hopefully. "Can you take the cub out again? I need to spend some time with Devil tonight before we try for a vision."

Dream Dancer inclined his head in agreement. "Sure, I need to be alone for a while anyway to get ready for the ceremony. After you are done with your horse, you need to go to the creek and bathe. Afterwards, put the buckskins that Raven gave you back on; make sure that your medicine bag is on as well."

Nodding, Golden Eagle turned away and went towards Devil's pen. Going to the shed, he took a couple armloads over and dumped them in then checked the stallion's water before climbing up to the top of the fence.

Golden Eagle murmured to the stud musingly. "Sorry for ignoring you boy, but a lot of things have happened today."

Sighing in frustration, Golden Eagle watched his horse walk over then eat absentmindedly for a minute before continuing. "I hope you don't mind if I talk to you while you are eating... I have a problem you see. I have come to know the people in this village and I like them, they have accepted me completely. Now I find out that if I don't get Raven to fall in love with me, they will die. I'm not sure if I want that woman to love me. I am not sure how I feel about her right now. If she falls in love with me, I would have to stay here."

The stud finished eating then regarded Golden Eagle intently; he didn't get any closer though.

Shaking off his confusion, Golden Eagle smiled at the stallion and called softly in Cheyenne. "Come here Devil, come boy."

The stud turned away then walked into the middle of the pen.

Chuckling, Golden Eagle grinned not discouraged before getting down. He went to the shed to get oats, and the last apples then went back to the fence... he climbed over. Devon took three steps then sat on the ground.

Looking at his horse expectantly, Golden Eagle put the oats with the apples in front of him before crooning the Cheyenne song Dream Dancer taught him. Devon watched hardly able to contain his glee when his horse came closer.

The stallion walked towards Golden Eagle then stopped just out of reach. Devil craned his neck and ate one of the apples.

Elated, Golden Eagle kept singing; he reached down then picked up an apple and held it out to the stud enticingly.

Devil reached out then sniffed the offered fruit in Golden Eagle's hand; he took the apple and ate it.

Golden Eagle kept his hand out so Devil could sniff at it.

Nuzzling the hand for another apple, the stallion snorted in rebuke when none was offered.

Chuckling, Golden Eagle reached down and picked up the last apple then held it out to Devil.

The stallion ate it and let his master stroke his nose for a moment before Devil turned away.

Knowingly, Golden Eagle stopped singing then got up and grinned in pleasure after the stallion as Devil went back to eating. He left the oats on the ground then turned and left the pen, elated at having touched him.

Quickly, Golden Eagle walked to the creek then stripped out of his clothing. The Englishman found a soap root, a clean bandage for his arm, the buckskins Raven had given him, and a new loincloth to wear with his buckskins waiting.

Undoing the bandages from his arm, Golden Eagle looked at it carefully. The swelling had gone down some; when he wiggled his fingers a bit. It hurt a lot... not as severe as it did yesterday, though. In another few days, the swelling should be down more then his arm would look almost normal again.

Satisfied at his arms progress; Golden Eagle, picked up the soap root and walked into the water then laid back to enjoy his bath. Devon thought about Raven and making love to her last night. Just the thought of her made his manhood rise in desire. Was it enough for a marriage though? The Englishman sighed unknowingly then started washing.

Hopefully, Golden Eagle would find out more tonight; Devon wasn't sure if he believed a vision would come, but it was worth a try. The Englishman lay back after he washed and looked up at the stars... he sighed in pleasure.

****

Jed stopped his horse; he turned to beckon everyone forward. When they all got within hearing distance, he sighed in relief. "Okay, the town is just ahead over that next rise. It should be about midnight when we get there. Everyone, stay together then follow my lead. I haven't been in this town since the time Giant Bear, and I passed this way. The town was only half finished and pretty wild so be careful."

Melissa nudged her horse closer in concern. "I think we should go to the sheriff's office first; even though it is out of our jurisdiction, just to make sure there is no real danger that we need to lookout for when we leave town."

Jed grinned already aware of Melissa's desire to go there first. "I know; okay let's go but stay close everyone."

They took their positions but crowded closer together.

Patricia called out in command. "Silver Tip, come here girl."

The dog waited for his mistress obediently.

Jed nudged his horse into a trot to cool them down. When they got closer, he slowed to a walk looking around cautiously. The town was bigger than the last time the deputy marshal was here. He noted the hotel on the right and saw three saloons before he found the sheriff's office on the left. There was loud music coming from the tavern... nothing seemed out of the ordinary. They halted at the hitching rail then dismounted.

Patricia looked down at Silver Tip. "Stay, guard the horses."

Silver Tip wagged her stub of a tail then settled down close to the animals keeping a close watch.

Everyone else gathered on the wooden sidewalk.

Instantly, Melissa took the lead; the others followed her into the building. She stepped inside then quickly looked around. Mell had brought her whip with her just in case. She relaxed when she saw the sheriff asleep behind his desk. In the cell's there were two men, one was sitting on the cot holding his head and another was apparently asleep.

Walking up to the desk, Melissa gently tapped her whip against it to get the lawman's attention.

The sheriff jerked awake and reached for his gun lying beside his hand, but stopped when a whip was put on top of it.

Cordially, Melissa smiled at the big man. "Sorry to startle you, sheriff."

Looking from her to the rest of her party, the sheriff glanced back at her and saw the marshal's badge. He lifted his eyes up to hers then raised his eyebrows in sarcastic surprise. "Well, a woman marshal, I never thought I would see the day!"

Melissa stiffened at his nasty voice; she straightened to her full height. "I'm sure you will see lots of us in the future. I'm Marshal Brown... this is my husband, Deputy Marshal Brown."

Gesturing to each, Melissa introduced the rest of her family; they nodded stiffly, none of them liked the looks of the dirty chubby sheriff.

Smiling nastily at Jed, the sheriff gestured unpleasantly. "How does it feel to be outranked by your wife?"

Jed's eyes turned hard in disapproval... he stared stiffly at the large sheriff. "Actually, it feels pretty good. You should give it a try someday."

The sheriff smiled insolently at Melissa. "I suppose she must be pretty good in bed to convince you to let her be the marshal."

Immediately, Jed took a menacing step forward but halted when Melissa lifted her hand to stop him. The marshal leaned forward; she grabbed the sheriff by the front of his dirty shirt then lifted him bodily out of his chair. "We didn't come here to trade insults with you, so keep a civil tongue in your mouth! Now, all I want to know is how things are in town and outside of it."

In disgust, Melissa let the sheriff fall back into his seat then straightened while she waited for his answer.

Shocked, the sheriff shrank back in his chair in fear; being a coward at heart... he didn't like being confronted directly. The fact that the woman, as old as she was, could physically lift his two hundred plus weight shocked him. "I have no idea what is happening outside of town. I don't go out of town often, only when I have to. The town itself is quiet."

Looking towards the cells, the sheriff snapped in anger. "Get away from there; they are none of your business!"

In surprise, Melissa looked in that direction then saw her son talking to a man sitting on his cot. The marshal turned to the sheriff, and motioned warningly. "He is a Baptist Pastor, if the man wants to talk to him; it is his right to do so."

Shrinking back, the sheriff didn't say another word.

When Daniel walked back to them, Melissa waved to Jed; everyone except Mell left. The marshal smiled at the sheriff stiffly. "We will be here for one night; we will be staying at the hotel if you recall anything."

The sheriff nodded with a scowl, but didn't comment.

Melissa turned her back on him, but loosened the coils of her whip; just in case he tried anything stupid then walked out of the sheriff's office.

Strategically standing at the edge of the door, so Jed could keep an eye on the offensive sheriff; he watched his wife apprehensively. Once out of danger, they hurriedly mounted then rode over to the hotel. After making sure the horses were looked after, they went inside.

Jed walked up to the counter. "We need three rooms, a meal, and a bath... all in that order."

Looking intently at the badge, the clerk nodded nervously. "Sure, Deputy Marshal glad to oblige you. I will have a lady show you to a private dining room while the boys get your things from your horses and fill tubs for you."

Inclining his head, Jed signed the register and tossed him a dollar.

The clerk's smile of appreciation was a little friendlier now, as he handed Jed three keys then rang a little bell.

A tiny, skinny, black-haired girl with dark brown sorrowful eyes came trotting around the corner. Her cheeks were sunk in which gave her a somewhat homely appearance; she halted in disbelief at the sight of them before she turned to the desk clerk. "Yes Sir."

Waving at the newcomers, the hotel clerks tone left no room for disobedience. "Take them to the private dining room; while they are eating have tubs put in their rooms then filled; rouse the boys to help you and have them bring in their packs."

The girl inclined her head in assent then beckoned to them.

Silver Tip was hidden behind the others, they didn't want her to be seen; Melissa, Daniel, Pamela, and Jessica stayed close to Patricia to keep her dog hidden while Jed kept the clerk busy.

When the girl saw the dog, she opened her mouth but closed it again when Patricia held up her finger to her lips for silence. Nodding, she motioned and they followed her down the hallway. She stopped beside a door then opened it and waited until they were all in... she closed the door behind her.

Everyone sat quickly. The girl waited until they were sitting then smiled shyly at them inquisitively. "What can I get you?"

Melissa beamed back at her encouragingly. "What was your special today?"

The girl sighed wistfully. "Beef stew, it smells delicious too."

Grinning in anticipation, Melissa rubbed her hands together eagerly. "Bring eight bowls of stew, coffee, as well as eight pieces of pie for dessert."

Raising her eyebrows in surprise, the girl counted them again... there were only six of them. "Eight bowls and eight pieces of pie; are you sure?"

Smirking teasingly, Melissa waved down at the dog before pointing at her next. "Yes, one for the dog and one for you!"

Surprised, the girl frowned hesitant unsure then motioned uneasily in panic. "You want me to eat with you?"

Trying to put the girl at ease, Melissa nodded decisively. "Yes, we are on a long trip and need information. I thought you might be able to help us, since we will be eating it would be rude of us not to share. Just put it on our room, we will pay for everything before we go. If the clerk asks, tell him the men want two helpings; also, let him know I want you to stay here so you can wait on us for the rest of the night. Please, don't tell anyone about the dog."

Eagerly, the girl inclined her head in anticipation not wanting to argue... too hungry to care. "Okay, I'll be back."

Once the girl left; Melissa turned to her son inquisitively. "Well, what did you find out?"

Daniel sighed in disgust. "It looks as if we have another crooked sheriff. The two men in the jail are brothers and wouldn't give him money for a bribe, so he locked them up. They run the store in town... but that isn't the worst of it; do you remember that gang of bank robbers you took to the capital last year?"

Daniel waited for Melissa's nod to continue. "They broke out of jail and are hiding here; plus, the sheriff's in with them."

Frowning in irritation, Melissa waved in aggravation. "Well, that's great! Are we going to have to fight crooked sheriff's all the way to Giant Bear's village; if we have to fight there and back, we might not make it home!"

Jed shrugged then gestured apologetically towards his wife... they didn't have any authority here. "What do you want to do, Mell? We have no legal right to interfere in Montana. I think we should keep going; at the next stop, we can wire the Montana marshal to let him know what is going on here."

Sighing resignedly, Melissa scowled dejectedly. "I suppose you're right, but I hate to leave a town in the hands of a crook."

Melissa was interrupted by a growl, as Silver Tip let them know someone was coming. Patricia shushed her, when Mell got up then walked to the door. When there was a soft knock, she opened it and peered out. The marshal saw the same girl holding a tray of food, so opened the door wider before beckoning to the waitress to come inside; she closed it then took her seat.

The girl handed everyone a bowl of stew.

Patricia took the extra bowl from the girl then put it on the floor for the dog first. Silver Tip sniffed it cautiously before eating it without hesitation. Everyone else dug in as soon as the dog let them know the food was safe to eat.

Sitting gratefully, the girl wolfed down her food... hardly even pausing for a breath between bites. She was done before everyone, so Melissa handed her a piece of pie. The others just finished theirs when the girl put her plate down.

Grimly, Melissa nodded her suspicions confirmed... just as she thought, the girl was half starved. She handed her another piece of pie then smiled encouragement as she fibbed a bit. "The dog doesn't eat pie so you might as well have this one."

The girl beamed in thanks; the rest of the meal was finished in silence.

Melissa waited until everyone was done before turning to the girl inquiringly. "What's your name and how old are you?"

Frowning hesitant, the young waitress was unsure why the marshal wanted to know about her... had she done something wrong. "My name's Black Rose, but around here they know me only by Rose; I will be seventeen in two days."

Caulking her head, Melissa smiled gently then pointed at her curiously. "And you are Cheyenne as well... are you not?"

Black Rose looked at Melissa in stunned surprise. "Well yes, how did you know? I've never told anyone!"

Everyone perked up at that, especially Pamela; she was slipping, she couldn't even recognize one of her own people.

Melissa frowned thoughtfully then motioned inquisitively. "It was only a guess at the nation, but I figured you were Indian right from the start. Where are your parents and how did you come to be in this town?"

Rose sighed sadly then shrugged grimly. "I don't know who my parents are! The couple who raised me said they found me beside a dying Indian woman; she told the couple my name was Black Rose and that I was from a Cheyenne tribe in the Bitterroot Mountains called the Eagle tribe. She died shortly after, so the couple took me in then raised me. Last year my adopted parents both passed on, so the hotel clerk gave me a job here because he felt sorry for me."

Thoughtfully, Melissa looked at Pamela inquisitively. Pam smiled in agreement aware of her mother-in-law's unspoken question. Mell looked at Jed next; he also nodded knowingly at the inquiry in his wife's eyes.

Not needing any more approval than that, Melissa turned back to Black Rose before gesturing curiously. "Do you like it here and wish to stay?"

Instantly, Black Rose shook her head no before waving in denial. "I hate it here; lately the leader of a group of outlaws comes over then tries to get me to going with him. I keep saying no, but one of these days he isn't going to accept that for an answer, and will force me to go regardless of my wishes."

In reassurance, Melissa reached over before taking Rose's hand in hers. "If you want come with us, we are going to the Bear Paw Mountains. I'm sure we can find a way to get you to your tribe from there."

Black Rose looked at Melissa then at the others in surprise. She turned back to the marshal incredulously before shaking her head bleakly. "I would like to go, but I have no horse, money... or proper clothes."

Grinning, Melissa let go of her hand then pointed towards her daughter, Pamela then Jessica as she explained. "You don't need money where we are going. As for a horse, we will take care of that. Now for clothes, I am sure the four of us women can come up with something to fit you."

Looking at Melissa in disbelief; Black Rose's voice wavered as she asked the marshal her hesitant question... she motioned skeptically. "You would really take me with you, but why?"

Melissa waved casually. "Like I said we happen to be going that way. I also hate to see anybody stuck in a town with a dishonest sheriff; plus, I like you."

Black Rose broke into a smile that lit up her whole face. It hid the gaunt malnutrition feature, giving her an attractive look. She reached out then hugged Melissa gratefully. "Yes, I want to go. Thank you with all my heart."

Hugging Rose back, Melissa looked at Jed over the girl's shoulder then winked at him.

Jed smiled back in delight at being able to help someone in need. Finally, they were in their room and able to relax.

*****

An hour later, sighing ecstatically; Melissa climbed into her bathtub after Black Rose finished washing her long hair then left. Mell laid back with a contented a sigh of relief, within minutes the marshal was asleep.

Finishing his bath, Jed got out of the tub to dry off before walking around the bathing screen that separated the two bathtubs. The deputy marshal looked towards Melissa then chuckled knowingly; remembering, all the times he had found her fast asleep in the tub.

Lifting Melissa out of the bathtub, Jed dried her off a bit before putting her in bed then climbed in. The deputy marshal cuddled close to Mell, and fell asleep with a loving smile.

****

Golden Eagle ducked into the tepee then stopped at the scene in front of him. Dream Dancer was sitting in front of the fire, he seemed to be in a trance; all he had on was a loincloth. His face was painted in different colours and patterns... as was his chest. He sat there rocking, chanting in Cheyenne.

The bear cub was cuddled up beside him asleep.

Walking to the fire, Golden Eagle sat down on a fur that was waiting for him... facing Dream Dancer. He inhaled appreciatively, when Raven's brother reached down then picked up a bunch of leaves with twigs then threw them into the fire; causing a pleasant scent of burning sage, it filled every inch of the tepee. Next, he picked up an eagle feather then waved it around sending the smoke towards his friend then reversed the motion. He inhaled deeply chanting rhythmically to the Great Spirit. Once satisfied that the sage was in every crevice in the tepee, he picked up his intricately designed pipe. Edward inhaled deeply on it. He blew the smoke into the air then down at the ground before turning his head first to the right then to the left... without hardly slowing his chanting. Without opening his eyes, he handed the pipe to Devon.

Golden Eagle copied Dream Dancer's actions before trying to give it back. He stopped when his friend motioned insistently for him to draw on the pipe again; obediently, he did so.

Still chanting, Dream Dancer got up with a hollowed-out portion of an antler then knelt down in front of his friend. Edward proceeded to paint designs on Golden Eagle's face. When finished, he picked up another antler and painted a symbol of an eagle on his cheek.

Dream Dancer grabbed his ceremonial bowl that was waiting; it had, intricate symbols painted on it then held it out for Golden Eagle to drink. His friend drank the dark liquid, and shuddered at the foul taste before handing the bowl back.

Putting it down, Dream Dancer picked up the pipe once again; he held it out for Golden Eagle to inhale one more time. He took it back satisfied, and sat back down in his place then made gestures for his friend to rock... as he was doing. He closed his eyes then reached out to Golden Eagle's mind to bring him on the vision quest for the answers he was seeking.

Feeling a bit dizzy, Golden Eagle's eyes became blurry. He closed them as he started rocking back and forth. Suddenly, the room started spinning faster then even faster... entirely out of control; he couldn't seem to stop it! He groaned in fear and acceptance at the knowledge that he was dying.

Abruptly, Dream Dancer's image took over every corner of Golden Eagle's mind... halting the spinning; the young shaman grasped him unexpectedly then without warning, he was lifted away from himself. He inhaled in shock as he felt himself flying away, but not moving. He saw himself arguing with his brother and storming out of his ancestral home, vowing never to return.

Immediately, the images changed; Golden Eagle saw himself through a funnel as he became cynical, dissatisfied with his life. Abruptly, he saw himself packing to leave England; it felt wrong, as if he shouldn't have come here. However, he was being pulled by another force to go now instead of when it was time. He saw his younger sister packing next, he knew instantly that she shouldn't have come... it had altered things.

The scene changed; he saw his older sister falling out of her saddle and watched his younger one go into a coma then die. He moaned in denial, as he was being beaten almost to death... he saw the Indians turn and leave. Next, he saw Giant Bear with his tribe looking for him as if they knew he was there.

With a lurch, Golden Eagle was lifted again as they moved through time... suddenly they stopped. He saw a ranch with lots of cattle and horses then he noticed a few old Indian women and men working around the homestead.

The scene changed again, now Golden Eagle was inside the house. He felt welcomed immediately, as if he belonged there. He looked around then saw Raven holding a child to her breast, and a little boy looking at the new baby.

Golden Eagle saw himself watching pleased; all of a sudden, the image was gazing directly at him and smiling in joy, as if he knew he was there.

With a sickening halt, Golden Eagle came back to himself; for a few minutes, he struggled to catch his breath in amazement. He opened his blurry eyes then looked across the fire at Dream Dancer staring fixedly at him. His eyes were enormous and black instead of dark green. Suddenly, they turned dark green for a bit then black as if unsure which shade they should be.

Sure, he was seeing things; Golden Eagle closed his eyes in bewilderment... wondering if he imagined it. Opening them again, Devon saw his friend's eyes change once more. He frowned puzzled waiting for Dream Dancer to come out of it, but he was still staring at him with a fixed expression not moving.

The cub sat up unexpectedly; he started bawling loudly, as he pushed up against Dream Dancer insistently.

Getting scared, Golden Eagle got unsteadily to his feet in fear then dropped to his knees in front of Dream Dancer... shaking him. When he got no response, Devon slapped Raven's brother in the face then shook him again, persistently. A hint of desperation entered the Englishman's voice, as he pleaded with his friend in anguish. "Dream Dancer, wake up; what's happening?"

Dream Dancer jerked in his arms without warning, and went limp against him. Golden Eagle was terrified now, as he held him close calling his friends name... urgently.

The cub stopped crying then stared at Dream Dancer intently for a minute; before curling up against him and went to sleep in unconcern.

Opening his eyes a few minutes later, Dream Dancer looked up into Golden Eagle's anxious face. "I'm all right now, but that was definitely a close call. If you hadn't kept calling me, I would have been lost and died."

Golden Eagle nodded shakily as he gazed down in relief at his friend's eyes, that were now a brilliant dark green. "I felt the same sensation earlier before you took me with you."

Taking a second to pinch the bridge of his nose, Dream Dancer sighed grimly. Finally, he pushed up into a sitting position. "I know, I felt you slipping away on me. You probably wouldn't have died, but your mind would have wandered the spirit world... lost. In desperation, I lunged at you; thankfully, I was able to catch you before you passed out."

Reaching over, Dream Dancer grabbed a pan of warm water and a soap-root. He took the cloth out of the water then put the liquid on it from the root before washing his face and chest. Edward rinsed the buckskin cloth then handed it to Golden Eagle to wash his face. He put his head in his hands, and shuddered in apprehension. "Did you feel another presence?"

Staring at Dream Dancer in shock, Golden Eagle had no clue as to what his friend was talking about. "No, I didn't! Why?"

Sighing grimly, Dream Dancer looked at the Englishman with an apologetic look. "That's why I had a problem reaching you. I think Raven was with us."

Gazing at his young friend in shock, Golden Eagle waved incredulously. "But Raven must be a hundred miles away from here by now! How could you find her, and pull her in at that distance?"

Rubbing his eyes tiredly with his finger and thumb. Dream Dancer dropped his hand in his lap before shrugging fretfully. "Like I said, I'm not sure. If she was, the only reason I can think of for being able to find her at that distance, is because I used her when I started learning to do this. Since I knew her intimately, it would be easier for me. That means, if I'm right... I will be able to find you now, no matter where you are."

Golden Eagle shook his head perplexed. "I'm still confused about this. How could you take my mind with you as you did?"

Dream Dancer frowned in concentration trying to explain. "It isn't really taking you with me that you felt. All I did while you were seeing your horse then bathing, was to meditate before asking the Great Spirit to help me show you your future. I can't always control what is shown yet. All I can do is go along and watch; that's why we saw past and future. When you drank the liquid then smoked the distinctive tobacco harvested for these purposes, it put you in the same trance I was in. The sage I burnt and we inhaled helps us to visit the spirit world, plus it keeps our spiritual selves strong. If you had been an Indian, the Great Spirit would have shown you the vision directly.

Since you aren't I was used as a guide, all I did was touch a part of your mind that is responsive to dreams and visions. When our minds touched, you were shown everything I was shown. Hundreds of years ago, shamans were able to read minds plus walk in others dreams, but we lost the ability... there hasn't been a spiritual leader able to touch minds in fifty years. When our shaman found out that I could, he didn't want me to leave. It wasn't until I reminded him that I was destined to go to England that he relented. Since it's been fifty years, we have no idea what to expect or how powerful it will become. Take Raven for example, since I touched her mind five years ago, I have felt her need for me every time she is in trouble or needs me. I am still sure that I felt her with us when we travelled to your past then your future. Because I can't control my powers yet, it makes it difficult for me sometimes to let go. I'm hoping to find a way to control what I do. Lately I have had the feeling that on my journey to England, I will find someone who will help me. I have no idea who it is or even their gender."

Golden Eagle frowned in confusion as he nodded. "I understand better now, but I think we should go to sleep and tomorrow we will talk about the vision. Right now, my mind is spinning; I can't make heads or tails out of anything we saw."

Dream Dancer sighed in agreement then let Golden Eagle help him to his bed, he was still weak. He dropped down onto his blankets and went directly into a dreamless sleep.

Covering his young friend up, Golden Eagle went to Raven's pallet; he slept curled up beside the cub.

****

Raven bolted straight up out of her blankets, with a cry of despair. Her heart was racing so fast it felt like it wanted to explode in her chest, she was perspiring a lot. Her breathing was ragged, she gasped urgently for breath. The warrior woman grabbed her breast, trying to get her heart to slow down... it hurt something awful. Finally, the pain eased; when her heart returned to its normal rhythm, she dropped her hand relieved.

Dream Dancer had reached out then touched her mind, but this time was different. It was so forcefully intense, that Raven hadn't been able to fight it off... even being so far away from him. She felt another presence, and knew instinctively it was Golden Eagle. The woman had sensed her brother's panic when he touched her mind, instead of

Devon's; then felt his frantic lunge to reach the Englishman before he passed out. The woman felt relief from Edward when Devon was brought in.

They travelled to England, and Raven watched Golden Eagle's life as an English Lord unfold before her. She also felt the two forces pulling at him then sensed that he had chosen the wrong one to follow. The woman felt the same as Devon as she watched his younger sister getting ready to leave... it was wrong, she shouldn't have come here.

Next, Raven remembered being in front of her house and going inside. She shook as she recalled seeing herself in a chair suckling a baby then saw Golden Eagle looking at her with love. Abruptly, she was outside; Devon's presence was gone, and only her with Dream Dancer remained.

Raven still connected to her brother; flew across the land to a field where she saw herself standing, waiting for something. She watched in puzzlement, as a horse galloped to her then understanding hit her as her dream lover rode towards her. He swept her up in front of him, she looked at him in disbelief... it was Golden Eagle. His hair was lighter than it was when she left, a silver blonde. His eyes were a stormy grey; she hadn't been able to see the colour because they were swollen.

Raven felt Dream Dancer slipping away as if he were dying, then nothing... that's what had made her sit up in horrified shock. Screaming her brothers name out, she tried to find him but couldn't. Suddenly, the woman got a sense of well-being and knew that Edward was all right. She lay back down too exhausted to think about what happened.

CHAPTER THIRTEEN

Golden Eagle woke to the smell of bacon frying and coffee brewing. He sat up before lifting his eyebrows in surprise. "I didn't know Indians ate bacon or eggs; I always thought that was a white man's characteristic."

Dream Dancer smirked in humour. "Well of course we do, if we can get it that is; besides, I'm part white too."

Chuckling not having thought of that, Golden Eagle sobered as he thought of last nights near disaster. "How are you feeling this morning? No after effects from last night I hope?"

Frowning, Dream Dancer shrugged dismissively. "A bit of a headache, but I took some medicine... it helped some."

Taking the pan off the fire, Dream Dancer dished out the eggs then bacon and handed it to Golden Eagle. While his own eggs were cooking, he sat back then eyed Devon. He pointed over in the direction of the clearing where they had spied on his uncle. "You will have to get dressed. We have to take the cub out and meet Uncle Black Hawk for our lessons."

About to put food in his mouth, Golden Eagle stopped then looked at Edward puzzled. He frowned as he waved grimly. "You aren't going to tell your grandfather about the vision, and he must not force us to marry?"

Scowling, Dream Dancer shook his head. "No, for two reasons! First, the shaman will say I'm wrong... he won't listen. For another, if I tell them what I did; I will be in big trouble then sent home."

Seeing Golden Eagle's angry face; Dream Dancer paused before smiling reassuringly. Edward waved towards the west dramatically in explanation. "Don't worry, someone is coming who will help us... so be patient."

Baffled, Golden Eagle eyed his young friend suspiciously. "Who is coming that can sway your grandfather or the shaman? Why would they believe this person and not you?"

Rolling his eyes, Dream Dancer leaned forward dramatically. He lowered his voice to a whisper. "White Buffalo comes!"

Dream Dancer sat back up then laughed at Golden Eagle's dubious gaze; he held up his hand to stop his questions. "We will talk about it later; hurry up and finish eating."

Golden Eagle frowned pensively at his friend's melodramatic light heartedness; he was taking this too casually. They finished eating in silence before getting dressed then headed out.

****

Raven woke and stretched; she got up then put kindling in the fire. Once the fire caught, she heated up the rest of her food from last night. Afterwards, the woman went to get her two snares then smiled at finding two rabbits in them. She took everything to camp; she threw one rabbit to the wolf and gave one to Bruno. Going over, Raven fed and watered her horses before sitting down to eat. She thought about the dream she had last night then sighed disgruntled. She should have known not to let her brother stay with Golden Eagle without her there. The woman was shocked at finding out Devon was her dream man, and angry that the Great Spirit would try manipulating her.

Finished, Raven broke camp, but her mind kept going over the vision. She was confused, who was the second group that pulled Golden Eagle here; it didn't make sense. She mounted then banished all thoughts.

****

Jed woke to the feel of someone feathering light kisses on his chest. He felt a wet tongue lap at his nipple, and gently bite it. He groaned then lifted Melissa up for a passionate kiss. He fondled her breasts before lifting her further, until Mell was lying on top of him. He pulled her up, so he could reach her nipples and sucked on one gently.

Melissa chuckled in delight then straddled Jed; she pushed up on her knees and lifted herself to sheath him inside her.

Jed gasped when Melissa sat on him, taking his full length inside her.

Melissa leaned back to draw Jed deeper into her depths.

Moaning in anticipation, Jed brought his hands up and teased Melissa's nipples for a moment; before bringing one hand down between their bodies then stroked Mell's bud of pleasure.

Panting in excitement, Melissa lifted herself until she had the tip of his manhood inside her before sitting down, just as Jed pushed up. They both gasped savouring the deep penetration.

Stroking Melissa's bud harder and faster as she ground her hips against him; Jed couldn't take it another minute... he grasped Mell's hips then pressed her down hard repeatedly.

Dropping down onto her hands, Melissa kissed Jed fervently.

Lifting his hips, Jed pushed up against his wife desperately.

Groaning in pleasure, Melissa peaked long and hard, which triggered Jed's release as her muscles contracted around his engorged manhood.

Feverishly, Jed thrust into Melissa one last time; causing them both to climax together.

Moaning, Melissa fell on top of Jed unable to support herself any longer and laid there breathing harshly... trying to catch her breath. Mell rolled off then moved onto her back with a smirk of gratification.

Rolling over, Jed propped himself up on his arm so he could see Melissa's face then laughed deep in delight. "Don't you look pleased with yourself?"

Unable to help it; Melissa's smile widened mischievously. "Well, we have been riding hard the last few days and we haven't made love since the day we left home. So, I figured since we will not see another town for a while we had better sneak a quick one before we leave."

Chuckling teasingly, Jed grinned at her shamelessly. "I must say you can sneak a quick one anytime, I wouldn't object. We better get up though before someone comes for breakfast."

Jed combed the knots out of Melissa's tangled hair lovingly... savouring every minute. The two of them giggled as if newlyweds, as each tried to help the other get dressed. They just finished when a knock sounded.

Jed raised his eyebrows comically, and wiggled them mischievously with a smug look on his face. "See, I told you someone would be coming; a minute ago, we would have been both caught with our pants down."

Melissa blushed just as Jed opened the door.

Patricia walked in then saw the blush on her mother's face; Pat rolled her eyes knowingly. "Don't you two ever quit, I could hear you next door giggling like children."

Unable to help it Melissa's flush deepened.

Laughing in delight, Patricia went over and sat by her mother. "It's okay Mom; I know you two are children at heart."

Pushing her daughter off the bed, Melissa hit her teasingly.

Snickering, Patricia chuckled. "Okay I won't tease you anymore, I promise. Are you ready for breakfast?"

Inclining his head at his daughter, Jed ignored Patricia's banter. "Yes, we are just grabbing saddlebags and heading down to the dining room. Is Black Rose ready to go as well?"

Nodding, Patricia smirked then couldn't help a touch of smugness from entering her voice. "Yes, she is! I got her a horse, tack, and a rifle while you two were busy playing. My clothes fit her good, she will meet us downstairs."

Knowingly, Melissa and Jed looked at each other then grinned at their daughter's teasing before grabbing their saddlebags; paying no attention to Patricia's mischievousness as they left.

They were close to the dining room when they heard a commotion. Melissa hurriedly passed her bag to Jed and rushed inside when she heard Rose's cry. She uncoiled her whip in preparation as she went in. The Cheyenne maid was trying to get away from a man, that Mell knew too well. "Jim, let her go!"

Jim dropped Rose's arm instantly before giving her a push, to get her out of his way. Cringing in alarm at that familiar voice, the outlaw went for his gun as he spun around. However, he wasn't fast enough as he felt Mell's whip coil around him for the third time in his life; he groaned in disgust.

Unrelenting, Melissa held the whip tight as Rose rushed to them. Mell walked up to Jimmy then grinned nastily; she shook her head, and clucked her tongue at him in disbelief. "Harumph, still terrorizing the women I see!"

Jim stopped fighting the whip, knowing it was useless then relaxed as he inclined his head in sarcasm. "Hello there, Marshal Brown!"

The outlaw looked behind Melissa, and saw Jed then frowned in annoyance. "Deputy Marshal Brown as well... really, what a pleasant surprise it is to see you both here!"

Melissa grimaced angrily then waved distastefully. "Well, I am not sure it is enjoyable, but it is a shock to see you here. How did you manage to escape from jail this time?"

Casually, Jim shrugged dismissively. "Bah, that was easy!"

Reluctantly, Melissa scowled in loathing as she uncoiled the whip from around her helpless victim. She put him in jail three times now, and he always manages to escape somehow. Mell knew that there was no point locking him up since he was in with the town sheriff. "Lucky for you we are not here to look for lawbreakers, but I will tell you this... leave Rose alone; now go before I change my mind and haul your behind to the next town to lock you up!"

Unhappily, Jim looked at Rose in regret cowering behind Jed. He nodded then left immediately in relief.

Soothingly, Melissa turned to Rose as she came out from behind Jed; Mell put her arm around the girl. "He won't bother you again."

Rose sighed thankfully then squeezed the marshal in gratitude.

Turning, Melissa gazed at the people staring at them with one eyebrow cocked inquisitively.

The townspeople turned back to their food. Melissa looked around and saw a table against the wall, so walked towards it as she coiled her whip back up. They sat and waited for the other three. Ten minutes later the others arrived.

Sitting back, Melissa smiled curiously at her daughter. "What did you do with Silver Tip this morning?"

Patricia waved towards the back of the hotel. "I took her out the back; our horses are ready, so I left her guarding them."

Smiling, Melissa inclined her head in approval. "Good."

After everyone ate, Jed went to settle the bill. The rest of them went outside to wait for him.

Jed came out a then looked his horse over. After they were all satisfied with the care the animals had received; they mounted then rode out of town without looking back.

****

Golden Eagle and Dream Dancer limped to Raven's painfully. They entered then dropped onto their blankets in exhaustion.

Groaning, Golden Eagle sighed as he lay back for a moment. "I think your uncle is trying to kill us!"

Dream Dancer chuckled, but didn't comment. There was a scratching on the tepee flap, so Edward called out glumly. "Come in."

Entering, Giant Bear looked at the two of them lying in their blankets. He turned to Golden Eagle then pointed at the end of the village. "The medicine man wants to look at your arm."

Unenthusiastically, Golden Eagle nodded before getting up.

Giant Bear raised his eyebrows curiously. "What's the matter you two? You both sound like a herd of horses ran over you?"

Sighing plaintively, Dream Dancer chuckled uncomfortably before moaning painfully. "Not horses Grandfather, but Uncle Black Hawk. He is teaching us how to fight with a knife."

Nodding in approval, Giant Bear smirked. "Good."

Hopefully, Golden Eagle turned towards his young friend expectantly. "Can you take the cub out; I have to go for lessons after I see the healer?"

Chuckling, Dream Dancer inclined his head resignedly; now the official grizzly sitter. "Okay, I will look after him for you."

The two men left without comment then turned towards the medicine man's tepee. The chief looked at Golden Eagle out of the corner of his eye. "You should start talking in Cheyenne whenever you possible can now."

Frowning, Golden Eagle shrugged dismissively. "I will try."

Harrumphing, Giant Bear waved encouragement. "We will help you when you have a hard time."

Golden Eagle inclined his head agreeably, but didn't speak again as they stopped in front of the medicine man's tepee.

Giant Bear scratched on the flap, and they waited to be let in.

The old man opened it then stepped aside for them to enter.

Going to the fire, Golden Eagle sat on the fur waiting for him.

The medicine man came over, and helped the Englishman out of his shirt then undid the binding from Golden Eagle's arm. He gently probed at it before smiling in approval. "The swelling is down, and the colour looks better."

In confusion, Golden Eagle looked towards Giant Bear so he would translate. He understood most of it, but not all.

Immediately, Giant Bear told him what the old man said.

Determinedly, Golden Eagle frowned in concentration then spoke hesitantly in Cheyenne. "Yes, it feels um, good."

Nodding, the medicine man grinned appreciating the white man's use of his language; he picked up an ointment then massaged it into Golden Eagle's arm. Devon looked at the healer in awe at a tingling sensation. "What's this?"

In satisfaction, the medicine man smirked in humour at Golden Eagle's amazement. "It will help your arm to heal faster. It relaxes muscles so you can exercise your arm. It absorbs through the skin to the bone; it will help arm become stronger."

Having no idea what was said, Golden Eagle turned towards Giant Bear to translate. He turned back to the old man when the chief finished then smiled in delight. "It feels good!"

Experimentally, Golden Eagle wiggled his fingers a bit; he sighed thankfully, at least he could move them more now.

Pleased by the movement, the medicine man grinned then re-wrapped the arm before speaking to Giant Bear. The chief nodded and translated. "He said to take the ointment, put it on before exercising your arm. Do finger exercises then stretch your muscles, but only twice a day."

Nodding, Golden Eagle took the hollowed out wooden bowl with the cream in it. "Thank you."

The old man inclined his head appreciating his gratitude.

Waving, Giant Bear sent the Englishman on his way.

Getting up, Golden Eagle left then went to Raven's to drop off the ointment. Dream Dancer and the cub were gone, so he hurried over to the corrals after putting the cream down. When Devon came around the corner, he saw his friend feeding Devil; so, he went for lessons.

****

Jed slowed then looked behind his shoulder with a scowl of anger; he might regret taking Rose with them. They placed her in the centre with Daniel and Pamela because she didn't know how to shoot a rifle or how to ride, so they needed to watch her.

Patricia was riding close to her, trying to give her lessons on how to handle a horse. Instead, of riding in her designated spot to watch for dangers as she was supposed to be doing.

Resignedly, Jed slowed to a walk in disgust then looked for a camp for lunch. He found the right spot and pulled up. Everyone helped except Rose; she was on the ground crying.

Grimly, Jed walked over to Pam then motioned in demand. "You will have to ride beside Rose now; I want you to help her. Patricia is supposed to be watching out for you guys, and the packhorses... not babysitting!"

Pamela inclined her head in agreement then sighed disgruntled, when her father-in-law stalked off angrily. Pam walked over to Melissa, and pointed over her shoulder at Jed. "Your husband is angry about Rose. Can you take her aside then talk to her? I have to give her horseback lessons on our way, so Pat can ride where she is supposed to."

Nodding, Melissa got up in irritation. She walked over to Rose then sat beside her. Mell motioned in compassion, and asked curiously. "Why are you crying; you can't be in pain already?"

Rose sighed dispiritedly then wiped the tears away before shaking her head in apprehension. "No, I'm not in pain, but your husband has been glaring at me since we started this morning. He is angry that I can't look after myself."

Melissa scowled knowingly, now furious with Jed. She put her arm around Rose comfortingly. "I'm sorry my husband has made you feel bad... ignore him; I promise, he will not do it again. The only way for you to learn, is for you to do it. Come with me, we will get your rifle so I can show you how to shoot it. Afterwards, I will teach you about protecting yourself. Pamela, will show you what to look for in edible plants when we stop for the night. She will also teach you the different medicinal properties of those plants. While you ride, Pam will give you lessons on how to handle your horse. Patricia can teach you how to identify the different tracks of an animal, as well as men then how to draw a gun if you like. We will be teaching you every day when stopped, so no more feeling sorry for yourself. Come on, let's get started."

Rose hugged Melissa gratefully before getting up.

*****

Jed shook his head irritably before sighing in annoyance, that girl was slowing them down. He couldn't do anything about it now, he watched Melissa take Rose for a bit of target practice.

Jessica brought her brother-in-law lunch then sat beside Jed to talk. Jess waved at the retreating Rose curiously. "You know, I never seen you act this way about someone's inability to do the things you do. You agreed to bring the girl, now you seem to be resenting the fact you did?"

Frowning, Jed sighed in exasperation. "I know I agreed, but I didn't think she was useless. She is slowing us down too much!"

Grimacing, Jessica nodded; she could see his point, but! Jess frowned cautiously, not wanting Jed to be angry with her too. "Do you realize that scowling at her, is making it worse?"

Not believing that, Jed grimaced then shrugged doubtfully. "No, I didn't know I was making it worse."

Poking Jed in the shoulder teasingly, trying to take the sting out of her accusation... Jessica smiled at him consolingly. "Well, you are; so please, try to control yourself. I know we are in a hurry but if we push the horses or ourselves too much, we might end up taking longer to get there because of exhaustion. One day taking it easy will not hurt. Especially, when we get to that river you were talking about; we don't want to be too tired for that!"

Jed nudged Jessica playfully, calm once more. "And how did you get to be so smart, Jess?"

Grinning in delight, Jessica taunted back. "I think your wisdom has finally rubbed off on me."

Jessica looked up then saw Melissa coming out of the trees. She saw her sister motion to Pamela, and they talked for a moment. Pam nodded then turned towards the trees.

Melissa spun around and stalked furiously towards them.

Knowingly, Jessica grinned devilishly at Jed as she got up not wanting to get in the middle of this conversation. "I think I had better go, Melissa's coming. She doesn't look pleased at all!"

Looking at the determined Melissa, Jed nodded forlornly then watched Jessica's hasty retreat. He sighed aggrieved then turned to his angry wife.

Angrily, Melissa stopped in front of Jed then put her hands on her hips as she snapped in irritation. "What do you have to say for yourself?"

Hastily, Jed put his plate down before getting on his knees; he put both hands together as if praying for mercy. He looked up at Melissa pleadingly. "I'm sorry; I promise, I won't do it again!"

Stoically, Melissa tried to keep her lip from twitching; her expression didn't change. "What are you sorry for?"

Nodding, Jed tried to look entirely humbled. "Yes, I'm a bad boy. I will never to scowl at Rose again, and I will try to find more patience."

Immediately, Melissa turned to look at Jessica then grinned at her in thanks so Jed couldn't see. Mell turned back with a straight face, not letting her husband off the hook. "What kind of penance are you going to do to make up for being a bad boy?"

Innocently, Jed smiled up at Melissa. "Well, I could apologize and teach her how to use the rifle, since I'm a better shot."

Playing along, Melissa looked down at Jed in outrage then shook her finger at him. "That sounds like insolence to me!"

Trying to keep a straight face, Jed bowed to Melissa solemnly. "Sorry mistress, it won't happen again... please don't hurt me!"

Giving in, Melissa couldn't help laughing; she reached out and slapped him for his impertinence. "Oh, get up, quit acting like an idiot. Yes, you can teach Rose about her rifle and apologize!"

Jed nodded glumly; he got up pretending that the apology would hurt. He finished his lunch in two mouthfuls then handed the bowl back. "Okay, but let's get going we can teach her tonight when we stop."

The camp was cleaned up, and they were on their way. A little slower, as well as a lot calmer than the morning had been.

****

Golden Eagle walked out of Giant Bear's tepee and headed for Raven's. He went inside then smiled at Dream Dancer and his uncle. He spoke in Cheyenne. "How are you, Black Hawk?"

Black Hawk smiled in approval at his nervous use of Cheyenne. He made sure to respond in the same language. "I am doing well. How are you? Any progress with your stallion?"

Shaking his head he walked over and sat, Golden Eagle sighed in disgust then switched to English. "I'm not good enough yet to converse in Cheyenne. I only understood part of what you said."

Trying to help, Black Hawk grinned consolingly and repeated each phrase in English then again in Cheyenne.

Eagerly, Golden Eagle beamed in delight but kept speaking in English. "I'm fine thank you. I am making good progress with my stud. He came to me and ate two apples out of my hand before allowing me to touch his nose."

Pleased at the Englishman's progress, Black Hawk chuckled impressed. "Good, today you should try walking up to him. If he stands for you, try touching him all over. If he doesn't let you; don't get discouraged just sit down... he'll come to you."

Nodding in agreement, Golden Eagle motioned curiously. "Okay, are you working with your mare tonight?"

Standing, Black Hawk inclined his head. "Yes, we were waiting for you; the mares already in the corral waiting for us."

Black Hawk led them out. He stopped at the corral then turned to them. "I am just going to repeat everything we did yesterday. She needs a break, but when you work with a horse you can't give them the whole day off; you have to keep at them, because they forget. Once fully trained, you don't have to worry about them forgetting anything."

Dream Dancer and Golden Eagle watched him enter, and shared a satisfied look as the mare turned to face Black Hawk. Not once did she budge, even when the stallion called to her.

****

Raven sighed tiredly, she shifted uncomfortably and slowed her horse... it was time to stop for the night. She started looking for a camp, but it was another half hour before she found one. It was more open than she liked, but it had a creek; she hoped it was deep enough for a bath.

Dismounting, Raven unsaddled her horses; she looked after them first. She decided to go fishing after then take a bath before cooking something to eat.

Walking to the edge of the creek, Raven stripped before looking for a fishing spot. When she found one, she dropped to her belly and put her hand in the water. She pulled out six fish. Finding a soap root, she immersed herself in the creek with a moan as she washed vigorously then got out and dressed.

Taking her fish back to camp, Raven gathered wood for a fire. She prepared two fish for herself and fed her wolves. She set her snares then made up a bed. For the first time in a long while, her sleep wasn't disturbed by dreams.

****

Jed sighed in frustration; Rose was riding better, but still slowing them down. At least she wasn't crying, and Pam was staying close to her... instead of Pat. His daughter was riding in proper formation, with her attention focused around her.

Rose was too inexperienced to ride in the dark, so Jed figured they would stop for the night. It would give everyone a break... especially the horses.

An hour later, Jed found an excellent spot to stay at with a nice-sized creek running through it so everyone could bathe.

It didn't take long to set up camp before Jed took Rose into the trees for target practice. Melissa with Pamela following went for a bath, since they had to wait for their turn with Rose.

Jessica with Daniel's help was cooking supper tonight.

Patricia turned in the opposite direction everyone else had gone, wanting to hunt with her dog; she walked away from the camp then looked down. "Track, Silver Tip."

Silver Tip wagged her stub of a tail and put her nose to the ground. She walked ahead cautiously, with Patricia following. The dog veered left before barking in anticipation as she looked to the right steadily.

Patricia spotted the two-year-old buck when he jumped out of the trees, startled by the bark. It only took her a second to aim; the bullet hit him perfectly. The buck staggered to a stop before falling dead. Pat smiled in approval at Silver Tip, and reached down to touch her dog in praise. "Good girl."

Silver Tip wagged her stub of a tail furiously.

Patricia went over then cut the deer's throat to let it bleed; Pat hoisted the deer up onto Silver Tips back before they turned heading to camp.

Melissa and Pamela were just getting back from their bath, when Patricia with her dog following walked out of the far trees.

Shaking her head in amazement, Melissa chuckled at the pair in humour; Patricia always used her dog to carry her kills for her... it looked funny. Mell, grinned at her daughter. "I heard the shot, so I figured you would be bringing something back."

Teasingly, Patricia smirked saucily then waved dramatically. "Of course, I never miss!"

Hooting in amusement, Melissa shook a chiding finger at Patricia in warning. "You're as conceited as your father is!"

Dramatically, Pat grabbed her chest as if pained then shook her head in denial. "No way... nobody, can top Dad for conceit."

"I heard that comment squirt!"

Chuckling, Patricia and Melissa turned to see Jed walking towards them with Rose. Pat put on an innocent look then waved decisively. "Only stating fact Dad; you wouldn't want me to lie, would you... not with a Pastor around."

Daniel broke in indignantly with a laugh; he put up both hands in surrender. "Don't get me involved in this Pat, you are on your own."

Patricia stuck her tongue out at her twin. "Spoil sport!"

Pamela grinned at her sister-in-law, and took pity on her when Patricia's twin brother refused to back her up. She winked at her then changed the subject... helping her out of a tight spot. "If you don't have any objections Pat, I would like to confiscate your buck to show Black Rose how to skin and dress a deer. I would like to use the hide to make her a pair of buckskins too."

Mischievously, Patricia inclined her head agreeably then pointed at Jed... volunteering him. "Okay, I'm sure Dad will be nice enough to carry the deer over to the trees out of the way for you. But you will have to give the intestines to Silver Tip, since she shared in the kill."

Pleased, Pamela nodded. "Okay, I have no objections to that."

Jed gave his daughter a dirty look for suggesting him then grinned good-naturedly; he lifted the buck onto his shoulders. He turned to Pam then swept his hand out in front of him dramatically. "Lead on ma'am."

Smiling at her father-in-law's dramatics, Pamela led the way with Jed then Rose following her.

Melissa beamed at her daughter enticingly. "You should go have a bath it's cold, but refreshing."

Nodding, Patricia rubbed her hands together gleefully. "Sounds like a good idea to me."

Jessica broke in hopefully. "I will go with you too; I'm sure your brother can watch supper on his own."

Daniel sighed dejectedly, with a long-suffering face. "Go you two; I can handle things… if I must."

In anticipation, Patricia and Jessica grinned at each other; turning, they sprinted to the creek with Silver Tip running beside them barking blissfully. Melissa and Daniel smiled at each other, as they heard the girls whooping in delight then a giant splash as they jumped in, clothes and all.

Sitting down to help Daniel watch supper, Melissa poured a coffee then smiled at Jed as he walked over and settled beside her. She gave it to him.

Taking the cup, Jed nodded his thanks.

Melissa looked at him intently, as she poured herself a coffee. "How long will it be until we reach the river that you were talking about earlier today?"

After taking a sip, Jed looked at his wife and frowned grimly before shrugging. "I was hoping to reach it tomorrow early. So, we could cross in the daylight and camp on the other side. But since we have had to slow down, we will not reach it until sometime after dusk. I don't want to chance crossing it in the dark, so we will camp on this side and go in the morning."

Melissa nodded thankfully. "That means we will be stopping early; good, we need another easy day before we get into Blackfoot country."

Jed scowled in warning. "Fording that river isn't going to be easy; especially with an unbroke stallion, plus a novice rider."

Reaching over, Melissa took Jed's hand reassuringly. "We will make it okay, don't worry so much."

Noticing movement, Melissa watched her daughter and Jessica sneak up behind Daniel suspiciously. Both smiled innocently at Melissa... Patricia called out hastily before she could give them away. "Silver Tip, shake!"

With that command, the massive longhaired black dog... shook her whole body vigorously. Water went flying everywhere; not only did Daniel get soaked, but Melissa and Jed got wet too.

Daniel followed closely by Jed jumped up in outrage, as they charged after the laughing girls.

Wiping the water off her face, Melissa stayed where she was; Mell shook her head in exasperation after the four of them, they were always teasing or playing tricks on each other.

Rose walked over and handed Melissa a large roast; Mell nodded her thanks then grabbed a spit before skewering the meat... she put it over the fire to cook. Afterwards, the marshal handed the young addition to their group a coffee when she sat beside her. "How are you doing so far?"

Enthusiastically, Rose grinned in pleasure as she motioned in excitement. "I'm doing well; I hit the target already. I helped Pamela skin and dress the deer, but I already knew how before. She described what parts the Cheyenne use and what they were for, it amazes me that they can find so many uses for everything... they don't throw anything away."

Chuckling at Rose's bemused look, Melissa nodded in agreement. "Yes, they use almost every part; plus, most of their food and their medicines get harvested as they move from one camp to the next, it's amazing to watch them. Where you and I would starve or die of thirst, they can find enough food or water to feed several families. Until the white man came, that is... now their lives are changing; I'm afraid it isn't for the better."

Rose gestured gratefully. "I'm so glad that I came with you, I have learned a lot already. But your husband is still upset because I'm slowing you down a lot, I can see it in his face."

Melissa smiled consolingly then waved in warning. "We will make up the time after we get across the river, once you have a couple more days of riding. Don't worry about it; we all needed a couple days of rest, so you helped us."

Turning to the task at hand, Melissa stirred the stew before turning the spit; Mell called out loudly. "Come eat everyone."

They all gathered around then ate; afterwards, they fell into their blankets in exhaustion. Now in better spirits to tackle the rest of the gruelling journey.

****

Golden Eagle followed by Dream Dancer left Giant Bear's tepee and headed for Raven's. He looked sideways at his young friend. "How's your headache?"

Dream Dancer shrugged irritably. "It's still there, but not as bad. I will make my medicinal tea then take the cub out, while you go see your stallion."

Nodding in agreement, Golden Eagle frowned in worry, concerned that his friend's headache was lasting so long. "Okay, I think we should talk about what happened last night."

Inclining his head in dread, Dream Dancer sighed before fidgeting uneasily. "Yes, I know; I have thought of nothing else all day. There is going to be a lot of truths come out that I have been forbidden to talk about, but now I must."

Exhaling grimly, Golden Eagle looked at Dream Dancer then frowned. He already guessed at some of the truths, but he didn't say anything. He figured he would allow his friend to speak of it in his own time. Just before reaching Raven's, they split up. Dream Dancer went in; Golden Eagle kept going.

*****

With a noticeable spring in his step, Golden Eagle walked back to Raven's an hour later with a smile of satisfaction on his face. He went in then grinned at Dream Dancer sitting there patting the cub. He sat across from his friend and sighed in contentment. "Devil wouldn't let me walk up to him, but after I sat down, he came over then ate the oats out of my hand."

Dream Dancer nodded and grinned encouragement. "Good, you are making progress; maybe, tomorrow he will let you."

Golden Eagle beamed eagerly. "I hope so."

Getting an idea, Dream Dancer pointed at the bowl on the ground enticingly. "Do you want me to put some ointment on your arm, so you can do exercises while we talk?"

Nodding, Golden Eagle inclined his head in thanks. "Please, it sure feels good when it tingles."

Smirking knowingly, Dream Dancer didn't tell his friend what the shaman put in it; or he would never let him put it on. Edward got up and helped Golden Eagle with his shirt then took off the bandage, he examined his friends arm critically. He nodded pleased with how fast the Englishman healed... he looked at him in praise. "Most of the swelling should disappear in another week, but it still won't be healed. So, you will have to be careful you don't overdo it. After it goes down, it will be susceptible to breaking again. It will take another two weeks before you can use it fully. After the swelling disappears, I will get flat sticks to brace it for you. That way you can use your hand, without straining the arm. It will also pad it, in case you hit it or something falls on it."

Inclining his head in agreement, Golden Eagle watched his friend apply the ointment. Dream Dancer was concentrating so intently on what he was doing; he didn't realize he was muttering. He was such an earnest young man, but with a mischievous nature at times... which was good.

Unexpectedly, Golden Eagle felt a sharp tingling start then looked at his arm in wonder... when a warm feeling spread through it. Devon looked at Dream Dancer in awe, as he listened to him chanting under his breath while massaging the arm. The warmth travelled from the tips of the Englishman's fingers, all the way up his arm past his elbow and into his shoulder.

Dream Dancer sat back feeling a bit light headed then stared at Golden Eagle's arm in shock... what had he done!

Golden Eagle looked at Dream Dancer in wonder. "What did you do?"

Shocked, Dream Dancer looked at his friend and shook his head startled. "I'm not sure; I was massaging your arm when I felt the need to chant. Heat entered my hands before seeping from them into your arm."

In amazement, Golden Eagle wiggled his fingers and moved his wrist around. The swelling was gone entirely, there was still some pain; nothing compared to earlier. "It feels good, not healed but like I had the break for six weeks instead of three."

Shrugging thoughtfully, Dream Dancer stared off into space thinking aloud as he mused fearfully. "They say that over a hundred years ago a medicine man could heal by touch. I never believed that, there is too much white blood in me for full belief of all Indian legends; now I'm not so sure. When I first learned that I had powers greater than any shaman alive now, I was scared out of my mind. I hate it that the Great Spirit would choose me for this burden. It would be so easy to misuse my gifts... if you want to call it that. As each one gets stronger or new ones appear, I get more terrified. I can touch minds now at immense distances. I can predict storms before they happen, and now I can heal. What will happen next? I don't think I want to know! What will I do if someone finds out, especially white people? They will try to use me!"

Gently reaching out, Golden Eagle turned Dream Dancer's chin towards him so he was looking at him. "Nobody can use you unless you want them to. The things you can do are a gift; don't ever think they are not. It will be a tremendous responsibility to use your powers for good, but the Great Spirit wouldn't have given them to you if there was any doubt you weren't strong enough to handle them. Fear is a natural emotion, always remember that if you are frightened of something you will use it more cautiously, which is a good thing. The only time you want to be truly scared of your gift is if you lose your fear of using it. When that happens, you could use your power without thinking then hurt yourself or others. That is when you better be terrified because you will be dangerous. Try to remember to think of every outcome that could happen if you do use your gift for something. Take healing me for instance. Think of what the consequences could be, the medicine man or shaman could find out about it then make you stay here in Montana. Or, since my arm is now better, I could try to escape. I won't, but what I'm trying to do is to get you to start thinking about all possible consequences. If you did this to a stranger when there are others around, the story will spread then you would have a line up of people wanting you to heal them. I want you to think of what will happen before you do it, remember that God makes things happen for a specific reason. So, for you to interfere would be wrong. Listen to your inner voice or your Great Spirit. They will guide you so you will know when to use your power... as well as when not to. I think you should rethink what you are taking in school. If you become a doctor, you can get away with healing if you are careful."

Golden Eagle was startled and pleased when his friend hugged him.

Dream Dancer smiled gravely before pushing himself away. He looked intently at Golden Eagle his face earnest. "Thank you! Now I know why you would be important to me too. I will never forget your words of wisdom."

Deadly serious, Golden Eagle frowned solemnly. "Remember, no matter where I am if you need me... I will come to you."

Without hesitation, Dream Dancer nodded before taking out Golden Eagle's knife then cut his left palm. He took Devon's hand and cut his too. They clasped hands to blend their blood as Ed vowed indisputably. "We are now blood brothers; if you ever have need of me, I will come to you or die trying!"

Finished, Dream Dancer ignoring the sting; got up then found two soft rawhides. He wrapped his hand, and walked over to wrap Devon's before wiping the blade then gave it back.

Earnestly, Dream Dancer sat back down across the fire; he took out his ceremonial pipe and tobacco then filled the bowl. He took a stick from the fire and lit the pipe. Edward inhaled deeply then blew smoke towards the Great Spirit, and at the ground to Mother Earth before turning to blow more smoke to the west then to the east, because that is where the sun rises and sets... it gives precious light, plus life in an otherwise dark world. He passed the ceremonial pipe over to Devon for him to continue the ritual.

When the ceremonial pipe was done, Dream Dancer sat forward then looked at Golden Eagle intently. "Everything I say must stay with us, I'm not supposed to tell you any of this; if Grandfather finds out, I will be in trouble. After the vision we had last night though, I concluded that the Great Spirit wants you to know. You are going to be angry with me after, but I want you to remember that I never lied to you. My English name is Edward William Charles Summerset the third... I am the person you came to see. Raven is Lady Raven Paulina Summerset. We are Earl Summerset's Grandchildren."

In dread, Dream Dancer watched Golden Eagle's expression closely. Edward was surprised to see no change.

Nodding, Golden Eagle smiled knowingly. "I figured that out the second day we met; we have three different portraits of your grandfather at home. You are the spitting image of him, especially with those unique Summerset eyes."

Instantly, Dream Dancer relaxed with a sigh of relief. "I'm sorry I didn't tell you. I wanted to, but my sister forbade it!"

Rubbing the back of his neck in confusion, Golden Eagle frowned thoughtfully then waved in bewilderment. "I understand; your grandfather threatened to cut my tongue out if I talked about the reason I came here. Although, I'm not sure why anyone but me would care?"

Dream Dancer motioned curiously. "Why did you come here?"

Dropping his hand, Golden Eagle shrugged. "I came to sell my land; because of the conditions of my grandfather's will, I have to live on the property for a year before I sell it. A man named Jed Brown wants it."

Immediately, Golden Eagle stopped short at the stunned look on his friend's face. "What's the matter? What did I say?"

Shaking his head in shock, Dream Dancer sighed in disgust. "Now, I know what the vision meant by two forces pulling you here. One was the Great Spirit, but he wasn't ready for you. My grandfather must have asked the Great Spirit to help him find someone for Raven, for whatever reason. Once the shaman saw you, my nam'-shimi would have asked his blood brother to contact you. That's the second force pulling you here."

Golden Eagle shook his head in confusion. "I don't understand; if the Great Spirit showed me to him, why was it too soon for me to come? Why show me at all, if he didn't want him to contact me?"

Frowning, Dream Dancer rubbed his forehead thoughtfully then lowered his hand and looked intently at Golden Eagle. "It is hard to explain, but I will try. The Great Spirit doesn't always give visions that are meant for others to act on. Sometimes he provides an image for reassurances, so let us use you as an example. My grandfather wants to help Raven find a husband, so he asks Ma'heo'o if someone is out there who is meant for her. The Great Spirit gives him assurances by showing the shaman you; regrettably, Grandfather had heard about you somehow... probably from my father. So, he decides to interfere by getting Jed to write to you to get you here. If things had proceeded naturally, it might have gone something like this. In the vision, we saw you argue with your brother then you vow never to return. Next, we saw you becoming dissatisfied with your life. I bet you were thinking about the property here as an escape from your life in England?"

Dream Dancer saw Golden Eagle nod in agreement then continued in satisfaction... he was on the right track. "The only thing holding you in England was your sisters. So, the Great Spirit is finding ways to bring you and Raven together. If you hadn't gotten that letter your younger sister would have died at home, that would have been the last straw for you. You would have come here on your own. Now, do you see what I mean by two forces? Both were well intended, but ended up contradicting each other. If what I think is true, Ma'heo'o had to find a way to fix things. Since your sister was fated to die on that day, a way to make it so had to be found. Although we don't think about it, when it's our time to pass on; we have no choice. So, the

Great Spirit uses the War Chief Howling Coyote to complete his plan. Now, other deaths will happen if things are not put right. The only way to fix things is for you to fall in love of your own free will with Raven, not by force!"

Frowning, Golden Eagle shook his head sadly. "I don't think falling in love will fix it now. I think it has gone too far for such a simple solution."

Dream Dancer smirked then motioned reassuringly. "I know, but remember when I said White Buffalo comes."

Golden Eagle inclined his head thoughtfully. "Yes, you said you would explain it to me later."

Sitting forward, Dream Dancer grinned in delight. "Well, do you remember Uncle Black Hawk talking about that woman sheriff who taught him how to fight with a knife?"

Puzzled, Golden Eagle shrugged in confusion. "Yes... why?"

Shaking his head in amusement, Dream Dancer chuckled at his obtuse friend. "That is White Buffalo; she is also married to Jed Brown. The good part is that Melissa is no longer a sheriff, but is thankfully a marshal... her husband is a deputy marshal."

Comprehending finally, Golden Eagle sighed in relief now understanding where this was going. "Oh, I see; she is going to come here, and help fix this mess we find ourselves in?"

In warning, Dream Dancer nodded then waved at Golden Eagle. "Yes, but not just her! It is going to take a combination of Raven, you, and the marshal to set things right."

Silently mulling over his friends warning, Golden Eagle frowned thoughtfully before inclining his head. "Okay, I will do my part. I'm not sure I will love Raven, but I'm willing to try. So, tell me about the ranch."

Grinning, Dream Dancer wasn't worried at all; he had seen that look in Golden Eagles eyes. They talked long into the night about Raven's plans for the ranch, and what adding his property to hers would do for the future of both of them.

CHAPTER FOURTEEN

Jed rolled out of his blankets at dawn. He stretched and yawned before looking over at the fire pit; Rose was making breakfast already.

Slipping behind some trees; Jed did his business in privacy then went to the creek with a pan and filled it with water, to shave and wash. Afterwards, the deputy marshal went and hunkered down beside the fire.

Feeling calmer, Jed grinned at Rose; he took the coffee she handed him. "Good morning, how are you feeling this morning... you're not too sore I hope?"

Rose shrugged negligently. "I am a bit, but not bad now."

Relieved, Jed nodded pleased then motioned enticingly. "That's good; as soon as we finish breakfast, we will go out and practice with your rifle for fifteen or twenty minutes."

Glad that Jed was not glaring at her, Rose inclined her head agreeably. "Okay, I found flour in one of the packs, so I made hotcakes with bacon."

Eagerly, Jed smiled in delight; he rubbed his hands together enthusiastically. "Sounds good to me, I love hotcakes."

Smiling, Rose dished Jed up some then handed him the plate. She saw Melissa and Jessica coming, so she made up two more. She beamed proudly before giving one to each of them then poured them a coffee.

Daniel and Pamela came next then helped themselves to coffee while Rose dished them up some breakfast. Patricia was the last one and smiled her thanks as she sat down then ate with gusto. The younger girl fixed herself up a plate and gave the extras to the dog. There was absolute silence as they all scraped their plates clean.

Full, Jed finished eating then sat back with more coffee. "We will take it slow today; tomorrow we will cross the river. Rose, can you swim?"

Hesitantly Rose nodded; she sighed dejectedly. "Yes, but it's been a while so not as well as I would like."

Sympathetically, Jed inclined his head and pointed at Pamela. "That's okay; some is better than nothing. I will double you up with Pam. I will take one of the packhorses across. Melissa, you can take the white colt since he has never had to cross water before and your horse is used to unbroken ones. Daniel, you can keep leading your packhorse. Patricia, I want you and your dog to go first to scout the area before we cross."

Everyone murmured assent, so Jed got up and motioned to Rose. "If you are ready, we can start your lessons now."

Rose jumped up enthusiastically then went to get her rifle.

Melissa watched them walk away with a laugh of humour; she used her thumb to point at Jed. "Have you noticed your father has managed to get out of cooking, and washing dishes since we started this trip?"

Patricia chuckled knowingly before waving in disbelief. "Of course, you didn't really expect Dad to cook or do dishes did you!"

Everyone laughed. Pamela got up then volunteered. "I will do the dishes; my husband can help me while you guys start breaking camp."

Daniel grumbled good-naturedly at his wife when Pamela volunteered him for the job. The others chuckled at the Pastor's exasperated expression then they all got up to get ready to leave.

****

Raven woke and got up to make coffee before reheating her fish from last night for breakfast. She checked her snares while she waited and threw a rabbit to the wolf as well as one to Bruno then put her snares away. The woman fed both her horses and went over to eat. She just sat down on her blankets when Bruno growled a warning then looked off to her left.

Brave Heart called out a challenge to the unfamiliar horses.

Snapping her fingers in demand, Raven called Bruno over to her. "Lay down here boy and watch."

Bruno settled close beside Raven's blankets obediently then watched the approaching men carefully, but without any more display of hostility.

As a precaution, Raven got up with her rifle and cocked it in preparation before cradling it in her arms. She smiled in relief when she recognized Chief Spitting Badger as one of the Indians. She released the hammer on her rifle then dropped her arms, but still held the gun unsure why they were here. What luck though to find him here!

Nodding a greeting silently, Raven waved an invitation for them to sit and offered them the rest of her fish. While they were eating, she went over to her packs. The woman took out her ceremonial pipe then tobacco and walked back over to the fire to make fresh coffee. She sat back before filling her pipe then lit it once the men finished eating.

Immediately, Raven passed the pipe to Chief Spitting Badger to begin the ceremony; if she had stumbled into their camp instead, the chief would have used his pipe. As the next important one, the pipe was passed back to her and finally given to the warrior.

Raven's status was a mystery, even to her. The Cheyenne considered her a notch below a chief, but more important than a shaman or medicine man. She never figured out why.

After the ceremony was finished and the pipe out, Raven looked at the leader musingly. "Chief Spitting Badger I was on my way to see you."

Spitting Badger nodded knowingly... his face impassive. "Yes, the shaman saw the Raven coming on a matter of great importance that we needed to discuss in private; he advised me to come to you instead."

Quickly, Raven masked her surprise; it wasn't a good idea to express your feelings to an Indian. They figure it's a sign of weakness.

Keeping his face blank, Spitting Badger sighed gravely. "I know why you are coming to see me Raven of the wolf tribe, 'protector' of her people."

Nodding, Raven sighed relieved then waited for him to go on.

Spitting Badger grimaced angrily, but only for a moment before his face became expressionless. "At the time of the last moon one of my warriors went hunting, he never came back. Squatting Dog has not returned in all this time. Our spiritual leader had a vision two nights ago about how he died; the shaman also saw you coming. So, the answer to your question is no. I didn't have anything to do with the massacre of the white people our spiritual healer saw in his vision."

Instantly, Raven nodded in relief with only a slight lift of her lips to show her pleasure... that was all the emotion she showed. She motioned in reassurance. "That is good; I know you have been approaching my nam-shimi' to join our winter camp. I will tell him that you didn't have anything to do with it, so you will be welcomed next winter."

Spitting Badger inclined his head before getting more coffee.

Excusing herself, Raven went over to her pack then took out the rabbit skin she had scraped the other night. She also took out a set of the grizzly claws and one of the eyeteeth, plus two molars of the grizzly she had killed. The woman walked back then nodded at the chief in appreciation. "Thank you for coming to see me. I have gifts for you both; although, your warrior will have to ask his wife to finish tanning his gift."

Raven offered Spitting Badger the claws and teeth from the grizzly. She gave the brave the rabbit-hide.

Chief Spitting Badger waved in pleasure pleased with the gifts before frowning disgruntled. "The Raven is extremely generous, but I did not bring a gift for the 'protector'!"

Quickly, Raven nodded solemnly at him not in the least upset over that... she motioned the apology away. She knew though, that she would have to help him keep his dignity by telling him that he had given her a gift of immense importance to her. "Coming here to meet me was worth more than the gifts I gave to you; may your journey be short and without hardships?"

The two men rose, Raven clasped arms with both men... the chief first of course. They turned towards their horses, but only went a few steps when Spitting Badger stopped suddenly and said something to his warrior.

The brave trotted to the horses instantly; he took out something from the saddle and turned back. The warrior hurried over then handed it to his chief.

In relief, Spitting Badger walked back to Raven gravely. "I do have something for you."

Dramatically, Spitting Badger held it out towards Raven impassively; it was a rifle with a fringed carrier.

Pulling the rifle out to inspect it dutifully, Raven nodded solemnly in approval... accepting it. "Thank you, it is beautiful!"

Inclining his head, Spitting Badger's lip curled in a semblance of a smile; that's all the pleasure he would show at Raven's approval. "It's a rifle I traded for yesterday with a ve'ho'e."

Pleased, Raven nodded in appreciation. "I will treasure your gift."

Lifting his lip a bit in a smile, Spitting Badger was satisfied that he had given the 'protector' of her people a gift worthy of her position, so was no longer shamed... finally, they left.

Raven frowned thoughtfully. She watched them leave pensively. A ve'ho'e; what white man? She hadn't asked him, knowing that Spitting Badger wouldn't know what the man's real name was. It wasn't good when the whites started selling the Indians rifles. It only meant trouble to come. She shrugged there was no use worrying about it now.

Turning away, Raven swiftly broke camp. She put her new rifle on her packhorse since she had no bullets for it and mounted. She headed towards the Eagle's summer camp... now ahead of schedule.

****

Dream Dancer left his grandmother's tepee with two bowls of porridge then walked to Raven's and slipped inside. Golden Eagle was up making coffee. Edward smiled then handed Devon a bowl. "How's your arm today?"

Golden Eagle wiggled his fingers experimentally. "Better, but it swelled up during the night so it's still a bit sore; I don't think I should use it too much yet. Can you re-wrap it for me please? I wouldn't want anyone to see it yet."

Nodding, glad his friend wanted to hide it for now; Dream Dancer frowned thoughtfully, wanting to see if he could do it again as he helped Golden Eagle with the bandages. "I'll put ointment on it tonight and see what happens."

Having no objections, Golden Eagle inclined his head when his young friend finished wrapping his arm before stepping back. "Okay, but we are running late, so we better hurry to the clearing for our lessons. I think we should take the cub with us; he can play in the field while we work."

Startled by that logic, Dream Dancer chuckled impressed. "That's a great idea, I never thought of that."

Snickering at the stunned look, Golden Eagle smiled at his young friend's praise but didn't comment as he asked in concern. "How's your head, is it any better this morning?"

Forlornly, Dream Dancer rubbed his temple irritably. "Yes, it's quite a bit better; unfortunately, still there though."

Taken aback, Golden Eagle scowled in apprehension then motioned in dismay. "Should you still have a headache?"

Dream Dancer frowned worried, but tried to hide it. "I don't know. I think I strained myself a little bringing both of you with me at the same time... I have never done that before. When I healed you last night, it made me light headed so that could be why it's still there!"

Thoughtfully, Golden Eagle nodded uneasily before grinning at an idea. "If it's still there tomorrow, you should go see the medicine man.

Or better yet, maybe try rubbing some of that ointment on your temples after you do my arm; the heat in your hands from healing me might help you as well."

Picking up his bowl to finish eating, Dream Dancer inclined his head in approval. "Good idea, okay I will try that tonight."

Golden Eagle watched the cub eat his breakfast, and looked over at his young friend curiously. "I forgot to ask you last night about the cub. He was acting weird after you had the vision. When I came out of the dream, you were staring at me fixedly... still as a statue. The cub jumped up then started crying loudly, that's how I knew you were in trouble. After you jerked in my arms then fell back with your eyes closed. The cub stopped crying unexpectedly, and just stood there staring intently at you. After a few minutes, he curled back up against you then went to sleep. Why did he do that? Was it my imagination, or did he actually help you somehow?"

Unsure, Dream Dancer shrugged pensively... he could only speculate of course. "The bear was our spirit totem at one time. We were called the bear tribe before my Cheyenne grandfather on my father's side died; but when they joined us, it was on the condition that we became the wolf tribe. The Great Spirit finds us through our spirit totems, that is why I told you to make sure you had your medicine bag on. It helped the Great Spirit to find you, and me when it was time. Ma'heo'o often uses real animals to give messages or warnings. Sometimes your spirit totem will show up at your greatest hour of need. Take the cub for instance. If the Great Spirit knew I would need extra help in the future, he could have gotten the mother grizzly to sacrifice her life. So, Raven would be able to bring the baby cub here. That way, when I was in trouble, the Great Spirit could help me through him."

Golden Eagle sighed grimly. "Your Great Spirit is as baffling as our God is."

Dream Dancer grinned consolingly then picked up the cub. "That's why they are Spirits or God's. We are not supposed to understand them, just follow their teaching as best we can. I always believed that Ma'heo'o and God are one and the same, just called by different names."

Startled by that thought, Golden Eagle shrugged and finished his food before getting up. "I suppose you could be right, let's go."

****

Jed slowed his horse to a trot to cool him down then looked around. He could hear the river clearly and knew they were close. They rode around a curve then slowed their horses to a walk as the river came into view. He started looking for a campsite; it was still early, but he didn't want to take a chance of being caught in the middle of the river at night.

Melissa rode up and pointed to the right; in the distance was the perfect place for a temporary camp. Jed inclined his head in agreement. Everyone dismounted then an encampment was set up for the night. Afterwards, they walked to the edge of the river and looked at the far shore in trepidation.

Fearfully, Rose stared in panic at the fast-moving water then shook fretfully... she pointed grimly. "We have to cross that; it's not possible!"

Soothingly, Jed walked over to Rose. He put his hand on her shoulder before smiling calmly. "Yes, we are going to cross that; don't worry, I have done it before it's not as bad as it looks. All you have to do is hold onto the horse."

Rose nodded relieved at Jed's assurance that he did it before, but she still looked doubtful.

They went back to camp soberly unsure what tomorrow would bring. All of them tried to push thoughts of what was to come away, wanting to enjoy the first early day they had since starting their journey. Unfortunately, their laughter was strained; with no pranks, or jokes this night to relieve the tension.

****

Raven slowed her horse to a trot then to a walk; they had ridden hard today, and she hadn't even stopped for lunch. Both horses, as well as their rider, were exhausted. It was still too early to camp, but she felt it was essential for her horse's sake. She started looking for a defensible one then finally found it up on a hill. Behind the ledge rose a cliff, which would be difficult to climb, it gave her some protection.

Raven rode up to it and jumped down off her horse. She unsaddled both horses then rubbed them down before she set up camp. She decided to look for fresh meat, so grabbed her rifle and walked cautiously through the underbrush around the base of the hill. The young woman spotted a doe in the distance, but it was too large.

Undeterred, Raven kept going until her wolf-dog raced after a bunch of pheasants. They were a perfect size, so she shot them before heading back to camp. Once at her fire pit, the woman threw one pheasant to each of her canine animals then sat down and cleaned her bird. She built up her fire then put the bird on a spit to roast.

Trying to keep her mind off her growling belly, Raven busied herself... waiting in anticipation for supper; she saddled the packhorse so it would be ready to go in the morning, and made her bed while the bird cooked; finally, the woman sat down to eat then sat back against a log to enjoy her coffee.

Letting her guard down, Raven let thoughts of Golden Eagle surface; she shivered remembering their night of lovemaking. She couldn't figure out what came over her that night... maybe it was the alcohol that did it. The woman could have easily used her training to get away from Devon, but didn't. Except for a brief half-hearted effort, she melted against him instead.

As much as she would like too, Raven couldn't blame it on Golden Eagle either; Devon had given her plenty of chances to tell him no, but she hadn't... she even encouraged him.

Unable to help it, Raven trembled in pleasure remembering the feel of his hard muscled body pressed against her. She had enjoyed every minute of their lovemaking and hadn't wanted to leave the Englishman in the morning.

Bringing the vision from the other night to the front of her subconscious; Raven frowned then sighed musingly. She recalled seeing Golden Eagle as a Lord in England, he looked good in his fancy clothes... he also seemed miserable. The woman remembered seeing herself suckling an infant, and had known before seeing Devon that he was the father. She couldn't help thinking about how good that had made her feel. She touched her belly with a frown, was she pregnant?

Raven shook of her foolishness, nah it couldn't be it had only been one night. She threw away her cold coffee; banked the fire and crawled into her blankets... trying to sleep. Try as she might though to banish images of Golden Eagle, her last thought before she slept was about him.

****

Golden Eagle and Dream Dancer walked towards the corrals then saw Black Hawk already there waiting for them. The mare was running around the corral nickering at the stallion.

Black Hawk motioned curiously at Golden Eagle. "How did your visit with Devil go last night?"

Shrugging, Golden Eagle grinned unperturbed that his horse was stubborn. "He let me walk up to him, but as I reached out to touch him... he moved away. When I sat down though, he came over to me and ate out of my hand again."

Pleased by that small progress, Black Hawk nodded then waved towards the paddocks enticingly. "Why don't you go over and try touching him again."

In anticipation, Golden Eagle turned quickly then walked over to the stud's corral and climbed in.

Devil turned to face him when he arrived then stood looking at him. Golden Eagle crooned to the stallion in urging and walked towards him. The horse's nostrils flared searching for a scent, this time he didn't move.

Thrilled, Golden Eagle stood beside him then reached out to touch the stallion in awe. Devil quivered in response at the feel of a human's hand on him, but didn't turn away.

Taking the opportunity, Golden Eagle scratched Devil's neck and proceeded to rub his hand all over him. He touched the stallion's legs, but didn't try to lift them yet or go behind him... unsure if the horse would kick. Devon stepped back not wanting to push him too fast then left the corral excitedly.

Gleefully, Golden Eagle couldn't stop smiling as he walked to Black Hawk then waved in wonder. "Did you see that? I touched him?"

Nodding, Black Hawk chuckled in humour at Golden Eagle's eager question. "Yes... congratulations. Tonight, and tomorrow, I want you to go in with the stud every chance you get and touch him; next time try picking up his feet then handle them too."

Golden Eagle inclined his head in exhilaration. "Okay."

They turned back to the mare, and Black Hawk motioned in explanation. "Today I'm going to saddle Lady again. I will put the sacks on her for a bit; when she stands for that, I will try lying on her back. If it doesn't take her long to get used to that, I will get up on her to get her used to having someone on her. Afterwards you both can come in with the noise makers"

Golden Eagle nodded; he watched Black Hawk keenly.

*****

In approval, Golden Eagle chuckled two hours later as he watched the mare follow Black Hawk like a puppy; as he walked back to them, finished for the day. "Your horse learns fast."

Black Hawk nodded pleased. "I'm not going to do anything more with her today; always end your lessons on a positive note. You two can go have an early supper if you want."

Inclining his head, Golden Eagle smiled thankfully. "Okay, I will go in with my stud first then we will take the cub out before supper."

Agreeing with a distracted nod, Black Hawk turned away without comment to brush down his mare.

Walking to the other pen, Golden Eagle followed by Dream Dancer went over to Devil's paddock.

Seeing the water bucket in the corral, Raven's brother took it out before turning away. "I'll get him water while you go in with him."

Not paying any attention, Golden Eagle nodded vaguely before climbing over the fence. He walked towards the stallion crooning softly. Devil let him touch him again, but this time Devon picked up his feet. He scratched the stud all over then turned and left still not wanting to push his horse too much yet, he might bulk then refuse to let him close again.

Dream Dancer came around the corner when Golden Eagle climbed over the fence. While his young friend put water into the stallion's corral, Devon went to the shed then took out hay.

Once they were done, they turned and went to Raven's together. The cub was awake when they entered, so Dream Dancer picked him up; leaving again, they went out back... into the trees. The grizzly cub went to the bathroom before ambling over to a tree that was dead and lying on its side. Cuddles scratched at it insistently, but was too small to move it yet.

Being helpful, Golden Eagle smiled then pushed it over for him. Underneath were grubs, worms, and insects. The cub ate while the two friends sat talking about England.

Dream Dancer frowned thoughtfully. "When my fathers will got read there was a list of estates; I was only eleven at the time, so didn't pay attention."

Golden Eagle nodded as he tried to remember back then he ticked them off on his fingers as he talked. "Hmm, let's see if I can remember. You have a townhouse in London, Oxford, and Windsor. You have two castles one is in West Summerset, thirty-five miles from Clevedon. You can see the coast of Wales from there. The castles built on the cliffs, which overlooks the mouth of Severn. It goes to the Bristol Channel then out to sea. You own all the land in Summerset and the serfs. You also have a castle in Wales at Conwy, not far from the border of Snowdonia. Your grandfather hardly ever went to his castle in Wales... they say that Snowdonia's haunted; people who go there never come back. You will probably spend the first few years at your townhouse in Oxford, that's where the best schools are. I would like to make suggestions on what you should do after you arrive in England; it might help you stay the Earl of Summerset, and not lose your title because of an angry Queen."

Eagerly, Dream Dancer smiled in thanks. "Please do, I'm not sure what to do when I get there so anything that might help will be appreciated."

Nodding, Golden Eagle frowned contemplatively. "Well, before you leave you will need to gather every document you have to take with you. Your father's birth, marriage, and his death certificate are imperative and must be with you. Yours plus your sister's birth certificates, with a copy of your grandfather's will is very important. Don't forget your father's death certificate also. Then the first thing you need to do when you land is to go to your townhouse in Windsor, and put in a request to see the queen. When she grants you an audience, make sure you take all the papers I have listed with you then give them directly to her. I wish I had my trunks here so I could show you how to dress properly, and give you some lessons on how to behave in the presence of the queen."

Waving, Dream Dancer smirked devilishly. "I know where your trunks are, Grandfather hid them; he said... 'if you are going to be living here you should be cut off from your old way of life, until you became used to the new one'."

Laughing, Golden Eagle chuckled at his young friend's best imitation of his grandfather's voice. "Okay, before you go, I will give you some decent clothes. Once you arrive, have your butler get new clothes made up for you. The queen will leave you sitting for a few days, so you should attend some of the parties while you are waiting. Stand up, you will be wearing a sword on your right side since you are left-handed as your grandfather was. When you walk into the room, where the queen will receive you... don't look around; stare straight ahead, and keep your right hand loosely on the hilt of your sword. When the person who is guiding you, probably the secretary stops. Drop on one knee then bend down with your hand on your sword hilt, like this."

Dream Dancer watched closely and imitated him.

Golden Eagle nodded satisfied. "Good, but you will need to practice so your movements are more fluid... not jerky. When you go to some of the parties or balls, you bow a bit to the host then take the host's wife's hand in yours and bend over it before saying, 'charmed my lady', then straighten and walk in. Remember you are an earl, so the only people more powerful than you are; is the queen, any children she has, her husband of course, and a duke. The queen is Victoria, her husband is Prince Consort Albert... we don't have a king at present. The prince is only as powerful as the queen allows him to be. The aristocracy in descending order is made up of... king or queen, prince and princess, duke as well as a duchess, earl with a countess, viscount with a viscountess, marquees with a marchioness, and baron with a baroness. All the offsprings of the nobles are called lords or ladies. Most likely, the queen will be in Windsor Castle since that is where they spend most of their time. If she isn't you will have to go wherever she is to see her. Your grandfather was out here because he was in exile; he angered the old king who at that time was King George the fourth. So be extremely careful what you say to any of the royal house. Like her father, Queen Victoria has a quicksilver temper it can flare up when you least expect it. Remember, she can let you have your estates back since they were never taken away or she can banish you just for being a Summerset. She can also send you to prison or cut off your head with a flick of her hand. In England, she is all powerful."

Shaking his head baffled, Dream Dancer scowled dejectedly. "I'm not sure I will remember all that, it's confusing."

Waving, Golden Eagle grinned decisively in promise. "You will I promise, from now on every night before we go to bed, I will tell you more then give you some history and etiquette lessons. I will have you so well versed in court manners nobody will suspect that you are part savage. Your light colouring will help, but make sure you are upfront with the queen nobody else needs to know, but she does."

Pleased, Dream Dancer smiled appreciatively. "Okay thank you, but we better get back supper should be ready."

Nodding, Golden Eagle took the cub back to the tepee.

CHAPTER FIFTEEN

Golden Eagle woke early then looked past the fire pit to where Dream Dancer was still sleeping. He smiled in delight; this was the first time he had woken before Edward.

Remembering last night, Golden Eagle wiggled his fingers experimentally and grinned wider. His arm was now healed, thanks to his friend's magical touch. They had gotten back from supper then Devon went to visit his stallion. Afterwards, they took the cub to the lake and they all had a bath before going back to Raven's for more history lessons on England's Royalty.

Dream Dancer had rubbed more cream into Golden Eagle's arm as they talked, with the same results as before. The heat sensation had gone from the tips of Devon's fingers all the way up into his shoulder. Raven's brother had rubbed some on his own temples afterwards; it seemed to help him too. Edward felt light-headed after healing him, so they pondered the possibility that the healing was coming from deep within him... so could be taking some of his strength from him. If that were the case, the young earl would have to be extremely careful; a severe injury might kill him!

Frowning in warning, Dream Dancer had cautioned Golden Eagle not to use the arm yet. If he tried using it too soon, Devon could damage it further. Maybe in another day or two, the Englishman would have full use of it again.

Shivering, Golden Eagle rolled out of his blankets then built up the fire; it was chilly and he could hear rain falling outside. The cub woke, so Devon passed him a cooked squirrel... which he wolfed down.

Quietly, Golden Eagle got dressed in his waterproofed buckskins then headed out the door. He went to the corral first, and fed his horse then touched him again. Devon finally turned away before going to Giant Bear's next to get their breakfast.

Scratching on the tepee flap, Golden Eagle heard a muffled reply. Devon ducked inside then grinned at Giant Bear's wife.

Grinning at the wet Englishman, Golden Dove smiled back and dished up some porridge as she asked him in Cheyenne. "How are you doing this morning... where is Dream Dancer hiding?"

Golden Eagle frowned in concentration as he answered hesitantly in Cheyenne. "I'm fine, is wet... it's raining. Dream Dancer is sleeping."

Golden Dove chuckled as she looked at the Englishman's dripping hair then handed him two bowls of porridge, and a folded piece of paper. "It looks as if it's pouring not just raining, you are soaked you know! Here, can you please give this to Dream Dancer for me."

Forlornly, Golden Eagle inclined his head in agreement then laughed with Golden Dove before switching to English. "You are right it is pouring out. I will give that to Dream Dancer, thank you for breakfast."

Smirking, Golden Dove beamed in delight. "You're welcome."

Carefully, Golden Eagle turned then left the tepee and walked to Raven's wondering what was in the note. He ducked inside before grinning at Dream Dancer cheerfully, pleased with himself for getting breakfast for his young friend for a change. "Good morning."

Accepting a bowl, Dream Dancer chuckled at his friends... soaked appearance. "Good morning to you too, you are up awful early today."

Boastfully, Golden Eagle laughed in satisfaction as he sat across from Dream Dancer with his bowl of cold porridge. "First time I woke up before you."

Dream Dancer smiled dismissively at his friend's smug look then pointed at the paper curiously in Golden Eagle's hand. "What is that you have there?"

Shrugging, Golden Eagle passed his young friend the note. "I don't know; your nis-gi-ii asked me to give it to you."

Distractedly, Dream Dancer nodded his thanks then opened it and read while he ate his breakfast. When he finished, he handed it back to Golden Eagle. "It is a list of supplies needed from the ranch, which means I will be leaving in a couple of days, but I will be back."

Nodding knowingly, Golden Eagle frowned thoughtfully reading the list contemplatively. "That's a lot of supplies... does Raven have enough? If your sister gives this yearly, how does she keep up and what about money for extras; I'm sure she doesn't charge your nam'-shimi for anything?"

Finishing his breakfast, Dream Dancer shrugged not worried. "Usually Nam-shimi' doesn't need so much. He only gets supplies in the winter, now that he will be staying for the year... they need extra. You are right, Raven doesn't charge them for anything, Grandfather makes sure the women make dream catchers, buckskins, Indian saddle blankets, and other products that the whites crave then gives them to her for payment. My sister sells them, and uses the money to get things like... coffee that we can't grow, or other essential staples that our people can't get. We have talked about the future though. Eventually, they will have to stay here year-round. It's getting too risky for them to move around now that the government is trying to drive the Indians onto reservations. So far, nam'-shimi has managed to stay away from them but as more whites come; they steal more land. It's not looking promising for the Indian Nations in the future."

Golden Eagle, handed the list back. He sighed grimly, what could they do it was a difficult situation. The queen had no real voice here; it was too far away for her to do anything about it. So going to her would do no good. Besides, there were too many people in England that wanted out... there was no way they could stop them. He shook off his thoughts not wanting to think about it anymore then got up. "Let's go for our lessons, dress warm it's pouring out."

Dream Dancer groaned half-heartedly and dressed as he asked his friend hopefully. "Do you think my uncle will cancel the lessons since it is raining?"

Smirking, Golden Eagle chuckled sympathetically before shaking his head negatively. "I hardly doubt it, but we will wait and see what he has to say."

Sighing forlornly, Dream Dancer scowled shrewdly without much confidence knowing his uncle the way he did. He picked up the cub then they headed out the door.

****

Raven woke and hurriedly dressed then broke camp; she didn't even take time to eat. She looked around for Bruno and his female, but neither was around. Grumbling under her breath, Raven nudged her horse into a canter then looked up irritably it was clouding up fast... she could see lightning in the distance. She knew she was in for a soaking; the woman shrugged in exasperation, nothing she could do about it then rode on.

****

Melissa woke up first so started breakfast.

Jed joined Mell and smiled his thanks when she handed him a coffee. He looked up then frowned in concern. "It looks as if it's going to rain; I hope it holds off until after we cross the river."

Nodding, Melissa scowled anxiously before waving decisively. "I hope so too, but we have to cross today we have already lost too much time."

Frowning, Jed heaved a sigh uneasily. He shook off his unpleasant feeling, not wanting to upset anyone; he smiled at Patricia and Jessica. "Good morning, how are you two feeling this fine morning?"

Jessica grinned good-naturedly. "We are just great!"

Patricia looked up at the sky wearily then smiled in thanks at Mell when her mother handed her some porridge... she turned to Jed. "I feel fine, but I don't like the looks of those clouds coming, Dad. I'm going to eat breakfast and cross the river right away with Silver Tip, so we can scout around. I think we better get across before that storm hits."

Sighing heavily, Jed nodded thoughtfully; he motioned in anxiety. "I was thinking the same thing! I will go with you as well. It will be faster with two of us scouting. Rose will have to forgo her lessons today. After we look around, I will come back across then lead the girls over."

Turning to Melissa, Jed waved around the camp expectantly. "Have everything and everyone ready to go!"

Feeling unsettled, Melissa inclined her head then handed Jed his porridge. She was getting forewarning feelings... Mell shivered in response; White Buffalo tried to ignore it as best she could, but failed. They had no choice but to navigate it today, time was running out!

Eating quickly, Jed and Patricia were just finishing their breakfasts when the others arrived; Melissa handed out bowls of porridge and coffee.

Without another word, Jed with Patricia a step behind left then saddled their horses; they mounted and rode to the edge of the river. Pat whistled for her dog then waited.

Melissa walked up beside them in concern, trying to ignore her foreboding feelings. "The river is getting rougher, please both of you try to be careful."

The two nodded and urged their horses into the water.

Frowning, Melissa stood there watching then looked around when she felt someone take her hand in support. She smiled at Pamela then her son before turning to watch apprehensively.

Jed led the way; he turned to look over his shoulder at Patricia in warning. "It gets deep ahead, and a little rough so get ready for a swim."

Scowling, Patricia nodded but didn't comment as she fought to keep her horse under control. Pat saw her father's mare plunge into the water, and saw him slip out of the saddle then swim beside her holding the saddle horn. She kicked her horse angrily before slapping him with the reins in rebuke. The gelding nickered in fear, and backed up a step before plunging in.

Patricia copied Jed and slipped out of the saddle.

Silver Tip swam up beside his mistress then foraged ahead.

Grimly, Patricia saw swirling water so tightened her grip on the saddle horn. She could tell that the undertow was stronger here, just by the way that the water was reacting. Pat got pushed up against her horse, but was prepared for that. A piece of driftwood floated towards her, so the young woman kicked it away from them before it could touch her gelding.

Thankfully, Patricia saw Jed climb back on his horse; Pat sighed in relief then waited a few minutes before getting back on her horse, as they stepped up into shallower water. Finally, they were across safely.

Standing up in his stirrups, Jed looked back at Melissa and waved in reassurance; knowing his wife would not leave, until she was sure they were okay then turned right to explore that part of the river.

Patricia and Silver Tip turned left to explore their side.

*****

Holding her breath, Melissa watched the whole ordeal from the opposite riverbank; she sighed in relief when Jed and Patricia reached the opposite side safely. Mell didn't relax though, until she saw her husband's signal that they were okay. She squeezed Pamela's hand in thanks for holding on to her. They turned, and started breaking camp to get ready for their turn.

****

Golden Eagle followed by Dream Dancer went into Raven's then both fell on their beds in exhaustion, wet clothes and all.

Plaintively, Golden Eagle groaned in agony. "I don't think I'm ever going to learn how to fight with a knife. You seem to be learning faster than I am."

Dream Dancer chuckled in sympathy. "Well, I have a confession to make. When I use to watch Black Hawk and Raven make their moves, I would go somewhere private then try to copy them. So, I already have a few years of doing this behind me."

Satisfied, Golden Eagle sighed reassured. "That makes me feel better."

Groaning in reluctance, Golden Eagle stood up and grimaced down irritably. "I'm soaked right through, but I have to go back out to feed my horse then go for lessons so I might as well stay in these clothes."

Without even a hint of remorse, Dream Dancer chuckled teasingly and added fuel to the dying fire. "I will stay here and dry out while you are gone."

Shaking his head in exasperation, Golden Eagle grimaced dejectedly at his young friend; he slipped out of the tepee as Dream Dancer laughed mischievously after him. Devon went to the shed for feed, after putting the hay in Devil's pen he went in then approached him.

Devil snorted at him forlornly as the stallion stood with his rear end turned to the fierce wind.

Moving slowly, Golden Eagle crooned softly to Devil in sympathy as he ran his hands up the stallion's neck. He moved his hands back down then touched the stud's sides before running his hand down the horse's leg... he lifted each foot. The Englishman brought his hand back up then down one side of the horses back. Carefully standing to the side in case the horse kicked at him, he scratched the stud's hindquarters above the tail then smiled in delight when Devil pushed against him for more.

Golden Eagle went to the other side then lifted each hoof on that side. Playfully he pulled his stallion's tail to see what he would do, but the stud just pushed against him wanting a scratch. The Englishman obliged him before walking up to Devil's head. He rubbed his ears, and patted his forehead before leaning forward then kissed the horse on the nose.

Devil snorted indignantly through his nostrils.

In amusement, Golden Eagle chuckled then held out his hand and let Devil sniff then nibble on his fingers looking for grain. Devon turned and clucked to the horse; the stallion obediently followed him. After giving the stud oats, the Englishman climbed over the fence then went to Giant Bear's for lessons.

****

Raven pulled up and jumped off her horse then went to her packhorse to get her rain slicker. She drew it over her head as the rain started coming down harder. The woman sighed in disgust before remounting.

Grimly, Raven decided to ride a bit further. If she remembered correctly, there was an old miner's shack ahead. It would give them protection from the pelting rain, and lightning that was drawing closer.

Forlornly, Raven hunkered under her rain slicker in misery then nudged her horse into a canter... continuing doggedly on.

****

Melissa and her group stood on the bank then watched Jed coming towards them... swimming beside his horse. It was only just starting to rain, but darker black and purple clouds were coming fast; they could also see lightning in the distance. The river was getting higher and choppier as the wind picked up.

Jed's mare climbed out of the water, he waved at Daniel and Jessica quickly. "You two can start crossing, watch for floating debris or water snakes. They don't live in fast water, but keep an eye out for them; sometimes they get caught as the river rises then swept downstream."

The two nodded at the information before nudging their horses. Daniel was leading a packhorse and Jessica led Rose's.

Jed jumped off his horse then went to join Melissa. He watched Daniel trailed by Jessica plunge into the rushing river. He lowered his voice, so only Mell could hear him before motioned in concern. "I don't know about this; the river is getting worse, and that storm is moving in faster than I thought was possible."

Melissa took his hand and squeezed it in reassurance. "We will make it love, don't worry so much."

They stood on the riverbank together then watched in trepidation, neither relaxed until the two made it safely to the opposite bank.

Swiftly, Jed turned to his horse and tied the packhorse to the back of his saddle before rummaging inside his saddlebag... he pulled out a small rawhide rope. He walked over to Pamela's horse; he tied the line to the back of the saddle then made a loop. He turned to his daughter-in-law and the newest member of their group in warning. "Okay, Pam when you get to the deeper water you will need to swim. Just hold onto the saddle horn. Rose, you grab this strap and hold onto it as you slide off the horse. All you have to do is kick your legs; the horse will do the rest. I will ride ahead; Melissa will be behind you. Push any debris out of your way. Whatever you do, don't panic. All you need to do is hold on. The horse will get you to the other side safely."

Pamela mounted then Jed lifted Rose so she was behind her.

Quickly, Jed mounted his horse before turning and looked back at Melissa in encouragement; he faced forward then nudged his horse onward. The deputy marshal walked into the deep churning water; he frowned when lightning flashed closer. The rain was now a solid sheet as it fell harder.

Suddenly, the wind howled fiercely; Jed looked upstream into the distance then saw the water moving faster as debris floated towards them. Horse and rider got to the edge of the drop off then plunged in; they were committed now, no turning back.

Keeping a tight hold on his saddle horn, Jed slipped out of the saddle and looked behind his shoulder to check on his packhorse. Once reassured he watched Pamela with Rose clinging tightly to her, jump in then successfully drop out of their saddle one on each side of the horse. The deputy marshal uneasily stared past them at Melissa fighting with the colt.

Reassured, Jed sighed in relief when both horses jumped into the water; he turned back just in time to push a piece of driftwood out of his way.

*****

Pamela and Rose successfully slipped off the horse one on each side. Pam yelled loudly in question trying to be heard above the rushing water, and the fierce wind. "How are you doing back there, Rose?"

Rose called back nervously. "I'm okay Pam."

Remembering Jed's advice; Rose kicked her legs hard as she pushed pieces of wood out of her way. She had a hold of the strap in a death grip then she shivered in panic as a lightning bolt flashed ahead on the distant shore, not too far away from them. A loud clap of thunder boomed out only split seconds after the lightning hit.

The horse squealed in fright and tried to turn.

All of a sudden, the strap Rose was holding came loose; she went under as the current pulled her down relentlessly. She squealed in shock, causing her to swallow water before struggling to try to rise to the surface desperately.

Grimly, Pamela held onto the saddle horn for dear life as the lightning flashed and the thunder boomed on the opposite shore. She grabbed desperately at the horse's reins as he turned, trying to bring him back around. Pam heard a frightened cry then pulled herself up enough to see over her horse; it was in time to see Rose get pulled under the water.

Without hesitation, Pamela hastily released the saddle horn and swam around then plunged in. She grabbed Rose by the shirt, pulling her upwards; once they surfaced, Pam grabbed the younger girl around the chest holding her backwards trying to keep them both afloat. She sighed in relief when the girl sputtered and took a breath.

Fearfully, Pamela looked around but couldn't see her horse anymore. She groaned apprehensively then tried to push against the current... she was unsuccessful. Pam knew she couldn't get them both across by herself!

Rose turned her head and looked up at Pamela in terror then shouted an apology. "I'm sorry, the rope broke."

Pamela smiled in reassurance, trying to keep the fear out of her voice as she pleaded desperately. "It's okay, but we need to get to the far shore, and I can't do it alone. I need you to turn over then hold my hand; I will keep you afloat, I promise. We both need to kick as hard as we can and try to steer towards the shore! Can you do that?"

Nodding grimly, Rose grasped Pamela's hand trustingly; she turned then kicked as hard as she possibly could, trying not to be a hindrance. They were making progress when a piece of wood floated by in front of them.

Feeling an unexpected painful pinch between her ribs, Pamela unexpectedly screamed in shocked surprise... unable to move.

Confused by her inability to go anywhere, Rose held onto Pamela desperately as she pulled herself closer to see what the problem was. "What is it... what happened?"

Panting, Pamela shuddered in agony. "That piece of driftwood is a tree under the water. A branch I didn't see pierced my side. I can't move; I'm stuck you will have to go on alone."

In shock, Rose saw the blood pooling around Pamela and shook her head in horror. "No, I will not leave you!"

Mind racing furiously, Rose looked around in despair trying to figure out how to help her new friend; she saw a log coming swiftly towards them. It was bobbing up and down, but staying above the water. She released Pamela's hand then lunged for it, hoping to catch it before it swept past them. Luck was with the younger girl when she got a hold of it, kicking her legs as hard as she could manage, she steered it towards Pamela.

Unfortunately, Pamela was still tangled up in the tree. It took several minutes before Rose pulling Pam backwards managed to get her loose. The injured older girl, grabbed onto the other side of the log Rose was clinging to; thankfully, they pushed away from the tree then both kicked their legs hard.

Without warning, Rose felt the log tipping and looked over fearfully to see Pamela sinking under the surface. She lunged towards her then caught her by the hair before she could drop out of sight. The younger girl heaved up with all her strength, and grabbed Pam around the waist once the older woman broke the surface; she pulled her up onto the log, amazed that she had managed to keep a hold of the tree.

Pamela coughed weakly then spit water out trying to clear her lungs before pulling herself up. "I don't know how long I can hold on!"

Holding onto the branch with one hand, Rose swung around so that Pamela was between her and the log. This way she could stabilize Pam against the tree limb with her body... plus still maintain a grip on the wooden slab. The young girl grabbed the branch on the other side of the older woman; helping to keep her in place.

Feeling protected, Pamela sighed in painful relief; closing her eyes, Pam lost consciousness.

Rose clung to the driftwood in desperation; in this position, she couldn't steer or lessen her grip to push obstacles away afraid she might lose Pamela for good this time. Jed would never forgive her if she didn't get Pam safely to shore. The younger girl looked up imploringly as she mumbled a prayer to the Great Spirit under her breath. Abruptly finding an inner strength that she didn't know she had, the girl kicked urgently trying to get to shallower water.

Pushing and kicking her feet harder; Rose watched in horror as a large branch came rushing towards them rapidly. She positioned herself so she could protect Pam, this way it would hit her instead. The younger girl grunted in surprise then gasped for breath when it connected under a rib. She heard a snap... she screamed in painful shock.

Fearfully, Rose tightened her grip urgently as she felt herself almost lose her hold on the log and Pam. The younger girl was starting to lose consciousness when she felt hands pulling her out of the water.

****

Raven looked around but didn't see anyone. There were no fresh horse droppings or footprints, so she dismounted then walked to the miner's cabin and pulled open the door. The woman nodded pleased, abandoned as she figured, so she took both horses in with her.

Satisfied, Raven was thankful to have a dry place to wait out the storm; she would get an early start tomorrow, she hoped.

Keeping to her routine, Raven unsaddled her horses first. Hearing a persistent bark at the door, she opened it and smiled at Bruno. "Decided to join me did you; well, come in make yourself at home."

Bruno trotted in then went directly towards the fireplace.

Raven watched him circling around and around in amusement, as he tried to find the best spot to lie in; he dropped down suddenly... promptly, he went to sleep. Shaking her head, the woman chuckled at her dog in amusement. She went back to work getting a fire going then ate supper before curling up in her blankets to sleep.

****

Golden Eagle with Dream Dancer following went back to Raven's and plopped down in front of the fire, in relief. Devon sighed irritably still soaked to the skin. "It has been a long, wet day but finally it's over; my arm hurts a lot tonight though! How is your headache?"

Dream Dancer added wood to the fire then smiled at the soaked Golden Eagle. "Strip to your loincloth; I will put cream on your arm."

Needing no second urging, Golden Eagle nodded then did so.

Touching his forehead, as he too undressed; Dream Dancer sighed thankfully... he answered Golden Eagle's earlier question. "My headache's gone, thanks to your advice about rubbing your ointment into my temples. Your arm hurting is because of the weather."

Glad to hear that good news, Golden Eagle inclined his head appreciating the praise as he sat down so Dream Dancer could unravel the binding. Devon stared down at his arm in wonder; it was difficult to believe that a couple days ago it had been swollen to twice its size.

Moving Golden Eagles arm around critically, Dream Dancer felt around where the breaks had been then grinned in satisfaction. "Your arm looks good... the swelling is gone now."

Relieved, Golden Eagle watched Dream Dancer rub the ointment into his arm; as had happened before his young friend started chanting and Devon felt the hot tingly feeling travel up his arm... into his shoulder. The Englishman closed his eyes blissfully as the heat warmed the rest of him.

Finished, Dream Dancer sat back pleased; he was only a bit light-headed. He could feel that Golden Eagle's arm would need only one more healing touch. Edward looked at Devon's ecstatic expression and laughed knowingly. "You can leave the bandage off tonight, but you should bind it during the day. At least for a few days then I think you can go without the bandage after that."

Golden Eagle opened his eyes reluctantly and nodded in agreement. Devon smiled gratefully at Dream Dancer then changed the subject. "Okay, let's get back to your lessons on England. The queen's full name is Alexandrina Victoria; she goes by the name Victoria though. She is the only child of Edward the Duke of Kent, and Victoria Maria Louisa of Saxe-Coburg. They were only going to call her Victoria, but George the fourth, her uncle who was next in line for the throne insisted that she be named Alexandrina. That way she would have her godfather's name as well; Tsar Alexander the second of Russia is his full name. She was born on the twenty-fourth of May, eighteen-nineteen. Her father, the king, died when she was eight months old. An ambitious Irish officer befriended Victoria's mother; his name is Sir John Conroy. He would be the power behind the throne once Victoria became Queen until she turned eighteen anyway. Lucky for England, her uncle King George the fourth didn't die until twenty-seven days after Victoria's eighteenth birthday. She became Queen in eighteen-thirty-seven; once queen, she banished Conroy from the Royal Court. Lord Melbourne was prime minister, so he took over Conroy's office then became the power behind the throne until eighteen-forty when she married her distant cousin, Prince Albert of Saxe-Coburg. Several attempts have been made on the queen's life so far, including two in eighteen-forty-two that I know of."

Dream Dancer listened raptly as Golden Eagle continued, unsure if he wanted to go to England now. It didn't seem as if it would be a pleasant place to be. Edward shrugged; the Great Spirit must have a reason for him to go there. Until told otherwise, the young earl would go.

****

Melissa made it to shore and rushed to Jed in fear. "What happened? The girls were in front of me then gone!"

Jed shook his head unknowingly. "It looked like Rose panicked and went under the water! Pamela must have gone after her."

Daniel grabbed Jed's arm urgently; pleading in despair. "Well, let's go find them!"

Shaking his head, Jed put his arm around Daniel consolingly. "I'm sorry, they could be anywhere at this point; we will camp here. It's too dark and pouring right now, we will look for them first thing in the morning."

Daniel wrenched away furiously. "I will find them by myself then, without your help!"

In anger, Daniel stalked away but stopped short when his twin sister grabbed his arm to stop him.

Patricia felt her twin's pain as her own, but knew it would be impossible to find them in this storm... urging her brother to reconsider. "Dad is right Daniel; besides, in the morning Silver Tip can track them. Unfortunately, she can't in this rain. It will be much faster that way, running around blindly in this storm right now would be a useless exercise. It is so dark we might ride right past them and never know the difference. We could be miles away before we even realized it then we would have to backtrack, which could kill them both. They are both in good physical condition, if they huddle together once on shore, they should be fine until morning. Pamela is Cheyenne even though you forget that sometimes, and can survive in this or worse!"

Grimacing, Daniel sighed in frustration when his mother walked over and took his hand; she too nodded her agreement with the others. "We will find them tomorrow, I promise!"

Sighing plaintively, Daniel scowled reluctantly... his sister was right to scold him. He did forget Pam was Indian and could look after herself. The Baptist Pastor inclined his head grudgingly.

Everyone turned back then went to the camp Patricia and Daniel had set up earlier. Nobody felt like eating so they all crawled into their bedrolls then tried to sleep.

Clutching his bible desperately, Daniel prayed feverishly begging God and Jesus to look after his wife. If Pamela died, he didn't know what he would do. He looked up imploringly. "Please Almighty, not her; I don't think I could handle that!"

Daniel fell into a restless sleep; his dreams were full of sardonic laughter. "Is your faith strong enough Preacher?"

Loud menacing taunting, made Daniel toss and turn all night. In the morning, the Baptist Pastor would be unable to remember his dream; only a vague sense of uneasiness, would follow him around for days.

CHAPTER SIXTEEN

Raven woke then smiled up at her horse, when he nudged her awake impatiently. She looked out the only window and sighed; thankfully, the storm was finished, since she could see the sun peeking over the windowsill. She pushed her horse's nose away with an amused chuckle. "Okay, I'm awake; give me a minute to get up!"

Brave Heart snorted as if to say it's about time.

Laughing at him, Raven got up reluctantly then went over and opened the door for Bruno. She saddled Brave Heart then tied the packhorse on a long rope to her stallion's saddle blanket, so he could eat; she took them over to the door then held it open for them. "There you go, out with the both of you. I will be a few minutes yet"

Brave Heart nickered, as if in thanks; he went out to eat, while he waited for his mistress patiently.

Knowing others would use this cabin, Raven cleaned up the mess; besides, she might need it on the way back... depending on what shape Janet was in. She ate a hurried breakfast before departing.

****

When Daniel got up, it was barely daylight. He rummaged around noisily, so everyone would get up. There were dark circles under the Baptist Pastor's eyes from lack of sleep. All of a sudden, he shivered in anxiety; wondering why he felt so agitated and edgy... was his wife dead!

Patricia was the first one to the fire then sat down. Pat regarded Daniel before frowning worried. "It is still raining; I don't know if Silver Tip can track very well in this. We will try it anyway and hope for the best."

Daniel scowled grimly; he made porridge but didn't comment. He was going dog or no dog... he didn't care. The Baptist Pastor looked up before wiping the rain out of his eyes. The older twin could see clearing off to the west, but it was still some distance away yet. He turned back to his cooking resolutely, not saying a word to anyone. He was beginning to feel real fear for the first time in his life.

Jessica then Melissa came next, followed a minute later by Jed.

Patricia looked at Melissa briefly, with a grimace of concern as she made coffee. She was really worried about her silent twin, feeling his panic... it was making her apprehensive.

Melissa smiled in comfort then reached over before squeezing Pat's hand calmly, to reassure her. "It will be fine dear, don't worry."

Inside though, Melissa was anything but calm; her outward appearance was only for show... everybody knew it. Mell was blaming herself. She had known it wasn't a good idea to cross, but she had pushed her nervousness aside then urged the crossing anyway. If anything happened to Pamela, she would forever be blaming herself.

Breakfast got eaten in total brooding silence.

*****

Rose got rudely awakened by a kick in the backside; she groaned in denial. Turning over, she looked up into the unsmiling eyes of a hideously painted warrior. Screaming in terror, she tried to roll away in desperation.

The Indian grabbed Rose by the hair cruelly, and hauled her back. He pulled the girls face up close to his then grinned in pleasure, at her fear.

Grimacing in panic, Rose cried out in pain as her injured rib protested at the sudden jerk; she looked up at the Indian in confusion when he spoke harshly to her. The girl shook her head uncomprehendingly. "I don't understand you!"

The Indian grunted in irritation and motioned to the fire before bringing his hand up then making a gesture for eating; he pointed at the fire pit once more in demand.

Nodding in understanding, Rose carefully got up holding her side as she limped over to the fire obediently. When she got closer, she could see a pile of furs on the other side. The bundle thrashed around then moaned pitifully. The young girl rushed over quickly in fear; she fell beside the sleeping fur then lifted the edge away from Pamela's face... she examined her critically. The Cheyenne maiden whispered distraught, as tears of terror streamed down her face. "I'm so sorry Pam, I tried to get us to safety but I think I made it worse!"

Rough hands grabbed Rose from behind and pulled her away.

Tearfully, Rose looked up in despair at the Indian standing above her; he waved angrily for her to move away from Pamela.

The Indian brave pushed a reluctant Rose to the dying fire.

Having no choice, Rose knelt down obediently in front of it.

The brave handed the young woman the remains of a rabbit.

Rose, ate hungrily not even pausing for a breath, she was starving. She saw three warriors come out of the trees leading horses; the girl sighed in relief when she saw one of them with a travois trailing behind him, at least they were not leaving the injured Pam behind.

Two Indians walked over and hoisted Pamela onto the travois.

The man standing above Rose beckoned her to come then he pointed at his horse in demand.

Nodding, Rose got up painfully then limped to the horses. She gasped in agony as the Indian lifted her roughly before leaping up behind her. The girl looked around at the grotesquely painted warriors; she figured that these must be the Blackfoot Melissa had talked about last night.

Looking back at the river in sorrow, Rose wished that she were still in it. The Indians nudged their horses into a trot, she prayed that Mell would find them. The girl had no hope though, as they got spirited further away.

****

Raven looked around and found a campsite for lunch. She had lost a half a day because of the rain, but the chief showing up had saved her three or four days at least... she was still ahead of schedule. The woman could see the mountains ahead now; she hoped to reach the Eagle's village sometime tomorrow evening.

Making a quick meal, Raven fed her horses before changing her bandage on her leg; another couple of days, and she could remove the stitches. She mounted again then rode on.

****

Golden Eagle and Dream Dancer entered Raven's tepee then both sighed in relief at being done that lesson for today. Edward put water on for tea then threw in a handful of leaves, while Devon fed the cub and changed into dry clothes; it had stopped raining finally. They sat down to have a quick cup to warm up their insides before the Englishman had to go for his lessons with Golden Dove. Suddenly, a loud scratching sound on the door flap was heard.

Unenthusiastically, Golden Eagle sighed plaintively then put his tea down. He went over to the flap, letting in Black Hawk and Giant Bear.

Dream Dancer handed each a cup of tea and sat back to sip his.

Giant Bear spoke first as he waved towards the opposite side of the village. "Golden Eagle, the medicine man wants to look at your arm again to see if the cream he gave you is helping it any."

Golden Eagle inclined his head; he looked towards Dream Dancer briefly then smiled in reassurance, at his frightened expression.

Black Hawk waited for his father to finish and spoke up next. "After you are finished your lessons, we are going to start training your stallion."

Forgetting everything else in his eagerness, Golden Eagle sat forward before motioning in anticipation. "Are you sure he's ready?"

Not worried, Black Hawk inclined his head decisively. "Yes, you have made good progress with him; soon, Raven will return so we must get him ready to ride before then."

Nodding eagerly, Golden Eagle drained his coffee.

Black Hawk rose then left.

Giant Bear beckoned for Golden Eagle to come.

Calmly, Golden Eagle spared another quick look of comfort towards Dream Dancer; he followed Giant Bear to the medicine mans. They entered, as before they sat around the fire.

The old man unwound Golden Eagle's arm then probed at it in shock; he looked at Devon in puzzlement. The healer turned, and spoke rapidly to Giant Bear in excitement.

Surprised by the healer's awe, Giant Bear looked at the medicine man in doubt before translating for him with a frown of uncertainty... he turned to Golden Eagle inquisitively. "Your arm has healed fast; way faster then is possible. Why isn't it still swollen, what caused it to heal so quickly?"

Protecting Dream Dancer, Golden Eagle kept his face impassive then shrugged carelessly. He stared at the medicine man with an expressionless face as he lied coolly. "I put the ointment that you gave me on three times a day, as you said I should; the tingling increased every time I used it, and the swelling started disappearing noticeably every day... I also heal fast."

The medicine man shared a dubious look with Giant Bear; the old man finally nodded reluctantly. Unsure, if he should believe him or not then put the wrap back on the arm... he frowned troubled. "You don't need the sling, but leave the bandage on two days and you can remove it as well."

Nodding in delight, Golden Eagle grinned at the idea of having more freedom without the sling.

Chewing the inside of his lip thoughtfully, Giant Bear scowled at Golden Eagle suspiciously. The chief didn't believe Devon's explanation that he healed fast; or that the ointment was the reason he improved quicker. What other reason could there be, though!

Golden Eagle left the two confused men, to try figuring out what was going on. Devon went for his lessons whistling in delight, at having outsmarted Giant Bear. It felt good, too darn good! He frowned thoughtfully; Dream Dancer wouldn't approve he was sure, but the Englishman shrugged with a grin... it didn't make him feel that guilty.

****

Daniel sat tensely in his saddle as they gathered around Patricia and her dog. The pastor wasn't leaving it up to them; he was murmuring a prayer to God under his breath asking for his assistance.

Taking a shirt from Pam's pack, Patricia held it out for her dog to sniff.

Silver Tip sniffed the shirt and looked up at her mistress.

Patricia squatted then grabbed her dog by her ruff; she brought Silver Tip's nose close to her face; trying to convey her urgency. "Find Pamela!"

The large dog yelped then turned up the river and raced off.

Mounting, Pat trotted after the dog staying close to her.

Melissa rode up beside Patricia in question; it was still drizzling a bit, but bright blue skies were getting closer. "Are you sure your dog can track in the rain?"

Sighing, Patricia shrugged unknowingly not sure, but it was worth a try. "I don't know, but the girls had to have left the river somewhere; if I know Pam it won't be too far away. Once we find where they exited the river, Silver Tip will have no trouble finding them."

Nodding satisfied, Melissa fell back; they trotted upstream, but stayed close to the riverbank looking for any sign of the girls. They spread out to explore a wider area. It took several hours before Silver Tip found the blood-soaked log, where the girls had exited the water.

Jed and Melissa jumped off their horses then walked around the area carefully, reading the signs.

In unease, Melissa came back a few minutes later with a look of fear on her face. She tried hard to hide it, but was unsuccessful. "It looks as if the girls were holding onto that log over there; one of them was hurt bad enough to bleed. We found many Indian tracks around here. It looks to me as if they had been here for several days... probably fishing. I would imagine that they thought it was a lucky day when the girls washed up to shore. Once they dragged the girls out of the river, they went southwest. Silver Tip has the scent now, so we will follow her then see where she leads us."

Patricia and the others nodded soberly then prayed hard as they followed Silver Tip deeper into the woods. Two hours later, they rode into a clearing where the Indians had camped for the night.

Melissa and Jed again dismounted searching.

Walking back, Jed waved so that everyone would dismount. "It looks as if there were four warriors. One of the girls slept by the fire, the other one over there. The one by the fire was hurt bad enough, that they had to use a travois to carry her. I want everyone to grab a bite to eat; it might be the last time we have a chance for a hot meal until we find them."

Everyone nodded in agreement and gathered around.

Jed got a fire going while Melissa started lunch. They all waited for hot coffee; still chilled to the bone from the rain earlier, but thankful it had stopped.

All except Daniel, he rummaged in his saddlebags until he found his holster and guns; he had brought them in case they were needed, but not necessarily by him.

Daniel stared at them undecided; that sense of foreboding returned stronger than ever. Shaking off his trepidation, the pastor strapped his gun belt in place before taking each gun out and checked them. He twirled them then dropped them into the holster. Like his mother, he could draw two guns at the same time and was a crack shot.

Quickly, Daniel grabbed both and drew them to get a feel. It had been a long time. Twirling them again, he dropped them back in one more time. The Baptist Pastor took out his rifle then checked it over as well; suddenly, the preacher turned hearing an ominous knowing laugh. The man cocked his gun reflectively looking around uneasily, but there was no one there... he let the hammer down confused.

Fretfully, Melissa and Jed exchanged looks; but Patricia was the one who walked over to her brother. Patricia put a hand on her twin brothers to stop him then frowned concerned. "You don't have to do that Daniel; we will find the girl's and get them back safely. You won't need your guns!"

Still hearing that ominous laugh, Daniel jumped in surprise not having heard Patricia coming; he flushed guiltily and sighed. He looked at his sister seriously. "I know, but if I have to use them to get my wife back... I will. The Lord knows I try to live my life by his word, sometimes it's not enough. I'm praying to God right now that I won't have to use them."

Patricia sighed sorrowfully; she knew there was nothing she could say now that would change Daniel's mind. Pat squeezed his hand in reassurance then went to sit beside her mother dejectedly, praying that her brother didn't have to do something he would regret later.

Seeing her mother's questioning look, Patricia shook her head. "Leave Daniel alone; it must be his decision to make!"

Nodding unhappily, Melissa ate quickly.

Everyone remounted and followed as Silver Tip led the way.

****

Golden Eagle walked back to Raven's after his lessons then ducked inside. Devon smiled at Dream Dancer as he walked over to the fire, and sat down then accepted a cup of coffee gratefully; he was getting use to the strong taste, but still preferred tea.

Dream Dancer frowned in agitation; he waved in demand wanting to know what Golden Eagle said. "Well, what did the medicine man say?"

Grinning reassuringly, Golden Eagle couldn't help chuckling as he remembered the two men's doubtful faces when he left. "He was surprised at how fast I heal; he said I could take off the bandage in two days. I told him that it was the cream he gave me that healed me. I don't think he believed me though."

Black Hawk stuck his head inside the flap. "Come, it's time!"

Draining his cup eagerly in anticipation, Golden Eagle got up with Dream Dancer then followed behind his young friend.

Stopping at Devil's pen, Black Hawk turned to Golden Eagle. "I put my mare, plus another stud in the other pen for a distraction; see how your stallion is prancing around then calling out a challenge, you must get his attention focused on you... just as we did with my mare."

Smiling, Black Hawk handed Golden Eagle the whip.

Eagerly, Golden Eagle nodded in anticipation; he opened the gate to start the first day of training. Devon whistled in demand as soon as he entered the paddock. Devil turned for a moment then moved away... calling out another challenge to the other stud.

Golden Eagle cracked the whip suddenly; Devil jumped in surprise then took off around the pen... with a squeal of anger. The determined Devon ignored his stallion's rage. He took a step, in front of the stud to turn him. The Englishman pointed the whip in the opposite direction so his horse would see it, but had to crack the whip twice before Devil would turn.

Two more times Golden Eagle turned Devil before lowering the whip then let the stallion rest.

The mare nickered; the stud turned abruptly to answer her.

With a flick of his wrist, Golden Eagle cracked the whip demandingly then started running Devil again relentlessly.

Dream Dancer and Black Hawk smiled at each other in approval, as Golden Eagle refused to relent. It took an hour for the stallion to stand for Devon. Both men were impressed at what a quick learner he was.

****

Jed called a halt as soon as Silver Tip started growling.

Patricia called her dog over then shushed Silver Tip hurriedly.

Everyone dismounted and gathered around.

Remembering back years ago, Jed frowned troubled then waved to the south. "There's a Blackfoot camp ahead; when I came this way with Giant Bear, we went around on the other side... I imagine that's where the girls are being held. Melissa and I will go scout out the village. I want you to set up camp, but absolutely no fire. After we look, we will plan a course of action."

Everyone nodded except Daniel; he stared at his father insistently with a stubborn look. "I'm coming too!"

Not sure if that would be a good idea, Jed looked at Melissa and saw her nod in agreement. The deputy marshal turned back to his son then pointed at him in warning deadly serious. "Okay, but no heroics; we are just looking right now. I want your promise that you will not do anything without our permission, or I will leave you here!"

Daniel frowned angrily, but inclined his head furiously not wanting to be left behind. "Fine, you have it!"

Patricia took their horses reins with a grimace of trepidation; Pat could feel her brother's resentment... it worried her.

Melissa took off her white buffalo robe; it was too easy to see then handed it to Patricia with a reassuring look. "He will be fine I won't let him do anything foolish, I promise."

The three slipped into the woods soundlessly, and cautiously walked forward... looking for sentries. Jed stopped periodically to listen then continued when he didn't hear anything. He held up his hand suddenly, and motioned them all down without saying a word.

They squatted immediately; there were no trees from here to a hill just ahead. Jed carefully slipped out then checked, but nobody was anywhere nearby. Waving the other two to come out. He kept low to the ground shuffling forward before crawling cautiously up the small rise. It would give them a good view of the whole encampment. The three lay flat and looked around vigilantly.

Not seeing any sentries here either, Jed leaned over then whispered in Melissa's ear first. Next, he turned to Daniel and pointed then leaned closer in explanation. "There's the travois; that must be where the medicine man or shaman is at, so we know where one girl is... I don't see the other one."

Calmly, Melissa leaned close to Jed and pointed to the left before gesturing to their right. "They have two sentries out that I can see."

Frowning, Jed whispered cautiously. "They don't need more; see the dogs walking around the camp they are trained to give warning of intruders. Come, I have seen enough."

They warily inched backwards, with their guard up. Rushing back into the trees, they headed back to the others... none of them said a word. when they got back, the others crowded around to hear what they found.

Rubbing his chin thoughtfully; Jed grimaced, thinking back again to his earlier days. "We know where one girl is, but we aren't sure how badly she is hurt or which one it is. We do have a couple of things to our advantage. First, the Blackfoot are highly superstitious, plus their sacred animal is a white horse... which we happen to have two of. Second, is that I have had dealings with the Blackfoot before. I saved a chief son once, but not with this tribe. I hope that they have heard about that incident. We will camp here tonight then first thing in the morning Melissa, Daniel, and I will go into their village."

Jed turned to Melissa inquisitively then waved towards the horses in question. "Which horse do you want to trade for the girls?"

Grimacing, Melissa sighed irritably at possibly losing two horses... both sons of Lightning on this trip. "I will give them the colt, if I have to lose one. I can't ride him the rest of the way since he is too young for such a gruelling ride. I can give Raven my horse when we get to Giant Bear's."

Thoughtfully, Jed inclined his head in agreement then motioned cautiously. "Okay, but you will have to ride one of the other horses into camp or you might lose both horses."

Melissa nodded grudgingly.

Unenthusiastically, Jed frowned as he gestured at their packs. "We can't have a fire so find jerky and whatever else that can be eaten cold.

Try to get whatever sleep you can; it's going to be a tough day tomorrow."

Solemnly, Jed turned to Melissa speculatively once they were alone. The deputy marshal knew these people extremely well from his earlier years in Montana. At that time, they had given him the name of Grey Wolf. He was also aware that his wife would be the key to their success or failure. "Mell, I want you to wear your white buffalo hide tomorrow; I need you to be as dramatic as possible. With their spirit animal... plus the Cheyenne's around you, combined with your white hair. I'm hoping we won't even need to trade your colt. It's too bad you couldn't ride him in, so you can rear him up at the appropriate time. Unfortunately, the colt's too unpredictable for that right now. I think we better put both our badges away. I'm not sure, but I think the army was searching for these Indians not too long ago. They might take exception to our badges."

Knowingly, Melissa eyed Jed keenly. She knew her husband was going to use her to scare the Blackfoot into voluntarily releasing the girls. Mell chuckled eagerly, she loved a challenge and leaned forward for a passionate kiss... it might be their last, so she made it count. White Buffalo pulled away breathlessly then took Grey Wolf's hand and led him to bed in determination, wanting to feel her husband inside her tonight; one never knows what tomorrow would bring.

****

Raven looked around then found a good defensible campsite... she dismounted and made camp. After eating, she crawled into her blankets. The woman thought of Golden Eagle; she couldn't seem to get him out of her head. She fell asleep, even in her dreams there was no respite from the Englishman as her dream lover came to her once again.

****

Golden Eagle sighed as he entered Raven's tepee for the night. He stirred up the coals before adding wood; he waited for Dream Dancer to come in with the cub. Devon thought of Raven as he waited then couldn't help wondering where she was, and if she was okay. He had dreamt about her last night. Actually, the Englishman had them every night. She was so beautiful, and their one night of lovemaking had been so intense... magical to him; thankfully, Edward came back in interrupting his thoughts.

Dream Dancer put the cub down.

The cub waddled over to Golden Eagle immediately; Cuddles curled up beside Devon then promptly fell asleep.

Snickering, Dream Dancer laughed. "I think he likes you."

Smiling, Golden Eagle nodded; he patted the cub's ebony soft curly fur lovingly. "I like him too."

Enthusiastically, Dream Dancer sat down before grinning inquisitively at Devon. "So, how does it feel to train your horse?"

Grinning in pleasure, Golden Eagle motioned in excitement. "It feels great; he is a fast learner too. It only took a little over an hour to get Devil to follow me around without a rope. But then my stallion was following me yesterday looking for grain, so I guess it doesn't really count."

Chuckling, Dream Dancer got up to put Golden Eagle's ointment on his arm. "Everything counts with a horse, looking for grain is different then following you around because he wants to. Here, let me put stuff on your arm and let's go to sleep. It is going to be a big day tomorrow."

Golden Eagle inclined his head in agreement then undressed, as had happened before the tingling heat started from his fingertips before going all the way up to his shoulder.

Dream Dancer sat back with a smile of satisfaction; he hardly felt any wooziness this time. Edward frowned thoughtfully, each time he healed his friend the light-headedness had gotten less as if he were not putting out as much power, maybe that meant Golden Eagle was fully healed. "I can feel that you don't require any more healing from me, your arm will be okay now. I don't know how strong it will be at this point, so go slow."

Golden Eagle wiggled his fingers and twisted his wrist before stretching out his arm. Devon opened then closed his hand into a fist and shook his arm, nothing... no pain at all. "I think you are right; I don't feel any pain when I move it, neither does it feel as if it was ever broken."

Golden Eagle impulsively reached over then hugged Dream Dancer ecstatically. "Thank you for helping me."

Dream Dancer pushed him away, pleased that he had been able to heal him. After all, his people had done it to him in the first place. "You are welcome, I'm glad I could help. Now go to bed!"

Golden Eagle smiled at Dream Dancer flush of pleasure then nodded without comment. Devon crawled under his fur with no bandages; he fell asleep immediately. As the Englishman slept, he dreamt of Raven.

CHAPTER SEVENTEEN

Rose was rudely awakened by a kick in the back; she screamed in pain then curled up protectively.

The woman standing above Rose snickered in pleasure. She reached down and grabbed the girl by the hair before hauling her to her feet.

Staggering after the Blackfoot woman, Rose held onto her tortured ribs; she was bent in half trying to keep her hair from being ripped out of her head. The young girl bit her lip to keep from crying out, not wanting to give the woman the pleasure of knowing she was hurting her. Black Rose was dragged out the tepee then pulled to a group of women.

The women parted; Rose was thrown to the ground between them. The woman that hauled her over pointed to a scraper then to the hides. The young girl nodded dejectedly; she picked up the crude wooden tool and got to work.

****

Golden Eagle woke and looked across the fire; Dream Dancer was just getting up. Devon smiled at his friend. "Morning."

Dream Dancer grinned back. "Good morning, my friend."

They both got dressed then Golden Eagle stoked up the fire and put wood in, to make tea.

Turning, Dream Dancer prepared to leave. "I'll get breakfast."

Distractedly, Golden Eagle nodded as he got a fish for the cub that was waking up then gave it to him. Devon sat and looked down at his arm in pleasure. It seemed strange not to have it wrapped or tied to his side. The Englishman flexed his fingers experimentally then twisted his wrist around in delight. He grinned relieved when he felt no pain or strain.

Walking in twenty minutes later, Dream Dancer handed Golden Eagle his porridge; they sat in tranquil silence eating.

****

Melissa woke first and hurriedly pulled out hardtack, as well as a couple cans of beans for their breakfast. They would have to eat everything cold; with no coffee to wash it down.

Jed walked over wearing his buckskins.

Daniel then Patricia arrived, with Jessica following.

They all grumbled about the lack of coffee.

Shrugging, Melissa just grinned placatingly; she handed out the cold food. They complained more, but everyone ate it.

Grinning in admiration at his wife, Jed looked Mell over with a chuckle. She had changed into the buckskins that Pamela had made for her, a couple of years ago. The front of the shirt was intricately designed with a buffalo done in hundreds of tiny white beads. A grizzly, standing on its hind legs done in black beading on the back of the shirt... gave it a dramatic look. Pam had told them that she made the buckskins to represent the relationship between Melissa and Giant Bear.

Wanting the Blackfoot to know what her totem was, Melissa had left her white medicine bag hanging in clear sight; her white buffalo hide was folded neatly beside her, waiting to be put on. She had braided her hair in two braids Indian style... they fell below her waist. The fact that her hair was pure white now added to the startling effect she created.

In approval, Jed smirked knowingly; Grey Wolf couldn't wait to see the effects Melissa had on the superstitious Blackfoot.

Looking up, Melissa saw the approving smile on Jed's face; she laughed at him in pleasure before getting up, and twirled around flamboyantly. "Do you like my look?"

Nodding, Jed chuckled in pleasure. "Yes, I think you will give the Blackfoot nightmares. Can you speak their language?"

Frowning thoughtfully, Melissa sat back down; it had been a long time since she had used it. "Yes, not as well as I used to though, but good enough to be understood I think."

Reassured, Jed continued eating quietly.

Once finished breakfast, Melissa put on her white buffalo robe before mounting Pamela's horse.

Patricia handed Melissa the lead rope to the white colt then scowled up in caution worried for them. "Be careful!"

Inclining her head, Melissa smiled grimly at Patricia in warning. "We will! I want you two to clean up this camp and stay hidden, be ready to go as soon as you see us coming."

Patricia inclined her head in understanding, as she watched the three most important people in her life ride out. Make that four as she saw Silver Tip trotting beside Melissa's horse. Pat opened her mouth to call her dog back then closed it without saying anything as the dog disappeared with the trio. The youngest twin turned to Jessica as soon as the others were out of sight. Without saying anything, they cleaned up all traces of them being there then hid with all the horses.

*****

Melissa looked down then saw Silver Tip trotting beside her horse. Mell opened her mouth to send the dog back to Pat, but closed it when Silver Tip looked up at her with a penetrating stare. It was as if the dog was saying I'm coming with you, and nothing you say can stop me. White Buffalo chuckled down at her then nodded her consent, with a smile. "Okay you can come too, but no fighting with the other dogs unless they attack you first."

Silver Tip yelped agreeing and Mell laughed in delight.

Jed snickered in glee. "I think she understood everything."

Nodding decisively, Melissa smirked. "I think so too."

Daniel, who was riding behind them never said a word or even cracked a smile. The Baptist Pastor brooded, fighting with himself and his beliefs; at times he swore he heard laughter.

They crested the hill that they hid behind last night then started down. The trio heard a shout, and saw the Blackfoot gathering as they watched them curiously.

The dominant female hound slunk forward; her hair was bristled in challenge at the strange scent of another female.

Silver Tip growled at her in warning.

The female hound, after taking a good look at the black bear of a dog; tucked her tail between her legs with a whimper of fear, and raced off.

Silver Tip just ignored her after that.

Melissa gazed down for a moment then nodded in approval at Pat's dog before looking back up.

Jed nudged his horse forward and took the lead. He stopped at the edge of the crowd then waited quietly. When all the Blackfoot in the village were gathered together, and silence fell; Grey Wolf called out in command, his face expressionless. "I wish to speak to your chief!"

A man stepped forward immediately; he crossed his arms before drawing himself up imposingly, his face impassive. "I am Chief Broken Horse! Why have you come to my village?"

The chief was relatively short, but he had a daunting stance; it made him look bigger than he was. His hair was mostly grey and done in two braids, which reached down to the middle of his back. His face was extremely weathered, with deeply embedded lines converging in many directions... showing that he had a tough life. He had a scar running from the corner of his right eye down his cheekbone then it curved until it reached his nose. It was shaped like the hoof of a horse. Whatever had caused the injury had also crushed the man's nose, which gave him a funny way of speaking.

Dismounting, Jed handed Daniel his horse's reins before he walked over to the chief. "I am called Grey Wolf."

Excited murmurs made Jed stop speaking... waiting for the crowd to hush. The deputy marshal smiled inward, showing emotions here could be fatal. Good, they had heard of him! Grey Wolf waved behind him, to introduce his family. "This is my wife, White Buffalo and our son Daniel."

Clucking to the white colt, Mell hoped he would remember.

The white stallion reared up then pawed the air dramatically.

Sighing in relief, Melissa watched the awed looks of the Blackfoot and secretly she grinned... just the effect she wanted. White Buffalo clicked her tongue again in demand, which was his cue to settle. She got down off her horse then handed the reins to Daniel before walking to Jed leading the colt.

There were exciting murmurs from the Indians, when they got a good look at Melissa and the horse she was leading. Several of them stepped back in fear, murmuring uneasily about a devil.

Silver Tip followed Melissa then sat when she stopped; she gazed around vigilantly. The fur on the dog's neck bristled in warning, but other than that... she showed no signs of hostility.

The whispers of unease started again, as the Indians stared in amazement at the massive black dog that looked like a miniature grizzly; she stayed close, protecting the white woman without any urging.

Daniel nodded at the introductions, but didn't get down; his job was to hold both his parent's horses, in case they had to make a quick getaway.

The chief grunted, impressed; he looked at Melissa and the white colt expressionlessly, trying not to show it. "I have heard of you Grey Wolf, but not for many moons. The Blackfoot in the south still talks about the time you killed ten warriors in their village, without them even knowing you were there then saved the chief's son... after killing so many of his warriors."

Jed nodded solemnly, remembering as well. "They had stolen my son! I was close to the chief's tepee when I heard a child crying in fear. A wolf came into camp and was trying to drag him away. So, I killed the wolf to save the child. I don't kill children, or blame them for their father's mistakes. I didn't know at the time; he was the son of the chief."

Chief Broken Horse inclined his head eloquently, but that is all the emotion he dared show; he waved in demand uneasily. "You were then named after the grey wolves, just as silent and deadly when stalking your prey. We have not stolen anything from you, Grey Wolf! So why have you come here?"

Cautiously, Jed shook his head guardedly. "No, you haven't stolen from me, so I came openly in peace! But your warriors did find an Indian woman, as well as a half-breed that got separated from us in the storm; they were swept away by the raging river. One is my son's wife; the other one, I was escorting to her tribe."

The chief nodded thoughtfully. "I know of the two you speak of. One I don't think will live; the other one is my son's slave."

Jed frowned, disturbed at the notion that one of them was hurt that badly. Grey Wolf kept his face unreadable; he pointed enticingly at the white colt. "We will trade our sacred white horse for the two women."

Melissa urged the colt forward then clucked, so he would rear again in a spectacular show. White Buffalo made sure that the horse's position, made it look as if the stallion was trying to strike out at her angrily.

Looking the colt over, Chief Broken Horse hid his admiration... plus a twinge of fear; he reached up then stroked the scar on his face. The horse reminded him of the white stallion that had almost killed him as a child. Unfortunately, it was not up to him, she was his son's slave. He finally shrugged impassively. "I will give you the one in the shaman's tepee, but you have to talk to my son about the other one."

The chief signalled out two warriors. "Go put the woman back on the travois and bring her here."

The two men trotted off immediately. The chief turned back to them then waved casually, trying to prove his generosity to the feared Grey Wolf. "I will give you this woman as a gift, since she will probably die anyway!"

Relieved, Jed gestured curiously. "Which one is your son?"

A man pushed forward proudly then drew himself up before folding his arms across his chest in refusal. "I am, I don't wish to give up my slave."

Frowning, Jed studied him closely; the man was taller than his father, but not as tall as Melissa. The warrior was fairly husky. He had imposing arm muscles for an Indian. The Blackfoot brave looked to be in his early thirties. His hair was past his shoulders and was worn loose in pride. With his dark brooding looks, he was quite striking.

Enticingly, Jed waved at the colt. "Not even for the horse?"

The Indian looked the colt over then eyed Melissa up and down insolently. "I will trade my slave for the horse, and your wife!"

In anger, Jed scowled furiously; he knew that the man would try something. He was too arrogant for his own good. Grey Wolf bent when Mell touched his arm then listened as she whispered in his ear.

Jed looked at his wife incredulously. "Are you sure?"

Melissa nodded decisively in reply; Mell knew the looks of the brave all too well... he would not trade. The man was too full of pride and arrogance to be fair when dealing with others, figuring he should get his way every time.

Expressionlessly, Jed looked back at the arrogant Indian... he flashed a brief smile in temptation. "I have a better idea, a knife fight between White Buffalo and you; if my wife wins, we take your slave and the colt then leave. If you win, you can keep your slave and the white colt."

The villagers all started talking at once in excitement; it was unheard of for a woman to fight a brave.

The chief held up his hands in demand for quiet. "Are you sure Grey Wolf, my son hasn't lost for many moons; plus, he is thirty years younger. I wouldn't want to see White Buffalo hurt or killed then have Grey Wolf stalk my warriors for revenge."

Instantly, Jed nodded expressionlessly before giving reassurances solemnly to the chief. "I'm sure! I will make a vow to you right now; no matter what happens, I will not take revenge. Besides, White Buffalo has never lost... I think your son needs a lesson."

Leaning forward, Jed lowered his voice so only the chief could hear him.

Chief Broken Horse looked at his proud son. He had tried talking to him several times over the years. The brave was too arrogant and full of pride; they were not good traits in a future chief... his son wouldn't listen. Maybe if the white woman beat him, he would become a better man then a good leader in the future. The older man nodded mind made up, and motioned in agreement. "If that's your wish, continue!"

Turning to his wife, Jed inclined his head in permission.

Smiling grimly, Melissa took the colt to her son and handed him the reins.

Daniel looked down at Melissa in dismay. "Are you sure Mom? I should be the one to challenge him to a fight, since it is my wife who is his slave."

Tenderly, Melissa put her hand over Daniel's leg in comfort then squeezed tenderly. "Yes, your job is to help people... mine is to hurt them!"

Daniel sighed resignedly, but in relief too. The Baptist Pastor looked up as the warriors came up to them bearing the travois between them. When the preacher saw his wife lying there looking as white as death; he cried out then jumped off his horse before rushing to her.

Melissa grimaced; at least she wouldn't have to worry about him doing anything stupid now. White Buffalo tied her colt to Daniel's saddle horn; the other horses were trained to not wander off before walking back to Jed and standing beside him.

Jed bent slightly before whispering in question. "Are you sure about this? He's way younger than you are and has impressive arm muscles for an Indian."

Sighing, Melissa nodded decisively. "It's the only way now!"

Knowing his wife was right, Jed scowled helplessly; they couldn't back out without severe penalty. "Okay, but remember... I love you."

Taking a moment, Melissa smiled up at Jed then cupped her husband's cheek lovingly with her hand. "I love you too."

Tenderly, Melissa gave Grey Wolf a quick kiss of reassurance and turned away before walking towards the man she was to fight. When she got closer, she assessed his strengths as well as his weaknesses quickly. The man was muscular in the arms, but weak on brains. He had a more extended reach then she did, but White Buffalo was taller and had longer legs. The brave should be easy to beat, as long as she stayed out of his reach. She didn't want to kill him then get the chief's back up, but she would do so if left with no other choice. The marshal stopped not too far away from him and heard Jed come up behind her, so she took off her buffalo robe then handed it to him. Mell tucked her medicine bag away under her shirt.

The Indians caught sight of the white buffalo on the front then the black grizzly on the back of the buckskin shirt. Excited whispers, of a she-devil started up again.

With an expressionless face, Melissa blocked them out of her consciousness needing all her attention on the warrior.

In satisfaction, Jed hid his grin of delight having heard them whispering fearfully of a devil. Grey Wolf took a piece of cord then tied Melissa's hair together in one long rope. he tucked her hair under the whip that she was wearing as a belt... to keep it in place. Mell had tied it loosely; with one tug, the whips snake-like coils would loosen and be ready for use.

Melissa took out her knife; she stood patiently, waiting for the chief's son to stop bragging to the other men about how fast he was going to put the white woman on the ground.

Jed feeling his wife's readiness backed away, praying silently.

All the other Indians formed a circle around the two combatants then waited expectantly. The Indian women clustered together whispering in anticipation, none of them had ever seen a woman and a man fight. Secretly, deep down they all hoped White Buffalo would win... none of them dared voice it aloud; every woman there had felt the wicked backhand of the chief's son at one time or another.

Chief Broken Horse came over then stood beside Jed regrettably. "Grey Wolf, as much as I would like to see my son lose some of his arrogance, I can still call this off and give you back your women."

Looking away from Mell, Jed shrugged at the chief's concern. "Thank you, it's too late now. Besides, you have never seen my wife fight. Watch and see why the Cheyenne named her, White Buffalo!"

Broken Horse nodded recalling his enemy's awe of the sacred white buffalo. For a white woman to be named, she must have powerful medicine. Now he was beginning to be afraid for his son; the chief turned to watch in dread.

Standing relaxed, Melissa waited for her foe to come to her.

The brave strutted towards the white woman arrogantly; he had no reason to believe that he would lose.

Instantly, Melissa turned her knife around so that the handle stayed tucked against her palm... with the blade resting on her arm. When the brave advanced, Mell bent her knees then lifted up on the front of her feet so her heels were off the ground. That way White Buffalo could pivot immediately.

The warrior stopped close; he smiled insolently at the white woman before lunging forward knife first.

Knowingly, Melissa had been waiting for this reaction... she sidestepped neatly; as the knife and the braves hand went past her; Mell brought her hand down hard against his wrist.

In disbelief, the man drew back in shock with a painful hiss.

Expressionless, Melissa waited patiently still relaxed as she watched the warrior's eyes narrow. She rocked back on her heels as the brave came at her again, but this time cautiously. White Buffalo paid close attention to his eyes, as they circled each other. It was not long before he gave himself away, as his eyes flickered down to her left shoulder. The marshal calmly waited as he lunged for her; at the last moment, she pivoted around his arm so that her back got pressed against it. Still turning... she thumped him in the back with her elbow. Mell continued rotating the rest of the way around, so she was now facing his back as he staggered forward incredulously.

The warrior growled in rage then swung around to find her.

Melissa figured it was time to end it. The brave was so enraged now, he charged her like a bull. Mell knew that if he got those muscular arms around her... he would crush her to death. White Buffalo patiently waited until the warrior was close enough; suddenly, she jumped up then kicked out with her long legs catching the brave in the face.

The kick toppled the warrior backwards; he landed in a dazed shock... he shook his head to clear it.

Instantly, Melissa seeing her opportunity to finish it jumped on the warrior, so her legs straddled his chest. She made sure that his arms were pinned before she held the bowie knife to his throat... dramatically. Mell sat like that for a moment breathing heavily. Swiftly, she grasped the handle of her knife in both hands and lifted it over his face then brought it down with all her might. At the last second, White Buffalo moved a bit. The blade went whistling past his head as she buried it to the hilt in the dirt. The hunting knife was so close to his head that it nicked an ear, making it bleed.

Calmly, Melissa stayed for a dramatic moment; letting the silence of surprise and shock intensify. Swiftly, Mell sat up before lifting both arms above her head then gave a blood-curdling scream of victory... White Buffalo yelled in the warrior's language fervently. "Now you are dead!"

Placatingly, Melissa lifted herself of him then stepped back before smiling down at the brave in approval. Mell held her hand out to help him up, hoping he would take it and there would be no hard feelings; White Buffalo also added praise hoping he would accept it too... trying to take the sting out of his lose. "You are good fighter, a fine warrior!"

In rage, the brave looked at the hand offered to him in disdain then rolled away without accepting her help.

Melissa shrugged in regret; she bent to pull her knife from the dirt. "WHITE BUFFALO, behind you!"

Confused, Melissa looked up in surprise as she heard her name screamed in warning by Jed. As Mell tilted her head towards the chief's son, the brave's knife stabbed down towards her face. White Buffalo turned her head away instantly... not fast enough; she felt the sting of the blade as it cut a deep furrow across her cheek.

The warrior's knife dropped to the ground in shock, as Silver Tip jumped for the Indian then toppled him backwards. The enormous dog grabbed him by the throat, squeezing slowly; not in any hurry to kill him... wanting him to suffer. Enraged at what he had done to the leader of her pack.

Quickly, Melissa ran over then grabbed the dog by the neck pleadingly; trying to lift her off the unfortunate warrior. "No Silver Tip, don't kill him!"

Silver Tip let go instantly, but not before leaving two holes in the warrior's throat; with a bit of blood on her muzzle, she backed away from the chocking Indian at the fervent note in her leader's voice.

Jed rushed over uneasily then studied Mell's face; Grey Wolf dabbed at the blood with a rawhide that was handed to him.

The shaman pushed through the crowd immediately, and looked at Melissa's cheek. "It will need to be treated; come with me White Buffalo... I will help you!"

With no hesitation, Melissa inclined her head in agreement; she gave Jed a reassuring look before trotting off after the shaman with Silver Tip following closely beside her.

Grimly, Jed looked at the man on the ground angrily but didn't say anything; letting his father handle it.

Chief Broken Horse stood over his first-born son silently; finally, he shook his head in disappointment. "You have shamed this tribe and me for the last time. I had hoped that time would curb your boastful arrogance then help you gain some wisdom before it was time for you to become the next chief. Now I no longer have that hope, you are no longer my son. You will live on the edge of our village as an outcast... never will you be welcomed in my tepee again."

Broken Horse turned to Jed shamefaced as he motioned in apology. "I'm sorry Grey Wolf, White Buffalo fought with honour. My wife will bring the girl; you and your family are welcomed here anytime."

Jed nodded solemnly then clasp arms with the chief. "I accept your apology; I would be honoured to revisit you on my return."

Instantly, Jed looked around when he heard his name; he smiled as Rose limped painfully towards him holding her side. Once close enough, the girl flung her arms around him eagerly.

Stroking Rose's hair in reassurance, Jed murmured encouragingly. "Daniel is seeing to his wife, go join him."

Rose nodded in agreement then slipped away silently.

Turning, Jed saw Melissa coming; he sighed in relief. Except for a paste on her cheek, White Buffalo looked unhurt.

Melissa walked up beside Jed and grinned teasingly. "I'm fine, a scratch shouldn't even leave a scar I'm told."

Appeased, Jed sighed in relief; he put his arm around his wife.

Concerned, Melissa turned her gaze to the chief. "The dog didn't hurt your son too much I hope?"

Chief Broken Horse shook his head negatively as he frowned decisively in anger. "He is no longer my son; he has dishonoured this tribe. You fought bravely and with honour, if it had been up to me, I would not have spared his life. You have your women back as promised... you are free to go in peace."

Nodding, Melissa inclined her head in farewell before clasping the chief's arm. "Thank you, Chief Broken Horse."

Followed closely by Mell, Jed went over to Daniel and Rose.

Quickly, Melissa bent down to her son then whispered encouragement. "We can go now; the shaman gave me some medicine for Pamela. I will tell you what to do later."

Standing up, Melissa turned to Jed calmly wanting to get out of there as soon as possible before something else drastic happened. "Bring your horse over; we will tie the travois on."

Nodding, Jed left then got his horse. After the travois was tied, Grey Wolf lifted Rose onto Melissa's horse so she was behind her.

Instantly, Rose cried out in agony as Jed lifted her.

Frowning, Melissa twisted to Rose in alarm. "What's wrong?"

Carefully, Rose took a hesitant breath; large ones were beyond her ability, as she held onto her side. "I think one of my ribs is broke!"

Grimacing, Melissa frowned in worry. "I'll look at it later."

Once everyone was mounted, Melissa and Jed waved to the chief then urged their horse's on... without looking back.

****

Dream Dancer smiled at his uncle. "Devil is learning fast!"

Black Hawk inclined his head in approval as he watched Golden Eagle turn the stud. He called out more instructions to the Englishman. "Let him go around again and stop him. When he comes to a halt, go up to him then touch him all over and coo to him to see if he will follow you around again."

Watching intently, Black Hawk nodding to himself impressed; the stallion was a fast learner and would be ready to ride soon. He watched Golden Eagle touch the stud then Devil followed him obediently. Tommy beckoned so Devon would come over. "That is enough for today, tomorrow we will do the same... we will bring our noisemakers too. If he responds fast, you can try putting a blanket then bridle on him."

Ecstatically, Golden Eagle smiled in anticipation and went back into the centre of the pen to gather his things.

Quickly, Dream Dancer opened the gate for him in excitement. "Wow, at this rate you will be on him in three or four days."

Chuckling, Golden Eagle grinned eagerly at Dream Dancer's enthusiasm. "I sure hope so."

Walking over, Black Hawk took his gear back. "You two are invited to my tepee for supper."

Concerned, Dream Dancer frowned in worry. "Are you sure Gentle Doe is up to the company?"

Nodding, Black Hawk waved in unconcern. "Mom is helping her prepare the supper, so she doesn't have to do much."

Eagerly, Dream Dancer grinned in agreement. "In that case we accept! I'll help Golden Eagle with the cub, we will be there shortly."

Satisfied, Black Hawk inclined his head then left.

In anticipation, Dream Dancer followed by Golden Eagle rushed to Raven's to get ready for supper.

****

Jed reached the area where they had left the two girls.

Melissa whistled to let them know it was safe to come out.

Jessica and Patricia hurried forward with the extra horses.

Swiftly, Melissa got off Pam's horse then helped Rose down. Mell turned to Patricia. "Help Rose on her horse, but be careful she's injured. I want to travel further before we make camp; we are going to need a fire."

Patricia nodded without speaking; questions could wait until later. Pat helped Rose up before mounting her horse.

****

Dream Dancer with Golden Eagle close behind got back to the tepee. Edward took the cub out while Devon made tea. They sat across from each other once he returned. Ed smiled sadly. "I have to leave tomorrow morning."

Sighing forlornly, Golden Eagle nodded dejectedly. "I know."

Frowning, Dream Dancer looked at Golden Eagle intently worried. "Will you be, okay? Do you want me to try healing your arm one last time? I noticed that you were favouring it earlier."

Golden Eagle smiled and shook his head negatively. "I'm fine; the arm is sore from using it today. The muscles have to work harder to catch up with my other arm; I will put more cream on. Besides, if I don't show some weakness to your nam-shimi', he would start asking me questions that I will not answer."

Nodding relieved, Dream Dancer grinned glad his friend wasn't in any pain then smirked. "Okay, I might see you in the morning; if not take care until I get back, no fighting with my nam'-shimi!"

Winking without comment, Golden Eagle chuckled at his young friends teasing then stoked the fire before putting on some cream; he went to his blankets to sleep, with the cub cuddled against him.

****

Jed found a good campsite then called a halt.

Patricia and Jessica hurriedly made camp, while Daniel helped Jed remove the travois then put Pamela beside the fire.

Melissa helped Rose down and took her behind the horse for privacy. "Lift up your shirt up before it gets too dark to see; I need to make sure your ribs are not broken."

Sympathetically, Melissa winced at the dark purple colouring then gently probed the wound. "Take as deep of a breath as you can, and exhale out as far as you can."

Melissa kept her hand on the wound as Rose did as instruct. Mell frowned then motioned for Rose to lower her shirt. "One could be broken or maybe cracked but I don't feel anything sticking out. Your lungs didn't get pierced, I don't hear any rattling when you fill them with air. So, I will bind them tomorrow before we start riding, to give them support from the motion. We don't want the jarring to move any jagged piece that might be near your lung."

Rose nodded glumly. Melissa waved towards the fire. "Go sit; I don't want you to move around much. I need to tend to Pam."

Dejectedly, Rose sighed in annoyance; again, she was useless. Holding her side, she limped painfully to the fire obediently.

Going over to Pamela's horse, Melissa removed the package the medicine man had given to her then went over to Pam. Mell knelt on the ground beside her daughter-in-law before opening it. White Buffalo smiled hopefully up at Jed. "Can you help the girls, while Daniel and I see to Pam? Rose might have a broken rib, so I don't want her doing anything until I wrap it."

Jed frowned anxiously; one hurt was serious enough; two would make travelling difficult. Grey Wolf turned obediently.

Calmly, Melissa smiled in reassurance at Daniel. "Can you remove Pam's fur, as well as her shirt please?"

Daniel nodded then did as instructed. While he was doing that, Melissa selected three packages of dried leaves and got up to see Rose. Heating water for them to make tea would not be too strenuous for her. Mell walked around the fire then handed two packets to her first, and finally the other one as she explained what she wanted her to do. "Rose, can you steep a pinch of these two packets in some water for tea... make enough for both you and Pam. I also need you to make a paste with this one; I need some warm wash water also."

Smiling in relief, Rose inclined her head; glad to be of some use at least. She got up to get water from the stream.

Going back to Pamela, Melissa knelt down so she could remove the bandage wrapped around her ribs; while Daniel lifted her carefully. Mell explained as she worked what the spiritual leader had told her. "The shaman said Pam has a broken rib, which is a bit of a cause for worry because it is protruding inward... close to her lung. He said she must be kept as still as possible, so that the rib doesn't puncture another hole in her soft tissue. Rose told me that in the river, your wife got snagged on a tree. A branch punctured a small hole in-between her ribs, which caused one to break. The shaman thinks the branch either scraped her lung or put a tiny hole in it, thankfully not all the way through. That's why she is wheezing a bit. If it had gone all the way in, she would be coughing up blood depending on how large it is. Since she hasn't yet, he doesn't believe it went all the way. If that rib moves though, it could pierce the same hole then make it bigger. Rose is brewing tea, when it is cooled off you must put some in your mouth and dribble it into Pam's. She should swallow reflexively. If not, you will have to stroke her throat to make her swallow. She must have the tea three times a day and water. Twice a day, she should have broth given in the same manner. Rose is making a poultice for Pam's wound. It needs to be washed before we re-wrap her ribs."

Daniel listened quietly to Melissa talking, while he gently held his wife up so his mother could remove the binding. When she finished speaking, the Baptist Pastor sighed in real concern. "But, will she make it Mom?"

Melissa looked at Daniel in sympathy before shaking her head sadly. "I don't know; all you can do is pray for the best, but prepare yourself for the worst. If she gets pneumonia... she probably won't survive it."

Fearfully, Daniel nodded bleakly without saying anything.

Rose came over with warm water and a cloth, so Melissa cleaned Pamela's wound; while Daniel gave her medicine then some water to drink. Once finished, they squatted around the fire to eat themselves. Everyone enjoyed the hot stew Jessica prepared immensely, but were all too tired to talk. They fell into their blankets in exhaustion, as soon as they possibly could.

****

Raven sighed in relief as she looked for a hidden defensible camp. The Eagle tribe was over that ridge; down into the trees for a bit before reaching a clearing. She wanted to scout them out first, but it was too dark to see.

Raven found what she was looking for and made camp. There was a stream behind her, so she went for a bath after finishing with her animals. Returning, the woman rummaged in her pack for supper. A fire this close to the Eagle camp wasn't possible, so she ate jerky with hardtack before crawling into her blankets; promptly, she fell asleep.

CHAPTER EIGHTEEN

Golden Eagle woke then looked around for Dream Dancer, but he was already gone. Devon got up and stretched then dressed before building up the fire to make tea. It was almost ready when Edward ducked into the tepee.

Relieved, Golden Eagle smiled enthusiastically; Devon was glad his friend was still around. "I thought you had left already."

Grinning reassuringly, Dream Dancer handed Golden Eagle his breakfast. "I couldn't leave without saying goodbye... now, could I?"

Pleased, Golden Eagle beamed in satisfaction. "Good!"

Dribbling honey in his porridge, Golden Eagle ate in silence. He was not all that hungry, so Devon only ate half and put the bowl down. He looked over at his young friend inquisitively. "Are you going to come for your lessons this morning before you go?"

Nodding decisively, Dream Dancer grinned. "Of course..."

Unexpectedly, Dream Dancer not quite finished what he was going to say... laughed in amusement instead; he pointed down at Golden Eagle's side, so he would look down.

Inquisitively, Golden Eagle looked and saw the cub eating the rest of his porridge. Devon looked back at Dream Dancer in disbelief, with a chuckle of amusement. "I didn't think he would like porridge."

Knowingly, Dream Dancer smirked in humour then pointed at the jar. "It's probably the honey, bears love it."

Delighted, Golden Eagle grinned in pleasure. "Good, I will give him porridge in the morning instead; one less thing to do at night before bed."

Liking that idea, Dream Dancer nodded in approval. "That's a good idea; now that the cub is done, we better go for our lessons."

Getting up with the cub, Golden Eagle followed his friend.

****

Daniel and Mell woke to the smell of bacon frying.

Melissa reached over to check Pamela; she smiled at her son in reassurance. "Pam's asleep, go eat then we will check her wound and give her medicine."

Nodding, Daniel sighed in relief; he yawned then got up.

Neither of them had gotten much sleep, since they both slept beside Pamela; Melissa on one side, and Daniel on the other... trying to keep her warm. Pam had woken several times groaning then thrashing in her sleep; they had taken turns throughout the night, administering to his wife's needs.

Daniel walked to the fire and smiled teasingly at his father. "You cooked?"

Jed grinned up at his son, ignoring his humour. "Well, we need to go slower; so, I figured I should cook since I was the first one up."

Hungry, Daniel hunkered down before accepting the plate of bacon, and flapjacks his father handed him in gratitude.

Jessica followed by Patricia came next.

Patricia smirked at her father incredulously, but didn't comment. "Everything is ready to go."

Pleased, Jed nodded then gave each of the girls a plate.

Rose and Mell came next.

Melissa looked at Jed disbelievingly before exclaiming in shock; she held onto her chest theatrically, as if having a heart attack. "You, made breakfast!"

The others all laughed at Mell's amazed stare.

Injured, Jed gave his wife a dirty look. "I do cook sometimes!"

Laughing in humour, Melissa smiled in delight at her husband's injured tone; she helped herself to coffee without anymore teasing.

Patiently, Jed waited until everyone finished eating then sighed grimly. "We are going to have to slow down, so I want to leave a bit earlier from now on, and we will ride further if we can. If we have no more problems, we can make the next town in four days. We are still in Indian Territory so keep vigilant; most of the tribes are not as friendly as the last one was. We will have to try keeping Pam as quiet as possible."

Waving, Daniel grimaced in dismay then motioned for everyone to go ahead. "Maybe, you should leave us behind; we can always catch up later."

Stunned, Melissa shook her head emphatically; surprised, that her son would even suggest such a thing. "There's no way that I would leave you or my daughter-in-law out here all by yourselves especially when she is hurt."

Frowning, Jed nodded decisively; reluctant to leave anyone behind, especially his children. "I agree with your mother. Besides, we were going to have to slow down anyway. Our horses need to stay in reasonably good shape just in case we have to outrun unfriendly

Indian tribes. We can tie the travois between my horse and Mell's, this way Pam is not bouncing around on the ground. If we have to make a run for it, we won't have to worry that she will get hurt anymore then she is now or fall off without our noticing. Tomorrow after we get out of the trees, it is relatively barren from there so it shouldn't be a problem for the horses to carry her that way. It will also be scorching hot with not much water or shade, be prepared for that too! I want everyone to fill up every container we have with water before we go."

Daniel inclined his head in relief; he hadn't wanted them to leave him, but the Baptist Pastor felt that he had to make the offer. "Okay, I will give Pam her medicine right away."

Melissa got up to help her son.

The others finished breaking camp and Pamela's travois got tied behind Jed's horse. Daniel put his gun belt on again before mounting. He frowned disconcerted when he heard that strange laughing, but this time it was different; it had more of a satisfaction sound to it now. The Baptist Pastor stared grimly at the others as they gazed at him in disapproval, but he refused to say anything... not ready to talk yet.

Confused, Melissa looked at Jed in bafflement but neither said anything. Respecting their son's decision to go back to carrying his guns; they turned their horses then they were on their way once more.

****

Raven woke just before dawn, so swiftly broke camp; she picketed the packhorse, so he could eat but couldn't wander off. The woman turned to Bruno in demand. "You stay here boy and guard the packhorse, while I go scout the Eagle tribe."

Bruno whined plaintively at being left behind, but obediently settled down then watched the horse.

Raven mounted Brave Heart before trotting away.

****

Golden Eagle with Dream Dancer walking beside him went back to Raven's... both immersed in their own thoughts. When they got closer to the tepee, Edward sighed dejectedly then waved ahead of them. "It looks like my grandfather is here already."

Forlornly, Golden Eagle looked up sadly then saw the wagon and horse waiting outside Raven's. Devon frowned in irritation. "I will miss you while you are gone; try to hurry back!"

Dream Dancer smiled at the sad note in Devon's tone. "I will."

Without another word, Dream Dancer ducked into the tepee before putting the cub down then started to gather all his things.

Golden Eagle walked over to talk to the chief.

Giant Bear smiled in greeting before motioning at his arm in doubt, still not believing the Englishman's reason for the fast recovery. "How is your arm doing today?"

Dramatically, Golden Eagle sighed in irritation as he put on a good show of being in pain; Devon held onto his wrist and slowly flexed his fingers. "It's fairly sore today from all the exercising I have been doing. I will put more of that amazing cream the medicine man gave me on it tonight."

In irritation, Giant Bear nodded with a frown of displeasure; still, he couldn't figure out how Devon had done it. "That should help it. How's it going with your stallion, any more progress yet?"

Enthusiastically, Golden Eagle grinned at the thought of his horse then dropped his arms. "Yes, Black Hawk figures we can put the saddle blanket and bridle on him tomorrow."

Pleased, Giant Bear nodded in satisfaction. "That's good."

Dream Dancer walked to his grandfather. "I'll see you soon."

Calmly, Giant Bear inclined his head. "Okay, you be careful."

Sadly, Dream Dancer turned to Golden Eagle next; the two clasped arms then embraced. "I will see you in a few days."

Teasingly, Golden Eagle chuckled in warning. "Yes, and don't get into any mischief while you are gone."

Shaking his head, Dream Dancer laughed as he recalled the jokes he played on his English friend. "Now that isn't something I can promise you!"

Smirking knowingly, Golden Eagle helped Dream Dancer put his things in the wagon before waving goodbye. Turning away, he walked into the tepee and gathered the cub. It wouldn't hurt to keep the little guy with him while at his lessons. Carrying his bundle, he walked sadly towards Giant Bear's tepee. The Englishman would miss Raven's brother and their talks. He reached the chief's tepee then ducked in for his lessons with Golden Dove.

****

Raven entered the edge of the trees and dismounted; she tied Brave Heart's reins together then put them over his head. If she had to call him, her horse wouldn't trip on the reins nor would they get caught in the underbrush, she hoped. The woman whispered in command. "Stand, Brave Heart!"

Turning away, Raven melted into the trees without a sound. She walked forward cautiously, so quiet not even the animals realized she was there. Every once in a while, she would stop to listen then go in another direction; the woman slipped past the sentries like a ghost... unseen and unheard.

Sighing relieved, Raven reached the edge of the trees without incident then cautiously peered out. The woman looked left, nothing interesting presented itself; she turned right then spotted what she was looking for. It was a hill overlooking the village. She could hide behind it while she watched them.

Warily, Raven backed away from the opening and angled to her right. Suddenly, the woman stopped then squatted down behind some bushes as she heard rustling off to her left.

Holding her breath, Raven waited. She watched two warriors walk out of the trees where she had been standing only a second ago. The woman remained unmoving as they vanished from view, when it was safe she moved ahead; judging that she was near the hill, she went back to the edge of the trees to look.

The hillside was ahead of Raven, she sighed in relief; so far so good. Now the woman had to cross an open space then she would be safely hidden behind the hill.

Cautiously, Raven looked around and didn't see anyone; she crouched in readiness. The woman was about to run out, when she heard a raven squawk loudly in rebuke. Instantly, she dropped down then waited.

Patiently, Raven stayed still for five minutes before she heard warriors trot past her. After they went by; the woman got up and reached for her medicine bag... thanking her spirit animal for the warning.

Again, Raven cautiously peeked out; not seeing or hearing anything more she crouched down then left her hiding place. The woman raced across the open area in a half crouch.

Once Raven reached the hill, she ran behind it before climbing up. She saw rocks ahead, so hurried behind them and stopped to catch her breath. Carefully she looked around; all she saw was more rocks to her left. They were higher up, past that was the top of the hill. It would be the perfect place to hide so she could watch the village.

Exploring the rocks carefully, Raven noticed a niche hidden in the back. If she had to hide, she could crawl in there... nobody would see her. Satisfied that she knew the area well enough, the woman warily made her way to the top of the hill. When she judged she was close enough; she dropped onto her stomach as she peered over the edge cautiously.

The view from up here was better then Raven at first thought... she could see the village and people. She identified the shaman's tepee, and the chiefs right away. Next, she looked for Howling Coyotes but didn't see it. The woman counted tepees before shaking her head in puzzlement when there were only thirty of them; there should fifty tepees.

Looking at the chief's again, Raven stiffened when she saw a white woman come out; she was blonde and didn't seem very tall from this distance. Sighing disappointed that she couldn't see her face... she wondered if that was Janet. She didn't want to get her hopes up though; the Eagle tribe had a couple of white women in their camp from before. That was the reason they were refused when they asked to stay on her ranch. Two of the white women hadn't wanted to get adopted, they wished to go home. The Indian braves who owned them refused to give them up, so the tribe had left.

Not discouraged, Raven backed off then went to her hiding place; she took out jerky and ate thinking. She decided to get her horses then she would come around on the other side of this hill, so nobody would see her. That way she could watch the village for the rest of the day. Hopefully, she could get the chief alone to talk to him. The woman sat back making plans.

****

Jed looked around contemplatively; it wasn't long before he found what he was looking for... a defendable campsite.

Melissa with Daniel's help unhooked the travois then moved Pamela over to the fire, while the others made lunch.

Melissa took off Pamela's shirt before washing the wound. She looked at Daniel with concern. "Pam has a fever; hopefully, it won't last. Go over and ask Rose if the medicine is ready."

Getting up, Daniel left; he came back a few minutes later and handed his mother the paste for Pamela's injury.

Carefully, Melissa put paste on before wrapping a bandage around Pam; she redressed her then covered her with a fur. Mell took her white buffalo hide and put it around Pam for warmth, hoping to sweat the fever out.

Sitting back, Melissa looked at her son and motioned to the cup he was holding. "Give her the medicine then come eat."

Daniel nodded vaguely after Melissa. Alone he bowed his head in prayer; urgently pleading to God and his son Jesus to help his wife. When the Baptist Pastor finished, he put tea in his mouth then dribbled it into Pam's.

Once the tea was gone, Daniel sat back and looked up imploringly. The Baptist Pastor felt a shiver flow down his spine as he prayed; he smiled when he felt another presence beside him, comforting him in his time of need. The pastor stayed that way for several long minutes, not wanting the feeling to leave him yet before reluctantly opening his eyes... once it disappeared. He felt lighter in spirit now, as the faith that he had thought lost was renewed.

Daniel recalled a passage in his bible that he had forgotten; it was in Romans five, verse three, four and five; *'We can rejoice, too, when we run into problems and trials, for we know that they help us develop endurance. And endurance develops strength of character, and character strengthens our confident hope of salvation. And this hope will not lead to disappointment, for we know how dearly God loves us because he has given us the Holy Spirit to fill our hearts with his love.'*

*****

Going to the fire, Melissa accepted a bowl of stew and ate.

Jed eyed his wife then frowned in concern. "How's Pamela?"

Uneasily, Mell sighed. "I'm not sure; Pam has a fever which worries me. If it turns into pneumonia, we could be in trouble!"

Everyone finished eating sadly and repacked to go.

Taking a bowl to Daniel, since he never came to eat; Melissa eyed her son's serene face curiously but didn't ask, only smiled in approval knowing he had found his inner peace again.

Daniel ate all of it except the broth then patiently fed his wife using his mouth. Thankfully, he got Pam to take all the nourishing soup in the bowl. When the Baptist Pastor finished, they reattached the travois to Jed's horse.

As Daniel walked over to his horse, he was undoing his gun belt. The Baptist Pastor put it away for good... his faith now stronger than it ever was; if his wife were to die today, it wouldn't ever get shaken again.

Looking around expectantly, Daniel smiled serenely when he heard a groan of regret; again, there was nobody around. Never again would the Baptist Pastor hear that mocking laughter. A few minutes later, he forgot about it as if it had never been.

Jed and Melissa exchanged relieved smiles; they had both been worried when Daniel had strapped the gun belt back on after retrieving Pamela.

Daniel's twin sister, Patricia rode towards him once he mounted; she winked at her brother in relief, having felt the pastor's faith when it became stronger. "It's about time... you had all of us worried for a while there!"

Nodding, Daniel sighed sadly before following the others. "I was worried too; my faith has never gotten tested before. I have watched my parishioners in my church, as one tragedy or another tested them. Some walked away stronger in their faith, others lost their belief in God. I have never understood how they could walk away from the Almighty. It frustrated me, being unable to help them to see that Jesus will forever stand by them. Now, at last I understand. I have always believed, but until now I felt unsatisfied. My first reaction, since I am a preacher should have been to trust in God and Jesus... but I didn't. I strapped my guns on instead, so I thought I lost my way for sure. Today, I realized that Jesus understood and was still standing by me regardless of my mistake. Just because I'm a pastor, doesn't mean I'm can't make errors in life... only God is perfect."

Patricia nodded as they continued riding in silence.

****

Golden Eagle ducked out of Giant Bear's tepee then walked to Raven's. Golden Dove had mentioned that he should start walking the cub around the village, so he could get used to people and dogs. She also advised him to take Cuddles to where the children were. That way they could play with the cub; to keep him occupied while he was at his lessons or working with his horse. Devon had expressed his concern about the dogs hurting the cub or one of the children getting injured. Mary reassured him that both were used to bear cubs in the village... this wasn't the first time they had one.

Golden Eagle ducked inside Raven's tepee then put the cub down before grabbing a fish to feed him. When Cuddles finished eating, the Englishman picked him up again then took him out back to his favourite tree.

After the cub finished, Golden Eagle called him to come. The five dogs eyed the cub curiously, but only one came to sniff him. Cuddles growled indignantly... the dog retreated satisfied. They walked past the shaman's tepee, out into the open where Golden Eagle could hear children laughing.

When the children caught sight of the vi'hoi coming with the cub, they quieted then gathered in a group.

Bending, Golden Eagle picked up the cub then walked to the children. When Devon was close, he stopped and smiled. "I am Golden Eagle."

The boy who brought water to his horse nodded. "I'm Little Beaver."

Smiling, Golden Eagle inclined his head at the introduction. "Dream Dancer has gone home; I am hoping you will play with the cub during the day so that he won't be by himself."

Little Beaver eyed Golden Eagle still holding the cub then huddled with the other children. He turned back to the Englishman, and nodded his head in agreement. "I will come for the cub just after the sun rises; I will bring him back to you before the sun goes down completely."

Nodding, Golden Eagle smiled relieved. "Good; his name's Cuddles."

Needing reassurance, Golden Eagle put the cub down to see what the children would do. Devon watched in satisfaction as each child went separately to the grizzly cub; introducing themselves. Little Beaver picked up the cub after introductions finished... they disappeared.

Turning, Golden Eagle went looking for Black Hawk.

****

Raven looked around cautiously, not seeing or hearing anything; she ran across the clearing back into the trees. When she was hidden again, she grinned pleased with herself. The woman moved ahead slowly. Sometimes she would stop then listen closely before veering around a sentry.

About halfway back to her horse, Raven stopped dead in her tracks and waited tensely... feeling the hair on the back of her neck rising in warning. She stood there perfectly still not moving a muscle for a good ten minutes. Only the woman's eyes shifted, as she looked for whatever was causing her reaction. She saw movement ahead; if she had kept going on her current course, she would have walked right into a sentry.

Raven backed away then turned to her right, and went around. She found where she had left her horse; swiftly, she mounted and rode off.

****

Jed stopped then beckoned Melissa forward. "The trees end ahead, after that it's open country. Even though it's early, I think we should camp here; it will give Pam a break. Hopefully the fever will be gone before morning."

Melissa sighed relieved then motioned decisively. "Yes, I think we need a good night's sleep before riding through unfriendly Blackfoot territory."

Quickly, camp was set up for the night.

****

Giant Bear walked to Black Hawk then stood there watching Golden Eagle work his horse. The chief turned to his son in concern. "How is Gentle Doe?"

Black Hawk smiled in relief. "She's doing fine so far."

Relieved, Giant Bear waved at the paddocks inquisitively. "Good! How's Golden Eagle doing; he seems calmer lately."

Nodding, Black Hawk grinned in agreement. "Yes, he is; Dream Dancer was good for him, training with me... plus teaching his horse helped too."

Pleased, Giant Bear gestured towards the Englishman. "He will start training with Running Wolf in two days also."

In approval, Black Hawk inclined his head. "That's good; now that Dream Dancer is gone it will keep him busy."

Turning, Black Hawk looked at Giant Bear inquisitively; he hadn't gone over since the night the chief told his wife what he did. "How's Mother?"

Giant Bear scowled in irritation then shrugged dejectedly. "I don't know, she still won't talk to me unless she has to. Which reminds me, you and your wife are suppose to come with Golden Eagle to eat?"

Black Hawk nodded distractedly then walked to the fence before calling out instructions. "Golden Eagle you can stop him any time, take him to the middle of the pen after and try to put the saddle blanket on him."

Golden Eagle waved in acknowledgement.

Backing up, Black Hawk moved closer to his father before frowning pryingly. "Have you changed your mind on forcing the two to marry?"

Grimly, Giant Bear shook his head decisively. "No, I have not!"

Angrily, Black Hawk sighed in exasperation then motioned in warning. "I wish you would! Forcing those two to marry is going to backfire in your face. It will cause a catastrophe, even you wouldn't want to contemplate."

Staring at his son in surprise, Giant Bear grimaced nervously and frowned in alarm. "What do you know that I don't?"

Shaking his head, Black Hawk shrugged in forewarning. "I'm not sure what will happen exactly; I just have a bad feeling."

Bleakly, Giant Bear stood quietly beside Black Hawk worried more than ever now. For some reason, their spiritual leader was apprehensive as well. The Great Spirit had been silent lately, way too quiet with no vision's forthcoming. Now Black Hawk was getting these feelings... it was time to talk to the shaman. He turned to his son. "I will see you later."

Shaking his head in disapproval, Black Hawk nodded and watched Giant Bear leave. Tommy knew his father wouldn't listen. The half-breed turned to Golden Eagle and watched him walk towards the stallion.

*****

Pleased, Black Hawk stepped up to the fence and called out. "Golden Eagle, get him to follow you around the pen then take off the blanket and rub him down. That will be it for today; we are going to moms for supper."

Waving, Golden Eagle inclined his head towards Black Hawk. Devon smiled when his stallion followed him, barely paying attention to what was on his back. Devon took off the saddle blanket and rubbed his horse down.

Black Hawk let him out then took his things. "Go get cleaned up and meet me at my fathers for supper."

Golden Eagle nodded then went to get ready.

****

Raven arrived at camp and un-hobbled her packhorse before tying him to Brave Heart then remounted. She looked at her dog. "Come, be quiet."

Riding around the village, Raven gave it a wide berth; she wondered what was going on. The Eagle tribe had twice the sentries then they usually do this close to their village. There were no whites here, being so remote.

The only time an Indian settlement had that many sentries out, was when they feared attack or were in enemy territory. So, who would attack them out here? The last she heard; the army was busy running after the Blackfoot for destroying a wagon train a month ago. Which meant that they were too busy running away from the military, so didn't have time to strike here.

Unless the chief feared that Raven would bring warriors here, which meant they knew about the attack.

With no outcry, Raven reached the hill she had watched the village from; she got off and walked ahead of her horse cooing in encouragement. "Come Brave Heart, you have to climb."

Brave Heart followed his mistress up the steep terrain.

Getting to her pile of rocks, Raven moved the horses in front of them so they would be harder to see. It was reasonably level here, so the horses would have no problem staying close to her. She went to the packhorse first, and took out hay then oats that she carried in case feed was unavailable. After feeding the horses, she took out jerky then cakes to eat and gave some to her dog.

Crawling up to the top of the rise, Raven peeked over. It was quiet and hard to see. The war chief hadn't returned either. She went to her horses then made a bed; hopefully, tomorrow she would get the chief by himself so she could find out what's going on. She rolled into her blankets to sleep.

****

Golden Eagle escaped Giant Bear's tepee and went back to Raven's place. The cub was asleep with a half-eaten fish lying beside him when he entered. The Englishman smiled at the cub then curled up beside Cuddles to sleep.

CHAPTER NINETEEN

Melissa woke first then checked on her patient; she shook her head in concern, Pamela's fever was getting worse. Mell reached over Pam and shook her son.

Daniel woke instantly then looked up at his mother in fear.

Holding her hand up, Melissa smiled reassuringly and crooked her finger for Daniel to follow her. They went over to the smouldering fire; he built it up again, while Mell got water then started the coffee. She made breakfast, while the Baptist Pastor put a pot of water on the fire to heat for Pam's sponge bath. Getting a bowl, he added water for his wife's tea. White Buffalo finished making the porridge before setting it on a rock in the fire to cook. She looked over at her son inquisitively. "Can you stir the porridge, while I go wake the others?"

Nodding, Daniel watched his mother get up then leave; he smiled in delight, Melissa was still in her buckskins... she looked remarkably striking. The Baptist Pastor stirred the porridge before adding the medicines to the boiling water for tea. He reached over to check the water it wasn't ready, so he left it on while he stirred the porridge.

Walking back, Melissa took over breakfast duties.

Jed and Jessica arrived with Patricia; Rose was not far behind.

Sleepily, Jed smiled at his wife. "How's Pam this morning?"

Uneasily, Melissa sighed in sorrow as she motioned grimly. "Not good; Pamela's fever is worse, but her wound is healing."

Worried, Jed frowned apprehensively and gestured inquisitively. "Will Pam be up to a long ride?"

Shrugging, Melissa grimaced nervously. "I don't know, but we need to get Pam to a doctor as soon as we can. We will have to tie her securely so that if we need to trot or run, she won't get bounced as bad."

Rubbing his chin in contemplation, Jed nodded calmly... even though he didn't feel it. Grey Wolf sensed time running out. "We will keep to a walk as much as possible today."

Agreeing, Melissa inclined her head in relief.

Getting up, Daniel took the bath water and tea to his wife.

Making the paste, Melissa heated the broth they saved from last night's stew while she ate; after, Mell took them over to her son.

Daniel smiled sadly at his mother when she knelt beside Pam.

Melissa sighed at her son's downcast face, and reached out then squeezed Daniel's hand comfortingly. "Go eat breakfast while I sponge Pam down, the tea and broth should be cool enough when you get back."

Nodding, Daniel finished undressing his wife before leaving.

Tenderly, Melissa washed Pam with the tepid water then checked her injury. Mell put more paste on and re-wrapped her ribs. She tightened the dressing more this morning, to give Pamela's ribs better support if they had to run then dressed her again. White Buffalo just finished when Daniel came back carrying a cup of coffee for her. She grinned in pleasure as she sat back and accepted the cup gratefully. "Thank you; everything should be cool enough now."

Silently, Daniel nodded then knelt down beside his wife.

Over her cup, Melissa watched as her son put his lips gently on his wife's then released some liquid into her mouth slowly. Mell sighed relieved when Pam reflexively swallowed the tea; Daniel did the same with the broth.

Sitting back in concern, Daniel waved anxiously. "Why has she not responded yet?"

Shrugging, Melissa frowned uneasily before shaking her head perplexed. "I don't know; the shaman couldn't find any other wounds or any bumps on her head. He figures when Pam's ready, she will wake up on her own."

Gently, Daniel absently stroked his wife's hair away from her forehead; he scowled in fear as he looked over at his mother in dread. "Pamela's fever is getting worse, is there something we can do for that at least?"

Thoughtfully, Melissa finished her coffee then sighed negatively and motioned reassuring. "We are already giving her medicine for fever. I will strengthen the dose a bit when we stop tonight, that's all we can do."

Relieved, Daniel nodded towards his mother; he smiled sorrowfully up at his father when Jed came towards them carrying some rope.

Jed handed it to Melissa. "Better tie her down, it's time to go."

Putting her cup down, Melissa inclined her head. Getting up, they cautiously secured Pam tightly to the travois. She put her buffalo robe around her for warmth.

Carefully, Jed with Daniel's help lifted it between them then carried Pamela to the horses.

Melissa brought her horse over beside Jed's. She held him still, while the other two women secured a rope on each saddled horn then a cord to the back of the saddles; this way the travois rested between Mell and her husband's horse... like a hammock that Jed had seen used on sailing ships.

The men eased the travois down slowly, holding their breaths uneasily.

Jed's horse threw his head back then snorted in uncertainty, at the unfamiliar weight; his saddle leaned awkwardly to the right.

Quickly, Jed stepped in front of him; he stroked his horse in comfort. "Easy, Two Socks!"

The horse bent down for a scratch before settling down.

Uncertainly, Melissa turned to Jed worriedly. "I think we better walk in front of them, to let them get used to walking together; especially, with the travois moving between them."

Agreeing, Jed nodded at that good idea; they led the horses out into the open warily. Keeping the horses evenly spaced proved no problem, since both horses travelled together a lot.

The travois bumped Melissa's horse's side, which caused him to jump in surprise.

Instantly, Melissa murmured reassurances to him; obediently, he settled down. After walking for half an hour with no problems, Jed nodded to Mell... they mounted. They tried to keep most of their weight on the opposite side of their leaning saddles, so they weren't tilted quite as perilously.

Daniel watched fretfully, unsure if this was a good idea; if one of them spooked, it could spell disaster. Despite his trepidation, the horses continued moving together with Pam strung in the middle precariously.

To be on the safe side, Jed kept the horses at a walk for an hour. He turned to look back at his son in warning. "We are going to trot for a bit, so the horses can get used to the travois."

Daniel nodded anxiously.

Calmly, Jed looked over at Melissa. "Okay ready."

When Melissa nodded, Jed gave the command. "Now go!"

In perfect sync, Melissa and Jed kicked their horses into a trot at the same time. The travois bumped against the horse's way too much, so Mell moved hers over a bit to tighten the ropes more. The travois steadied as the horses got into a rhythm that kept them at an even distance. She sighed in relief as both horses adjusted to the travois, with no real fuss.

Happy with their progress so far, Jed turned to Melissa again. "Okay, let's canter for ten minutes then go back to a walk."

Biting her lip nervously, Melissa nodded as she waited.

Jed gave the order; simultaneously, they kicked their horses into a canter. Grey Wolf's horse tried to surge forward, past Melissa's then the travois bumped into Mell's horse.

Daniel watched in dismay as his father fought with his horse then finally got him under control. The Baptist Pastor saw the travois hit his mother's horse in fear. He held his breath anxiously; praying, he watched Melissa trying to keep control of her horse before heaving a relieved sigh as both adjusted and the travois steadied between them.

Not wanting to push their luck, Jed sighed in satisfaction as he called out to his wife. "Okay, a trot first... then walk."

Again, Melissa waited and together they pulled up as they slowed then went into a walk. Jed smiled in approval at Mell. "We will stay at a fast walk until just before we stop for lunch, and we will try it again."

Sighing resignedly, Melissa frowned in relief but nodded in agreement; glad she didn't have to do this again for a while, as they continued riding.

****

Raven woke then sat up; she looked up at the sky, but it was still too dark to see. The woman got up to feed both her horses before rummaging in her pack for breakfast.

When Raven judged that it was light enough, she climbed back up the hill then looked down. The village was beginning to come awake; she watched the women coming out first to start their chores.

In excitement, Raven saw the white woman leave the chief's tepee; she was carrying two buckets to fill with water. The woman disappeared towards the creek in the distance.

Standing up, Raven decided to slip down and intercept her. In disappointment, she dropped back down as two other women followed Janet to the river.

Sighing in disappointment, Raven settled back to continue watching the chief's tepee; finally, she saw the chief's wife with their daughter come out then leave.

Getting up, Raven looked down the hill speculatively. If she slipped down to her left, she could sneak up to the chief's from behind. The woman dropped down in irritation when the chief came out of his tepee then went to the shaman's. She frowned in irritation, and settled back to wait for another opportunity.

****

Golden Eagle woke to a cold nose stuck in his face, nudging him awake impatiently. Devon laughed in delight before pushing the cub away. "Okay, I'm up Cuddles; what's your problem this morning... you hungry already?"

Yawning, Golden Eagle rolled out of his blankets then got dressed; he walked over to the corner where the bucket of fish was, and took out a small one. He hit it with the butt of his knife before giving it to the cub, to keep him busy while he went over to get them some porridge. The Englishman left the tepee then walked towards Giant Bear's.

Halfway there, Golden Eagle unexpectedly heard horses galloping into the village. Looking up, he jumped out of the way when two white men almost knocked him down. He hurried after them curiously. Devon slowed when he got to Giant Bear's tepee then watched the two men storm in.

Black Hawk came running up to Golden Eagle. "Come on, it looks like trouble."

Nodding in relief at being included, Golden Eagle rushed after Black Hawk. Once inside, Devon immediately stepped into the shadows so he wouldn't be noticed then listened.

*****

Giant Bear jumped up when the two white men stormed into his tepee. The chief scowled in angry reproach as he waved in demand. "What is the meaning of this Jake, you are supposed to be at the ranch?"

Jake shook his head urgently. "I'm sorry Giant Bear, but the sheriff and half a dozen men are on their way here right now. We raced ahead of them to warn you as soon as we found out!"

Uneasily, Giant Bear scowled. "Raven isn't here!"

Grimly, Giant Bear looked up when Black Hawk came in. In his agitation, he didn't see Golden Eagle slip in too. "The sheriff is on his way; it will be at least another two weeks before Raven gets back... any suggestions?"

Black Hawk thought for a moment then nodded coldly. "First, we will have to hide Golden Eagle; if they see him, they are going to want to know what happened to his guides. Since the sheriff only came with six men, he is probably just here to look around and ask questions; we will let him know that Raven is looking into the matter. I will try to stall him until she returns."

Giant Bear inclined his head in relief. "Okay, I will let you handle it."

Turning, Giant Bear eyed Jake speculatively. "Are you going to stay and help convince the sheriff?"

Jake grimaced in agreement then gestured sharply in reassurance. "You will need us here as back up; I will help any way I can. I already posted men all around, to make sure nobody comes in or out of these hills without me knowing. I left Shorty in charge at the ranch until I return."

Immediately, Jake turned to the ranch hand beside him and waved towards the entrance. "Dan, go take your position but stay hidden for now."

Dan nodded then left.

Golden Eagle stepped forward wanting to help. "I can tell them it wasn't your village that attacked me. I can explain that you saved my life!"

Black Hawk looked at Golden Eagle in surprise; he had forgotten he was there. Tommy shook his head negatively. "No, they wouldn't care. If they saw you, it would give them an excuse to drive us out; Raven too, for harbouring us."

Gesturing vaguely, Golden Eagle nodded with a worried frown. "Okay, I will hide over where we train in the morning."

Surprised, Giant Bear looked at Golden Eagle in shock. "You will hide without a fight or us needing someone to watch you?"

Sullenly, Golden Eagle scowled at the chief's incredulous look; apparently, he didn't know him well. "I promised Raven I would wait for her... I always keep my word! Besides, I don't want to jeopardize my sister's only hope of rescue!"

Turning to the Englishman, Jake looked him up and down speculatively. "So, you are the man who is causing all the fuss."

Nodding with a smile, Golden Eagle looked the foreman over. Dream Dancer told him Jake looked after the ranch when Raven was gone. He stuck out his hand. "Name's Devon Rochester or Golden Eagle."

Raven's foreman inclined his head in greeting then clasped Golden Eagle's hand in a firm handshake. "I'm, Jake Shannon."

Inquisitively, Golden Eagle frowned thoughtfully wondering how much time he had. "When will the sheriff arrive?"

Jake sighed disgruntled. "About, half an hour or so I think!"

Golden Eagle nodded then turned to Golden Dove. "Is there breakfast?"

Smiling in encouragement, Golden Dove waved down at the waiting food. "Porridge is ready whenever you are."

Golden Dove had seen Devon come in, but hadn't said anything; she watched him knowingly. Mary guessed some time ago that the Englishman knew everything, by the way he had been acting lately.

The fact that Golden Eagle never showed any surprise or asked questions when he saw Jake, had confirmed it for her. What the Englishman was going to do with that information worried Golden Dove, he was so hard to read. Mary knew Devon was biding his time until his sister was returned to him, what would happen after that was anyone's guess.

Calmly, Golden Eagle walked to the fire; he dished up two bowls of porridge.

Immediately, Golden Dove lifted her eyebrows in surprise.

Grinning, Golden Eagle shrugged with a chuckle of delight as he explained. "The cub likes porridge with honey."

The chief's wife inclined her head, but didn't say anything as she watched him go.

****

Raven sighed in aggravation; this wasn't working at all. She had sat in this spot all morning and watched the village. Not even one occasion had presented itself, to get the chief or the white woman alone. She went back to her horses then rummaged in her packs for something to eat. The woman sat with her back to the rocks, thinking as she ate her lunch and fed her dog. She could take a chance then ride in, so she could confront the chief directly; time was running out she knew.

If the sentries were out watching for her, Raven could be dead before she reached the village. Then another idea came to her, she got up to tie the packhorse to her stallion's saddle. "Come, Brave Heart."

Carefully, Raven led her horses back down the hill; once at the bottom, she turned to the stud. "Stand, Brave Heart."

Immediately, Raven snapped her fingers in demand to her wolf-dog. "Come with me Bruno... stay close."

Warily, Raven and Bruno inched their way around the hill; she crouched and cautiously looked around. Not seeing anyone, she raced out of her hiding spot then into the trees for cover. The woman crouched there listening, but not hearing any outcry cautiously made her way back to the place that she saw one of the sentries posted. When they were close enough, she drew her knife then crouched in readiness. She put her finger to her lips, to show the wolf that he needed to be quiet.

Raven held her knife tucked against her arm... in case she needed it. They inched their way forward, but when she got to the location she was looking for; the lookout was gone. The woman frowned irritably. He had to be here. She spotted movement to her left, so went in that direction.

The sentry Raven was searching for, was standing beside a tree... relieving himself. She motioned the wolf to stay then crept soundlessly up behind the man. The woman stood up behind him, and put her arm around the warrior's throat; she held the knife up threateningly so he could see it. "Why are there so many sentries around the village?"

The warrior looked to the side and saw the wolf crouched, ready to jump at him if he threatened the woman that held him in any way. He held up his hands showing he was no threat; he answered her calmly, already knowing who she was. "The chief has banished our War Chief Howling Coyote. He has threatened revenge against us."

Easing her grip on the sentry in relief, Raven stepped back.

The warrior flipped his loincloth back, covering himself; he turned to face the woman. He nodded impassively, as his suspicion was confirmed before he pointed at her. "The chief has also been waiting for the Raven, 'protector' of her people!"

On her guard, Raven stiffened instantly in surprise. "Why?"

The Indian shrugged. "I don't know; the chief told us that when you come, we are to bring you to him immediately... with no harm done."

Dangerously, Raven's eyes narrowed. "Not if, but when?"

The warrior scowled knowingly. "The chief seemed certain that you would come here, since he has something... you want."

Nodding, Raven waved an invitation for the brave to go first. The woman snapped her fingers in command; Bruno obediently walked beside her, watching the Indian cautiously. When they reached the open area then exited the trees, she whistled for her horse to come.

Brave Heart galloped around the hill and ran to his mistress, leading the packhorse. He stopped beside her then followed.

The Indian brave looked at the horse in admiration. "I'm going to come see you when we get to our winter camp, to trade for one of your horses."

Raven, not caring about horses or trading right now; still answered distractedly... not wanting to discourage him. "I have many for trade."

The warrior inclined his head then continued to lead the way.

****

Jed and Melissa slowed their horses to a walk. He waved towards Mell's right. "There's a hill over there with large rocks at the bottom, for protection; we can camp there for lunch."

Melissa looked at where her husband was pointing then looked over her shoulder at the others. "You guys go ahead of us, and start setting up camp; we will be there shortly."

They galloped away, while Melissa and Jed followed slowly.

****

Golden Eagle watched from his hiding place as the sheriff, with six men rode up to the village. All the Indian's gathered behind Giant Bear, Black Hawk, as well as Jake curiously.

To be on the safe side, Golden Eagle had kept the cub with him; instead of letting him go with the children this morning. The cub wiggled in his arms trying to get down. Devon held him tighter then whispered consolingly. "Quiet now Cuddles, you can play later."

Thankfully, the grizzly cub settled down; Golden Eagle turned his attention back to the meeting.

*****

Giant Bear, Black Hawk, and Jake stood in front of the villagers then watched impassively... as the seven vi'hoi rode towards them. When they were close; Black Hawk and Jake stepped forward.

The sheriff took the lead then called a halt.

Black Hawk nodded at the brown haired, brown eyed, man cordially. Tommy didn't know him, since he stayed away from towns as much as possible; even though he grew up with his Aunt Melissa, his experiences with white men wasn't good. "What can we do for you, Sheriff?"

Searchingly, the sheriff looked at all the faces in the crowd; when he didn't see the Englishmen or the guides he was looking for, he turned to Black Hawk. "We are looking for three white men, and two white women that disappeared recently. I was hoping you would have seen them?"

Black Hawk shook his head negatively; he kept his face impassive. "Why, would they come here?"

Waving in explanation, the sheriff frowned in suspicion. "They were not coming here, but were on their way to Raven and Edward Summerset's place then vanished without a trace."

Dismissively, Black Hawk shrugged unknowingly. "I'm sorry, they didn't stop here on their travels."

Sighing in irritation, the sheriff inclined his head expecting that answer; he looked around curiously. "I was led to believe, that there were more of you here then Raven was telling us?"

Calmly, Black Hawk smiled before motioning behind him. "All the wolf tribe is here, there's no more of us."

The sheriff nodded and frowned thoughtfully. "Why are you still here, shouldn't you be gone for the summer?"

Shrugging, Black Hawk gestured dismissively. "Raven asked us to stay until she comes back. She said if you come here, we are to answer all your questions truthfully. We are also supposed to tell you that she will be back in two weeks, with news on what has happened to the people you are searching for; she said for you to come back at that time."

The sheriff looked around again at all the faces; he stiffened suddenly in question then turned back quickly to Black Hawk. "You have a white woman here? I was led to believe that you don't steal women anymore!"

Reassuringly, Black Hawk shook his head negatively. "She was never stolen, that is my mother; a white preacher married the chief and Golden Dove legally. You can contact him at Smyth's Crossing in North Dakota... if you want to check."

A man off to the sheriff's left urged his horse forward impatiently. "He is lying!"

Quickly, Black Hawk whispered to the foreman. "Who's that?"

Jake sighed softly in annoyance. "His name is Charles; he's our neighbour... unfortunately. After Raven's parents died, the man tried to get her to sell out to him but she refused. When Raven was old enough, he tried to get her to marry him. She laughed in his face in public. Since that day they have been enemies. He still keeps harassing her, hoping she will sell it."

Black Hawk nodded; he turned back to the conversation. He assessed the man as he sat there arguing. His horse was taller than the sheriffs, yet the man still only reached the lawman's nose in height. He was in his late forties... almost entirely bald. He had a sharp beak of a nose that he held at a lofty position, so he could look down at people. He reminded Tommy of a weasel; his voice was high pitched, with a whining aggravating tone.

The sheriff frowned angrily at the annoying Charles. "I told you that I would handle this; if Raven says that she will be back in two weeks with news, it is good enough for me! Since both the guides were her friends, I'm sure she will do everything in her power to find them."

Charles scowled back furiously then pulled his gun. "If you can't do your job, I will!"

In shock, Black Hawk froze when the vi'hoi pointed his gun at him.

****

Raven and her prisoner reached the village then walked to the chief's tepee. The brave scratched at the door and stood back for Raven to enter.

Frowning, Raven waved at her horse anxiously. "Can you make sure nobody gets too close to him? He goes crazy when people go near him; I wouldn't want anyone to get hurt."

The warrior nodded as the chief's wife opened the flap.

Relieved at his nod, Raven ducked inside then looked around quickly. The chief was sitting in front of the fire, with the white woman she had seen earlier sitting quietly behind him.

Chief Red Eagle waved inviting Raven to sit across from him.

Dutifully, Raven sat then waited as the chief lit his pipe.

Red Eagle blew smoke in the air to the Great Spirit, and down at the ground to Mother Earth before blowing smoke to the right then left. The chief passed the pipe to Raven, so that she could repeat the ritual.

The pipe got put down before Red Eagle looked at the warrior woman solemnly. "Raven of the wolf tribe, 'protector' of her people... you are welcomed here. I have been expecting you!"

Continuing the ritual, Raven nodded impassively. "Chief Red Eagle is also welcomed at the wolf tribe's fire anytime. You know why I have come?"

Red Eagle inclined his head in relief then pointed behind him. "You have come for the vi'hoahi?"

Raven nodded decisively. "Yes, and for the war chief!"

Chief Red Eagle frowned in anger. He gestured sharply in finality. "I banished Howling Coyote, and all his followers when I got told what they had done. In these troubled times with the whites killing many of our people, it is not good to call attention to ourselves. Already the whites outnumber us; if we don't learn to live in peace with them, the Cheyenne will be no more. We must stand together at this time, not bicker among ourselves. Had I known what Howling Coyote had planned I would have put a stop to it. Unfortunately, I did not find out until after. When I banished the war chief, I wouldn't let him take the vi'hoahi with him. Now he has turned on us. I fear he has an evil spirit inside him, causing him to hate anyone who goes against him."

Inclining her head, Raven's lip curled up in approval. "Chief Red Eagle is wise... he sees the true future. I have been to a white school; they taught us that for every white person here now, they have more where they come from. If we are to survive, we must learn to live in peace. The Badger Tribe has also seen the future, so wants to join me. If you wish, you can also stay with us. As long as you live on my land, nobody can drive you out. I have approached other chiefs, but only the two of you see the truth. The rest wish to kill whites to drive them away, this will not happen. Unfortunately, they will all die."

Frowning, Red Eagle nodded. "You speak passionately, as well as honestly. I have been approached by other chiefs on banding together to drive the whites out. I have tried to talk them out of such a foolish plan, but they refuse to listen."

Gesturing in frustration, Raven inclined her head grimly. "We too were approached; only one tribe broke away from us. They left to join the war against the whites, it saddened me when I heard they died."

Grimly, Red Eagle sighed in understanding then pointed as he gave directions. "When Howling Coyote left, I sent one of my warriors to follow him. He said that they are only one and a half days towards where the sun sets then a half-day towards where the sun rises. They took fifty tepees with them in total."

Raven scowled thinking quickly; she almost walked right into their camp. Well, at least they are back the way she had come, and it would be closer to her village then here. She smiled at the chief's wife when she handed her a bowl. "Thank you."

The chief's wife smiled back shyly at Raven, and handed her husband some lunch then the white woman a bowl before sitting herself; they ate in complete silence.

Not once did Raven talk to the white woman; except for a cursory glimpse when she first entered, did the Cheyenne warrior woman pay any attention to Golden Eagle's sister... not wanting to offend the chief. Until Janet was given to her, she was still his slave.

****

Jed turned to make sure no evidence of their presence was left. When he was satisfied, he nodded then they moved off. Grey Wolf motioned for Patricia, and Jessica, to take the lead.

Melissa and Jed were now in the middle with the travois between them, plus both packhorses were tied to their saddles now. Rose with Daniel brought up the rear; he was leading Pamela's horse while Rose led the white colt. They rode now in complete silence, carefully watching as well as listening vigilantly for any hint of danger.

****

Golden Eagle listened intently to the discussion going on with the sheriff from his hiding place, sounds echoed in these mountains. He smiled in approval at Black Hawk's answers, he hadn't told any lies. It was true that they hadn't visited the village; they found him elsewhere else. Raven would be back in two weeks with answers that was also correct. He even told the truth about the wolf people all being here. The sheriff didn't ask if other tribes were living here. He put the squirming cub down then whispered. "Okay, but stay close."

Distractedly, Golden Eagle turned away then frowned in concern when a white man started arguing with the sheriff; the Englishman couldn't catch everything they were saying from this distance. Devon jumped up immediately outraged. He took a step forward, as the man pulled his gun then levelled it at Black Hawk threateningly.

Shocked, Golden Eagle squatted; he watched the grizzly cub that he just put down, go streaking towards the horses bawling loudly. Devon held his breath, as he watched the sheriff's horse rear in fright.

*****

Black Hawk stared in amazement when the cub raced towards them... crying loudly. The horses reared and screamed in terror; throwing some of their riders then bolting with others.

Charles landed hard on the ground before rolling a few times. When he stopped, he levelled his gun at the cub.

Immediately, Black Hawk and Giant Bear ran forward to grab Cuddles... it was too late; as a gunshot rang out then the cub fell to the ground dead.

The only one still on his horse was the sheriff. After getting his horse under control, he jumped down and raced forward. He was the first one to reach Charles; the lawman kicked the gun out of his hand then reached down to haul him to his feet.

When the sheriff kicked the gun out of Charles's hand; Black Hawk and Giant Bear stopped to see what would happen.

Charles growled at the sheriff heatedly, as he sputtered angrily. "How dare you touch me?"

Squeaking indignantly, Charles's words were cut off as the sheriff's fist connected with his jaw; he landed on the ground groaning in pain. The lawman stood over Charles seething. "I have a mind to throw you in jail!"

The sheriff turned to two of his men then pointed down at Charles in disgust. "Get this riffraff back on his horse and out of my sight!"

The two men hurriedly did as they were told; the sheriff watched them gallop off in satisfaction. He had wanted to do that for a long time now... the lawman grinned in pleasure. He sobered, and turned to Black Hawk in apology. "I'm sorry!"

Sighing grimly, Black Hawk walked over to the cub then knelt down beside him sadly; Tommy turned the cub over, but the animal was dead. He looked up at Giant Bear, and shook his head bleakly. "He died saving my life, as I saved his."

Giant Bear nodded in sympathy, but didn't say anything; the chief looked at the sheriff intently. "You give that white man a warning, if he ever comes here again... he is a dead man!"

The sheriff nodded not blaming the chief. "I will warn him. Again, I'm sorry. Tell Raven, if she gets here earlier than two weeks to come see me. If she doesn't, I will be back."

Black Hawk inclined his head in agreement; silently, he watched the sheriff and the rest of his men leave.

*****

Golden Eagle sat down hard on the ground in horror, as he watched the cub race towards the horses then die; as the bullet meant for Black Hawk, killed him instead. Devon wanted to applaud the sheriff, when he punched the man in the mouth.

As soon as the sheriff left, Golden Eagle raced to the baby grizzly and knelt. "I'm sorry, I tried to keep a hold of him but he kept squirming to get down. I was afraid if I didn't, he would cry then they would find me."

Not blaming the Englishman, Black Hawk put his hand on Golden Eagle's shoulder consolingly. "It's okay; he gave his life to save me, as I saved him. I will skin and stuff him so that Raven can keep him always. The Great Spirit has plans for all his creatures, be they human or animal. Now we know why the cub was put in my path... it was not my time yet."

Sighing, Golden Eagle nodded; it was the same thing Dream Dancer believed. "You might be right, but I'm going to have two angry people on my hands when they return."

Smiling, Black Hawk shook his head negatively. "They will understand. Go get lunch then we can work on the stallion after."

Nodding, Golden Eagle followed Golden Dove to her tepee.

****

Raven finished her second lunch of the day then sat back.

Janet finished her lunch a few minutes later.

Looking at over at her, Raven waved for her to come sit with her.

Fearfully, Janet walked over and sat with her head lowered.

Tenderly, Raven put her finger under Janet's chin then raised her head up so she could see all of her. The woman hissed in anger when she saw the white woman's face, and turned furiously to the chief. "Who did this?"

Shrugging, the chief scowled. "The white woman was like that when she came here, only worse; some swelling has gone down already. I would guess Howling Coyote did it. The shaman said that her cheekbone got broken, other then that there doesn't seem to be any more wounds."

In relief, Raven turned back to Janet. Her left eye was black and blue; just under that was a cut on her cheekbone, she would have a scar. The white woman's lower lip had swelled then cracked; the blonde looked like her brother, only feminine. She sighed in sympathy then motioned knowingly before switching to English. "Is your name Janet Rochester?"

Frowning in surprise, Janet nodded eagerly. "It was, but I got married; its Lady Janet Clevedon now, how did you know?"

Nodding, Raven smiled. "I came looking for you; you have an anxious brother waiting in my village for your return."

Janet's face lit up in disbelief. "My sister, is she there too?"

Sadly, Raven shook her head. "I'm sorry, your sister's heart couldn't take the shock... it stopped beating."

Bowing her head, Janet covered her face as she grieved.

Reaching over, Raven sighed and stroked her hair in sympathy. Janet was older than Devon, but the young woman knew by looking at the Englishwoman that she was far from experienced. The white woman's inexperience might become a problem on their way back to her village.

The chief scowled in puzzlement. "Why is the woman crying?"

Gesturing in explanation, Raven smiled. "This is the way white people mourn for their dead. I told her that her younger sister died!"

Accepting that, the chief nodded. "I will have a horse saddled, and supplies gathered for your trip. Tonight, you can share our tepee."

In apology, Raven shook her head. "Thank you, but I must get back."

Chief Red Eagle frowned in regret then turned to his wife. "Get Raven whatever she needs, and a horse for the vi'hoahi."

Anxiously, Raven turned to Janet. "Wipe your tears, you will have to grieve later; if you have anything here, go get it."

Sniffing, Janet shrugged mournfully. "I have nothing, except this dress."

Grimacing at the rag, Raven turned to the chief. "Do you have a boy who is the white woman's size? She will need buckskin pants and a shirt."

Red Eagle nodded then got up. Instantly, Raven rose and pulled off her necklace then handed it to the chief. "Give this to him in trade; tell him it is from a grizzly that I killed recently."

Pleased, Red Eagle tried not to show it; it would add to his grandson's standing within the tribe... the chief left.

Raven sat down to wait impatiently.

****

Spotting a possible campsite, Jed called out to his daughter. "Patricia there is an outcrop off to your left, go check it out see if it will make a good camp for the night; since there is no moon out, we will have to stop or risk injuring one of the horses."

Inclining her head, Pat rode off with Silver Tip following.

Patricia came back a few minutes later. "It's a good place, there is even a little stream behind us for water."

Jed nodded thankfully. "Okay, let's stop for the night then."

****

Raven looked at Janet and sighed in annoyance. The white woman failed to mention that she could only ride side-saddle. Lucky for them, the chief made sure the saddle blanket had a girth and stirrups. She made them special for the ladies then provided each horse she traded with one.

Irritably, Raven moved closer to Janet to give her lessons. "You have to relax, there's no difference riding astride... move with your horse and use your legs, not just the reins."

Janet frowned painfully. "It feels odd riding like this; in England, ladies don't ride astride. At home, horses have bits to control them and we don't use our legs... it's unseemly."

Scowling, Raven nodded irritably then waved grimly; she only fibbed a little, since some women in town still rode side-saddle. She didn't have the time though or the inclination to get a spoiled white girl a side-saddle. "That is true in England, but not out here. Now take a deep breath and let it out then relax. Good! Now squeeze with your legs gently as she walks, so she picks up speed. Okay, now close your eyes and feel her under you. Slowly move with her, not against her."

Nodding, Raven watched in approval as Janet relaxed then started to move in time with her horse. "Good, open your eyes and squeeze a bit harder with your legs to get her to trot."

Pleased, Raven smiled as she watched the mare pick up speed. "Okay, now inhale then exhale and relax. Feel her move then rock your hips."

Janet loosened up, and grinned in delight at Raven. "That feels much better, not so jerky."

Raven started looking around for a campsite. It was getting too dark with no moon. She saw what she was looking for a few minutes later, so turned to Janet. "Okay, to slow your horse lean back; relax in the saddle and ease back on the reins gently, don't jerk them."

Pleased, Raven watched in satisfaction as Janet did as she was told. The mare obediently slowed to a walk. The younger woman nodded, and turned her horse to the camp she had picked out. She dismounted then went over to help Janet... she looked up at her. "All horses I train and this so happens to be one, can be mounted or dismounted on either side. Or you can push yourself back over her hindquarters then slide down her backside; she will not kick or move."

Shaking her head, Janet laughed at the mental image of herself sliding backwards; she just knew that she would end up landing on her rump, on the ground. "I think I will stick to dismounting on the left side, thanks."

Chuckling, Raven nodded not surprised. "Okay, stand up in your stirrups and lift your left leg over the horses back; lower it, until you can reach the ground."

Janet did as instruct and smiled relieved at doing it right.

Grinning, Raven nodded in approval. "Do you know how to unsaddle a horse then rub them down or check their hooves?"

Shrugging in apology, Janet shook her head negatively. "No, we had stable boys who did that for us."

Frowning, Raven shook her head in disbelief at how useless women in England were. "Okay, you can watch me tonight but afterwards you have to tend to your own horse. The first thing you need to learn out here is that your horse is your life. Without a reliable horse... you are helpless. Some Indian's can outrun a horse at long distances, so for you to try to running from an Indian on foot is futile. Before you eat, sleep, or get yourself a drink of water; your horse must be seen to."

Every once in a while, Raven would look over at Janet to make sure she was paying close attention. She turned back to the mare, satisfied at the English woman's intent concentration. "Now, watch as I take the bridle off the horse and the saddle. Once removed, put them somewhere clean; that way you don't get any dirt on it. Anything that can cling to the saddle blanket can dig into the horse, causing her to buck. Usually, I find a low hanging branch or a log to drape them on."

Janet nodded, watching the Cheyenne woman closely.

Raven smiled at Janet, once she finished. "The second important thing to do for your horse is to check their hooves. Indian horses have no shoes, so are considered barefoot or unshod. Always stand beside your horse, facing backwards. Run your hand down her leg, and pull up on the hair just below her fetlock. She will lift her foot for you when you pull. This horse is well trained though, so all you have to do is touch her leg then say 'up'; see how she automatically lifts her foot without any fuss. Now, look at the grooves in her hooves you need to clean them out. A rock in her hoof would make her lame. If it's left to long, it could damage her hoof and cause her to become crippled."

Intently, Janet watched Raven clean the hooves without any fuss from the horse. The Englishwoman then helped unload the packhorse.

Next, Raven took out oats then showed the Englishwoman how much to give them; Janet was shown how to hobble a horse, so they wouldn't stray. She dug into one of the packs then pulled out a brush that she made, and handed it to the older woman. "I use this to curry my horses."

Pleased, Janet grinned in relief. "I know how to use that."

Thankful, Raven nodded satisfied. "Good, I will let you brush down your horse and the packhorse. Oh, before I forget... stay away from my stallion; he was wild when I found him. Only a few besides me can get close to him. While you are combing the horses, I will make supper. Tomorrow, I'll show you how to set up camp."

Quickly, Janet nodded then did as instructed without fuss.

****

Golden Eagle walked back to Raven's and ducked inside. He looked around expectantly; forgetting for a moment then sighed in dismay, when he remembered that the cub was dead.

Dropping onto his sleeping fur dejectedly, Golden Eagle sighed as he gazed around at the empty tepee; it seemed so bare now. First Raven left then Dream Dancer, and now the cub. The Englishman laid back to sleep thinking about Raven.

****

Melissa smiled in relief when done bathing Pam. "The fever's down."

Daniel sighed thankfully. "Well, that's good news, anyway."

Sitting back, Melissa nodded at her son before smiling up at Jed when he handed her a bowl of stew. "Thank you."

Jed handed one to his son. "I heard you say the fevers down?"

Nodding, Melissa smiled. "Yes, enough to give me hope."

Relieved, Jed grinned thankfully. "Good, we made better time today than I thought we would; so tomorrow we will keep to the same routine."

Silently, Melissa inclined her head distractedly. Jed left, so she finished dressing Pamela then sat back to eat her supper.

Eating all the meat and vegetables, Daniel fed the broth to Pamela before giving her water and medication. Finished, they covered Pam with furs then went to the fire for a coffee.

Melissa gave the good news to the rest of them, and sat back then listened to everyone talking. It was the first time, since they lost Pam and Rose that the atmosphere around their group lightened; quite a bit of chuckling was involved. Grateful for that, Mell banked the fire before bed.

CHAPTER TWENTY

Golden Eagle woke and rolled out of his blankets; he dressed then looked at the dying embers in the fire pit. Devon shrugged, and left the tepee; since the cub was not there anymore, he didn't have to come back until tonight.

Giant Bear had informed Golden Eagle last night that after he had his breakfast, he was to train with Black Hawk; then Running Wolf would come for him afterwards, to teach him how to... track, wrestle, hunt, shoot a bow, and to live off the land.

Now, Golden Eagle's lessons with Golden Dove would take place at night... after supper. Devon reached Giant Bear's then tapped on the flap, and entered when permission was granted.

****

Melissa was jerked awake by a moan of pain; she rolled out of her blankets then knelt beside Pamela. Mell felt her forehead, and grimaced uneasily; her daughter-in-law was burning up.

Daniel sat down across from his mother. "What's wrong?"

Trying to hide her fear, Melissa looked at her son earnestly then waved towards the creek. "Go get some cold water. Pam is burning up; I need to bathe her to cool her down. Wake the others while you are doing that."

Nodding grimly, Daniel jumped up and hurried away.

Anxiously, Melissa bent then murmured soothingly to Pamela while she took off the furs and undressed her. Mell looked at Pam's healing wound. There were no red marks around the injury, so there was no blood poisoning. Nor was there any pus to indicate that there was an infection. White Buffalo was baffled entirely, why did she still have a fever; could the small swelling in her stomach be the cause?

Rose came over then squatted down in concern.

Seeing her upset look, Melissa smiled at her reassuringly. "I need more medicine, but add an extra two pinches of the powder to strengthen it."

Jumping up, Rose nodded and left.

Returning, Daniel brought the cold water then knelt.

Shaking her head baffled, Melissa looked at her son in dismay... extremely confused. "It's not the wound that is causing the fever, thank God! We need to sponge Pamela down to cool her off; after she gets her medicine, we need to pile blankets on her to sweat out the fever. It would be a good idea if you stripped then crawled in with her as well, the extra body heat might make the fever break sooner."

Daniel nodded desperately praying as they worked on Pam.

****

Raven got up out of her blankets, and added kindling to the dying embers. She looked over at Janet, but the white woman was still sleeping; she made coffee then started breakfast.

Janet rolled out of her blankets with a groan of pain, and looked over at Raven as she shook her head dejectedly. "I'm never going to get used to sleeping on the ground."

Chuckling in disbelief, Raven smiled consolingly then waved her over. "Yes, you will; now come over and have a coffee."

Sighing grimly, Janet obediently did as she was told.

Stirring the porridge, Raven got up then went to one of her packs and dug inside until she found the two packets she was looking for; she went back to the fire then opened them. The younger woman grabbed a handful of each before throwing them into the pot with the porridge to cook.

Gesturing, Janet asked curiously. "What did you put in there?"

Smirking, Raven smiled. "Nuts and raisins, of course!"

Not expecting that, Janet dubiously enquired in surprise. "Where do you get raisins or nuts out here?"

Stirring the porridge, Raven shrugged dismissively. "In the fall, we harvest the nuts ourselves; I trade for the raisins or have them shipped in from Boston once a year."

Thoughtfully, Janet nodded; that made sense and sipped her coffee with a grimace... tea was preferred.

Picking up a bowl, Raven began adding porridge to it then looked at Janet intently... hesitating to ask, but needing to know. She was married, so being a virgin isn't the issue. "Your face is pretty swollen; he didn't hurt you in any other way, did he?"

Reaching out to take the bowl, Janet hesitated; she looked at Raven in confusion before blushing then shook her head emphatically. "No, he was going to but the chief took me away from him before he could!"

Raven sighed in relief, and gave her the porridge. They ate in silence, both immersed in their thoughts.

****

Melissa looked down and sighed at her son in relief then beckoned him to come out. "The fever has broken; you can crawl out of there now. Bring me some warm water after you dress so that I can sponge the sweat off her, and we can go."

Daniel nodded then rolled out of the furs as the sweat poured down his face in rivulets. The preacher put his pants on, but not his shirt and went for water; He badly needed to cool off.

Jed walked over with two bowls of porridge then handed one to his wife. "How is she?"

Taking the bowl, Melissa grinned pleased. "The fever broke; I want to sponge the sweat off before we go."

Sighing gratefully, Jed stood back when his son came over then put the warm water beside his mother. Grey Wolf handed Daniel a bowl of porridge before looking at Melissa. "I will tell the others to get ready."

Silently, Melissa inclined her head distractedly then finished her porridge before taking the furs off Pam again, to wash her.

****

Golden Eagle sat down and sighed in exhaustion.

Black Hawk walked over then squatted down beside him... inquisitively. "How is your arm doing?"

Putting on a show, Golden Eagle grimaced as he moved his fingers experimentally. "Not too bad, only a little sore."

Pleased, Black Hawk nodded in approval. "You are doing well, and you learn quickly. In another week or two, you will not need anymore instructions. You should be able to continue on your own then you can put your dance together, whenever you feel that you are ready. From that moment on, you will start using your... knife, tomahawk, coup stick, and bare hands."

Enthusiastically, Golden Eagle smiled in thanks at Black Hawk's praise. "I boxed for years in England, plus I like to fence; I think that helped in my training, but do you think I will be ready that soon?"

Inclining his head, Black Hawk grinned decisively. "Yes!"

Thrilled, Golden Eagle beamed in pleasure then got up as Running Wolf walked into the clearing.

Nodding, Black Hawk stood and smiled at the young warrior. "Don't be too hard on him today; he has been training hard."

Running Wolf grunted evasively, but didn't say anything. The brave handed Golden Eagle a bow, a quiver full of arrows, plus a rifle. "The bow is yours to keep; I made them for you. The rifle is my nam-shimi', you can return it later."

Golden Eagle inclined his head in pleasure. "Thank you."

Running Wolf turned impassively, without saying a word then beckoned Golden Eagle to follow him. Devon frowned in disapproval after the unpleasant, rude Indian brave; the Englishman shrugged dismissively, and did what he was told.

****

Raven looked over at Janet then smiled in approval. "You are riding well today; how do you feel?"

Janet grinned at the praise before chuckling in pleasure. "I feel good; I'm even starting to like pants and riding astride."

Smirking, Raven inclined her head... not surprised. She spotted the outcrop that she stayed at a few nights ago. The younger woman turned to Janet before pointing for her to look. "You see that ledge over there?"

Patiently, Raven waited until Janet saw it then asked. "Look at it, and tell me why it would make a good spot to camp."

Biting her lip in concentration, Janet studied the area then smiled in triumph. "The hill behind the ledge is straight down, so nobody would be able to sneak up from behind."

Pleased, Raven nodded encouragingly. "Good; what else?"

Caulking her head, Janet frowned in concentration and brightened. "There are lots of trees below on both sides, so it would be hard for someone to sneak in without giving themselves away. Which would mean that there is only one good way in or out? That would make it easy to defend."

Hooting in approval, Raven grinned impressed. "You are right; there are two other reasons. One is that even though you can't see it from here, there is a stream for water. The trees again are the other reason, if there is vegetation around there are animals for food. If you are hiding from someone, you could defend that ledge for a while. Always look for camps that are only accessible one way, preferably with water close and food."

Smiling shyly at the approval, Janet changed the subject curiously. "When will we get to your village?"

Frowning in concern, Raven sighed grimly. "I have to find the Indian's that attacked you first, and scout them out. We will find them tomorrow night, if we have no difficulties; it should take us one day for scouting or possibly two. So, hopefully we will be at my grandfathers in about eight days... I hope."

Surprised, Janet shuddered in disgust. "Do we have to go there? Can't you just take me to my brother first?"

Sighing, Raven shook her head negatively. "No, I am running out of time as it is. I didn't come just for you. My whole tribe is in danger; if I don't find the killer's, the army will come into my village and kill everyone in it."

Distressed, Janet sighed. "I wouldn't want that to happen."

****

Jed held up his hand to stop everyone then sat, listening. He turned and motioned silently to Daniel, so he would come forward then they both dismounted. Grey Wolf handed his reins to his son before leaning forward to whisper guardedly. "Get up on my horse; keep everyone quiet... if Pam makes noise, you will have to smother it!"

Daniel nodded uneasily then mounted his father's horse.

Turning, Jed untied Pamela's horse from Daniel's saddle. He offered the reins to Melissa; she dismounted grimly then handed the white stallions reins to Rose before mounting Pam's darker horse. Grey Wolf beckoned Patricia to come forward next. "Stay here with your brother; if we are not back in twenty minutes, lead everyone southwest... as quickly as you can."

Patricia nodded then took out her rifle. Jessica followed her lead tensely. The twins and Melissa's sister weren't sure what was up, but something had spooked the older couple.

Jed mounted Daniel's horse then turned north.

Melissa waved silently in reassurance to the others, and they galloped away. Mell had listened to Jed's instructions, but knew better then to talk; sound travels far out here.

Jed led his wife to a hill, about ten minutes from the others and to the north of them. They crested the hill then stopped in disbelief.

Melissa gazed down in horror at the carnage-taking place.

Moving his horse closer, Jed whispered in worry. "Are you okay?"

Grimly, Melissa nodded mutely as her horrified stare swept the valley. The army had come across a Blackfoot camp; they were killing everyone... including women and children.

Helplessly, Jed looked around in disgust then stiffened in surprise before leaning close to Melissa furiously. "There are no warriors down there... only old men, women, and children."

Miserably, Melissa gazed around grimly then nodded before pointing to the north. "The braves are coming, they are over there; I can't count them from this distance, but there's at least a hundred."

In frustration, Jed looked in that direction and turned to his wife urgently. "Let's get out of here; it's too late to help now!"

Knowing her husband was right, Melissa nodded. They turned before racing back; both jumped off the horses then Daniel remounted his own, after tying Pamela's horse onto his saddle.

Silently, Jed mounted and pointed so that Patricia would precede further south away from the carnage that was occurring. Grey Wolf let her head south for half an hour then waved her back to them.

They all gathered close together in order to be able to hear.

Furiously, Jed sighed dejectedly. "The army is north in a valley murdering women and children again; as we watched about a hundred braves were galloping to save their families. I want to get as far away from here as we can so we will not stop for lunch today, but keep on riding."

Gesturing, Jed turned to Patricia but included everyone. "We are far enough now so you can start going straight west again; keep your rifles out... in case!"

They all nodded tensely in agreement then they were off.

****

Raven pulled up and pointed to her left. "We will camp there for lunch. I want to show you how to use a rifle when we stop."

Janet frowned grimly, but finally nodded in agreement.

Dismounting, Raven hobbled the packhorse so he could graze. The younger woman turned and motioned so that the Englishwoman would follow her.

Janet dropped the reins of her horse; she was trained to stay then helped Raven gather wood before watching avidly as her rescuer built a fire.

Raven pointed to the packhorse. "Grab the bacon and beans out of the left saddlebag, please; while I gather what I need."

Inclining her head, Janet jumped up to do what she was told.

Getting up, Raven went to the right saddlebag then took out a coffee pot, coffee, and two skillets. She put the coffee, plus the beans on to cook... once she returned to the fire. Afterwards, she grabbed her rifle, a box of bullets then waved so that Janet would follow her before walking into the trees.

Immediately, Raven found a good-sized tree and took out her knife then made a sizable X in the centre; she walked back to Janet. The younger woman showed the Englishwoman how to load, as well as unload the rifle. "Always make sure your safety is on when working with a gun, or you might accidentally shoot someone! Here, you try it."

Grimacing in distaste, Janet didn't like guns then tentatively took the rifle from Raven and slowly loaded then unloaded it.

Nodding, Raven smiled pleased. "Good! Do it some more but try to be faster, while I go stir the beans and put the bacon on."

In no hurry, Raven took her time then walked back to Janet; who was reloading again. She smiled at the Englishwoman teasingly. "How many times have you loaded since I left?"

Boasting, Janet smiled proudly. "That was my second time."

Pleased, Raven chuckled impressed; Janet was a quick study. "Not bad, I want you to put the gun to your shoulder. Make sure it is held tight, or you will bruise badly from the recoil."

Warily, Janet frowned attentively; she tucked the gun against her shoulder then waited tensely for further instructions.

In explanation, Raven put her hand out and touched the sight on the rifle. "This is what you want to line up to make your shot. Centre this in the middle of the X on the tree then gently squeeze the trigger when ready."

Earnestly, Janet did as she was told and jumped in stunned shock at the pain in her shoulder; the Englishwoman almost dropped the rifle in amazement, as she staggered back a bit. The deafening noise reverberated through her skull, causing her to cringe as she bit her lip accidentally.

Raven laughed at the astonished look on Janet's face. "You have to hold the rifle tighter against your shoulder. Sadly, you missed the target but you manage not to fall... that's excellent; try a few shots then come for lunch."

Janet sighed unwillingly, but didn't refuse as she repeated her efforts; until she felt that her teacher would be satisfied.

****

Golden Eagle limped towards the corrals, and sighed plaintively. He was beat, but he still had to work with his horse then eat; afterwards, he had lessons with Golden Dove before he could even contemplate going to bed. Devon walked around the corner then forgot all about his pain and fatigue, as his stallion neighed at him in greeting. The Englishman smiled, as he walked over to join Giant Bear's son by the fence.

Black Hawk smiled teasingly, at the late Golden Eagle. "Your horse has been standing exactly in that position for the last half hour, watching for you... without moving a muscle."

Golden Eagle laughed then shrugged in apology. "Sorry I'm late, but your son is hard to please and wouldn't let me leave until I got it right."

Grinning knowingly, Black Hawk nodded curiously. "What were you having trouble with?"

Waving in emphasis, Golden Eagle sighed dejectedly. "Walking soundlessly through the underbrush; the bow is giving me lots of trouble too, mostly because my arm can't hold it steady. Since it's still weak, I couldn't hold the string long enough to hit the target."

Shrugging in regret, Black Hawk chuckled consolingly. "Well, I can't help you with being stealthy that will come with practice; so too, will the strength in your arm return as you use it more. As for the bow, when you first pick it up you have to relax. Take a few deep breaths, and blow them out through your mouth. As you are blowing each breath out, think of another part of your body relaxing. After you are completely loose, lift your bow then sight on your target. Think of the arrow as an extension of your arm with the tip as your finger, decide where you want it to touch then visualize the arrow touching that spot. Make sure to exhale slowly as you let the arrow go gently, no jerking the string! It might seem strange and slow to do this at first, but once you hit your target a few times it gets easier. After a while, you will automatically relax when shooting... without even being aware that you are breathing properly."

Eagerly, Golden Eagle grinned in thanks. "I will try that."

Nodding pleased, Black Hawk waved him to go in. "Good, now get in with that stud then get to work; he's been waiting for you patiently. If everything works out today, tomorrow you should be able to get on him."

Excited by that prospect, Golden Eagle smiled in anticipation; he picked up the equipment before going into the pen.

****

Patricia rode back to the others; she had been scouting ahead with her dog. Pat went straight to her mother and father then waved to their left. "About an hour from here there is a decent campsite with water. Behind that is a steep hill with trees on one side for cover, but the rest is pretty much open which I don't like. I climbed it to look around... I didn't see anything better. I suggest we make camp there, even though it's a little early since we didn't stop for lunch."

Jed looked at Melissa for her opinion and turned back to his daughter at his wife's nod. "Lead on."

Turning, Patricia rode ahead as everyone followed her.

****

Raven looked over at Janet. "We will stop soon so that you can practice with the rifle. I also want to teach you how to move around a bit quieter. Tomorrow we will reach the outskirts of Howling Coyotes hiding place, so I will not be able to give you any lessons until after we leave there."

Janet nodded relieved then sighed with a painful grimace. "An early camp sounds good to me."

Knowingly, Raven chuckled in sympathy and the two rode on.

****

Black Hawk turned when he heard footsteps behind him then smiled at the foreman. "Hello Jake, where were you hiding?"

Jake stopped beside Black Hawk and watched the white man curiously, as he worked with his horse. He didn't speak for a bit then turned, and answered Black Hawk. "I was out seeing to my men. One of them saw Charles break away from the ones escorting him then head north."

Rubbing his chin, Black Hawk frowned. "That's where Raven went."

Scowling, Jake inclined his head. "Your father just told me!"

Turning, Black Hawk called out to the Englishman. "Put the saddle blanket on him; if he doesn't fuss, add the sacks."

Golden Eagle waved in acknowledgement.

Looking at Jake again, Black Hawk sighed inquisitively. "Do you have any idea, why our neighbour would go that way?"

Thoughtfully, Jake finally shrugged unknowingly. "He could be going around, so he wouldn't meet up with the sheriff again."

Black Hawk chuckled as he nodded. "You could be right; the lawman gave him quite a wallop."

Nodding, Jake watched Golden Eagle for a moment before turning to Black Hawk curiously. "What is going on around here, anyway? Your father has hardly said two words to me! Who's the white man?"

Grimacing, Black Hawk told Jake everything he knew. When Tommy finished, the foreman shook his head uneasily. "Giant Bear is making a mistake if he tries forcing Raven to marry!"

Resignedly, Black Hawk snorted in agreement. "Don't I know it, but he will not listen to anyone."

Reflectively, Jake scowled in contemplation. "I worked for the Summerset's since before the older earl died. I helped raise that girl... she's like my daughter. I taught her everything she knows about cattle, plus running a ranch. She is as stubborn and pigheaded as her English grandfather was; if she refuses to marry this Englishman, I will stand behind her all the way!"

Well aware of that, Black Hawk smiled in appreciation at Raven's foreman... he was as reliable as they come. "You are a good man, Jake; I know you care for my niece. I have to tell you though that your protégé is falling in love with the Englishman, but because of my interfering father she will never admit it."

Surprised by that, Jake grinned thrilled. "Are you sure?"

Gesturing, Black Hawk nodded decisively. "They have already spent one night together, but like you said Raven is obstinate."

Pleased, Jake's smile widened. "Well, it's about time she fell in love; I'll have a talk with the man to see if I approve."

The two men chuckled in conspiracy towards Golden Eagle.

****

Jed looked around then nodded in approval at his daughter's choice. Everyone dismounted; a camp was hastily set up. Grey Wolf with Daniel's help unhooked the travois then set it beside the fire before helping the others.

Melissa built up the fire and put water on to heat for Pamela's bath, while Daniel bent over his wife to undress her.

Moaning, Pam opened her eyes.

Daniel smiled in relief down at her then smoothed his wife's hair back tenderly. "How are you feeling love?"

Pamela moistened her dry, cracked lips before whispering painfully. "Thirsty and I hurt something fierce!"

Nodding knowingly, Daniel smiled tenderly before turning to his mother. "Pam is awake; will you bring some water, please!"

Relieved, Melissa grinned in delight and filled a cup with water. Mell handed it to Daniel before kneeling, and watched as he tenderly lifted his wife's head so she could drink.

Slowly, Pamela drank before shifting with a groan of pain. Daniel eased his wife down, and sat back.

Pleased, Melissa smiled at her daughter-in-law teasingly. "You gave us quite a scare young lady! How do you feel?"

Shrugging, Pamela grimaced uncomfortably. "My side hurts; other then that I feel okay I think... what happened?"

Turning to her son; Melissa gestured towards the fire. "Will you bring the tea and warm water, while I check Pam's wound?"

Daniel nodded then left.

Undressing Pam, Mell explained everything that happened.

Thoughtfully, Pamela sighed grimly when her mother-in-law finished. "I don't remember much, except going after Rose and getting tangled in a tree."

Not surprised, Melissa inclined her head. "You were unconscious for most of it."

Looking up, Melissa smiled at her son when Daniel handed her the bowl of paste for the wound. "Thank you."

Carefully, Melissa washed the injury then looked at it critically and nodded pleased. "It is healing nicely, but it's turning some interesting colours!"

Wanting to see, Pamela lifted her head to look as best she could; she grimaced at the pain movement caused. Quickly trying to be sneaky, Pam looked at her belly then away with a relieved sigh. "It sure doesn't feel as if it's healing."

Soothingly, Melissa grinned and put the medicine on it then re-wrapped Pam's ribs. "It might not feel that way right now, but believe me it was a lot worse a couple of days ago."

Finished, Melissa redressed her daughter-in-law and smiled at Jed then the others as they gathered around. "Looks like Pam is going to make it after all."

Smiles of relief appeared on all their faces.

Looking at Rose, Pamela whispered gravely. "Thank you for saving my life!"

Rose smiled at Pam teasingly. "You saved mine first!"

Pamela snickered, unable to laugh. "I guess we're even."

Relieved, Rose inclined her head in agreement.

Once reassured that Pam was okay; everyone went back to their chores light-heartedly. It wasn't long before the relieved teasing laughter that had been missing, returned to the group.

****

Finished with his horse, Golden Eagle grabbed the rifle out of his tepee and walked to Giant Bear's for supper. He scratched on the door and waited politely for permission to enter.

Golden Dove smiled at him as she pushed open the flap; she spoke in Cheyenne slowly. "How are you doing today?"

Golden Eagle grinned back. "Tired; what about you?"

Nodding in approval when Golden Eagle carefully answered in Cheyenne, Golden Dove chuckled sympathetically. "I'm feeling good; come, sit then eat."

Instantly, Golden Eagle propped the gun against the tepee wall and walked over then sat by the fire.

Giant Bear and Jake walked in next then sat across from him.

Giving reassurances, Golden Eagle waved so that Giant Bear would look in the corner. "I brought your rifle back."

Looking at the gun, Giant Bear harrumphed in unconcern. He turned to Golden Eagle then shrugged. "Keep it; I have more."

Irritated, Golden Eagle frowned angrily at the abrupt tone but his good manners prevailed; he mumbled crossly. "Thank you!"

Ignoring the atmosphere between the two men, Golden Dove handed out bowls of stew; quite descended as they ate.

****

Raven kept cooking pretending she didn't hear Janet approaching behind her. At the last moment, the younger woman turned. "Better, but it's still not good enough!"

Janet sighed dejectedly with a shrug. "When did you first hear me?"

Pleased, Raven grinned in approval. "About ten minutes ago."

Sighing, Janet smiled forlornly then propped the rifle against a tree; she sat down across the fire from Raven before grinning in pride. "Better than last time though."

Chuckling, Raven inclined her head in agreement. "Much... how did you make out with the rifle?"

Shrugging, Janet grimaced... unsatisfied. "I hit the tree three times, but not even close to the X."

Beginning to dish up the food, Raven beamed in encouragement at the disgruntled Janet... she tried too hard. The younger woman couldn't figure out why either, but shrugged inwardly to herself it wasn't her business. "That's an improvement; if you want, I can teach you how to shoot a bow?"

Excited, Janet's face lit up. "Could you? I would like that."

Smiling, Raven nodded and handed Janet her supper. "Yes, I can, but not until after we leave the war chief's hiding place."

Not liking that reminder, Janet nodded soberly then ate.

****

Melissa smiled at her daughter-in-law, and bent over then kissed her forehead. "Go to sleep Pam; we will talk tomorrow."

Pamela nodded and grinned up at Mell. "Goodnight, Mom!"

Turning to Daniel, Pam pleaded earnestly. "Stay with me!"

Daniel inclined his head before lying down then carefully put his arm under Pamela, so that her head was on his shoulder. The Baptist Pastor kissed the top of his wife's head, and sighed in contentment. "Goodnight... I love you!"

Pamela snuggled closer contentedly. "I love you too."

Turning away, Melissa left the two of them alone and walked to the fire then sat down across from her husband. "Where are Jessica and Rose?"

Jed smiled then waved at the creek. "They are doing dishes."

Knowingly, Melissa snickered teasingly.

Shaking his head, Jed's expression became injured. "What! I tried to help... they refused."

Grinning, Melissa ignored Jed's look. "I'll take first watch."

Jed nodded thoughtfully. "Okay, I will take second; Patricia can take the third watch, and Jessica will have the last one."

Melissa inclined her head in agreement then smiled when the three girls walked over. Mell gave two of them their schedules.

Jessica nodded before pouring Rose then Patricia a coffee.

Rose cleared her throat hopefully. "Can I take a watch?"

Immediately, Melissa shook her head negatively. "No, you are still learning; besides which your rib hasn't healed enough yet. If it makes you feel better, you can cook breakfast."

Nodding, Rose sighed dejectedly. "Okay."

Needing to stay awake, Mell refilled her coffee before getting up. "Goodnight, pleasant dreams everyone!"

Turning away, Melissa sauntered to a large tree; sipping her coffee.

Watching his wife leave, Jed banked the fire for the night.

****

Golden Eagle got up to leave.

Jake stood hopefully. "Mind if I sleep at Raven's with you?"

Looking at Jake, Golden Eagle shrugged in consent. "No, I don't mind."

Pleased, Jake smiled in thanks. "I will collect my bedroll."

Turning, Golden Eagle nodded and left without comment.

Giant Bear got up worriedly. "Jake, I don't want you to talk about the ranch to the Englishman, he doesn't know about it."

Smirking, Jake inclined his head thoughtfully. "As you wish, but I think that man knows more than you think."

Suspiciously, Giant Bear scowled. "What do you mean?"

Shrugging, Jake waved dismissively. "Just a hunch I have; nothing that I have heard definitely."

In agitation, Giant Bear sighed. "Watch what you say to him."

Nodding, Jake turned and noticed the rifle propped against the tepee. "Golden Eagle forgot his gun I will take it with me."

In disinterest, Giant Bear nodded then sat back down.

On his way out, Jake picked up the rifle and went to get his gear then walked over to Raven's; he scratched on the flap.

Quickly, Golden Eagle lifted the door out of the foreman's way and took his rifle from Jake. "Thank you, I forgot it."

Jake nodded then put all his stuff down opposite to Golden Eagles, and made his pallet there. Devon put more wood on the smouldering coals then made coffee and tea. The foreman walked over, and sat across the fire from the Englishman before accepting a cup for his coffee. After drinks were poured, the two men sat there eyeing each other speculatively.

Golden Eagle was the first to break the silence, as he motioned inquisitively. "So, you are Raven's foreman?"

Shaking his head knowingly, Jake chuckled and nodded. "I guessed that you knew more then you were letting on."

Smirking, Golden Eagle shrugged dismissively. "Well, I could understand Cheyenne after a week, if they didn't talk too fast. I had a harder time speaking it. When I saw Dream Dancer, it didn't take long to figure it out; he looks like Earl Summerset!"

Caulking his head inquiringly, Jake eyed the Englishman. "That he does; I take it you don't want Giant Bear to find out you know."

Sighing, Golden Eagle smirked grimly. "No."

Confused, Jake looked at Golden Eagle. "Why haven't you escaped?"

Frowning, Golden Eagle shrugged hastily. "I made a promise to Raven; and I want to know what the chief is up too."

Snickering, Jake harrumphed in disbelief then couldn't help tease Devon a bit. "Are you sure that's the reason? It doesn't have anything to do with a raven-haired she-devil... would it?"

Instantly a picture of Raven came to mind; Golden Eagle instantly hardened. The Englishman shifted to hide his arousal from Jake. Devon grimaced reluctantly. "I have not spent enough time with her to decide yet."

Smiling knowingly, Jake drained his coffee letting the uncomfortable Englishman off the hook before going to bed.

Golden Eagle banked the fire and went to his sleeping pallet.

****

Raven turned on her back for the fifth time, and sighed as she looked up at the stars. She couldn't sleep; every time she closed her eyes an image of Golden Eagle would appear. Finally, sleep overtook her. Instantly, a horse and rider appeared on the horizon riding towards her. The man reached down then swept her up in front of him. He bent his head to capture her lips in a searing kiss before stopping his horse, and swung down with her in his arms. Devon tenderly placed her on the ground; he started making love to her. The woman sighed in pleasure then gazed up at him as he stood up.

Raven cried out suddenly in denial, when Golden Eagle started shimmering before fading. She jumped up and rushed towards him... Devon was gone. The woman looked around in desperation; she was now standing on a dock watching a ship leaving port, as tears of loneliness streamed down her face.

Urgently, Raven jerked herself awake with a cry of despair. She looked around and saw Janet sleeping. The woman curled up in a ball then wiped tears away before sighing anxiously; finally, she slept.

****

Melissa looked around and frowned, something was bothering her but she wasn't sure what. She undid the whip from around her waist before coiling it in her hand loosely then walked into the trees. Mell decided to make a circle around the camp. White Buffalo learned a long time ago to trust that voice inside her head; plus, the shivers of warning flowing down her spine that said something wasn't right.

*****

Jed woke abruptly; he lay there rigidly, until he was sure the threat wasn't immediate. Grey Wolf reached over then grabbed his gun belt that was always close to his head, in easy reach. He got up cautiously and strapped it on. The deputy marshal bent next to pick up his rifle, that was never far from his side when not at home before going to Rose first. He put his hand over the young girl's mouth, so she wouldn't cry out then bent down to whisper urgently. "Grab your rifle and slip behind the trees off to your right... please, stay hidden there until I tell you it is safe!"

Rose fearfully gave a nod before doing what she was told.

Looking towards Jessica... Jed saw Patricia already talking to her; Grey Wolf started towards his son then stopped suddenly, as four men walked into the camp with rifles trained on him.

The largest of the four growled. "Don't do that, put it down."

Slowly, Jed knelt and put the rifle on the ground then stood up with his hands in the air. "What do you want?"

The leader scowled at the man incredulously as he watched him carefully put his rifle down. "What do yah think I want? Your horses are what we want and supplies."

Cautiously, Jed discreetly looked but didn't see Melissa or Patricia's dog. He brought his attention back to the four men, not wanting to give anything away. Grey Wolf eyed their dirty, ripped uniforms; immediately knowing that they were survivors of the infantry attack they had seen earlier. They had wild, desperate looks on their faces. The deputy marshal figured that they were going to kill them, they couldn't leave witnesses.

Seeing movement behind the men; Jed tensed in readiness.

A whip whistled eerily in the silence... 'SNAP!'

The burly man cried out a warning to his men; just as he heard the loud crack of a whip... he was too late. Snake-like coils curled around him, locking his arms against his sides.

Silver Tip attacked the fourth man in the line.

Jed's gun cleared leather; two shots fired... one right after the other. The third man, too stunned to react fast enough turned to run. Instead, he dropped his weapon with a shriek as he grabbed his shoulder in pain.

Turning, Jed saw Patricia standing with a smoking pistol.

Rose came running then stopped beside the deputy marshal.

Swiftly, Jed smiled at her in reassurance. "Grab some rope out of my saddlebag, so I can tie these men up."

Nodding, Rose ran off with Jessica following to help.

Patricia gathered all their guns before calling her dog off.

Teasingly, Jed grinned in relief at Melissa standing behind the stocky man keeping tension on the whip. "Well, it's about time; what were you waiting for... one of them to shoot me?"

Melissa chuckled jokingly. "I thought about it!"

In concern, Mell's expression sobered. "Is everyone okay?"

Sobering, Jed nodded placatingly. "Everyone is fine, love."

Grimly, Melissa frowned before jerking on the whip. "What do you want to do, we don't have time to take them with us."

Biting his lip, Jed scowled thoughtfully in indecision before shrugging. "No, we don't; thankfully we are only about a day or two at the most away from the next town, which is where the army is based... if I remember correctly. So, we will doctor the two up who are bleeding then tie them securely, so the army can come and get them after we report this incident."

The burly man grunted in fear as he tried to fight the whip.

Silver Tip squatted then growled menacingly in warning.

The big man instantly stopped fighting, and took a step back.

Patricia looked at the man before grinning in warning. "I wouldn't move if I were you."

The leader suddenly froze then watched the dog warily.

Walking up to his father, Daniel frowned at the men.

Jed motioned in concern. "How's Pam doing?"

Daniel smirked with a grunt. "She slept through it all."

Pleased, Jed sighed relieved. "Good, she needs her rest."

Rose and Jess ran up to Jed then handed him the rope.

In thanks, Jed inclined his head in approval before walking up to the leader and uncoiled the whip from around him. Grey Wolf marched the man over to a tree then tied him securely.

Trooping back, Jed gestured towards Rose in hope. "Can you reheat the stew then feed all these men; when you're finished you can go back to bed."

Nodding, Rose left; Jessica followed her to help.

Walking over, Jed grabbed the other outlaw; he took him to a tree a few feet from the leader and tied him.

Going to the third man, Daniel checked the hole in his hand; the bullet had gone straight through. The Baptist Pastor grinned with a knowing look towards his mother. "I suppose this was father's handiwork?"

Melissa chortled as she coiled her whip. "Of course it was!"

In approval, Daniel sighed in admiration; his father was not as fast as his wife or son with a six gun, but his accuracy was way better. "Will you grab some bandages so I can wrap this?"

Agreeing, Melissa inclined her head then trotted off.

Leaving that outlaw; Daniel went to the last man and ripped open his shirt then examined the wound.

With no regret, Jed walked up. "The bullet has to come out."

Frowning in agreement, Daniel pointed at the fire. "Can you put your knife in the coals to heat it please?"

Nodding in agreement, Jed went over obediently and shoved the knife blade in the coals.

Returning, Melissa expertly bandaged the man with a hole in his hand. When Mell finished, Jed pushed him to a tree and tied him with the others.

Taking the last man over to the fire, Daniel pushed him down. The Baptist Pastor took the glowing knife out of the coals. He grabbed a thick twig on the ground so the man could bite on it; that way he wouldn't accidentally bite off his tongue.

Rose, Jessica, and Patricia took a bowl of the stew then went over to feed the other three.

Daniel beckoned his father to hold the man down for him.

None to gently, Jed pushed the man on his back then held him; Daniel dug at the wound with the tip of the knife.

Unrelenting, Daniel grunted in exertion when the man lifted up in pain... trying to get away from him. The Baptist Pastor managed to grasp the bullet, despite the soldier's unwillingness to cooperate. When he pulled it out, the man mercifully lost consciousness; not once had the rebel cried out. The preacher applied some paste that was left from Pam's poultice earlier then wrapped the shoulder.

When the soldier came to; Daniel fed him then gave him some tea before Jed took the man and tied him up with his comrades.

After banking the fire Melissa smiled at the others. "Good job everyone... now go to bed! Jed will take over the watch."

Smiling, Melissa kissed Jed passionately. "Goodnight, love."

Jed hugged Mell then smacked her bottom. "Go to bed."

Grinning saucily over her shoulder at Jed; Melissa made sure to give a little wiggle as she turned away with a teasing giggle.

CHAPTER TWENTY-ONE

Raven woke then sighed disgruntled; she hadn't slept well last night; nightmares of Golden Eagle going back to England had awakened her. She couldn't afford to have dreams this close to the war chief's camp. If someone heard her last night, the two of them would be in big trouble.

Shaking off her thoughts; Raven got up before adding wood to the last of the embers. She put coffee on then made some porridge. The woman left it to thicken; it gave her a chance to check on the traps she set last night.

In satisfaction, Raven found three rabbits; she threw one to the wolf, and one to Bruno then took the third one to camp.

Janet was already pouring coffee, so she poured a second one and handed it to Raven. "Good morning."

Nodding, Raven mumbled irritably. "Morning!"

Sitting down with a weary sigh, Raven took a sip of her coffee. Feeling better, she skinned the rabbit.

Intrigued, Janet watched her take off the hide; before reaching over she stirred the porridge.

Fashioning a spit, Raven put the rabbit on it to cook.

Since her rescuer was busy, Janet dished up their breakfast.

Scraping the skin, Raven rolled it up then gave it to Janet; she needed to give older woman something to do after they stopped. "Put this in your saddlebag; I'll teach you to cure it."

Nodding, Janet stroked the silky rabbit fur. "Thank you."

Glad the Englishwoman liked it, Raven smiled before she sobered in caution as she waved in forewarning. "We should find Howling Coyote tonight, so you won't be able to practice with the rifle until we are back on the trail."

Shuddering in fear, Janet sighed dejectedly; she didn't want to go anywhere near that terrifying Indian and risk being caught again. She reached up to feel her healing cheek, remembering the pain before dropping her hand grimly.

Eating silently, Janet peaked over at Raven figuratively. The younger native woman was quite intense... so strong; unlike any woman she had ever met. Even the queen of London fell short, but not by much. After the attack, the white woman would have given anything to go home to England. Now though, the Englishwoman wasn't that sure.

In England, Janet's older husband had pampered her; she loved it in many ways, but hated it too. When her husband died, her father stole everything from her... she had been powerless to stop him. Unfortunately, that meant the widow was at the mercy of her father's whims, it was degrading.

Janet never wanted to feel that helpless or dependent on anyone ever again. Looking at the independent Raven so sure of herself; without a man telling her what to do or what to wear... the Englishwoman wanted to be just like her. Strong, unconventional, completely fearless!

****

Golden Eagle woke first; he stirred up the embers before adding more wood. Devon put on coffee then left the tepee and headed to Giant Bear's to get breakfast. He scratched on the flap then entered when it got lifted for him.

Golden Dove beamed cheerfully in delight. "Good morning."

With a smile, Golden Eagle nodded. "Morning, is breakfast ready?"

Inclining her head, Golden Dove grinned before motioning curiously. "Yes, it is; is Jake still sleeping?"

Nodding, Golden Eagle gestured. "He is; I will take him a bowl as well."

Chuckling, Golden Dove waved him over in invitation. "Okay, help yourself."

Filling two bowls, Golden Eagle turned. "See you tonight."

Walking over, Giant Bear's wife opened the flap. "Okay, see you for supper."

Ducking out, Golden Eagle hurried to Raven's. He pushed his way inside then smiled at Jake, who had just gotten up. "Morning, did you sleep okay?"

Jake inclined his head as he accepted the porridge. "Yes, I did... thank you."

Sitting across from Jake; Golden Eagle put honey on his porridge then extended the jar. "Would you like some?"

Shaking his head, Jake refused. "No, thank you."

They ate breakfast in silence.

Draining his coffee, Jake got up to go. "I have to check on my men; I will see you tonight."

Golden Eagle nodded goodbye, and put his empty bowl down; he doused the fire before leaving for his lessons with Black Hawk.

****

Rose finished making breakfast; she smiled across the fire at Daniel, who after making the paste and tea for his wife, was waiting patiently for the porridge. He wanted to feed Pamela before his mother came to administer the medication. "Can you wake everyone please, breakfast is ready!"

Daniel inclined his head then left; he came back to the fire when done, and dished up porridge for the two of them.

Melissa and Jed walked over then helped themselves to breakfast, and coffee before eating hastily.

Patricia followed closely by Jessica came last.

Finished breakfast, Rose took a bowl with a cup of coffee to one of the men. Pat and Jess followed the younger girl's example before walking over to help feed the deserters.

Smiling at her husband, Melissa waved optimistically. "You said last night we should reach the next town soon?"

Jed nodded thoughtfully before rubbing his chin irritably; he needed another shave. "We should be there really late tonight, or tomorrow morning sometime. It was just an army outpost at first, but a town grew around it. We can find a doctor there to look at Pam and Rose then wire the Montana marshal, and let him know about that sheriff in the border town. I think we should spend one night in town as well for a much-needed break, even if we have to stay an extra day."

Grimly, Melissa frowned in agreement; she didn't want to lose an entire day though then shrugged resignedly. "I don't like that idea, so hopefully we can reach it tonight instead. The horses are exhausted... so are we. Guess it will have to do. I better give Pamela her medicine then we can go."

Without comment, Jed watched Melissa pick up the paste and tea. He drained his coffee then got up to help break camp.

****

Golden Eagle fell on the hard ground then stayed there as he laid back breathing deeply in exhaustion.

Black Hawk chuckled in sympathy as he sat down beside the Englishman. "My son is coming. Did you bring your rifle, bow, and arrows?"

Golden Eagle groaned dejectedly before sitting up reluctantly. "Already! Yes, they are leaning against a tree to your left. Your son doesn't say much."

Shrugging, Black Hawk smiled in agreement. He gestured in reassurance. "He takes his responsibility of being the next chief seriously; too much so sometimes. Don't take it personally... he's like that with everyone."

Surprised it wasn't Black Hawk as the next chief, Golden Eagle grinned then motioned teasingly. "Well, by the look of your father it's going to be a long time before that happens."

Disagreeing, Black Hawk shook his head negatively. "No, my father is talking about handing leadership to Running Wolf next year."

Intrigued, Golden Eagle looked at Black Hawk in astonishment. "Why, is he sick or something?"

Shaking his head, Black Hawk shrugged negligently at the surprised look on the Englishman's face. "No, he isn't sick... just tired he says. My mother wants him to give it up as well."

Quickly, Golden Eagle stood up without commenting on Giant Bears retirement; just as Running Wolf walked into the clearing, and beckoned impatiently for Devon to follow. The Englishman waved goodbye to Black Hawk before collecting his things. He walked behind the brave obediently.

Running Wolf led him to the same target area they had used yesterday, and pointed to the rifle wordlessly.

Nodding, Golden Eagle put down the bow and quiver of arrows. He lifted the rifle then aimed and fired; Devon shot ten times before hitting the centre on the eleventh shot... thankfully, he never missed the target. The Englishman was better with a pistol or a sword, never having used a rifle before.

In England, the preferred method of duels was with a sword or duelling pistols. You and your opponent were placed back-to-back then walked until told to turn by a third party. Quickly, spinning around as fast as you can you shoot your opponent. Marksmanship was essential to survival; he had been one of the best with a pistol.

It was different out here Golden Eagle had been told; they used a gun holster. To use the gun, you had to get the revolver out of the pocket. Devon had tried it a couple of times, but he had a hard time with getting it out first. He shook off his thoughts, as he turned to his teacher inquisitively.

Running Wolf grunted in approval before pointing at the bow.

Smiling proudly, Golden Eagle was undeterred by Running Wolf's silence now that he knew it wasn't personal. It had taken five shots less than yesterday, to hit the centre. He took out ten arrows and stuck them in the ground, making sure they were in easy reach then took one and notched it.

Golden Eagle remembered what Black Hawk had told him yesterday; he stood there for a few minutes relaxing his body. He breathed in then out before lifting the bow, and sighted down the shaft. He imagined the arrow already in the centre of the target then gently let go of it, and watched in amazement when it hit the mark. It didn't go where Devon had aimed, but at least the Englishman had hit the target this time.

Frowning angrily, Running Wolf crossed his arms in front of his chest in disgruntled disapproval. "You have been talking to my ni-ho-ii."

Unrepentant, Golden Eagle grinned in delight as he nodded in satisfaction. "Yes, he gave me some advice last night."

Snorting in irritation, Running Wolf uncrossed his arms and pointed to the rest of the arrows without a word; but the look on his face told Devon he would be giving his father an earful.

Chuckling knowingly, Golden Eagle resumed his lessons.

****

Raven slowed her horse; turning right she rode into the trees.

Janet followed silently; she dismounted when Raven did.

Frowning, Raven turned to Janet in warning. "We will have lunch before continuing. Once we leave here, until I tell you there will be no talking unless it's an emergency. Keep the rifle with you at all times; you can lay it across your saddle, but make sure the safety is on. Don't shoot at anything, unless it is impossible to avoid it. Try to be quiet, sound travels far here."

Grimly, Janet nodded soberly before helping her with lunch.

****

Jed and Melissa stopped their horses then looked at each other uneasily. He sighed in agitation as he asked his wife's opinion. "How many?"

Melissa shrugged thoughtfully. "I would guess fifty horses."

Frowning, Jed nodded his head in agreement. "I figured that."

Dismounting, they changed horses again.

Walking over to Pat, Jed pointed south. "There are a few trees off to your left, it's the only cover for miles out here. Take everyone over there... have lunch. Your mother and I will wait for the horses that are coming this way. Keep your guns handy, but don't shoot unless you have no choice."

Patricia nodded calmly; she waited for Daniel to mount their father's horse before taking Mell's reins. Pat looked at her dog. "You stay with Mom."

Silver Tip whined plaintively then obediently went to the leader of her pack, and sat beside her horse.

Melissa leaned down from Pam's horse to smile in comfort at her daughter's dog. "We won't be that long girl."

Yipping at Melissa, Silver Tip dutifully followed. Jed and Mell moved their horses further away from the others then stopped to wait.

Squinting, Melissa shaded her eyes then turned to Jed. "Army."

Jed frowned before waving knowingly. "Looking for deserters, or trying to find out what befell his men. Do you have your badge on?"

Quickly, Melissa nodded that she did; they lapsed into silence while Mell checked to make sure her badge and guns were visible. White Buffalo checked the fur behind her. Satisfied, she waited patiently.

About a quarter of a mile off, the man in the lead called a halt. He left everyone behind before riding towards the pair waiting... with only one other person curiously. He had seen the others veer off, so wanted to check it out; although, he guessed that they were just taking precautions. It never hurt to be careful out here.

The major eyed the man and woman waiting for him. He noticed the marshal badge on the woman then the deputy marshal star on the man. He smiled in delight, then waved towards them before looking at his aid. "Well... a woman marshal; doesn't that beat all Simmons."

The man beside the major snorted in disdain, but didn't comment.

Overhearing, Melissa narrowed her eyes in anger.

Instantly, the major lifted his hands in apology seeing the angry look... not wanting to offend anyone. "I meant no disrespect ma'am. It's just a bit of a novelty to see that's all."

Nodding, Melissa relaxed at the major's rueful tone; she eyed him.

The major looked at Mell boldly before smiling in approval at the picture she made, wearing those buckskins. The man noticed the white fur behind her; grinning he motioned hopefully. "Mind if I see the robe behind you."

Melissa inclined her head in agreement then lifted the buffalo skin so he could look at it.

Impressed, the major whistled in awe never having seen a white buffalo before. "You must have done something pretty spectacular, for the Indians to award you a white buffalo hide; especially, being a white woman and all."

Shrugging dismissively, Melissa ignored the request to talk about it... she tucked it securely behind her. Mell pointed at herself then Jed, introducing them. "I'm Marshal Brown from North Dakota; this is my deputy marshal and husband, Jed Brown."

Inclining his head respectfully, the major returned the introductions in kind. "I am Major Sinclair, and this is my aid... Simmons. What are you folks doing out here, so far from your home; if you don't mind my asking?"

Smiling amiably, Melissa answered vaguely. "We are heading to the Bitterroot Mountains to visit friends and family."

Eagerly, the major sighed in relief before waving towards the east. "Well, maybe you can help me then; I'm looking for an army squad of about thirty. They were supposed to be back two days ago, but nobody has seen them."

Instantly, Melissa shared a knowing look with her husband.

Jed was the one who answered the army officer before pointing behind him with a grunt of anger. "As a matter-of-fact Major, we saw them from the top of a hill about two days back."

Snorting in disgust, Melissa took over the telling. "Your squad had come across a Blackfoot summer camp, and they were killing everyone in it. Unfortunately, there were only women, children... plus a few old men in it; they found easy prey."

In rage, the major's face turned purple in anger. "Damn that Tucker, I should have known better then to send him on a scouting expedition. I will kill him when I find him."

Sadly, Jed shook his head regretfully. "Well, I don't know if very many of your men lived; we saw about a hundred braves riding to help their families. I do however know that at least four survived... we left them tied to a tree after they came into our camp last night, and tried to kill us for our horses!"

The major grimaced angrily in hope "One wouldn't happen to be a burly black-haired man with slightly curly hair, would it?"

Melissa nodded decisively. "Yep, that was the leader."

Major Sinclair grinned then turned to his aid in satisfaction. "Tucker is alive. Now I can hang him for insubordination, plus the deaths of innocent women and children. We will find out if anybody else survived. Thank you for the information, I need statements if that is possible?"

Knowingly, Melissa nodded in agreement before gesturing towards where the rest of her family gathered. "We were just stopping for lunch; would you care to join us?"

Quickly, the major shook his head negatively. "No thank you; if you are going to be in town tomorrow, you can drop off your statements at the sheriff's office instead of at the army barracks... if you prefer."

Turning, Melissa pointed in the direction they had just come from. "They are south of here, about six hours... good luck."

The major tipped his hat cordially in farewell. "To the both of you also, fair thee well... Marshal and Deputy Marshal Brown."

Melissa watched Major Sinclair ride back to his men then leave with a salute. Mell looked down at Silver Tip. "You were not needed, go find Pat."

The dog barked happily and raced off towards her mistress.

Jed chuckled in grim approval. "The major was not looking too happy with his man that's for sure. I definitely wouldn't want to be in Tucker's place right about now. I might have ended up liking Sinclair, if I stayed around here for any length of time. He hadn't said squaws, but women."

Nodding, Melissa smiled in agreement; as they rode towards the others, she motioned inquisitively at her husband. "Will we ever be without prejudice against the colour of people's skin?"

Shrugging, Jed gestured grimly. "Hopefully one day, Mell."

They rode back to their group in silence after that.

****

Sighing tiredly; Golden Eagle came around the corner, but perked up as his stallion neighed at him in greeting. He walked up to Black Hawk, and leaned against the fence for a break.

Black Hawk smiled enticingly; with a wave, he gestured at the stallion watching them. "Are you ready to get on that horse today?"

Golden Eagle nodded eagerly; he straightened forgetting all about his weariness in his excitement. "I sure am."

Knowingly, Black Hawk chuckled as Golden Eagle's face lit up. "Okay, I want you to put him through his paces then saddle and bridle him. Lead him by the reins again, make sure he understands you when you say... 'whoa'; when you are satisfied, put the sacks on him. If he doesn't balk too much, I want you to stand up in the stirrup and get down again. If you feel confident, you can sit on him then dismount and take the blanket off then lay on him bareback. Afterwards, you can call it a day if you want."

In excitement, Golden Eagle gathered everything he would need before going to work without complaining once about being too tired.

****

Raven rode ahead of Janet quietly, keeping a vigilant watch.

Janet followed with the packhorse, so that Raven's horse was unfettered; that way, he could react promptly when his rider needed.

Frowning pensively, Raven looked around for a place to hide Janet so she would be safe while she scouted. Howling Coyotes camp should be half an hour to forty-five minutes from here; the younger woman judged from the chief's description of the area. She didn't want to get any closer than that.

If Janet wasn't like a child out here, Raven would have camped closer to their encampment, but this would have to do. She turned into the thicker trees, and followed a game trail... satisfied she stopped before dismounting.

Waiting for the prearranged signal, Janet got off also.

Quietly, Raven walked over close to the Englishwoman and spoke softly. "We can murmur now, but no loud talking. I want you to unsaddle the packhorse, rub him down then feed him. After he is finished eating, saddle him again just in case we need to make a hasty retreat. Do the same with your horse and make sure to tie both of them securely, so they don't wander off. You can have half the rabbit I cooked this morning, with some cakes that are in the saddle packs on the packhorse... absolutely no fire. Set out three or four traps like I showed you, I'm going scouting. If you get bored, you can take the skin I gave you out. Take four sticks, and stretch the hide out before scraping it; leave it like that, till I get back."

Nodding silently terrified, Janet watched Raven disappear with her wolves. The older woman shook off her fear, angry with herself for allowing her emotions to gain control and did as she was told.

****

Golden Eagle stood beside the stallion murmuring reassurances as he put his foot in the stirrup. Devon lifted himself up and waited. The stud looked back curiously but didn't move, so the Englishman stood up all the way. The stallion shifted uneasily, not liking that then snorted in warning.

Stroking Devil's neck, Golden Eagle crooned softly. The stud stood still, so he got down then stood up again. His horse didn't object, so he got down and went to the other side then stood in the stirrup on that side. When his horse didn't move, the Englishman lifted his leg and straddled him.

The stallion shifted uncertainly, but Golden Eagle rubbed his neck then talked to him soothingly. Devil stood still, so Devon dismounted. The Englishman repeated his actions before stripping the saddle blanket off the horse, and took the bridle off; he walked over to Black Hawk in elation.

Black Hawk grinned as he watched the stallion following Golden Eagle; he didn't need to ask the Englishman the question, since it was written all over his face... he did anyway. "Well, how do you feel?"

Ecstatically, Golden Eagle smiled in pleasure as he gestured enthusiastically. "Great, did you see that? He hardly even fussed when I sat on him."

In approval, Black Hawk nodded with a chuckle. "Yes, rub your horse down then meet me for supper at my tepee; we will have to celebrate."

Eagerly, Golden Eagle nodded and went back to work.

****

Jed looked around in concern before turning to Melissa. "We will camp here, I never noticed anything better. At least we will have a steep hill behind us, with water available. We were delayed too long this afternoon by the major; with hardly any moon, it's not a good idea to continue."

Melissa inclined her head in agreement then sighed in disappointment; Mell had hoped to get to the town tonight.

Everyone dismounted and helped set up camp.

Rose started supper; it wasn't long before everyone gathered around the fire, except for Daniel and Pam.

Pouring two coffees, Melissa went over to them.

Pamela scowling at Daniel in angry demand, harrumphed in irritation. When she saw Melissa coming; Pam motioned entreatingly in hope. "Mother, tell this lummox that I want to get up and sit with the others."

Shaking her head, Melissa chuckled at the two of them. "Well, if you are feeling good enough to argue with your husband... I guess it will be all right."

Trying to appease her son, Melissa turned to Daniel then compromised. "Pick Pam up, and set her on the log; that way she will not be walking yet."

Daniel nodded in relief before lifting Pamela effortlessly then walked over, and gently put his wife on the log.

Jed smiled in delight at his daughter-in-law. "It's nice to see you are feeling good enough to join us, Pam. We missed you since you got hurt."

Pam grinned at her father-in-law. "I'm glad to be feeling better too."

Looking up, Pamela inclined her head in thanks to Rose when she handed her a bowl of stew. She ate, enjoying the laughing and joking going on around her; she sighed content, when her husband put his arm around her.

****

Raven moved ahead soundlessly; she grimaced in apprehension. They camped closer to Howling Coyote's camp then she thought. The younger woman only walked for fifteen minutes then almost stumbled into a sentry.

Lucky for Raven, Bruno sensed him and growled softly in warning. Holding up a silencing hand. She dropped to her stomach then slithered forward. At the edge of the trees; she stopped and looked out. The young woman saw the war chief's tepee in the centre, and the others positioned around it.

Nodding to herself in satisfaction; Raven knew this would be an excellent spot to watch. She slithered backwards then got up and headed back to camp. It was getting too dark to see much of anything, but the younger woman now knew where they were. Tomorrow, she would come for the day to watch them. She walked around the sentry then broke into a trot.

Making a face, Raven knew she needed to move them further away; especially, if she was going to have another nightmare. The sentry would have heard her for sure, if they had been this close last night.

*****

Janet jumped up in fear then pointed her rifle in the direction of the rustling noise. She sighed in relief when Bruno walked in first, to give her warning before her rescuer showed herself.

Warily, Raven walked out of the trees; she had used her dog, so the inexperienced Janet wouldn't kill her by mistake.

In relief, Janet dropped to the ground shakily; glad Raven was back.

Squatting beside the older woman, Raven accepted the canteen of water... plus, a plate of cold food that Janet had made her. The younger woman sighed plaintively; she looked at the Englishwoman in warning, as she whispered. "The sentries are only about fifteen minutes away... no talking. I want to move us further away, so let's eat then you can follow me. Afterwards, I will show you how to tan your hide before we go to bed."

Nodding wordlessly in fear, Janet got up and stayed close to Raven.

****

Golden Eagle went to Black Hawk for supper; unfortunately, Gentle Doe wasn't feeling well, so he left with Black Hawk to eat at the chiefs instead.

An hour later, Golden Eagle slipped into Raven's then smiled at Jake when the foreman handed him a cup. "When did you get back?"

Jake shrugged in unconcern. "About twenty minutes ago."

Pleased he hadn't waited long, Golden Eagle nodded and sat across the fire from Jake then asked curiously. "How are your men doing?"

Jake smiled in reassurance. "So far they are okay; nobody has tried to slip past them to get in here yet, but they will try sooner or later... I am sure."

Golden Eagle frowned thoughtfully in worry; he didn't have any food available here. "Did you eat?"

Jake inclined his head. "Yes, how did your training go today?"

Golden Eagle grinned eagerly. "Better, I even sat on him; he didn't buck."

Jake nodded impressed then banked the fire for the night. "That's good! I will see you in the morning."

Golden Eagle nodded as he drained his coffee before going to bed.

CHAPTER TWENTY-TWO

Golden Eagle left Raven's tepee then walked to Giant Bear's. He scratched on the flap, and entered when it got lifted. He looked at Black Hawk's worried expression then frowned. "What's the matter?"

Black Hawk sighed in despair before running his fingers through his hair in distress. "Gentle Doe complained of back pains last night. So, the medicine man and shaman are with her, she might be in labour."

Halting, Black Hawk stopped talking fearfully then turned to the door as his mother walked in. "How is she, Ni-go-i?"

Golden Dove sighed grimly; she shook her head in worry. "Not good, our suspicions were correct... she is in labour."

In agony, Black Hawk motioned in fear. "It's too early! She won't be in her eighth month for another week."

Sighing grimly, Golden Dove nodded sadly. "It could still turn out to be false labour, we will not be sure for a few hours yet."

Shoulders slumping, Black Hawk grimaced but he knew deep down that it was fruitless. He started his pacing once again in agitation. He stopped suddenly and turned to Golden Eagle, as if recalling why the Englishman was there. "You will have to practice on your own today."

Frowning, Golden Eagle inclined his head having already guessed that before grabbing two bowls of porridge then left.

****

Melissa walked over to her daughter-in-law, and helped her stand up in alarm. "Are you sure you can walk?"

Pamela chuckled teasingly at her mother-in-law before nodding decisively. "Yes, my right-side hurts like the dickens but my legs are fine... they are not broken you know."

Scowling, Melissa nodded still concerned then kept a firm grip on Pam as they walked to the fire for breakfast.

Quickly, Pamela sat down before sighing in annoyance at the pampering. "Honestly, I am feeling better."

Jed and Daniel walked to the fire then dished up porridge.

Nodding without commenting, Melissa handed Pamela a bowl before sitting down with the others.

Patricia, Jessica, and Rose came together talking and giggling. Everyone was in high spirits, knowing a night in a bed was only a few hours away.

Jed included everyone in his smile, as they all sat down to eat. "It is about five hours to the next town at this pace. We will stay one night there then it will be a two to three-day ride to the town just before Raven's place... I think. We will stop at the ranch first, and see if anybody is home. Then two days to Giant Bear's winter camp, so we should be there in five or six days at the latest. If nobody is there either, we will have to find Giant Bear's summer camp. That might be a little difficult, without someone to help us find it. However, we will cross that bridge when we come to it; no use worrying now about it now. Even with all the delay's we have had, we are still making excellent time."

Pamela sat straighter confidently, as she motioned pleadingly. "I would like to ride now."

Daniel and Melissa both shook their heads in denial, but Mell was the one who spoke. "No, when we get to town, we will take you to see a doctor... Rose too. If he says it's okay, you can ride after we leave town but only if he agrees."

Wilting unhappily, Pamela nodded grudgingly. "Okay."

Melissa smiled encouragingly at her daughter-in-law before turning to the others. "Okay everyone, let's get going; the faster we get there, the sooner we can have a hot bath!"

Everyone chuckled at Melissa's ecstatic expression at the thought of a bath. They all nodded eagerly agreeing; but couldn't help teasing Mell unmercifully about her inability to stay awake in a tub, as the camp got quickly dismantled.

****

Raven rolled out of her blankets and looked towards Janet, but she was still sleeping. She went to the packhorse before taking out cakes then grabbed her extra canteen. The younger woman slung it over her shoulder, nibbling on one of the cakes as she quietly left... with Bruno following closely.

Giving the rest to Bruno, Raven broke into a trot as soon as she finished eating; she slowed when she got close.

Silent as a whisper, Raven skirted the sentries. She slipped back to the hiding place that she found last night. She parted the bush in front of her, but everything was quiet. If she didn't see anything by tomorrow, the two of them would have to leave. She settled comfortably then watched.

****

Golden Eagle sighed tiredly; he laid down on the ground for a moment hoping. He waited for Running Wolf, but finally decided that he wasn't coming. He got up before grabbing his rifle, bow, and arrows then headed to the practice area.

Putting everything down except for the rifle, Golden Eagle started shooting. After the sixth shot, he hit the centre; elated, he shot another ten bullets. Unfortunately, he only ended up in the centre twice more before lowering the rifle then picked up the bow.

In preparation, Golden Eagle put ten arrows in front of him tip down in the dirt before breathing deeply relaxing. He lined up his shot; carefully, he let the arrow go. Devon hit closer to the centre with his first attempt then he had with all ten arrows yesterday. The Englishman jumped around in excitement then stopped in embarrassment. He looked around. Of course, no one saw him. Shrugging, he quieted and continued calmer now.

****

Jed raised his hand in warning before stopping his horse. Everyone halted, as Jed pointed ahead in relief. "There it is! It is called Little Rock because of the mountains behind it, which are called the Little Rocky Mountains. It is about an hour away; as soon as we get into town, we will drop off... Pamela, Rose, and Daniel at the doctors. The rest of us will go to the sheriff's office. I hope that we will find it calmer then the last two towns we have been in, is everyone in agreement?"

They all nodded with smiles of anticipation. Jed chuckled at the eager looks on all the faces turned to him. "Good, let's go."

Melissa and Jed kicked their horses into a trot. Mell looked at her daughter-in-law encouragingly. "Not much further."

Pamela sighed in irritation as she swayed between the horses. The movement was almost making her sick to her stomach. "Good, I am getting tired of staring up at the sky all day."

Melissa laughed in sympathy, but didn't say anything more.

****

Golden Eagle walked to Raven's then dropped off the rifle, bow, and arrows. He hit the target ten times with the arrows today, but only one got close to where he was aiming. It was still a better improvement from two days ago, when he couldn't hit the target.

Going to the training pens next, Golden Eagle smiled at his stud as the horse trotted over to the gate then nickered at him in greeting.

Since Black Hawk wouldn't be here today, he decided to play with his stallion for a bit; since he didn't have any equipment to work with, anyway. He walked into the corral, and raced across the paddock playfully.

Devil chased him then turned away uninterested.

Waiting until the stallion moved, Golden Eagle snuck up behind him and grabbed his tail; giving it a yank, he ran to the other side of the pen.

Spinning, Devil chased him to the other side of the paddock before nudging him playfully with his head.

Laughing, Golden Eagle fell on the ground playing dead.

Snorting, Devil pushed his master in uncertainty before dropping onto his knees and lying down beside Devon.

Curious to see what his stallion would do. Golden Eagle turned, and put his head up on the stallion's neck; promptly, he fell asleep.

****

Raven sighed irritably; she shifted, so she could get to her cakes and canteen. She took a drink then cupped her hand and poured water into it, for her dog. The young woman broke the cake in half then fed some to Bruno before eating hers.

Settling back, Raven pushed the brush over to re-assume her watch. The only excitement was the changing of the sentries, other than that there was nothing. The young woman would wait until dusk before going back to camp. She shifted to get comfortable as she laid there without moving.

****

Jed and Melissa eased their horses to a walk as they entered the town. They got a several curious looks from the townspeople, but nothing threatening. Grey Wolf pointed to a man sitting on the steps of the general store whittling, so they headed towards him. He smiled down at him then tipped his hat cordially. "Excuse me sir; can you point me towards the doctor in town?"

The man nodded then pointed with his knife ahead of them, but didn't look up even once. "Sure can, three doors down on the left-hand side."

Jed tipped his hat politely once more. "Much obliged."

The man grunted before going back to whittling, uninterested.

Melissa and Jed turned up the street then pulled up to the hitching rail, everyone dismounted. Grey Wolf with Daniel's help unhooked the travois, Mell opened the door for them; she waited until Rose went in then shut it.

The man behind the desk looked up inquisitively before jumping out of his chair; he hurried to a door to his left. "In here please!"

Jed and Daniel followed him then laid the travois on the bed.

Pamela frowned in aggravation. "I could have walked!"

The doctor smiled at the irritated young woman, placatingly. "You let me be the judge of that young lady! I am Doctor Michael Andrews."

Michael shook Pamela's hand before turning to the others.

Stepping forward, Melissa shook the doctor's hand making introductions.

In explanation, Melissa smiled at the handsome doctor when he turned back to her before pointing to her son. "We will let Daniel explain while we go to the sheriff's office, we will return after to see how the girls are."

The doctor nodded as he pointed in the general direction. "The sheriff's office is up two buildings."

Thankful to have that information, Melissa and Jed left.

The others waiting followed behind, wanting to show a unified front in case they encountered another unlawful sheriff. Patricia also wore her sheriff's badge, as they walked up the street with Melissa and Jed leading. Mell unhooked her whip then coiled it in her hand as she took the lead.

A man of about fifty, with a badge looked up and smiled in welcome. "How are you folks today, what can I do for you?"

Thoughtfully, Melissa eyed the sheriff... quickly assessing him; she relaxed and put her hand with the whip down, at the unquestionable integrity she saw in his eyes. Mell introduced everyone then tensed for a scathing remark.

The man nodded knowingly; he smiled in pleasure, as he pointed at Melissa then Jed. "I know who you both are. Although, you are older now. I only saw you from a distance, but I still remember seeing you use those guns once."

Melissa lifted her eyebrows in surprise; she shook her head baffled. "I don't remember you!"

Not surprised, the sheriff hadn't wanted anyone to see him at that wild time in his life. "I was passing through one of your towns; when you and at that time your fiancé, took down two hired guns that were looking to take over your towns. Miller's Creek, I think the town was named. You both inspired me so much that I quit the gang I had just started riding with then came home here, and became the next sheriff. It was the best decision I ever made."

Pleased by that, Melissa shared a look with Jed then both turned back; they grinned in delight at the sheriff.

The sheriff sighed remorsefully at his lack of manners; he stood up then shook everyone's hands before chuckling. "Well, I guess I should give you my name, I'm Sheriff Peterson. Please have a seat, and tell me how I can help you? I'm curious to hear what brings you so far from home, to my humble hometown?"

They all found seats then Melissa explained about the sheriff in the border town, and the massacre at the Indian village.

****

Golden Eagle woke suddenly then jumped up incredulously; he looked up at the position of the sun, Devon must have slept for a good hour... not once had the stallion moved.

Devil lifted his head to look up at his master then laid his head back down, as if to say he didn't want to get up yet.

Agreeing, Golden Eagle chuckled and knelt down before lying across Devil's neck then scratched him all over. The stud snorted through his nostrils gently in pleasure, and didn't move a muscle enjoying the scratching immensely.

Inspired by a thought, Golden Eagle laid full length on his horse then clucked for him to get up. "Come on boy, up you go!"

Reluctantly, Devil lifted up onto his knees.

Straddling the stallion, Golden Eagle leaned forward then put his arms around Devil's neck so he wouldn't fall off. "Come, up you go."

Devil surged up with his master clinging to his neck.

Smiling in elation, Golden Eagle whistled so the stud would walk. After one round, the Englishman sat up and let Devil wander where he wanted.

Golden Eagle grabbed a fistful of his horse's mane then whistled for a trot. Immediately, Devil responded; he let his horse go his own way not trying to lead him yet. The Englishman whistled again, but this time asked for a canter.

Leaning back, Golden Eagle halted him finally and jumped down; Devon gave his horse a giant hug in thanks before heading for his tepee.

****

Raven sighed in disappointment and slithered back; it had been a fruitless day. It was getting dark, so she headed back to camp. Stopping, she crouched at a rustling ahead. A warrior walked by close to her hiding place.

The sentry stopped suspiciously, instantly on guard as he felt another presence. The Indian looked around cautiously; Raven held her breath then grasped her knife before taking it out of her pouch, in readiness. The woman and the lookout both heard a growl of anger off to their left.

The brave seeing a wolf ahead with a rabbit in her mouth, chuckled at being so jumpy... the man continued walking.

Raven breathed a sigh of relief before she slipped around him soundlessly. The brave was unaware that the wolf just saved him from certain death.

*****

Janet jumped up in fright, she pointed her rifle in the direction of the rustling. Again, she saw Bruno first before Raven stepped out; the Englishwoman sighed in relief before lowering her gun.

Raven's eyebrows rose in surprise.

In Explanation, Janet shrugged in embarrassment. "I was starting to get worried, which made me a little jumpy."

Thoughtfully, Raven nodded then looked down at her wolf. "I will leave Bruno with you tomorrow to keep you company."

Comforted, Janet inclined her head appreciatively; several times today, she had almost shot her rifle in reflex. The Englishwoman didn't tell Raven that though, knowing her rescuer would be very angry at her foolishness. "That will make me feel so much better, thank you."

Raven smiled hopefully; she was starving, the younger woman motioned eagerly. "Did you catch any rabbits today?"

Janet beamed before wrinkling her nose with a shudder of distaste. "Two, I gutted and skinned both of them... it was absolutely disgusting! I scraped the hides after and staked them out like you showed me."

Unable to help herself, Raven laugh softly at the unladylike face Janet made; she went and looked down at the hides. She noticed a few slices where the Englishwoman punctured the skin, but for her first time she did well. She smiled in approval then turned curiously. "Good, did you reset the snares?"

Regally, Janet drew herself up at the compliment before inclining her head haughtily, trying not to show her pleasure. "Yes, I figured you would want me to."

Raven chuckled at Janet's attitude, but wasn't fooled. "Good girl, go check the snares; I will show you how to build an underground oven, so that there is no smoke."

Eagerly, Janet grinned in delight at the thought of hot food then did as she was instructed... quickly in anticipation.

****

Doctor Andrews finished with Rose before walking into the room where Pamela was waiting. He looked at Pam solemnly. "Hi there, let's get your shirt off first; I need to have a look at you."

Pamela nodded before sitting up so the doctor, and her husband could help her remove her shirt.

The doctor unwrapped her ribs, after Daniel moved back; he draped the cloth across Pam's breasts when she laid down, to spare her any discomfort.

Carefully, Doctor Andrews ran his hands across her ribs then down under the rib cage before going across the top of her stomach. He looked closer at her belly; he smiled in delight. "Expecting are you, I would say six months."

Immediately, the doctor stopped talking when Pamela glanced at her husband before biting her lip uneasily.

The doctor moved back out of the way knowingly. Daniel marched up to the bed then glared down at his wife in anger. "You're pregnant, and you didn't tell me! How could you endanger yourself; with a baby on the way?"

Pamela sighed in apology; she lifted a beseeching hand before placing it on her husband's arm. "I wanted to tell you! I went to the doctor the day I stopped to see your mom, that's when we compared dreams. With all the rushing around to get ready to go, I just never got the chance. Besides, I knew that if I told you... you wouldn't have let me come."

Furious, Daniel scowled then waved in frustration. "You are quite right; I wouldn't have let you leave the ranch!"

Daniel turned to look at the doctor grimly before motioning in fear. "She hasn't hurt the baby, has she?"

Doctor Andrews smiled reassuringly. "I don't think so, but let me finish my examination and I'll let you know."

Frustrated, Daniel nodded briskly then backed off.

Taking out his stethoscope, the doctor bent towards Pamela then mouthed silently. "I'm sorry."

Shrugging, Pamela smiled reassuringly at his apology; her husband would have noticed sooner or later.

Intently, Doctor Andrews listened to Pam's lungs first before putting the scope on her stomach, and listened with a frown of concentration. He stood up with a touch on her shoulder in reassurance. "Well young lady, you are pretty lucky. Your lungs are clear no rattle or wheezing, so it wasn't punctured all the way. Your baby has a strong, healthy heart rhythm. Your third rib is broken, but it's healing nicely. I took out the stitches, it looks good; I don't think you need a travois now. Just be careful mounting or dismounting; no heavy lifting while you are pregnant. Keep bandaging your ribs for another week, for the support while you're riding."

Uneasily, Daniel walked up to the doctor in question; he gestured inquisitively. "Should she be riding in her condition?"

Decisively, the doctor chuckled with a nod of amusement at the anxious father to be. "Of course she can, I'm a firm believer in lots of exercise until the seven and a half... even the eighth month. After that no riding, but walks as well as light exercise are still needed."

The doctor bandaged the ribs then helped Pamela with her shirt. He was helping her to sit up when Jed and Melissa entered. Mell smiled at Pam hopefully then turned to the doctor. "How are both girls' doing?"

Doctor Andrews started with Rose first. "Rose's rib was fractured. I would say a sliver of bone was still attached, so it kept the rib in place. Wrapping it, helped to stop it from getting damaged further. She doesn't need the binding anymore, as long as she is careful not to re-injure it."

Pointing at Pamela next, the doctor grinned of satisfaction. "This young lady can ride again, as long as she keeps her ribs tightly bound for another week. Since you are her mother-in-law, congratulations are in order on the upcoming birth of your grandchild; in three... to three and a half months."

Melissa grinned knowingly then nodded in delight, at hearing that the child she had suspected Pamela was harbouring was okay. That was what had kept the fever from abating for so long; it wasn't the injury causing it, but the baby. "I know; I couldn't help noticing."

Daniel sucked in a shocked breath in anger; he waved incredulously. "Mother, why didn't you tell me?"

Grimly, Melissa shrugged. "It wasn't up to me to tell, and I wasn't sure for a while there that Pam would survive; I didn't want to make it worse."

In approval, the doctor inclined his head. "You are very wise. If you don't mind, could you tell me where you are going?"

Inquisitively, Melissa smiled. "We're headed to the Summerset ranch in... Malta, I think it's called; on the border of the Milk River, why?"

Relieved, Doctor Andrews sighed; he hoped that was where they were heading. He motioned eagerly. "No kidding, I'm headed that way tomorrow too. Mind if I ride along with you, it's not safe going alone."

Looking at Jed for permission, Melissa saw him give a nod. She turned to the doctor in warning... motioning in caution. "You can come if you like Doc, but we are in a bit of a hurry so we will be riding hard. We are hoping to make the next town in two days, at the most. Earlier if we can, we'll be riding at seven in the morning; if you still want to come, meet us at the hotel."

The doctor nodded decisively. "I'll be there."

Melissa inclined her head in goodbye before they left.

****

Golden Eagle walked to Giant Bear's; He ducked inside, when the flap was opened. Devon looked around then spotted Black Hawk. "How is she?"

Black Hawk turned an anguished look to Golden Eagle. "I was just in there. I had to choose between saving my wife or my son; she was in so much pain, I could only stay for a few minutes. I left after telling them to save the baby."

Sadly, Golden Eagle walked over and put his hand on his friend's shoulder in comfort. "If you need to talk come see me."

Without comment, Black Hawk nodded then turned away.

At the scent of food, Golden Eagle sniffed in appreciation. He walked to the fire and dished up stew. He decided to take extra, in case Jake was back and hadn't eaten. Devon grabbed another bowl then left.

****

Raven walked over; with Janet's help, they opened the underground oven then lifted the rabbits out. Plus, the tiny potatoes they had dug up earlier. They rapidly filled in the hole, so no smoke escaped.

Janet inhaled at the heavenly smell; she sighed in hunger. "I'm starving!"

In agreement, Raven chuckled; she cut one rabbit in half and put it on Janet's plate then put the rest on her own. The younger woman split up the few potatoes they had managed to find before they dug in enthusiastically.

Groaning in pleasure, Janet bit into the rabbit and juice squirted down her chin. "I will have to remember how to cook this way... it's delicious."

Satisfied at the ecstatic look on Janet's face, Raven grinned in delight as she nodded. "A lot of times we cook... deer, pig, or cattle this way; it's gutted and skinned, but otherwise whole then we have a feast."

Janet sighed blissfully. "I hope I am around the next time you cook this way; it is fantastic!"

Raven laughed knowingly, hoping she would stay as well; the young woman had never had a female friend before, they both finished their meal in silence.

****

Jed ushered everyone into the hotel before walking up to the desk. "We need three rooms, please. We also have a dog."

The hotel clerk looked at the animal, and his eyes widened in fear. "I think you mean a bear is with you; is it trained?"

Reassuringly, Jed smiled. "Yes, she is."

Looking at the badge on Jed's shirt in reluctance, the clerk handed him three keys. "Sure, you can keep the dog but she isn't allowed in the eating room."

Knowingly, Jed inclined his head in thanks before signing the register. "That sounds fair enough. I would also like to know if we could have supper in our rooms, and a bath would be nice."

The clerk pointed in explanation towards the back of the hotel. "There are bathing rooms out back. We do have tubs in the rooms for the women behind a partition; if there is more than one lady, they will have to use the ones out back. I will send the boys to fill them. I can send up supper right away."

Jed turned back then nodded in thanks; he flipped the clerk a silver dollar. "Much obliged, sir."

Expertly, the clerk caught the coin; his smile widened in gratitude. He shook a bell hidden under the counter, which was only used when a tip was given.

A boy of about fifteen rushed into the room in disbelief; it wasn't very often he got called by that bell. "Yes sir."

Giving instructions, the clerk pointed to Jed. "Get these folks their luggage and show them to their rooms."

Nodding in greeting, Jed smiled at the boy. "You can show us our room's first then go to the stables and ask for our saddlebags, but don't take anything from the packhorse."

The boy beckoned to them, so they followed him gratefully.

****

Golden Eagle walked back to Raven's then shouldered his way inside. He smiled sadly at Jake then handed him a bowl.

Jake frowned knowingly. "Gentle Doe is worse?"

Grimacing, Golden Eagle nodded grimly. "Yes, Golden Dove thinks she will die in the early morning... if she lasts that long. I was leaving the tepee when she stopped to tell me not to come back tonight for lessons. She was just on her way to go get Black Hawk; his wife was asking for him."

Sadly, Jake sighed gloomily... they ate in silence.

Finished eating, Golden Eagle got up; too tired and depressed to talk. "I'm going to bed. Goodnight."

Nodding before banking the fire, Jake followed Devon's lead.

****

Raven sighed in irritation before looking at Janet in annoyance. "There was no activity today. I will watch tomorrow again, but if I don't see anything useful; we will have to leave, regardless."

Janet nodded forlornly, not looking forward to another day sitting around waiting then lay down disgruntled. "Okay."

Uneasily, Raven grimaced; hoping not to have a repeat of the nightmare from the other night. The younger woman yawned and dropped down onto her pallet. Exhausted, she fell into a dreamless sleep almost immediately.

****

Waving goodnight to Daniel, Jess, and Pat; all of them had went to the bathing area. Jed turned to his room, walking in he chuckled. He stared at his wife in the tub asleep. Grey Wolf stripped then went and picked Mell up before putting her in bed. He climbed in beside her.

CHAPTER TWENTY-THREE

Melissa woke then purred in pleasure; when Jed ran his hand down her chest and belly. From behind, he teased the curls at the junction of her thighs. Mell pushed back in encouragement.

Jed arched his hips, and pushed his engorged manhood against Melissa's buttocks enticingly. Grey Wolf scooted closer then lifted Mell's leg over his, and pushed up then entered her moist womanhood from behind.

In encouragement, Melissa groaned then rotated her hips.

Eagerly, Jed pushed up inside his wife harder before nibbling on her neck. Grey Wolf put his arm under Melissa's head, so he could bend his arm and play with her breast at the same time. The deputy marshal continued stroking her bud of pleasure gently, as he ground his hips against Mell faster.

Moaning in satisfaction, Jed felt Melissa's first tremors of ecstasy peeking. Once Grey Wolf felt his wife let go of her control, the deputy marshal released his.

Melissa cried out in pleasure, as she felt the tremors inside her strengthen; gasping in gratification, Mell felt her husband lose his control as well.

Panting in exertion, Jed dropped his head on his pillow then disentangled himself from his wife and turned onto his back.

Groaning, Melissa twisted around before curling up against her husband then purred deep in her throat... like a contented cat, in approval. "Hmm, that's a nice way to say good morning."

In agreement, Jed chuckled then nudged his wife playfully in humour. "Sit up, I will comb your hair before we go."

Aggrieved, Melissa groaned but not in pleasure this time; it was now a gasp of agony at the thought of her hair. "I fell asleep in the tub again, didn't I?"

Sympathetically, Jed nodded before laughing at his wife's pained expression. "Pass me the brush, love; I will get the tangles out."

Plaintively, Melissa sighed then reached towards the nightstand and passed the brush to Jed. Mell sat up before turning her back to her husband; White Buffalo put on a stoic expression, as Grey Wolf methodically attacked the stubborn knots in her long white hair.

****

Raven woke then sat up reluctantly. She wasn't looking forward to another day of lying perfectly still, and watching; hoping to hear, or see something that might give her a clue as to why they had attacked Golden Eagle's party. The young woman sighed perturbed before going to the packhorse then grabbed her canteen, more cakes, and half the rabbit from last night.

Looking down at Bruno when he trotted over, Raven shook her head. "You stay with Janet!"

Bruno whined plaintively, but instantly went to the sleeping Janet before lying down close to her; he watched Raven disappear... forlornly.

****

Piercing shrieks of grief shattered the silence of predawn unexpectedly... waking Golden Eagle instantly; he jumped out of his blankets in fear, thinking they were under attack as more screams filled the teepee.

Jake looked up at Golden Eagle sadly then handed him a cup of coffee. "Gentle Doe died a few minutes ago."

Distressed, Golden Eagle dropped down across the fire in shock. "Are we under attack as well?"

Negatively, Jake shook his head reassuringly. "No, they are grieving! I guess I should tell you before you go out, that Indians don't grieve as we do; we usually mourn most of our lives... depending on the death. The wolf tribe will grieve for two days, today they will shriek out their grief and cut themselves. Depending on how close a relative or friend you are, is how many slices you put on your body! For some, it will only be two or three shallow cuts. Running Wolf will probably slice himself up to seven times, since she was his mother. Black Hawk will cut himself up to ten times or more. I have seen Indian's die because their grief was so strong, that they sliced themselves one too many times then bled to death. Tomorrow, they will keep shrieking but not as powerful or severe. There will be no more cutting themselves, thankfully. In the evening, they will have a funeral... with everything she needs to go to the spirit world placed around her, so it can be burned at sunset with her. The ones closest to Gentle Doe will cut off their braids during the burning of the pier. After the fire dies, they will not mention her name again for one full moon. It is disrespectful for others to mention her, since she has reached the happy hunting grounds. In the morning, it will be as if the death never occurred unless someone else dies of his or her wounds. In the old days, this tribe would have left here fearing ghosts; neither would they have burned the dead. At that time, the dead were left in the open or in a tree with everything that they needed in their journey... Raven and her family have brought many changes to this tribe."

Golden Eagle sighed uneasily. "I'm glad you warned me, Golden Dove did talk about their funerals, but she never told me about cutting themselves. Should I go out there then follow their example?"

Jake shook his head negatively. "No, you wouldn't be welcome there; you did not know her that well. Just do what you did yesterday, but slip around the back. Tomorrow you will be expected to attend the funeral, but that is all they will want from you. Golden Dove brought left over stew for us to eat later, so come back here after you finished for the day."

Golden Eagle nodded grimly in relief as he finished his coffee then grabbed his stuff before leaving.

****

Melissa and Jed left their room then headed down to the dining room. They entered and looked around expectantly; spotting the kids sitting in the corner, they went over.

Glad to see the doctor, Melissa smiled warmly at him in greeting. "Decided to join us did you, Doctor Andrews?"

The doctor beamed at her enticingly. "Please call me Michael."

In agreement, Melissa inclining her head before sitting. "Only if you call me Mell... have you met everyone?"

Michael nodded then motioned curiously. "Yes, I did. Do you mind if I ask why, you folks are going to Earl Summerset's?"

Not minding that question, but not telling him everything... Melissa pointed at her daughter-in-law. "Pam happens to be Raven and Edward's aunt; since she married our son, we wanted to celebrate with them."

Glad it wasn't anything dire, Michael grinned over at Pam.

Everyone sat quietly waiting for the waitress to finish their order then pour coffee. After she left, Jed cleared his throat inquisitively. "Why are you headed to Malta, Michael; if you don't mind me asking?"

Michael shook his head... it was no secret. "They have no doctor in town, so I go out there every two weeks and administer to the sick."

Jed nodded at this simple explanation then silence descended.

****

Raven slipped into her hiding place and parted the bush; she did a survey, but nothing changed since last night. Everything still seemed quiet, so the woman settled comfortably then continued her vigil.

Dejectedly, Raven sighed; it was going to be a long day.

****

Golden Eagle sighted on his target; the Englishman let go of the shaft, and watched in dismay as it flew past the target then hit a tree some distance away. He sighed miserably and gave up; he couldn't concentrate with all the wailing in the distance.

Sitting down, Golden Eagle thought of his own mother. She died giving birth to his younger sister, so he knew what it would be like for Black Hawk's son. Devon still missed her; it left a hole in his life when she died.

Unfortunately, Golden Eagle's father changed for the worst after that becoming harsh and demanding. Sometimes Devon wondered if he were wrong in his reasoning; maybe his father had always been that way, but his mother had kept him from seeing it by sheltering him.

Shaking his head grimly, Golden Eagle pushed memories of his parents away then turned his thoughts to Raven instead. Her coal black hair and dusky skin made the misty green of her eyes even more vivid... her beauty was unmistakable. Devon wished she would hurry back so he could see her again. The Englishman treasured their one night of lovemaking; even dreamed about it often.

Once Raven returned, Golden Eagle hoped that he would still feel that tingling sensation when she was around. Devon was praying hard that he did so; wanting it to be love, not just lust! The Englishman frowned thoughtfully still thinking of her; he got up then collected all his gear, and headed for the tepee.

****

Jessica rode up to the doctor; she smirked knowingly. "You are not a very good rider, are you? I see you do not wear guns, but have a rifle. Do you even know how to use it?"

Michael looked at Jessica calmly then smiled in aggravation; he answered her disdainfully. "I'm not the greatest horseman, and not too proud to admit it. I usually go by buggy, but I can still keep up if that's what you are worried about, miss. As for not wearing a gun, I'm in the business of saving lives not taking them. The rifle is for wild animals... yes, I know how to use it."

Angrily, Jessica scowled at his sarcastic tone then kicked her horse into a gallop and surged ahead.

Plaintively, Michael sighed; watching as Jessica expertly manoeuvred her horse. The doctor shook his head regretfully then wondered why the young auburn headed Jess didn't like him. Nobody else seemed hostile towards him... only her.

Thoughtfully, Michael smiled wickedly. He couldn't help thinking of the challenge Jessica would make. The doctor contemplated the possibility of getting past her hostility. Jess was a beautiful woman; an itch began unexpectedly. He wanted to see what she was hiding beneath those baggy men's clothing she was wearing... he loved challenges.

*****

Jessica slowed her horse before walking him to cool him off. Her brow puckered in puzzlement; she sighed perplexed, why did the doctor annoy her? When Michael looked at her with a frown of disapproval at her attire, it irritated her to no end. Men were not her favourite people these days, not since she called off her wedding to that cheating womanizer. Jess turned then sighed grimly as the object of her displeasure rode up.

Michael smiled smugly before pointing behind them. "Mell said to let you know we are stopping for lunch; you are to wait for everyone else."

Aggrieved, Jessica nodded testily then stopped her horse to wait for them.

Unable to help himself, Michael looked at Jessica teasingly before smirking devilishly. "You ride well, and I see that you have a rifle as well as guns. Do you know how to use that rifle? If you don't, I can teach you."

In aggravation, Jessica frowned angrily then tossed her head haughtily. "Yes, I know how to use my rifle. I wear guns, but I don't usually use them; I have other ways to protect myself."

Michael snorted in disdain, as he looked Jessica up and down suggestively. "I bet you do!"

Hiding his smirk, Michael fell silent as the others caught up.

Melissa grimaced at Jessica in confusion before shaking her head in disapproval. "You shouldn't have ridden off like that Jess, you are supposed to be protecting Pam!"

Stiffly, Jessica nodded at the rebuke. "Sorry, it won't happen again."

In forgiveness, Melissa inclined her head at the apology.

Jessica glared at Michael, for having witnessed the reproach of her beloved sister; she jerked her horse around before falling back into place, without another word to the doctor.

Pamela smiled sympathetically at Jessica, but didn't comment.

Finding the perfect spot, Melissa stopped and dismounted then a hasty lunch was eaten.

****

Raven sighed in irritation, another useless day; the young woman was about to move back when a disturbance occurred at the war chief's tepee. Howling Coyote came out then stood with his arms folded, staring off to his left. The two sentries who had caused the uproar, stood behind the war chief and waited.

Puzzled, Raven watched then tensed as she heard three horses approaching. The young woman saw one man, and two packhorses loaded with goods ride up to Howling Coyote. The white man dismounted on the far side before a heated debate occurred, but strain as she might she couldn't see who it was.

Thoughtfully, Raven eyed the vi'hoi horse's... they looked familiar. The young woman stared at the white man, when he stepped in front of his horse; she sucked in a shocked breath when he turned, giving her a better look at him. She knew that man... it was Charles, her neighbour.

What was Charles doing here, anyway; he hated Indians with a passion! Raven's neighbour raised his voice angrily, enough for the woman to hear him this time. "I'm telling you the white man wasn't there... you were not supposed to kill him. That Englishman wouldn't know the difference between one Indian and the next!"

Howling Coyote spoke again, but too low for Raven to hear. Charles scowled grimly; he answered loudly frustrated. "I couldn't get them to do anything. It seems the sheriff talked the townspeople into waiting until Raven returned. Damn it since it didn't work, I want you to attack the ranch and Raven's grandfather. I brought you more rifles; I want them off that property now... I need that gold!"

Raven inhaled in disbelief; she watched the war chief shake his head no. Not needing to hear more, the woman knew Howling Coyote didn't have enough men to attack her ranch... or the wolf tribe. She slipped out of her hiding place then past the sentries before rushing to camp.

In warning, Raven made a lot of noise so Janet wouldn't shoot her before rushing up to her. The younger woman whispered urgently before beckoning the Englishwoman to hurry. "Get on your horse quickly; we have to leave now!"

Janet nodded fearfully before doing as she got told without asking any questions. Afraid her nightmares were coming true, and the war chief was coming after them.

****

Golden Eagle whistled to his stallion then smiled in delight, when the horse obediently came over to him. Devon led him to the fence and climbed up before laying on Devil's back; confident now, after yesterday's playing around. When the stud didn't fuss, the Englishman turned so he was facing front then grabbed his horse's mane and sat up.

Softly, Golden Eagle whistled his command to walk but didn't direct the horse; wanting the stud to become familiar with him on his back without any pressure at first.

Devil pranced a bit, but calmed after a few minutes.

Golden Eagle smiled in pleasure as they walked around the pen then he whistled for a trot, and finally a canter before asking for a walk again. Devon dismounted then played with his horse; he laid down to see if his horse would lay with him again. When he did, the Englishman put his head on Devil's neck. Promptly he fell asleep, but not for long this time.

Turning over, Golden Eagle straddled Devil after giving him a good scratch; he urged his horse to get up with him clinging to his neck. Devon put him through his paces before jumping off, and headed towards the tepee. The Englishman was starving.

****

Melissa looked over at her husband in aggravation then frowned in disapproval. "Jessica is acting weird; I have never seen her so distracted."

Jed smiled knowingly before winking suggestively. "I think it has something to do with a good-looking doctor."

Sadly, Melissa sighed; at least she wasn't moping about that no-good cheat, she almost married. "You could be right. I think we should stop?"

In agreement, Jed inclined his head before pointing to the left. "Over there looks like a good spot, and it's not far."

Gazing in that direction, Melissa nodded in agreement and called to her daughter. "Pat, go scout out those trees off to your left; if it is okay we will camp there tonight."

Patricia nodded then whistled to her dog... they raced off. The others followed, waiting for Pat's signal that it was all clear.

Relieved, Jed sighed when his daughter beckoned them to come. They all dismounted before setting up camp.

****

Raven pushed their horses hard, but slowed as dusk descended; she walked the horses for half an hour, to cool them down. There was only half a moon tonight, so not bright enough to see to keep riding. The younger woman turned to the right, and left the main trail before dismounting in a grove of trees.

Janet not saying anything, helped Raven set up camp. When supper was cooking, the Englishwoman sat across the fire from Raven then eyed her curiously. "Well, what happened?"

Heatedly, Raven frowned before waving furiously. "It seems that my neighbour; was the one who arranged the attack on you and your brother."

Thoughtfully, Janet frowned... thinking back. Finally, she nodded angrily. "Yes, I remember now. I was still dazed, so thought I was seeing things when a white man came into our camp two days after the attack; what did you hear?"

Grimacing, Raven told her everything she had heard.

Anxiously, Janet shook her head furiously. "Are you sure they won't attack the ranch or your people?"

Thoughtfully, Raven grimaced before nodding decisively; the war chief wouldn't be that stupid... would he? She finally shook her head confidently. "They can't, without the rest of their tribe they don't have enough warriors for an assault. Plus, my ranch is too close to the town for Howling Coyote to take the chance that the army would show up. Even though the war chief used the white man to get back at me, he knows I'm too powerful for him to fight openly. I have too many chiefs on my side, so he will not risk challenging me openly. As for Charles, he has been after me to either marry him or sell out to him since my parents died. I have walked those hills around my grandfather's all my life, and I have never seen any hint of gold anywhere."

Janet frowned in thought. "Could it be at my brother's place instead, that's why they took me as a hostage?"

Raven started to shake her head negatively, but stopped suddenly and scowled grimly. "Not on Devon's land, but up against it there might be a place that borders both properties... it could have gold. I suppose he would need both places in that case, but since your brother was selling the land; Charles didn't feel threatened by him. I imagine they took you as insurance that he would sell the place cheap, in exchange for your life."

Distastefully, Janet nodded all too familiar with greedy men. "He probably figures if the gold is on the border of both places, it's likely that some could be on ours, or it might be a cave; it could run between both places."

In agreement, Raven inclined her head then dished up supper. "Eat, it's still four days back to my people; we will be riding hard only stopping when we have no choice. We must hurry in case I'm wrong, and Howling Coyote decides to attack. Starting tomorrow, we will start your lessons again."

Nodding, Janet ate quietly lost in thought.

****

Golden Eagle sat across the fire from Jake then smiled his thanks as he handed him a bowl of stew. They ate before sitting back to enjoy coffee.

Worried, Golden Eagle sighed grimly. "Did you find out whether the baby lived or not?"

Jake nodded relieved. "He lives, but he's tiny. He'll make it though; one of their women agreed to feed him."

Thankfully, Golden Eagle sighed; he waved vaguely around. "Well, that's good news. Did you go see your men today?"

Jake inclined his head that he had before waving. "So far everything's quiet, no sign of Raven yet. How's the training going with your horse?"

Golden Eagle smiled in delight at the thought of Devil. "Good, I was up on him yesterday and today. I walked, trotted then cantered him around the paddock with me on him, but I didn't try to guide him yet. I will work with him more tomorrow before the funeral."

Jake nodded in approval. "Good."

Banking the fire, Jake waved. "Goodnight."

Going to bed, Golden Eagle's last thought was for Raven to hurry home.

****

Jessica sighed and strolled towards the small lake, trying to figure out what it was about the doctor that made her so uncomfortable; unsure of herself. Paul never made her feel that way. She reached the edge of the lake then looked down at the inviting water. Jess looked around, not seeing anyone decided to take a swim.

Slowly, Jessica removed her hat letting her wavy fiery red hair cascade down her back to just above her hips. She took off the oversized men's vest then removed her boots, and pants before standing straight. Jess looked at herself contemplatively. What was wrong with her that men found unappealing, Paul said she was too ridged, with too many morals.

In aggravation, Jessica continued her inspection... she wasn't skinny, but not fat either. Her backside was more prominent than she liked, but her hips and waist were just right. Jess's breasts were small, but she was sure they would fit nicely in any man's hand. They were pretty perky, thrusting up invitingly; with a touch of a rosy colour in the centre.

Looking down further in approval, Jessica's liked her long shapely legs. Jess also had nice firm muscles in the calves, but they were not overly muscled. Her feet were bigger than she would have wished for, but the fourth toe curled to the side which made them look cute.

Jessica sighed and walked into the water. She ducked under the surface then swam under the water for a few minutes before surfacing. Jess went around the trees that were on the edge of the lake, and stopped in surprise. She treaded water as she watched the man of her thoughts earlier, he stood on the beach gloriously naked.

Michael's hair was dark brown with a slight curl at the ends. It was pretty long, brushing the top of his shoulders. His neck was muscled, but not too thick. Doctor Andrews' shoulders were broad which tapered down to a muscled chest, with surprisingly large arm muscles for a doctor. There was a light dusting of hair in the middle of his chest, but that was it. His waist was narrow which emphasized his nicely rounded firm buttocks. The doctor's legs were long and muscled. It was the sight of the appendix at the juncture of his thighs, which had Jess squirming in embarrassment, as it jutted up from the foundation of brown curls.

Sucking in a shocked breath, Jessica's eyes widened when the doctor's shaft started to grow. She jerked her eyes up, and saw a knowing smile cross Michael's face; he watched her blush grow, until her face was the same shade as her hair. Jess spun then swam towards her clothes.

Gracefully, Michael dove into the water; with powerful strokes he caught Jessica as she was leaving the water. Doctor Andrews ran behind her before turning Jess around then he was kissing her hungerly.

Instantly, Jessica grabbed onto the doctor's broad shoulders to hold herself up; when her legs buckled, from the sheer pleasure.

Easing Jessica down onto the soft sand, Michael followed her. The doctor lay on top of her before pushing his knees between her legs, so Jess would open them wider to accommodate him.

In denial, Jessica groaned in passion when Michael left her lips and captured one of her breasts in his mouth; suckling gently, but urgently.

Propping himself up, Michael brought his hand down between their bodies so he could touch Jessica's most intimate secrets.

In shock, Jessica cried out in delight when the doctor stroked her bud then arched her hips up for more.

Michael moved to Jessica's other breast, and gently lapped at it as his fingers pressed her bud harder. His mouth left her chest then went down Jess's belly nibbling all the way, slowly moving towards his goal. Doctor Andrews pushed her legs up and dipped his head to taste her nectar.

Jessica arched up before crying out, in surprised pleasure then felt a pressure building inside her. It was almost painful, but at the same time... it felt pleasurable. Unable to keep it at bay, Jess let go; she saw stars as she cried out her intense gratification.

Instantly, Michael scooted up before kissing Jessica then probed; until his engorged manhood found her moist opening. The doctor lifted his head and looked at Jess, with desire. "I want you, but only if you want me too!"

In denial, Jessica shook her head before pushing weakly against the doctor's shoulders half-heartedly... trying to get away.

Closely, Michael watched Jessica then waited until she looked up before pleading desperately. "I need you!"

Shocked by that, Jessica met Michael's gaze; she gloried in the blaze of passion she saw in the doctor's light golden-brown eyes. She had never seen that look in Paul's, in all the times he tried to seduce her. Unable to resist the desire any longer, Jess nodded in agreement.

Relieved, Michael sighed; he pushed his manhood deeper inside Jessica. The doctor held himself still, so that her body would adjust to his intrusion.

Once Michael felt her relax, he entered her more; until he felt the narrowing of her vagina that he had known would be there. When a woman was sexually active, this would be open and accessible... not so tight.

Holding himself in check, Michael's intense gaze kept Jessica prisoner for a long moment until the doctor dropped his head then kissed her tenderly.

Relaxing, Jessica's body lost its tension at the tender kiss then she arched her hips; just as Michael entered her fully. Jess whimpered in pain, and pushed against him trying to get away.

Quickly, Michael held still then brought his mouth down to Jessica's ear and whispered soothingly. "There will be no more pain, trust me!"

Hesitantly, Jessica nodded then felt Michael move his hips. When there was no pain, just pleasure... Jess groaned arching against him.

Relieved, Michael felt Jessica's response; he thrust into her fully. When Jess moaned in surprise and peaked, the doctor lost control then captured her lips again in a demanding kiss... his hips slammed into her repeatedly.

Gasping in pleasure, Jessica wrapped her legs around Michael as he drove into her. Feeling the pressure building inside her, Jess didn't fight it this time as she soared among the stars.

Michael, feeling Jessica's release let his control evaporate as he spilled his seed inside her. The doctor dropped on top of her, and tried to get his breathing to normal. He had slept with a few women, but Doctor Andrews never felt this level of satisfaction before or this sense of well-being.

Anxiously, Michael lifted up then looked at Jessica. The doctor had gone further than he had planned, right now. She was looking so vulnerable. Jess had her eyes closed and her head tilted away from him, as if trying to hide.

Grimly, Michael sighed; hoping that Jessica didn't regret this before rolling off her then gathered her close. He stroked her hair in contentment. Doctor Andrews frowned uneasily. "I'm sorry, I never meant to go so far."

Tensing in Michael's arms, Jessica sat up.

Sitting up, Michael moved so that he would be facing Jess.

Saying nothing, Jessica looked away from the doctor.

Finally, Michael put his finger beneath Jessica's chin then turned her head... so Jess was looking at him. Doctor Andrews saw her lips tremble; he grimaced uneasily. "Are you okay? I didn't hurt you too badly, did I?"

In denial, Jessica shook her head emphatically.

Confused, Michael's scowl eased. "What's the matter then?"

Forlornly, Jessica sighed and shrugged dismissively. "You must think me pretty clumsy, if you regret taking it this far."

Shocked by that, Michael looked at Jessica in disbelief then roared with laughter. When Jess frowned at him, he laughed harder... Doctor Andrews couldn't help it. He got himself under control before wiping the tears away. "I didn't mean it like that. I hadn't wanted it to go this far yet! I wanted to woo you first, for us to get to know each other. You weren't inept; I have never felt such intense pleasure in my life. Nor have I ever lost control like this, or had a woman make me want her so much."

Jessica frowned in relief. "You are not sorry or disappointed?"

Michael shook his head negatively. "No, I'm not sorry; I thought you might be though because it happened so fast, plus you were a virgin. I figured you would be upset with me."

Confused, Jessica shrugged. "I'm not sure yet how I feel; like you said it happened so fast."

Knowingly, Michael nodded. "Fair enough, how about a swim."

Nodding, Jessica followed the doctor into the water. When it reached the inside of her thighs; the water stung, but the discomfort soon faded.

They played in the lake for a bit before Michael took her hand leading Jess into shallower water. Doctor Andrews proceeded to make love to her one more time, but this time slowly.

*****

Melissa paced back and forth, mumbling under her breath furiously.

Jed reached over then took Mell's hand in comfort before standing trying to appease his wife. "It was bound to happen."

Stopping his sentence, Jed stepped back when his wife rounded on him.

Angrily, Melissa drew in a fierce breath. "Later would have been preferable, when they were married or better yet with someone closer!"

Knowingly, Jed sighed then nodded grimly. "Oh, so that's the real problem... is it? Love doesn't always choose someone close to home. You knew that eventually Jess was bound to find someone to love, and not necessarily close. You must let her find her own way. Paul was a disaster; he hurt her badly."

In sorrow, Melissa bit her lip then turned away dejectedly. "I waited my whole life to have a sister; now she will probably move far away, and I will not see her again."

Frowning, Jed shook his head sadly. "You know that Jessica is more of a daughter than your sister! It's your daughter you are upset about losing. If it were Pat moving that far, you would feel the same way."

Unhappily, Melissa frowned before turning. "I suppose you're right."

Michael and a giggling Jessica chose that moment to come into the firelight. They stopped short at the angry glare they received from Mell.

Melissa folded her arms across her chest grimly then stared daggers at the two of them. "Where have you two been?"

Jessica eyed her sister uneasily, and knew that she was already aware of what had happened. Jess straightened before stepping forward furious now herself. Melissa was always trying to be her mother, instead of her sister. "We were down at the lake swimming, if it's any of your business... you are not my mother!"

Instantly regretting that outburst of defiance, when Jessica read the pained look that flashing across her sister's face; unfortunately, it was too late to take back her words.

In despair, Melissa turned away before marching off.

Grimly, Jessica sighed in regret then turned to Michael. "I better go talk to her, stay here!"

Worried, Michael nodded and watched Jessica hurry away.

Jed drew himself up to his full height then waited.

Uneasily, Michael tensed when his prospective brother-in-law towered over him.

Smiling reassuringly, Jed waved at the fire. "Relax; I'm not as upset about this as my wife is, so how about a strong cup of coffee? No better yet, a shot of whisky will calm our nerves."

Relieved, Michael sighed and relaxed as the two men headed to the fire; it was going to be a long night.

*****

Remorsefully, Jessica hurried after Melissa. She found her sister sitting on a stump at the edge of camp. She hesitantly advanced then perched on the other end. Jess sighed and motioned in apology. "I'm sorry; I should never have said what I did. You have always been a mother to me, it caught me off guard that you knew before I had a chance to talk to you."

Sighing, Melissa shook her head grimly. "You don't need to apologize, you are right; I am not your mother."

Curiously, Jessica frowned. "How did you find out?"

Melissa grimaced in anger. "Jed and I went to the lake."

Dejectedly, Jessica sighed then turned to Melissa imploringly. "Oh, Mell; it happened so fast, and I'm so confused. Do you think you could be my sister, instead of my mother this once?"

Fighting a sob, Jessica felt Melissa engulf her in her arms; Jess let her confusion take control as she sobbed.

Once Melissa's sister stopped crying, Mell let Jess go before picking up her hand and gave it a tug. "Come, let's go for a walk while we talk."

Relieved, Jessica nodded; the two women walked and talked for an hour. Melissa had to struggle with herself at first... the motherly instinct in her was strong. Eventually, she did manage to let go of it then they chatted like sisters for the first time. Both exhausted mentally. They went to bed sharing a relationship that they had needed and found at last.

CHAPTER TWENTY-FOUR

Golden Eagle woke then sat up; he listened intently. He heard only occasional outbursts of grief, but it was more subdued... less frantic. He sighed in relief, and got up then built the ember up into a good fire before putting tea and coffee on.

Silently, Golden Eagle poured Jake a coffee when he joined him by the fire. Devon just finished pouring a tea, when he heard a scratching on the tepee flap.

With a clutter, Golden Eagle put his cup down then jumped up to open the door; hoping to see Golden Dove or Black Hawk.

An old Indian woman thrust two bowls of porridge at Golden Eagle before leaving... without speaking. Devon sighed disappointed then carried the oatmeal to the fire; he handed one to Jake. They ate then sipped their drinks reflectively.

Thoughtfully, Jake sighed before giving Golden Eagle warning. "There will be a feast tonight, after the funeral to honour the dead; it's more a celebration of life."

Draining his tea, Golden Eagle inclined his head before getting up. "I will see you at the funeral tonight then."

Gesturing at Golden Eagle's clothes, Jake cautioned. "Make sure you dress in your ceremonial clothing, if you have any."

Nodding, Golden Eagle turned to leave. "Yes, I do... see you."

****

Melissa woke then stretched and reached over for Jed, but remembered he was on sentry duty. She sighed before thinking about last night, and her new relationship with Jessica... she smiled in relief. They had chatted then giggled like sisters; Jess in all likelihood would marry the doctor then move here, but they could visit once the railroad made it this far.

Getting up, Melissa went to the lake to wash her face then hurried over to the fire. Mell grinned at Rose hopefully. "Is coffee ready yet?"

Rose handed Melissa a cup before pointing behind her. "Jed just left to wash up and shave, said he would be back soon."

Nodding, Melissa poured coffee into her cup then sat back.

Michael strolled into view; he halted when he saw Mell. The doctor, continued on. Nobody liked a coward he couldn't help thinking.

Hiding her smile behind her cup, Melissa ignored the doctor.

Jed was followed by Jess; next Pat arrived with her dog.

Daniel and Pamela came last.

Quickly, Michael jumped up then hurried to Pam needing to get away from Melissa's disapproving stare. "How are you feeling this morning? Did your fever return or any more pain?"

Pamela smiled reassuringly before shaking her head negatively. "No, I'm fine. Just stiff from riding that's all."

Relieved, Michael nodded and went back to his coffee.

They all sat around waiting for breakfast, when everything was finished, they all helped themselves. After eating, the group quickly broke camp then continued on their way.

****

Golden Eagle eyed the target and smiled proudly. Three arrows were on the edge of the bull's eye; he was getting better. Devon took three more out before putting them in front of him; he wanted to try firing rapidly. The Englishman took out a fourth arrow, and shot it then grabbed another... shooting it too. He seized the third arrow waiting for him, quickly.

Just as Golden Eagle pulled the bow string back, he heard a rustling to his left. He turned, he spotted a buck watching him curiously. he never even hesitated; Devon lined up then let the arrow go. He watched in fascination as the tip entered the deer behind his front leg, in-between the ribs... embedding deep.

The buck made one more gigantic leap then fell dead.

In amazement, Golden Eagle whooped in delight before running over; he took out his hunting knife to slit its throat. Devon chanted the Cheyenne thank you, to the Great Spirit then to the buck's spirit. The Englishman had only learned this song recently. He wasn't sure he even got it right, but he continued doggedly.

Golden Eagle cut open the buck's stomach then pulled out the insides, being careful not to break open the stomach or the intestines; not wanting to taint the meat. Devon got everything out without damaging anything, and he grinned in relief before cutting the liver and heart away from the intestines. Remembering Running Wolf's instructions, the Englishman sliced the liver in half. One-half he cut again... still chanting, he buried two pieces.

Grimacing in distaste, wondering if he could do it; Golden Eagle took a bite of the last piece then almost gagged at the warm salty metallic taste. Blood ran down his chin, but Devon managed to eat it all.

Carefully, Golden Eagle put everything that Running Wolf had told him they used back into the cavity of the deer. Devon sat back, and sighed in pleasure at making his first kill; unexpectedly, he frowned thoughtfully wondering how to get the deer back to his tepee. The Englishman thought for a minute before untying the rawhide rope from around his waist; he would tie it around the antlers and drag it back.

Dejectedly, Golden Eagle sat back again then sighed grimly. That wouldn't work at all; if he dragged it the hide wouldn't be any good afterwards. Devon grimaced reluctantly, but knew he had no choice... it needed to be carried. The Englishman tied the rawhide rope around the buck's stomach, to keep everything inside until he could get it back to camp. He knelt and hoisted the deer up onto his shoulder then cringed in discomfort as blood dripped down his neck before slithering under his shirt.

Resignedly, Golden Eagle shrugged and stood up; trying hard to ignore the warm blood, now coating his chest. The deer was heavier than it looked, and the white man's legs almost buckled from underneath him. Hoisting it in a better position in determination, Devon trudged back to camp knowing it wasn't far. The Englishman was practically ready to fall over from exhaustion, when he stepped out of the trees then walked into the centre of the village.

Four Indian women, and two braves rushed to him. The men lifted the deer; they grunted in exertion, as they lifted the carcass clear of the white man's shoulder. The warriors looked at Golden Eagle with new respect, at having carried the deer all the way on his own.

One of the women stepped forward. "We will use the deer for the feast tonight, if you have no objections."

Golden Eagle bowed in pleasure. "I would be honoured."

One of the women inclined her head solemnly then asked curiously. "The hide, do you want it when we finish with it?"

Thoughtfully, Golden Eagle pointed towards the chief's tepee. "Please give it to Golden Dove as a thank you gift, for teaching me your language and customs."

The woman nodded in approval then turned and disappeared.

Relieved, Golden Eagle hurried to the tepee before entering.

Jake was pouring coffee for himself; the foreman looked up in surprise before arching his eyebrows in shock, at the blood all over the Englishman. "What happened to you?"

Exhausted, Golden Eagle fell down and sighed. Devon explained what had happened then accepted the coffee.

In respect, Jake smiled when the Englishman finished and chuckled before holding out his hand for a shake. "Well, congratulations on your first kill."

Gratefully, Golden Eagle shook the offered hand. "Thank you! I came to change before I went out to work with my horse."

Chuckling, Jake shook his head negatively. "Don't change yet, go out as you are. Your horse needs to learn to work with the smell of fresh blood; this will be good for him to learn."

Grimacing, Golden Eagle nodded unhappily not looking forward to staying dressed in these clothes; he drained his coffee cup and got up to go. "Good idea, see you later."

In approval, Jake waved before smiling after the retreating Englishman. Yes, Devon showed considerable resolve at carrying a buck around. He was sure now, that Golden Eagle would be the right partner for Raven.

It just so happened, that Jake liked him; the foreman knew if the old earl were alive, he would highly approve of Golden Eagle. Raven's hired man banked the fire then left to check on his men.

****

Melissa slowed her horse and let the doctor catch up.

Michael tensed when he got closer to Mell. He knew this would happen eventually, but he hoped it would be later.

Decisively, Melissa looked at the doctor out of the corner of her eye. "You are going to marry her, of course!"

Michael stiffened uneasily then gestured in appeasement. "If that is what Jessica wants?"

Melissa looked at the doctor for the first time since this morning, with a hard glare. "And is it not what... you want?"

Frowning, Michael cringed at Mell's menacing voice but answered evenly not backing down. "We need some time to get to know one another before we make that decision."

Leaning forward, Melissa's scowl was dangerous. "Are you telling me you are willing to bed my sister, but not marry her?"

Swiftly, Michael shook his head then held up his hand apologetically. "No, that is not what I'm saying. I said if Jessica wants to get married, I will gladly marry her; but I will not force her into marriage, if she doesn't want it!"

In anger, Melissa frown deepened grimly before waving in angry demand. "What if she's pregnant?"

Relieved, Michael sighed now on firmer ground being a doctor and all. "It isn't likely Jessica got pregnant from a first encounter. Although, it does occasionally happen; if she is, I will come up with something."

Decisively, Melissa nodded before gesturing at him in warning. "So, there will not be a repeat of last night then?"

In apology, Michael shrugged grimly... still not backing down. "I can't promise you that; it's up to Jess."

Furiously, Melissa grimaced.

Calmly, Michael held up his hand to forestall Melissa from interrupting him. "All I can promise, is that we will not make love again until after we have discussed the possibility of a child first. That is all I can assure you of at this time."

In warning, Melissa stared intently at Michael before pointing at him threateningly. "If Jessica becomes pregnant, I promise that you will marry her whether either of you likes it or not. My father will be down here in no time with a rifle if you don't; believe me... you won't like the results. If you think my husband is big, wait until you meet my dad!"

With that threat hovering in the air, Melissa kicked her horse ahead then caught up with Jed.

Jed looked over at his wife, and saw the angry frown on Melissa's face then sighed forlornly; obviously, Michael hadn't appeased Mell's rage... only made it worse.

Grimacing, Jed looked up at the sky then looked around for a campsite for lunch. Grey Wolf finally beckoned Patricia forward, when nothing seemed promising. "Please go find us a camp, it's going to rain soon; I would like to eat before then."

Patricia nodded and whistled for her dog then galloped off.

Melissa looked up at the sky before grimacing uneasily. "Last time it rained we almost lost two of our party."

Jed smiled reassuringly. "At least we don't have to cross any water this time."

Relieved by that, Melissa inclined her head without speaking; they urged their horses into a trot when Pat waved that it was safe for them to come.

****

Golden Eagle whistled in demand a second time at his stud; Devil hadn't liked the smell of the fresh blood right from the first, and was still showed his displeasure.

Annoyed, Golden Eagle had gone over to Giant Bear's to get some equipment so he could saddle his horse. The Englishman knew, he wouldn't get anything done with his horse at this rate.

Devil frisked before finally obeying the whistle; with a loud snort of unease, he walked up to his master.

Relentlessly, Golden Eagle put Devil through his paces spending over two hours with him; satisfied, the Englishman stopped his horse then jumped down and gave him a good rub down in appreciation.

Once done, Golden Eagle headed back to Raven's to drop off the horse equipment, then grabbed his ceremonial buckskins. Devon left the tepee before heading to the creek for a bath.

****

Raven and Janet put on their parkas before mounting their horses, it wasn't raining yet but it would soon. The younger woman waved the Englishwoman up beside her. "While we are riding, I will give you some Cheyenne language lessons then tell you some of our histories to pass the time."

Janet inclined her head eagerly, bored by herself. "I would like that."

Pleased, Raven nodded before continuing Janet's training.

****

Melissa and the others pulled their parka's on then mounted before leaving camp. They only rode for about half an hour when the skies opened up; within minutes... they were soaked to the skin. Mell sighed grimly. "I suppose we will have to stop early."

Jed nodded thoughtfully. "Probably before dusk, I would imagine. Tomorrow we will ride hard, no stopping for lunch so we should reach Malta around supper time if all goes well."

In agreement, Melissa inclined her head. "Sounds okay to me, but I would like to go as far as we can today."

Nodding, Jed smiled knowingly as they urged their horses on.

****

Golden Eagle walked back to his tepee and sighed when it started to rain. He ducked inside then smiled dejectedly at Jake. "It's raining out, not a good night for a funeral."

Inquisitively, Jake nodded as he eyed Golden Eagle's buckskins in surprise. "Where did you get those?"

In delight, Golden Eagle looked down. "Raven gave them to me; she said if I have to marry her, at least I could do so in decent clothing instead of the rags I was wearing at the time."

Chuckling, Jake smiled in appreciation. "Well, they certainly fit you good; almost as if she had made them for you. The eagle on the front also suits your new name."

Nodding, Golden Eagle smirked devilishly; remembering Raven's reaction to his Cheyenne name. "I know, she was furious when I wore them to my adoption then was named Golden Eagle."

Shaking his head, Jake grinned at the image of Raven mad. "I can imagine; I have seen her like that plenty of times, let's go."

Golden Eagle nodded before following Jake out.

****

Raven sighed plaintively, she was soaked and the horses also. The younger woman chuckled softly to herself, as she looked over at Janet fugitively; the Englishwoman looked like a drowned rat. They had quit talking about an hour ago, too wet and miserable to continue.

Enticingly, Raven motioned at the unhappy looking Janet. "We will stop early; tomorrow, we will have to skip lunch to make up time."

Janet nodded wearily without argument; she followed the younger woman into the trees, thankfully.

Quickly, Raven showed Janet how to build a shelter of tree limbs with a layer of twigs. After eating, they curled up under the cover to sleep.

****

Jed nodded to the right. "We will camp over there."

Everyone sighed in relief thoroughly wet right through.

Daniel, Jed, and Michael made a hasty shelter; large enough for everyone to crawl under for some protection. After eating jerky and cakes, they fell into their blankets then slept.

****

Golden Eagle stood, watching as the fire burned down on Gentle Does pier. It had been a magnificent display of skill, by the shaman and medicine man as they danced asking the Great Spirit to receive Gentle Doe's spirit.

Curiously, Golden Eagle looked at the things on the pier that were burning with Gentle Doe; this was done to help her with her journey. Some items surprised him like food, flint, and a knife. He would have to ask Golden Dove later what the meaning of those items was.

Black Hawk, Running Wolf, Giant Bear, and Golden Dove all stood in front of the crowd.

Watching, Golden Eagle saw them cut off their braids as they chanted; Giant Bear and Mary, cut theirs to their shoulders. Black Hawk then his son cut theirs above their shoulders, that would be the last show of mourning for Gentle Doe. They threw them on the pier, with a whoosh the braids vanished.

Giant Bear and Black Hawk took the lead, everyone followed as they headed to the tepee that was used for special occasions; they had used it for his adoption. It was the main building in the village, and could seat up to a thousand people. Raven built it in the style of a tepee, with hides covering it. It was a permanent structure, being too large to move.

Golden Eagle made his way over to Black Hawk then sat beside him. He shook his head, to remove some water before slicking his wet hair back.

Black Hawk was staring off into space in sorrow. He was not paying attention to anybody or the fact that he was soaking wet, with little rivulets of red dripping down his body.

Fugitively, Golden Eagle looked over before grimacing in sympathy; Black Hawk was only wearing a loincloth, since his whole body was full of cuts... some were still bleeding.

A woman walked over with a bundle in her arms then tried to give it to Black Hawk, but he turned away.

Lifting his arms, Golden Eagle smiled. "I'll take him."

The woman looked at the white man intently; unsure if she should let him have the baby, but finally nodded and handed the boy to Golden Eagle. "I will return soon to feed him."

Nodding, Golden Eagle held the baby tentatively at first before easing the blanket away so he could see the boy's face. Devon peeked at Black Hawk, and saw him staring at his son with an anguished look.

Knowingly, Golden Eagle uncovered the rest of the baby before Black Hawk could look away. Devon smiled at Tommy in pleasure. "He has blonde hair like your mother's; although, it will probably go dark later. What are you going to call him?"

Reaching out, Black Hawk touched the baby's golden fuzz then his expression softened. "Little Buck."

Golden Eagle nodded in approval; he handed the baby to Raven's uncle before he could move away.

Black Hawk took his son, and cradled him in his arms; he watched as the baby opened his eyes, and regarded his father for the first time. Tommy smiled tenderly then watched puzzled wondering if his son were going to cry when the baby's face scrunched up, but he promptly farted.

Unable to help it, Golden Eagle laughed in delight at the look on Black Hawk's face. The baby, his job done closed his eyes and went to sleep.

The woman came then took Black Hawk's son, as supper was brought into the tepee and passed around. She gave Golden Eagle a grateful look, having seen him hand the baby to his father. She took him from Tommy.

In approval, Black Hawk looked at Golden Eagle inquisitively. "I heard you shot a buck today, and carried it all the way here on your shoulders. That is why I named my son, Little Buck."

Grinning, Golden Eagle nodded pleased by that then explained what happened. Black Hawk ate listening to the Englishman's story. When Devon finished, Tommy inclined his head in appreciation. "Congratulations, you are now a Cheyenne and have earned your name."

Drawing himself up, Golden Eagle smiled at his friends praise then ate. Once the food was removed, the shaman stood up and walked to the fire; he turned and beckoned to the Englishman to come to him.

In confusion, Golden Eagle looked at Black Hawk curiously. Tommy smiled in reassurance then waved for Devon to go.

Still unsure, Golden Eagle walked hesitantly to the shaman; he frowned in puzzlement, when the spiritual leader shaking his ceremonial staff... circled him chanting.

The shaman finished his dance then turned to Golden Eagle... he pointed at the crowd; he looked at the Englishman intently. "You will tell the story of your first kill as a Cheyenne."

Relieved, Golden Eagle finally understood; to the Cheyenne he was now a man, and earned his name. The Englishman remembered Raven as she told her story, so Devon not only explained the story but acted it out too. When he finished, they cheered in approval.

The shaman walked over to the Englishman then waited for silence before chanting again, and held open his hand. Inside was a tine off the tip of the deer's antler. "This is a piece of the antler, off your first kill; you will put it in your medicine bag then keep it with you always."

Golden Eagle pulled out his medicine bag, and opened it. He took the antler. With a grave expression that befitting the occasion; Devon solemnly put it in his white elk bag. The ceremony over, the Englishman walked back to Raven's uncle proudly. He sat down beside him with a smile of delight.

Black Hawk grinned in respect. "You learn quick; your dance was good for your first time. Have you been working with your horse?"

In excitement, Golden Eagle inclined his head eagerly. "Yes, I did; I have ridden him three times inside the paddock."

Motioning in warning, Black Hawk waved towards the pens. "I will be with you tomorrow."

Relieved, Golden Eagle smiled in pleasure. "Good."

Getting up, Black Hawk turned away. "See you tomorrow."

Nodding, Golden Eagle watched him go before getting up to leave. Devon entered his tepee, but Jake was already asleep. The Englishman stripped out of his formal clothes then slept.

****

Raven jerked awake, at the low intense growl her dog was making; she grabbed her gun before reaching over, and touched Bruno in question. The dog whined at his mistress, when she bent and whispered. "What is it, boy?"

Suddenly, Raven heard a loud growl coming from the trees where the female was sleeping. She tensed in fear, when she heard a vicious scream to her left. She saw a streak of grey, as the female ran towards the sound.

Urgently, Raven tried to hold onto Bruno; he broke her hold then raced after his mate. She lunged for her dog; it was too late. "Drat!"

Janet woke in confusion, when she heard screams and growls getting louder than Raven's savage curse. "What's happening?"

Instantly, Raven jumped to her feet and looked down at Janet. "Stay here, keep your rifle ready."

Raven barely waited for Janet's nod of understanding before she took off after her animals. She followed the sounds through the trees then slowed when she came to an opening; she peered out cautiously.

It was a good thing the rain had stopped, with a three-quarter moon Raven was able to see quite clearly into the clearing.

Staring, Raven grunted in amazement as she watched the two wolves fighting a cougar. What was it doing here at this time of year? Usually, about now they were higher up in the mountains having their cubs. If it were a male, he would remain close to the den to protect the female. They only came out of the hills in the winter, when hunting was scarce.

Confused, Raven watched as Bruno went behind the cat then attacked from the rear; as the female tried to get at the cat's throat. She was puzzled by the wolf's actions. Usually, wolves didn't challenge a full-grown cougar.

Lifting her rifle, Raven finally got the opportunity to shoot the animal; she knew it was too late to save the female wolf, though. As the cougar sprang on top of her before the bullet hit, and the cat fell over dead.

In trepidation, Raven trotted out of the trees; she called to Bruno, immediately concerned. "Come over here, boy."

Once Bruno was beside her, Raven walked to the cougar. When she was close, she nudged the animal with her rifle but it was dead. The young woman pushed him over, and saw the female wolf lying there with her eyes staring... dead. She sighed sadly then patted Bruno in sympathy as he nudged his mate. He sat back on his haunches, howling out his grief.

Leaving him to grieve, Raven took out her hunting knife and walked over to the cougar. Before skinning him, the young woman used her knife to check his mouth then scowled in fear. Immediately, she stabbed her knife into the soft dirt several times cleaning any saliva that might have got on it; putting her hunting knife away, she hurried to Bruno.

Grimly, Raven ran her hands through her dog's thick fur... looking for any scratches or open sores. Finally, her inspection complete she sat back then sighed in relief. The young woman checked Bruno's mouth next, to make sure he hadn't bitten through the cat's thick hide. Seeing no sign of blood on her dog, she got up and checked the animal's hind end where he had been attacking the cat, but saw no puncture wounds.

Relieved, Raven sat back then sent a silent prayer of thanks to the Great Spirit for saving her wolf-dog. If she even found any evidence that the cat had scratched or bitten Bruno, she would have had to put him down.

As it was, Raven would still have to keep an eye on her dog for a couple of weeks. The young woman sat for a moment, staring in disappointment at the beautiful cat grimly before sighing dejectedly.

Raven would have to bury both the cat and the wolf. Rabies was highly contagious, even to humans so the hide would be useless. "Come Bruno!"

The wolf-dog whined, and nudged his mate then followed Raven.

Giving warning, Raven called out to Janet as she got close to camp before walking out of the trees.

Janet sighed in relief, lowering her rifle. "What happened; what was making that screeching noise? I have never heard anything make such a hair-raising sound before."

Tiredly, Raven sighed then went to the packhorse to find something to dig a hole with. "It was a sick cougar that came out of the mountains. He killed Bruno's mate before I could shoot him."

Not expecting that, Janet sighed sadly at losing the beautiful wolf that had shadowed them all this time but refused to come closer. "Can I see the cougar? I have never seen one before?"

Finding what she needed, Raven inclined her head as she turned with her axe and a shovel that she always carried, plus two rawhide ropes. "You can help me bury them too."

Surprised, Janet frowned puzzled. "Why are you burying them, won't the scavengers eat them?"

Sighing, Raven tone was grim. "The cat has rabies."

Janet frowned before getting up to follow Raven. "Oh, that's horrible; we had a mad cow once."

Raven stopped then looked down at Bruno. "You stay here!"

Bruno whined dejectedly, but dutifully went back to the fire.

Raven started walking as she explained. "It's the same thing I think, rabies is highly contagious. Usually, the carriers are dogs, wolves, bats, raccoons, or skunks here. They pass it on by biting or passing fluid from their body to other animals. Humans can catch rabies; the result if not treated immediately is an unpleasant death."

Raven stopped at the edge of the trees then turned to Janet cautiously. "Do you have open sores or cuts on your hands?"

Janet put her hands out so Raven could examine them.

Checking them carefully, Raven didn't see anything and nodded. "They look okay. We will dig a hole under this tree big enough for both animals. I will show you what to look for in a rabid animal too."

Two hours later, Janet sighed in relief then sat down hard on the ground. Raven walked over and sat beside the Englishwoman. "That should be deep enough. We will tie the front legs then back ones together before dragging the cat over. Do not touch him if you can help it; don't whatever you do, scratch yourself on his claws or touch any place that has blood or fluid."

Uneasily, Janet frowned then took the rope Raven handed her; they both walked over to the cat. The Englishwoman stepped closer when she was called over.

Waiting for Janet to kneel; Raven squatted beside the cat's head then pointed to his muzzle. "See the foam and saliva around his jaws; this is what you would look for. When you see an animal foaming at the mouth like this, don't hesitate to shoot it. Another indication of rabies is an animal's willingness to attack anything it gets close to... take the cat for example. If he had come into our camp, he would have attacked us immediately. Usually, a cougar will not come close to humans unless it's starving, feels threatened, or has cubs close. Rabies causes animals to go crazy so never trust one with this disease, just shoot it. Okay, let's get these animals into their grave."

Frowning, Janet nodded grimly; they carefully tied the rope around the cat's legs then dragged him over to the grave and dropped him in. Then they went back for the wolf.

Not seeing any fluid, Raven grabbed the wolf's tail; Janet grasped a hind leg. They hauled her to the grave then threw her in. The younger woman frowned thoughtfully staring down at the shallow grave, not liking the fact that another animal could uncover them easily. She turned to the Englishwoman. "Go get a burning branch out of the fire, I think we should cremate them as a precaution."

Janet nodded and raced back to camp, while Raven grabbed wood plus a few armloads of underbrush then threw it on top of the animals. Smiling in thanks when the Englishwoman returned, she took the burning branch then threw it down; they watched in satisfaction as both animals burned. Once done, both women stumbled back to camp exhausted... plus, extremely filthy from soot.

Grabbing the extra canteen, Raven wash her hands and face; with no water it would have to do, before handing it to Janet. "We have an hour until dawn. Get some sleep, tomorrow we will camp early."

Nodding, Janet sighed in relief; once in bed, she fell asleep instantly.

CHAPTER TWENTY-FIVE

Raven stirred the porridge before getting up and walked into the trees. She searched then found a straight sapling that was not too thick. The young woman used her axe to cut it at the base. She headed back to camp, stripping the branches off as she walked. The young woman walked over then sat by the fire; she took out her hunting knife to peel the bark off.

Janet dished up porridge then handed a bowl to Raven.

Putting the branch down, Raven accepted the bowl. After she ate; she retrieved the limb to smooth it, so no notches were evident. She stood then turned to Janet as she motioned up. "Stand, so I can measure this."

Nodding, Janet put her bowl down. "What are you making?"

Thoughtfully, Raven put the branch against Janet and made a mark where she wanted. "I have an extra bow string with me, so I'm making you a bow."

Excited, Janet grinned widely in pleasure. "Thank you."

Curiously, Janet frowned in puzzlement then sat down again. "I heard Indian women were not allowed to handle weapons."

Shrugging, Raven frowned thoughtfully. "You are right and wrong at the same time. Earlier in our history women were not allowed, but we have become more resourceful as our people dwindle. The older women don't want to change, preferring the old ways. Many of the younger women go with their husbands when they are on the warpath. They participate, if the battle goes bad. I'm an exception; I have been training as a warrior since I was a child. I will explain while I make this bow. It's only to practice with. Later one will be made for you, if you wish."

Fascinated, Janet nodded vigorously in anticipation as she listened eagerly to Raven's life story.

After Raven finished, she watched Janet practice loading and unloading her rifle then got up with a satisfied nod at the Englishwoman's progress; she started breaking camp.

****

Golden Eagle stirred up the fire then made tea and coffee.

Jake got up with a sniff. "Hmm smells great, it is always a good omen when you wake to the smell of coffee brewing."

Nodding, Golden Eagle laughed. "It's only good when you don't have to be the one who is up to make it. I prefer tea, but it doesn't smell as good."

Jake smiled contentedly. "Well, you could be right."

Halfway to the fire, Jake stopped and changed directions at a scratch on the tepee. The foreman opened it before stepping aside. "Howdy, Golden Dove. You brought breakfast, thank you; let me help you with those bowls."

Without protest, Golden Dove handed the bowls over then walked inside; she smiled at Golden Eagle as she came towards the fire. "Good morning."

Grabbing a cup, Golden Eagle poured Raven's grandmother a tea and handed it to her after she sat down. "Morning, thanks for breakfast."

Golden Eagle accepted his bowl of porridge from Jake, with a nod of gratitude. "Thank you."

In satisfaction, Golden Dove grinned as she watched the two men eating with gusto. Both absorbed entirely in their breakfast, they did not hear the scratching on the door.

Putting down her tea, Golden Dove got up. "I will get it."

Surprised, Golden Eagle looked up and smiled sheepishly.

Lifting the flap out of the way, Golden Dove nodded in pleasure. "Good morning, Black Hawk... come on in."

Black Hawk ducked inside then kissed his mother's cheek. "Morning."

Hastily, Golden Eagle put the last spoonful in his mouth before grabbing another cup and poured Black Hawk a coffee. "Glad to see you this morning; how is the baby today?"

Half heartedly, Black Hawk grimaced with a chuckle. "Is it a good one? In answer to your question, he is letting me know who rules the tepee."

They all laughed at Black Hawk's pained expression.

Eagerly, Golden Dove stood up then grinned down teasingly. "Well, I must go; I have to finish tanning my new deer hide, and watch my new grandson while you boys get to play."

Curiously, Golden Eagle asked Golden Dove. "Do you like it?"

Nodding, Golden Dove beamed down at him in pleasure as she gestured in delight. "Of course I like it! I already know what I'm going to make out of it. First, I am going to make the baby an outfit then a small pair of moccasins before making a pair for you, Jake, and myself. I should have enough left over to make a pair for Black Hawk then for my husband."

Three eager identical nods of pleased agreement, were answer enough for her. Satisfied, Golden Dove grinned before waving goodbye.

In gratitude, Black Hawk turned to Golden Eagle after his mother was gone. "Thank you for giving the skin to my ni-go-ii. You should have seen her face when she was given the hide, and told it was from your first kill."

Pleased, Golden Eagle beamed then gestured earnestly. "It was the least I could do; she has taught me so much about your language and customs."

Standing, Black Hawk got up when Jake rose to leave. "We have to get going; if you come to the corrals Jake, we can go for a ride before supper."

Jake nodded, happy to be included. "Sounds good to me, see you."

Golden Eagle waved at Jake then banked the fire; grabbing his stuff, he followed Black Hawk out.

****

Jed walked over to Rose's blankets, and slightly moved her shoulder... not wanting to give her a fright. "Wake up Rose."

Immediately, Rose turned over with a yawn. "I'm awake."

Chuckling in disbelief, Jed smiled as her huge yawn drowned out her declaration. "Will you make breakfast please, while I wake everyone else?"

Rose rolled out of her blankets in agreement then got up.

Going to Jessica next, Jed noticed an extra body lying beside her. He shook his head in disapproval; he was glad that he had found them, instead of Melissa. Grey Wolf pushed on Jessica's shoulder, more forcefully than he usually would have.

Jessica jerked awake and looked into Jed's grim face then blushed when she realized Michael had turned in his sleep... cuddling against her. Jess turned from her brother-in-law then mumbled grumpily. "I'll wake him up!"

Grimly, Jed grunted in anger before marching off.

Dejectedly, Jessica sighed in exasperation before sitting up; she nudged the doctor impatiently.

Michael woke then smiled up at Jessica. "Good morning."

Jessica scowled before waving grimly. "You rolled over in your sleep, Jed found us together; if it had been Mell, she would have been furious."

Apologetically, Micheal grunted irritably. "I'm sorry."

Getting up in aggravation, Jessica put some space between them as she finally shrugged dismissively. "Forget it, come on I can smell breakfast."

Quickly, Michael rose and rolled his blankets up solemnly as he eyed her curiously. "Have you thought about my proposal?"

Uneasily, Jessica nodded; she wasn't sure if she wanted to accept or not. "I have, but I haven't made up my mind yet."

In annoyance, Michael motioned in bewilderment. "What's the problem; either you want to get married... or you don't!"

Confused, Jessica interrupted with a shake of her head. "It's not as simple as that. You refuse to move to Dakota with me, but you expect me to leave everything and everyone I love behind to move here with you!"

Grimly, Michael sat down and put on his boots. He sighed in defeat. "I told you I have responsibilities; I can't leave both towns with no doctor!"

In exasperation, Jessica harrumphed in anger then bent over and rolled her own bedding up. "You make it sound as if you are the only one with obligations, but I have them too. It's a big decision; I need more time!"

Exasperated, Michael got up angrily in disappointment. "Fine, we will be in town soon then we will be going our separate ways. If you come to a decision; you know where to find me."

Grabbing his bedding, Michael stalked off to his horse angrily.

Swiping at her face impatiently, Jessica watched him go then wiped her eyes so no one would notice the tears. Jess left her bedroll there before turning; she headed to the fire dejectedly.

Rose handed Jessica a bowl before pouring her a coffee.

Everyone sat quietly, trying to pretend that none of them had heard the argument between Jessica and the doctor.

Jed looked at Michael inquisitively when he arrived. "How far is Malta?"

Not really caring, Michael frowned in thought anyway then looked around. "We travelled further and faster than I usually do. I will say three or four o'clock if we hurry."

Frowning, Jed grimaced as he nodded his head. "That's what I figured; I have decided to change our plans. Melissa, Doctor Andrews, and I will go to town. Patricia, I want you to skirt it then take everyone a few miles before making camp. We will take Silver Tip, that way we can find you."

Melissa scowled then motioned curiously. "Why, the change?"

Jed shrugged before rising. "It's just a precaution, let's go."

Everyone nodded; soon not a sign was left of them.

****

Golden Eagle looked around swiftly, not seeing Running Wolf anywhere he cautiously took a step forward. Devon saw a brief flicker of movement off to his left, so he dropped into a crouch then waited. Not seeing or hearing anything; the Englishman shifted his coup stick and moved to his left, sure the warrior had gone in that direction.

Warily, Golden Eagle took another cautious step then froze. Quickly, he dropped to the ground; he rolled and brought his stick up, but wasn't fast enough as Running Wolf hit him first with his coup stick.

Satisfied, Running Wolf nodded impassively at Golden Eagle. "Better!"

Running Wolf held out his hand to help the Englishman up.

Impassively, Golden Eagle hid his smile of elation then accepted the assistance offered. Devon stood up and absently rubbed his shoulder, where the coup stick had struck him.

Unable to help it, Running Wolf smirked as he watched the Englishman rub his shoulder. "Go, no more lessons today."

Aggravated, Golden Eagle noticed the smug look in irritation then quickly dropped his hand. "It's still early yet?"

His face once more expressionless, Running Wolf shrugged. "It is, but my ni-ho-ii wants you to go see your horse early."

Eagerly, Golden Eagle nodded; remembering Black Hawk's statement about going riding. "I will just go grab my things."

Waving dismissively, Running Wolf shook his head negatively. "Go! I will put everything in your tepee."

Without arguing, Golden Eagle inclined his head before going back.

Black Hawk was waiting impatiently at Devil's paddock. Tommy let Golden Eagle catch his breath before waving for the Englishman to look at the equipment. "This is a gift from me and my mother. We started making these things for you when you first started training your horse."

Surprised, Golden Eagle stared in disbelief. The saddle blanket had eagles embroidered on both sides with his family crest below them, they even included stirrups. The saddlebags had a wolf with ravens stitched to represent his relationship with the wolf tribe and their 'protector'. The rifle cover had eagles on it... beaded. The bridle was beautiful in its simplicity. The headstall was a supple leather; the reins were two thin strips of leather braided. One was died black, giving it a unique look. Devon ran his hands over the reins and knew the braid would keep his hands from slipping, when wet.

Unable to hide his pleasure, Golden Eagle turned to Black Hawk before grinning in appreciation. "These are absolutely beautiful, thank you! I will cherish them always."

Black Hawk smiled satisfied at Golden Eagle's expression. "I'm glad you like your gift. Now get in with your stallion. I want you to ride him at a walk, trot then a canter. If you have no problems, we will go with Jake."

Golden Eagle nodded and gathered his equipment then went in.

****

Jed stopped his horse and turned to the others. "Okay, this is as far as you go. Patricia will lead you now."

Jessica moved her horse forward pleadingly. "I need a moment with Michael before we go."

Not surprised, Jed inclined his head in assent knowingly.

Immediately, Jessica turned her horse then beckoned Michael to follow. When she was sure, they were far enough Jess dismounted; she put her horse between her and prying eyes.

Michael followed Jessica's lead then dismounted expectantly.

Jess smiled hesitantly, unsure. "Can you wait for my decision?"

Grimly, Michael sighed in disappointment; he had hoped for more. The doctor stared at Jessica's pleading look before nodding. "I don't have a choice! Be careful out there. I'm not sure what is going on, but I have the feeling since I started this journey with you; that this visit is not just a social call between friends or family. Try to stay out of trouble if you can."

Unable to answer that, Jessica just smiled reassuringly; she stood on tiptoe then kissed the doctor goodbye. Michael drew Jess closer, and deepened the kiss... reluctant to let her go.

Jessica broke away then mounted; she looked at the doctor in earnest. "I promise to have an answer for you when I return."

Michael nodded grimly before mounting. The doctor looked at Jessica solemnly before letting his love for her blaze to the surface, so Jess could see it. "Just remember that I love you."

Sighing forlornly, Jessica turned away before galloping back.

When Michael rode up, everyone was gone except Melissa, and Jed.

Scowling, Michael shrugged dejectedly at Mell's look. "Jess still hasn't given me an answer, maybe you can talk to her."

Thoughtfully, Melissa shrugged undecided; she didn't think she should interfere... at least not yet.

****

Black Hawk watched in satisfaction as Golden Eagle and Devil cantered past again; he turned expectantly... hearing footsteps behind him.

Jake walked up and smiled eagerly at Black Hawk. "Well, it looks as if we will be going for that ride after all."

Inquisitively, Black Hawk nodded thoughtfully then turned back to watch Golden Eagle. "Your horse is a gelding... right?"

Smiling, Jake inclined his head reassuringly.

Thankful for that, Black Hawk grinned. "Good I will use a gelding, also. We don't want the stud to act up today."

Nodding, Jake chuckled in agreement. "My horse is ready to go; I left him saddled and tied to the other corral."

Stepping up to the fence, Black Hawk beckoned to the Englishman. "Okay, Golden Eagle you can stop over here."

Impatiently, Black Hawk waited; he waved when Golden Eagle stopped. "Give your horse a rest, while I go saddle mine."

In excitement, Golden Eagle jumped off his horse

Once Black Hawk left; Jake went over to his horse then untied him before walking back towards Devil's pen.

Golden Eagle walked his horse until he saw Black Hawk coming. Devon opened the gate and led Devil out.

Trotting up to Jake, Black Hawk stopped to wait as Devil decided to neigh a challenge to the other horses.

Pulling down sharply on the reins, Golden Eagle slapped Devil on the nose lightly. "None of that allowed!"

Devil snorted then lifted his head away, but he did settle.

Mounting, Golden Eagle walked his horse to the others.

Black Hawk chuckled in satisfaction; he turned his horse to take the lead. Devil didn't like that, so he tried to surge ahead.

Instantly, Golden Eagle pulled on the right rein until Devil's head was touching his foot. It caused the stallion to spin in circles, until he felt Devil relax then Devon released it so they could walk behind Black Hawk.

Devil tried again to take the lead, so Golden Eagle pulled the right rein in. The stud snorted in anger, when he was finally allowed to go forward.

Jake rode up beside Devon. "Doesn't like to follow, does he?"

Grinning, Golden Eagle laughed in delight. "No, why don't you drop back and follow us to see what he does?"

Intrigued, Jake nodded before slowing until Devil was far enough ahead that if he kicked; he wouldn't hit them then fell in behind the stallion.

Immediately, Devil tensed angrily and tried to stop; when that didn't work, the horse decided to back up.

In rebuke, Golden Eagle kicked Devil in the ribs hard. "No nonsense out of you... let's go!"

Irritated, Devil shook his head with a loud irate snort but he obeyed.

They rode like this for ten minutes then Jake trotted beside Devil.

Giving Golden Eagle a break, Black Hawk kept this pace for a while before kicking his horse into a trot. The stallion tried to leap forward, but his master reined him into a circle instantly.

The two men stopped to wait again patiently before starting out at a trot again when Devil settled down.

Again, Black Hawk maintained the trot for a while before kicking his horse into a canter.

Thankfully, Devil behaved this time; not once did he try to take the lead. Golden Eagle reached down then patted his stallion in praise.

Pleased, Black Hawk slowed his horse after about ten minutes before halting. He turned to the others. "We will go back now; this time I want everybody together nobody out in front."

Jake and Golden Eagle turned their horses around. They walked for a few minutes then Black Hawk nodded for the trot.

Devil promptly tried to take the lead, so Golden Eagle had to rein him into a circle. Once the stud settled down, they went back to a walk before picking up the trot again. He behaved, so Black Hawk maintained the trot for a moment before he nodded, and they picked up their pace.

They were close to the paddocks, so Black Hawk called out. "Walk."

Black Hawk smiled at Golden Eagle as they slowed. "That's it for today put your stallion away; meet me for supper at moms."

Golden Eagle smiled pleased with his horse then turned away.

****

Jed slowed to a walk before entering the outskirts of town.

Melissa undid her whip before coiling it loosely in her hand.

The first row of houses was dark, but they weren't concerned until they passed the store that was also black and empty.

Immediately, Melissa and Jed exchanged uneasy glances when they heard the murmur of people talking excitedly ahead. They rounded a corner then stopped in surprise; staring at the group of people that were shouting with displeasure at something a man standing on a wagon said.

Not liking the mood of the crowd, Jed looked around uneasily then spotted the sheriff standing on the porch in front of his office; he had a rifle cradled in his arms. Grey Wolf pointed him out to Mell. They turned to the hitching rail then dismounted.

Quickly, Melissa stepped up onto the porch before looking at Silver Tip in demand. "You stay and guard the horse's girl."

The dog obediently dropped down, watching them closely.

Shocked, Melissa stopped before taking a step as the sheriff turned to them. Mell gestured at Jed with a scowl. "I know that man, wait here!"

Frowning, Jed watched his wife go back to her horse then dig around her saddlebag for a moment; she took a packet out that Mell had brought along with her, to surprise Giant Bear and Mary.

Tuning back, Mell took the lead as she whispered to her curious husband. "I will explain later."

A bit unsure, Melissa approached the sheriff cautiously. She wasn't sure if this was what the white buffalo was supposed to tell this man, but she was almost positive. "Good afternoon, Sheriff, mind if we talk?"

The sheriff measured Melissa and Jed; the only sign of surprise at seeing a woman marshal, was one eyebrow lifting.

Smiling in surprise, the sheriff of Malta looked at Michael. "Hello Doc, didn't expect to see you out this week."

Michael shrugged dismissively then returned the sheriff's smile. "It was too quiet; since these folks were on their way here, I tagged along."

Grimly, the sheriff looked one last time at the crowd of townspeople. He sighed uneasily before turning to his guests with a pleasant nod. "Come on in folks, I have coffee on."

Melissa followed and took a chair where the sheriff indicated.

They waited as the sheriff handed coffee out then sat behind his desk, with a sigh of relief. The lawman sipped his, eyeing his visitors curiously before sitting forward. "I'm Sheriff Lane; what can I do for you folks?"

Gesturing at herself; Melissa smiled, making introductions. "I'm Marshal Brown and my husband is, Deputy Marshal Brown. We're from North Dakota, on our way to the Summerset Ranch for a visit."

Sheriff Lane sighed in worry. "I figured that; regrettably, you might be riding into what could be a fight between the town and Raven's family."

Not liking the sound of that; Melissa grimaced in uncertainty then waved gravely. "Can you tell us what's going on?"

Nodding, the sheriff sighed solemnly. "Four weeks ago, an Englishman with his two sisters got off the stagecoach then asked around for a guide to lead them to Earl Summerset's Ranch. Two brothers from town, who are friends of Raven's agreed to take them. They never came back, all traces of the five of them vanished. Some of the townspeople blamed Raven's people for killing them, and are trying to rouse the others into action. I took men out to the village; Raven was gone looking into the matter... they said. We didn't see any white people except for the chief's wife, plus some half-breeds. I managed to stop the townspeople from calling in the army, but as you can see from the crowd. I can't keep them from going themselves."

Glad she brought this packet; Melissa handed it to the sheriff to look at... she had been right. "Sheriff, I can promise you that Giant Bear didn't have anything to do with it. Nor would he allow his people to do it."

The sheriff shrugged before opening the package, inquisitively. "You were not out here, so how would you know whether he did or not?"

Melissa smiled before waving to the papers. "There are two reasons I know he wouldn't. First, as you can see from the documents; twenty-seven years ago, I deputized Giant Bear as a deputy sheriff. He was never released from that oath, because of a mistake I made he swore for as long as he lived... instead of as long as he wore the badge. I never told him; he is still under oath. The second, is that the Englishman who came here was Devon Rochester from England. It's because of Giant Bear that he is here. We got in touch with Lord Rochester for the chief, so he would come here. The chief was hoping Raven and Devon would fall in love and get married. He wouldn't do anything to jeopardize that."

Thoughtfully, the sheriff frowned. "For years I heard rumours that Giant Bear was a deputy at one time. I think it was from a friend of Raven's who told me, but I had no proof."

Having one more piece of evidence, Melissa reached into her pocket and pulled out a letter then handed it to the sheriff. "Thankfully, I brought this along. It's a letter from our present mayor's office in North Dakota, where Giant Bear was deputized. It not only confirms that he is still a deputy in the books in North Dakota, but that he was legally wed to his wife, Mary."

Quickly, the sheriff nodded as he bundled up the papers and handed them back then took the one from the mayor. "That was a good idea; I asked who the white woman was, since the agreement was no white captives were allowed to be taken. Do you need this one? If you don't, I will keep it. I need to show it to the townspeople to calm them down."

After getting Melissa's nod of agreement, he took a key out of his pocket; the sheriff unlocked a drawer before putting the letter inside, and re-locking it. He sat back up then eyed Melissa before gesturing in warning. "If you are going to help your friends... I would hurry if I were you. I can only hold the townspeople here one, maybe two more days if we are lucky."

Melissa inclined her head in thanks, and stood up then shook his hand. "I appreciate all the information, Sheriff; we will see you again soon."

The sheriff nodded and shook hands with Jed.

Turning to the doctor, Melissa inclined her head. "We will probably see you as well in a few days; take care of yourself."

Michael scowled grimly; he knew there was more to this story then what they let on, now he was worried. "You take care of Jess for me."

Nodding, Melissa smiled reassuringly before going out to her horse while Jed said goodbye. Finally, they were on their way out of town with Silver Tip leading. The dog led them to Pat without wavering in her path.

Jed and Melissa dismounted; Daniel saw to the horses while his parents ate. Mell repeated the conversation with the sheriff, in-between bites.

Finished eating first, Jed gestured impatiently. "Okay, let's pack up; if we hurry, we can reach the ranch. The sheriff told me where to find a trail that is passable by a horse. We will stay at the ranch for the night, and head out to Giant Bear's first thing in the morning."

Within minutes not even a hint of them was visible.

****

Raven slowed her horse before turning to Janet. "The horses are beat, so I want to stop early; plus, I'm disgustingly dirty."

Janet nodded forlornly. "Good, they are not the only ones."

Chuckling knowingly, Raven turned into a grove of trees to her left. She stayed here before and knew a creek was back in the trees.

Thankfully, Janet familiar with Raven's routine helped set up camp. After eating the fish, the younger woman showed the Englishwoman how to catch with her hands, they went to the creek for a bath.

Once in camp, they rolled into their sleeping furs and fell asleep instantly.

****

Golden Eagle handed Jake a coffee and yawned. "Wow, am I ever tired."

Jake chuckled at Devons enormous yawn that drowned out his words. "You look tired too. Why don't you go to bed; I'm hot, so going for a soak!"

Agreeing, Golden Eagle nodded and drained his tea.

Jake finished his coffee before leaving.

****

Jed slowed his horse wanting to cool him down; all the horses were foam-flecked. It hadn't taken them long to get through the hidden trail then into the open, so they could pick up speed... he figured it was best to slow down. He turned to Mell. "The ranch is ahead, there should be sentries."

Melissa nodded knowingly keeping a sharp lookout, it wasn't long before they saw a horse and rider approaching cautiously. Mell waved so everyone would stay back, while only the two of them rode ahead to meet him.

The man stopped in front of Melissa then smiled pleasantly in greeting. "You must be Mell and Jed Brown. Edward told me to keep a lookout for you; he said to tell you that he couldn't wait any longer. When you arrived, I was to take you to the ranch, then provide you with anything you needed."

Chuckling, Melissa smiled in delight; Dream Dancer was up to his tricks. "All we need is a bed and directions to Giant Bear's village."

The guard nodded then turned back up the trail. "My name is Eric Johnson. Please follow me."

Turning, Jed waved to the ones waiting; the rest caught up. Grey Wolf turned to Eric curiously, not asking how the young earl knew they were coming; Giant Bear had done plenty of bragging about his grandson's predictions. "When did Edward leave?"

Eric smiled apologetically. "Yesterday morning, the earl with two wagons left carrying supplies up to the village."

In frustration, Jed inclined his head in irritation; if the rain hadn't stalled them, they might have made it. Arriving at the barn they dismounted.

Melissa handed the white colt to the head stableman. "This is Raven's new stallion; we brought him along, since she will need him this year."

Steven nodded relieved; he would put the stud in with the mares in case some of them weren't bred. "The name's Steve, and you are correct we do need him... thank you! I will take care of your horses. They will be saddled and ready to go in the morning. Johnson will take you to the house then show you to your rooms. There is food waiting for you, and breakfast will be ready in the morning."

Before leaving, Melissa smiled at Steve. "Thank you."

CHAPTER TWENTY-SIX

Jake woke first, so built up the fire; it was a bit chilly in here this morning. He warmed himself and put coffee on. Leaving, he headed for Giant Bear's tepee. He looked up at the sky grimly then scratched on the door. The foreman waited before sighing in irritation, and scraped on the flap again... hoping for permission to enter. When the door was lifted, he ducked in.

Golden Dove beamed at Jake cheerfully. "Good morning."

Grimacing, Jake smiled forlornly in warning. "Morning, I'm not sure if it is good though; it looks like it might rain, and it's downright chilly out there!"

Shrugging, Golden Dove smirked without comment then dished up some breakfast for the two men.

Accepting the bowls gratefully, Jake nodded. "Thank you."

Walking over to the tepee entrance, Golden Dove held it open for the foreman. "Say good morning to Golden Eagle for me."

Inclining his head in agreement, Jake left. He immediately broke into a trot; grumbling irritably, as the wind picked up and threatened to cool off his breakfast. The foreman reached his destination then ducked inside.

Golden Eagle was pouring himself a coffee; he hadn't bothered with tea needing something stronger. Devon looked up, and smiled at Jake before pouring him one too.

Quickly, Jake handed Golden Eagle his bowl then accepted the cup of coffee in return. "Thank you; Golden Dove said to say good morning."

Nodding, Devon smiled his thanks for the message. "You're up early?"

Sighing, Jake grimaced miserably. "The wind woke me, it's getting worse."

Grimly, the Englishman scowled irritably. "That just figures!"

Dejectedly, Golden Eagle lifted his cup to take a sip of his coffee... he jumped in shock; when a booming clap of thunder sounded, right above him. Devon sloshed coffee down the front of his clean buckskins, he grimaced angrily.

In sympathy, Jake hooted when he noticed coffee dripping off Devon.

The flap opened swiftly before Black Hawk stumbled in. "This will be a good day for staying in today. I told Running Wolf not to expect you, Golden Eagle."

Wiping at the front of his shirt, the Englishman smiled delighted. "Good, I could use a day of rest. I haven't had one since my arm healed."

Black Hawk nodded in sympathy before squatting down beside the fire; he smiled his thanks at Jake, when he was handed a cup of hot coffee.

Jake sighed in disappointment. "Well, some people have all the luck. I still have to go out in this to do my rounds."

Watching the Englishman smile smugly at Jake, Black Hawk cleared his throat at an idea. "On second thought, we will ride with you. It will give Golden Eagle a change of scenery, plus... be a good test for his stallion."

Smirking, Jake watched the smug look disappear on the Englishman's face; he grinned at him in satisfaction.

Golden Eagle sighed in vexation before grinning good-naturedly. He poured them another cup of coffee, trying to forestall the inevitable; not looking forward to a soaking.

****

Raven jumped out of her blankets in fear before rushing to Janet then shook her awake... in panic. "Get up; we have to get out of here now!"

Janet sat up then stared at Raven in shocked surprise, at having been awakened so rudely. "What's wrong?"

Swiftly, Raven grabbed everything that was loose and started stuffing it in the saddlebags... even dirty dishes. "There's a lightning storm coming, we have to get across the creek now; if we are lucky, we can get to the cabin that I used on my way here before the storm hits, no more questions hurry!"

Hearing the panic in Raven's voice, Janet didn't argue; swiftly, she rolled her blankets up then saddled her mare.

As fast as possible, Raven threw the packsaddle into place before whistling for her stud.

Bruno raced to Raven, and whined in urgency then ran off before returning to his mistress; the wolf-dog barked impatiently.

Nodding grimly, Raven threw her saddle blanket on her horse. "I know Bruno; I am going as fast as I can!"

Brave Heart neighed loudly... uneasy; his nostrils flared in fear before pawing the ground nervously.

Mounting in record time, Janet beat Raven but had no time to gloat.

Raven turned one last time to the Englishwoman. "Stay as close to me as you can, and whatever you do... don't get separated from me; we are now in a race for our lives. Remember to trust your horse, if you get into difficulty she can find her way."

Janet nodded in alarm then rode up beside the packhorse that Raven tied to Brave Heart's saddle. Hopefully, she would be able to stay close to him; which in turn, would keep the Englishwoman near the younger woman.

Raven rushed them as fast as she dared go through the trees.

****

Melissa and the rest of her party all met in the hallway.

Johnson stumbled into the house as everyone was dressing. "We are in for a big storm. You might want to stay another night and leave in the morning."

Thoughtfully, Melissa and Jed looked at each other before both shook their heads... Mell was the one who spoke. "No, we need to get to Giant Bear's as."

Shrugging, Johnson nodded not arguing with them. "Okay, your horses and supplies are all waiting for you. I will accompany you to the trail that Dream Dancer took it's not the fastest way to go, but you might be able to catch up to him. Once on the trail, keep following it because it will lead you right to Giant Bear's winter camp. You will see cairns of rocks periodically, there are supplies in the ground under them... if you get into any trouble."

Jed inclined his head in thanks as they headed out.

****

Jake led them up a steep incline then whistled three times.

Instantly, a man stepped out of the shelter of trees and gestured for them to follow him. They soon found themselves in a hidden camp, so they dismounted in relief at being out of the wind. They hunkered down beside the campfire then accepted cups of hot strong bitter coffee.

Black Hawk smiled across the fire at Golden Eagle as Jake talked to the sentry. "Your stud is behaving better today; he hasn't tried to take the lead even once. This storm doesn't seem to be bothering him much either."

Golden Eagle nodded, pleased before chuckling in disagreement. "Yes, he's doing well but the storm is bothering him a bit. A couple of times I thought for sure he was going to buck... especially with that lightning flash and the thunder we had a couple miles back. His whole body twitched; I could feel his muscles bunching under me, I thought for sure I was in for it. I kept stroking his neck keeping him distracted. As long as I talked to him, he behaved."

Pleased, Black Hawk drained his coffee as Jack beckoned them to follow.

They remounted, and Jake turned east heading up higher into the hills. The foreman sighed in relief then motioned... thankfully. "No problems here, we will circle around until we come to the trail heading to Raven's ranch. We can go up that trail until we get back to the village."

Black Hawk sucked in a shocked breath at Jake's reference to Raven's ranch. He quickly looked at Golden Eagle to see his reaction. Except for a raised eyebrow at his stunned intake of breath, no surprise was evident on the Englishman's face. He gestured grimly. "You already know about the ranch?"

Golden Eagle grinned perceptively. "I have known almost as soon as I met Raven's brother, we have many portraits of the late earl when he was younger. Dream Dancer is the spitting image of his late grandfather. I also saw the ranch in a vision that Dream Dancer helped me have."

Black Hawk sighed in disgust. "I told my father you knew a lot more than you were letting on."

Grimly, Golden Eagle shrugged dismissively. "I also know it was your dad who brought me here to begin with."

Uneasily, Black Hawk eyed the Englishman intently as he waved curiously. "And this doesn't upset you?"

Shrugging, Golden Eagle frowned as he shook his head resignedly. "At first I was outraged then Dream Dancer helped me have a vision. In it, I was shown the ranch... Raven, a boy, and a newborn baby before I saw myself smiling proudly at my wife. I'm still not sure that's what I want, but I'm willing to try."

Jake called to the sentry while the two men continued talking.

Glad to have this out in the open, Black Hawk nodded then sighed sadly before gesturing resolutely. "At least you're willing, that's all anyone can ask."

****

Raven looked back then saw Janet's horse slowing; she reined in her own, until the Englishwoman was even with her. "Why are you falling behind?"

Janet sighed wearily, unsure why there was such a need for haste. The Englishwoman motioned in exhaustion. "She is too tired; I don't know how long she can keep up this pace."

Grimly, Raven searched behind them... grimacing in panic. She turned back to Janet anxiously as she pointed over her shoulder, the way they had come. "I'm sorry, but she has got to keep going there is a forest fire raging behind us! If we can get across the creek, it will keep the fire from following us further; there's not much vegetation on the other side for several miles; hopefully, it will prevent the flames from spreading to that side."

Startled, Raven looked up as she felt the first raindrops falling then scowled in relief. "This rain will help with the fire, but not much. It has been burning too long; this forest has many dead trees, and a lot of old growth to keep it fuelled. It's not much further... please try to keep up."

Shocked, Janet glanced back in surprise; not realized what was behind them. She saw the smoke before hastily turning to Raven, and nodded with a stark look of fear on her face. They kicked their horses hard, pressing on.

****

Jed stopped beside their guide before grimacing in irritation. "Is the weather like this all the time out here?"

Johnson shook his head negatively. "Not really, sometimes a storm will blow in from the Rocky Mountains, but they never last for long. I will be leaving you here, about six hours up the trail there is a camp set up for this type of emergency. I would suggest you stay there tonight; it's about halfway between the ranch and the village. This lightning and wind will only get worse before it gets better, so be careful. You don't want to lose a horse or one of your companions if lightning hits a tree that is in your path."

Grimly, Jed looked at Melissa then saw her nod agreeing.

Turning back, Jed held out his hand. "Thank you, we will take your advice."

Warmly clasping Jed's hand, the sentry tipped his hat to the women before turning and galloped away.

Jed turned back to the trail before following it grimly, keeping a close lookout for trees leaning precariously... possibly hit by lightning.

****

Jake slowed for their last stop then whistled before waiting... nothing happened. Suddenly, they heard two shots ring out and a scream of pain.

Quickly, Jake spurred his horse forward in anxiety; Black Hawk was beside him in an instant as they galloped towards the gunshots.

Golden Eagle stayed behind them, letting the skilled warriors remain in the lead; when he saw both men take out their rifles... he did as well.

Black Hawk veered right then went after someone that was racing away.

Jake swerved left after another man.

Undecided at first, Golden Eagle was about to follow Black Hawk when he noticed a horse standing alone. The animal was riderless, with a man lying beside him face down. Devon immediately went to the injured man in concern; when he got close, the Englishman jumped off his horse. He knelt beside him then gently turned him over.

Shocked, Golden Eagle sucked in a harsh breath; it wasn't a man at all, but a sandy-haired youth about seventeen or so. He immediately ran his hands over the boy looking for wounds. Devon found two, one in his left shoulder and one in his right leg. The Englishman checked the shoulder injury first then noticed that the bullet had gone through and out the back.

Quickly, Golden Eagle got up before rummaging in one of his new saddlebags; he found two clean doeskin cloths that Black Hawk had put in, they carried it for just such an emergency Devon got told. The Englishman knelt and wrapped the shoulder in a hasty bandage, to stop the bleeding.

Satisfied, Golden Eagle turned to the leg wound after. He used his knife to cut away the pants then expertly probed at the wound. The bullet was lodged in the fleshy part of his leg, and would have to be dug out... not here though. The Englishman wrapped the leg; he looked up when the two men returned, with the criminals tied to their saddles.

In trepidation, Jake grimaced in guilt and dread. "Is he okay?"

Preoccupied, Golden Eagle nodded as he tied the bandage. "Two bullet wounds, neither fatal; one will have to be dug out. He's out from shock."

Black Hawk scowled as he eyed the boy. "Is that your son, Jake?"

Uncomfortably, the foreman nodded forlornly. "His mother is going to kill me for leaving the boy alone on guard duty. I didn't think anybody would try anything here; it's the worst place to reach the village from."

Black Hawk frowned thoughtfully. "You're right, this is the wrong place for anyone trying to sneak into the village... its way too open. The camp where Raven fought that grizzly bear is not far from here; the herbs that I need are close to it. Golden Eagle, lift the boy up to his father then take the prisoner's horse so Jake can hold his son until we reach the camp."

The Englishman did as he was told; he gathered the reins of the prisoner's horse after. Golden Eagle stared up at the men who had shot the kid and glared angrily up at him. The man was staring at Devon with a horrified, stunned look on his face. "You are supposed to be dead!"

Surprised by that, Golden Eagle scowled grimly. "I don't know you; how do you know if I'm dead or not?"

The man visibly gulped as he realized he had spoken aloud.

Pensively, Black Hawk grimaced then shook his head warningly. "Later Golden Eagle, we must see to the boy first; questions will have to wait!"

Nodding, Devon grabbed the lead rope and walked to his stud.

Devil snorted then pranced as his master got closer with the mare.

In disapproval, Golden Eagle frowned at his horse ominously. "I'm not in the mood for your antics Devil, behave yourself!"

Horse and rider stared at each other intently for a bit; Devil, snorted softly as if in apology before standing quietly as Golden Eagle mounted.

Stifling a chuckle, Black Hawk watched and shared an amused look with Jake as Devil settled without a fuss. He jumped down then grabbed the reins of the kid's horse before picking up the reins of the man's horse, that he held captive then vaulted back onto his own... taking the lead.

****

Raven pointed up ahead in relief.

Janet nodded as she saw the fast-moving water ahead; it didn't look like a stream. The Englishwoman slowed to a trot, and looked behind her before frowning uneasily. The rain was coming down harder, but the forest fire still raged behind them closer than it had been. All morning, while running for their lives they saw wild animals racing in every direction... mostly in panic.

Raven turned back to the creek that should have been a trickle, but was three times its size and getting higher. The younger woman slowed to a walk. "The stream is running pretty fast, but shouldn't reach up to the horse's bellies yet. Give your mare her head then hold on to your saddle horn, and her mane. She will follow the stud with no direction from you."

Janet nodded nervously and did what she was told. The horse had a remarkably long mane, so the Englishwoman wrapped a handful around her hand twice... to be on the safe side. As Raven's stud stepped into the water, the mare obediently followed him without even a hesitation.

Urgently, Janet clung to the saddle horn with a death grip; she held her breath uneasily, as the horse cautiously walked into the middle of the stream.

The mare's, left front foot slipped out from under her... she stumbled.

Teetering, Janet managed to brace herself against the saddle horn. With the hand that was wrapped in the mane; she managed to stay in the saddle.

Thankfully, the mare righted herself and scrambled over the edge onto dry land; she stood there quivering for a long moment. Janet had to wait until she settled down before she could get her to move forward.

Unexpectedly, Raven's head jerked up in shock as she listened intently at a roaring sound in the distance. She cupped her hands around her mouth then shouted at Janet, desperate to be heard. "Get out of this gully... HURRY!"

Suiting words to action; Raven dug her heels into her stallion's sides, and bent low over his neck.

Without too much urging, Janet's mare galloped beside the packhorse.

In trepidation, Raven sucked in a shocked breath as she turned her head then saw the wall of water rushing towards them. The younger woman looked forward hastily; she saw the edge of the gully coming up fast. If they could make it up that hill, they would survive. It was as if everything was happening in slow motion. The closer they got to their goal, the quicker the water got to them... they weren't going to make it!

****

Jed pointed to his left; Melissa looked at the campsite that Johnson had recommended then nodded in approval. The wind was so strong now that the trees were bending alarmingly. The rain was coming down so hard, that they couldn't see more than two feet in front of them.

The campsite was a sanctuary, not only for themselves but also for the horses. Quickly, they tended to their animals first then went into the shelter, and saw to their own needs.

****

Thankfully, when Raven's stud started straining upwards; the slow-motion feeling stopped suddenly, and everything began speeding ahead again. The stallion gave a tremendous leap, clearing the lip of the gully.

Brave Heart came to a dead stop abruptly before sliding backwards... slowly; as the packhorse tied to the saddle, slipped at the lip. The gelding started pulling them back to the edge of the gully.

Raven grabbed her knife out of its sheath then reached over to cut the line... to save herself and her horse. Before she could, the packhorse managed to keep his feet then lunged upward to safety.

Janet and her mare reached the rim of the gully, at the same time as the packhorse. Her horse also slipped then started sliding backwards. The Englishwoman screamed in terror as the mares two front legs buckled under her, and was almost thrown from the saddle for the second time.

Immediately, Janet thanked God for the fact that her hand remained wrapped in the horse's mane. She remembered what Raven had said about trusting her mare, so she dropped the reins on her neck; letting her horse find her footing. The Englishwoman clung to her saddle horn desperately.

The mare struggled to her feet then tried to jump over the lip. After the second failed attempt, she squealed in rage and surged up. Once on flat land, the horse raced full out in terror; with a clinging Janet unable to stop her.

Neighing in demand, Brave Heart called to the mare; she slowed then turned, trotting back to him before standing against the stud quivering.

In awe, Raven sat on her horse staring down in wonder.

Bemused, Janet looked then gasped in disbelief. The tidal wave that had tried to catch them, had swept everything in its path ahead of it... trees, rocks, and animals; nothing was immune to its power. The Englishwoman shook in delayed shock then turned to Raven, in amazement. "How is that possible?"

Raven sighed in relief that they had made it in time, and turned her horse before trotting off. The younger woman looked over at Janet and shrugged dismissively, as the Englishwoman kept pace with her looking for answers. "Sometimes a rock slide will dam up a creek, which is why it gets smaller over time. Then nature takes a hand, and rain will fall so heavily in the mountains that the rocks can't contain it. Soon the water starts seeping through the rocks, until they break loose then all that water comes rushing down to fill in the stream. Normally that stream behind us is so deep you have to swim across, but about five years ago it started diminishing... now we know why."

Janet shook her head in wonder. "This is a strange land you live in; I'm not sure if I want to stay here long."

Shrugging reflectively, Raven grinned in comfort before nodding in agreement. "This land is savage and brutal at times, but it has incredible beauty too. You just have to know where to look. If you and your brother decide to stay, I will show you many wonderful things; plus, I can teach you how to survive out here... if you like."

Shyly, Janet smiled at Raven. "If I stay, I'll take you up on your offer."

In relief, Raven pointed ahead enticingly. "The cabin is over that rise. We will stay there; with any luck, the rain will stop during the night."

Reflectively, Janet beamed in pleasure to herself. She might have lost one sister, but she felt like she now had another in Raven. This sister though was not sickly! The Englishwoman felt guilt and sorrow; she sent a silent apology to her younger sister. Still, she couldn't help feeling elated at the same time.

In birth years Raven was much younger, but her experiences far exceeded Janet's; it made her feel like the younger sister now.

Instead of making Janet angry, it actually felt good; she might decide to stay here after all. The Englishwoman followed the younger woman towards the cabin, happier than she had ever been in her entire life.

****

Black Hawk held up his hand then cocked his head, and listened. He rode over to Jake then handed him the lead rope to his prisoner's horse. "There's someone ahead. If either man calls out shoot them."

Jake nodded and took his revolver out of his holster then pointed it at the man beside him.

Black Hawk looked at the Englishman before lifting an eyebrow.

Golden Eagle grimaced at Tommy, but quickly followed Jake's example; taking out his rifle, he pointed it at the other man.

Satisfied, Black Hawk jumped off his horse before disappearing.

After what seemed like an eternity to Golden Eagle, Black Hawk returned; he grinned up at Jake. "Looks like our supplies have arrived, but one of Dream Dancer's horses pulled up lame; they are camped here."

Relieved, Jake tossed the rope to Black Hawk before holstering his gun.

Sighing in relief, Golden Eagle put his rifle away. Thankful, he hadn't had to use it; not that he wouldn't have to help his friends.

They both followed Black Hawk eagerly.

Dream Dancer jumped up in shock when horses entered the clearing. Edward hadn't seen his uncle sneak into his camp. The two hands lowered their guns and grinned at Jake.

Jumping down, Golden Eagle pulled Dream Dancer into a hug.

Right behind the Englishman, Black Hawk hugged his nephew when Devon retreated. "It is good to see you boy."

Jake cleared his throat noisily. "Can one of you mind giving me a hand?"

Turning, Black Hawk grimaced in apology. "Sorry Jake; Golden Eagle take the boy, while we secure the prisoners."

Surprised, Dream Dancer looked at the prisoners behind Black Hawk speculatively then turned away. Seeing Golden Eagle gently lifting Jake's boy down, Edward motioned for his friend to accompany him. The young earl led him over to a shelter, and motioned for the Englishman to go ahead of him. "Put him in here, please! How bad is he hurt?"

Immediately, Golden Eagle ducked down. He had to kneel to go in then carefully placed the boy on the furs. Fortunately, he was able to stand once inside but not all the way. "He was shot twice; a bullet went through his shoulder and out the other side. The second bullet is in his left leg in the fleshy part, so it shouldn't be a problem taking it out. Neither of the wounds is life-threatening unless infection sets in. He hasn't come too yet, so I suspect he might have hit his head when he fell or it could be the shock."

Thankful for that information, Dream Dancer waved towards his wagon. "Under my seat is a saddlebag, bring it to me... please. Oh, put your knife in the fire to heat it as well."

Golden Eagle nodded then did as he was told.

Jake walked over and ducked under the shelter.

Dream Dancer moved so the foreman could kneel by his son's head.

Without protest, Jake watched Raven's brother administer to his son; he knew that Dream Dancer had helped the medicine man, his sister, and the doctor in town since he was a child.

With a start, Dream Dancer looked up in surprise as a light appeared beside him then saw Black Hawk grinning. Edward smiled relieved. "I forgot I had an oil lamp. I need you to put your knife in the fire too."

Turning back to his patient, Dream Dancer probed at the shoulder injury. Jake slid forward and lifted his son, so Edward had his hands free.

Distractedly, Dream Dancer nodded his thanks but didn't say anything. Edward probed at the wound in the boys back before grunting in satisfaction. The hole in his back was larger than the hole in the front, which told him that the bullet went through. The wound looked clean, but he wasn't taking any chances it would have to be disinfected; sometimes a piece of cloth or debris gets caught on the bullet and stays inside the wound... even if the shell exits.

Returning, Golden Eagle handed Edward his saddlebag.

In thanks, Dream Dancer nodded then dug into the bag and took out a bottle of whiskey. He sat it beside him before taking out a packet of leaves. Edward opened the package, and looked inside; satisfied he had the right one, he put it down beside the whiskey. He rummaged around then pulled out some bandages. The young earl grabbed a packet with a red ribbon tied around it then looked up at his uncle in warning. "Put some of this in some water to steep. Only a pinch mind you, it is quite strong and we don't want to kill him. I will need you to take Golden Eagles knife out of the fire and bring it please."

Nodding, Black Hawk took the package then left.

Turning, Dream Dancer looked at Jake in warning. "I'm going to put whiskey on his wounds to clean them, so hold him tight."

Queasily, Jake grimaced; he got in a better position after helping Dream Dancer remove his son's shirt before nodding that he was ready.

*****

Half an hour later, Jake gently lowered his son onto the blankets.

Dream Dancer sighed, grateful to have one injury done with before moving down. With the help of the two men, he pulled the boys pants off. Edward unwound the bandage then probed at the wound, and found no muscle or bone injury. The young earl sat back. He smiled at the Englishman in respect. "You are right, the wound is not serious; he should heal without a limp. How did you get to be so knowledgeable?"

Golden Eagle grinned as he remembered back. "I used to fight a lot of duels in England. My aim wasn't good, so every week I ended up at the doctor's getting a bullet out; or having stitches from being stuck with a sword. Fortunately, none of my duels was to the death just first blood."

Jake stroked his son's hair, trying to calm him since he was awake. Relieved by the news that his boy wouldn't have a limp. The foreman absently listened as Golden Eagle replied to Dream Dancer's question before grinning; he looked at the Englishman in challenge. "The Earl taught me to fence; if you want, I will be happy to poke holes in you."

Teasingly, Dream Dancer laughed in jesting. "You better watch him Golden Eagle; he is good, he even taught me."

Crowing in delight, Golden Eagle rubbed his hands together in glee then smiled challengingly. "Well, I have two foils in my trunks at the village; if you two want to try me... I will oblige both of you."

Not expecting that, Dream Dancer and Jake looked at each other incredulously then at Golden Eagle; both spoke together. "You're on!"

Black Hawk brought the tea, so Dream Dancer got down to business.

*****

It took another hour, but once done Jake lifted his son again so Dream Dancer could give the boy some tea. The young earl put furs around the boy before grabbing the whiskey bottle, and handed it to Jake. "Here, take this; I want you to go get drunk with Black Hawk."

Jake smiled sickly at Dream Dancer. "Do I look that bad?"

Dream Dancer chuckle. "Go! We will stay with him."

Jake crawled to the entrance; he left with Black Hawk.

Pleased, Dream Dancer grinned at Golden Eagle. "Jake did better than I expected him to do. But I don't want either of them to see what I was going to do next. Can you move back and block their view please?"

Golden Eagle nodded before doing what Edward asked.

Dream Dancer checked to make sure the boy was sleeping. Satisfied, he started chanting quietly before putting one hand on Kevin's injured shoulder and one on his leg wound. Edward began to rock; he could feel the heat radiating from his hands then he stopped. The young earl didn't want the boy to recover too quickly, and raise questions. He gave the boy enough to prevent any infection from developing and start the healing.

Standing, Dream Dancer had to lean on the Englishman.

Knowingly, Golden Eagle steadied him before smiling in sympathy. "Come on; let's go get some whiskey before the others drink it all."

Chuckling, Dream Dancer smirked teasingly. "I wouldn't worry about that; I have another bottle stashed away."

Knowingly, Golden Eagle laughed before leading Edward to the wagon to grab the other bottle.

They all sat in the pouring rain then got roaring drunk before staggering into the shelter and passing out.

CHAPTER TWENTY-SEVEN

Raven woke and listened intently for a bit, not hearing anything she got up then opened the door before peering out. It was still drizzling, but she could see the clouds breaking up in the distance. She sighed in relief and let the animals out. The young woman closed the door then added wood to the last of the glowing coals, to make a better fire. She made coffee and porridge; when it was ready to eat, she woke Janet. Once finished, the two women saddled up and after making sure no trace of them remained... they left.

****

Golden Eagle groaned in agony before sitting up slowly. He closed his eyes quickly then dropped his head in his hands, trying to stop the world from spinning. When the rain had quit, he had stumbled out of the shelter unable to stand the snoring inside and had slept near the fire. The Englishman massaged his temples trying to alleviate some of the pounding pain.

Dream Dancer smiled in sympathy; he poured him a cup of tea. He had made the hangover concoction knowing that everyone would need it. Edward got up and walked around the fire then squatted in front of the Englishman, holding the cup out enticingly. "Have some tea; it will help, I promise!"

In agony, Golden Eagle opened one bleary eye and stared at Dream Dancer's smiling face warily; he reached out then took the cup. Devon took a swallow and choked in surprise. "Ague... this stuff is awful!"

Nodding, Dream Dancer laughed before getting up. "The cure is always worse than the illness. It will help, now drink it while I see to breakfast."

Jake moaned in pain as he stumbled to the fire. "Did somebody say food? I couldn't eat even if I wanted to."

Unsympathetically, Dream Dancer grinned teasingly and poured Jake some tea. "Here, have some it will help you too."

Shuddering, Jake grimaced knowingly. "Your famous remedy, it tastes worse than the hangover makes me feel."

Dream Dancer chuckled. "It might taste bad, but it works."

Not looking forward to drinking it, Jake held the cup tentatively; trying to get the courage to down it. "I know, I have had it a few times. How is my son doing this morning?"

Dream Dancer smiled in approval. "Good, he's already had breakfast. I gave him something for pain, so he is sleeping. There is no infection so far, which we should be thankful for."

Jake sighed in relief then couldn't put off drinking the tea any longer; he took a deep breath in preparation before lifting the cup... he downed his tea in one swallow. He shuddered in response at the bitter, sour taste.

Golden Eagle finished his tea then smiled up at Black Hawk as he came stumbling towards the fire. "Good morning."

Black Hawk dropped down beside the fire and poured himself some tea then downed it. He shuddered before turning to Devon grimly. "Morning, now I know why you white men called that excuse for alcohol rotgut."

Unable to argue with that statement Golden Eagle nodded.

Dream Dancer dished up bacon and eggs for everyone then they all sat back enjoying their breakfast, now able to eat. Edward especially took pleasure in the laughing teasing jokes they were handing out.

****

Melissa was up first, so decided to celebrate their last day on the trail with the bacon and eggs that the ranch hand had given them. With the last of the flour, she also made flapjacks.

Jed walked over and poured coffee. "The others are up already."

Pleased, Melissa inclined her head without commenting on it; she finished making the batter before pouring some into the steaming pan. "It will seem strange when we get there to be able to stay in one spot for more than a day."

Jessica and Pat strolled up to the fire then sat together. Patricia poured them a coffee and sat back. "I agree with Mother it will seem strange, but I'm not going home for at least two weeks... I need a rest."

Jessica chuckled knowingly then sipped her coffee without comment.

Pam and Daniel strolled up to the fire before sitting on a log.

Rose sauntered in last.

Daniel reached over then poured all three of them a coffee.

Finished breakfast, Melissa handed out the plates of food. Everyone ate quickly eager to get to Giant Bear's village.

****

Golden Eagle put out the fire and walked to the lead wagon then joined Dream Dancer and his uncle.

Black Hawk frowned at his nephew in caution. "The big bay mare balked when I put her in the traces to pull the wagon, so I will ride beside her for a bit to make sure she doesn't act up. I split the prisoners up one in each wagon. Your horse is not badly hurt but he picked up a rock somewhere, so his front foot is bruised. Jake with Golden Eagle's help can scout ahead. When we get back to the village, I think we should send out two braves to guard this entrance. We better be prepared in case there is still vi'hoi lurking about."

Dream Dancer inclined his head at his uncle in agreement then asked curiously. "Did they tell you anything?"

Shaking his head in annoyance, Black Hawk scowled grimly. "No, but one of the prisoners recognized Devon. Golden Eagle says that he has never seen the man before last night."

Curiously, Dream Dancer looked at Golden Eagle; Devon shrugged baffled. Ed sighed perplexed. "Did you check their saddlebags?"

Shrugging, Black Hawk shook his head. "No, I figured I would wait until we got back to the village for that."

Turning away, Dream Dancer sighed in aggravation before climbing into the driver's seat; he called over his shoulder impatiently. "Let's go then!"

Golden Eagle and Black Hawk grinned at each other in amusement, at the sound of the irritating growl... in the young earl's voice then mounted.

****

Jed held up his hand to stop everyone as he sat listening and sniffing the air.

Silver Tip growled, but hushed when Patricia told her to.

Immediately, Jed turned in the saddle in caution. "Mell, come with me; everyone else take out your rifles, but stay here."

Turning back to Melissa, Jed nodded when she took out her whip in precaution, they moved forward warily. Silver Tip invited herself along and walked beside Mell's horse. They went around a bend in the trail then came to an empty camp.

Silver Tip walked around sniffing the ground curiously.

Melissa and Jed dismounted; she walked over to the fire pit then put her hand on the rocks, but quickly snatched her hand off again when the rock almost burnt her fingers.

Vigilantly, Jed walked around looking at the signs before turning to Melissa. "It must have been Edward, looks as if he stayed in this spot last night. Over to your left six horses came into camp in the night; one was carrying a heavy load. There is a bullet on the ground with blood on it, so someone was hurt. They left not long ago."

Melissa inclined her head in agreement and pointed at the fire pit. "The rocks in the fire are still hot since this spot is sheltered from the wind; I would say about two hours, maybe three at the most."

Jed nodded thoughtfully. "I'll get the others before we discuss if we want to stay here for lunch, or try catching the wagons."

Waiting, Melissa continued to look around until the rest of her party gathered in the clearing.

Riding up, Jed beckoned to his wife. "They want to press on."

Relieved, Melissa mounted immediately.

Urging his horse forward, Jed led them out of the clearing.

****

Raven beckoned to Janet. "Do you want to stop or press on; if we don't stop for lunch, we will stop early for the night."

Janet nodded preferring the early night to food right at this moment. "Let's keep going I'm not hungry, anyway."

In agreement, Raven silently kicked her horse into a fast trot.

****

Black Hawk galloped past the two back wagons then slowed beside Dream Dancer's wagon; he jumped off his horse onto the seat without stopping. His horse stayed beside the wagon patiently waited for his master. Tommy pointed behind them. "We are being followed, a large party maybe an hour behind us. They are riding pretty fast. It could be the sheriff again."

Dream Dancer looked back then squinted in concentration before turning back to Black Hawk with a smile of relief. "No not the sheriff, its White Buffalo and Grey Wolf!"

Surprised, Black Hawk's eyebrows rose in amazement. "Your powers are getting stronger if you can tell that from this distance! Tell me, why are Aunt Mell and Uncle Jed here?"

Grimacing, Dream Dancer shrugged uneasily then frowned in concern not wanting his uncle to know how much his powers had grown... he fibbed. "I had a dream they were coming awhile back. Afterwards, I could sense them getting closer; now I don't feel them so they must be here."

Thoughtfully, Black Hawk nodded not suspecting his nephew was telling him an untruth. "Well, since you are sure it's them; I think we should stop here then make lunch and wait for them. Do you happen to know why my Aunt Mell is here?"

Dream Dancer smiled in relief as his uncle accepted his explanation. "White Buffalo has come to save us!"

Black Hawk frowned then eyed Dream Dancer in confusion. Knowing he wasn't going to get a straight answer by the stubborn look on his nephew's face; he vaulted back onto his horse. "I'll get Jake and Golden Eagle while you set up camp."

Unrepentant, Dream Dancer grinned in amusement at his uncle's annoyed look then stopped the wagon.

Galloping ahead, Black Hawk spotting Jake... he whistled.

Jake looked behind him curiously and saw Tommy coming, so called out to the Englishman to get his attention. "Black Hawk wants us to stop."

Golden Eagle trotted towards Jake immediately to wait.

Pulling his horse up, Black Hawk pointed over his shoulder the way they had come. "We are stopping for lunch; we have company coming."

Surprised, Jake frowned. "Do you happen to know who it is?"

Nodding, Black Hawk scowled in irritation. "Dream Dancer says its White Buffalo and Grey Wolf."

Taken aback, Jake's eyebrows rose. "I didn't know they were coming."

Shrugging, Black Hawk turned his horse and they walked towards camp. "Nobody except Dream Dancer knew I guess."

Guiltily, Golden Eagle looked away.

Catching the look on the Englishman's face, Black Hawk scowled in exasperation. "Well, maybe not only my nephew."

Startled, Jake looked at Devon in doubt. "You knew they were coming?"

Golden Eagle sighed anxiously; he nodded in apology. "Yeah, I knew."

Grimly, Black Hawk threw his hands up in the air in vexation. "Secrets, everyone seems to have them lately."

The rest of the trip finished in silence.

****

Silver Tip growled in warning but was too late, as three shadows stepped out of the trees.

Jed and Melissa cleared leather in an instant.

A grinning Black Hawk threw up his hands in mock surrender. "I give up... don't shoot!"

Melissa smirked at Jed before they re-holstered their guns.

Patricia called Silver Tip over so she wouldn't attack the men.

Instantly, Melissa jumped off her horse then raced to embrace Black Hawk eagerly. Tommy swept his foster mother into his arms and twirled Mell around in pleasure, laughing.

In delight, Melissa squealed like a child then pushed away to look Black Hawk over. "My darling Tommy, I have missed you all these years! How are you and your wife doing; is your father and mother okay?"

Immediately, Melissa stopped her questions at the look of sadness that appeared on Black Hawk's face; it wasn't until then she noticed his shorter braids. Black Hawk smiled sadly in reassurance. "We set up camp when Dream Dancer told me you were coming. Why don't you wait till we get back there before I answer all your questions?"

Subdued, Melissa nodded already guessing that Tommy's wife had died; they walked back to her horse, she mounted.

Turning, Black Hawk and the others went into the trees for the horses.

Golden Eagle's stud called a challenge to Melissa's stallion and tried to rush forward. Devon cursed at his horse angrily... he just about ran him over. The Englishman pulled down hard on the reins; until the stud's nose was even with his master's chin. "Stop that this instant!"

Devil snorted furiously and tried to throw his head back up.

Quickly, Golden Eagle stepped to the side then pulled Devil's head with him. The stallion refused to budge, so the Englishman swung the end of the reins in a circle; he slapped the stud on the hind end, until he turned.

Pulling insistently, Golden Eagle took another step to the side; this time Devil followed without any prompting. Devon kept turning until he was back to where he had started.

Releasing the reins, Golden Eagle held them loosely waiting for his horse to act up again. When Devil behaved himself then stood quietly; Devon sighed in relief before mounting.

Knowingly, Melissa chuckled before giving the beautiful stallion an admiring gaze. "Training a new horse, are you?"

Inclining his head, Golden Eagle grimaced in aggravation. "Yes, this is only his third day out of the corrals."

Shrewdly, Melissa smiled. "You must be Devon Rochester."

The Englishman inclined his head. "It is Golden Eagle here; you are Melissa Brown or White Buffalo as Dream Dancer calls you."

Melissa nodded then rode the rest of the way in silence. She dismounted once they entered the temporary camp, and shook hands with everyone as introductions were handed out. Seeing two prisoners sitting in the wagons, she wisely ignored them for now. They all sat around the fire talking excitedly... waiting for lunch. Mell let everyone eat before turning to Black Hawk inquisitively. "So, tell me what happened to your wife?"

Black Hawk sighed sadly then told her everything.

Listening to the whole story, Melissa grimaced in condolence before reaching over and hugged Black Hawk. "I'm sorry for your loss, has the baby taken some pain away at least?"

Black Hawk solemnly nodded once Melissa released him. "More than I thought was possible; at first I didn't even want to look at him... it just hurt too much. Golden Eagle wouldn't let me get away with that though."

Relieved, Melissa smiled at Golden Eagle in thanks; before turning to Dream Dancer, and patted a spot beside her invitingly. "Come sit over beside me."

Dream Dancer smiled shyly then got up from across the fire before walking over to White Buffalo. "I heard a lot about you from grandfather."

Spontaneously, Melissa hugged Dream Dancer. "I have heard about you too and your rare gifts; now tell me how did you know we were coming?"

Biting his lip indecisively; Dream Dancer pushed away from Melissa then eyed her pensively before looking at Golden Eagle for permission. The Englishman understanding the questioning look, nodded in agreement.

Still, Dream Dancer held back a little as he turned back to Melissa. "I dreamt that you were coming to save us; after I had the dream, I could feel that you were getting closer. Not exactly how close though until you were right behind us, but closer from one day to the next."

Amazed, Mell frowned. "Your grandfather never revealed that gift."

Trying to alleviate suspicion, Dream Dancer shrugged sadly. "I don't think I could do it again; I think this was a special case, sort of once-only event."

Melissa listened grimly to Dream Dancer's account of his dream before sighing pensively. "Well, it goes with the dreams Pamela and I both had."

Dream Dancer smiled over at his aunt then turned back to Melissa. "Can you describe your dream for me?"

Thinking back, Melissa sighed grimly. "I thought it was just a nightmare at first. It wasn't until Pam told me she had the same dream that I paid more attention to it. I kept seeing a white buffalo turning away from a village one minute and deaths would happen. The next I would see the white buffalo going towards Giant Bear then saying, 'they must not be forced to marry.'; the white buffalo would repeat the saying over and over... in a chant. But I don't understand, who isn't supposed to be forced to marry?"

Triumphantly, Dream Dancer smiled widely in pride at being proven right. Edward shared a look with the Englishman then turned back to Melissa. "My grandfather is trying to force Raven and Golden Eagle into marriage. If I had more knowledge of what my nam-shimi was thinking; it might help to give me a better picture of what's happening, but all I can do now is to speculate."

Black Hawk cleared his throat as he interrupted. "I can help you with that; Father confided in me the day Golden Eagle started his training."

Excited, Dream Dancer nodded pleased. "Good. You start then I will finish with what I know."

Jed got up and poured everyone coffee as they all listened attentively to Black Hawk tell his story.

Intently, Dream Dancer listened closely; occasionally, he would nod as if he knew what was going to be said next. When Black Hawk finished, the young earl sighed grimly in relief. "Now I know my theory was sound. I had the same dream as the shaman, but after talking to Golden Eagle we decided that the dream meant something different."

Confused, Melissa frowned in bewilderment. "How can you both have the same dream, but have different answers?"

Shrugging, Dream Dancer tried to explain. "It is complicated, but like I told Golden Eagle a shaman is not infallible. The Great Spirit gives us visions to help us. Sometimes, a vision is meant to be acted on and sometimes it is only a reassurance that something... will happen. There have even been a few spiritual leaders that only interpret dreams they like; they ignore anything else. It's up to the shaman to decide whether to act or sit back then wait. Only time and experience can say whether he interpreted the dream correctly."

Taping her chin, Melissa grimaced thoughtfully. "I think I understand now; what you are saying is that we shouldn't have interfered in this situation. If we had not contacted Golden Eagle, he would have come here on his own."

Dream Dancer grinned pleased that White Buffalo figured it out. "Correct, that's exactly right; let me tell my story then you be the judge."

Melissa listened carefully; she was nodding at the end of Dream Dancer description. "Yes, I agree with you and Golden Eagle. I don't think the deaths we see are physical, though. They will not die per say, but it could be the loss of your beliefs or the Cheyenne as a whole."

Thoughtfully, Dream Dancer frowned then sat straighter in excitement. "That would make more sense since all the other Indian Nations, even the Cheyenne that's not living here, are being driven onto reservations. The few that are still free, only want to continue fighting the whites, so they too will be killed. So, if the Cheyenne here lost Raven's protection, they would end up dying on reservations. Or as you say, it could be our beliefs since we are different from the other Cheyenne tribes. We believe in living in peace instead of trying to drive the whites away. We have adopted a lot of the white man's ways of thinking knowing the only way to survive is through adapting to the changing world. Many of our people don't even consider us Cheyenne. They call us, 'friendlies'; thinking it's a degrading thing to us, but it isn't."

Jed interrupted. "So, what can we do to stop Giant Bear from making such a fatal mistake then losing Raven's protection?"

Sighing, Dream Dancer shrugged grimly. "I'm not sure, I couldn't go to my grandfather and the shaman myself; because to them, I am still too young and untrained. Our spiritual leader would say that I was wrong then all that would have done was to separate Golden Eagle and me. I think at the time, Devon needed me as much as I needed him to understand the situation. Between us, I think we learned more plus accepted more of what was happening then if we wouldn't have been able to get to know one another. That is why I think I had the dream about White Buffalo saying to hold on she was coming; or I might have been tempted to try interfering right away, which would have caused additional problems."

Golden Eagle smiled fondly at Dream Dancer. "He is right, at first all I wanted was revenge. My hatred was growing daily at being forced to stay here, and marry someone not of my choosing. I feel no hatred now, I'm willing to work things out. I think we need to go to the village then talk to Giant Bear and the shaman. Now that you are here, they will listen."

Melissa sighed contemplatively. "I agree; if that doesn't work, we will have to come up with a better plan."

Dream Dancer stood up quickly. "Okay, let's try it."

Camp was clean up, mounting they continued riding towards the village.

*****

Golden Dove watched her husband pace for a moment, and picked up a moccasin she was working on before trying to ignore Giant Bear. Finally, Mary could stand it no longer, as she growled in frustration. "Will you sit down or go do something!"

Giant Bear frowned down at his wife in aggravation. "I can't help it; they have been gone for over a day... anything could have happened!"

Reassuringly, Golden Dove looked up calmly. "They are fine, probably holed up somewhere to wait out last night's storm."

Unconvinced, Giant Bear stomped to the door before turning to his wife in disbelief. "That might be true, but they should have been back this morning. I am going to go look for them!"

Grimacing, Golden Dove sighed plaintively when Giant Bear left. She was a little nervous herself, but hid it better than her husband did. Mary turned back to her sewing to distract herself from her apprehension.

Anxiously, Giant Bear was organizing a search party when one of the sentries came galloping in. "There is a large party approaching."

Relieved, Giant Bear nodded then frowned hopefully. "Is it Black Hawk?"

The lookout inclined his head solemnly. "He has three wagons with him and some vi'hoi. Two are prisoners."

Thoughtfully, Giant Bear scowled in surprise. "Put the horses away then one of you bring the shaman."

Giant Bear walked to the edge of the village, waiting uneasily. The chief saw them coming and grimaced as he counted. Well, the three wagons must be the supplies, but who were the others. The shaman arrived a minute later then stood beside his chief grimly.

Cocking his head listening, Giant Bear heard a familiar war whoop; he turned to the shaman in delight. "Send Little Coyote to get Golden Dove. White Buffalo and Grey Wolf are here."

The shaman nodded apprehensively then left.

In excitement, Giant Bear turned to the galloping rider and grinned in pleasure when Grey Wolf jumped out of his saddle in front of him. "Blood-brother, it is good to see you again."

Warmly, Giant Bear embraced Grey Wolf then stood back to look at him keenly. "I see you are finally starting to get a few grey hairs."

Jed laughed in glee as he pulled one of Giant Bear's short braids. "Not as grey as you, old man!"

Melissa pushed her husband aside in demand. "Let the rest of us say hello."

Grunting, Jed staggered in exaggeration.

Chuckling, Giant Bear smiled knowingly before enfolding White Buffalo in his huge beefy arms. "Still pushing your husband around, I see."

Impishly, Melissa chuckled as she squeezed her blood-brother warmly. "Of course, and he wouldn't have it any other way."

Pushing away, Melissa stepped back. "Look who I brought."

Knowingly, Giant Bear smiled in pleasure; he gave his daughter a lingering glance before gathering her in his arms. "Morning Star, you look so much like your mother."

Pamela laughed as she cried. "I have missed you fiercely ni-hoi."

Stepping back, Pamela beckoned to her husband. "You remember my husband, Daniel."

Pleased, Giant Bear nodded and clasped his son-in-law's arm in greeting. "Of course I remember him."

Daniel beamed solemnly; the older twin didn't know Giant Bear well. He had preferred to stay home when his parents, and sister went to the powwows at the border of Montana and North Dakota. "It's nice to see you again, sir."

Waving, Giant Bear shook his head in distress. "No, please call me Giant Bear or ni-hoi which means Father."

Daniel nodded in pleasure then moved away.

Patricia squealing in delight flung herself at Giant Bear. "Uncle Bear, I have missed you; it's been way too many years."

Giant Bear laughed in humour as he lifted Patricia of her feet. "Little Owl, you are the only one who dares to call me Uncle Bear. But you have grown so big; I will have to think of another name for you."

Chuckling, Patricia stepped back with a shake of her head in denial. "Oh no you don't, I love the name you gave me."

Nodding, Giant Bear grinned in pleasure. "Good, from now on your Cheyenne name is Little Owl."

The chief turned to Jessica next as she stepped up; a bit more reserved than the others... she hugged him. "How are you Giant Bear, it has been a while since I have seen you?"

Grinning, Giant Bear stepped back. "Hello Red Sparrow, you are still the spitting image of your mother. You can call me Uncle Bear too if you like."

Jessica nodded pleased. "Okay, I would like that."

Seeing movement, Giant Bear looked over Jessica's head. He had never seen the native woman behind Red Sparrow before. "Who is that?"

Red Sparrow turned before introducing her new friend. "This is Black Rose. We helped her leave a white town and brought her with us, she is Cheyenne. We figured you could help her find her family."

Taking Rose's hand, Giant Bear nodded. "I will see what I can do."

Rose smiled shyly. "Thank you."

Curiously, Giant Bear turned to Jed. "Why are you here?"

Jed leaned forward forebodingly. "Remember you told me that the white buffalo was supposed to save you in the future."

Puzzled for a moment, Giant Bear thought back; he inclined his head slowly, having forgotten about the conversation they had before he had left Melissa's ranch to come home.

The others wandered off to give them some privacy.

Nodding, Giant Bear sighed grimly. "Yes, I remember."

Motion in forewarning, Jed frowned. "Well, now is the time!"

Taken aback, Giant Bear scowled incredulously. "You have come to save us from the whites?"

In warning, Jed shook his head negatively. "No, we have come to save you... from yourself!"

Giant Bear scowled in confusion, but before he could ask what Jed meant by that his wife trotted around the corner; squeals of joy, drowned him out.

Jed smiled in assurance then leaned forward. "We'll talk later."

Thoughtfully Giant Bear nodded, watching Grey Wolf trot over to Golden Dove for a hug. The chief heard an angry shout then turned to see Golden Eagle holding something, shaking one of the prisoners. Black Hawk and Dream Dancer grabbed an arm then held the irate Englishman.

Immediately, Giant Bear trotted over; he arrived at the same time as Grey Wolf and White Buffalo. "What is going on here?"

Golden Eagle shook free of the restraining hands. "This piece of scum has a shirt, brush, plus several other articles of my sister's. There is even a bloodstained shirt sleeve that was ripped off me."

Surprised, Jed frowned as he eyed first one then the other prisoner. "Evidence, they were planning on hiding proof in or around your village."

Melissa nodded agreeing with her husband. "You are probably right since the sheriff and villagers will be here tomorrow. If they found all that evidence here, they could call in the army without questions asked."

Shaking loose of the restraining hands, Golden Eagle scowled angrily. "They didn't find me when they came here last time, so whoever is trying to frame Raven's people must be getting desperate. Where did you get this stuff?"

The prisoner that had first recognized the Englishman looked away mutely. Golden Eagle grabbed the prisoner again then shook him violently. Black Hawk stepped forward to stop him, but stepped back again when White Buffalo held up her hand... motioning him away.

Unrelenting, Golden Eagle shook the man in a rage. "You will answer me, or I will skin you an inch at a time until you do! Believe me, living with the Cheyenne has taught me how to do it and keep you alive while you suffer."

Black Hawk choked then coughed to hide his amusement, and Dream Dancer had to turn away to hide his smile.

The prisoner paled visibly before trembling in terror. "I don't know anything. I was told to plant these things in the village."

The other prisoner broke in hurriedly. "Shut up you, idiot."

Melissa stepped in front of the prisoner then pushed her jacket away from her marshal's badge. "I would be quiet if I were you. There are witnesses to your crime and talking might save you from a hangman's noose."

The man scowled. "You can't hang us for carrying stuff we found."

Nastily, Melissa smiled. "Oh, but I see you still don't understand! Since you shot Jake's son, who happens to be white; we can use the evidence you have, to convict you of the murder of Devon's sister and the guides."

The man frowned angrily then turned away mutely.

Turning, Melissa waved at the Englishman. "Continue please."

Gratefully, Golden Eagle nodded and turned back to the other prisoner. "Who told you to put these here?"

Dream Dancer turned to look at the man White Buffalo was talking to then stared thoughtfully. His forehead smoothed when he remembered where he had seen him before; he interrupted Golden Eagle's question. "I know you!"

Golden Eagle whirled around at Dream Dancer's statement.

The man grimaced in denial at Dream Dancer then shook his head in fear. "I don't know you?"

Angrily, Dream Dancer nodded decisively. "You don't remember me; I was a lot younger. You came to the ranch with Charles when he was trying to get Raven to marry him. You kicked my dog and broke his rib."

The man scowled uneasily then hurriedly looked away. "You have confused me with someone else."

Convinced, Dream Dancer shook his head negatively. "No, I'm right; I distinctly remember that scar under your left eye."

Black Hawk frowned thoughtfully. "Charles is the same man who shot the bear cub instead of me."

Sadly, Dream Dancer inclined his head. "Golden Eagle told me about that. Charles is our neighbour and a pest; when Raven laughed in his face after he proposed to her, he kept coming over trying to get her to sell."

Speculatively, Melissa eyed the prisoner pensively. "Why?"

The man shrugged irritably. "I'm just a ranch hand, I don't know anything; I do what I'm told to do."

Nodding, Melissa turned to Giant Bear. "I don't think they know anything. Do you have a place to keep them until the sheriff shows up tomorrow?"

Giant Bear scowled grimly. "Yes, I will put a guard on them."

Golden Dove walked over. "Come, the women want to put the supplies away. Another tepee is going up for our guests. We can talk at supper."

Agreeing, Giant Bear sighed in aggravation knowing he wouldn't get any answers. Mell motioned curiously. "Do you have a place to bathe?"

Inclining her head, Golden Dove waved. "Come, I'll show you."

Immediately, Giant Bear waved to some braves standing off to the side then gave them instructions for the prisoners and their guest's horses.

Melissa went to her horse then grabbed her saddlebags before following Golden Dove, talking excitedly. The others followed Mell's lead, while the braves led the horses away.

Uneasily, Giant Bear watched his guests following Golden Dove with a frown of trepidation then turned when the shaman walked up to him. "What do you think of that?"

The shaman shrugged apprehensively. "I didn't foresee this; only Morning Star and her husband were supposed to come."

Grimly, Giant Bear nodded in confusion then turned to go help his braves. "I guess we will wait to hear from them, why they are here."

Nodding, the shaman followed his chief; extremely disturbed.

****

Raven pulled up then turned to her left. "We will camp here; if we get up early, we can be in the village around two or three if we don't stop for lunch."

Janet nodded in relief and followed Raven. They quickly set up camp together. When finished eating, they slept.

****

The newcomers sitting in the ceremonial tepee talked excitedly, while eating supper before drinks were handed out.

Giant Bear frowned at Golden Eagle dismissively. "We will be speaking privately now, so you can go back to your tepee."

Golden Eagle shook his head with a stubborn, mulish look on his face, but Melissa was the one who spoke. "No, he will stay; this concerns him."

Scowling angrily, Giant Bear addressed Melissa. "He doesn't know anything and must not know for now!"

Melissa smiled in sympathy at Giant Bear. "Devon knows everything; he knew before we arrived."

Angrily, Giant Bear grimaced before looking at his son.

Black Hawk shrugged defensively. "Don't look at me, I only just found out yesterday that he knew."

Giant Bear then turned his heated gaze on Dream Dancer.

Dream Dancer smiled in apology at his grandfather. "Yes, he knows; although, I didn't tell him everything."

Confused, Giant Bear turned to the Englishman and looked at him.

Golden Eagle smirked slyly, but refused to answer.

In rebuke, Dream Dancer elbowed his friend in the ribs.

Unexpectedly, Golden Eagle grunted as his young friend's elbow connected hard then sighed in apology. "Well, he made me suffer enough."

Waiting, Dream Dancer lifted an eyebrow in reproach.

Sighing in surrender, Golden Eagle shrugged in irritation. "Oh, very well; I have portraits of the late earl at home, Dream Dancer is the spitting image of his English grandfather. I put the pieces together on my own."

Rubbing the back of his neck, Giant Bear sighed aggrieved. "I knew it was a mistake letting Dream Dancer come here."

Disagreeing, Dream Dancer shook his head. "No, it was because of me that Golden Eagle learned to accept the situation you put him in."

Unable to refute that, Giant Bear nodded. Turning, he looked at Melissa inquisitively. "Why are you here?"

Grimly, Melissa smiled. "I came to save you, of course."

Uneasily, Giant Bear frowned. "Come to save me... how?"

Melissa sighed then eyed the chief trying to decide how best to answer. White Buffalo chose to be direct. "I have come with a message from your Great Spirit; I'm to tell you... 'they must not be forced to marry'!"

The shaman jumped up in disbelief, he waved furiously in denial. "That's a lie! My dream shows that if they don't marry the whites will kill everyone... even Raven and the vi'hoi! What does a vi'hoahi know; the Great Spirit would never tell her that?"

Defiantly, Dream Dancer shook his head then stood up as well... pointing at the shaman. "You are wrong; I had the same dream as you did, what you saw was Raven turning away from her people because you forced her to do something that you shouldn't have. The deaths of our people are only a forewarning of what will happen if Raven withdraws her protection. The death of the raven and the eagle above them meant that their Indian spirits would die within them, not that they would be killed."

Giant Bear stared then turned to the shaman confused. "Is he right?"

The shaman harrumphed in contempt before stopping thoughtfully... recalling his dream. He sat back down staggered; never had he been so wrong, he nodded reluctantly. "Yes, it could be interpreted that way."

Curiously, the shaman eyed Dream Dancer with new respect. "We have never had the same visions before now; how did you reach your conclusions?"

Dream Dancer sighed grimly before sitting down too. "I know my sister very well; she is as stubborn as they come. If you try to make her do something she doesn't want to do, Raven will find a way to get back at you. When she got hurt by that grizzly, she told me if forced to marry she didn't think she would be able to continue helping the Cheyenne."

Knowingly, Giant Bear grimaced furiously at the shaman. "I told you something was wrong!"

Agreeing, Dream Dancer nodded. "Yes, you shouldn't have interfered when the Great Spirit gave you that vision about Golden Eagle."

In trepidation, Giant Bear frowned apprehensively; things were going from bad, to worse. "How do you know about that??"

Grimly, Dream Dancer waved. "I only guessed at first, until Black Hawk confirmed it earlier. We figured that the Great Spirit gave you the first vision as a reassurance that somebody had already been chosen for Raven... not for you to interfere. Golden Eagle told me he was thinking of coming here years before. Since his youngest sister had a weak heart, we figured if things had progressed as they should, she probably would have passed on in England. It would have been the last straw for Devon then he would have moved here on his own. But because you drew him here before his time, things changed. He got drawn unwillingly into a fight that wasn't his own."

Giant Bear scowled, looking at the shaman. "What do you think?"

The shaman's face creased in thought as he ran through all his visions. He remembered seeing the golden eagle at Raven's naming ceremony. He shrugged... skeptically. "He could be right; although I am not entirely convinced yet, I will have to think about it some more."

Now even more convinced that they had made a tragic mistake, which had ended in unforeseen deaths... Giant Bear nodded; he turned to his grandson curiously. "What do you suggest?"

Dream Dancer smiled in satisfaction at being asked his opinion. "I think you should withdraw your request for Raven and Golden Eagle to marry; let them work it out on their own."

Relieved, Giant Bear sighed; he had wanted a way out of this since the beginning, anyway. He turned to White Buffalo next, but already knew the answer. "And your opinion is?"

Melissa inclined her head in concurrence. "I agree with your grandson."

Turning to Jed, Giant Bear saw him nod his agreement. The chief looked at the shaman last. "Do you agree?"

Unwillingly, the shaman sighed pained. "Yes!"

Waving towards Golden Eagle, Giant Bear released him. "You are free to go; if you do not wish to marry Raven, so be it."

Golden Eagle grinned in delight, pleased to have a say as he released the breath he had been holding. "Do you mind if I stay and finish my training?"

Surprised, Giant Bear's eyebrows lifted. "I figured you would leave if the opportunity presented itself."

Dismissively, Golden Eagle shrugged. "In the beginning, I probably would have jumped at the chance; now I have made many friends here so would like to stay if it is okay with you?"

In consent, Giant Bear inclined his head in surprise. "You can stay as long as you wish; it's the least that we can do, keep all your gifts too."

Jed sighed glad to get that over with. "Now that this situation is cleared up; I think we better talk about the sheriff. He should be here tomorrow with some of the townspeople."

Nodding, Melissa frowned grimly. "Grey Wolf is right; although we don't think the dreams of your people dying is connected, he still poses a threat."

Golden Eagle frowned in worry. "I don't like the fact that Raven's neighbour is the one who tried to shoot Black Hawk; plus, he sent his men to plant evidence against you. How did he get it in the first place."

Dream Dancer scowled sceptically at an alarming thought. "Do you think he had something to do with the ambush? I know he's been getting nasty with Raven because she refuses to sell, but killing people isn't like him"

Giant Bear grimaced angrily. "Maybe, but he didn't have to kill anyone; he could have just paid the Indians to do it. I wonder what's so important about Raven's land that would drive him to such desperate measures."

Melissa pondered grimly before turning to her husband. "Remember about ten years ago we had a similar situation. It was a drought year, and water was getting more precious than gold. One neighbour had a natural spring that came out of the hills through his land and onto the neighbour's land. They ended up in a war over it; one neighbour kept trying to buy out the other, but he wouldn't sell. Suddenly, his cattle started dying then his ranch hands started vanishing. We had to step in and put a stop to it."

Jed nodded remembering. "Yes, the neighbour got desperate enough he ended up killing a few people; later he was hung for his crimes."

They all turned and looked at Dream Dancer expectantly. He shrugged unknowingly. "As far as I know there is no problem with water for anyone. We do have good grazing land for cattle, but nothing to kill for."

Shrugging, Melissa sighed dejectedly. "It could be anything."

Golden Dove stood up satisfied at how events had turned out, maybe now she could let her husband back into her bed. "It's late; tomorrow we should send out a hunting party for fresh meat, so we can cook a feast for the townspeople coming."

Agreeing, Giant Bear nodded. "That's a good idea; we can roast a pig in the underground oven too."

Getting up, Melissa grinned eagerly not having had a roasted pig in a long time; she turned to Dream Dancer in demand. "If you think of anything that might cause your neighbour to go after the land let me know."

Rising, Dream Dancer nodded decisively. "I will; goodnight."

Hugs and kisses got exchanged then everyone went to bed.

CHAPTER TWENTY-EIGHT

Golden Dove smiled in sympathy when Pamela told her all about their trials to come here. Occasionally, Melissa or one of the others included more details. It was so nice to have her best friend and daughter, Morning Star around. The men went hunting, except four braves who were sent out to guide the sheriff and townspeople here.

The Indian women of the village were preparing an enormous feast. Golden Dove felt guilty sitting here talking, instead of helping. The women shooed Mary away, letting the chief's wife visit with her friends.

Ecstatic, Golden Dove hugged Pamela in pleasure at having another grandchild. "Congratulations, how far along are you?"

Pamela smiled in delight at her mother's thrilled expression then hugged her back. "The end of my sixth month, Daniel thinks we should stay until the baby is born."

Unable to contain her joy, Golden Dove nodded in excitement at being present for the birth of her grandchild. "We would love for you to stay here with us; if you two decide to go to the ranch instead, we can go stay with you when it is getting close to your time."

Nodding, Pamela grinned pleased. "I would love that."

Curiously, Golden Dove turned to Mell. "How long can you stay?"

Melissa sighed hopefully. "I'm not sure, at least two weeks. I have to wire the marshal's office then see if they need me."

Knowingly, Golden Dove smirked teasingly. "How long are you two planning on staying Marshal and Deputy Marshal?"

Shrugging, Melissa chuckled in delight. "Still as perceptive as ever. We have not made it official yet, but we are thinking of retiring next year."

Patricia shared a stunned look with Jessica at this revelation.

Smirking, Melissa smiled at the two's surprised looks. "What... did you think we would never give it up?"

Jessica laughed in delight. "We were wondering. Who's your successor?"

Mischievously, Melissa grinned before pointing at her daughter. "I will be recommending Pat; Dusty is our second choice."

Patricia scowled furiously. "That stuck up piece of work; he will wreck everything you have done."

Melissa's eyebrows rose startled at the angry answer. "You used to like Dusty, what happened?"

Frowning grimly, Patricia waved in annoyance. "He got too big for his britches, is what!"

Golden Dove and Melissa shared a meaningful glance; Mell nodded knowingly towards her friend. White Buffalo's daughter was in love.

Seeing the look the two shared, Pat glared at both of them in vexation.

Wisely, Melissa changed the subject.

****

Raven frowned impatiently at Janet then mounted. "Hurry up! We are close now; I want to get there before supper."

Janet sighed in frustration; Raven had been irritable all morning. Twice, she snapped at her. The Englishwoman mounted, trying not to feel hurt at the younger woman's tone. Reminding herself, that Raven wanted to check on her people. She followed without commenting.

Unable to help feeling an urgent need, Raven grimaced. She was aware of Janet's hurt feelings, but couldn't shut off her worried thoughts. What would she find when they arrived at the village? The younger woman sighed to herself apprehensively then tried to shake off her mood. Once they were on their way again... her irritability improved. She started giving the Englishwoman lessons; trying to appease the pain her friend was feeling.

****

Dream Dancer smiled fondly at Golden Eagle before laughing boisterously at a joke Black Hawk was telling them. Devon looked more comfortable now, with the angry lines that had been his constant companion since Edward met him gone. It made him look elegant or maybe nobler, would be a better word. The Englishman's hair had lightened considerably, since he was spending more time in the sun. A lock kept falling into his eyes, which gave him a rakish air.

Jake and Running Wolf were behind them pulling a travois; they were both loaded with a buck. They had broken off from the main hunting party then went west instead, much to their good fortune.

Dream Dancer saw dust ahead; he looked at Golden Eagle, and Black Hawk before pointing. "Others are coming!"

Black Hawk shaded his eyes; he squinted to see better. "It looks like the other hunting party is on their way back. We should meet up soon."

In excitement, they kicked their horses into a trot.

*****

Golden Dove looked then called out at a discreet scratching. "Come in!"

Little Badger poked his head inside. "The hunters are back."

Eagerly, they all got up and followed the boy outside.

Whooping in triumph, the braves galloped into the village.

Giant Bear smiled in satisfaction at Golden Dove when he rode up then dismounted. "We got two buffalo; Black Hawk's party has two bucks."

A smile of appreciation lit up Golden Dove's face before she grinned pleased then hugged her husband in congratulations; turning away, she beckoned the hunters to bring the animals to the butchering area.

Melissa embraced Jed eagerly. "I haven't had buffalo in a long time."

Overhearing as she was passing by, Golden Dove stopped. "Well, we will just have to cook some for you."

They all turned eagerly before looking as they heard a horse galloping in. Giant Bear and Jed walked over to meet the rider.

The sentry jumped off his horse in excitement. "The vi'hoi is coming; they should be here just past the sun's highest point."

In approval, Giant Bear nodded as he looked up towards the sky. "About three hours, do you know how many are coming?"

The lookout shook his head negatively. "No, most are men with only two women, there is no children. It is taking them longer because of the wagons."

Solemnly, Giant Bear frowned then turned to Grey Wolf. "It will be the wives of the guides who got killed."

Jed sighed in agreement and smiled at the guard before they turned away then headed back to the others.

Grimly, Melissa listened to Jed as he repeated the sentry's message... once he rejoined them.

Melissa nodded sadly, but didn't comment; she turned to Mary inquisitively. "Do the women need help?"

Golden Dove grinned in delight at the offer. "I was just on my way; anyone who wants to can come along, to help out."

All five visiting women nodded before following Golden Dove.

Giant Bear looking more relaxed than he had been in a long time smiled at all the gleeful hunters. "The hunt was such a success we have a surprise for you all; please follow me."

Golden Eagle looked inquiringly at Dream Dancer, but Edward just shrugged perplexed before following his grandfather.

Dream Dancer watched his nam-shimi' closely today before they broke off to go their own way to hunt. He noticed that the worry lines on his grandfather's old craggy face had vanished. Edward knew he was relieved at having released Golden Eagle and Raven from their forced union.

Reaching the sweat lodge, Giant Bear turned then faced the men. "We will have a purifying ritual to thank the Great Spirit for providing us with food. For those that have never done this before you strip to your loincloth; the shaman will perform the ceremony on each of us as we enter."

With a smile, Golden Eagle looked at Dream Dancer enthusiastically. "This will be a new experience for me. I've never been this way before; I didn't know these were here."

Vaguely, Dream Dancer pointed behind him as he undressed eagerly. "There are more buildings on the other side of this hill for the women. These are permanent structures and are built to resemble the lodges our ancestors used in what is now North Dakota along the Lakota River... at that time the Cheyenne were farmers so never moved; unfortunately, the Sioux and the white man changed all that. They are used mostly in the winter months when bathing is seldom. Sometimes we have a communal sweat bath with both men and women, but usually it's separate."

Understanding the need for cleanliness, Golden Eagle nodded then finished undressing. He watched the shaman chant and shake a ceremonial staff around Jake; the spiritual leader was dressed in a loincloth with a wolf pelt draped over his shoulders. His face was painted in intricate detail, it wasn't quite the same style as Dream Dancer had on his face the night they had visited the spirit world together.

Golden Eagle stepped up next then listened as the shaman chanted, but he could hear no recognizable words. Finally, the Englishman ducked inside and gasped in shock as a wave of heat hit him full force. It took him a moment to catch his breath then another minute to be able to see vague shapes ahead of him through the wall of steam. Dream Dancer entered behind Devon; he led his friend to a seat.

The shaman entered last then immediately sealed the opening closed, so nobody else could come inside. The spiritual healer walked over to the hot rocks and poured more water on them to increase the moisture, as well as the heat as he continued chanting.

Dream Dancer leaned towards Golden Eagle so he could whisper. "After we finish, we run to the creek then jump in; it's a cold shock when the water hits your hot flesh. Clean clothes will be waiting when we get out."

Without answering, Golden Eagle nodded before looking down in fascination as the sweat and dirt ran down his body in rivulets. Devon was finding it a tad hard to breathe though.

****

Raven jumped off her horse then bent, looking curiously at the deep horseshoe indents she had been noticing since this morning; whoever it is, is following the same trail they were... she looked up at Janet in concern. "Somebody, leading a horse came by this way last night. They were in an awful hurry. See how far apart the tracks are, that means they were galloping. If you look closely, you can see the indent of a shoe which means the horse has a white owner. Indians don't shoe their horses."

Janet got off her horse then scrutinized the tracks before looking at Raven, and nodded that she understood.

In interest, Raven walked further studying the ground closely; she beckoned and pointed out more intriguing tracks for Janet. "Look at these here, see how close together they are all of a sudden. It looks like the horse stumbled then picked up the gallop again. Whoever it is; is in an awful hurry and doesn't care if he kills his horse."

Frowning, Raven thoughtfully mounted disgruntled. Janet followed her lead after looking curiously at the tracks.

Grimly, Raven kicked her horse into a canter then looked at Janet when she caught up. "It's probably my neighbour, Charles! It wouldn't surprise me in the least, that he would run his horse into the ground and not care."

They rode silently for an hour then Raven slowed... again; she pointed into the sky so Janet would look up at the birds circling above. The younger woman took out her rifle, so the Englishwoman followed her lead then draped the gun across her saddle.

Cautiously, Raven nudged her horse into a trot but kept her rifle ready. The younger woman heard a shriek of fear; it meant, that whatever the birds were after was alive. She kicked her horse into a gallop.

Janet caught her breath in horror, as they crested a ridge then saw a horse lying on its side kicking feebly... trying to get up. The vultures too impatient to wait for the horse to die; tried to get close to eat.

Lifting her rifle, Raven shot into the air; which gave Bruno permission to drive the ugly vultures away. The ungainly birds lifted into the air with heated squawks of anger, at being deprived of their dinner by the barking wolf-dog and his companions.

Dismounting, Raven knelt beside the horse and felt along his legs for any breaks. Not finding any; the younger woman put her hand on his heaving side then one on his chest.

Rushing over, Janet knelt beside the horse's head before rubbing his nose to keep him calm as Raven examined him.

Swiping at the sweat on her forehead, Raven looked at Janet before pointing at the packhorse. "On the right of the saddlebag there's a halter; please bring it here. We need to get him up and walking."

Quickly, Janet nodded in concern then jumped up; she hurried to the pack horse. The Englishwoman rushed back, and handed Raven the halter then a lead rope. "Will he be, okay?"

Grimly, Raven shrugged not sure yet; she slipped the halter on. With the two women pushing him, the horse got to his feet reluctantly... standing, he trembled in exhaustion. The younger woman sighed as she looked up at the sky and frowned. Another couple of hours, they would have been back at the village. Unfortunately, with the exhausted horse it would take longer.

Raven sighed grimly then looked over at Janet. "I'm going to walk him around slowly; while I do that, I want you to make a fire and cook us something to eat. I hope if we walk for a bit, he will make it back to the village where he can be tended to properly. He was winded badly, but he's salvageable. He's a nice-looking stud, that is all he will be now. The horse is Charles's prized stallion. He has won many races with him, but he will never be able to race again. A few months in a pasture with light exercise he will be rideable, at a walk or slow trot... not for long though."

Janet nodded; she watched Raven patiently persuade the horse to take a trembling step then another. The Englishwoman turned away.

****

Golden Eagle shivered as he dressed in the ceremonial clothing that had been left for him. He looked at a shivering Dream Dancer then laughed as he hopped on one foot, trying to get his pants on as fast as possible. "That's something I wouldn't want to do everyday. I thought my heart was going to stop when I jumped into that cold water."

Dream Dancer grabbed his shirt, and immediately put it on before answering. "We don't do it often in the summer, it's more of a winter thing... once the ice freezes our bathing area."

Shivering, Golden Eagle nodded as he followed Dream Dancer up the path. Everyone had already left; they were the last ones.

Swiftly, Dream Dancer topped the hill first then waited for the Englishman when he spied dust in the distance. He pointed it out to Golden Eagle when he reached him. "Looks like the townspeople are almost here, let's hurry!"

In agreement, Golden Eagle nodded; the two broke into a trot. Dream Dancer saw his grandfather with the others as they gathered at the edge of the village, so he headed that way.

Giant Bear looked at his grandson then at Golden Eagle in disapproval for their tardiness as they stopped beside him on his left, but didn't comment. The chief turned around so that he could watch the townspeople coming towards him.

Jake, Running Wolf and Black Hawk stood on the right of Giant Bear. Melissa with Jed moved closer to Devon so they would show a united front to the sheriff; both had their badges pinned on. The shaman, Golden Dove, with the rest of Mell's party was behind the chief. The villagers surrounded them but stayed at a discrete distance.

Black Hawk pointed off to their left. They all turned to look towards the dust; a horse was galloping full out... racing towards the townspeople. Whoever was riding the horse reached the sheriff before stopping then a heated discussion took place.

Dream Dancer harrumphed angrily before waving towards the exhausted horse. "It's my neighbour Charles. I wonder where he's coming from, and look at his poor horse."

In disapproval, Black Hawk frowned in concern at seeing such a beautiful animal in such distress. The tall leggy mare had slick sweaty foam covering every inch of her, making it almost impossible to distinguish her colour. Her sides heaved in agony as she tried to draw in a breath... her head hung in exhaustion; she looked as if she were ready to fall over dead.

*****

The sheriff watched Charles gallop towards him; he didn't stop, until the man pulled up in front of him and wouldn't let him pass.

In irritation, the sheriff scowled angrily before eyeing the man's horse then shook his head in sorrow at the animal's condition. "Where have you been, and why did you ride your horse into the ground to get here?"

Charles frowned angrily at being rebuked in front of everyone, but let it go. "Two of my men snuck into the village then found evidence of the massacre in their possession."

Dubiously, the sheriff scowled in doubt as he eyed Charles's horse speculatively; the man hadn't come from his ranch or his horse wouldn't be in such a condition, so how would he know.

Searching, Charles looked around the lawman for his men but couldn't find them. He grimaced in annoyance; the two men were supposed to be here to back up his story.

Harrumphing irritably, the sheriff moved his horse around Charles. "Don't worry, if there is any evidence I will find it."

Frowning at the sheriff's tone, Charles walked his mare beside him.

*****

Giant Bear turned to Melissa. "That is Raven's neighbour, Charles."

Melissa frowned in disapproval; she eyed the man coming towards them speculatively. She shook her head in pity for the horse... disliking the man instantly, as she took his measure. White Buffalo had an uncanny way of measuring people, and rarely was she ever wrong in her assessment. It had given her an edge as a sheriff then as a marshal. What Mell saw in Charles was an avid, greedy don't care about anybody but yourself individual. He had a cruel streak hidden, but noticeable if you looked at his horse's sides closely. There were wicked spur marks some old, with several new ones.

*****

The sheriff walked his horse slowly to allow Charles's horse a chance to cool down, but it wasn't long enough; he pulled up in front of Chief Giant Bear before dismounting respectfully.

Melissa and Jed walked up to the sheriff then shook his hand.

Charles frowned in puzzlement as the two white people greeted the sheriff; he scowled in concern when he noticed the badges pinned to their shirts. He jumped off his horse then waited for introductions.

Not all the townspeople had come, but the ones that did dismounted before milling around waiting anxiously. The mayor with the town councilmen were here, with the wives of the missing guides. There were also relatives of the two women; plus, supporters of Raven's.

The townspeople refused to believe Charles's men when told that Raven's family murdered the Englishman, his family, and the guides.

Giant Bear impassively stepped forward then waited for quiet before speaking loud enough to be heard. "Sheriff, if there are no objections my braves will take the horse's and look after them; they will put them in the two corrals off to your left to wait for you, since you are all welcomed to a feast in your honour that we have prepared. We have a ceremonial tepee, where we will all be able to eat together and talk about your concerns if it is agreeable."

The sheriff looked at Melissa then saw her nod approval. The lawman turned back to face the chief. "I will be honoured to share your feast."

Relieved, Giant Bear nodded and beckoned to Little Badger then spoke in Cheyenne. "I want you to take the big mare the little man is riding and give her special attention."

Little Badger nodded solemnly before walking over to Charles then reached for the horse's reins.

Charles jerked them away. "No dirty Indian will touch my horse!"

There were shocked intakes of breath, even from the villagers at such an ignorant comment.

Golden Eagle, took an angry step forward but stopped short as Dream Dancer grabbed his arm to stop him.

The sheriff calmly passed his reins to a brave, who walked up to him before turning with an angry frown to Charles. "That's fine with me, you can stay here and guard the horse's while the rest of us go eat!"

Hissing, Charles scowled furious at being outmanoeuvred before thrusting the reins of his horse at the boy... without further protest.

Little Badger, not understanding any of the words the vi'hoi said; just stood there waiting patiently before leading the mare away.

Giant Bear grimaced in anger, and turned to the sheriff. "That man is not welcome here!"

Knowingly, the sheriff inclined his head in apology then motioned in conciliation before explaining. "He is under my protection this once; after we leave here, he will not return!"

Looking towards Black Hawk, Giant Bear saw him nod in agreement; it was his right to demand Charles leave, since he had almost shot him once already. The chief turned back to the sheriff impatiently. "My son has agreed, but only if he is relieved of all weapons will I allow him to go any further."

Irritably, Charles frowned at being ignored but was smart enough to allow the sheriff to handle this. He was sure that the lawman wouldn't leave him unarmed; he was shocked, when he saw the sheriff nod.

The lawman turned to Charles and held out his hand in demand. "You will give me your gun."

Instantly, Charles shook his head furiously. "I will not!"

In demand, the sheriff stepped in front of Charles ominously. "You will give me your gun now; or, you will get on your horse and leave!"

Charles nodded angrily before taking out his gun and handed it to the sheriff.

Relieved, Giant Bear nodded in satisfaction when the sheriff handed the gun to his deputy for safekeeping; he beckoned the lawman to follow him. "Come, we will eat before we discuss unpleasantness."

The sheriff nodded before beckoning the villagers to come as he followed the chief. The lawman looked around curiously; he liked what he saw. The tepees were in good repair, with no garbage lying around. He could see that several buildings were permanent. The children were all clothed with only a few running around naked... mostly toddlers.

Over the years, the sheriff had been in a few Indian villages but had never seen them so well fed; they looked in good health too. He turned to the chief inquisitively. "Your people look happy here?"

Giant Bear nodded proudly. "That is all thanks to Raven, since we moved here nobody has gone hungry or died of diseases. She built us a cold room for our meat, to keep it away from disease-carrying flies; it used to be that the meat would spoil, which caused more deaths in the old days then we care to think of. She also provides us with medicines we cannot get ourselves, and immunizes us against some of the diseases we are susceptible to... since the white man came."

Thoughtfully, the sheriff frowned before waving around curiously. "You are lucky to have her, but what do the other tribes think of you?"

Shrugging sadly, Giant Bear sighed. "Regrettably, most don't consider us Indians; they say we have become white, so they call us... 'friendlies'."

Sympathetically, the sheriff grimaced before waving. "Yet you still leave every spring then go to your summer camp."

Sighing resignedly, Giant Bear nodded grimly. "Yes, we have been, but I don't think we will be going any longer. Since all the Indian tribes are getting herded onto reservations, it will not be safe to leave soon; his was supposed to be our last year at our summer camp."

Relieved to hear that, the sheriff inclined his head in approval. "I think you have made a wise decision to stay here permanently; word has just come that the army will be arriving in force by fall, to drive all the Indians they can find onto reservations before winter hits."

Uneasily, Giant Bear scowled. "It was bound to happen."

Falling silent, the sheriff frowned in agreement... they walked part of the way in silence. The lawman eyed the building the chief was leading him to in surprise then smiled; it was shaped like a tepee but made out of wood, with hides covering the entire structure. It must have taken them over a hundred hides to cover the entire building.

The sheriff turned to the chief in approval. "Nice building you have."

Giant Bear smiled in satisfaction. "Yes, it is. Raven built it for us after we moved onto her land. It took us a long time to gather enough hides to cover it all. Unlike a regular tepee, which uses one hide to symbolize who owns it; we used a hide of every animal to symbolize the people as a whole. The women stitched it together then we all gathered to put it up as one. Usually, it is the women who take down then puts up our camps, but this building is different. We all helped build it, so we all needed to finish it. Every person had an opportunity to put their totem on a hide, as you can see there's still room for more. Every child who reaches manhood then wishes to stay puts his symbol on one of the hides."

The shaman was waiting at the entrance; he held the drape wide open, chanting softly as Giant Bear and the sheriff went into the tepee.

Black Hawk relieved the shaman of the drape then held it so everyone could enter. The spiritual healer had lit the oil lamps then started the fire.

Satisfied at the startled intake of breath, Giant Bear smiled at the look of awe on the sheriff's face as he looked around. "The inside is decorated by the shaman, medicine man, Raven, Dream Dancer, and me because we are the spiritual leaders. It symbolizes our spirit world; the walls also tell the story of our ancestors and how we came to live here... plus why."

In approval, the sheriff grinned as they walked to the centre then sat. "It's beautiful; maybe you can explain what the drawings mean."

Beaming, Giant Bear nodded glad the sheriff was interested. "I will be happy to explain it to anyone who wishes to hear."

Dramatically, Giant Bear waited until all found seats before clapping his hands sharply. Several Indian maids entered and handed out cups to everyone... then two walked in with water bags and filled everyone's cup.

Carefully, the sheriff took a sip of his drink then nodded. "It's good!"

At the praise, Giant Bear chuckled in amusement. "We make our own alcohol, which isn't as strong or deadly as whiskey."

The sheriff smiled, pleased that Giant Bear's group stayed away from whiskey. He watched as the older Indian women came in and handed out bowls of stew. More came in then passed around plates heaping with different meats. There were several varieties of vegetables available, but you could tell that they were from winter storage or bottled.

Warily, the sheriff tried the stew first then smiled as he turned to Giant Bear. "This is beef, is it not?"

Pleased, that the sheriff guessed correctly. Giant Bear nodded in agreement. "Yes, it is; there are three types of meat on the plate. They were cooked in an underground oven. One is buffalo, the other is a deer, and the last one is a roasted pig."

Experimentally, the sheriff tried all three then smiled in approval. "It's good, with the different textures pleasing my taste buds."

Everyone finished eating, and the women collected all the dishes then left quietly. More mead was poured for those who wanted some before the sheriff turned to Giant Bear. "Has Raven returned yet?"

Giant Bear shook his head sadly. "No, we have had no word from her yet, and I'm getting worried; she should have been back by now."

Grimly, the sheriff sighed; he turned to Golden Eagle; his eyes narrowed astutely. "You are Sir Devon Rochester from England?"

Golden Eagle nodded decisively. "Yes, I am."

Knowingly, the sheriff scowled in anger. "You been here all along?"

Decisively, Golden Eagle nodded again. "Yes; I got beat up pretty bad and didn't remember much at first!"

Hopefully, the sheriff looked around expectantly. "The rest of your party, are they here also?"

Regretfully, Golden Eagle sadly shook his head. "My older sister was taken captive; the rest didn't make it, including my youngest sister!"

There were cries of anguish from the back of the crowd; Golden Dove, Patricia, and Pamela rushed over to comfort the women. The three had been waiting for that announcement.

Twisting, the sheriff looked back; seeing the women being taken care of, he turned back to Golden Eagle then motioned around in demand. "Are these the Indians that attacked you?"

Golden Eagle shook his head negatively. "No, when I first woke up and found myself here, I thought they were; after I talked to Raven then saw two of the Indians who were responsible, I realized that they weren't the ones."

Charles jumped up in anger, wondering how Devon escaped getting discovered before. "That's a lie; there's evidence here that says they did!"

Giant Bear clapped his hands sharply; two braves walked into the tepee with two white men... obviously prisoners. Then a couple more stepped into the shelter helping a teenage boy hobble inside.

The sheriff eyed the boy and turned to Jake. "That's your son... isn't he?"

Jake nodded in agreement. "He was on sentry duty when those two men showed up then put a couple of bullets in him, as they tried to sneak into the village. It was a good thing for my son that we were on our way there and heard the shots. It was also fortunate for us that Dream Dancer was close by to dig out the bullet."

Eyeing the two prisoners, the sheriff looked up at Charles who was still standing. "Those are your men... are they not?"

Biting his lip, Charles sat down slowly then sputtered in desperation. "I fired them a few days ago."

Both prisoners gaped at their employer in disbelief then shouted out loudly. "He lies!"

Signaling, Giant Bear waved to one of the braves to bring the saddlebags over. He took them with a gesture of thanks before handing the bags to the sheriff. "You might want to look in their saddlebags yourself. Marshal Brown was here when we opened them, so is a witness to the fact that we didn't tamper with them."

Opening both bags, the sheriff pulled out the evidence the two were supposed to hide inside the village; the lawman turned to Charles in demand. "Can you explain why your men have all this stuff on them?"

Jumping up, Charles looked around wildly; he tried to think of something to say or to find a way out, but he was trapped.

Instantly, the sheriff stood up then faced him in accusation.

The lawman's two deputies stood up and surrounded Charles; the room hushed instantly in shock.

CHAPTER TWENTY-NINE

Raven frowned fearfully; she looked around in agitation. No guard had greeted them, so the closer they got to the village... the more agitated she became. The younger woman stood up in her saddle before gazing around the deserted village wildly; not a soul was in sight.

Looking towards the paddocks, Raven grimaced uneasily at all the horse's milling around. The young woman sat back in fear then kicked her horse into a trot before jumping down; she eyed the strange horses. She spotted the sheriff's horse then spun around... was she too late!

Janet dismounted and stared at Raven in dismay at the panic on her face. "Are you okay?"

Cocking her head, Raven held up her hand for quiet when she heard the sound of a horse walking towards them; the young woman spun around then stared at Little Badger hopefully... with one of Charles's horses.

The boy's face broke into a grin of welcome; Little Badger pulled the reluctant mare into a faster pace. "Raven you're back!"

Kneeling, Raven smiled at the youngster, trying hard to hide her fear from the boy. "Where is everyone?"

Not noticing anything amiss, Little Badger pointed over his shoulder. "They are all in the ceremonial tepee."

Relieved, Raven sighed as she calmed herself. "Can you take the horses then put them in the big pasture, be careful of my stud... okay; just lead the mares away and he will follow you? I will unsaddle them later."

Eagerly, Little Badger nodded solemnly. "I remember."

Pleased, Raven grinned then ruffled the boy's hair affectionately before standing up and beckoned for Janet to follow her; the two hurried towards the tepee. The young woman rushed in expecting to find the townspeople in an uproar. Instead, she saw the sheriff tying Charles's hands behind his back and everyone calmly sitting talking in excitement at this turn of events.

Pushing past Raven at a shout, Janet smiled in relief when her brother rushed towards her.

Golden Eagle pulled his sister into a hug. "Are you okay?"

Janet cupped her brother's face adoringly. "I am now!"

Relieved, Golden Eagle couldn't help holding her for a few moments longer before reluctantly setting her down. Devon kept his arm draped around her though, to keep her close. The Englishman turned and eyed Raven in appreciation. "Thank you for finding my sister, I will be forever in your debt."

Walking over, Giant Bear hugged the mystified Raven. "It took you long enough to get here! You should have been back days ago... what happened?"

Raven hugged her grandfather before pushing away and shrugged grimly. "I had a few delays, nothing to worry about. What's going on; I expected to see something different when I got here, was the vision wrong?"

Aggrieved, Giant Bear shook his head then sighed sadly. "No, it wasn't wrong only misinterpreted; I will explain later."

Confused, Raven glared at that piece of news and looked around puzzled then spotted Mell and Jed talking to Dream Dancer. The young woman turned back to her grandfather confused then both eyebrows creased in shock. "When did White Buffalo and Grey Wolf get here?"

Giant Bear smiled at his granddaughter. "They just arrived yesterday."

Leaning closer, Giant Bear whispered so that nobody else could hear them. "I am sorry that I tried forcing this marriage on you, so I have released you and Golden Eagle from having to marry!"

Shocked, Raven's mouth dropped open in stunned surprise at that statement; she snapped it shut with an audible crack, but before she could ask why... she was interrupted.

Sheriff Lane walked over and offered Raven his hand. "Well met Miss Summerset, you are looking good as usual."

Reluctantly, Raven turned to the sheriff; wanting to continue the conversation with her grandfather, but not wanting to be rude. She took his hand then smiled curiously. "Thank you! I see you arrested Charles; how did you figure out he did it?"

The sheriff let Raven's hand go before hooking his thumbs in his gun belt. "Black Hawk and Lord Rochester caught two of Charles's hands trying to sneak into the village to plant evidence. They shot Jake's son in the process; thankfully, he wasn't hurt badly. We don't know why yet?"

Not wanting anyone else to hear the reason, Raven beckoned for the sheriff to follow her so they could speak privately.

The sheriff listened thoughtfully then nodded in disgust. "I should have guessed it had something to do with gold, Charles has always been a greedy son of a gun. Pardon the language, what are you going to do now?"

Frowning, Raven shrugged unknowingly. "I do not know yet? I will talk to Devon later and see what he wants to do, since it is on both of our lands. Can you keep it quiet, until we decide?"

Sheriff Lane nodded then waved decisively. "You bet I will, that's all we need is a bunch of gold-hungry vultures in our town with gold fever."

Decisively, Raven inclined her head resolutely. "We agree on that; I need to go see the widows; I will talk to you later."

Raven walked over to Pamela and the two grieving women. Both widows turned when she approached. She reached out then took their hands in comfort. "I'm so sorry for your loss."

Colleen always being the stronger of the two women spoke for both of them, as they squeezed Raven's hand in gratitude at the sympathy. Both of them had already known the men were gone deep in their hearts; they had come out more to find out why. They also wanted to see where they were buried or if she knew where the bodies were. "You buried them here I am told; we would like to see where, if you don't mind?"

Knowingly, Raven sighed sadly having expected that then nodded decisively. "Of course, my grandmother will take you. I want both you ladies to know that I promised your husband's I would look after you. Whatever you need just let me know; if you want to go back to Scotland, I will help you. Or if you both want, you can move out to the ranch and stay with me... I could always use some extra help?"

The women looked at each other in amazement, not having expected that then both turned back to Raven. Colleen reached out and hugged the younger woman. "That's very kind of you; we will discuss it and let you know."

Extremely glad there was no hysterics; Raven was relieved that the two women were taking this better than she would have. The younger woman stepped away from Colleen and reached out then hugged Priscilla. "Let me know soon, okay?"

They both nodded before Golden Dove led them away.

Grimacing upset, Raven turned to her aunt and hugged Pamela in greeting. "What brings all of you here so suddenly, Aunt Morning Star?"

Pam smiled mysteriously; she led Raven over to her mother-in-law, as she waved jokingly. "We came to save my father from himself, of course!"

Raven frowned in bafflement, but didn't have a chance to ask any questions before Melissa was enfolding the younger woman in her arms in greeting. "Don't you look as beautiful as ever, what took you so long?"

Grinning in pleasure, Raven hugged White Buffalo back. "I had a few delays I'm afraid; it's sure good to see you!"

Mell stepped back as her husband elbowed her. "Don't I get a hug?"

Unable to help it, Raven laughed then squeezed Jed next.

Pat squealed in pleasure and pushed her father aside in her eagerness to get to Raven. "I'm so glad to see you, do I ever have a lot to tell you!"

Enjoying Pat's melodramatics, Raven chuckled at her cousin by marriage as she hugged her. "I'm sure you do."

Jessica was next, but she was more reserved as she hugged Raven then whispered in her ear. "I need to talk to you about something important."

Perplexed, Raven frowned but nodded. She stood back before including both girls in her invitation. "You both can stay with me tonight."

Pleased, Jessica smiled as she stepped back to give Daniel his turn. "Okay, I would like that."

Daniel lifted Raven right off her feet as he hugged her enthusiastically. "We miss you guys you know!"

Grunting at the ardent hug, Raven smiled. "I missed you too."

Welcoming hugs finished at last, Raven was able to sit down by the fire. Melissa and her family sat on her right then Golden Eagle with his sister and Jake sat on her left. Dream Dancer, Running Wolf, Black Hawk, her grandfather and the sheriff sat on the other side of the fire facing them.

Looking up, Raven smiled of thanks when two of the women brought the newcomers food... plus some mead. While she ate hungrily, she told them about the Badger Tribe being innocent; as well as Red Eagle's banishment of Howling Coyote.

Earnestly, Raven looked at the sheriff. "I can take you to where the war chief is hiding out!"

The sheriff shook his head negatively then motioned in reassurance. "It will not be necessary now that you have Devon's sister back safe and sound. We have Charles in custody; he will be tried as well as his men then probably hung. If you want, later when you get home you can come to my office and give me a written description of where they are at right now. I will send it to the army; they can round them up if they wish."

Raven frowned uneasily as she gestured around at her people in fear. "What about my family, will the army come here too?"

The sheriff smiled placatingly then shrugged calmly. "Not that I'm aware of; excuse me, I must talk to the mayor I'll be right back."

Confused, Raven nodded; she watched him leave before looking at her grandfather curiously. She frowned grimly as she gestured sharply in demand wanting answers now. "Okay, what is going on around here?"

Giant Bear leaned forward earnestly in apology; he raised a hand in entreaty. "I'm sorry Raven, I was wrong to try forcing you and Golden Eagle to marry... I hope you can forgive me!"

Grimly, Raven scowled forbiddingly in anger as she thought over the last month; was it all for nothing then! She leaned forward intently before waving in aggravation. "Are you telling me the vision was wrong?"

Shaking his head grimly, Dream Dancer took over the telling. They all decided it would be best for him to tell her; he agreed knowing how upsetting this would be to her. "Not wrong Raven, but misinterpreted!"

Dream Dancer told the flabbergasted Raven... everything.

*****

Michael stood at the back of the crowd watching Jessica longingly. He had not gone anywhere near her after he arrived. The doctor knew she was aware that he was here, but kept his distance not wanting to push her. Doctor Andrews sat down dejectedly then tried hard to ignore the need to go to her.

*****

Rose frowned uneasily; she turned her head away from the intense stare of the young buck, sitting beside Black Hawk. He had stared at her fixedly the whole evening... it was making Black Rose very uncomfortable. Suddenly, he was sitting beside her. She jumped, not having heard a sound.

Running Wolf moved closer, until their legs were touching.

Intrigued, Rose peeked at him through her lashes pretending to ignore him; the young man looked quite impressive, with the smaller headdress proclaiming him as a chief in training. The warm tingly sensation where their legs touched, made her smile a wee bit in invitation.

Running Wolf's face softened as he looked at the beautiful young woman. "What is your name?"

Rose shook her head in confusion, not understanding the language quite yet. "I don't know how to speak Cheyenne."

Perplexed, Running Wolf scowled; she was Cheyenne also, how could she not understand him? He switched to English. "I will teach you then."

Eagerly, Rose smiled and nodded. "I would like that."

Leaning towards her, Running Wolf whispered in her ear.

Unable to help it, Rose giggled; they got up, leaving together.

*****

Black Hawk had watched his son curiously off and on throughout the afternoon. Tommy grinned knowingly, when Running Wolf stared intently at the girl his aunt had brought with them. His son finally got up the courage to go talk to the tiny Rose before they left together. He nodded in approval; it was about time that his son found a mate.

Later, Black Hawk would have to talk to White Buffalo to find out where Rose came from... a formal offer for her must be made. Tommy turned back to the conversation between Raven and the others.

Incredulously, Raven scowled at her grandfather then waved furiously in reprimand. "I can't believe you would think I need help to find a mate. I have been turning down offers for year's nam'-shimi, I was not ready!"

Giant Bear visibly wilted as his favourite granddaughter berated him in front of the others.

Golden Eagle had been listening quietly not wanting to interfere. This was the first time since meeting the formidable chief, that he showed his age. Devon had thought he would be delighted to see the older man brought down a peg, but surprisingly he felt no satisfaction... only pity for Giant Bear.

"RAVEN, that is quite enough now!"

Raven looked up in surprise as her nis-gi-i towered above her.

Golden Dove frowned down grimly at her granddaughter before motioning sharply in rebuke. "We will speak later in private!"

Turning, Raven gazed at her grandfather's subdued appearance then sighed and nodded as she looked up. "Sorry Grandma, you're right."

The sheriff came back then sat, oblivious to the strained silence around him; he grinned at Raven elatedly. "I talked to the mayor, the town council, and the townspeople that are here. When we get back, the mayor is going to start procedures with the Government to make your land a reserve for your people. I hope that eases your mind about the army."

Startled, Raven stared at the sheriff speechless for a moment in amazement. "I didn't think that would be a possibility!"

Sheriff Lane grinned in delight as he nodded in reassurance. "Of course it is! Now, I'm not saying the Government will agree to this, but if the whole town is willing to support you... I can't see why not! Of course, Devon will have to agree as well since he is your neighbour; once he gives his approval we can get started right away. Since Charles will be hanged, his land will be confiscated so the town will add it to the reservation as compensation for his crimes against you and your people."

Raven stood up in a dazed shock; the others sitting around her got up as well. They turned to face the grinning townspeople. She smiled then motioned hopefully. "Are you sure that's what you want?"

The mayor stood also, so he could speak for the others. "Raven your people have been here for years and never caused any trouble. Some of us were unfortunately ready to drive them out when we found out about the guides, but we were wrong so wish to apologize by giving you a gift."

With tears in her eyes, Raven went to the mayor first; the others all followed her as hugs with handshakes of thanks were passed around.

Giant Bear clapped his hands for quiet in demand... he turned to his braves. "Bring out the drums; we will have a great celebration."

A cheer arose from the braves as they quickly raced out.

Beckoning to several women that he knew could speak English, Giant Bear waved towards the townspeople before giving them instructions.

The shaman built the central fire higher, until it was almost touching the top of the tepee then one by one the braves danced for the spellbound townspeople. The women the chief talked to sat among the villagers and interpreted the meaning of each dance, so they would not miss anything.

*****

Jessica aware of Michael's longing gaze couldn't take it anymore; she managed to corner Raven then motioned to her pleadingly. "I must talk to you; it is extremely important!"

Raven looked at the intense redhead curiously before crooking her finger, so Jessica would follow her to the back of the tepee; away from the noise. She frowned at the confused worried expression on Jessie's face, as they sat. "What is the problem Red Sparrow, you seem upset?"

Forlornly, Jessica nodded as she explained about Michael; and his refusal to consider moving to North Dakota. "I don't know what to do?"

Reached over, Raven took the bewildered redhead's hand and asked the vital question. "Do you love him, Red Sparrow?"

Nodding grimly, Jess motioned decisively. "Yes, I do!"

Delighted, Raven grinned. "Well then there should be no problem, if you love somebody that is all that is important."

Unhappily, Jessica frowned as she shook her head miserably. "But my family is all in North Dakota!"

Understanding her dilemma perfectly; Raven had that fear herself not long ago when she thought she would have to move to England. She couldn't afford to lose the doctor either so she decided to tell Jess about Michael, something only she knew. Hopefully, that would help her decide to stay here. "That is a problem, regrettably the doctor is right... he can't leave his responsibilities here. Let me tell you a secret about Michael. All the townspeople here suspect, but don't know how many Cheyenne stay here. Doctor Andrews on the other hand has known since he started doctoring here five years ago, do you know how he knows that?"

Baffled, Jess shook her head; unsure where this was going. "No!"

Intently, Raven tried to explain how dedicate to the people the doctor was. "Michael knows because he comes in the winter then immunizes my people against the white man's diseases. Do you know how much money it takes to get enough vaccine for all of them? Or what he charges us?"

Jessica frowned; unsure, what this has to do with her decision. "No!"

Raven chuckled at the bewildered Jessica; she held her thumb then her index finger in a zero before putting it up to show Red Sparrow. "Nothing... he will not accept a single penny for the vaccine or his time, which is how dedicated he is to all the people in both towns. I supply him with all the food that he needs in return. In the five years that he has been with us not once have I seen him with a woman either. Believe me, there are many in both towns that would gladly be his life partner. I have thought of it myself especially since he looks after my people, but deep respect we have. Regrettably, no love is there."

Knowingly, Raven laughed at the jealous look that crossed Red Sparrows face before continuing. "If he left what would my people do then? I know your family is important, but someday the train will get to Michael's town. We think in a couple years, afterwards you can visit your family. Besides, it's not as if you don't know anyone here; grandmother and I can visit you or you can come here, when you feel lonely."

Pensively, Jessica thought about everything Raven said then reached out before hugging her. "I am grateful for your advice, and you are right; I wouldn't want to deprive you of Michael's generous heart."

Teasingly, Raven pushed Jessica away with a laugh of pleasure then waved for her to go. "You better hurry before I change my mind, and go after that good looking Doctor myself."

Chuckling not worried, Jessica nodded. She got up and raced across the room searching for Michael. When she found him, she threw herself in the doctor's arms then looked at him adoringly; she framed his face lovingly. "Yes, I will marry you!"

Michael whooped ecstatically before grabbing Jessica's hand, and they escaped out of the tepee to be alone.

*****

In amusement, Raven chuckled as she walked away then sat beside Melissa before nudging her; she pointed at the door as the two lovebirds vanished. "I think you lost your sister to one good-looking doctor!"

Melissa looked then sighed in relief. White Buffalo turned and smiled at Raven sadly. "Good, I was hoping she would give in; I will miss her."

Raven nodded then motioned in reassurance. "I heard that the railroad was starting up, someone bailed them out of bankruptcy. They should be here in a few years depending on Indian raids and workers."

Startled, Raven looked up in surprise as the braves started chanting for Golden Eagle insistently. She swung her gaze towards him in shock, as Black Hawk motioned for him to go.

Golden Eagle rose, ignoring Raven's curious look then walked to the fire before dancing of his killing the buck... becoming a Cheyenne brave. Devon walked away when finished then smiled down at his sister in delight, explaining to her what that was all about as he took a seat! The chanting started again, and Black Hawk rose next then went to the fire to dance about the capture of the two white men who had shot Jake's son.

Janet had watched the chief's son fugitively all night in fascination. As he danced, her eyes became dreamy; she looked at her brother seriously then pointed towards the brave firmly. "I'm going to marry that man!"

Sceptically, Golden Eagle looked at his sister dubiously. "Black Hawk... are you serious?"

Musingly, Janet trying out his name in her head; she liked it. She inclined her head decisively at her brother. "It suits him."

Pinching the bridge of his nose, Golden Eagle dropped his hand; he stared at his sister in disbelief before motioning in caution, knowing Black Hawk would never leave. "You are willing to stay in this village?"

Calmly, Janet nodded as she waved not upset by that. "Yes, I am!"

Shaking his head grimly, Golden Eagle had a hard time imagining his pampered sister sleeping on the hard ground and living in a tepee. Devon gazed into her determined face then frowned... his sister had changed; he could see it in her eyes. The Englishman gestured in warning. "His wife just died a few days ago in childbirth, but the baby lived!"

Sadly, Janet sighed at his lose before smiling in delight at the thought of a child; the Englishwoman was unable to have any and had lamented that fact for years. "I will give him a month to mourn before I tell him!"

Golden Eagle laughed in delight; he watched the unsuspecting Black Hawk make his way towards them then sit. Absolute silence fell as the drums quit for a few... heart-pounding seconds. Abruptly, the banging of rocks and spears then the chanting for Raven began relentlessly.

Raven sighed; she got up obediently to the cheers of the waiting braves. Once in the center she began to dance, as had happened before Golden Eagle couldn't take his eyes of her.

Dream Dancer moved over to interpret the dance for the enthralled Englishman. "Raven is describing the screams of a cougar..."

When Dream Dancer's sister finished. He concluded the story. "Now she's showing their struggle to get to safety then their triumph, as they prevailed so the white woman can be reunited with her brother."

Startled, Golden Eagle looked at his sister after Raven finished and hugged Janet; thankful that she had survived all that. Devon turned to Dream Dancer with a nod. "Thank you!"

The braves, done showing their stories to the townspeople settled among them; the shaman allowed the fire to die down. Later several Indian women came in with furs then passed them out.

Giant Bear stood and addressed them solemnly. "It is getting late. You are all welcomed to stay in here tonight. Tomorrow, my people will make you breakfast; afterwards, my braves will escort you safely part of the way back. Anyone who wishes to come with me to examine the walls of this tepee before bed is more than welcomed too. I will explain what the symbols mean to anyone who wishes to hear. Goodnight, to all of you and may your dreams be filled with nothing but pleasantness."

The sheriff with most of the townspeople following him; went to hear Giant Bear eagerly as they listened intrigued.

Standing up, Raven looked at Golden Eagle then away guiltily. "You will have to get your sleeping pallet, and go to my grandmother's tepee to sleep tonight with Dream Dancer; all the women will be sleeping in mine."

Golden Eagle frowned angrily having wanted to be alone with Raven, but obviously, he wasn't going to get his wish. Devon nodded grimly then got up and left sullenly.

Golden Dove stood up then faced Raven reassuringly. "We already have a tepee set up for White Buffalo and her family."

Raven shrugged dismissively. "Okay, but Little Owl and Red Sparrow want to stay with me. Janet can too if she wishes."

Knowing there was no use arguing, Golden Dove nodded; it was obvious to her that Raven wanted to avoid Golden Eagle. "Okay, goodnight girls."

Jessica and Michael came back in just as they were leaving for bed. Jess spotted Daniel so went over to him before grabbing his arm pleadingly. "Will you marry us tomorrow?"

Daniel smiled thoughtfully. "Is Michael going to stay here with us for a bit, or is he leaving with the others?"

Michael inclined his head decisively. "I will be staying; Jessica wants to remain until her sister leaves, so I will stay with her."

Relieved, Daniel grinned placatingly. "I'm not sure we will do it tomorrow; I need to talk to my mother and Giant Bear to see when the best time is, but I promise I'll marry you in the next couple of days."

Looking at Michael inquisitively, Jessica turned back to her uncle as they nodded reluctantly. "We will wait if we must."

Chuckling at the downcast looks, Daniel pulled his younger aunt into a huge hug. "I promise only a day or two; and congratulations to both of you."

Melissa walked over; she waved at Michael. "You can stay with us."

Sighing dejectedly, Michael followed Mell out obediently.

Janet, Patricia and Jessica all followed Raven.

Spotted Owl having returned with Dream Dancer, walked up to Raven then waved towards the large corral reassuringly. "I unsaddled your horses for you; everything is in your tepee."

Appreciatively, Raven nodded thanks before turning away. The girls followed her dutifully to the tepee, but just before they entered; Golden Eagle waylaid them. "Raven, I need to speak to you please!"

Raven turned to the girls; she pointed at the entrance to her tepee in reassurance. "Go, I will be there in a minute."

Once they were gone, Raven turned to Golden Eagle.

Golden Eagle shifted nervously, unsure what to say now; Devon cleared his throat before gesturing hopefully. "What do you want to do now that we don't need to get married to save your people?"

Raven sighed in irritation, not having thought about it until now. She shrugged grimly not wanting to talk about it, but she could tell by Golden Eagle's face that he wanted an answer tonight. "Go our separate ways, I guess. I'm sure you and your sister want to return to England."

Frowning angrily, Golden Eagle waved in amazement. "What about our night together, can you pretend it never happened?"

Shrugging, Raven scowled decisively. "Of course, it was the alcohol!"

Turning away in finality, Raven was brought up short in disbelief as Golden Eagle grabbed her. He ground his lips against hers, in demand. As had happened before her struggle was half-hearted then she melted against Devon involuntarily.

Mercilessly, Golden Eagle didn't relent until he felt her body respond to his. Devon wrenched himself away and stood breathing heavily. Without another word, he spun before marching off his point made.

Stunned, Raven stood there touching her tender lips when Golden Eagle left abruptly; she shivered in desire as her body tingled wanting more. She ignored it in disgust at its traitorous betrayal of her feelings. She didn't want to love that man, that was final! She went into her tepee her mind made up.

The four girls talked then giggled for an hour; finally, they fell into their furs around midnight for some much-needed sleep.

*****

Abruptly, Raven sat up with an anguished cry as her nightmare returned. She looked around, but thankfully she hadn't bothered anyone. She wiped the tears away; Golden Eagle had left her again.

Forlornly, Raven rocked herself. What would she do if he did go; deep down did she want Golden Eagle to leave? Just thinking of the anguish that she felt in her dreams, as well as the empty hopeless feeling that she would have to live with... made her shiver. Maybe she should give her and the Englishman another chance now that there would be no interference from others. She couldn't live with herself if she didn't, at least for a month. This resolution in mind, she settled down then dropped into a dreamless sleep.

CHAPTER THIRTY

Raven woke with a feeling of inner peace thinking of her decision last night. It was as if a burden had lifted off her shoulders; she got up eagerly, looking forward to the future.

Quickly, Raven made coffee; just as she hoped the smell roused the others.

The four girls sat around the fire laughing as they enjoyed each other's company; talking excitedly about how bright the future looked for Raven and her Cheyenne tribe.

Turning, Raven called out in exasperation at a scratching sound on her door when it interrupted them. She didn't want to go out yet; enjoying the company of women for a change, instead of men. "Come in."

Golden Dove poked her head in then beckoned them to come out impatiently. "Come, the townspeople are waiting for you."

The girl's jumped up before rushing out as they followed Golden Dove.

Instantly, the sheriff then the mayor got up to shake hands with Raven. Afterwards, they found seats and coffee was handed out to the latecomers.

Trying not to miss anyone, Raven smiled around as she included them all in her look. "I hope you slept well last night."

The sheriff spoke for the villagers. "Yes, we did, thank you."

Food was brought in by the women and passed around. There were smiles of delight at the eggs, bacon, slices of pork, and Bannock that was being handed out. Absolute quite descended as everyone ate with gusto.

Looking around, Raven frowned in surprise; Golden Eagle, Jake, Black Hawk, and her brother were all missing. The young woman shrugged inwardly, they were probably out somewhere training or knowing her brother the way that she did... causing mischief somewhere.

Pleased, Golden Dove smiled at Raven in approval; she looked different... relaxed. Without the angry scowl she had since this mess started. Mary looked at her husband, her expression softened. She had let him back in her bed. Giant Bear's face also showed relief at having everything right again.

Golden Dove frowned in concern. Mary wondered if Raven knew about Golden Eagle, maybe that's why she looked happy.

After they finished eating, the sheriff finally stood; he shook hands with Raven, Giant Bear, the marshal, and everyone else as goodbyes were said.

Giant Bear led them to the paddocks then gestured at the sheriff. "My brave's saddled your horse's and hooked up the wagons for you."

The sheriff inclined his head in approval. "Much obliged."

Colleen walked over to Raven then touched her arm to get her attention. "We decided to accept your offer and stay at the ranch."

Raven reached over then hugged Colleen. "Good, I will have cabins built for both you right away. As soon as they are ready, I will let you know."

Nodding in relief, Colleen went to Priscilla. They got into their wagons with no worries about the future. The three prisoners were put in the wagons with an armed guard riding behind the carts, watching them.

Sheriff Lane mounted; he looked at Raven to confirm the conversation they had yesterday. "Come into my office when you can, since Sir Devon has given his consent for the reservation. The Englishman said you have full authority to do anything on his land that needs done, now that he has gone back to England. Whatever you decide to do is fine with him. He said for you to send him a letter in Sussex, he will sign any legal forms you need from there."

Tipping his hat cordially, the sheriff turned away without further discussion; eager to get the villager's home. Unaware of the bombshell he just dropped on the unsuspecting Raven.

Frowning baffled, Raven turned to her grandmother mystified as she motioned in unease. "What did he mean by that?"

Grimly, Golden Dove sighed resignedly. Well, her granddaughters face answered the question she had asked herself earlier... Raven didn't know. Mary reached over to take her hand in sympathy, but there was no easy way to tell her. "Golden Eagle left last night, he said he was going back to England. Dream Dancer, Jake, and Black Hawk went with him to Malta; he is catching the stage there. Devon instructed the sheriff that he was giving the land to you in trust; you can do anything you want except sell it."

Raven scowled incredulously; she hadn't even considered the fact that Golden Eagle would leave during the night, without his sister.

She waved over at the Englishwoman in bewilderment. "But he can't be gone, Janet is here!"

Janet stepped forward with an angry grimace; she gestured sharply furious at Devon for his desertion. "Well, I did tell him last night that I was planning on staying here, but I didn't think he would be leaving in the middle of the night either... without saying goodbye to me at least!"

Looking at White Buffalo in panic; Raven wondered what to do, as the sense of hopeless despair settled over her instantly.

Melissa sensing Raven's desperate desolation and understanding, stepped forward quickly. She pointed towards Malta in demand. "Well, don't just stand here; go get him!"

Confused, Raven shook her head undecided; she couldn't force him to stay if he wanted to go... could she?

Jessica grabbed her friend's arm in pleading. When Raven turned to her, Red Sparrow squeezed her arm in encouragement. "What did you tell me just last night, if you love him that's all that matters; I agree with my sister, go get him before it's too late!"

Giant Bear stood helplessly, watching his granddaughter's anguished expression not sure if he should say anything. Afraid to interfere again... as the minutes ticked by, he couldn't take it anymore. The chief stepped forward when Jessica released her then grabbed Raven's arms, he shook her trying to get her to see sense. "You must follow your heart! I wasn't going to say anything because I messed things up for you once, but now I must! When you were a child, the shaman saw you as the 'protector' of our people. He also saw a golden eagle by your side. We didn't know what it meant at the time; I now know that you and Devon were fated to be together from birth. Please don't throw away that love because this old fool made a mistake. Your mother had that love with your father. I have that love with your grandmother. Now go, before you regret this for the rest of your life!"

Raven stared at her nam'-shimi grimly then suddenly she threw her arms around Giant Bear; giving him a fierce hug before racing towards her tepee. As she ran, a whistle of urgency pierced the air calling her stallion to come.

Brave Heart's head lifted at the urgent request then raced towards the fence at full gallop. Clearing it in one leap, he ran towards his mistress.

Gathering her things from the tepee; Raven came out and quickly saddled her stallion. Lucky for her, the saddlebags were still full not having gotten around to emptying them. She vaulted onto Brave Heart's back before galloping out of the village, without looking back. A life without Golden Eagle would leave Raven miserable for the rest of her life. She anxiously prayed to the Great Spirit that she wouldn't be too late.

Golden Dove reached over then took her husband's hand as she smiled at him in praise. "You did well love, that was a very nice speech you made."

Giant Bear hugged his wife in appreciation. He looked around at all the admiring grinning faces. The chief stood straighter; his dignity now restored.

They all turned away, each of them prayed that Raven would make it in time as they went back to the ceremonial tepee. Already they were discussing when the best time for a triple wedding would be. Since Daniel wouldn't only be marrying Jessica and the doctor now, but Running wolf wanted to make Black Rose his wife. Hopefully, Devon and Raven would be wed also.

****

Dream Dancer frowned uneasily before looking at Golden Eagle as they approached the stagecoach building. "Are you sure this is what you want?"

Golden Eagle gestured resolutely. "I'm sure!"

Grimly, Dream Dancer looked at his uncle then over at Jake, afraid of what would happen next.

Black Hawk shrugged at his nephew's sad expression. "It is his choice; we can't force him to stay. That was tried with almost disastrous consequences!"

Dream Dancer wilted in agreement before sighing forlornly... his uncle was right. They dismounted before following Golden Eagle inside and waited while he paid for his ticket. They took seats beside him reluctant to leave him.

Turning to Golden Eagle inquisitively, Black Hawk gestured curiously. "Are you taking your stallion with you?"

Devon fretted in caution, unsure if it was a good idea to expose his horse to ship life. "I don't know, do you think he'll be okay?"

Leaning forward, Dream Dancer nodded in reassurance as he looked around his uncle so that he could talk to the Englishman.

"Sure, he will; I will be taking my horses with me. Just tie him to the back of the stagecoach."

Golden Eagle sighed in relief. "Good, I would hate to leave him."

They got up as the stagecoach driver beckoned them to come; it was time.

Once outside, Jake stepped forward first as he clasped the Englishman's hand firmly in parting. The foreman shook his head sadly in sorrow. "You take care of yourself; I'm sorry it didn't work out between you and Raven."

In warning, Golden Eagle scowled grimly then motioned in anxiety. "You take care of her for me; if Raven needs anything you have my address, just send me a letter or telegram."

Jake sighed unhappily in agreement, as he stepped back to let Black Hawk say goodbye next.

Hugging Raven's uncle, Golden Eagle finally released him.

Sadly, Black Hawk thumped Golden Eagle on the back then stepped away. "Keep up that training now, you hear."

Nodding, Golden Eagle gestured decisively. "You bet I will!"

Impatiently, Dream Dancer waited for his uncle to finish before grabbing Devon in a fierce embrace. "I'll miss you blood-brother, take care of yourself."

Chuckling, Golden Eagle stepped back as he grinned fondly. "I will; I'll be seeing you next fall in England… remember."

Dream Dancer nodded sorrowfully; he stepped back watching his friend tie his stallion to the back of the stage before disappearing inside.

The burly driver cracked his whip loudly in demand before snapping the reins; he bellowed insistently. "Get up there!"

Jake turned to the others with a dissatisfied smile then waved up the street in invitation. "Come on you two, I will buy you guys a drink so we can drown our sorrow in alcohol. They say it is the best medicine for broken hearts."

Dream Dancer and Black Hawk agreed gloomily before untying their horse's as they walked down past the sheriff's office and into the saloon.

****

Raven took the short cut; the sheriff couldn't because it was impassable by wagons. Even with this shorter route, she still wouldn't get to Malta until midnight… if she was lucky.

Unfortunately, Raven knew that she wouldn't find Golden Eagle there; he was probably on the stage by now. She did hope to catch Devon in the next town though; if Golden Eagle got on a boat before she could get to him, it would be too late. The determined woman bent closer to her stallion's neck, asking for more speed at the idea that she might never see him again.

****

Jake eyed Black Hawk blearily. "I think were a tad drunk!"

Black Hawk laughed uproariously in amusement as he slapped Jake consolingly on the back. "I think we are beyond Dat friend. Whets da time?"

The large red-headed Irish saloon keeper chuckled; he refilled their glasses. "It is eleven or thereabouts."

Dream Dancer groaned as he stared at the whiskey in his glass, as if it were going to jump up and bite him. Edward wasn't even sure if he could drink it without falling over. "I think we should go or I will fall on da floor!"

Snickering, Black Hawk put on a stoic expression; he raised his glass to his companions in a toast. "Errs to Devon, may is trip back be with no ardships."

The other two nodded decisively in agreement then reluctantly downed the whiskey before turning for the door... they waved goodbye to the saloon keeper. They were about halfway across the room weaving badly when the doors flew open violently; a desperate Raven rushed in having seen their horses tied outside.

The three men stopped guiltily, as Raven rushed up to them in a panic. "Where is he?"

Dream Dancer wobbled a bit as he tried to focus his blurry vision on his sister. "Gone, took stage at noonish."

Raven eyed the three men in disapproval. Apparently, they had been here all this time since they could hardly stand. Angrily she beckoned them to follow and walked to Sam. "We will need coffees, and something to eat."

Sam nodded with a grin of understanding. "Sure Raven, coming right up. By the way, what happened out at your place; I haven't seen hide nor hair of the sheriff or townsfolk's?"

Shrugging, Raven waved in reassurance. "They should be here tomorrow sometime, probably late; depending on how often they stop."

Inclining his head in relief, Sam didn't ask more questions knowing he would hear about it from the sheriff as soon as he got to town. The saloon keeper turned away then went into the kitchen to see if there was stew left.

Impatiently, Raven motioned to the three men to come with her; she led them to a table in the back where they wouldn't be disturbed. She sat forward intently then pointed at the three of them in anger. "One of you could have woken me to tell me Golden Eagle was leaving. Or better yet, you could have stopped him... at least until morning!"

Black Hawk shrugged grimly. "What yaw want us ta do, hogties am!"

Drunkenly, Dream Dancer chuckled at that thought since he wanted to earlier; he sobered, as his wild-eyed sister swung her gaze towards him. Edward raised his hands placatingly. "Devon said you no want am to stay."

A plump black-haired barmaid brought the stew; she peeked over at Dream Dancer longingly.

Jake, seeing the look elbowed Black Hawk knowingly; he tipped his head for him to look discreetly so that Raven wouldn't notice.

Black Hawk smirked then nodded at Jake in drunken humour.

Raven waited until the barmaid left before motioning in annoyance, not having seen the byplay between her uncle and foreman. "Well, none of you are sober enough to come with me, so stay here until I get back."

Dream Dancer hiccupped then smiled eagerly in foolish delight. "Yous change your mind bouts Devon?"

Curtly, Raven nodded decisively. "Yes, I did!"

Foolishly, Black Hawk and Jake grinned at each other.

Jake snickered knowingly; he poked Raven's uncle hard in an... I told you so manner. He leaned over then whispered conspiringly, or thought he did anyway. "Women, day always change Deir minds at de last instant!"

With a snort, Black Hawk laughed in agreement.

Raven scowled furiously at the two drunk men, having heard that loud whisper; she leaned forward in demand as she pointed at them in challenge. "Is that supposed to be funny?"

The two men looked at Raven, with identical innocent looks.

Impatiently, Raven harrumphed in disgust as she finished before rising angrily. "I must go, wait here until noon; if I'm not back by then go home."

The three nodded as Raven rushed out.

Knowingly, Black Hawk chuckled. "Did no pay de bill ider?"

Shrugging, Jake laughed before nudging Black Hawk; he pointed at the waitress at the bar. She was sending longing looks at Dream Dancer.

Agreeing, Black Hawk nodded in permission; Jake got up and walked over to her then discreetly passed her some money.

Lily slipped the money in her bodice with an incline of her head then walked to Dream Dancer. "Come honey; I will show you to your room."

Looking down at his uncle and foreman in confusion, Dream Dancer gestured drunkenly. "What's about Yau's?"

Waving for Edward to go, Black Hawk chuckled. "You go with Lily."

Watching Edward leave, the two laughed drunkenly in delight when Dream Dancer stumbled on the stairs.

Using his glass, Jake yelled out to the barkeep as he banged it on the table insistently. "More whiskey Sam, were now celebratin!"

Sam snickered in approval when his barmaid went upstairs with the earl.

****

The sun was coming up when Raven reluctantly slowed her horse; they all needed a rest as much as she could wish differently. She looked down at Bruno. "We will walk for half an hour then stop to eat."

Bruno yelped tiredly in agreement. Raven laughed as she looked down; Bruno's tongue was hanging out on the left side of his muzzle... it looked hilarious. She reached down then patted Brave Heart's sweaty neck in apology. "How're you holding up boy?"

Brave Heart blew hard in a loud woof through his nostrils, almost in rebuke as he breathed heavily in exhaustion.

Sighing, Raven grimaced in agreement nearly asleep in her saddle. She crested a hill and saw a valley below with a creek. It wasn't a big one so easily fordable; she decided to cross first then make camp for something to eat, and some sleep. It was a bit to open for her liking, but with Bruno around to give warning of any danger or strangers coming... it would do. She shrugged resignedly then trotted down the hill, and across the creek.

Unsaddling her horse, Raven rubbed him down. Afterwards, she checked his legs and hooves... satisfied she fed him. The young woman rummaged in her pack for food; she finally sat on her bedroll then fed half to Bruno.

Suddenly, Bruno growled and got up before looking up at the top of the hill intently that they would be climbing after a rest.

Jumping up with her rifle ready, Raven looked up. Pausing at the top of the hill, a horse and its rider stopped before staring down intently at them.

The sun, an abnormally large orange ball of fire just rising over the opposite hill shone directly on the man. The position of the sun and rider made the horse he was sitting on appear white just like his hair.

Raven inhaled in shock then dropped the rifle before racing towards the hill and to the man of her dreams.

****

Devon looked down speculatively, but the sun was blinding him... he couldn't see. The coach Golden Eagle took yesterday had reached the next town early this morning. He went to the hotel to eat after being informed that it would be an hour or two's wait as they changed the exhausted horses. The Englishman tried sleeping in the coach, but every time he closed his eyes an image of Raven would appear making him groan in agony.

Out of sorts, Golden Eagle had walked into the hotel grumpy but felt much better after he ate. He just finished his cup of tea when a woman walked in; the Englishman caught his breath in anticipation, until the black-haired lady turned then met Devon's grey eyes with her blue ones.

Golden Eagle's heart plummeted instantly in disappointment, so he got up and paid for breakfast before leaving. Devon walked to the stage then stopped in excitement; a woman with black hair done in two Indian braids stood arguing with the driver. She turned away angrily, and stared at the Englishman disgruntled before stalking away furiously. He wilted, as the brown-eyed woman marched passed him without giving him a second look.

Walking to his horse, Golden Eagle stroked him soothingly. Devil shifted uneasily before nudging his master anxiously; he craned his neck, staring longingly back the way they had come.

Sighing forlornly at his horse, Golden Eagle looked back. Suddenly, without hesitating; he untied Devil then turned him around before jumping up and galloped out of town... heading back the way they had come.

Now here the Englishman sat looking down hopefully, again at another black-haired woman. Squinting, Golden Eagle had to shade his eyes to see anything. Devon saw the woman running abruptly then he was kicking his horse in excitement down the hill... screaming her name. "RAVEN!"

Raven stopped when the horse got closer before lifting her arms; Golden Eagle bent and hauled her up in front of him. Devon instantly sealed their lips in an ecstatic kiss as she clung to the Englishman.

Stopping his horse, Golden Eagle jumped down before holding his arms up for Raven. The Englishman knew if she accepted him now... it would be forever. No longer would he be called Devon; from this day forward, he would be known as Golden Eagle a Cheyenne brave of the wolf tribe.

Without any more hesitation, Raven slid into his arms gladly.

Golden Eagle gently laid her down in the grass, whispering love words.

Raven clung to him crying in relief, refusing to let Devon go; afraid he would disappear as he had in her dreams. They made love fiercely unable to get enough of each other. After, they fell asleep unable to stay awake.

As sleep claimed them, a grinning ecstatic Dream Dancer chanting a love song entered their dreams. In his hand was a dream catcher with their likenesses painted inside. They both knew that this was no illusion, as the most powerful shaman in history lifted the dream catcher towards the heavens. Shooting stars danced all around him as if in celebration as if God, Heammawihio... their Great Spirit, was pleased!

EPILOGUE

Boston, Massachusetts

Edward was jerked awake by the loud call of the conductor as he yelled out so everyone could hear him above the noise. "One hour to Boston folks!"

Smiling in anticipation, Edward sighed thankfully before giving a giant yawn; finally, he was here. Dream Dancer mind wandered back to his journey. Leaving his sister and Lily had been one of the hardest things he had ever done. He had ridden across Montana into North Dakota with Melissa and her husband. The young earl had stayed with them for two days, but Mell was too busy getting her towns back in shape after being gone for two months.

Rousing himself, Edward pushed thoughts of home away as he looked out the window in anticipation not wanting to miss anything. Dream Dancer's first sight caused him to sigh in disappointment; it looked exactly like the towns close to the ranch except it was bigger and disgustingly dirty.

The Great Spirit had promised Edward in a dream that he would get help here; how he was supposed to find anyone in this huge place was beyond him. Why Dream Dancer needed help from someone not of his people baffled him, but he knew it would be revealed to him when the time came.

The train slowed, so Edward shook off his reflective mood then grabbed the gear he had put on the seat beside him so nobody could sit with him; he headed towards the rear compartments where his horses waited. Dream Dancer arrived in time to hear his stallion scream in anger then saw him rear. The young earl ran towards the idiot trying to lead his stud out. "Stop, get away from that horse before you get yourself killed!"

The tall, burly man backed off immediately as the young fellow grabbed the lead rope away from him.

Immediately, Edward's voice lowered soothingly before talking calmly in Cheyenne trying to quiet the distressed stallion! The stocky black stood trembling and blowing hard; his ears perked forward, listening attentively to his master's reassurances as he calmed once more.

Frowning angrily, Edward heard the man mumble under his breath as he shook his head. "Damn Indians and their horses!"

Furiously, Edward frowned at the man's prejudice comment but didn't criticize him. It wouldn't help anyway, he knew.

Once the train came to a halt, the large door dropped to the ground. Edward led his stallion out then tied him securely to the hitching rail; even though, he knew the stud would not stray unless spooked. Theres too much noise and people to take that chance. The young earl raced back up the platform then went to get his mare. Dream Dancer tightened her packs before leading his horse out to stand beside the stallion.

The man who tried to lead his stud out, came with his more passive gelding. Edward nodded his thanks then tied him up before heading to the train station. Once Dream Dancer had directions; he went back out and tied his stallions lead rope to his gelding then tied his mare on the opposite side of his saddle. The young earl finally mounted and headed north.

Raven with the help of their lawyer had made all the arrangements for him. Edward would stay in Boston for three days before catching a ship to England, where he would be met by another lawyer then taken to one of his townhouses. There, the young earl would be outfitted in the proper clothing so that he could be brought before the queen to be introduced.

All the arrangements were made for his schooling. Edward was to start at Oxford in the fall. His English grandfather on his father's side had attended the same school. Hopefully, in a few years he would be a full doctor. At first, the young earl had wanted to be a lawyer but his blood-brother advised him to become a doctor instead; that way, Dream Dancer could help people with his powers and they wouldn't be any the wiser.

Curiously, Edward looked around as the buildings got smaller then cruder with a lot more garbage lying around. The young earl noticed a group of men standing together, so he slowed intrigued. Dream Dancer had never seen people like them before. Jed had warned him that he probably would see them here; Grey Wolf had called them Orientals. They had coal black hair done in a long braid down their backs, some almost to their hips. They were dark skinned like his people, but their skin had a bit of a yellowish tinge. Their eyes were anywhere between a deep brown to black with a tilt some upward and some downward, depending on where they lived. Most of them wore beautiful robes or colourful, unusual clothes.

Jed told Edward that they were treated worse than the Indian tribes, most laboured in mines or on the railroad. Grey Wolf said they were treated like slaves, so most died from starvation or diseases. The young earl rode on shaking his head; at times Dream Dancer was ashamed of his white blood.

Edward turned onto his street and continued going. As he rode along, the houses got better kept as well as more expensive. The young earl saw the hotel, so turned left into the stables before dismounting then led his horses inside.

A large bulky dark-haired bear of a man in an apron bustled up to him; he knuckled his forehead in respect. "What can I do for yah, young sir?"

Smiling, Edward nodded cordially back. "I'm booked at the hotel for three days; can you look after my horses for me? Be careful of the stallion."

The man inclined his head in agreement then turned and bellowed loudly to someone in the back. "Hey, Chink... comes out here den take dese hoses and stable dem!"

A small Oriental walked out of the back room then shuffled towards them. He put his two hands together as if in prayer and bowed just a bit, but not once did he look directly at the brawny stableman. "As you wish!"

The short, four-foot nine-inch man was really slim... almost too skinny; he walked to the black then unhooked his lead rope.

The stallion rolled his eyes angrily and backed away, with a warning snort ready to rear up. The Oriental reached out then touched the stallion's nose calmly before talking soothingly to him, in a strange language. The stud's ears perked up; he calmed immediately as he followed the man docilely.

Amazed, Edward shook his head in disbelief that was the first time his stallion had allowed anyone near him without hardly any fuss. Satisfied his horses were in good hands, the young earl pulled off his main saddlebag that had some of his clothes in before turning to the stableman; he tossed him a half dollar. "Please have the rest of my packs brought to my room."

Edward waited until he saw the nod of agreement from him before turning to the Oriental when he came to take the mare. The earl slipped him a coin; Dream Dancer made sure to hide what he was doing from the stableman.

The Oriental bowed again with his hands pressed together, but a little deeper this time. "Thank you, my Lord."

When the Oriental stood up, he looked at the young man then stared into his eyes intently for a moment assessingly. A bit of a curve of his lip was all that showed his approval before he took the mare's rope; he unhooked her then led her away without comment.

Eyebrows furrowing, Edward frowned in puzzlement; when the Oriental had looked into his eyes, the young earl had felt a tingle of something. Almost of recognition and anticipation, but he had never seen the smaller man before that he knew of. Dream Dancer shrugged uneasily... disconcerted, he left.

Going to the front door, Edward entered the lobby... he looked around curiously. The counter was on his left; to his right was a stairway leading up to the rooms. Just past that was a door that the young earl assumed led into the dining room? Dream Dancer walked up to the counter, not seeing anyone he frowned then saw a bell so he rang for service.

A huge barrel of a man came out of the back rooms, and nodded in acknowledgement. "Yes sir, may I help you?"

Startled, Edward smiled in surprise; the man was enormous, at least three hundred pounds if not more. He was much shorter than the young earl was. He resembled the stableman, so Dream Dancer guessed that they were probably related.

The hotel clerk was assessing Edward just as intently; he eyed the light brown auburn-streaked hair, and dark green-eyed young man curiously. The clerk wondered if this was the earl he had been instructed to watch for. If it were, he was tall for sixteen at six feet. The clerk liked the honest, straightforward expression the young man gave him.

Without hesitation, Edward reached across the counter so he could shake the hotel clerk's hand. The clerk approved of the firm, but not crushing handshake the young man gave him as he grinned. "Names, Edwin Burke."

Immediately, Edward inclined his head before releasing Edwin's hand. "I'm Earl Summerset, but everyone calls me Ed."

Edwin nodded his suspicion confirmed. "I was expecting you."

Edwin reached under the counter then pulled out a particular key, that only a few were ever privileged to use before walking around the desk. The clerk beckoned the young earl to follow.

Edward dutifully trailed the clerk; he was led towards the door of the dining room. Edwin turned right then walked under the central stairway that led up to the rooms. The earl hadn't noticed the hallway at first glance. There was one door down the hall, the massive clerk almost didn't fit.

Unlocking the door, Edwin opened it with a flourish then waved for Edward to precede him. The clerk handed the key to the young earl as he walked past.

Walking in, Edward's eyes widened in surprise; the room was done up in royal blue colours... it was enormous. It even had its own bathtub off to the right partially hidden by a screen. The bed was round, it would hold three people comfortably without crowding each other... he was sure. The young earl turned to the fireplace then smiled in satisfaction; they had clearly expected him today since a fire was already crackling cheerily inside. Dream Dancer turned with a grin of pleasure and appreciation to the innkeeper. He dug out a silver dollar for a tip in thanks. "It is beautiful!"

Quickly, Edwin waved off the tip with a smile of pleasure at Edward's obvious delight in his room. "No need for that it has already been taken care of, so under no circumstances are you to tip anyone here. Your lawyer made sure that everyone was looked after. Now Susan will be here soon, she will take care of all your needs while you are here. The rest of your saddlebags will be delivered directly, so enjoy your stay with us Earl Summerset."

Glad he wouldn't have to worry about that, Edward nodded pleased. The young earl watched the stout innkeeper close the door then dropped down on the bed with a satisfied sigh; he fell asleep almost instantly.

*****

It was late when Edward left the hotel to walk to the saloon Edwin recommended. The young earl had turned seventeen yesterday, but had been unable to celebrate on the train. Dream Dancer decided to do so tonight. He was about halfway there when he felt a prickle of warning on the back of his neck. His hand dropped to his gun; he spun around looking for whoever was watching him so intently... nobody was there.

Edward frowned perplexed as he looked everywhere, but to no avail. That feeling of being watched didn't go away, however. He shrugged dismissively then turned back around and continued going.

The young earl released his gun then chuckled at his foolishness. The weapon was a new addition to his wardrobe, a gift from Melissa; she had insisted on teaching him how to use it. Mell had even given him additional pointers on the training Grey Wolf had given him. Dream Dancer knew deep down that he wouldn't be able to kill anyone, unless given no choice. He was a healer... not a killer.

The faint sound of a piano made Edward forget about the feeling of being watched. As it got louder, the sounds of singing and laughter joined in so he knew he was getting closer. Unexpectedly, he heard a woman scream in terror off to his left. The dreadful sound came from an alley between two buildings. Instantly, without thought, the young earl raced in that direction so he could help whoever was in trouble. Dream Dancer was halfway down the alleyway when the call for help was cut off abruptly... his pace quickened. He saw two men struggling with a young woman; she was on the ground sobbing hysterically, as one man held her down while the other one was in the process of raping her.

Not even hesitating for a second, Edward grabbed the man lying on the woman and heaved him bodily across the alleyway.

The man holding the woman down jumped up in surprise.

Much faster, Edwards left foot rose rapidly... connecting, under the rapist's jaw. Instantly, the man dropped stunned to the ground.

The man Edward had thrown across the alley raced back towards them. The young earl crouched; readying himself as both arms came up in a fighting stance, that he had learned from his uncle and Mell.

Wanting nothing to do with the towering stranger; the other man got to his friend then helped him up before both rapist's turned tail and fled.

Cautiously, Edward waited to make sure that they were not coming back. Once positive they were gone, he relaxed his stance then dropped down beside the sobbing girl. The young earl looked around, making sure nobody was around before eyeing her in contemplation.

Edward knew he was too late. She had been raped more than once. He frowned angrily; maybe he should go after those men... Dream Dancer couldn't help thinking, as he looked at the girl closely. She couldn't be more than fifteen. Judging by the coal black hair and dark yellow skin; she was Oriental, like the man in the stables.

With another swift look around, Edward moved closer to the girl. He rubbed his hands together chanting in Cheyenne.

The girl stopped sobbing as she listened to the man above her singing. She couldn't understand what he was saying, but it calmed her to listen to him. As she watched curiously, he continued to rub his hands together before reaching out to her. Automatically, she flinched thinking he wanted to hurt her too.

Not wavering or stopping his chanting, Edward brought Dream Dancer to the surface. He reached out with his tingling hands towards the girl... not allowing her fear to stop him. The young earl laid one hand on her forehead then one on her stomach, chanting in Cheyenne. It was the third time he had done this; the first was by accident. Dream Dancer wasn't sure he could even do it here, away from his people and homeland. He didn't let that stop him, as he tried to help the girl's body heal itself.

When Edward's hands touched her, he was surprised to feel a burning jolt race up his arms then continued down into his body. It took all his concentration to continue, as the young earl felt his healing powers reluctantly come to life; this feeling was different. Dream Dancer had not felt it with the other two. Was her body stealing something from him?

Thankfully, Edward felt the power in his hand's wane; he released the girl abruptly. The young earl sat back on his haunches, rubbing his hands together painfully. Dream Dancer dropped his head in his hands for a moment, hoping the woozy feeling in his head would not last long. He sighed in relief when the feeling subsided after only a few minutes, she had not been hurt that badly.

The girl smiled gratefully at the young man sitting in front of her. She wasn't sure what he did, but she felt warm and tingly. Suddenly, her eyes widened in stunned disbelief at something behind him. Instantly, the girl got to her knees then knelt with head bowed. Her hands came together in a prayer-like position; she started speaking in her language uneasily.

Edward spun around quickly then crouched; unsure what had her so upset. The young earl looked up in surprise at the slight man from the stables, that had looked after his horses.

The Oriental stared down at the girl in disapproval as she babbled incoherently. Finally, his hand came down in a sharp silencing motion as he spoke harshly to her in his language.

Instantly, the girl quieted as she bowed deeper. Now, her forehead was pressed against the Oriental's feet as she listened respectfully.

Jumping up without warning; the girl bowed to the Oriental man before turning to her rescuer with a grateful dip. Without looking at them, she scurried away as fast as she could go.

The man stared after his granddaughter reflectively; she had disobeyed him again; this time with disastrous results, he would deal with her later.

Thoughtfully, the Oriental turned and regarded the young earl intently. He stared down into the dark green eyes relentlessly; waiting for him to turn away, like every white man had done since he arrived here searching for his destiny. To his surprise, the boy's gaze never wavered.

The older man watched in fascination as Edward's eyes darkened from a deep green, to such a dark green that his eyes appeared black. He had watched the young earl kick his opponent then crouch in a fighting stance, when saving his granddaughter; he had been pleased to see that.

Even though Edward had a gun; he never made one move towards it as he had earlier, while the Oriental was watching him so intently. It was good the boy had decent instincts.

Now that Edward's eyes were completely black, with not even a hint of green anywhere; the Oriental could feel the chaotic power radiating from him. The older man had felt it earlier in the stables, which was why he had looked at the earl so intently.

Dream Dancer forced to the surface, stared up just as fixedly refusing to relent. He felt his power surge inside him as his eyes changed colour. The power tingling in Edward's body wanted to be released... it scared him badly. This had never happened to the him before; the Oriental was doing something to him. It wasn't the same feeling he had with the girl, though.

Dream Dancer refused to look away, knowing deep down if he did... it would be hazardous for him. Edward knew he had to bury his power somehow; it was almost beyond his control. Chanting softly, he slowed his heartbeat down a little at a time. The young earl could feel the blood in his veins slowing as he relaxed every part of his body, one muscle at a time.

Black Hawk had taught Dream Dancer to do this when using his bow and arrows. When his body then his heartbeat relaxed, so too did the power within him; the young earl could feel his eyes changing back to their deep green. Still, Edward refused to look away from the man.

Unexpectedly, the older man released Edward's gaze. He stepped back before clapping twice in admiration then bowed deeply, with both hands pressed together in respect. The Oriental's bow this time was more profound than it had been this afternoon. "You have saved my granddaughter; I owe you a debt. To repay it, I will accompany you on your travels and teach you how to control your powers, your mind, as well as your body. This is my destiny... I have been waiting a long time for you!"

Edward frowned confused then stood up to his full height. He looked down at the smaller man, who still stood bent over. "You can't come with me; I'm going to England in a couple of days!"

The Asian stood up then inclined his head at Edward shrewdly. "I have knowledge of this; even if I have to pursue you from a distance, I will follow. Your powers are strong, but without my help you won't be able to use them correctly. Without me, they will become unruly!"

Rubbing his forehead, Edward grimaced in anxiety. He had been afraid of that for so long now. The young earl smiled before nodding pleased. The Great Spirit had not steered him wrong; he found the help he knew deep down he needed. Raven had been worried because it had been so long since they had a shaman with Dream Dancer's ability. There had been no one to teach him how to manage the power that had begun to grow stronger. He felt instant relief as the two walked out of the alleyway.

Edward peaked at the Oriental. "What should I call you?"

The Oriental smirked in amusement. "Dao Ba Zevak Hajime. The meaning of my name is complex; Dao means sword in Chinese. Ba is Vietnamese, and it means third. Zevak is Hebrew it means, sacrifice. Hajime is Japanese... it means beginning. To make it easier for you just call me Dao, or teacher if you prefer."

Thoughtfully, Edward smiled curiously; trying to figure out why the Oriental would have a name that means so many things. If his people were anything like theirs, a meaning or warning would be hidden in his name... but a sword, third, sacrifice, and beginning didn't make much sense to him. "I take it you are not full Chinese then? Is there a reason for your name?"

Dao shrugged as he looked at Edward. "You are correct; I'm not full blood of any nation, but a mixture of cultures. Why this is so, has not been revealed to me yet. Our names have great meaning, but why is not always revealed to us until the end of our lives."

Pensively, Edward nodded obligingly. "I will call you Dao and teacher when alone. Call me Edward or Dream Dancer that's my Cheyenne name."

Grinning, Dao chuckled in amusement. "I will call you Earl Summerset in public and Dream Dancer in private; it suits you best."

When Edward took his teacher back to the hotel, he arranged to purchase Dao's bondage papers then freed him. In the morning, he would seek out all the documents for Dao's family and release them too.

Without hesitating, Edward had a cot put in his room for the mixed Oriental. As predicted, Dao refused to leave his new student's side; always, he stayed one-step behind respectfully in public. In private, he became Dream Dancer's shadow teacher.

Here ends Raven and the Golden Eagle

Coming soon in my White Buffalo (New Beginnings) Series...

Revenge of the Silver Fox

After a pack of outlaws, viciously kill her parents and twin brother while looking for her. Tiffany; the lone survivor at a ranch in Montana, mysteriously disappears... only to resurface years later. Now grown and bent on revenge, she is looking for those responsible! Finding out they had relocated to Canada to hide from the law... the determined Silver Fox follows.

A BRIEF NOTE TO MY READERS

Raven... Lady Raven Summerset, to the Cheyenne she is their 'protector', also Cheyenne warrior woman.

Edward, Ed for short... Lord Eward Summerset, known to the Cheyenne as Dream Dancer, Earl Summerset.

Tommy, Giant Bear's son... Black Hawk to the Cheyenne.

Mary, Giant Bear's white wife... known to the Cheyenne as Golden Dove.

Pamela, Pam Giant Bear's & Mary's daughter... known as Morning Star.

Melissa, Mell, marshal... known as White Buffalo to the Cheyenne.

Jed, deputy marshal... known as Grey Wolf to the Cheyenne and the Blackfoot.

Devon... Lord Devon Rochester, also known as Golden Eagle to the Cheyenne.

Here is a list of some of the research material that I found quite interesting.

- ➤ https://en.wikipedia.org/wiki/Stetson
- ➤ http://www.snowwowl.com/swolfNAnamesandmeanings2.html
- ➤ https://en.wikipedia.org/wiki/List_of_wars_1800%E2%80%9399
- ➤ http://www.naylors.com/blog/natural-horsemanship-versus-traditional-horse-training/
- ➤ https://en.wikipedia.org/wiki/Equine_anatomy
- ➤ https://truewestmagazine.com/fighting-blades-of-the-frontier/
- ➤ https://en.wikipedia.org/wiki/Timeline_of_United_States_railway_history
- ➤ https://en.wikipedia.org/wiki/Montana
- ➤ https://adventure.howstuffworks.com/outdoor-activities/hunting/traditional-methods/knife-hunting1.htm
- ➤ https://en.wikipedia.org/wiki/Gold_rush
- ➤ https://www.warpaths2peacepipes.com/native-indian-weapons-tools/bows-and-arrows.htm
- ➤ https://truewestmagazine.com/fighting-blades-of-the-frontier/
- ➤ https://www.salon.com/2013/05/11/the_modern_history_of_swearing_where_all_the_dirtiest_words_come_from/
- ➤ http://www.angelfire.com/ok3/dogg/language.html

BIOGRAPHY

I was born in Dalhousie, NB, but I have lived most of my life in Alberta. Presently, I am living in Falher; it is a town in Northern Alberta, known as the honey capital of Canada... plus the home of the largest bee.

I married a wonderful loving man, Michel Pelletier; I have two daughters, a stepdaughter, and two stepsons. So far, I have four grandsons, several step-grandsons, and step-granddaughters. I now have 2 great granddaughters.

I love to golf, dance and fish... above all is to write. Writing has been a passion for me since I was in my early twenties. It quickly became an addiction; I find hard to stay away from for any length of time.

I am now self-published; with the help of Page Masters Publications based out of Edmonton.

I have 3 series planned with at least three books in each set. If all goes as planned, I am hoping to have a full trilogy saga in the near future. Possibly, with more on the way... if the writing bug continues to bite me.

The first set of books begins the journey that will tie my three series together; they start from early to the mid 1800's in the USA as a western romance.

The second series is my transition from romance to fantasy, it will become a western fantasy; it's set in the late 1800's and continues into the late 2000's, which starts in England then bring you into Canada, where I will stay until the end!

My third series will be full fantasy. It will be the beginning of a new world and reappearance of magic in its full glory; including forgotten creatures, evil villains, different cultures, and unlikely people. With several surprises that even I'm unaware of!

www.ingramcontent.com/pod-product-compliance
Lightning Source LLC
Chambersburg PA
CBHW051940020726

47501CB00001B/213